A DISTURBANCE
OF FATE

Mitchell J. Freedman

SEVEN LOCKS PRESS

Santa Ana, California

Seven Locks Press
P.O. Box 25689
Santa Ana, CA 92799
(800) 354-5348

Individual Sales. This book is available through most bookstores or can be ordered directly from Seven Locks Press at the address above.

Quantity Sales. Special discounts are available on quantity purchases by corporations, associations, and others. For details, contact the "Special Sales Department" at the publisher's address above.

Printed in the United States of America

Library of Congress Cataloging-in-Publication Data
is available from the publisher
ISBN 1-931643-22-9

Cover and Interior Design by Heather Buchman, Costa Mesa, California
Cover photo courtesy of Corbis, Inc.

To Phil Ochs and Michael Harrington, who believed in the Kennedys,
and to my father, who still believes.

Each time a man stands up for an ideal, or acts to improve the lot of others, or strikes out against injustice, he sends a tiny ripple of hope, and crossing each other from a million different centers of energy, and daring those ripples, builds a current which can sweep down the mightiest walls of oppression and resistance.

— Robert F. Kennedy, Address to the
University of Capetown, South Africa,
June 6, 1966, two years to the day
before his death from an assasin's bullet

TABLE OF CONTENTS

Acknowledgements

It is said that no man is an island. It is also said that it takes a village to raise a child. These clichés apply to the process of book writing. A book is mostly, if not solely, written alone. However, its success depends upon the book writer's family, friends, editors, publishers, and the service personnel at libraries, bookstores, copy shops, and post offices, both private and public, and the works of previous writers. This book is yet another example of that insight.

I wish to acknowledge the following people who have helped make this book possible:

Although I dedicate this book to Phil Ochs, Michael Harrington, and my father, I wish to first thank my wife and two children. They have continued to suffer the loss of my time from them because of this book. To their everlasting credit, they have always supported my deep desire to bring this book to the world.

I thank my parents who encouraged my efforts in writing this book from the first lines that were written in October 1998. In the past, they had usually demanded I stick with my day job and forget about the creative side of my life, whether it was drawing cartoons, composing music, or writing. This time, however, they said it was okay to indulge my creative side—at least before or after my day job hours.

I would also like to explain the dedication to my father. My father, who served in local government in New Jersey from the 1960s to the dawn of the 1970s, instilled in me a belief that citizens have rights and duties toward each other and that a civilized society must provide an economic base of support for all of its citizens. Even today, in his spare time, he teaches a civics class to immigrants who are completing their citizenship requirements. My father truly believes in the continued power of John and Robert Kennedy to inspire people to do good deeds for their neighbors, their country, and the world.

Outside my family, I thank Jim Riordan, publisher, of Seven Locks Press, in Santa Ana, California. Mr. Riordan continually gave me encouragement to bring my book to print and continues to teach me about the world of book publishing. I also thank my editor, Kathleen Florio, who immediately understood the essence of this novel and has helped refine my prose through the editing process. While Ms. Florio used the Chicago style of grammar for her editing, if there are any grammatical inconsistencies, the exceptions or . . . ahem . . . errors must be deemed all mine due to my own *post*-Kathleen editing.

Rafer Johnson and Peter Edelman, two men close to Robert Kennedy, graciously agreed to review parts of my novel in earlier stages, despite not knowing me at all. Their positive comments gave me confidence that I was on the right track in pursuing this project. Dr. Kevin Starr, the California State Librarian and leading California historian, and one of the greatest living writers of non-fiction prose, read the entire novel and helped me reformulate the book away from its original science fiction opening (The original opening came complete with a future civil war based upon super-bacteria, terrorism, computer hackers, corporate dominance, the disparity of wealth distribution, and a time machine. How's that for complications?). He gave me constructive and authoritative advice when he did not have to bother talking with me, a relative stranger, at all. And for that, I will always be grateful.

I finally wish to thank those family members, friends, and acquaintances who read and commented on the book in its various stages, or otherwise helped me in a variety of ways. These include, but are not limited to, my uncle Maurice J. "Mitch" Freedman (2002 president of the American Library Association), Dave and Trish Kidd, Shirley and Irv Kornfeld, Brad Hutchings, Kimberly Scully, Barbara Ehrenreich, Marilyn Barrett, Esq., Professor Philip Melanson of U. Mass. (Dartmouth), Megan Rosenberg, and Sean DiZazzo.

In all, I thank everyone who helped me shepherd this book through to publication.

ROBERT F. KENNEDY AND ALTERNATIVE HISTORY

On March 18, 1968, just two days after announcing his candidacy for president, United States Senator Robert F. Kennedy delivered a speech that is sometimes called "The Measure of a Nation." It is a speech no mainstream politician would dare deliver today. Speaking in his usual nasal Boston tone, but with a powerful and earnest delivery he summoned for live audiences, Kennedy said:

> Too much and for too long, we seem to have surrendered personal excellence and community values for the mere accumulation of material things. Our gross national product, now, is over eight hundred billion dollars a year. But that gross national product, if we judge the United States of America by that, that gross national product counts air pollution and cigarette advertising. And ambulances to clear our highways of carnage.
>
> It counts the special locks for our doors and the jails for the people who break them. It counts for the destruction of the redwoods and our loss of natural wonder, and chaotic sprawl. It counts napalm. And it counts nuclear warheads—and armored cars for the police to fight the riots in our cities. It counts Whitman's rifle and Speck's knife. And the television programs which glorify violence in order to sell toys to our children.
>
> Yet the gross national product does not allow for the health of our children, the quality of their education, or the joy of their play. It does not include the beauty of our poetry or the strength of our marriages, the intelligence of our public debate or the integrity of our public officials. It measures neither our wit nor our courage. Neither our wisdom nor our learning. Neither our compassion nor our devotion to our country. It measures everything, in short, except that which makes life worthwhile. And it can tell us everything about America, except why we are proud that we are Americans.[1]

For those who ask why we might want to save Robert Kennedy from assassination in June 1968, "The Measure of a Nation" is at least one reason. There are other reasons that are as varied as the man's constituency through all these decades after his assassination. Jack Newfield, a journalist and Kennedy supporter in 1968, once quoted the philosopher Pascal in describing Kennedy's ability to gain the support of both Chicago "Boss" Mayor Richard Daley and 1960s' radical Tom Hayden: "A man does not show his greatness by being at one extremity, but by touching both at once."

Regardless of his having such contradictory and polarized supporters, it is nonetheless fairly clear where Robert Kennedy stood on political issues in 1968. He opposed the war then raging in Vietnam and opposed most American leaders' support for military dictators around the globe. Kennedy was also strongly committed to helping those who were impoverished and was concerned about the inequalities of wealth in American society and the world. He supported new laws regarding environmental protection. He was sympathetic to union organizing, though he believed many union leaders of the time were out of touch with their rank-and-file members. On the topic of civil rights, Kennedy, of course, supported housing and school integration among the various races. However, he was also wary of integration becoming a substitute for creating jobs and pursuing direct government action to revitalize American urban and rural areas.

Robert Kennedy, in the 1950s as a senate aide, and in the early 1960s while working for his brother as attorney general, had supported Cold War establishment assumptions. He had been tepid on civil rights for blacks and other minorities and doubtful about the ability of government to ameliorate poverty in any significant sense. However, as a senator and presidential contender during the mid- to late 1960s, his beliefs had evolved into a world view quite radical by today's standards, though less so at the time.

Kennedy approached many things in his life with an intense passion. While this intensity sometimes came across as "ruthlessness," it was also, when combined with his ideals, a very magnetic and charismatic force. It is Kennedy's magnetism—and his belief in the ultimate goodness of American society—that has stayed with the many Americans, liberal, conservative, left and right, who claim his mantle today.

In the last years of his life, Robert Kennedy often paraphrased a quote from George Bernard Shaw when debating people who could not imagine overcoming real and entrenched obstacles while striving to create a better society. He would say:

Some men see things as they are and ask, "Why?" I dream things that never were and say, "Why not?"

I wrote this book to dare to dream about "things that never were"—about what would happen if the man known to the world as "Bobby" was saved from assassination in 1968. And as we live the "reality" of this dream expressed in the pages that follow, I hope to promote a deeper understanding of the forces shaping our *current* society and to reinvigorate the vision that was lost in the aftermath of Robert Kennedy's tragic death.

In writing "alternative" history or historical fiction, one is always conscious of those who would claim that certain "facts" within the narrative are "wrong." But history books are just as capable of containing "wrong" information, especially when one relies upon human recollections of conversations and events. Often in real life, two or more witnesses contradict one another. And, as anyone who writes biographies can attest, contradictions may emerge in how a biographical subject has related events over his or her lifetime.

Even the single event of Robert Kennedy being shot just after midnight on June 5, 1968, at the Ambassador Hotel in Los Angeles is mired in controversy. Witnesses disagree as to whether Kennedy or Paul Schrade, a union organizer and Kennedy aide, was shot first. Witnesses disagree as to whether Kennedy fell forward *before* he was shot or fell forward as a *result* of being shot. Some argue that Kennedy fell *backward*, and then disagree with each other as to whether he fell backward before or after being shot.

A couple of witnesses told police and investigators that they saw the convicted assassin, Sirhan Bishara Sirhan, talking to a young woman in a polka dot dress a couple of hours before the shooting. Several others told police that, just after the shooting, a woman wearing a polka dot dress was seen running out a door of the hotel yelling, "We shot him!" or words to that effect. Sirhan says he recalls speaking to a woman in a white dress, not a polka dot dress, earlier in the evening.

The physical evidence surrounding the assassination has been little better at providing a conclusive answer as to what happened that night at the hotel. Some investigators and historians say this was due to less than stellar police investigative work. Others believe the police work was so bad it had to be part of a larger conspiracy and cover-up. Did bullet marks penetrate the ceiling or were there simply marks or indentations resulting from other causes? Was the fatal bullet fired from Sirhan's gun or the gun of Thane Eugene Cesar, the hotel security guard who was next to Kennedy at the time? Reasonable testimonies, evidence, and analysis support both sides on these subjects.

Cesar himself has been the subject of controversy—and his own words and conduct have only deepened that controversy. Cesar owned two guns in June 1968—a .22 caliber and a .38 caliber. The gun Sirhan owned and used that night was also a .22, although a different manufacturer produced it. Did Cesar lie when he told police and others that he left his .22 at home but brought his .38

with him to the hotel that night? During the time Sirhan was shooting, did Cesar shoot his gun—or did he merely draw his gun but not shoot, as he has said? Cesar admits he initially told the police he had sold the .22 *before* June 5, 1968. Yet, he willingly produced a receipt to private investigators within a year or two after the assassination showing the gun was sold in *September* 1968. What particularly concerns some investigators and historians is the fact that Cesar strongly opposed Kennedy's political views. More ominously, Cesar was a supporter of former Alabama governor George Wallace, who was also running for president at that time on a platform that included incendiary racist views towards blacks and other minorities.

An investigative reporter, Dan Moldea, set up a polygraph exam for Cesar in the early 1990s. During the exam, Cesar said he never fired his gun at the scene with Sirhan and Kennedy. He also said he had his .38 on him at the hotel and that he left his .22 at home. The polygraph examiner, who had extensive credentials and experience, concluded Cesar was telling the truth. Still, those who believe in Cesar's culpability have raised questions regarding the polygraph expert's credibility. And so on.[2]

Moving beyond the assassination, one may also rightly ask, "Could Kennedy have won the Democratic Party's nomination, let alone the presidency in 1968?" There are those who believe Kennedy, by winning the California primary, had a real opportunity to win both the nomination and the presidency based upon the political, economic, and cultural forces existing in American society in 1968. Others, however, disagree with that assessment.[3]

The following questions are what ultimately frame this "What if . . .?" novel:

> *What* really *would have happened if Robert Kennedy had survived in 1968?*

and

> *If Robert Kennedy had survived and won election as president, in what ways would our politics, economy, culture, and place in the world as a nation and a people have been altered?*

In developing this book, I relied upon almost two hundred other books on American and world history, including biographies of various historical figures of the mid- to late-twentieth century—and nearly every biography of Robert Kennedy (by friends, foes, doubters, and mythmakers)—and a myriad of articles in magazines, journals, and in cyberspace. For the discerning non-fiction reader, I have hugged, as much as I deemed possible, the "agreed upon" historical facts of our time, to borrow the novelist Gore Vidal's phrase.

In addition to the "agreed upon facts," I also kept in mind the interplay between individuals and institutions. Here are several postulates that guided me in structuring this book: (1) one president may respond differently to events than another person who might have held that office; (2) people and political parties in and around government, business, and throughout our society respond to one president and administration differently than they do to another; (3) two different presidents or executives may follow the same policy, but with different results and responses, depending upon the advisers around them and their own personalities; and (4) a different dynamic may sometimes—often?—affect the timing of events, or whether such events will ever occur.

This book has been written so as to feel "real." It is not a "novel" in the "modern" sense. It is only a novel because it is about altered history. Yet, in writing this work, I also paid respect to a wise old saying, "Truth is stranger than fiction." Therefore, the novel describes not only events that many of us might have expected, but also—as a result of the altered dynamic—various events that are unexpected, ironic, and sometimes strange or funny. Kind of like real life.

And in case anyone harbors illusions of objectivity, let me state early and clearly that *A Disturbance of Fate* contains some rather strong polemics. For how can a work of this nature *not* be polemical when its purpose is to deal with ever-relevant political, economic, and cultural issues? Or when it concerns giving renewed life to a political leader who was martyred during a time of great controversy?

On the other hand, in a strong nod to the goddess of objectivity, I allowed the altered history to unfold in ways that, from time to time, surprised the polemicist author.

I should perhaps mention something about the book's prose, now that I may have conjured up the image of libertarian novelist Ayn Rand with all that talk of objectivity and polemics. Most of the novel is written in an active voice and with a relatively fast pace of dialogue and action to satisfy post-modern sensibilities. And what I shorten in pace I lengthen in space—meaning pages.

Somewhat paradoxically, today's most demanding readers want their stories to be fast-paced, but they also want works that reflect multiple layers of reality. To meet those demands, I made an effort to blend not merely actual "traditional white guy's" Western history, but also women's history, black history, labor history, business history, technological history, and world history. This reflects the fact, as more and more people understand, that there are all sorts of histories going on simultaneously, not just one "history."

I also blended political science, economics, anthropology, sociology, philosophy, and the physical sciences the way novels used to do in the nineteenth and early twentieth centuries—and are starting to do again.

As a final guide to the contents of this book, the reader may wish to note the following:

1. Most of the people identified by name in this book actually existed and were part of our history from 1968 through 1987. My goal has been to render their statements, conduct, and values in this work of fiction in a way that is either fair or at least reasonable. One expects, however, that others will have their own opinion of how well that goal has been achieved. The only purely fictional characters mentioned in this book are Ivan Gavenenko, General William Ignatius Herron, and Professor Julian Lewis. They appear briefly and are based upon no person in particular. Yet, they represent individuals who would likely appear at some point within a particular altered history. Yasha Aron, Suha Fayed and the Flores family are additional fictional persons mentioned once in news stories.

2. At the end of the book, I have provided source notes that deal with various events, people, and ideas. The notes compare and contrast our time and the time in which RFK survived, and are intended to contribute to the reader's sense of reading actual history.[4]

3. The main text deals almost solely with the time in which RFK survives assassination in 1968 and the years following his survival. If a comparison of time periods is made, the time in which RFK survives is called "the RFK timeline." Our actual history is identified as "the first timeline."

Whew! I, along with my patient editor and indulgent publisher, personally thank the reader for taking the time to read these opening comments before proceeding.

Part I:

A Disturbance of Fate

Chapter 1

A HOMICIDE AT THE
AMBASSADOR HOTEL

Sirhan Bishara Sirhan, armed with his .22 caliber Iver Johnson gun, spent most of Tuesday, June 4, 1968, practicing his shot at a gun club shooting range in a dusty town called Duarte, California. Although Duarte was culturally as far from Los Angeles as Kansas, it was only about a half-hour's freeway drive from downtown L.A. at most times during the day.

Sirhan was twenty-four years old at the time and was unemployed—with little or no prospects for landing any decent job. He was living east of Los Angeles, in the city of Pasadena, with his mother and two of his brothers. Sirhan and his family were Arab Americans, which at that time constituted a relatively rare ethnic group within America. Sirhan was himself born in the famed city of Jerusalem in 1944. His parents, born in Jordan, lived in Jerusalem with Sirhan and his siblings until they emigrated to the United States in 1957. Sirhan's father, however, never adjusted to American life and, within a few years, left his wife and family to return to Jordan.

Sirhan, now fatherless, attended high school in America, where he not only graduated, but also performed well enough in his studies to attend college. He did not last long in college, however, dropping out following his sister's death from leukemia in 1965. It was from this point that Sirhan's life took a slow, but steady downward turn. First, Sirhan tried working in a few different jobs related to horse racing, starting with some gofer-type positions involving the exercise and care of horses. Later, at the Santa Anita racetrack, he tried to become a horse jockey. With his five-foot-two, 115-pound frame, Sirhan seemed to have potential. But after falling from race horses several times—once, injuring his head to the point of being briefly hospitalized—Sirhan washed out and was told he was not jockey material.

Unlike horse racing, the art of shooting a gun revealed a real talent in Sirhan. Those who saw him at the gun club, including a husband and wife who were at the shooting range on June 4, and others who saw him before that day, were of the opinion that Sirhan was an "expert" at shooting targets.

Sirhan was quiet and moody to people who knew him, but his private thoughts were vivid and increasingly violent. He had been keeping a diary filled with random thoughts about women he loved who didn't love him, his frustrations and dreams, and more and more during the previous few weeks, expressions of his desire to kill Robert Francis Kennedy, who at the time was a United States senator seeking to become the next president of the nation. At one point, Sirhan wrote what became the most infamous phrase in his diary: "R. F. K. must die!" In other parts of his diary, he wrote of wanting to be paid for making this happen. But who would pay him for killing Senator Kennedy remained a mystery.

Sirhan left the gun club around 5 P.M. and drove his beat-up '56 DeSoto back to Pasadena. Over the next couple of hours, he met with a few of his Arab American friends, first at a hamburger restaurant and then for a while at Pasadena College, where he and his friends engaged in that perennial male sport of watching women walk by.

As Arab Americans, they had begun to feel the growing weight of Israel's triumph in the 1967 war against Egypt, Syria, and Jordan, the leading Arab nations surrounding Israel. In 1968, most Americans—including both Christians and Jews—were deeply sympathetic toward Israel. They saw Israel as a tiny "underdog" nation that had defeated a large, alien, and hostile Arab world. Most Americans were not, therefore, favorably disposed toward Arab Americans, and less so to Arabs in foreign lands. This disapproval proved to be a relative constant in the United States over the succeeding decades in our time, even as Americans often voiced displeasure at the Israelis for failing to do their best to end the cycle of violence in the Middle East.

Reacting to this social environment, Sirhan became increasingly vocal in his opposition to the state of Israel during the year spanning June 1967 through June 1968. It is not clear whether Sirhan's opposition to the nation of Israel was based upon religious, ethnic, or political grounds—or all three. But one thing was certain. Sirhan was not an Islamic fundamentalist, as some might assume in our time. Sirhan, in fact, was brought up as a Christian, specifically in the Eastern Orthodox religious faith. Sirhan strayed from that particular Christian faith in the mid-1960s, but first experimented with other Christian faiths, including the Baptists and the Seventh Day Adventists. From there, Sirhan drifted toward the Theosophical Society and developed an interest in the occult and self-hypnosis. He had, by 1967, abandoned most so-called traditional Western religions, including Islam.

On June 4, Sirhan was carrying within him his despair and anger at being unemployed, his belief in self-hypnosis and the occult, his opposition to Israel, and his growing obsession with Robert Kennedy. And, of course, he was carrying his gun. He also had just over $400 in his pocket, which was a lot of money to have in one's pocket at that time. However, it was all that remained of the lawsuit settlement he had received after the fall from the horse that sent him to the hospital. His mother had been holding the settlement money for him, but without any fruitful job prospects, he had begun to spend it in the months leading to June 4.

Sirhan was therefore not in the best of moods and quickly grew tired of watching young women walk by on the Pasadena College campus. He convinced one of his friends to leave the others, and together, the two young men returned to the burger restaurant. Sirhan then left his friend a short time later. While walking to his car, Sirhan picked up a newspaper and saw something that caught his eye. He read that a parade and fair was to take place in the Miracle Mile section of Los Angeles, near downtown, to celebrate the one-year anniversary of Israel's victory over the Arab nations.

Deciding at once to go to the parade, he drove to the Miracle Mile section of town only to learn that the celebration was scheduled for the next day, June 5. Sirhan, dejected at first at this news, went back to his car. While in his car, he looked again at the newspaper and realized that June 4—today, he thought to himself—was the day of the California primary elections.[1]

The primary elections that year took place in a highly charged atmosphere. Americans were polarized and frustrated over the nation's continuing war in the Southeast Asian country of Vietnam. Anti-war demonstrations had increasingly become scenes of violence between the anti-war protestors and the police. Racial riots were continuing to break out in various American cities, largely as a result of angry, young black males lashing back at racist, white-run city police departments. Further polarizing racial relations, just two months before June 4, 1968, a white assassin killed the most famous civil rights leader of the 1960s, the Reverend Martin Luther King, Jr. King had consistently preached a message of love, tolerance, respect, and non-violence. But King's murder instead sparked further rioting, anger, and fear around the nation. On top of this, Americans had become divided not only by race, but also increasingly by age and by cultural values—in terms of clothing worn, music and the arts, hairstyles, and even entire lifestyles.

Political observers at the time recognized that 1968 was a year of controversy, heightened further by it being a year where nationally-known candidates were seeking to become the next president of the United States. In the state of California, those seeking the Democratic Party's nomination for president included, among others, Eugene McCarthy, the U.S. senator from Minnesota and Robert F. Kennedy, the U.S. senator from New York. President Lyndon Johnson remained on the ballot even after announcing he would not seek reelection. After Johnson withdrew, Vice President Hubert Humphrey entered the race as a "moderate" on the Vietnam War.

Humphrey had personally refused to enter any state presidential primaries in seeking the nomination. He preferred instead to gather party delegates the old-fashioned way: in the back room, a handful at a time, or gaining support from many Johnson loyalists. In 1968, primary presidential elections were still considered an unusual way to run for president, as various state political parties were still choosing convention delegates at party caucuses and meetings.

Sirhan put down the newspaper and left his car again. He began to walk around the Miracle Mile area looking for some politically related event. He kept walking until he came upon the campaign headquarters of the then U.S. senator from California, Thomas Kuchel. A victory party was supposed to be taking place at the liberal Republican Kuchel's headquarters, but Kuchel was losing in the primary to his right-wing challenger, Max Rafferty. Not terribly interested in hanging around with a losing candidate's supporters, Sirhan took the advice of someone there and walked across the street to the Ambassador Hotel to check out the partying going on for the victorious campaign of . . . Max Rafferty.

At this point in the evening, Sirhan did not even know Kennedy was having his victory celebration at the same hotel. Sirhan was interested in the Rafferty campaign party because he had gone to high school with Rafferty's daughter. After arriving at the hotel, he walked into the ballroom housing the Rafferty celebration. While there, he guzzled down four Tom Collins drinks, saying at one point that they tasted like "lemonade."[2]

After trying unsuccessfully to start a conversation with a hostess at the Rafferty party, Sirhan started back to his car. Entering his car, he realized he was feeling too drowsy—drunk?—to drive. Sirhan then decided to return to the hotel to get some coffee. For a reason not yet apparent to the world, he took his gun out of his car and brought it with him, putting it in his pocket or under his coat.

It was now close to 9 P.M. Once back at the hotel, Sirhan decided to remain there. He talked with various people, including, for at least a moment, a woman wearing a polka dot dress. Sirhan told one person he spoke with that he was a proud Democrat. To another person, he played the cynical radical, saying that Kennedy was "a son-of-a-bitch . . . millionaire . . . [who] just wants to go the White House . . . But even if he wins, he's not going to do anything for you or any of the poor people."

Around 10 P.M., a woman who ran the Teletype machine inside the hotel saw Sirhan staring at the machine without saying a word. She asked him if she could assist him in any way, but Sirhan just kept staring before finally walking away.

He then entered the Embassy ballroom where the Kennedy campaign festivities were in full swing. Asking where he could get some coffee, he was directed to the kitchen or pantry behind and to the right of the stage where Kennedy was expected at some point to address the assembled. Sirhan, however, did not go to the kitchen. He instead walked in and around the ballroom trying to start conversations with Kennedy supporters.

By 10 P.M., Senator Kennedy had already known for a few hours that he had won the California presidential primary election over McCarthy and

Johnson (really Humphrey) and that he had scooped up the delegates from the most populated state in the nation. Kennedy was also pleased with his primary election victory earlier in the day in South Dakota.

Despite these victories, however, Kennedy was exhausted from the frenetic pace he had maintained since announcing his candidacy for president in March 1968. Kennedy had hoped to be able to rest and be away from crowds for at least one full 24-hour period. He had called some reporters earlier in the day and said he would make what he believed would be his victory statement from the wealthy beach community of Malibu, where he and his wife, Ethel, had been staying with a friend, movie director John Frankenheimer.[3]

The media, however, refused to oblige Kennedy, and Frankenheimer advised him to greet his supporters gathered at the Ambassador Hotel. Kennedy, wearily agreeing with Frankenheimer, realized that if he wanted media coverage, he would have to appear at the hotel victory celebration. Frankenheimer drove Kennedy to the hotel that evening. On the way, Kennedy told Frankenheimer not to drive so fast because, he said, "Life is too short . . . "

Sirhan, meanwhile, finally entered the kitchen behind the Embassy ballroom at around 11 P.M. Securing at last that somehow elusive cup of coffee, he told a dark-haired woman that he liked his coffee with sugar. According to one witness, he also asked around that time, "Is Kennedy coming this way?" The witness responded, "Yes"—and Sirhan smiled. He obviously realized he was now right where he had wanted to be, at least according to his diary notations over the previous weeks. And what better way to strike a blow for the Arab world, on the anniversary of the Six Day War, than against a pro-Israel politician like Robert Kennedy?

At 11 P.M., Kennedy was already at the hotel and had spent quite a while in his campaign suite with his family, his aides, and his most well-heeled or well-connected supporters. Shortly before midnight, Kennedy left the suite to go to the ballroom to deliver his victory speech. He walked into the ballroom and up to the dais with Ethel, and his usual entourage of aides and local area friends. Once on the dais, Kennedy basked in the applause and screams of victory from the crowd.

Kennedy then spoke to the television cameras and radio microphones and those gathered in the Ambassador Hotel ballroom. The victorious candidate began by thanking his supporters, his advisers, Ethel, and even the family dog, Freckles. With the magnanimity—some might say arrogance—of a general who believes he has won not only a battle but the entire war, Kennedy invited Eugene McCarthy and his supporters to join him in mending "the divisions within the United States," including the divisions over the war in Vietnam.

McCarthy was obviously not in the ballroom. He was miles away, licking his wounds from the day's defeats. Watching the television, McCarthy angrily said to his advisers that he had no intention of giving up the fight for the

Democratic Party's nomination. McCarthy reminded himself that he, not Kennedy, was the original "peace in Vietnam" candidate. And it was McCarthy who took on the incumbent Democratic Party president, Lyndon Johnson, in November 1967, after Kennedy refused entreaties from anti-war and other Democratic Party activists to run for that office. Kennedy had also promised McCarthy that he would not run for president in 1968. When Kennedy broke that promise and announced, in March 1968, that he was running for president as a "peace" candidate, McCarthy had some reason to be angry and even bitter. McCarthy vowed that night there would be a show-down between them later that summer at the Democratic Party national convention in Chicago, Illinois.

Kennedy, speaking in the ballroom of the hotel that night, was oblivious to how McCarthy or anyone else viewed him. He was, instead, seizing his moment. As he ended his speech, he said to the people in that hotel ballroom and around the nation:

> What I think is quite clear is that we can work together in the last analysis, and that what has been going on within the United States over a period of the last three years—the divisions, the violence, the disenchantment with our society, the divisions, whether it's between blacks and whites, between the poor and the more affluent, or between age groups or on the war in Vietnam—is that we can start to work together. We are a great country, an unselfish country, and a compassionate country. I intend to make that my basis for running over the period of the next few months.

After a pause, he concluded:

> So, my thanks to all of you, and now it's on to Chicago, and let's win there!

Jeremy Larner, one of Eugene McCarthy's campaign managers, later said Kennedy made his best speech of the campaign that night at the Ambassador Hotel. Although many outside observers might have disagreed, the crowd loved it. A feeling swept the ballroom that Bobby Kennedy, a man the press had often called "divisive" during the primary season, *would* persuade hard-hat steelworkers to work for peace with their radical college-age children, *would* cause white workers to want to work alongside black workers (even in the American South), and *would* successfully convince loggers to join hippie tree-huggers in protecting the forests. Yes, they believed, Bobby Kennedy would make the lions lie down peacefully with the lambs.

The feeling around the room enveloped Kennedy as well. Almost jumping off the platform in the ballroom, he was feeling more alive than he had ever been during the campaign—and, more than ever, he believed he had finally grasped the "luck" he always thought was necessary to ensure any political success. He knew he needed to return to his suite to begin making calls to various politicians, first and foremost Mayor Richard Daley of Chicago, who was known in those days as a Democratic Party king-maker. Kennedy had been told by his aides to go through the hotel kitchen next to the ballroom, and then take the freight elevator back to the suite.

Kennedy bounded ahead toward the kitchen with the adrenaline of victory. As he did so, he was well in front of his "unofficial" bodyguards, Rafer Johnson, Roosevelt Grier, and former FBI agent Bill Barry. At least two of those guards, not realizing Kennedy was heading quickly toward the kitchen, stayed behind to help a pregnant-with-her-eleventh-child Ethel Kennedy off the dais.

In June 1968, the federal government did not provide bodyguards for any presidential candidate, not even Robert Kennedy, whose brother John F. Kennedy had been assassinated while president less than five years earlier. Worse, when the mayor of Los Angeles, Sam Yorty, offered Kennedy police protection just before June 4, Kennedy vehemently refused. Worst of all, Kennedy prohibited his unofficial guards from carrying guns. This directive seemed especially ridiculous in the case of Bill Barry, who was an expert at using a gun to protect the lives of those he guarded.

Kennedy's guards, even without guns, were very strong and agile men. Rafer Johnson was an Olympic Gold Medal decathlon winner from 1960 and still in great shape. Roosevelt "Rosey" Grier was in his prime as a football player, a defensive lineman with the then Los Angeles Rams. Bill Barry was a highly respected and decorated ex–FBI agent. Barry let people know he was devoted to the Kennedy family in the same way a Rosary Society lady was devoted to the Virgin Mary.

Kennedy now entered the kitchen surrounded by a burgeoning crowd, including those waiting for him inside. From the swinging doors where Kennedy entered the kitchen, there was a row of steam tables on the left side. On the right were ice machines, freezers, and carts to hold serving trays. The rest of the room had the usual cookware, ovens, and other accoutrements of a kitchen. The middle section where people walked through the kitchen was narrow and long, and led eventually to the freight elevator.

As Kennedy began to make his way through, the only person close to him who seemed capable of protecting him from harm was the hotel's part-time security guard, Thane Eugene Cesar. Cesar, then in his twenties, hated the Kennedy family and was supporting the racist governor of Alabama, George Wallace, in the presidential race.[4] He was not supposed to be working that night, but had been called at the last minute to assist with crowd security services at the hotel. Unlike Kennedy's guards, Cesar carried a gun as part of his security work.

Cesar entered the kitchen just behind Kennedy, pushing his arms in front of Kennedy to guide the candidate through the crowd. The Kennedy people had made it clear to the security company and hotel before that night that nobody was needed to guard the candidate. This was communicated to Cesar, who was glad not to have to bother. But there he was, guiding Kennedy into the relatively cramped passageway of the kitchen. On the other side of Kennedy, also helping navigate through the crowd, was the maitre d' of the hotel, Karl Uecker.

Busboys, waiters, and supporters swarmed toward Kennedy to shake his hand, touch his shirtsleeve, his hair, anything. It had been that way since Kennedy's announcement seeking the presidency nearly three months before—and this night was no different.

Sirhan, standing toward the back end of the kitchen, now began to move through the crowd to meet up with his prey. Almost immediately, he began pushing people out of his way, moving closer and closer to Kennedy. As Sirhan neared the political leader he so desired to kill, he pushed a woman who, in turn, fell against a young hotel waiter named Vincent DiPerro. DiPerro was standing to Kennedy's right, near one of the ice machines. Despite the woman falling into him, DiPerro kept his ground. DiPerro then noticed Sirhan on the opposite side of the aisle, and also saw something shiny near Sirhan's belt loop on his jeans. He was already suspicious of Sirhan, whom he believed to be the same scrawny, seedy-looking man he had seen earlier in the evening talking with a pretty woman in a polka dot dress.

DiPerro yelled over to the maitre d', Uecker, "Hey, watch that guy! It might be a . . . "

Before DiPerro finished the sentence, Uecker's eyes met Sirhan's. As Uecker said later, "I just felt something—just looking at him."

Sirhan, recognizing the suspicion in Uecker's glance, started to pull out his gun from his pocket. Uecker, a hefty but quick fellow, pushed Sirhan back, and then immediately knocked Sirhan hard against the closest steam table. Just as quickly, Uecker jumped on Sirhan and started pummeling him. Sirhan tried to protect himself from Uecker with one hand, while using his other hand to reach again for his gun.

Rafer Johnson came running up and pulled Kennedy away from the center of the room and pushed—some said threw—Kennedy down between an ice machine and the partition that went about halfway through the aisle. Right behind Johnson was Rosey Grier who, upon arriving at the scene, ran over to help Uecker.

Seeing Grier and Uecker on Sirhan, Johnson looked toward Kennedy. He saw Kennedy on the ground on the side of the ice machine, holding his ankle and wincing in pain. Johnson also noticed Kennedy slightly bleeding from the forehead, a result of Kennedy hitting his head on the edge of the machine. Johnson instinctively jumped onto and covered Kennedy with his muscular, decathlon-trained body. He told Ethel Kennedy later, "That bastard was gonna have to shoot through me!"

Some people heard Sirhan scream, "Son of a bitch!" when he initially locked eyes with Uecker. But Uecker told reporters afterward that he never heard anything from Sirhan at that point. As Sirhan struggled against Uecker and now Grier, Sirhan's gun suddenly fell onto the table, next to Sirhan's waist. Somehow, Sirhan was able to grab the gun. Uecker continued hitting him while Grier grabbed Sirhan's wrist and twisted his hand almost palm-up trying to take the gun away from Sirhan. Despite wincing in pain from the powerful football player's grasp, Sirhan managed to fire off two shots, with the bullets blasting directly into the ceiling.

After the two shots fired, Kennedy aide and union organizer, Paul Schrade, joined Uecker and Grier. Schrade had been trying to hold back the crowd, but now realized that Sirhan was armed and aiming to kill. He joined Uecker in punching Sirhan in the face, neck, and stomach, while Grier continued to try and wrestle the gun from Sirhan's hand. A few people started yelling, "Break his hand! Break his hand!"

Grier, explaining later to Johnson how difficult it was to remove the gun from Sirhan, said, "He had a demon's look in his eyes."

Sirhan was somehow able to hold on to his gun. He got off another two shots, but both missed their target. One bullet lodged near the top of the opposite wall, and another ricocheted off the partition near the ice machines—and then lodged into the floor just inches from Johnson, who was still covering Kennedy's head and body with his own massive form.

Kennedy was dazed from the pain in his ankle and from being floored, then jumped on, by Johnson. Kennedy felt the blood from his forehead running down his cheek to his shirt, but later said he was not quite aware what was happening around him.

Thane Cesar, the hotel's security guard, fumbled to pull out his gun for what seemed to him like hours instead of less than a minute. Then, finally focusing well enough to get a bead on Sirhan, he yelled at Grier, Schrade, and Uecker, "Back off! Now!" Schrade and Uecker immediately pulled back from Sirhan, but Grier stayed to the side holding down Sirhan's hand and gun.

Sirhan was now reeling from the beating he had taken. He was also blinded by the kitchen ceiling lights shining in his face. Looking dazed, he began making a slight shaking motion that seemed like the start of an epileptic spasm. This gave Cesar enough time to fire his gun almost point-blank at Sirhan's neck and head, instantly killing the would-be assassin. Grier jumped further to the side at the sound of Cesar's gunfire before letting go of Sirhan's hand.

Sirhan's now lifeless body slid off the steam table onto the floor, his head shattered in a bloody mess. Rafer Johnson, hearing the gunshots, looked over at Sirhan's body and knew the danger had passed. He called out to Schrade and Grier, "Over here!" The three men carefully assisted Kennedy up off the ground.

Bill Barry, the third bodyguard, had arrived on the scene shortly after Grier and Johnson. But all the while, he was shielding Ethel Kennedy, who kept struggling to get to her husband. Ethel finally broke free of Barry's protective grasp as she saw her husband begin to stand with help from the others. Kennedy was writhing in pain, first from the effort of trying to stand, and then again from his wife's strong but fearful embrace.

Once Kennedy was standing, Grier and Schrade helped him as he limped toward the freight elevator. A lone photographer was a few feet in front of them snapping photographs. Ethel was just behind her husband, darting her eyes every which way. As Kennedy and the others approached the elevator, the television news cameras were finally able to get past the ballroom crowd and enter the middle of the hotel kitchen to shoot—with cameras—the now dead assailant.

The time was 12:18 A.M. on June 5, 1968, and a homicide had occurred at the Ambassador Hotel. Except this time, fate had found itself thwarted—at least for now.[5]

Chapter 2

RESURRECTION

The assassination attempt hit the nation and the world with the force of a heavyweight champion's punch. The photograph that most burned into people's minds was that of Kennedy being carried on one side by Rosey Grier and on the other side by Paul Schrade, toward the freight elevator. In the photo, Kennedy's arms were spread out over the shoulders of the other two men as though he was on a cross. His face reflected a mix of relief and somberness. Poor blacks and Hispanics, as well as Irish and Polish Catholics, saw in that photo a new Christ-like figure defying death. Some Italian Americans, also Catholic, who had not warmed to Kennedy in the past, were stunned into thinking they had liked him all along.

One of the first to call Kennedy's suite, within an hour after the assassination attempt, was Chicago Mayor Richard J. Daley. Kennedy had told his staff before the California primary that he could not win the nomination without Daley. Daley was the boss of bosses in Chicago and Illinois politics at that time. Daley also had a national network among other boss mayors and could deliver votes in any election, no matter what the situation. Daley was widely credited with tipping Illinois to John F. Kennedy in the 1960 presidential election, with voters who had addresses located in cemeteries and who, in the words of New York's Tammany Hall, "voted early and often."

Daley was an Irish American, as were the Kennedys. In 1968, Daley was in his early sixties, a generation older than Bobby, and suffering from a weak heart. He was almost as wide as he was long, breathing hard while carrying his weight. To describe Daley would be to describe the classic looking "backroom" or "machine" politician. Although he talked as if he had no formal education beyond elementary school, too many foes had gone down to defeat because they underestimated Daley's appeal and his savvy in winning elections. It wasn't all corruption, and Daley was very intelligent. He also had an ability to charm anyone, from presidents to housewives. When people walked into Daley's office, he made them feel "like dey wuz royalty," and that's how he talked them into doing what he wanted them to do for "da city."

Daley, unlike other big-city mayors, had relatively friendly relations with the minority community—despite his bouts with the Reverend Martin Luther King Jr. during the latter's civil disobedience marches and sit-ins in 1966 and 1967, and despite the fact that Chicago had racial segregation in housing and education as bad as, or worse than, any American southern city. The segregation was enforced through the realtors' board and the police. It was so acute that the only positive thing one could say was that the separation of the races appeared to have prevented race riots from occurring in Chicago, while other cities with less pervasive discriminatory housing patterns, such as Los Angeles, went through one or more such disturbances. But this lid of segregation wasn't going to hold forever, warned more than one observer—and it had already begun to break open. In April 1968, after the assassination of King, a mini-riot broke out, but the police kept things under control with brutal precision.[1]

What also separated Daley from other big-city white boss mayors was his devotion to his religion. Daley went to daily morning Mass on his way to work. Considering the corruption he allowed all around him and his willingness to accept the racial oppression of black Americans, it would be fair to question whether Daley understood the meaning of Christian charity and justice as opposed to the mere ritual of attending Mass. But Daley's devotion to his conception of Jesus, and the pacifism that animated some of Jesus' sentiments, began to spill over into Daley's political views.

By 1968, Daley became one of the few traditional establishment politicians to oppose the Vietnam War. One may argue, though, that his timing coincided with the fact that his sons Michael and Richard were of draft age. Nonetheless, like a true insider, Daley kept his opposition private but pushed President Lyndon Johnson for a peace commission as a way to honorably exit the war. The proposed commission died because Daley insisted that its chair or co-chair should be Robert Francis Kennedy, the senator from New York—a choice Johnson rejected.

Daley had been rooting for Kennedy to win the nomination but refused to commit himself before the California primary results. Daley had no respect for Humphrey ("Dat spineless Boy Scout!") and hated Eugene McCarthy, whom Daley saw as passionless. "Da way he talks an' acts," said Daley to his wife, whom he called "Sis," "you'd t'ink McCarthy wuz Episcopalian! Gene McCarthy's got no soul, Sis. No soul for people or his party!"

Daley had another reason to dislike McCarthy. Daley worshipped the Kennedys as though they were gods. McCarthy, on the other hand, was the equivalent of an "atheist" when it came to the Kennedys. Daley never forgot McCarthy's remark in 1960 that Jack Kennedy was "an amiable lightweight." McCarthy, during the 1960 presidential campaign and up through the Democratic National Convention in Los Angeles that year, had supported first Humphrey, then Stevenson, and even considered Lyndon Johnson for a moment—in short, anyone but a Kennedy. This was, in Daley's view, treasonous, especially for an Irish American.

Daley was gentle, almost fatherly, when he was finally able to reach Kennedy by telephone. Daley spoke first. "You alright, Bobby? I said a prayer for ya just before, an' I'm followin' up wit' a big one for Mass later this mornin'."

Kennedy replied, "Yes, Mr. Mayor, I'm fine, sir. Only my ankle's a little sore after being knocked down by Rafer Johnson. Lucky Rosey Grier didn't fall on me!" Johnson and Grier, who were in the room with most of Kennedy's main staff, laughed with the others.

The mayor then turned into a gruff and angry father who now knows his son is safe after a dangerous fall. "Damn it, Bobby, I don't want no jokes! You'z better take better care o' ya-self! Get a damned professional bodyguard service, if ya gotta. I hear Lyndon's finally gettin' dat bill goin' ta have Secret Service agents protectin' candidates—an' you're takin' as many as ya can get! Plus one! Enough o' yer superman stuff already! I already called my Department o' Investigation ta beef up security here for da convention—what wit' dat radical scum comin' ta da city ta protest an' all . . . I got more agents among dose smart-assed, snot-nose college kids dan dey'll ever know! So does da FBI an' even da army! Bunch o' book-smart bums ain't gonna outsmart us!"

Kennedy paused, smiled, and then spoke into the phone receiver. "Mr. Mayor, I have been getting the same speech from Ethel—well, not quite as eloquently—and I'm hearing it from my brother-in-law Steve, and everyone down to Sam Yorty, who told me he's still not supporting me. I have to say, Mr. Mayor, I will be more careful, but I won't go into a bulletproof glass cage. I gotta stay out there, seeing people, letting them touch—"

"Bull! Ya want my support, Senator?" Daley was serious. Calling Kennedy "senator" was a strong indication he meant business.

Kennedy softly replied, "Yes, Mr. Mayor."

"Well, ya got it. But only on da condition ya stay away from crowds for a couple o' weeks, t'rough da New York primary at least. I'm gettin' word out ta make sure ya get da support ya need ta take dat nomination. Ya wanna make speeches ta people? Make it a meetin' hall wit' total security—if people wanna listen on da outside, let 'em hear it over loudspeakers or sump'in. I got calls ta make in Ohio, Michigan, and New York for starters. An' don' t'ink it's over in Pennsylvania, neither. Dose people aren't as committed ta Humphrey as ya might t'ink. I, I, I can't promise first ballot," Daley paused, "but . . . " He paused again.

What Kennedy didn't know at the time was that Daley was on the verge of tears. "Bobby, I'm so glad dey didn't get ya," he said in words chopped up while trying to clear his throat. "I wanna see ya in my office first t'ing Monday. I'd ask sooner, but I got a family too, and I understan'. One more t'ing. Ya need anyt'ing right now? Ya okay? 'Cause just say it an' it's done. I loved your broddah more dan life—an' I ain't losing you, ya got dat?"

Kennedy smiled and said, "I got that, Mr. Mayor. And you know something, sir? I deeply appreciate the support you have given our family over the years. I can't thank you enough for your support this morning and everything you've said. I'll be there any time you want me. See you Monday. Goodbye, Mr. Mayor."

But the mayor wasn't quite finished. "Bobby, I jus' got one more t'ing ta say! Ya betta listen ta your wife more, hear me? She's right about da protection, an' she's prob'ly right about a lotta other t'ings, too! My wife, Sis, an' I, we always talk about politics an' t'ings, an' she knows t'ings about people, bein' a woman an' all, dat I can't see. Okay?" He paused.

Kennedy didn't respond.

Daley yelled into the receiver: "Bobby, okay?"

"Okay, Mr. Mayor!" Kennedy yelled back, the way a new recruit answers his drill sergeant.

"Fine," said Daley. "See ya, kid!" Click.

After hanging up the phone, Kennedy turned to Frank Mankiewicz and Joe Dolan, two of his trusted advisers during the primary election season. He said, "Well, if I can stay alive until the convention, we just got Mayor Richard J. Daley's support and—wait! We still have to chase Hubert Humphrey's ass all over the country for delegates!"

Screams and jumps of joy swept through the suite. Nobody heard anything Kennedy said after the word "support."

Kennedy held a press conference early the next morning that was carried live by all the networks. He thanked those who called throughout the night. President Johnson didn't call Kennedy's suite until 7 A.M. West Coast time, not too long before the press conference. President Johnson could be as persuasive as Daley, if not as charming, when he needed to be. Johnson told Kennedy he was announcing an executive order to provide Secret Service protection to all viable presidential candidates.

"Now, Bob," began President Johnson, who hated Kennedy about as much as Sirhan Sirhan ever did, "Ah know you don't lahk anyone thinking you need 'protecting' lahk some little boy in a big supermarket,"—Kennedy winced, wanting to tell the president to go to hell—"but Ah've signed an executive order that orders the Secret Service to start protecting you, Senator McCarthy, Vice President Humphrey, former Vice President Nixon, New York Governor Rockefeller, and maybe even Ronald Reagan, that movie star governor out there, through the Democratic and Republican conventions in August."

Ethel, who could hear President Johnson's voice booming through the telephone, smiled and made the Catholic sign of the cross when she heard Johnson speak of ordering secret service protection for her husband.

"Thank you, Mr. President," said a most formal Robert Francis Kennedy, junior senator from the great state of New York. Kennedy gulped down his own bile, not knowing the president was himself doing the same.

Johnson was trying to be civil, although, with others, he often referred to Kennedy as "that little shit." Johnson then said, "Ah wanted your permission, Bobby, 'cause Ah know you have consistently refused police protection in the past, and Ah didn't want you to think Ah was doing anything to embarrass you. With this vicious attack last night, Ah think your wife, at least, is gonna be on my side right now on this one—"

"You're right, Mr. President, she is."

"Good. So Ah can announce this and start the wheels rolling?"

"Yes, sir. I appreciate your concern—and respect your leadership—in announcing this order."

"Ah'm just glad you weren't hurt—or worse—by that madman. Now, Senator, when you get back home, back here, Ah'd lahk you to come and see me for a friendly chat. You, maybe Larry O'Brien, and Frank Mank-witz. Let me know in a couple of days if that's okay with you, will you?"

"Sir, would you mind if I also brought Joe Dolan?"

"Not at all, Bob, not at all."

"It will be an honor to meet with you, Mr. President. I'll call your office directly to let you know our schedule. Thank you again, sir. Goodbye."

"Goodbye, Senator." Click.

"That son of a bitch is up to something," he said to Ethel after he hung up the phone. Ethel, still floating between shock and joy at seeing her husband still among the living, said, "Bob, I wish you and Mr. Johnson"—in the Kennedy household, when speaking of Lyndon Johnson it was rarely "the president"— "would get over this horrible contempt you have for each other. It's going to hurt you more than him now. Remember, he's not running for anything anymore. He at least had the decency, and concern for you, to call before announcing the executive order regarding the Secret Service."

Kennedy shook his head. "Ethel, if I went on my knees to him and asked him to forgive me for every sin he thinks I ever committed against him, he'd just chop my head off. It's far too late for any 'kiss and make up' with that guy. Whatever I did during any campaign is nothing compared to what is considered 'normal' in Texas politics. I just don't get it and never will. I only wonder what he'll do to help Nixon if I get the nomination—"

"Bob, how can you say such a thing? Mr. Johnson wouldn't dare help a Republican, especially Nixon, and you know it! Nixon would undermine the civil rights programs, the poverty programs, all things Mr. Johnson fought so hard for and—"

Kennedy shook his head again. "I don't know, Ethel. All I hear coming out of that White House this past year, especially after McNamara resigned as defense secretary, is that Johnson decides whether he likes you or not by where you stand on the war and where you stand with me. And he feels betrayed by the black leadership's embrace of my candidacy on top of everything else. Look, Ethel, can we change subjects? We need to get back to Washington, plot our strategy for visiting a few states, and the New York primary's in two weeks— Oh my God! Why did I say 'on to Chicago' last night? Damn!"

"Bob, nobody's noticing that remark at all!" She and other intimates called him "Bob" much of the time. He, in fact, hated being called "Bobby." Ethel hated it, too, because it sounded less than respectful of him as a great man, not someone's "younger brother." To the rest of the world, though, he was still "Bobby."

She continued. "If anything, people want to hear from you—" She paused suddenly, fighting back a rush of tears, ". . . about . . . that . . . man who tried to—" Ethel sat down, put her hands over her head, and started to cry with heaving, deep sobs.

Kennedy, sitting next to her, hugged her around her shoulders, kissed her hair, and said, "Honey, honey, I am right here, right next to you now. I'm okay. I'm—"

She pushed him. "'Okay' isn't good enough! I . . . I . . . I can't stand the thought of losing you! I kept praying you wouldn't get hurt or shot at for all these months. All I see now is that someone's gonna try it again—and again and again and again—*until they get you!*" She was going to cry again but fought back her tears.

"Bob," she said softly, "maybe . . . maybe you ought to stop this campaign altogether."

The candidate started to stand up, shocked at what he had just heard.

"Stop!" she said, holding up her hand in case her voice was not strong enough.

He continued to try to stand, but his ankle hurt, and she pulled him back down next to her on the bed.

She continued, more boldly than before. "Now, listen, just for once, listen to me. I'm not saying this from some housewife point of view. And you know I backed your running, even last year when you were trying to make up your mind! I just talked with Joe Dolan, Bob. He says Humphrey's still four hundred delegates ahead of you and only needs three hundred more for the nomination. If you call it off now, nobody cares about shooting a senator like they do a presidential candidate or a president. There's always 1972 or 1976."

Kennedy was holding down his anger as he said, "Ethel, I can't see how you can say—"

"I said it and I'll say it again," Ethel said sharply. "I know I supported and even pushed you to go ahead with this chase before, but I did it clenching my teeth—because I knew *you* really wanted it. But your children and I . . . *We need you at home. Alive!*"

Kennedy was stunned by his wife's demand, for most husbands don't listen to their wives very carefully, in any era, and husbands usually miss any number of hints before a wife has to spell it out, usually screaming. He now asked plaintively, "Ethel, why didn't you say something before?"

"Because you blew up whenever anyone—Frank, Joe, Steve, Teddy—you name it!—even hinted you needed professional bodyguards, for one thing. How am I supposed to say don't run at all?!"

"I have Rosey, Bill, Rafer Johnson . . ."

"Who cares? You wouldn't even let Mr. Barry, an FBI man, have a gun! If it wasn't for that security guard with the gun, you would've been killed! You ran past all the guys last night and didn't care for anything that might have been—

and was—out there. And you're still missing my point! We have ten children now and one more on the way, and you're running around—"

"Ethel, we're only talking a couple of months to the convention. Don't you believe I can win this thing?"

Ethel shook her head. "Bob, I can't get through to you, can I? Why won't you just think of us, of our family—" She stood up, pointed at her swelling belly full of baby, and sighed, tears filling her eyes again.

The husband finally stopped being the candidate and saw the wife as a human being he loved, not a walking mannequin called "potential first lady." The husband saw the wife was not only serious, but demanded and deserved an explanation—or something. But all he could come up with was: "Look, Ethel . . . I—I don't know what to say. I really feel I can win this nomination. Daley's on board, we're sure to win New York in two weeks, and we're getting momentum from the California victory. Humphrey's stalled now, and I know I can win on the second ballot at least. McCarthy's through, and his supporters know that already. The convention will be here quicker than we can imagine. I will do anything for you—*anything!*—but I must finish this out."

She was starting to sob again, softly this time. The wife realized the husband would never understand. "You'll do 'anything'?" she asked.

"Yes, anything." The husband was almost laughing, but held back, not knowing his wife's state of mind—and knowing there wasn't "anything" he'd have to do that would be significant.

Ethel suddenly composed herself. She looked him in the eyes, and said, "Fine, Bob. Then what I want is for you to stop messing around with all these damned floozies and harlots who go after you like you're Elvis Presley!"

Bob edged away from her slightly, indignant. "What? What are you talking about, Ethel? I never . . . I l-l-lo—"

"Oh, Bob!" She pushed him further away from her. "You haven't *really* said you've loved me in years. No wonder you can't even say it out loud to me! I never told you I knew about these women, and whenever anyone ever said anything, I always denied it to them—and myself. But last night, when I saw you on the ground, and that madman . . . "—she clenched her fists to steady herself—"that man firing that gun, I vowed that if you got out alive, I wouldn't let you leave me for anyone—nowhere, no-how! Not for an office—and especially not for any other woman!" She stood up and almost screamed into his face: "I'll be *damned* if I let you go!"

She steadied herself and sat back down. He tried to hold her hand, but she pushed his hand aside. He then looked to the floor, wondering what else Ethel was going to say.

"You know," she said as she looked straight at him. "Bob, you *look* at me!" Kennedy looked up, his face more like that of a choirboy caught looking at nudie pictures than of a future leader of the free world.

Ethel continued. "I've given you a big family—something we both wanted, though you sometimes make it sound like it's only me who wanted it. I even isolated myself from my own family and became one with yours. I keep being told of your trysts—not as bad as your brother's cheating on Jackie, mind you—and some people were even telling me you were fooling around with Jackie after Jack's death, but I know Jackie wouldn't have done that."

Ethel was starting to cry again but got back on track. "Yet, I always defended you, and I denied every damned story up and down! And last night, Bob, did you realize you thanked the stupid *dog* before you got around to thanking me? I know you caught yourself, but really, doesn't that just show you where I stand? How do you think that makes me feel? Can you ever *begin* to understand that?"

Kennedy listened without saying anything. After some silence on both sides, he said, "I'm sorry, Ethel . . . I . . . I'm so sorry." He paused a few moments before suddenly blurting, "If I told you all the times I didn't do anything, with all these women throwing themselves at me, but I could have—"

"And that's supposed to make me feel better? That you could have been *worse?* I know a lot of men do this, whether in company offices or in government or where ever! God knows there are enough women out there who want to bed power, but there are more than enough men who manage to keep their marriage vows, Bob Kennedy, and you know it."

Ethel was angry, but she was also speaking with more confidence than she'd done since before their marriage. As a result of feminist "consciousness raising," as it was called in the late 1960s, this type of discussion had begun to occur more and more among married couples across America.

"Ethel, I . . . I am not going to talk about this." He suddenly recovered himself, stood up, and said, "All right, Ethel." He then realized he needed to touch her, not lecture her. He sat down next to her, stroked her cheek, and kissed it.

Then he said, "I'm sorry. I love you. See, I said it. And I mean it. I really *do love you.*"

But the gesture wasn't enough, and Ethel pulled away from him.

He persisted, grabbing and holding her hand with a firm tenderness to keep her from moving further away from him. "Ethel, I love our family, and I have loved, and will love, our life together. For too long I've been trying to be one of the boys, like Jack—like my father, for goodness sake—and I knew I was wrong. I knew that. Always! That man last night, whoever he was, and why he tried to do what he tried to do, it affected me, too. Not as much as those around me. It's strange to say, but I felt like something or someone wanted to protect me—besides Rafer and everyone. I don't know why. I have my own doubts, too, God knows." Ethel nodded and began to smile as he continued. "And maybe I owe it to you and the children to live up to their— your—view of me on my best days."

"Bob, I didn't mean to—"

"Ethel, you're right. Don't back down now. I've been a jerk, and I love you too much to deny that now. I . . . " He kissed her lips and caressed her as he hadn't since they were dating. "I love you, darling." They sat, kissing each other with a passion born of a second chance. They held each other close, finally falling back on the hotel bed and then laughing at themselves.

"Look at us, a couple of kids, and you're pregnant!"

"No, Bob. *We're* pregnant! It isn't just me, and it never is. And I do love you. And now," she said with a teasing smile as she pulled herself up slowly, "as you said, 'It's on to Chicago, and let's win there!'"

"New York, my dear. New—"

"I know that, you sweet fool. *I* didn't forget about the primary in the state you're senator from!"

"Oh my God! Now I feel even worse for saying 'Chicago' last night! My own state's primary is coming up, and I can't remember it!"

"And Bob?" Ethel was now walking toward the bathroom to do what ladies of the time called "freshening up."

"Yes, my love."

"You're firing Kristi Witker."

Kennedy looked shocked—again. "She was just with the kids last night. She was helping you, too. She—"

Ethel turned back toward him. "I mean it, Bob. Today."

Waving his hands in surrender, the candidate smiled weakly and said, "Yes, Ethel. Today." Of course, he left it to Frank Mankiewicz and Steve Smith to gently tell Kristi Witker, a twenty-two-year-old blond and shapely beauty, that her services were no longer needed at this time. Frank made a phone call to the Democratic National Committee to secure a position there to keep her quiet for a while. She later became a newsreader for a top metropolitan television station.[2]

Meanwhile, polls the next day showed "Bobby"—the press and the public continued to use that moniker—surging ahead around the country, even in parts of the South. People began defecting from the McCarthy campaign. Kennedy spoke only at town halls around the state of New York over the next two weeks before the primary there, while Dolan, Mankiewicz, and "Da Mayor" went around the nation gathering delegates. Kennedy spoke with confidence—albeit with a shield around him made from a new product called "Plexiglas"—and with an eloquence that people noticed and responded to more deeply than before California. He wasn't saying anything different than before. If anything, he was even less specific in his policy statements. The difference was in perception. People wanted to get a glimpse of and be a part of—and support—the man who had cheated death.

Jack Newfield, a journalist and adviser to Kennedy, watched with fellow newspaper reporters as 20,000 people shouted and applauded Kennedy's speech inside New York's Madison Square Garden, just before the New York primary. Newfield sighed and said, "Some day Robert Kennedy will lead his legions—the young, the black, the alienated, the romantic, the educated—to Armageddon and final victory."

Jack Nelson of the *Los Angeles Times* laughed at Newfield and said, "Jack, Bobby's just a rock and roll star like the Beatles. Even if he wins, he'll have to deal with a Congress filled with Strom Thurmond, Sam Ervin, Wayne Hays, and Wilbur Mills. Those rascals will eat him up so quick and easy they won't even burp."

Another reporter piped in. "I don't know, Nelson. Bobby stirred up the public like the Beatles even before he was shot at. Now it's like when John Lennon said the Beatles were 'bigger than Jesus.' Except here, Bobby *is* bigger than Jesus!"

Nelson shot back, "Yeah. And Newfield's talking about Armageddon when Bobby hasn't even got the nomination yet! You guys are no better than the public—your hearts are controlling your brains. This thing will blow over, maybe with a vengeance when people see his feet are made of clay. The higher he's up in the polls this week, the more people will switch at the first sign of trouble next week—or next month. You watch."

"Hedging your bets, Mr. Nelson?" asked a smiling Newfield.

They all agreed on one thing, though: Kennedy's chances for at least a second-ballot nomination by the Democratic Party were looking better and better by the hour. Conservative and Republican columnist William F. Buckley's prediction two years before about the "inevitability of Bobby" did appear to be coming true. Gone were the reporters' innuendoes in their stories of Bobby Kennedy's ruthlessness and cynical calculation. Gone, too, were those polls in states such as Indiana and California that showed him being seen by half the respondents as a "divider, not a healer."

The win in California wasn't as large as Kennedy's own staff had expected just a week before, but the assassination attempt wiped away most of the negatives. Even without the attempted assassination, the way the press and television had been covering the campaign as if it were a horse race, with constant talk of "momentum," the win in California was itself enough to turn the momentum his way.

All Mayor Daley and other political types needed to know was whether Kennedy could defeat both Humphrey and McCarthy. And the victory in California, with the largest delegate count of any state in the country, was enough to convince them—even without Sirhan's act of madness.

A week after the assassination attempt, a reporter asked Kennedy to comment on reports that Sirhan's diary said "RFK must die" because of Kennedy's support of Israel. The candidate replied: "I've not seen the diary, so-called. However, one can never truly know what is in the mind of a person who would do such a thing as to try to commit murder. My views on Israel are hardly controversial. I, along with many other senators and members of Congress, support a strong and safe Israel—as well as peace in the Middle East. I doubt any of the presidential candidates really differ here—well, maybe George Wallace has a different view!" The reporters broke up with laughter, and the quip, of course, was never included in their stories. What was quoted was Kennedy's parting line on the subject: "I simply can't comment any further. I'm not a psychiatrist."

Privately, he spoke with Frank Mankiewicz, his press secretary, and his long time adviser, attorney Joe Dolan. Kennedy told them, "The biggest irony is the Jewish vote in New York has finally swung my way. It's strange, really strange. The Jews never listened to me when I explained my strong record on Israel. Some called me a calculating politician for wearing a yar-mulker, or whatever—like I was the first non-Jewish politician to wear one! They keep punishing me because of my father, who admittedly wasn't very supportive of Jews in his days as ambassador to England. Now a nut from Jordan thinks I'm too pro-Israel and . . . and suddenly, I'm 'kosher!'"

Mankiewicz, who was Jewish, laughed with Dolan at Kennedy's largely unintended joke. But Mankiewicz stopped laughing long enough to say, "Just take the support, Bob, don't analyze it! And next time, it's 'yarmulka'! There's only one *r*, not two!"

Mankiewicz laughed again and said, "Bob, you're such a goy!" Now the two aides really cracked up, and Kennedy, realizing the word "goy" maybe didn't mean he was a "genius," laughed, too, but not as hard as the other two men.[3]

Kennedy, his momentum stronger than ever, swept more than 80 percent of the delegates in the New York primary election on June 18, 1968. McCarthy, angrier than ever at what he saw as the Kennedy mystique, said to a couple of reporters, "Well, maybe I would have done better if some nut took a shot at *me*!" McCarthy, who had been known to make funny, though often sarcastic comments, had finally crossed the line. A reporter with the Associated Press put it over the wire, and the comment became political dynamite, exploding in McCarthy's face.

Mayor Daley and Tom Hayden, former leader of the now-radicalized Students for a Democratic Society, strange bedfellows indeed, each said in their own way that McCarthy's comment had no place in American politics, and it showed McCarthy was out of touch with America. People were outraged at McCarthy's comment. President Johnson declared to his young assistant Doris Kearns, "What a loose cannon that McCarthy is. Even Bobby wouldn't be that stupid and mean—not with a goddamned reporter, anyway!"

McCarthy's natural reaction to adversity was passive detachment, which didn't help in the first twenty-four hours after he made the statement. His aides pleaded with him to apologize for making the comment. Instead, McCarthy dithered and became even angrier at Kennedy's political machine, which he said was behind the criticism. Jeremy Larner, by now McCarthy's most trusted adviser, prepared an apology for him.

McCarthy read it and rejected it. "I'm not groveling, Jeremy. The Kennedys tried to kill Castro, and let Diem and Trujillo get killed. Malcolm X knew more than he realized when he said of Jack's murder that 'the chickens had come home to roost'! And then, I make an offhand remark about *me getting shot— not Bobby! Me! And I'm supposed to apologize?* Ridiculous." By the time the next polls were out, McCarthy was dropping like a rock in a lake, with nothing but a few barely perceptible ripples left on top.

Finally, McCarthy's own staff came to him and said he should withdraw for the good of the antiwar coalition. McCarthy, by this point not only bitter, but frustrated with the glowing aura surrounding the Kennedys, called a press conference for the next morning. There he announced his withdrawal from the race for the presidency. When asked if he was endorsing Kennedy, he replied, "I endorse nobody today nor will I in the foreseeable future. It appears I might hurt whomever I endorse, so why bother? I am, however, freeing up my delegates to vote for whomever they please starting with the first ballot at the August convention. Thank you." And that was the end of Eugene McCarthy's candidacy.

Within forty-eight hours, it was clear that most of his delegates were going to vote for Kennedy, even those who had vowed they would never support the "usurper" of Gene McCarthy, who had had the courage to take on LBJ when Kennedy had initially failed to respond to the challenge. Most McCarthy delegates realized that ending the war in Vietnam was too important to stand in the way of personal loyalties—and consistency.

Tom Hayden and Allard Lowenstein[4] were very instrumental in making sure McCarthy delegates didn't coalesce around another potential antiwar candidate, such as Senator George McGovern of South Dakota, or Vice President Hubert Humphrey, who had made noises that he was interested in ending the war now that he was running for president. However, Humphrey, in deference to President Johnson, wouldn't make a public statement opposing the war, and that was enough to convince most McCarthy delegates to switch to Kennedy.

Kennedy's staff had prepared a chart, the day of the California primary, showing what it would take for a first-ballot victory at the Democratic convention set for late August in Chicago. They thought they could reach the magic winning number of 1,312 delegates through a strategy of gaining Daley's endorsement, making "pork-barrel" promises to key state office holders in the Midwest, begging some McCarthy and Humphrey delegates to switch, and conceding most of the South to Humphrey. More than likely, they believed, a win would come only on a second ballot, again with the hope that some other compromising middle-ground candidate did not come forward.

By the time of McCarthy's withdrawal on June 24, 1968, Humphrey saw the writing on the wall. Humphrey, who had grown to admire Kennedy's commitment to the poor and the minorities, asked one of his most trusted aides, Ted Van Dyk, to approach Larry O'Brien at the Kennedy campaign headquarters for a meeting. Humphrey had told Van Dyk, on the day of the California primary and before the assassination attempt, that he hoped Kennedy would "win decisively" in California, even if that improved Kennedy's chances for the nomination.[5] After the assassination attempt, Van Dyk continued to travel with Humphrey, but found his candidate had "lost the fire in his belly." Humphrey's momentum had stalled even in the first timeline. Here, with

Kennedy racing toward the Democratic convention, Humphrey was starting to lose the delegates he had picked up outside the primaries.

Lyndon Johnson was furious when he found out what was happening from one of his White House advisers, Joe Califano, who was also advising the Humphrey campaign. Johnson immediately demanded that Defense Secretary Clark Clifford, a well-entrenched Democratic "fixer" from the days of Harry S. Truman, find anybody—*"Anybody!"* screamed Johnson—to challenge Kennedy at the convention.

Johnson talked with Clark Clifford about setting up a "Draft LBJ" movement. The president did his best to start acting like a candidate, but finally Clifford said to his longtime friend, "Mr. President, I could find somebody to push this movement if I looked hard enough, but it would not in the least stop Bobby's coronation in August in Chicago. And right now, as you told me just before the California primary, even Nixon could work better with this Democratic Congress than you can. As you also said, sir, and I must be blunt here, you already told the country you won't run again."

The president, frowning, muttered, "Clark, everyone's deserted me."

There just wasn't any fight left in the president, which was saying a lot about a tough and fearless politician like Lyndon Baines Johnson.

On July 8, 1968, Humphrey announced in a press conference that he had decided he would rather take a "rest from active politics for awhile" than create a divisive convention for the Democrats. Lyndon Johnson was apoplectic, even though he'd known this was coming for almost two weeks. He shouted at Joe Califano, who was leaving the administration to join Kennedy's campaign, "Joe, did you watch that press conference of Humphrey's today? Ah lost all respect Ah ever had for him. How the hell could Humphrey give up without a fight? Ah always said he had no balls. No balls at all! Why, the Vietnamese would have walked all over him! Damn it, Joe! That little shit Kennedy is gonna be the nominee—and win! Then he's gonna pull us out of Vietnam, with the reporters talking about how brave he is—not that their editors and publishers will let that shit go out too strong, being good Republicans and all—and people will blame *me* for the damn war, when it was *the Kennedys' goddamned war to begin with*!"

The president covered his head with his hand for a moment, then released it, yelling, "But great God-all-mahty! Kennedy versus Nixon—*again?* Ah can't wait to see *that* debate, the two tight-assed bastards!"

Joe Califano could only shake his head and bow out quietly from the Oval Office.

President Johnson may have been as bitter as McCarthy, but he was right about one thing, at least: Bobby Kennedy had, indeed, defeated all his rivals in the Democratic primary without firing a shot. Well, maybe with a few misplaced shots fired in his direction.[6]

Chapter 3

TRYING NOT TO LOSE

The only people more depressed by Kennedy's resurrection than President Lyndon Johnson were those running the Nixon for President campaign. Frank Shakespeare, on leave from the CBS television network, and Roger Ailes, a twenty-eight-year-old whiz-kid television producer, were handling media strategy for Nixon. They didn't like what they saw on the television screens every night, with people screaming to get a look at, let alone a touch of, Robert Francis Kennedy.

The two of them were at Shakespeare's home, having lunch with Harry Treleaven, Nixon's advertising director. Treleaven had been a reporter for the *Los Angeles Times* before becoming a major advertising consultant for a large New York ad agency.

Shakespeare spoke first. "Gentlemen, the latest polls show we're down big with Kennedy. Even Humphrey, had he stayed in the hunt, would be making it a race."

"Kennedy's the nominee, guys. Let's stay focused," said the youthful yet somewhat portly Ailes. "Right now, he's got the highest TVQ," which meant that Kennedy scored big with voters when he went on television.

"Fine, Roger, fine. I know the score," said Shakespeare. "The problem is we prepared this campaign for Nixon as one where we watch the Democrats continue to shoot themselves in the foot, head, and other vital body parts, keep Wallace voters thinking a vote for Wallace is a vote to elect a civil rights Democrat, while we keep Dick Nixon under careful and tight media control. Then we squeak out a victory this November. If we're behind, and we've got Kennedy uniting Democrats, then we have to change the script, don't we?"

Harry Treleaven sat back and said, "Nonsense, Frank. Just a little change, don't you think?" He looked around and saw Ailes looking, at best, neutral. "It's simple, guys," said Treleaven. "We just go negative. Negative ads against Kennedy. Not pro-Nixon. We run it through outsiders so they don't think it's from our campaign, at least not until it's over. We need to deflate the Bobby love-in with a few well-placed and well-phrased ads. That will start to do the job. Remember, guys. Dick Nixon isn't running against Jack Kennedy—Mr. Glamorous, Mr. Smooth. This is ruthless Bobby, the always-says-the-wrong-thing-and-pisses-people-off *little brother* Bobby Kennedy. And what some people call his 'growth,' we'll call his inconsistency. He was for the Vietnam War; now he's against it. He says he's for blacks' civil rights, but last month, debating McCarthy in California, he says he's against integrating them with white people in Orange County. I was talking with Len Garment, our best legal guy outside of John Mitchell, and he says it's pretty well known in the Capitol that LBJ hates Bobby with a passion. There isn't any Rose Garden strategy expected to come out of the meeting Bobby had with LBJ last week. Far from it!"

Reports in the press said that Kennedy and three of his advisers did meet with President Johnson. The meeting was inconclusive. Kennedy's campaign had him pose for a photograph with a semi-smiling, tense-looking Lyndon Johnson. There was no specific endorsement. Johnson simply said in a public statement from the White House, "I expect and hope that people will vote Democratic from top to bottom." Kennedy pointedly told reporters that no promises for a specific endorsement were asked for or received.

Johnson had privately told Doris Kearns, whose help he wanted in writing his memoirs, "The little shit may make a good president, Doris. He seemed more grown up in this meeting Ah had with him. God knows neither he nor Ah were ever meant to be vice president to anyone. Ah just can't get behind him, though. And," smiling, "Ah wouldn't get in front of him either."

Treleaven was not aware of the inside workings at the Johnson White House, but it wasn't hard to figure out from the scuttlebutt around town. He continued his presentation to Ailes and Shakespeare. "We don't need Johnson to endorse Nixon. We just need him neutral and telling other Democrats to be less than supportive of Kennedy at the top of the ticket. Again, I think with some well-placed negative advertisements—I already spoke with Kevin Phillips on our staff about how we should set this up. Have you seen Phillips' analysis of how you win an election by knowing 'who hates who'? He says that exploiting white fears—and, yes, that means using racial appeals if we have to—that's the vehicle we use to gain strength in the South and parts of the West. A more subtle George Wallace approach, where we do it through code words, winks, and nods. You know, talk about welfare, welfare queens, law and order. Great stuff. It's genius, fellas, just genius! The ads we do have to be different, though, in different parts of the country. For the Northeast, where there are too many minorities, we just show Bobby's inconsistency on Vietnam and race issues. The point is to make people say, 'We don't trust Bobby.' In the South, we highlight his consistency, not his inconsistency, on civil rights with his brother and in the Senate. In the West, we highlight his antimilitary stance on Vietnam and his wanting to cut the defense budget— remember, there are a lot of union defense workers there. Through the ads, we bring Bobby back to earth and then exploit the differences in the Democratic coalition just like we were planning to do with McCarthy or Humphrey."

Roger Ailes was nodding and starting to feel better enough to eat lunch. Shakespeare wasn't convinced, however. "Harry, that takes you part of the way, but not all the way. I won't underestimate the power of the Kennedys, nor will I underestimate LBJ's loyalty to Democratic Party machines and congressmen. The presidential election isn't the only election this year, as you well know. I don't think Johnson hates Bobby enough to screw up the Dems' hold on Congress—"

"Frank, do you think the Dems are vulnerable enough in Congress that LBJ can't screw with Bobby and still get his pals in Congress elected?" asked Treleaven. "You can't be serious! There isn't a chance in hell the Republicans can take the House, let alone the Senate, for chrissakes!"

"Harry, this isn't about whether Congress stays Democratic this year. I know it's Democratic, and it will stay Democratic for quite a while. But if LBJ is seen as screwing over Bobby for personal reasons, it could start a civil war among Democrats that will be the equivalent of a nuclear bomb with mutually assured destruction within the entire Democratic Party. LBJ doesn't want to lose a war and blow up the Democratic Party at the same time—at least I don't think so— and we can't think like that anyway."

"Why not?" said Roger Ailes with some reticence. Ailes, who would normally be aggressive and confident with a mere politician, had been the equivalent of a church mouse listening to these immortal television and advertising men.

"Because," said Shakespeare, "Johnson's gotta play too cagey even for him if he wants to start telling people to split ballots, one vote against Kennedy and one vote for the local congressman, around the country. It's one thing to try to beat your political rivals. It's another thing to piss off the party money men, people like Clark Clifford, Jack Valenti, Averell Harriman, people like that. There are lots of jobs to fill in the executive branch, Roger—always remember that!"

"But what does Lyndon Johnson have to lose if he's going back to Texas anyway?" asked Treleaven. "I say this. Let's at least make it our strategy to neutralize Johnson to the point where he doesn't do anything for anyone. Let him look presidential and above it all. That can only help us. Kinda like what Ike did to Nixon in '60."

"Harry, we're already on that," said Shakespeare. "We've got Billy Graham, one of them big-time evangelical southern preachers who's in love with Nixon. Ever see his TV show crusades for Jesus? They're great ratings grabbers! Anyway, he's getting chummy with LBJ on our behalf. Nixon tells Graham how much he respects Johnson and all, and Graham, who is our best diplomat to the Southern vote—Phillips calls it the Yahoo Belt—goes and runs to LBJ and tells him what Nixon said. We hope it will soften LBJ up, and with more statements by Nixon that he wants an 'honorable peace' in Vietnam, and telling Graham privately that he would also be seeking victory, that may be enough to keep Johnson from helping Bobby."

Ailes loved the way Shakespeare and Treleaven fed off each other, when they weren't otherwise clashing in the last two weeks.

But Shakespeare was back at Treleaven again. "There is one major problem, Harry, I have with your negative ad strategy. It will always get back to our candidate and—I hate to say it, but I will—the press will seize the chance to say the old 'Tricky Dick' Nixon is back. The press hates Nixon because Nixon hates the press. I wish Dick would just get it that he needs to schmooze with these guys. He just won't, and so they work hard to make him look bad. I wish it was because of the liberal bias, like Dick says, but it isn't. The reporters and editors love Rockefeller, Romney, and when they get to know him, they even like Ronald Reagan. The one thing I'm sure about the press isn't whether they're liberal or conservative. It's that they're vain, lazy, and always looking for flattery. And flattery gets you nearly everywhere with those whores!"

"Harry, remember—" Shakespeare stopped suddenly and turned sharply to Ailes. "Roger, never take notes at meetings like this. You never know how things would look to outsiders who aren't here, just reading someone's cold mental notations. Now Harry,"—a pause—"and Roger, you might not remember the flack LBJ took on that ad with the girl holding the flower and the A-bomb going off during the last election campaign. You think the press will let Nixon off easy? We've spent a year talking about 'the new Nixon,' and negative ads will wipe that out, I can almost guarantee it!"

Ailes nodded again, looking as somber as when the meeting began. Although his candidate's prospects were not terrific, Ailes was feeling better about his own prospects. Since the mid-1960s, Ailes had been the successful producer of an afternoon talk show hosted by a former second-rate, 1940s-era crooner. Ailes was a firm believer in success in America, and here he was now, the son of a blue-collar worker from Ohio, sitting in New York City with two powerhouses of television and advertising. Ailes knew, like these two executives, that television was the new way to run campaigns and mold public opinion—with Nixon being as good a lab rat as any to test that theory. Nixon, with his ever-present five o'clock shadow and general creepiness in front of a camera and especially crowds, was being transformed into a "new" and "friendly" Nixon with the use of the same camera.

"The camera never lies," most people believed at the time. Ailes, however, knew better. The camera tells people what the producer wants them to see, and it could be the "truth," whatever that was, or anything else the producer wanted to have someone else believe. To make the transition from the old Nixon to the new Nixon, in the minds of voters, Ailes had helped script "interviews" for Nixon during the primary season to make it appear Nixon was spontaneously answering questions from "folks on the street." The questions and answers were as carefully scripted as any *Playhouse 90* TV series from the 1950s. The people were carefully chosen—often including at least one Negro, but not more than one. "Don't want to upset the white voters," said Ailes. And Nixon spent more time in makeup than Bette Davis or any other aging Hollywood actress.

The strategy had been working up to the time of the attempted assassination of Bobby, and Nixon was more than grateful. He had, by June 1968, become almost completely dependent on Ailes, Shakespeare, and Treleaven. It had not taken Ailes long to realize that, while working on Nixon's campaign, he wasn't just polishing up his Rolodex. He was becoming someone people wanted on *their* Rolodexes.

"Gentlemen," said Shakespeare, "we've got a problem, and we better get to solving it or else we're looking at a second Kennedy administration—and it won't be pretty for Republicans or most institutions and people we hold dear."

"It's still not even the Fourth of July. We just have to be ready by Labor Day in September," said Ailes, trying to be hopeful.

"No, Roger!" Treleaven was sharp. "We've got to have these attack ads out now if we're going to be ready by the end of August. We have got to take the risk of ruining Dick Nixon's new image. I understand your concerns, but," he hesitated, and then, after an awkward silence among them, he finally said, "I didn't want to say this, even to you fellas, because it's supposed to be as quiet as one gets in these things, which we know is never quiet enough. Anyway, in just a few weeks, Bobby Kennedy's campaign might well implode in any event."

Treleaven's voice was down to almost a whisper. "What I want you to keep really quiet about is this: I just spoke to a publisher friend at Simon and Schuster. He said there's a book coming out on Bobby Kennedy by Victor Lasky, a good Republican operative with CIA ties to boot. He was basically done with the book, and it was in final galleys, when that Ay-rab tried to shoot Bobby. Lasky initially agreed to delay the book, thinking the attempted hit was a ruse by ol' Joe Kennedy and his cronies to put his boy over the top. I thought so initially myself. I mean, all those shots fired and nobody's hit, not even the 'magic' waiter who saw Sirhan's gun?"

Ailes said, "You mean, a publicity stunt, kind of like what some people said about Sinatra's son's kidnapping?"

Harry Treleaven answered, "I never knew what to make of that one, either. But this time, I was so convinced it was a set-up that I even asked my own contact at Simon and Schuster, what kind of dumb assassin would think Bobby Kennedy would be so pro-Israel that he should kill him? *Too* crazy, right? Well, Lasky, to his credit, saw that lead was not gonna go anywhere, even if it made for a good mystery novel. He decided he'd better make sure the book got published sooner rather than later, what with Bobby's numbers and stuff. The publisher is not Simon and Schuster, but one of their subdivisions. But it will get wide distribution. I heard about this because, when Lasky told the publisher to publish, the publisher started fighting Lasky, saying that publication should be delayed further, maybe after the election, in light of the shooting attempt. Lasky got pissed and called in his friends from the CIA, including CIA 'assets' in the publishing business, and friends of friends at the top of Simon and Schuster. He threatened to take the book to other publishers—he could always shop it to Regnery Press, which is close to Bill Buckley's *National Review*. Plus, Simon and Schuster knew that Lasky's book on President *John* Kennedy was a best-seller for the last few months of Jack's life. So even a liberal outfit like Farrar Strauss or Grove Press might scoop it up if given the opportunity. Needless to say, the division publisher caved, and the book is coming out in a few weeks."

Shakespeare thought a moment and smiled. "Yes, this Lasky book could prove interesting. Lasky could give Nixon the screen we need. Yes. Yes, indeed."

Ailes basked in the glow of the two fixers but wondered how it would all play on television. Who cared about books, anyway?

The three media operatives for Nixon knew the Democratic Party had significant fissures—and Robert Kennedy knew it, too. Kennedy knew the New Deal coalition was crumbling in the face of the war and the continued march for civil rights. And while he was often at odds with the late Mrs. Eleanor Roosevelt, the widow of the saintly Franklin Delano Roosevelt, and even more at odds with most of the New Deal political types in New York and elsewhere, he saw the importance of maintaining that coalition by refocusing on an aggressive domestic agenda that favored jobs more than "hand-outs." He desperately wanted to move forward with his jobs program and Marshall Plan–like assistance to overcome rural and inner-city poverty. He also saw the need to pursue environmental protections and other far-reaching, technologically based policies to continue the job train so that it reached all Americans.

In just a few years since his brother's murder, Robert Kennedy had become an almost Popular Front-type of New Dealer, even as he voiced doubts about "handouts" and "welfare." In speeches at home and abroad, he wondered aloud on more than one occasion about whether he might have become a follower of the Latin American revolutionary Ché Guevara if he had been born poor instead of rich.

Kennedy, after receiving word that Humphrey was bowing out, huddled with his advisers to strategize for the convention and unite the Democrats for the fall campaign. He was worried about the radical young group known as the Yippies, and their plan to disrupt the Democratic Convention. But in truth, he now had little to fear from these radicals, who were reeling with defections from their "counter-convention" plans. First, Tom Hayden, who had been part of the early Yippie movement planning, dropped out to formally join the Kennedy campaign the morning after the assassination attempt. Next to join the Kennedy camp were longtime SDS member Rennie Davis and the radical folksinger Phil Ochs.[1]

Dave Dellinger, an older radical who was friendly with the SDS and the Yippies, was starting to hear his labor roots call to him that this was no longer the moment to attack the Democrats. Dellinger was fairly convinced that Kennedy would end the war. He also saw that respected black leaders viewed Kennedy as genuine, even if Dellinger still had some doubts. There was a time to disrupt and a time to join. Suddenly, this was not the time to disrupt, at least not the way the Yippies had been planning. Dellinger opted out of the Yippie counter-convention, too. Without these influential activists, thousands of would-be volunteers also dropped out of the planning effort.

Kennedy, who had organized his brother's senate and presidential campaigns, as well as his own, knew not to be too passive when bringing strange bedfellows into a candidate's coalition. To bring student radicals and Daley together was going to require direct dialogue. Kennedy was not satisfied to hear from Allard Lowenstein that the Yippie counter-convention plans were falling apart. He wanted, he told Lowenstein, to put another bullet in the body to make sure it was dead. Lowenstein winced at the imagery coming from Kennedy, but he had heard that, since the assassination attempt, Kennedy seemed to be unconsciously using shooting metaphors, to the discomfort of everyone around him. With his closest advisers and Ethel warning him about such metaphors, Kennedy had begun an effort to break the habit, but with mixed results at best. Luckily, he hadn't gone public with any of the metaphors—yet.

Tom Hayden was specifically invited to attend the convention strategy meeting at Kennedy campaign headquarters in Washington, D.C., to discuss Abbie Hoffman and Jerry Rubin and their Yippie plans to disrupt the Democratic Party convention. Hayden showed up at the headquarters dressed in a shirt, suit, and tie, trying to be "Clean for Bobby" after being "Clean for Gene" McCarthy. His wavy black hair was combed as best he could manage.

Hayden still looked like a post-acne, pock-marked Irish Catholic choirboy from the Midwest. It was hard for him to fully ignore not only his Irish roots but also the family's politics. His father had been an anti–Franklin Roosevelt Republican, a surprise to outsiders who only knew Tom Hayden the radical. Once one went past this superficial family rebellion, one could also see that the son had maintained his father's instinctive distrust of liberals and progressives who denied the mysteries of faith—religious or secular—which, in turn, led the son to associate himself with radicals and even Communists.

Regardless, Hayden hadn't spoken with his father for the past two years. His father was in no mood to speak with him, either, since he was a former marine who couldn't accept his son's opposition to any military action taken by the United States. Lacking any current relationship with his father, Hayden had begun to see Robert Kennedy as a father figure, replacing his other now-fallen father figures, Jack Kennedy and Martin Luther King Jr.

The meeting Hayden attended consisted of all Irish Americans—except for the Jewish, and anything but Irish, Allard Lowenstein. The Irishmen included, in addition to Hayden and Kennedy himself, Kennedy advisers Joe Dolan and Larry O'Brien. Dolan was a long-time Kennedy friend and aide going back to Jack Kennedy's run for the senate, even before the successful 1960 presidential campaign. O'Brien was not only a Kennedy mainstay, but managed to stay friendly with Lyndon Johnson, becoming U.S. Postmaster General under Johnson before joining Robert Kennedy's presidential campaign in April 1968.

As Hayden entered, Kennedy extended his right hand and said, "Nice to see you, Tom."

Hayden shook hands like a hearty Mayor Daley pol trying to keep the senator and likely presidential nominee from knowing how nervous he really was. Hayden was nervous because he had been taking heat from SDS radicals for being a turncoat and a traitor to "the cause." Even after radical McCarthy supporters went over to Kennedy after the New York primary win and McCarthy's implosion, their intense hatred for Hayden actually increased—for being a "premature" Kennedy supporter.

The new phrase coming into vogue, "The personal is the political," largely used by women feminists against men who wanted their girlfriends to make coffee while they made revolution, was already taking on a more ironic meaning as the student movement descended into the same personal sectarian fights that had broken out on the Left and within the labor movement in the 1930s and 1940s.

Kennedy was nervous about possible wiretaps at the meeting and ordered the campaign headquarters debugged before the morning of the meeting. He wondered if Hayden had followed the instructions given him for how to come to this meeting. He plunged ahead, however, saying, "Tom, please. Sit down."

Kennedy kept speaking, departing from his script when Dolan and O'Brien were supposed to speak. "Tom, we asked you to come today to see if we can mediate between Mayor Daley and the Yippies, and see if we can just call off this planned counter-convention or make sure hardly anyone shows up on their behalf. We thought you'd be a reasonable choice to represent the students' interests in a meeting we're going to propose to Mayor Daley. The mayor, to whom we've briefly spoken, has indicated a willingness to talk, at least tentatively."

Hayden gulped. He would be the representative? Boy, these guys don't get it, do they? he thought to himself. Hayden knew that if he met with Mayor Daley and did anything other than call him a fat, freakin' racist pig, he'd be burning more than bridges with regard to any political future he could ever have with the wine-and-cheese liberals who were hanging on to the words of any and all radical elements in the SDS and the Black Panthers at the time. Kennedy couldn't read Hayden's mind but saw his hesitation.

"Tom, what is it? Are we asking for the impossible?"

"No, Senator, not the impossible. Just, uh . . . " Hayden couldn't tell Kennedy what he really felt, but then he did. "It's just that you don't really know how radicalized the students are, Senator. They've been beaten up mercilessly for over three years, and all they get is crap—as if they were the ones beating up the cops! They're spit at by old Legionnaires and the union guys like nothin' better than cursing at us as we walk by construction sites, calling us names and stuff."

Allard Lowenstein, the New York political activist who had connections with the civil rights and student antiwar movement and yet maintained close ties with mainstream Democrats such as Humphrey and Kennedy, said, "Tom, we know that. You know we're looking to bridge the gaps here. That's why we asked you here today."

"No, Mr. Lowenstein, you're still not getting me," Hayden said. He knew him well enough to say "Allard" or even "Al," but this was a formal meeting, it seemed to Hayden. "What I'm trying to say is that I don't think even if Mayor Daley came out and said he loved the student radicals that they'd listen—*as long as I'm there.*"

"What?" said Lowenstein and Mankiewicz in unison. Kennedy was dumbfounded. Lowenstein said, "What do you mean, Tom, as long as *you're* there? How could you have no credibility with student leaders? Is that what you're saying? I've not heard that! Ever!"

"Look, Al—I mean, Mr. Lowenstein—"

"Cut the formal stuff, Tom. It's okay to call me Al in front of the senator."

"Okay. As I said. Look, Al. You don't know what goes on inside the SDS, any more than I know whether George Ball is supposed to be really opposing the war in Vietnam when it looks like everyone's all in agreement in the Johnson administration. I have been saying to movement people since March—at least the ones speaking to me—that if the Democrats nominated Gene McCarthy or Bobby—uh, the senator here—we should go into the Democratic Party and work together to bring the war to an end after November's elections. We supported the Democrats in helping pass civil rights legislation, and while we didn't get what we wanted in total, we got a heck of a lot. Here, all we're asking for is pulling out of Vietnam, and Senator Kennedy will do that as president, I believe. Al, I'm getting called a cutthroat politician and a turncoat worse than what you and I called each other following Freedom Summer a couple of years ago."

Lowenstein remembered, and smiled wanly. The candidate forced a smile, wondering what the hell he was going to do if there was any disruption in Chicago.

Joe Dolan decided he needed to take over the direction of the meeting. "Tom, who should we get to represent the students' interests with Mayor Daley? We have to think strategically here if we want to create a coalition that will defeat the Republicans this November—and end this war in Southeast Asia, right?" Dolan, a lawyer for over twenty years and closer to Hayden's father's age than to Hayden's, did his best not to sound like a parent, but he was not of this generation and never would be, even if he wore a loud tie, grew his hair below his ears, and listened to the Grateful Dead for three straight days while smoking marijuana. Hayden ignored the condescension lurking deep in Dolan's tone of voice.

"Mr. Dolan, you need someone like Rennie Davis, even though I'm not sure he's enough. Maybe Phil Ochs, too, based upon him being a celebrity of sorts to the student movement leaders."

"Ochs? Phil Ochs?" asked Kennedy. "Is he the folk singer?" Lowenstein nodded. "The one who wrote the song about my brother? I can't recall the name of the song, though . . . "

"I know the song," said Hayden. "The song was . . . " He hesitated, realizing the name of the song, "uh . . . um . . . it was called 'Crucifixion.'" Hayden quickly pushed aside his embarrassment over the name of the song and said, "But, Senator, if I might . . . I mean, even Ochs has problems among movement people. Bernadine Dohrn, she's a *real* radical in the SDS. She said to someone I know recently, 'Ochs is a sucker for any Kennedy'—uh—um, as I am, I guess, too. I—" Hayden's face turned beet red as he said this, all the more so because it was true.

Kennedy smiled and turned away briefly to give Hayden a chance to recover.

"Tom," Kennedy said gently as he looked back at Hayden, "it's clear we can't stop everyone from coming, but stopping most will do. Can this Ronnie Davis fellow make a difference?"

Lowenstein spoke confidently. "Uh, it's Rennie, Bob. Yes, Rennie Davis can do it. Davis is a respected antiwar protestor and still high up in the SDS, right Tom? His dad was an economics professor who worked on Truman's Council of Economic Advisers, so we can tell that to Mayor Daley. And—"

Hayden broke in, more confident than Lowenstein, but challenging him. "Al, it's still not enough. You need Dave Dellinger, too. Ochs won't be taken seriously enough, even though he is strong on the issues. He's loved, but he's still a singer, not an organizer. Dellinger's the key. You'll never get Abbie Hoffman and Jerry Rubin to back away from this counter-demo anyway. However, the more you isolate them, the more they scream their 'Politics of Ecstasy' and 'Fu'—I mean— 'Screw on the Beaches'—and other slogans. If Rennie Davis and Dellinger stand there and say something like 'There must be peace in the peace movement,' that could be more than enough to defuse the situation."

Larry O'Brien, ever the strategist, asked, "But can we get Dellinger to talk with us?"

Hayden sat back and smiled. "That's up to you guys. Dellinger is one tough pacifist. I never know when he's to the left of me or the right of me. Maybe Al will have better luck than I've had."

Lowenstein laughed knowingly and said, "I don't care where Dellinger stands. I just want him on the inside of the hall pissing out, not outside pissing in."

Kennedy laughed at the two young men. "Tom, Al, you guys are already starting to sound like Daley!" The older men laughed a lot harder than the two young men, who looked warily at each other and wondered what kind of bargain they were entering into.

Hayden called Rennie Davis, who was more than glad to agree to meet, seeing the nihilism creeping into the Yippie movement Rubin and Hoffman were creating. Lowenstein had a student intermediary friendly with Dellinger approach Dellinger. Dellinger was reluctant but was clearly worried about Rubin and Hoffman, who he believed were beginning to resemble ad men more than revolutionaries.

Dellinger, a half century old in 1968, was a pacifist and a leftist who had agitated against World War II—spending time in jail as a war resister—agitated again during the Korean War, and now was in charge of the national committee that had mobilized against the Vietnam War. Dellinger had seen agent provocateurs before—the guys who were the most gung-ho for the cause turning out to have been spies—but concluded Hoffman and Rubin were too wild to be anyone's agents. That really made them dangerous to serious organizers such as Dellinger. Dellinger agreed to meet, but only after making Kennedy wait for two days.

Davis and Dellinger met with Kennedy, Lowenstein, and Larry O'Brien at an apartment owned by a friend of Frank Mankiewicz's in New York City. Dolan was in the Midwest working the delegates and told Kennedy that O'Brien was more than up to the task of keeping the meeting in order. Kennedy and O'Brien knew this was a very dangerous meeting. There was always the possibility of an LBJ or Nixon campaign wiretap. After initial pleasantries, Dellinger immediately turned to matters of substance, not strategy. He wanted to get to the heart of the matter of Kennedy's commitment to end the war.

"Senator, I do believe you are genuine in wanting to end the war in Vietnam. I do believe that. I must ask, though, are you ready to do so even if you are blamed for 'losing' Vietnam, which you will be in some powerful corners, if not the mainstream? And I know you know what that means. That means one term for you. I hate to be blunt, but I want to know why I shouldn't put my body on the line against you and Nixon both."

Kennedy smiled, trying to hide his rising anger. "Mr. Dellinger, I have every intention of pulling our troops out of Vietnam, come what may politically at home. I know the populace is pretty volatile on this subject and could be led to believe that I, or my administration, 'lost' Vietnam, as if it is ours to lose in the first place, and as if we aren't losing already among our allies and many people in America. I know the consequences of being perceived as weak, too, and plan to be aggressive in helping to rebuild Vietnam, helping them have meaningful elections, as we did with Europe."

Dellinger winced at that last statement because he knew American post-war involvement in Europe didn't begin and end with the Marshall Plan. The Marshall Plan was seen by Dellinger and some revisionist historians as a screen for the millions of dollars used to bribe officials and even voters in Italy, France, and West Germany away from voting for Socialists and especially Communists. Dellinger also knew the United States supported and paid for the Gladios, armed men from the surviving Fascist and Nazi movements in Europe who, after World War II, harassed, and sometimes killed, not only Communists, but also non-Communist labor leaders and resistance fighters—the same labor leaders and resistance fighters who had fought on the same side as the United States against the Gladios' heroes, Hitler and Mussolini.

Kennedy ignored Dellinger's wince because he didn't understand what Dellinger could possibly be thinking about. Kennedy continued. "And I plan to be aggressive in working to create a thaw in the Cold War with both the Russians and the Chinese. Unlike my brother and me the first time around, we're going to listen to nationalist leaders in third world nations who want to improve their nations' well-being even if they want to do it in ways that we don't approve of from an *economic* standpoint. We will, however, insist on, encourage, and support movements dedicated to democracy. If people vote not to have a two-car family and a television in every room of their homes, then that's their vote."

Dellinger was impressed overall, despite Kennedy's innocence about American foreign policy after World War II. Dellinger pressed on, however. "I'm a union supporter, believe it or not, Senator. I just have no use for boss union-ism as practiced by the likes of George Meany and even Walter Reuther."

Now it was Kennedy's turn to wince. He thought to himself, I can take criticism of Meany—that old bastard's making noise that he may support Nixon. But, geez! Reuther, too? I always have to defend Reuther from being called a Commie—and now, this radical tells me Reuther's a "boss unionist"?

Dellinger was being a bit rough. Reuther, although he was publicly silent on the matter, was known to oppose the war. And unlike some union leaders, he let his lieutenants in the union he led, the United Auto Workers, publicly voice their opposition. Reuther allowed this freedom to voice anti-war opinions despite the fact that the UAW not only covered autoworkers, but also workers in the military weapons industry. Reuther did not officially endorse Kennedy until late June 1968. He wanted to make sure he could be somewhat clear of Lyndon Johnson's vindictiveness. Kennedy understood as he was very close to one of the Reuther lieutenants, Paul Schrade.

Reuther had more than enough enemies at the moment. Besides fighting battles from both the left and the right within the UAW, Reuther in 1967 had broken completely from George Meany and the largest association of unions, the AFL-CIO. Besides the usual personal reasons for the split, a significant policy dispute separated the two union leaders. Reuther openly called for unions to organize the South to maintain labor's power against corporate America. Meany, on the other hand, believed such an organizing effort was neither wise nor possible to achieve.

Dellinger noticed Kennedy's reaction to his Reuther remark and dared Kennedy with his eyes to challenge him directly. Kennedy, not one to easily back down, decided to take Dellinger on.

"Mr. Dellinger, I think it's important to note that I asked you here to listen to you. However, I also wanted to gauge your willingness to be part of a coalition that will bring important changes to this country and end a war that is being fought over the wishes of many people, not just students, but even some corporate leaders." Here Kennedy was thinking of his friend Thomas Watson, who was head of IBM, a giant corporation. "We know there is a planned counter-demonstration during the Democratic convention in Chicago next month. We asked you here because we are interested in having you speak with Mayor Daley and reach some sort of rapprochement to not disrupt the Democratic Party's convention in a way that is counterproductive to everything you wish to accomplish regarding the war in Vietnam.

"But, honestly, Mr. Dellinger, if you speak and act with Mayor Daley the way you are speaking and acting with me, we won't get anywhere. I applaud your pacifism, even though I am not a pacifist, but I also applaud the ability of those who work with people they may not like in order to achieve a common goal that is good for our nation. I am never going to live up to your expectations, and if I did, I'd be more surprised than you. I just want to do a few things as president. I'd like us to get out of the war in Vietnam and lessen if not alleviate the tensions in the Cold War. I'd like to reform labor laws so farm workers, textile workers, and steelworkers, particularly in the South and the West, can more easily form unions and have better benefits for themselves and their families. I'd like to see us live up to President Truman's platform and secure a program of health care for all citizens. I'd like us to start cleaning up our rivers and forests and limit the pollution we are suffering from in our cities, and even suburbs. Maybe even promote public transportation. Now that may not be radical enough for you, but it is radical enough for most people, I'd say."

It was certainly too radical for O'Brien. If this room is bugged, he thought to himself, we're dead screwed. Lowenstein, who hoped to hear Kennedy talk about these things in concrete terms, at least after the election, was happily shocked. He knew Dellinger would not have a comeback other than "What do you want from me, Senator?"

Dellinger, reeling from Kennedy's words, said, "What do you want from me, Senator?"

"I want you to have a civil discussion with Mayor Daley, who, if you have any contacts out there leaking information from his office, you already know is against the war in Vietnam, too—and, this may surprise you, has a better relationship with important black leaders in Chicago than you'd ever know. Daley may be old politics, but if we're going to change things, we can only do it by bringing along the old politics with us as far as we can. The more we bring pols like Daley along, the more chance we'll have to succeed and not go out too far where we're cut off from the mainstream of America. And we owe it to the country to try to do that, don't you think?"

"Senator, I won't argue with you on that one, even though I want to. Except I don't understand the meaning of any meeting with Mayor Daley. We're already willing to tell whomever we can not to disrupt this convention next month. I understand that. I am just concerned that you think I'm gonna go to a meeting with a boss mayor and grovel to him, or apologize for being an activist trying to make this country better than the racist fiefdom he runs in Chicago—"

Lowenstein jumped in for Kennedy, who he thought was going to lose his temper and blow up the entire meeting. "David, David," Lowenstein said, waving his hand in front of Kennedy and Dellinger across the table. "I completely understand your feelings on this, I really do." Kennedy gave a look that showed that he didn't understand and didn't share any of those feelings. Dellinger noticed this, too.

"David," said Lowenstein, "the point of this meeting is to look for common ground: your opposition to the war in Vietnam. You're a union supporter, as you noted to us before. I am, too. So is Mayor Daley—I know it's not the same type of support, but it's still about paying people a good wage, raising the minimum wage, about jobs and free health care for everyone. It's important just to let him know that you can talk to him and that his beliefs about you, the antiwar movement, and all are . . . uh . . . " He struggled for the right words. " . . . um . . . uh . . . not complete. Yes, that's it. His viewpoint of you is not complete."

Dellinger shook his head. "Al, this is precisely where you and I always go our separate ways. I don't get what I'm supposed to talk about with a guy like Boss Daley. I told you. I will break my usual rule and try one more time to support a Democrat who promises to end what I consider to be an illegal war since all war is already immoral. I also recognize I'll be in a 'coalition,' as you would call it, with Daley, and maybe a few other people like him, a prospect that disgusts me, truth be told. I just wanna know: What am I supposed to talk about with Daley, if I'm not just kissing his ring?"

O'Brien broke in with a mature authority. "We want you to tell him, face to face, you're not going to disrupt the convention and that you'll tell others to do the same. We want you to tell him that you want him to do nothing in return. *Nothing!* All you want in reality is that he show your group some respect at the convention—"

Dellinger shook his head and sighed. "What makes you—*any* of you—think I'm gonna want to be on the inside listening to silly-assed convention speeches? What makes you think I'm a damned Democrat?" Dellinger was starting to get out of his chair as he said this.

O'Brien was working to keep his cool but was losing that battle. "Mr. Dellinger, please *sit!* Thank you! Now look. When I say 'show your group some respect,' I'm talking about *you* in terms of the entire antiwar protest movement! There will be McCarthy delegates there who hate the mayor as much as you, if not more than you. There will be the Hollywood set there, Paul Newman, Warren Beatty, you know, those folks, and Daley's had no use for any of them— ever! Bob—I mean, the senator—has got to bring these elements together to make sure he can get elected to end this damned war once and for all—and, I might add, bring a little more racial harmony to this nation before we have any more race riots."

Rennie Davis, with his thin build, Buddy Holly–1950s' eyeglasses, and boyish brown-blond wavy hair, was so quiet he was barely breathing throughout the meeting as he watched these "titans" battle for position. After gasping for enough air to speak, he stood up, figuring correctly it would give him more power. He then spoke slowly but clearly. "I'm willing to go to Chicago, I mean, to the convention there, and support the senator. I'm willing to sit with the mayor and give him some sense of ease that we aren't here to embarrass people unnecessarily—"

"Rennie," said Dellinger sharply, also jumping up, "what the hell are you saying? *Of course we are there to embarrass people!* That's the whole *idea* of agitation, damn it!"

"I know that, Dave, I *know!*" said Davis. "But this time, we gotta pay some respect to get some respect. If I don't get respect back, I figure nothing is lost at this point. Last year I never thought we'd get the Democrats to nominate a peace candidate for president. Tom didn't really think so, and neither did anyone else I know. Did you?"

"No, but it's only another promise—"

"I know that, too, Dave! But this promise is a lot better than LBJ's promise to let the local Vietnamese 'boys' fight it out." Davis turned sharply to look down at Kennedy as he said this. Kennedy nodded and smiled in approval. Davis looked back at the old pacifist, Dellinger, and said, "It's like love, man, . . . isn't it? You gotta take the risk to love again, even if you've been burned. If you don't, the hate will consume you."

Dellinger sighed, put his hand on Davis' shoulder, and said, "You kids never cease to amaze me. One moment I gotta stop you from grabbin' a gun and try-ing to shoot it out with police—that was you and Tom a couple of months ago in April!—and next, I feel like I gotta keep you from falling in with the old, tired, corrupt, machine-boss party hacks. I dunno." He sank back into his chair and turned to the senator, saying, "I'm willing to give all this a try. I'm on board. I just hope my mentor, Saul Alinsky, back in Chicago understands."

Davis sat back down, beaming.

"Sal who?" asked Kennedy.

Allard Lowenstein and Rennie Davis laughed the loudest on that one, while Dellinger was not a little disgusted.[2]

Chapter 4

DALEY MEETS THE RADICALS

Kennedy left it to Larry O'Brien to mediate the meeting of Dellinger, Davis, Mayor Daley, and one of Daley's most trusted confidantes, Thomas Aquinas Foran. As part of the promise to meet with "dose radical bums," Daley demanded that Foran be present with him—"Just so there's no mistakin' what's said." Foran was the U.S. attorney for the Northern District of Illinois at the time and was formerly a senior lawyer for the city of Chicago.[1]

The date of the meeting was set for Thursday, July 25, 1968, but Kennedy was unable to go to Chicago at that time. Instead, Kennedy and his top aides had decided that he would begin his foreign trip—to Europe, the Middle East, and the Soviet Union—a trip that had been planned in the days just before the California primary. Kennedy and his advisers now called the foreign trip his "presidential trip" because it was designed to reaffirm Kennedy's status as a world leader.

O'Brien nervously accepted his assignment to be the mediator between Daley and Foran and the two radicals. The first thing he did was to tell Dellinger and Davis to come separately, to tell nobody where they were going—to maintain deniability for all sides, if necessary—and to meet early in the morning at Daley's office after Daley went to Mass.

On the morning of July 25, O'Brien opened the meeting with introductions. Daley was on his best behavior, as if greeting a ward alderman whose support he needed for a library project that wasn't being built in the alderman's ward. Daley, however, had his own strategy for the meeting. He had told Foran to play "pit bull" in case things got out of hand or if the radicals needed a lesson in what Daley called "respect." Foran could play that part, not only because he was a federal prosecutor but also because he looked more like a young, '40s-era, white heavyweight boxer than a lawyer.

Daley and Foran did not realize, of course, that they were dealing with David Dellinger, who knew a thing or two about negotiation strategy. Dellinger had already discussed with Davis the same strategy of "good cop, bad cop," with Davis set to play the good cop while Dellinger played the tough cop role. O'Brien was also ready for the "good cop, bad cop" routine with both sides, even though neither he nor any of the others let on. It was too obvious, O'Brien reported to Kennedy beforehand, that this was how the meeting was likely to go.

O'Brien, after the introductions, reminded Dellinger that the mayor had strong doubts about continuing the war effort in Vietnam, and wanted a bombing halt and negotiations to begin immediately for a withdrawal of U.S. troops. Daley nodded in approval at O'Brien's statements. Foran was a little surprised that Daley let O'Brien speak for him. Daley, however, respected O'Brien's savvy. He also wanted to gauge where O'Brien was going.

The mayor and Kennedy had their own discussions before this meeting, and Daley was now waiting to hear O'Brien confirm what was expected of him, if anything. Daley was initially upset when he heard that Kennedy was not going to be at this meeting. Kennedy called the mayor and truthfully told him he was keeping his promise to Ethel that he would be a "homebody for a few weeks" after the New York primary. This promise to stay home for awhile, he told Daley, had resulted in the delay of the presidential foreign trip, which also meant that he could not attend the meeting in Chicago.

"Home" for Kennedy was not just the place where the wife and kids lived. It was a place that was also called Hickory Hill, and it contained the house Bob and Ethel had purchased from his brother Jack Kennedy in the mid-1950s. It was a house with a long and distinguished history. During the first two years of the nineteenth century American Civil War, it had been the headquarters of Union General George McClellan. It later became the home of former Supreme Court Justice and Nuremberg Tribunal Justice Robert Jackson. Hickory Hill was about a half-hour's car ride from Washington, D.C., but was a world away as far as Bob, Ethel, and their brood were concerned. The five-and-a-half-acre property was nestled in a particularly lush, green, elite suburb not too far from the secluded CIA headquarters in Langley, Virginia, and was just northwest of Arlington, Virginia, where Jack Kennedy's remains rested under an eternal flame.

Sitting in his home office talking on the phone with Mayor Daley, it was not easy for Kennedy to keep the mayor from entirely canceling the meeting. Kennedy said, "Mr. Mayor, when you think about it, nobody's asking you to agree to anything. You just have to talk with these fellas about how you're all working together to make sure there aren't any counter-demonstrations during the convention. You'll find these fellas, even though people call them radicals, are reasonable as well—"

Daley huffed at Kennedy. Then he said, "Bobby, I don't need deeze guys for nut'in'! I got my informants in der movement tracking der every screwed-up move. Dey ain't got nut'in' goin' right now, I'm tellin' ya! An' even if dey did, I got my police officers in trainin' for riot control an' shuttin' down demonstrations before any trouble starts. Deeze wise-guy bums can come wit' a hunnert t'ousand kids an' we'll shut 'em down so fast nobody in da press will notice a t'ing."

"My advisers indicate, Mr. Mayor, that national television networks are expecting, and want, to see action, even blood, and they'll report whatever your forces do, just like the networks covered the demonstrations for civil rights in the South. And that would be bad—"

"Bobby, ya goin' soft on me? What is dis garbage! We can shut down *any* press, includin' TV! I squeeze da local networks an' dey squeeze der bosses in New York an' L.A. We done it before, Bobby. You wan' me ta meet wit' deeze bums, I will. But dey're nut'in'. Jus' nut'in' but bums! Like I said, I'll meet wit' 'em. But I ain't agreein' ta nut'in', an' dey better not try ta push me aroun' with der college-kid, book-smart crap tellin' me I gotta be a goo-goo or sump'in!"

"Goo-goo" was a phrase Daley and some other politicians used to denigrate people who stood for what was called "good government," or government electoral reforms such as open public meetings, conflict-of-interest disclosures, and the like. Daley thought such views were naïve or childish.

"Mr. Mayor, I appreciate your willingness to meet me halfway on this one. I understand your points well, but if my campaign is about anything besides the war, it's about getting the generations to talk with each other—and having students learn to work with government officials and union leaders to make a better place for all of us. You weave your usual charm with these kids—one of 'em isn't a kid, but an older fella who's a pacifist and—"

"A Commie! Bobby, whaddya *doin'* wit' deeze characters? Are we goin' crazy here?"

"Mr. Mayor, we're not here to invite them into our administration. We're not even here to make friends with them." Bobby paused here, knowing maybe he *was* starting to make friends with them—well, he was friends with Allard Lowenstein, who was friendly with them. He said before Daley spoke again, "We're here to make sure they don't deliver the white suburban vote to Nixon this fall with any demonstrations. That's what I'm talking about. No more, no less, sir."

"Awright. I know, I know. Ya been dere before, dealin' wit' dem Southern governors an' radical Snick people.[2] I guess we gotta deal wit' deeze bums— an' dey are bums, Bobby. Long hair, don' bathe regular, don' go ta no church, an' Jews, Bobby, an' not even Jews who are like da Jews I know, who go to der church or temple or whatever an' work hard at der jobs—most Jews I know are good people, but not deeze odduh guys." He stopped for breath and started again. "Bobby, I wouldn' do dis for nobody else but you an' ya family. I guess it's betta ta stop 'em by talkin' 'em out of it. But I ain't beggin', Bobby! Got that? I ain't beggin' ta *nobody*!"

"Mr. Mayor, I can't thank you enough. We'll try this meeting. If it doesn't work, then you and your finest men in blue are gonna have to do what they have to do to protect the convention and your fair city." He gulped at what he was saying, but made the best of it. "Thank you, Mr. Mayor. I'll have Larry O'Brien contact you to set up the date and time."

A tense Kennedy spoke that very afternoon with O'Brien, who visited Hickory Hill to discuss the meeting and a couple of other matters related to the August convention. Kennedy was screaming, mostly at himself, for having given too much room to Daley to blow up the meeting with the radicals. If the meeting with the radicals blew up, Kennedy told O'Brien, it would allow Daley to try out his forces' riot control against student radicals coming to Chicago seeking vengeance against the Establishment. Kennedy, straddling both sides, could simply be swallowed up in the resulting chaos, if not violence. "Larry, this meeting between Daley and the radicals has got to succeed. There's no failing on this one—*no fail!* Got that?"

Kennedy sat down at his desk and ran his hands through his thick brown hair. "I'll be gray before this is over, Larry. Before I used to think I'd get killed, but now I think I might die of a heart attack like Stevenson. Nah! I'll just turn gray, maybe have a stroke, kinda like Dad . . . " Then he looked up at O'Brien and said, "The thing I don't get is, why aren't these kids going to protest at the damned *Republican* convention? Why us?"

O'Brien, who knew this was coming, having wondered this himself for some time, said, "Senator, the president who is in office right now is a Democrat, not a Republican. The president before him was a Democrat. The war started, with ground troops at least, on their watches. And the Congress is Democratic controlled, even if half of them, especially in the South, vote like Republicans with the Republicans. And it isn't as if electing a Republican will end this war like Ike did in Korea. Republicans have supported this war in Vietnam every step of the way and continue to call for expanding the war, whether it was Nixon—at least before his 'secret plan to end the war'—and Goldwater before him. But at the end of the day, they weren't in the president's chair when this thing really got rolling."

"But Larry, I'm the *peace* candidate! This doesn't make sense! They ought to be protesting at that other convention, especially if it's Nixon or Rockefeller—or whoever becomes the Republican nominee for president."

"The only other thing I can figure, Bob, is they expect the Democrats to listen—and not beat the shit out of them for protesting. I dunno. I'm just going with my gut here."

"Larry, they're in for a rude surprise if they think Mayor Daley is gonna give them any breaks, other than breaking their arms, legs, and faces, and maybe even doing a Bull Connor right out of Birmingham, Alabama. This meeting has to succeed or else we give the election to the Republicans—or God knows, Wallace! I want you to give a full update to Ethel so she can call me when I'm on my trip abroad."

"Mrs. Kennedy, sir?" O'Brien was trying not to look shocked, but still looked surprised.

"Yes. Mrs. Kennedy. Don't ask me why right now. Just do what I say."

"All right, sir. I'll call Mrs. Kennedy. Isn't she going with you, sir?"

"Larry, she's four months pregnant and has ten kids at home! She isn't getting on a plane to go to the Middle East and the Soviet Union!"

"Right. Right, sir. I forgot. I'm just surprised you want me to call—I mean—I just thought—I—I . . . " He gave up trying to look like he understood. "Sorry, sir."

Kennedy sighed and let a few moments of silence pass. Then he said, "You know, Larry, when Jack ran, I took care of all the headaches that go with a campaign—and lived with the headaches, too, if I couldn't get rid of them. And people called me an asshole. Well, *you* try to be the guy who says no all the time and deals with people who don't take no for an answer. *You* try to get people who hate each other to commit to working together for a common purpose. And *you* work with people who want you to fail, even though they say they're on your candidate's side. See how *you* look after a while when you're dealing with the high and mighty Eleanor Roosevelt crowd, the Stevenson supporters, the Paul Newmans, the Norman Mailers, and that damned faggot Vidal out there. All I wanna know is this: Where's *my* Bobby? Don't I get to have a Bobby when *I'm* running for president?"

"What about Teddy?" O'Brien couldn't believe he was actually responding at all. He put his hand to his mouth as if to say to himself, Shut up, idiot. Can't you see the senator's just blowing off steam?

Kennedy, meanwhile, shot O'Brien a glance that said, in effect, Teddy? Are you kidding? Neither man had to say a word on the subject of Edward M. "Ted" Kennedy, senior senator from Massachusetts.

Kennedy waved O'Brien out of the room, but then called him back. "Larry, you have got to make this goddamned meeting a success and get those radicals to see they better not screw up this moment. We're hanging on a thread here. I don't care what the polls say right now. Nixon's running his campaign like a TV show, and it was damned good before and may be again. And I know this: If Nixon wins the nomination, and then loses a close one this year, he's not gonna roll over like he did after the 1960 election. He's playing for keeps, including recounts. And God knows Johnson's gonna come after me one way or the other before this election's over. Sometimes I think I'd rather take that Sirhan fellow over Nixon and Johnson and their friends in the Establishment. The weird thing—well, maybe not so weird—is those Establishment people were friends with my father and brother, but they aren't too crazy about me, and never were for the most part."

Kennedy thought to himself again: Where's my Bobby? Where is my goddamned Bobby? Damn it!

Larry O'Brien left the room thinking, If the Daley meeting's successful, Bob might make me his "Bobby," and I don't want *that* job. If the Daley meeting fails, though, I'm dead meat and so is the campaign. God almighty, I'm *already* his Bobby! I knew I should have gone off begging for delegates like Dolan! He took the easy way out, the son of a bitch!

And a few days later, O'Brien was mediating between two radicals and the Mayor of Chicago and his leading legal adviser. After O'Brien's opening comments at the meeting with Daley, Rennie Davis spoke first. Davis said how pleased he was to meet directly with the mayor. He wanted the mayor to know personally that not only were many in the student movement supporting Senator Kennedy for president, as was the mayor, but he was pleased the mayor and the students had common ground in their opposition to the war in Vietnam.

Daley said, "Yeah, but I don' go paradin' around about it, makin' trouble."

Dellinger, barely concealing his disgust, said, "I never made trouble in my life. It's people who don't want to work together for everyone's interest who make the trouble. By the time I show up, trouble's already there. And, with all respect, when you stand up for what you believe in, that's not making trouble." He stopped, then leaned a bit across the table and said, "You know what 'makin' trouble' is? 'Makin' trouble' is backroom deals that freeze out the poor and oppressed in favor of real estate developers who line your pockets—"

Daley, forgetting his promise to be charming, exploded. "Ya listen ta me, ya Commie son of a bitch! I never took a cent from nobody! From nobody! Ya unnerstand? Ya talk big, but where are ya? I stood up ta President Johnson ta say we need ta stop da war, too. An' when I stand up, it counts! Yeah, sometimes it's behind closed doors, in *my* office. But I'm wit' people a helluva lot more important den you little turds! I make t'ings happen. I get t'ings done!"

Dellinger smiled, thinking to himself, Yeah, like making the trains run on time, as Mussolini used to claim. He held back, though. Davis and Foran feared the worst was still coming. Dellinger dropped his smile, leaned further toward Daley, looked at him straight on, and said, "Mr. Mayor, you stood up—and I stood up to stop this war. Yet, the war is still going on. And it's still going on despite your supposed deals behind closed doors and even despite my agitation with Saul Alinsky." Dellinger had to throw that one in, even though he hadn't agitated on the war with Alinsky.

Dellinger then sat back and let his smile return gracefully to his face. "So maybe, Mr. Mayor, we better try to get together and elect Senator Kennedy as our next president, okay?" Dellinger folded his arms, indicating "I'm done" to O'Brien.

Daley looked at Foran, then at Davis. Davis looked at Daley, then at Dellinger. Everyone looked at O'Brien, who had been sweating through his shirt thinking of what a riot by student radicals during the convention would look like on television and what the polls would look like afterward.

O'Brien looked back at Daley, then Dellinger. He spoke as calmly and as confidently as he could. "Gentlemen, I am glad we are having an honest talk, and most glad to hear Mr. Dellinger indicate a willingness to work together for our most important common goal." God, he thought to himself, I sound like some hippie shrink here, but what the hell? Whatever works! "Mr. Mayor, if I understand correctly from my discussions with Mr. Davis and Mr. Dellinger, they are willing to make sure most—they can't guarantee all—people in the student and antiwar movement stay away from any counter-demonstrations in Chicago during the convention next month—"

Davis broke in and erased what was left from the script he had with Dellinger. "Mr. O'Brien? I must interject here." Davis thought, Geez, I sound like one of my pompous professors! "Mr. Daley, Mr. Foran, there is no organized movement in the sense either of you may think. People come in and out. New leaders seem to come forward every few months. Neither Mr. Dellinger nor I can speak for a majority of the movement with any certainty—"

Foran interrupted Davis, saying, "Then why are we talking with you and this other guy here?"

"Because," said Davis evenly, "you should talk to at least a couple of people who have influence at least; and David and I—I mean Mr. Dellinger—are two people that others will listen to, or at least consider listening to."

O'Brien breathed deeply and then said, "Yes. That's all I meant, Mr. Davis. The key word here is 'influence.' That is a good word, Mr. Davis." Davis nodded, as did Daley. If there was one thing Mayor Daley understood, it was the meaning of the word "influence." Daley used that word often to answer critics who thought he was a "boss" of a "machine," a charge he took careful pains to deny in words, at least. Daley was getting comfortable again.

Foran spoke once more. "Okay. So you fellas use what Mr. Davis calls 'influence' that keeps people from sleeping in the streets and parks of Chicago during the convention. That's great. So what else are we here for? What do you guys want?"

Dellinger smiled and said, "Nothing, Mr. Foran. Nothing."

Daley looked suspiciously at Dellinger, then back at Foran with a shrug. But Foran wasn't satisfied to leave it there. "Mr. Dellinger, what do you mean by 'nothing,' if I may sound ignorant to you?"

Dellinger smiled again. Foran had just asked "the one question too many," as any good trial lawyer, especially Foran, knew. But Foran knew he had to ask it in this situation. This wasn't a courtroom filled with jurors. And with the convention coming up, Daley wanted to avoid any unpleasant surprises.

Dellinger put down the glass of water he'd just picked up, and said, "Counselor, I am so glad you asked that question. When I say *nothing*, I mean this: When Fred Hampton Jr. of the Black Panthers puts together a free after-school program serving milk and cookies, you and your friends in the police department do *nothing* to stop him. When Saul Alinsky needs a permit to lead a demonstration in front of a store or some slumlord, you let him have the permit like you would for the Shriners, and then, do *nothing* to stop him. And when a black lawyer or doctor wants to move into a white neighborhood, you, the Realtor Board, the police, you all do *nothing* to stop them—and yes, maybe do *some*thing to *keep* nothing from happening to that black lawyer or doctor and his family. Should I go on? Are you getting my drift?"

Daley kept his cool this time. He looked hard at O'Brien, who had missed this coming all the way. Daley then looked at Foran. He whispered in Foran's ear, then Foran whispered back. Daley sat back in his chair, looked at Dellinger and O'Brien, ignoring Davis—who hadn't been expecting Dellinger's remarks either and was now feeling as if he were in grade school watching rival senior high school gangs "duke it out."

Daley said, "Gentlemen, I'd like ta confer wit' da U.S. attorney, Mr. Foran, for a few moments."

Daley lumbered out of the room, with Foran following respectfully behind. O'Brien, after the two men left, turned violently to Dellinger and in an angry whisper said, "Are you out of your fu—eff'in' mind, man?! What the—*who* the hell do you think you are to talk to one of the most powerful elected officials in the whole damned country like that?" O'Brien was almost shouting out of his whisper by the time he finished his question, for which he wouldn't accept any answer except "I'm sorry, Mr. O'Brien. How rude of me to say such a thing."

Dellinger was not about to give any such answer to O'Brien or anyone else. Instead, he leaned into O'Brien's face and said, "Who the hell do I think I am? Well, Larry, I'm just a 'crazy mothah' agitator who wants to make sure the good people who demonstrate for the things that should come naturally in a free society don't have to keep getting their asses kicked in every big town in America." He sat back and continued, in a slightly softer tone. "I don't ask for much from the mayor, and I'm willing to deal. I want the police department to declare a truce in their war against black people, at least for a little while, and even act with some caution or *respect* for once. Okay? So maybe we cool our demos for the rest of the campaign season. But the harassment of the Black Panthers, at least Hampton's people, must stop *now*. Let the boss mayor send one of his black aldermen down to Hampton on a peace mission—let 'em see what's *really* happening there. And I want Alinsky, after the elections in November, to get better treatment from the permit department so he isn't having to quote chapter and verse, and having to keep sending out for lawyers to get what everyone else gets for free—you know, Kiwanis, the Lions, Knights of Columbus? I don't think I'm being too out of line here when you consider we're supposed to be working together, right? Well, working together doesn't mean I have to watch my friends get their asses kicked like what happened right here in Chicago three months ago in April after Martin Luther King was killed, or two or three years before that when King was marching through a white neighborhood in Cicero."

O'Brien breathed a deep, sad, frustrated sigh. Rennie Davis perked up at Dellinger. Now why didn't I think of that? Davis thought. And why didn't he tell me about it beforehand? Davis knew Dellinger hadn't trusted him or Tom Hayden since the spring, when the two younger radicals were screaming that the movement should arm itself for the final revolution after Martin Luther King was assassinated. Back then, it was Dellinger who insisted on remaining nonviolent. Now, when they were dealing with mainstream politicians and big city bosses, it was Dellinger who was talking about giving support to the Black Panthers. As Hayden said to Davis when he first broached the idea of this meeting with Daley, you never knew where Dellinger was going to be—to the left or to the right of you. And there was Dellinger, going from the right to the left of them once again. Those old labor pacifist lefties . . . a strange breed, thought Davis.

Daley came back into the room ten minutes later, looking somewhat upset but trying to smile. Foran was seething, playing the pit bull with conviction this time.

Daley spoke first. "I've t'ought over da definition o' da word *'nut'in'* after discussions wit' counsel," nodding twice, sideways, to Foran. He then smiled directly at Dellinger. He opened his arms and the palms of his hands as if he was showing Dellinger he had nothing to hide. "Mr. Dellinger, I can assure ya dere's no problem with dis Alinsky fella, whoever he is—"

Dellinger held back a laugh, but the laugh sniffled out a bit, as though he had sinus problems.

Daley repeated himself, this time deliberate and clear. "Dere . . . will . . . be . . . no . . . problems . . . for . . . dis . . . Alinsky . . . fella . . . accordin' ta my office staff, who I jus' checked wit'—" He paused a moment, then switched gears, awkwardly and painfully. "As for dis Black Panther fella, I'll ask Harold Washington, a Negro alderman in our city, ta check up on dis person, listen an' see what da boy—er, young man—is doin', an' provide a report ta me for consideration."

"Fred Hampton is the *man* your Mr. Washington will want to see, Mr. Mayor," said Rennie Davis, who deeply respected the work Hampton was doing with inner-city children.

"Fred Hampton, eh?" said the mayor. "If he agrees ta renounce da use o' weapons—guns, I mean—an' is truly helpin' people—an' is willin' ta work t'rough one of da charities dat's recognized in da community, or maybe t'rough a city agency, he shouldn' have no problems."

"And," said Dellinger, quietly but firmly, "you're forgetting the other thing . . . "

"What udder t'ing?" Daley's eyes flashed with anger.

Dellinger hated himself for gulping, but he did—not because he was afraid of Daley, but because he didn't want the meeting to blow up at this point.

"There's a lot of really good people, including, I'm sure, you and Mr. Foran, who know it is wrong that Negroes don't have a right to live where they want to live in the city of Chicago—"

Daley relaxed and answered, "Mr. Dellinger, you should know I don' have control over where people wanna live. I can refer you ta da Ree-la-tor Board ta see what dey know about dis. I t'ink, in dis day an' age, people oughta be able ta live where dey want, unless it's dangerous for dem—but even den." Daley shrugged his shoulders and dared Dellinger.

Dellinger looked at O'Brien, then at Davis, and decided he had gone as far as he could today. "Thank you, Mr. Mayor, for that advice. I'll check around."

Foran was not happy, and neither was Daley. Dellinger tried to look satisfied. But inside, he was concerned because he couldn't put anything in writing, knew it wasn't enforceable anyway, and would still have to explain to people in the movement why they should work for Bobby Kennedy, who was clearly in bed with the odious Boss Daley. He believed, however, he had made his point with O'Brien that the movement was not going to lie down for long and would be back right after the inauguration of the thirty-seventh president, whom he assumed at this point was going to be Robert Francis Kennedy.

O'Brien happily—and quickly—adjourned the meeting. After he left City Hall and sent Davis and Dellinger on their way, O'Brien looked up at the sky and thanked God and Bobby Kennedy, in that order. In doing so, O'Brien wondered just who, or what, was in the sky, or at least in the air, these past six weeks. This all seemed like a string of political miracles, one after the other. Maybe Bobby had his own Bobby after all. If he did, it wasn't anyone visible to O'Brien or anybody else.

Davis, Dellinger, and Hayden got the word out across the country through the universities, where summer school was more or less filled because of students making up classes after a year of demonstrations and election campaigning. The refrain to the faithful was clear and succinct as stated by Rennie Davis: "Last year, we didn't think we'd ever get the Democratic Party to listen to us, right? Well, the party did. Even an old-politics boss like Daley is against the war in Southeast Asia! He couldn't stop it alone, and neither have we. This is not the time to disrupt things. It's a time for coalitions. We have a choice now: We can support Robert Kennedy, or continue to agitate, or vote for a third-party peace candidate. But anything we do besides supporting Senator Kennedy will simply result in a win for someone like Nixon—and four more years of war, no matter what Nixon is saying about his 'secret' plan. It's time to give peace, love and a Kennedy another try!"

That refrain worked in most cases because people knew that Robert Kennedy, as a senator at least, had the credentials. He had sat and marched with Cesar Chavez and the farm workers. He had responded to the concerns of poor black people in the inner cities. Even his answer about not wanting to move inner-city blacks to Orange County was grounded in a strong desire to help poor black folks directly, so they didn't have to leave their communities. And, unlike any other mainstream politician, Kennedy had attacked apartheid inside South Africa itself. The student movement knew Kennedy had publicly called for a bombing halt and making peace with the Vietnamese Communists, unlike Humphrey and Nixon.

Rubin and Hoffman were devastated when they heard Davis, Dellinger, Hayden, and Ochs were now actively opposing the Yippies' planned demonstrations in Chicago. The two Yippie leaders vowed to disrupt the convention no matter what, and made additional overtures to the most radical elements of the SDS. But the SDS was in sectarian disarray, looking for heretics, not coalition partners. Worse yet, no rock performers or folk singers of any note were willing to come to Chicago to play or sing for the Yippies, especially now. Money from the culturally elite Left, starting with Leonard Bernstein and others, had dried up as Davis, Dellinger, and Hayden stepped up their counter-campaign against the demonstrations. Most people in and out of the movement saw the coronation of Kennedy as not only inevitable, but they also saw cause for hope that the political wounds and cultural gaps existing in America would heal or close with his victory in November.

Robert Scheer, then editor for the New Left magazine *Ramparts,* summed it up for many student activists in the August 1968 issue of that magazine. Scheer wrote that Robert Kennedy was still a "liberal" who would "let people down" where it mattered most on issues of economic equality and redistribution of the nation's wealth. However, Scheer also wrote:

> I do discern in Bobby Kennedy a sense of duty, an intense and burdensome duty, to meet the best hopes and expectations of most Americans. The duty springs from the very mythology that has been built up around his late brother, John F. Kennedy. And this younger brother wants to finish what the myth says the older brother was just starting, before being slain in Dallas five years ago. The younger brother wants to create a country that is united, tolerant and accepting of people of all colors and races. He wants to guide our country to peace not only with itself, but with the world, particularly in southeast Asia. He believes he can, through merely "liberal" policies, bring economic bounties and political freedoms to people in all nations, east and west, north and south.
>
> Some say Senator Kennedy is merely opportunistic, cashing in on his brother's martyrdom for his own greater glory. This is definitely true, but this tells us very little about this man. For if Senator Kennedy were not opportunistic, he would not be a politician. He would also not be a Kennedy. During this election campaign, I have

seen Senator Kennedy up close and I had occasion to question him on a variety of subjects. There is, I have found, an intensity in him that is genuine when he talks about the poor, the farm workers, the minorities in this country, and yes, the war.

If it is a myth that the late President John F. Kennedy was really beginning to accomplish any of the things his supporters believe he would have accomplished, and there is no doubt it is a myth, it may not matter. Many of Senator Robert Kennedy's supporters, including those who are prominent antiwar activists, believe the myth. You can hear it in these activists even when they deny it. But regardless of whether they believe in the myth or not, there is something more important that feeds their optimism. And that is that Bobby Kennedy appears to believe the myth himself, when he, of all people, should know better.

The belief in the myth of President John Fitzgerald Kennedy is helping to liberate many activists from the weight of their often-isolating agitation. It is leading them back into the mainstream of politics in America with at least some of their more important goals intact, though many of the risks of joining such politics remain. It is also forcing labor leaders, such as Walter Reuther of the United Auto Workers, to remember their roots in the 1930s before they became more interested in fighting Communists than the bosses who run the lives of their workers.

While this is quite possibly all to the good for the Left, for Bobby Kennedy, the myth surrounds him the way a prison fence surrounds a prisoner. He feels he cannot escape until he finishes what he thinks his brother started. Again, it is *his* belief in the myth of an unfulfilled promise that should give hope to those of us who, throughout this decade, have directly challenged racism, poverty, and the war.

In concrete terms, I am defining "hope" to mean at least three things: First, the senator, if elected president, will work to quickly end the war in Vietnam with little or no further bloodshed. Second, he will be dedicated to overcoming racism at a variety of levels in our society. And third, he will continue to make fighting poverty a major policy priority in his administration, albeit in a typically liberal way of programs designed to supplement, not supplant private enterprise. These are, I repeat, hopes, not predictions.

While some of us continue to disdain fighting for merely partial loaves of bread in American politics, these three hopes are, nonetheless, significant. There is a choice to be made this November. It is a choice between a false and "freeze-dried" Richard Nixon and a fallible, yet still searching Robert Kennedy. Four years ago we chanted, "Part of the way with LBJ." We refused to blindly accept Johnson's slogan "All the way . . . " because we sensed something was not right with Johnson's policy in Vietnam. This year, we may be able to go *more* of the way with RFK, despite the disappointment and despair of the last four years.

Jack Newfield read most of Scheer's article and called Allard Lowenstein. Newfield said, "You gotta hear this, Al! We got Scheer and *Ramparts!* Can you believe it? *Ramparts!* Now if we can only get Izzy Stone on board!"[3]

Instead of being ecstatic, as Newfield was, Lowenstein said solemnly, "Maybe this election is our country's redemption." Robert Kennedy's candidacy had a way of affecting otherwise cynical people that way, it seemed, particularly after the assassination attempt in June.

Newfield, however, had neglected to read to Lowenstein the part of Scheer's essay where he criticized the candidate for having anything to do with Mayor Richard Daley. Nor had Newfield read Scheer's warning to his readers that demonstrations would not become a thing of the past under a second Kennedy administration.

By the end of the first full week of August 1968, it was clear there were not going to be any significant demonstrations during the Democrats' convention in Chicago. The Yippies' demonstration plans had almost completely collapsed. Lowenstein called Larry O'Brien and said to him, apropos of a then hit television show, "Larry, all I need to say is this: *Mission Impossible? Mission Accomplished.*"

O'Brien thanked Lowenstein, to which Lowenstein replied, "Don't thank me, Larry. You and I, and Senator Kennedy, should all thank the kids. They didn't have to trust the Establishment again, like they did in 1964 with Lyndon Johnson. Maybe if we showed them more respect, this generation could become the best generation this nation has produced in a long, long time. They want to do right, Larry, and we gotta do right by them, too."

O'Brien, knowing his mission was, in fact, accomplished, was already back to his cynical, political operative ways. He replied, "Al, let's just win the damned election this fall, and then we'll wax our thoughts about posterity, okay?"

Lowenstein was disappointed by O'Brien's response but not surprised. He smiled at his end of the telephone and said, "Okay, Larry. We'll win the election this fall. But just remember. The election isn't the end, it's the beginning."

Chapter 5

LOOKING PRESIDENTIAL

The day before O'Brien sweated through the meeting between Daley and the radicals, Robert Kennedy left on his trip to Europe, the Middle East, and Soviet Russia. Kennedy's plan was to meet various leaders in order to provide voters with solid evidence that he wasn't just an antiwar candidate—just in case, thought Kennedy, President Johnson tried to arrange a quick peace before the election to possibly help Nixon.

Kennedy's itinerary was to go first to Moscow, then to Czechoslovakia, and then, via Italy, to Israel. After that, it would be on to West Berlin, then to Paris, and then home. Kennedy also planned to return to the United States just before the publication of his book on the Cuban missile crisis, *Thirteen Days,* which was scheduled to appear around the start of the Democratic national convention.

It was all part of his strategy to look presidential, appear tough as a war hawk, and maintain support from antiwar doves. "Gotta keep the 'beards' in line," said Kennedy to his aide Milton Gwirtzman in late June. Gwirtzman later asked himself, Aren't I a "beard?" Is he talking about me, too?

It did not take long for Kennedy to plan the trip once it was finally decided upon—he was a Kennedy, after all, and nearly every foreign leader was interested in accommodating him. Kennedy's traveling party included his campaign adviser Frank Mankiewicz, one of the young speechwriters, Adam Walinsky, and renowned economics professor and former ambassador to India, John Kenneth Galbraith. Galbraith, a close Kennedy family friend, initially supported McCarthy when Kennedy said he wouldn't run for president. However, he formally left McCarthy after the New York primary. "I'm glad to be back with you, Bob," said Galbraith.

"I understood your dilemma, Ken. You were the consummate gentleman during the primary. You never attacked me, and, with McCarthy looking for heretics in his own camp, I can only say that your willpower in not attacking me was the sign of a true friend."

Almost immediately testing his friendship with Kennedy, Galbraith convinced him to speak with Chester Bowles, the current ambassador to India, about joining them on the "presidential" trip, particularly the first stop, which was Moscow. Bowles was a successful businessman who joined the

State Department during World War II, served later as governor of Connecticut, and worked in and out of the State Department diplomatic corps. In a series of lectures at Harvard in the mid-1950s, published in a book entitled *American Politics in a Revolutionary World*, Bowles outlined the need for the United States to stress self-determination not just in Eastern Europe, but in Latin America, Africa, and Asia. He believed the United States' mission was to expand economic and political opportunities in less-developed nations. He strongly believed in the inculcation of democratic values in the post-colonial world, even if it meant tolerating "radicals." From his progressive yet business-oriented view, Bowles believed it was necessary to know the customers' story, in this case, the history of the peoples of Asia, Africa, and Latin America. This, he believed, would be the best defense against the United States' "clumsy militaristic and unimaginative" reactions to the threats posed by the Soviet Union and Red China to "world stability." Bowles longed for a Marshall Plan for various poorer nations, but complete with all the strings the United States normally attached, including some protection of corporations that would reap profits during and after development.

Bowles was so respected a figure in the late 1950s that he was given to understand, by then candidate John F. Kennedy in 1959, that he might serve as secretary of state in a future JFK presidential administration. Bowles jumped aboard John Kennedy's bandwagon early but wound up as a mere undersecretary of state. In that position, he was ignored and then not so tactfully told to leave—ironically, for not being sufficiently "gung-ho" with regard to fighting Communist insurgencies in Southeast Asia, particularly in Vietnam. Robert Kennedy, who was the "unofficial" head of the National Security Council within his brother's administration, had been particularly disrespectful to Bowles around the time of the disastrous Bay of Pigs invasion of Cuba in April 1961. Bowles had doubts about the Bay of Pigs plan all along, and Bob Kennedy was more interested in punishing Bowles and others for being "weak" than in admitting Bowles and others may have been right from the start.

Bowles never forgot the treatment he received from a younger Robert Kennedy at the time, and he was reticent, to say the least, about meeting him and the others in Moscow, even when it was clear Kennedy was going to be the Democratic Party's nominee, if not the next president. Galbraith convinced Bowles to speak with Kennedy, which he did. Bowles, like others, found a more mature Robert Kennedy who was willing to learn from his mistakes. Kennedy had impressed—flattered?—Bowles because, during their discussion, he apologized to Bowles for not seeing the nationalist impulses of so many third world leaders, particularly in Vietnam.

This was not the first time Kennedy had humbled himself in the past year. In late 1967, Allard Lowenstein called him a coward for refusing, at the time, to challenge Lyndon Johnson for the presidency. Most people expected Kennedy to forever banish Lowenstein from the Kennedy circle, as he had done to several others who had dared criticize any Kennedy.

About six months later, after Kennedy finally announced his candidacy, he saw Lowenstein at a political gathering. Lowenstein was working for McCarthy and still refused to join Kennedy. After speaking briefly with Lowenstein, he wrote a note on a scrap of paper and handed it to Lowenstein. The note read: "For Al, who knew the lesson of Emerson and taught it to the rest of us: 'They did not yet see, and thousands of young men as hopeful, now crowding to the barriers of their careers, did not yet see if a single man plant himself on his convictions and then abide, the huge world will round to him." When Lowenstein joined the Kennedy campaign in June, the candidate welcomed him with, literally, a gracious hug.

Kennedy, two days after speaking with Bowles, conferred with Galbraith. Kennedy had told Galbraith that Bowles was most likely "the best man" for the position of secretary of state in his administration. Galbraith responded by reminding him of Jack's "broken promise" to Bowles when Jack ran for president. Then Galbraith said, "I believe it is important to tell Chet now whether he will be the secretary of state or not. As I've said, Chet was a devoted believer in your brother. He is an excellent judge of diplomats and was damned right about why we should have avoided that mess in Vietnam."

Kennedy decided right then, said Galbraith to Bowles, that he would make "an unbreakable promise" to Bowles if he would join him in Moscow and for the rest of the trip abroad. Bowles agreed to join the campaign, but only after some further discussion with Galbraith and with his own wife, who remained skeptical about trusting any Kennedy, particularly Bob Kennedy. Bowles then called President Johnson's secretary of state, Dean Rusk. Rusk, who served under JFK and Johnson, asked Bowles about the rumor that he was considering "taking a ride on Bobby's junket." Bowles said it was true, but, he added, "I wouldn't put it quite that way." Bowles told Rusk he was planning to meet Kennedy in Moscow. He then asked Rusk whether or not he should resign his post in India. Rusk, a loyalist to Lyndon Johnson in a way he never had been to Jack Kennedy, suggested Bowles should resign, and Bowles did. Bowles did not expect to stay on long if the Republicans won the election.

In the back of Kennedy's mind, he had always hoped to convince Robert Strange McNamara, the former secretary of defense for both his brother and Lyndon Johnson, and now with the World Bank, to join him in his campaign. Kennedy still idolized the man he called "Mac," despite McNamara's fingerprints all over the war and Mac's blind trust in antiseptic reports of numbers, numbers, and more numbers—not to mention the antiwar movement's view that McNamara was no better than a war criminal. Mac, for his part, knew he wasn't well loved in nearly any part of the country. He told Kennedy early in the 1968 campaign that "a detailed political pulse" needed to be taken before he would ever return to national politics or any cabinet position in a new Kennedy administration.

Kennedy once floated the idea of Mac being his vice-presidential candidate for 1968, an idea all of his advisers rejected. He kept in almost constant telephone contact with Mac and made him a secret, unofficial adviser. When told of Bowles coming on board the campaign and probably becoming secretary of state should Kennedy win, Mac told Kennedy he had some doubts about Bowles but believed he would, if watched carefully, be an excellent secretary of state who would command the respect of the State Department and third world leaders.

Averell Harriman was another unofficial adviser to Bob Kennedy. During John Kennedy's administration, Harriman had been a rival to Bowles, and the two men did not get along very well at the time. However, Harriman always respected Bowles' knowledge and experience as a diplomat and grew sympathetic to Bowles as Harriman's own doubts about Vietnam grew. After speaking with Galbraith and Kennedy, Harriman made a personal call to Hamilton Fish Armstrong, then editor of the prestigious magazine *Foreign Affairs,* to suggest that Bowles write an article for the journal. When Bowles was publicly revealed as an adviser joining Kennedy on his trip abroad, Bowles suddenly received an invitation to write a panoramic overview of American foreign policy for *Foreign Affairs.*

It was said at the time that a person who wrote a leading article for *Foreign Affairs* during an election year was a likely candidate for secretary of state, or National Security Council adviser, in a new administration. The magazine, in this regard, operated as an American version of the Soviet Union's *Pravda,* where readers could tell "who's up or who's down" according to who appeared in the journal.

Kennedy's advisers were a bit apprehensive because the trip was getting underway just before the Daley meeting with the radicals in Chicago. In the period between the announcement of the trip and the trip itself, Kennedy's poll numbers began to slip from the "resurrection highs" to a more human—and mortal—level. Quite a few people thought it was presumptuous for a mere candidate, even Kennedy, to go on a foreign trip—the type of trip only incumbent presidents take—during an election campaign. Respected Establishment writer Joseph Alsop wrote: "This arrogant trip is reminiscent of the 'can't lose' attitude of Republican Thomas Dewey in 1948, who, in fact, did lose to Truman." Luckily for the Kennedy campaign, polls showed little if any movement to Nixon.

The trip began with a long plane ride to the Soviet Union, with a meeting with Premier Alexei Kosygin. Kosygin was one of the top two leaders at the

Soviet Politburo at the time. He was attempting to introduce "liberal" economic reforms, which in the Soviet Union meant market reforms, and was meeting some resistance from his rival, Leonid I. Brezhnev, the general secretary of the Communist Party. Any economic reform was easier said than done in a society that had learned to make peace with a brand of "socialism"—really bureaucracy—in which Igor, at the bakery, gave a few loaves of bread to Raisa, at the shoe factory, and Raisa gave Igor shoes. It was a lousy system, people in the Soviet Union whispered to each other, but they were getting what they needed enough of the time.

Kosygin said, in private discussions with Kennedy, Galbraith, and Bowles, that the Soviets were interested in improving relations with the United States and engaging in more meaningful strategic arms limitation talks. However, Kosygin also indicated that talks to end the war in Vietnam were progressing much too slowly, which, in his view, hindered both nuclear arms limitations talks and Kosygin's economic reforms. He pressed the senator to use his influence with the White House to move things forward toward a resolution of the American involvement in Southeast Asia. After the meeting, Kennedy said to Galbraith, "Kosygin's spies must be poorly informed if they think I have any influence with Lyndon Johnson!"

Kennedy, who had been briefed on the tentative democratic reforms occurring inside Czechoslovakia, asked Premier Kosygin during their meeting if the Soviets were prepared to allow events to take their "natural course toward freedom" in that Eastern European nation. Kosygin was visibly displeased at the question, but responded by saying, "The Czechs have the freedom to make their own decisions." He further stated the Soviets would respond to the Czech government's request for assistance should anarchy become a problem in that country. Kennedy showed equal displeasure at that last statement, but indicated his hope that the Dubcek regime in Czechoslovakia would act responsibly as well. Kennedy thought to himself, I hope Dubcek can at least hold on till after I become president. Kennedy was gladdened overall by Kosygin's willingness to develop better relations with the West.

Next Kennedy met with Leonid Brezhnev, whom most outsiders perceived as the co-ruler of Soviet Russia, if not the sole leader of the Communist Party Central Committee. Since the death of Joseph Stalin in 1953, the committee had led the Soviet Union and jealously guarded against another Stalin arising from the committee by constantly seeking "consensus." After meeting Brezhnev for merely a half hour, Kennedy became more concerned about future U.S.-Soviet relations. Brezhnev was fairly gruff with Kennedy, complaining about the United States beginning a program to develop multiple warheads on existing nuclear weapons. He warned the American presidential aspirant that this development would represent a new arms race and further chill already cooling relations.

After the day of meetings, Kennedy walked around the courtyard of the American embassy with Galbraith.

"Ken, the Russians act so afraid of us, so defensive. We're not invading Eastern Europe. We're neither the Nazis nor Napoleon. Why do they continue to act the way they do?"

"Well, there are those in Washington who talk about expanding NATO right into Poland if they thought they could get away with it. The Russians, in turn, listen to these very belligerent statements that come out of our most ardent right-wingers and think that's the policy of our country." Kennedy looked surprised but said nothing. Galbraith sensed Kennedy was not satisfied with the answer and continued. "Senator, I didn't say that people like us, or even Lyndon Johnson, listen to such crackpots, but they're out there, and the Russians have sensitive ears—"

"—and spies," smiled Kennedy.

"Well, that's what you get with spies, I suppose. Spies tend to look for the most salacious information, even if it's often bad information, with the sad result that those in the home country clamor for more. You remember how you treated Bowles and Stevenson, who doubted the assessment by Max Taylor and Bob McNamara about the level of support we had in Vietnam?" Kennedy smiled wanly while Galbraith continued. "There's another factor, too. If you were a Russian spy, where would you rather live? Moscow or the United States? You have a better chance of staying in America by providing salacious information as opposed to information that says 'Everything's fine. Let's start peace talks.' You know, Graham Greene was quite good on the lies and exaggerations of spies in *Our Man in Havana,* even though it was a novel, of course."

"I haven't read it, Ken."

"You should, if I may say so, Senator. It's not long and quite amusing, and definitely enlightening. In any event, Party Secretary Brezhnev is quite right about the multiple warheads issue, although this program of ours began much earlier than Brezhnev thinks."

"Didn't we start research on that program under Jack?"

"Yes, under Bob McNamara, if you recall. The MIRV program is almost ready for deployment, according to Clark Clifford. Clark's doing a great job running the Defense Department, meaning that he's holding Lyndon in line, at least much of the time. Clark believes it would be politically impossible to stop the MIRVing of our nuclear weapons—and he's right, of course— because not only has the Pentagon bought off on it, but so have the unions, including Walt Reuther's United Auto Workers, who have representation in many of the defense contracting companies. On the Soviet side, I understand from Soviet Ambassador Dobrynin that the Soviets are running more than ever by committee. Kosygin is seeking accommodations with the West and is implementing, as best he can, some economic reforms. But Brezhnev is taking a harder line toward the western nations—and maybe even against China. What we learned today was consistent with what Dobrynin was saying. Brezhnev and Kosygin are clearly rivals, and the noise coming out of Czechoslovakia could be a wild card in all this. I don't get the sense that President Johnson is concentrating on this right now, what with the peace talks currently frozen and the continued bombing campaign in Vietnam. And with this election year going into overdrive, neither is anyone else in Washington."

"Where does Chet Bowles stand on this?"

"Chet, as you may know, is an expert on Asian and African countries and has been less focused on the Soviets in recent years. He is usually pretty mainstream, for better or worse, on the Soviets and the Chinese. He is still a quick study, and, unlike Rusk and some of the others, he will listen and learn very quickly what is happening in those great nations—and I say 'great' because of their size and strategic importance to everything we do in our foreign policy, Senator, as you know. Plus, you always have George Kennan and whatever Soviet experts he recommends to lean on."

"Yes, Ken. Let's set up a meeting with Kennan as soon as possible when we get back to the States. Right now, I'm very interested in seeing what we find in Czechoslovakia tomorrow." With that, Kennedy turned in to his room for the night.

Before going to bed each night, Kennedy called Ethel, gave her a general summary of the day, and made sure he asked about the state of her health, her pregnancy, and the children. Ethel was on air every time he called because he rarely called her while on trips—at least before their "little talk," as she told her mother-in-law, Rose Kennedy. The Kennedy matriarch, who had silently endured her husband's pathological infidelity, was pleased to see that Ethel was strong with her Bobby. "Times are changing, dear, and I believe you were right to do what you did." Ethel, who wanted always to be the favorite daughter-in-law, which was in large part the motivation for the large family she and Kennedy had created, could not have been happier that Rose supported her on such an important "domestic" issue.

The next morning, Kennedy and his retinue were off to Prague, the capital city in Czechoslovakia. In July 1968, Prague was a city in revolution. The Communist bureaucrats were up in arms as Alexander Dubcek, the country's prime minister, continued to allow open political discussions and artistic freedom. Prague, looking more like San Francisco than Vienna, had become a gathering point of literary and cultural radicals. These radicals included the playwright Václav Havel and musicians such as Joseph Janicek and Milan Hlavsa. Janicek and Hlavsa were in two of the most outrageous local rock bands of the time, The Primitives and Hlavsa's Fiery Factory. The two musicians would eventually be united in the rock group known as The Plastic

People of the Universe, which band, in the first timeline, became a lightning rod in the Chartist movement in Czechoslovakia in the 1970s and 1980s against Communist government oppression.[1]

Discussion of a "generation gap" was not as common a lament in Czechoslovakia as it was in the United States. The young Czech literary and music radicals had elders whom they deeply respected. These elders included not only Dubcek, but also the eminent philosopher Jan Patocka, a survivor of both Nazi and Communist persecution who exemplified the radical democratic tradition in Czech society.[2]

Americans, including policy experts, referred to the Eastern Bloc countries as if they were all the same. But Czechoslovakia was as different culturally from Poland, for example, as Lima, Ohio, is different from New York City. Czechoslovakia included the region of Bohemia, from which the word "bohemian" is derived. The Czechs loved their artists and philosophers in a way that American society never had, because of certain American populist, anti-intellectual impulses.

Neither Kennedy nor his advisers had any idea about Czech culture, save perhaps Ken Galbraith—who himself didn't have a clue about Havel's writings nor the rock and roll wave currently engulfing Prague. All Kennedy knew as he stepped off the plane was that there had been a Communist coup in February 1948 that caused the Czechs to fall fully into the Soviet orbit, and now there were some political reforms going on. Kennedy was interested not only in meeting the prime minister but also in walking the bustling streets during this so-called "Prague Spring," referring to the reforms that began during the early part of 1968.

The most important thing Kennedy did *not* know was that Soviet Russia, by the time of his arrival, had already called up more than five hundred thousand officers and ground troops, mostly reservists, who were massing along the eastern borders of Czechoslovakia, ready to invade. The Politburo, made up of the most powerful members of the Soviet Central Committee, was under intense pressure from the other Communist-run dictatorships in Eastern Europe to invade. The Politburo knew its troops' readiness was severely lacking, however. What if the Czechs resisted? Would it lead to more bloodshed than had occurred in the Soviet invasion of Hungary in 1956? The Politburo was loathe to invade, remembering the world's criticism following the invasion of Hungary. The members were also aware that, unlike in Hungary, no Russian troops were currently stationed within Czechoslovakia. The Soviets, as a precaution, had decided to test the Czech's own military prowess by engaging the Czech military in joint exercises throughout June and July 1968, the better to determine weaknesses on both sides and regroup for a later invasion.

Brezhnev himself had been on the phone regularly with Dubcek, imploring him to move slowly on the reforms, even to the point of asking Dubcek to suspend the reforms to give the hard-liners throughout the Eastern European nations and in the Soviet Union itself some time to digest the changes. Brezhnev, as a leader of the hard-line faction at the Politburo, considered his request to Dubcek to be conciliatory, not threatening.

Dubcek was now, however, facing pressure from reformist elements because, in their eyes, he was not moving fast enough with reform. In a heated conversation with Brezhnev in mid-August 1968, Dubcek threw the responsibility back to Brezhnev, saying at one point that the Politburo would have to do what it thought "appropriate." Brezhnev was shocked at Dubcek's failure to take action himself and called Dubcek's remarks "flippant." He sadly hung up the phone after that conversation and reported to the Central Committee that an invasion might well be necessary, if only to placate the other Eastern European Communist leaders.[3]

Kennedy, Galbraith, and Bowles met with Dubcek about two weeks before the latter's momentous call with Brezhnev. Dubcek was already feeling the pressure from the Communist hard-liners and the reformers but was not yet convinced there was any crisis that couldn't be resolved in a way that was reasonably tolerable to both sides. Kennedy spoke first at the meeting, commending Dubcek for his reforms. Kennedy stated—very naïvely, according to Galbraith—that if the reforms being undertaken in Czechoslovakia could succeed, the United States and the Soviet Union might be able to begin talking about true nuclear arms control and maybe even withdrawal of their respective troops from all of Europe.

Dubcek strongly agreed with Kennedy, which made Galbraith more nervous. Dubcek said, "You know, Senator, I was always disappointed in the way the Americans reacted from 1945 through 1947, just after the war ended in Europe. There were coalition governments in Poland, Hungary, Czechoslovakia, the East German zone, and Yugoslavia, if not quite in Albania or Romania. There were more non-Communists than Communists in the coalition governments, at least early on. The Americans treated the non-Communist leftists, who merely sought land reform against the reactionaries and the church interests, as if they were no better than Communists. Even Jan Masaryk[4], before his untimely death in May 1948, was confused and ultimately disheartened by the Americans' attitudes. When Prime Minister Winston Churchill of England made that horrible speech in 1946 about 'iron curtains,' there weren't any 'iron curtains' surrounding our nations in what we still like to call Central—not Eastern—Europe. The Berlin Wall didn't go up until fifteen years later, in 1961, as you know. We were shocked, back in the 1940s, by how all the American leaders, starting with your fascist agents—pardon me for speaking so bluntly—such as John Foster Dulles and his brother, Allen Dulles, wrote us off as 'lost' to Communism even before we Communists succeeded in gaining control."

Dubcek's statements shocked Kennedy, Galbraith, and Bowles. What was he talking about, wondered Kennedy? Galbraith himself had heard something akin to that from the Czechoslovakian ambassador to the United States at one of the many Georgetown cocktail parties he'd attended over the years. The ambassador told Galbraith that although the Communists' "committees" were exercising more and more control in Czechoslovakia throughout 1947, Truman's growing desire for a showdown with Russia pushed events toward the1948 Communist coup as much as anything else. Galbraith wondered, as did Bowles, whether the American bipartisan anti-Communist coalition had missed the opportunity to avoid the capture of Eastern Europe. This thought, however, was too "radical" to think about and therefore quickly forgotten.

The meeting ended with Kennedy asking if he could set up some meetings with some of the more politically minded cultural trendsetters who were emerging in Czech society. Dubcek answered, "You may ask to see them yourself. We are, despite what some say, a free country."

As they were leaving, Dubcek said, "I don't know if you know this or not, but my parents met each other while they lived in Chicago in America. My older brother was born there, although they came back to this area of the world by the time I was born. It's funny. If my father had not protested against America's entry into World War I, and had he not supported the Bolshevik Revolution—which is why they left—I might be a politician in Chicago today!"

The Americans were stunned.

Dubcek, seeing their shocked faces, said, "It's true! It's true!"

Kennedy said, "President Dubcek, I am very hopeful that this East-West rivalry can come to a peaceful end. I am very glad to have met you and hope your reforms continue." He went over to Dubcek and warmly shook his hand.

After leaving, Kennedy said, "Imagine that, guys. Dubcek could have been a ward politician under Daley. Geez, he could have been Daley's rival!"

"I wonder if he would have been a 'reformist' in Chicago, too!" quipped Galbraith.

Kennedy had Galbraith scout out some prominent cultural shakers in Prague. Galbraith quickly found Václav Havel and set up a meeting with Havel and the rock musician Joseph Janicek in a flat near the center of town. Janicek was only nineteen at the time, but already a seasoned political veteran and musician. Havel, before the meeting, asked if any younger people were going to be with Kennedy. Kennedy said he would bring his younger speechwriter, Adam Walinsky.

After the meeting's initial introductions, Janicek, who thought all Americans were in agreement about all cultural trends in America, immediately sprayed Kennedy with statements in broken English, saying, "Man, I am BEEG FAN AMERICA! I love Frank Zappa! 'Plastic People' song, great! GREAT! Love Doors, Grateful Dead, the Fugs! My band, Primitive Group, play their music—people love it!"

Galbraith was shaking his head in confusion. Kennedy himself had no idea what this kid was talking about. Walinsky, however, was laughing at the elders' discomfort and was very happy to hear what Janicek said. Although Walinsky's taste ran to folk music—he loved Bob Dylan, Phil Ochs, and Joan Baez—Walinksy knew all the people and bands Janicek referred to. He responded, "Yeah, in America, younger kids like them, but our parents *hate* them!" He shook his head as he said the words "hate them" so that Janicek would definitely understand.

"Yeah, us parents, too," said Janicek, and searching for words, turned to the interpreter Havel had brought along, who translated Janicek's next words as, "but our parents know it's all about freedom."

Kennedy was nervously silent as Walinsky said, "Our parents don't quite see it that way, I'm afraid."

Havel, who worshipped Zappa as one of the leading musical and socially conscious minds of the time, was as surprised by Walinsky's response as Janicek, but said nothing. Walinsky then asked Janicek and Havel, "You guys like Bob Dylan?"

Havel nodded strongly in the affirmative, but Janicek, through the interpreter, said, "Well, yes, but . . . Dylan is not *music man*. Zappa music man . . . um . . . uh . . . Hendrix music man! Great! I love Hendrix! I play guitar! Hendrix!"

Havel put up his hand in front of Janicek to stop this conversation from becoming nothing more than a review of the music scene. Havel's goal in meeting was to speak to a very important world leader from America and discuss the Prague Spring reforms. Havel hoped to better determine whether America would protect the government and people of Czechoslovakia from the Russians. From Havel's outsider view of America, Kennedy was something akin to an "assistant" president. Havel had no knowledge of the hatred between Johnson and Kennedy. Nor did he realize that when the senator and his entourage landed in Prague, Kennedy had all but ignored the U.S. ambassador to Czechoslovakia after the ambassador, incurring the wrath of Johnson, graciously set up the meeting with Dubcek.

Havel said through the interpreter, "Mr. Kennedy, we are honored to meet you and your fellow countrymen from America. We are, here in Czechoslovakia, very interested in renewing the freedoms you have in America. The freedom to speak, to write, and to have the *feeling* of freedom. As Joseph said, we do love Frank Zappa—"

Kennedy was thinking to himself, Who *is* this Frank Zappa fellow they keep mentioning?

" . . . and American writers Philip Roth, Norman Mailer, Terry Southern—"

Kennedy almost choked. Roth? Mailer? Next this guy's going to tell me he likes Vidal! Are these literary people, these musicians, the same everywhere?

"But," said Havel, as he finally got down to business, "we are most concerned that the reforms in our country continue. I understand from Mr. Gul-ge—"

"Galbraith," said Galbraith.

"Yes, Galbate, that you have met with Prime Minister Dubcek. Do you believe, Mr. Kennedy, that the prime minister is committed to continued reforms?"

Kennedy was tentative now, wondering just how radical Havel really was. "Well, Mr. Havel, he appeared to be a most reasonable man who is interested in the free expression of ideas. I can see, however, that although he is under pressure from people inside and outside of his government, he does want the political reforms to succeed."

"Did he talk of free and open elections?" asked Havel.

Janicek jumped in. "And to stop raiding our music halls and places we play?"

Kennedy sat back, surprised at the way the young man, Janicek, sounded exactly the same as the young people he had met in the elite universities back home. "Well," Kennedy answered, sounding more as if he were being interviewed on American television, with Mayor Daley watching in the wings. "Mr. Dubcek did not say anything specific about such things. I am confident, however, that reason will prevail and that reforms will take place relatively soon."

Havel felt some anguish. He had been hearing rumors of Russian troops massing at the Czech border and he was already aware of the joint military exercises between Czech and Soviet troops. He feared Dubcek was weakening. Dubcek had offered nothing in response to Communist hard-liners' raids of reformers' meeting places in the countryside. More ominously, Havel remembered the invasion of Hungary twelve years earlier and the failure of the Americans to assist the Hungarians in any way. He feared the same could happen again, although the Czechs, unlike the Hungarians, had their own army, with no Soviet troops inside Czech borders—yet.

Havel decided to end the meeting, and the senator and Galbraith were relieved. Walinsky asked, in front of everyone, if Janicek and Havel could take him to a nightspot.

Janicek said, "Yes! We go now! Not wait for night!"

Havel smiled in gentle acquiescence. Havel thought perhaps he'd learn more about American intentions from the young man, who might be willing to talk. Needless to say, all he got that evening was youthful exuberance and the hope of utopia just around the corner, although, by relative standards, Walinsky was not the most naïve waif among Kennedy's young speechwriters.

Kennedy had planned a speech later that day before a crowd gathered in one of the main parks in Prague, but Dubcek said there was not enough time to plan a speech. Dubcek was really concerned about Kennedy making a speech that further ignited the reformers. Kennedy told Walinsky he could throw out the draft of the speech he'd written for the candidate. In that draft speech, Walinsky included references to Bob Dylan and Frank Zappa which Kennedy and Chet Bowles vehemently rejected.

Bowles, who was as far removed from rock and roll music as one could get, was offended by Walinsky's insertions. Speaking alone with Kennedy, he asked, "Doesn't Adam exercise any discretion or precaution when he's conjuring up those speeches? I simply do not understand these younger—"

Kennedy waved his hand, "Chet, I know what you're saying. I don't get the kids *anywhere* today. Every time I think I understand them—wham! They go off talking about guitar players with weird names who I don't know *at all*."

"Senator, I agree with you, of course, but I'd like to ask something about the support we seem to be seeking in America with reference to college-age youngsters. What I don't understand, in all candor, is this. The voting age in the United States is twenty-one, which means most of the college kids we would see on the campuses can't vote for us even if they wanted to. Why bother seeking their support, if I may be so bold?"

Kennedy thought a moment, ran his fingers through his still-too-long hair, and replied, "Chet, if we're going to work together, you can always speak your mind. Really. Not like last time." Pausing a moment, he then said, "I guess I'd like to answer your question this way. The kids, *if* they support you, work hard stuffing envelopes. They make calls to voters, and they have the most time to show up and fill out rallies that need filling out. They bring enthusiasm and excitement. There's also something else. There's a generation gap right now in our country, as you and I both read about constantly. When kids went 'clean for Gene,' they also went 'clean' for me. I have this continuing belief that if the kids and their parents can unite on a candidate, and I believe I am that candidate, they might start up a dialogue with each other that is needed now more than ever. I might have felt that was silly a few years ago, and maybe it is—"

Bowles was quick to reply that it was not silly. "I see what you are saying, Senator," he added.

"Thanks, Chet. But you got me thinking even more about this. With the kids' support, my hope is to end the war in Vietnam, rechannel the energy of the colleges away from protests and instead, get them to help us fight against poverty and racism. I don't know how we do that with a detailed policy yet— I mean, we have the Peace Corps and the domestic version, VISTA . . . But I don't quite know. Your question, though, is valid. We have to concentrate on voters more than non-voters—most of the time."

Kennedy smiled at Bowles in a way that told Bowles things really would be different this time with Robert Kennedy.

The next day, the Kennedy entourage flew to Rome, and then on to Israel. Frank Mankiewicz, however, had had enough of the entire trip. He had spent most of his time on the phone to O'Brien in Washington and was constantly wondering, How is this gonna play back home? Mankiewicz had only come along in the first place to give practical political advice, which Kennedy basically ignored anyway. Mankiewicz figured he now had better things to do than gallivanting around like a diplomat, which he wasn't and didn't want to be. He returned to the States, where he found O'Brien very happy with the coverage the U.S. press had been giving the trip. "Frank, Bobby looks absolutely presidential! I mean it! Presidential!"

Mankiewicz shook his head and said, "So far, Larry, so far. I think Bob should come back home while he's ahead. But he won't."

After Kennedy and his remaining group arrived in Israel, Kennedy was disappointed to learn that Prime Minister Golda Meir was unable to meet with him as previously promised. Instead, she sent Moshe Dayan, the Israeli general and defense minister, who was the military hero of the Six-Day War, to meet with the traveling candidate.

Meir begged off, claiming illness, but truthfully, she had spoken with President Johnson the day before. He told her, "Mrs. Prime Minister, if Ah may say, although Ah am a Democrat like the senator, who is a great and good man in mah opinion, it might be better for your nation if you did not speak to him raht now in light of the election campaign going on. Although Senator Kennedy is ahead in the polls, former Vice President Nixon, who is likely to win the Republican nomination for president, is a man with a long memory—and is not to be counted out. I think all would understand, even the senator, if you were unable—for whatever reason—to meet him on such . . . short . . . notice."

Kennedy, when he learned Meir had canceled, knew something was up. "That bastard Johnson's behind this. I know it!" he said to Bowles and Galbraith. Both men knew not to disagree, even if they doubted it. Meir, they both thought, was a woman, and she claimed illness. Maybe she really was ill.

Kennedy was, nonetheless, glad that if he could not meet Prime Minister Meir, he was at least meeting Dayan, a real war hero and someone he thought was an influential minister. Kennedy met with Dayan for an hour, clearly enjoying the general's stories of the quick and almost perfect war the Israelis had won in 1967 against the Arab nations.

Chet Bowles had tried to brief Kennedy beforehand as to how the U.S. State Department viewed the 1967 Middle East war, but Kennedy brushed Bowles aside, saying he wanted to rest before seeing Dayan. Neither Kennedy nor Bowles discussed, for example, the fact that the Israelis had struck first against Egypt, with the Israelis calling their actions a "defensive maneuver." While Egypt's President Gamal Abdul Nasser had made menacing noises of war against Israel a few weeks before the Israelis invaded, it was also true that Nasser had let the Russians talk him into not striking Israel first. The Russians, in turn, thought Lyndon Johnson had the Israelis under control, which Johnson did not. The Israelis, during the six days of war against Egypt, Jordan, and Syria, had even gone so far as to bomb a U.S. naval vessel, the *Liberty,* which the Israelis said was an accident, but which some observers inside the U.S. government thought was deliberate. There was still a dispute raging in both the U.S. military and the State Department as to whether the *Liberty* attack was deliberate or accidental.

Kennedy was pleased to have spent time with Dayan, while Bowles and Galbraith were disappointed that nothing of substance came out of the meeting. O'Brien, watching the media back home, saw the photograph of Kennedy with Dayan in the *Washington Post* and the *New York Times* and grinned. As far as O'Brien was concerned, that photo, with a smiling Dayan clasping his two hands onto Kennedy's right hand and Kennedy beaming, was worth more than millions of dollars in campaign ads and meetings to get the Jewish vote in New York, Florida, and California.

"Ball game on the Jewish vote!" O'Brien said to campaign advisers William vanden Heuvel and Milt Gwirtzman, who were eating breakfast with O'Brien in the Kennedy presidential campaign headquarters in Washington, D.C. O'Brien added, "This day can't get any better now unless Lyndon Johnson calls me and asks what he can do to help Kennedy win this 'sum-bitch' election!"

Kennedy reacted the same way as O'Brien when he saw the photo on the front page of the *International Herald-Tribune.* Kennedy, too, understood that "being presidential" was at least as much about image as substance.

"Now it's on to Germany, and let's win there—*again!*" joked an exuberant Kennedy.

Kennedy, on the way to Germany, took the time to speak with Bowles about the State Department's report on the Middle East. Kennedy said at one point, "It seems, Chet, that if we can get the Arabs to agree to what is said in United Nations' Resolution 242, we can really make progress towards peace."

Bowles tried to be kind as he responded, "But Mr. President, Resolution 242 was essentially written by the American government—even the Israelis had some problems with it. So far, talking about Resolution 242 is largely about talking to ourselves and what we want to see."[5]

It was true that the Jewish organizations in the United States had been unhappy at first with that United Nations' resolution because Israel was in no mood to give up most or all of the land it had just won from Jordan (the West Bank area), Egypt (the Sinai desert and Gaza), and Syria (the Golan

Heights). However, since Resolution 242 demanded the Arabs recognize the Israeli government as legitimate, the Israelis didn't worry about the resolution very much, for recognizing Israel was pure acid to Nasser and to the other pan-Arab nationalists, while the more feudalistic and conservative Arab governments were too afraid of their precarious hold on their populace to recognize what all the Arabs called "the Zionist entity."

Joe Dolan, who was following the newspaper and TV coverage about Kennedy's trip abroad while on the road digging for convention delegates, could not eat breakfast until he saw that the morning media coverage was benign. "Phew!" he said to himself every morning. "No gaffes." While Kennedy was away, Dolan continued lining up previously committed Humphrey delegates in Pennsylvania, Ohio, and Michigan, and in the border states, including Tennessee and Kentucky.

As the privately-chartered jet landed in Berlin, Kennedy said to himself that he was glad to be back in Europe. Kennedy had decided, however, that he needed to make a speech in Germany, not simply take a photo with top German officials. President Johnson, meanwhile, continued to try to neutralize Kennedy's trip in any way he could. Just as Kennedy was landing, Johnson called the German chancellor with the same speech he had given to Golda Meir. While the chancellor understood Johnson's message, he reminded the president that he had, in effect, a co-chancellor due to the coalition among various parties in Germany's parliamentary system. The chancellor told Johnson he'd have to speak with that assistant chancellor, who was the former mayor of West Berlin and leader of the Social Democratic Party, Willy Brandt. And Brandt, unlike the chancellor and Golda Meir, was enamored with Robert Kennedy.

Brandt convinced the chancellor that the American president was asking them to be rude to a long-standing friend of West Germany. The chancellor therefore called back President Johnson and told him that Brandt was going to be greeting Senator Kennedy in West Berlin, where Brandt had been mayor. Johnson was not pleased, but was glad the chancellor was not going to be there to greet Kennedy.

Brandt, upon meeting Kennedy, told him about Johnson's maneuverings, which sent Kennedy into orbit. "I'll show him," he said to a somewhat confused Brandt. Then, after taking a deep breath to remain calm, he said to Brandt, "Willy, I've been thinking on the way here that I'd like to speak to the people of West Berlin. I think it's important that while I'm here, I reaffirm my brother's commitment to you all."

Brandt enthusiastically agreed. He told Kennedy he could speak near the Berlin Wall, exactly where President John F. Kennedy had spoken in 1963. In that speech, John Kennedy uttered the famous phrase *"Ich bin ein Berliner"* ("I am a Berliner") as he stood on a platform near the barbed wire and concrete making up the infamous wall. It was a speech that Berliners and Europeans recalled with warmth and pride for decades.

When Kennedy told Galbraith and Bowles, they immediately warned him that there would be comparisons to his brother's speech and reception—and that such comparisons could leave the candidate looking less than presidential. Kennedy, however, remained adamant that he would speak at the wall. He worked for hours and hours on his speech with Walinsky, Bowles, Galbraith, and finally, alone.

The next morning, Kennedy made his way in a West German government limousine to the huge platform from where he would speak to the German people—and, with television and radio, to the world. As the limo approached the platform, Kennedy began to think about his martyred brother. He fought back tears, partly because he admitted to himself that he hadn't thought as much about Jack, as he still called him, in recent weeks. Punishing himself for this transgression against his brother's memory, he also recalled his brother's cool nature under any adversity. He recalled his brother's valiant but silent fight against Addison's disease. He recalled the way Jack charmed people in ways he, Bob, never could.

I never received the accolades for my speeches that Jack received for his, he thought to himself. Why can't people get over the fact that I was just playing an enforcer role for my brother? That wasn't the real me. I'm the real me now. I know people tell me I'm the best thing since sliced bread since that nut took his shot at me. But I know one thing. People come to see me to see if they can be there when someone tries to shoot me again. I'm like a walking car race. That's the adrenaline I feel out in the crowds way too often.

Kennedy started to panic. Why did I agree to speak here? Chet and Ken are right. The press will compare my speech to Jack's speech, find it lacking even if it's great, and I'm helping the sons of bitches who want to bring me back to earth . . . permanently! Damn! If Mankiewicz had been here, he'd have just canceled it and let me yell at him. Damn it to hell!

Tears welled up in his eyes. He looked up to the top of the inside of the limousine, and then, in his mind's eye, past the roof of the limousine into the sky, looking for Jack.

Mankiewicz, meanwhile, was in Washington, working with O'Brien on final arrangements for the convention in Chicago. Mankiewicz was, as Kennedy thought, "pissed" at what Kennedy was doing. "Larry, why the hell didn't he speak, if he's got to speak at all, at someplace more neutral? Is he out of his mind? Is Galbraith that much of a naïve academic that he can't see what this could mean to the campaign? Doesn't he remember the crap Bobby got for his comments in Chile two or three years ago? I thought Galbraith was smarter than this! Christ, I thought *Bobby* was smarter than this!"

In 1965, Bob Kennedy had visited a mining area in Chile as part of a tour of several Latin American countries. After seeing the horrible conditions there, he said to a *New York Times* reporter, "If I worked in this mine, I'd be a Communist, too." On the same trip to Latin America, Kennedy had spoken to a group of radical students, saying in part:

> This is the time of trial. Throughout the hemisphere, men and nations argue the great questions, and freedom hangs in the balance. Throughout the hemisphere, entrenched privilege resists the demands of justice. In every American land, the dispossessed and the hungry, the landless and the untaught, seek a better life for their children. In every American land, in yours and mine no less than in others, a revolution is coming—a revolution which will be peaceful if we are wise enough, compassionate if we care enough, successful if we are fortunate enough—but a revolution which will come whether we will it or not. We can affect its character; we cannot alter its inevitability.

The American press, most mainstream politicians, and even Democratic Party leaders attacked Kennedy, at the time, not only for being soft on Communism, but also for essentially sympathizing with violent revolution!

O'Brien shuddered. "Don't remind me, Frank!" He shook his head and said, "I don't get why he wants to make a speech at the Berlin Wall either. It's crazy! How's he gonna top his brother? If we get out of this speech with only a few jokes and some minor criticism, I'll be flying to Chicago without a plane." Both men looked down at the floor of the headquarters in disgust, expecting the worst.

Halfway across the world, Kennedy arrived at the Wall and was hurtled through a crowd of what seemed like a million people but was "only" half that, at least by official counts. The East German government, perhaps the most hard-line in the Eastern European "captive" nations, had extra security on hand on the other side of the Wall. The government there had declared a curfew and took the extraordinary step of jamming all possible radio frequencies to keep what-ever Kennedy had to say from reaching East German ears. Czech radicals, however, were able to broadcast the speech through their "underground" radio stations, whose transmissions filtered back to those parts of the more coura-geous population of East Germany willing to listen to the speech.

Kennedy met Vice Chancellor Brandt, who embraced his American friend with a deep bear hug, then shook Kennedy's hand and introduced him as a brother in the international struggle for world peace and, "just as impor-tantly, freedom and justice!" The crowd was acting as unruly as screaming kids at a Beatles' concert, and Kennedy hadn't even begun to speak. Most people couldn't make out the vice chancellor's final words in introducing the senator because the screaming and applause were so loud. Kennedy approached and finally reached the podium and was shocked that, try as he might, he couldn't even begin his speech. The cries and cheers of the audience were overwhelming. He thought of the biblical story of the battle of Jericho and the walls crumbling to the sound of trumpets. He quickly tried to kill that thought, which, ironically had been Walinsky's original idea for his speech.

Kennedy kept motioning the crowd to be quiet, yet the crowd refused. The people's emotion at seeing the slain president's brother at the hated Wall dividing Berlin—dividing the West from the East, dividing the freedom to speak from the oppression of that freedom—needed its release in this moment. Kennedy stepped back and bowed his head—and the noise reached its peak. Kennedy struggled unsuccessfully to prevent some tears from forming. Then, finding his strength, he wiped his eyes, looked up at the audience, and put his hands up in a firm gesture, in effect ordering the noise to cease. Suddenly, a silence enveloped the air, almost suffocating the throng.

Kennedy stepped up to the podium and leaned into the microphone. His hair was waving slightly in the soft wind that had been blowing all morning. He finally began, with a German translator standing next to the podium with his own microphone:

> There is a wall in Jerusalem that has withstood war, wind, pestilence, sorrow, joy, and time. It is a wall of an old Jewish temple, built over two thousand years ago. People of all faiths go to the wall, called the "Wailing Wall" by those of the Jewish faith, to pray. People pray for their own sins to be banished. They pray for the health of loved ones. They pray for peace and, at long last, for justice and freedom to come strong and complete into the world.
>
> We stand here today before another wall. This wall is a product of a war of sorts, not in the sense the Israelites and Romans had in their day, but a wall of war all the same. And while people may sometimes come to pray at this wall, those who come to pray at this wall pray that it falls down into rubble. They pray that it breaks apart and scatters to the winds. Or that the wall be picked apart, piece by piece, with picks, with shovels, and by hand, by people of all faiths working together in a communion of freedom.
>
> The political leaders on the other side of this wall, the ones who built this wall, think they can stop time with stone, mortar, barbed wire, and checkpoints. They think they have won with this wall because friends are kept apart from friends, children from parents, brothers from sisters, parents from children. Time, they believe, will make people forget each other the way an eraser removes a pencil's mark. The slight mark that remains will not be clear enough to mean anything, they believe.
>
> Those political leaders, however, are wrong.

Kennedy pounded the podium in rhythm to the next five words:

THIS WALL WILL NOT LAST! I say it again. THIS WALL WILL NOT LAST!

There were enough Germans who spoke English, as a result of fifteen years of American influence from television broadcasts to American soldiers stationed in Germany, who needed no translator for those words. The audience erupted with a sound that started with a moan, then a roar, and then a scream, with stomping feet. They began to chant, "THIS WALL WILL NOT LAST! THIS WALL WILL NOT LAST!"

Kennedy tried to stop the chant to continue his speech. He failed. As the chant itself continued, he realized he was losing control of the crowd. He thought to himself, My God, what do I do now?

He took his right hand off his speech notes, just for a second. That was all the wind needed, however, as it snatched them into the air. Kennedy gasped as the notes flew up in the air, up over the dais, above trees, and—now, it was the crowd's turn to gasp—over the Berlin Wall. Another cheer went up, people laughed, many crying with laughter, and Kennedy relaxed a bit and smiled. He knew the wall of Jericho was not going to crumble and lead to World War III, at least not that day. The crowd, with this last upsurge of emotion, finally lost a bit of its noisy energy—enough to allow him to continue. And luckily the rest of the notes contained no more than an outline. There were no secrets, nothing controversial for KGB agents to leak to their friends in the CIA. He was well aware that the KGB hated him only slightly less than the CIA at this point in his political career. He decided, without the speech notes, to wind up, trying to remember Walinksy's words.

My friends, this wall stands today, and will stand the rest of this day and into tomorrow. It will, however, come down in our lifetime. It will not last the generation. It is not the "Wailing Wall" in Jerusalem and will never be such a wall. The wall will come down because it *must* come down. And when it comes down, it will *not* come down because people have changed their nature. It will not come down because people have given up war forevermore.

It will come down, instead, because it does not belong here and never did belong here. And it will come down because people *cannot be at war all the time*. There must be freedom to move, to go from one place to another. There must be freedom for people to see their friends and family. The crumbling of this wall will not bring utopia, but it will be a sign that human nature is capable of love as well as hate, of tolerance as well as intolerance. It will be a sign that people need at least some world justice, some world peace, and a lot of freedom. And those conditions do prevail over time.

I say to the Russian leadership, the East German leadership, today, at this moment, We cannot hide behind walls from each other. We cannot resist peace with guns and tanks for too long. The spirit of Hungary in 1956, the spirit of the youth today in Prague, our youth, our children, here in Germany, in France, and even in my land of the United States, are no longer accepting of the limits imposed by those who would undermine the freedom to speak one's mind or to travel as one pleases.

My brother once said in this very city, *"Ich bin ein Berliner."*

The crowd's energy had returned as they applauded and shouted, until their voices became a roar again as Kennedy finished saying the German phrase. He forcefully put up his hands in a gesture that momentarily mesmerized the crowd. At that moment, Walinsky, realizing Kennedy was trying desperately to end the speech, handed his boss a small piece of paper with the German sentence he wanted to say. Kennedy took the paper and concluded his speech:

My friends, we can begin today to take down this wall by saying to those East German and Russian leaders, and to the people in the East, in the West, and in the North and South of our planet, *"Die Menschenliebe macht uns zu Brüdern und Schwestern!"* ["We are all brothers and sisters in the human family."]

Thank you, and may God bless us with justice, peace, and love toward our neighbors throughout the world.

The last sentence, not surprisingly, was drowned out in the frenzied joy of the crowd.

Vice Chancellor Brandt leaped from his seat and hugged Kennedy. There were hats flying everywhere amid thundering screams and cheers. The podium and dais shook from the movement of a million feet. The vice chancellor then looked back at the crowd and saw it was on the verge of deciding to blast through the Wall at any moment. Brandt jumped to the podium and said in German, "We cannot accomplish everything we want in one day, my friends! Violence must be avoided at this moment at all costs. We are not ready today! We are not ready today!"

Kennedy joined Brandt, who told Kennedy what he said. Kennedy then said, "The vice chancellor is right!"

Someone yelled from the crowd, in English, "Brandt's a coward! We must fight *now!*"

Kennedy's face reddened with anger. But he knew from his stint in the American South that anger is just what the heckler wanted. He breathed a cleansing sigh and then said, in loud measured tones, "Vice Chancellor Brandt is one of the bravest men I have ever met. He fought in the Resistance when others decided to wait things out. We are not prepared today to storm that wall. We will not be making a statement for freedom if we cause violence today. *Today is not the day."*

"When?" "Why not?" The demands came from seemingly all quarters of the crowd.

"It is coming, one step at a time," Kennedy answered, again in measured tones. This experience was new to Kennedy, who had worked so hard to move people through rhetoric, as did his brother. Now Kennedy had to calm them. "In a world filled with nuclear weapons, we cannot run and break down this wall in a sudden rush. We must diffuse, as leaders, the threat of nuclear war before, not after, we tear it down. The wall will come down only when we replace this wall of fear with a building of trust. Trust is the foundation here, not anger, not more violence."

The crowd caught its breath and then hushed. The Berliners, seeing their own emotions threatening them, realized, after all, that today was not the day. American reporters who covered the day's events said they had never seen anything like this before. An old journalist among them, from the Hearst newspaper wire service, said he recalled another American leader who had so captivated a German crowd: Woodrow Wilson just after the Armistice ending World War I. "This is a dangerous time," said the old reporter. "I can't say whether we're on the brink of annihilation, the brink of world peace, more chaos, or more muddling. Bobby," he said, and the younger reporters could only agree, "is an almost primordial force. But like Wilson, who also seemed invincible, he could burn out like a comet in the atmosphere."

O'Brien and Mankiewicz, watching Walter Cronkite and the other evening news' shows the next day, were in open-mouthed shock at what they saw and heard. "Who wrote that speech? Who wrote that?" yelled Mankiewicz. "That was un-effin'-believable! The Jews—shit, everybody!— have got to love the . . . the *balls* of talking about Jews and Jerusalem in . . . goddamned Germany!"

O'Brien was just as effusive. "That was amazing! It was hard-line so even Nixon can't touch it. And the peaceniks had to love the last bit—that was even better than the remarks Bob made after Martin Luther King was killed. He's scary when he goes off the cuff, but sometimes . . . it's just golden! Perfect!"

Mankiewicz turned a bit more somber, however. "Yeah, but anyone can play this into anything they want. Too sentimental. Or better yet for Nixon, it shows Bob gets people riled up, and maybe people have had enough riling up."

O'Brien suddenly looked like a four-year-old whose balloon had burst. "You—you're right, Frank. It's the emotional side here. I'm drained just thinking about the roller coaster nature of it. Shot it up sky-high and then slammed it back down. Remember that poll before the California primary showing people thought Bob divided people more than united them? We gotta get out there and see what people's reactions are."

They didn't have to worry. Nixon's staff thought they could attack on just those grounds, but they were stymied. Kennedy's timing was astonishing. His speech occurred right near the beginning of the Republican National Convention, set to nominate Richard Milhouse Nixon for president for the second time in less than a decade. Yet, Kennedy had the headlines and the coverage. The Gallup Poll showed Kennedy nearing his initial highs following the resurrection.

Worse, Nixon did not, as he and his advisers had hoped, get the "bounce" of popularity in the polls that a nominee normally receives after a nominating convention. With Kennedy's speech in West Berlin, and last minute infighting among the Republicans, particularly the Republicans' "liberal" Rockefeller wing, Nixon's campaign received a two-point bounce that disappeared three days after the Republican convention.

But all was not perfect for Kennedy, either. Despite positive coverage of his Berlin Wall speech from both U.S. and European media, when Kennedy and his entourage arrived in Paris, the last leg of the trip, he received a chilly greeting from the French government. The French officials, who had just gone through the cataclysm of the May Day riots under a student leader who called himself Danny the Red, wanted no speeches from this particular American senator. Ironically, there was no call from Johnson either way by that point. Kennedy had thought of defying the French, but realized he risked sending the wrong message—the brash, arrogant Bobby—to foreign leaders. He said to Galbraith, "Ken, let's just smile a few more times for the cameras and go home. We've got a convention ahead of us, and a campaign to run."

Chapter 6

ANOTHER CONVENTION

On August 21, 1968, less than a week after Kennedy arrived home, the Russians, with the Eastern European nations of the Warsaw Pact, invaded Czechoslovakia, putting a violent end to the Prague Spring.

In the weeks leading up to the invasion, the White House had been in contact with the Soviet ambassador to the United States, Anatoly Dobrynin. Dobrynin gave Johnson reason to believe that the Russians were far more interested in better relations with the United States. On the evening of August 20, Johnson was putting the finishing touch on his announcement of a peace mission to Moscow to push for an expanded nuclear nonproliferation treaty, when Ambassador Dobrynin came to the White House with the news that the Soviets were going to invade Czechoslovakia. Johnson, through Secretary of State Dean Rusk, informed Dobrynin that there would be no mission to Moscow and none by this president—ever.

Dobrynin muttered sadly to Rusk, "I understand, Mr. Secretary. Tell President Johnson I understand his feelings on the matter—off the record, of course."

The news of the invasion stunned Kennedy. However, he immediately grasped that the political fallout would likely fall against any candidate calling for "peace" in the face of "totalitarian aggression." He called a press conference late in the day and made a forceful statement condemning the Soviet Union as the enemy of freedom, the enemy of peace, and the enemy of human decency. He called for an immediate grain embargo against the Soviets, knowing this could be politically dicey in the grain-producing states of the Midwest, including Illinois, a key state for the fall election.

Sitting in his home at Hickory Hill with his longtime friend Kenny O'Donnell, Kennedy said, "What else could we do to register our protest? Bomb Cuba? I saw where that led back in '62. We were lucky then, and I wouldn't want to tempt fate again, Kenny. The only thing we export to the Russians of any value is grain. We'll deal with the political fallout in six weeks or so."

O'Donnell asked, "Bob, isn't that a little long to wait—"

"Ken!" Kennedy interrupted sharply. "The Russians invading one small country may not seem like a lot, but it affects *everything* I'm trying to do in this campaign. Clark Clifford tells Larry O'Brien that the North Vietnamese have dug in their heels at the Paris peace talks. Le Duc Tho, the North Vietnam spokesman, came out with a statement that shows support for what the Russians did. Can you believe that? Johnson is feeding people the same line as Nixon's people: Kennedy is going to cave in to the Vietnamese—and the Vietnamese Communists are waiting for me to get elected and won't do anything to stop the war. And you know what that bastard Johnson did last month just as I left on my trip? He met with Nixon! Just as I have been saying all along, he and Nixon are on the same side in this war question and . . . and . . . " Kennedy shook his head with a deep sigh of frustration. "They're gonna milk this Russian invasion with everything they've got. We could be heading into a new Red scare, Kenny. I really mean it."

It was true that Nixon and Johnson had met on July 26, 1968. It was true that the Vietnamese had "dug in their heels," but all they wanted was the United States to stop all bombing of South Vietnam before they made any peace concessions, a position they consistently adhered to for the past three years.

Yet, despite Kennedy's misgivings, things were so bad for Nixon that he couldn't get a positive bounce from the Russian invasion of Czechoslovakia. Kennedy managed to play hawk and dove at the same time, condemning the invasion and expressing the hope that the Czech people would remain strong—and then saying the time to speak with the Soviets over arms control was coming no matter what those in the Soviet Union might currently think. Kennedy's "hawk and dove" statement infuriated Nixon to no end.

Nixon exclaimed to John Mitchell and another aide, John Ehrlichman, "How does Bobby Kennedy get away with it? When will the press people see through that son of a bitch?" These rhetorical questions were couched less in fury than in frustration.

Nixon took out his frustration by calling a press conference without alerting his campaign's media staff. In classic Nixon style, he agreed with the senator's earlier point that the Berlin Wall must come down, but pointedly noted that the wall had gone up during a particular *Democratic* administration. "Now some may say that President John Kennedy might have been able to stop that wall from going up, but I, Richard Nixon, don't believe that by that point, at least, there was little to do short of war." Nixon then concluded by saying that he knew "the American people will see that I have the experience in these important matters of foreign affairs, and just as President Eisenhower and I brought peace in Korea and the world, so, too, will we bring peace again with a Republican administration."

Nixon refused to take questions after his statement and simply left the podium. This merely reminded the reporters of why they did not like Nixon in the first place. Nixon's remarks hung in the air, and the reporters convinced themselves that the remarks were "typical Nixon innuendo of attacking an opponent by talking about what *others* say," as columnist Meg Greenfield put it in the *Washington Post*.

"We just farted," said Ailes the morning after the press conference. Ailes' only comfort was that none of the three television and radio advisers to the Nixon campaign had called the shots on that conference.

President Johnson recognized the frivolity of reading presidential tracking polls in mid-August in the face of serious foreign and domestic concerns. Yet Johnson, a natural political animal, couldn't get away from talking about the election. He spoke, as he did more and more frequently, not with Clark Clifford, but with his young "official" historian, Doris Kearns. "Good speech Bobby made in Berlin—and that press conference on Czechoslovakia was pretty good too, Ah gotta admit. He knows we can't put an embargo on grain in an election year. Smart politics, though. Everyone will forget that next month when the election carnival is in full swing. Maybe the little shit is worth more than Ah give him. Ah dunno. A leopard can't change its spots, can it?"

Kearns responded, "I can't see how a leopard changes its spots, Mr. President. Maybe we're just seeing a side of the senator that is simply coming better into focus." She was careful, however, knowing Johnson could quickly turn into what press secretary Bill Moyers had once described to her as "a teed-off snake in the corner of the kitchen."

Johnson continued. "You know, we knew the Russians were gonna invade Czechoslovakia the way they did Hungary in 1956. We just didn't know precisely when." This, of course, was not quite true. "Unlike us, them Russians don't mess around like we have in . . . well, you know—"

The president actually believed the U.S. war in Vietnam was a "limited" war, although by then, the tonnage of bombs dropped on that small nation was rivaling what the United States had dropped in World War II over *all* of Europe.[1] And that didn't include the half-million American troops fighting against Vietnamese farmers and peasants, most of whom saw the United States as a "foreign invader."

In the spring of 1968, North Vietnamese president Ho Chi Minh had issued his ultimatum to President Johnson: "Stop the bombing and then we'll talk of resolving this war." Johnson responded to the "intransigent demand" of Ho, the North Vietnamese, and the Viet Cong in South Vietnam with the largest aerial assault of B-52 bombers since the bombing campaign had begun in 1965. Johnson also significantly increased the search-and-destroy missions against both the Viet Cong resistance fighters and the North Vietnamese troops.

Vietnamese casualties continued to mount, which would have been "good news" for American war aims in any other war. However, U.S. reporters were now becoming cynical at U.S. military spokespersons' efforts to reclassify civilians as the "enemy" simply because they were now dead. If these civilians were now the enemy, reasoned the reporters, then weren't the previous low estimates of enemy support among the peasantry understated? And if the enemy count is that large, and getting larger, where is our support among the Vietnamese people that required us to enter the war in the first place? There was a growing understanding among reporters and the elite of American politics that the political goals of the war in Vietnam were not the same as the political goals in World War II. In World War II, the idea was to smash an aggressive Nazi Germany and fascist or military regimes in Japan and Italy, not help civilians in those countries overthrow their dictators. In Vietnam, it was about helping civilians defeat the Communists within one country, South Vietnam, and bombing another, North Vietnam, to keep it from helping Communists in the South. The problem the American government faced was that lots of people in South Vietnam seemed to be for the Communists. Thus, the military got stuck playing games with "enemy dead," and the reporters became cynical.

The reporters were now finding "grunts"—regular soldiers, and even officers—who were feeling the same way. And worse for the Cold Warriors in Washington, D.C., major business leaders from the halls of Chase Manhattan, Standard Oil, General Motors, and IBM were starting to ask the same questions as reporters and soldiers.

Larry O'Brien, just before the Democratic convention was to begin, was now getting it from both sides on what the presidential nominee should say about the Vietnam situation. He was, like it or not, considered Kennedy's new "Bobby." From one side, O'Brien heard from Clark Clifford about the supposed "intransigence" of the Vietnamese. From the other side, he had to endure Tom Hayden talking about U.S. imperialist murder. O'Brien wanted to be curt with Hayden in the same way Lincoln had been curt with abolitionists in his own nascent party a century before. O'Brien thought to himself, Damn that Hayden! He doesn't understand that we gotta win the election before we can get out of the war! Hayden was clueless regarding the political maneuverings between Nixon and Johnson—and O'Brien wasn't going to tell him. O'Brien simply bit his lip and told Hayden that he would talk with Kennedy about making a statement during the convention.

O'Brien was also working overtime reading and trying to stop any political fallout from the new book by Victor Lasky, *RFK: The Myth and the Man*. The book Harry Treleaven had talked about a month or two earlier was now released to the public—on the eve of the Democratic convention. Luckily for Kennedy, the book was released the day of the Russian invasion of Czechoslovakia and was essentially ignored in the broadcast media, where more and more Americans learned "the news," rather than turning to newspapers.

Further adding to O'Brien's—and Kennedy's—luck, Lasky was not a sympathetic person in the eyes of major news editors and publishers. He was a gruff, older reporter, which made him "gauche" to those refined, elite souls.

Worse, the media elite projected a "ghoulish vampire" image onto Lasky as they recalled his earlier book, an attack on JFK published shortly before the president was assassinated in 1963. Now, they reasoned, just two months after Robert Kennedy was almost murdered, here comes Lasky again, trying to make this younger Kennedy brother seem like the devil incarnate. This was par for the course for the elite media because Lasky, though an insider with the CIA and the FBI, was an outsider among the Beltway and New York media powers.

Ironically, Lasky's book was well researched, if partisan in its conclusions. The book chronicled Kennedy's hardball tactics, his flip-flops on issues over the years, his inexperience as a lawyer and as attorney general. In its most explosive sections, the book hinted at Bobby's sexual relations with the late Marilyn Monroe. Lasky picked up where another far-right journalist, Ralph de Toledano, had left off in the latter's *RFK: The Man Who Would Be President,* published the year before. Like Lasky's book, de Toledano's had not fared well with the press, despite having a respected publisher. Besides the fact that de Toledano was seen, among even the mostly Republican editors and publishers across the nation, as a highly partisan "right-winger with an axe to grind," the book was released in late 1967, right after Kennedy had told everyone he would not run for president in 1968. The book immediately ceased to be newsworthy and failed to register with much of the public.

The only people poring over the Lasky book with more vigor than O'Brien, Mankiewicz, Galbraith, Arthur Schlesinger Jr., and a few others around the Kennedy camp were Nixon's men. Frank Shakespeare said to Harry Treleaven, "This is great stuff, Harry. It's as if we got the chance to publish de Toledano's book all over again."

Treleaven was happy to be vindicated, but replied, "Yes, but the book's going nowhere. Even when it's reviewed, it's the same bullshit: 'Nothing new except a little more innuendo and venom from a known Kennedy-hater.' That's not enough, Frank. And with the Russian invasion of Czechoslovakia and Bobby taking a tough stance—God! He called for embargoing grain against the Russians, for chrissakes!" He paused and took a deep breath before starting again. "Did you know we asked Republican Senate candidate Bob Dole of Kansas, a big Nixon supporter, to float that idea to Archer Daniels, the big agribusiness company in his state? And you know what? They went ballistic! Who'da thought a big corporation would be softer on communism than Ché Bobby?"

Frank Shakespeare was quick to answer: "Archer Daniels and those grain companies are not soft on communism, Harry. And you know that, too. They're just greedy asshole businessmen—the kind of people we like to work for! What pisses me off is they refused to even let us *talk* tough. After the election, we could forget about the embargo—and everyone else would have forgotten by then.[2] Harry, we need to keep focused here. I love this stuff from Lasky. It gives me what Roger and I need to prepare some hard-hitting campaign ads. We must—"

Roger Ailes walked in on the conversation, refusing to wait his turn to speak any longer: "Thank God those ads are running now! We're still behind in the polls, Wallace's support is still strong. And it's almost Labor Day! We gotta increase Kennedy's negatives, which are *natural* negatives if we play it right. But I'm startin' to wonder if we're gonna come in third behind Wallace if we don't knock Kennedy down to earth!"

Shakespeare said, "Okay, okay, Roger! But calm down! The ads are great, but we gotta be real careful here as to how much we do. Remember, we just spent the past year talking to everyone about the 'new' Nixon. We blow that and there's no hope whatsoever. And it'll be *our* ass! We can't make Nixon look like an attack dog because there isn't any underdog sympathy for an attack dog, even when he's down. Am I clear?"

Ailes and Treleaven nodded.

Back in Chicago, a subdued hope filled the city as the opening day of the Democratic Party's national convention approached. Bobby Kennedy's nomination was already assured. The antiwar college kids and activists, despite their anger at Johnson's increased bombings and the continuing draft, were also in a sanguine mood, for they realized they were getting what they had asked for last year—a peace candidate for president. In the summer of 1967, nobody could have predicted that Johnson would decide against running again and that Kennedy would be walking into a convention as the presumptive presidential nominee a year later, arm in arm with antiwar activists and, of all people, Boss Daley.

The presidential nominee had decided upon a choreographed, but quiet and unifying, convention. The Soviet invasion of Czechoslovakia underscored the need for unity in the Democratic Party and to look like hard doves as opposed to weak hawks, or worse: weak doves. Kennedy's advisers for the convention included Mayor Daley, of course, Lane Kirkland from the AFL-CIO, Walter Reuther of the United Auto Workers union, and Allard Lowenstein. This was in addition to the usual aides and advisers: Joe Dolan, O'Brien and O'Donnell, Lowenstein, Mankiewicz, Steve Smith, Ted Sorensen, and the "intellectuals," which now consisted of Bowles, Harriman, Galbraith, and Arthur Schlesinger Jr.

On the opening night of the convention, Kennedy made a brief appearance to hold hands up high with Hubert Humphrey and Richard Daley, with a smiling and clean-cut Tom Hayden and Rennie Davis in the immediate background for all the college kids to see. There was Allard Lowenstein speaking late at night about leading youth to help workers around the nation eradicate poverty, with Walter Reuther standing just behind him, embracing him when he was finished.

Reuther and his union, the UAW, while clearly favorites of the presumptive Democratic presidential nominee, found themselves in a strange position in the weeks leading to the convention. For Reuther, after storming out of the AFL-CIO in 1967 after his dispute over labor strategy with George Meany, decided to ally himself with the Teamsters Union. The Teamsters, at least, were interested in organizing labor in the South. But the Teamsters was the union of Jimmy Hoffa and organized crime, the twin nemeses of Bobby Kennedy during most of Kennedy's public life. The Teamsters, who hated Kennedy as much as Kennedy hated them, had already endorsed Nixon at the Republican National Convention. Reuther was forced, just before the Democratic convention, to suddenly break off relations with the Teamsters and to reaffirm his support for Kennedy.

To add to the confused personal politics among the union leadership in America, Meany, an ardent cold warrior who saw Kennedy's "peace" candidacy as nothing short of treason, was quietly letting people in his kingdom of labor know it was "okay" to vote for Nixon. He was barely at the Democratic convention before he left and let his loyal assistant, Lane Kirkland, represent the association of labor unions. Reuther, now officially on the outs with Meany and the Teamsters, spent many hours with the other union leaders in the AFL-CIO. He found that his union's warm embrace of Bobby Kennedy was allowing him back into the union movement's fold.

But Reuther was not ready to lead the UAW back into the AFL-CIO—at least not yet. Reuther was simply betting on Kennedy to defeat Nixon so he could help Kennedy and "the kids" lead an organizing drive through the American South that would rival the civil rights movement. After the organizing began, he figured he could then come back to the AFL-CIO with the power to neutralize, if not overthrow Meany. Reuther was always known as a man who thought big when it concerned union organizing.

Kennedy, after that first night, decided he needed to stay away from the delegates and the television cameras. He was working hard with his speechwriters to write a speech that was more programmatic than filled with memorable rhetoric. He wanted—to put a more cynical spin on things—to promise significant programs or subsidies to every section of the country. The strategy was to blunt Wallace in the South and force Nixon to the right toward Wallace to the point where Nixon could not claim he was the "moderate" his campaign had been making him appear to be. Kennedy also told reporters, off the record, that he was champing at the bit to debate Nixon. O'Brien, also off the record, said to reporters that Nixon was not "debate-ready because he's been so insulated by his television-savvy campaign staff." O'Brien refused to go "on the record" because, he admitted years later, he did not want to embarrass Nixon into debating. As Gene McCarthy had pointed out long ago, the Kennedys loved to play football, but if you noticed, it was always "touch" football.[3]

None of the reporters reminded Kennedy to his face that he was no Jack Kennedy when it came to debating. Also, although the reporters liked that Kennedy was talking to them more openly than Nixon, a few veteran reporters never forgot that Kennedy was very much like Nixon. Both tended to be distant from reporters, particularly when tough questions were asked, and both Nixon and Kennedy were always willing to drop innuendos about their opponents while surrogates engaged in direct attacks.

The big—and only—mystery of the 1968 Democratic convention was whom Kennedy would pick as his vice-presidential running-mate. Seeing that Humphrey was not interested in continuing as vice president, Kennedy decided he wanted a regional choice, outside the Northeast, in order to "balance" the campaign ticket. This was proving impossible, however, because the Southerners were too "conservative" for Northerners and Midwesterners, and the Northerners and Midwesterners were too "liberal" for Southerners. The more people Kennedy, Dolan, Mankiewicz, and O'Brien talked with, the harder the decision became.

Delegates and political bosses alike were adamant about getting every-thing they wanted in a vice president. The great unspoken point beneath each constituency's refusal to compromise was that "some nut out there" would eventually take a shot at Kennedy again. The liberals and the leftists didn't want a repeat of a Kennedy-Johnson type of ticket—even though one could easily argue that Johnson was more effective and—yes!—"liberal" in fighting poverty and racism than Jack Kennedy had been. Northern liberals and left-ists detested the idea of any Southerner on the ticket and made their prejudices against Southern accents known early.

Daley, seeing the tension, began thinking he might make a good vice pres-idential candidate himself. Daley's wife reminded him that the national media hated him only slightly less than he hated the national media—and unlike the local press in Chicago, Daley couldn't easily cajole or buy off the national media. Kennedy, who learned of these aspirations from "da Mayor's" aides, breathed a deep sigh of relief when Daley called to say he was not interested in the vice presidency.

There was talk, from a Wisconsin Democratic operative, about drafting the most famous football coach in America at the time, Vincent Lombardi of the Green Bay (Wisconsin) Packers, for the vice presidential slot. Lombardi was already a hit on the business convention circuit with his brilliant though perhaps boosterish pep talks on teamwork, duty, competition, and playing hard and fair. Ironically, Nixon—a football fanatic of the first order—originally asked John

Mitchell to contact Lombardi with the suggestion that Lombardi run for vice president with Nixon. The Republicans, however, found out Lombardi was a New Deal Democrat and a Kennedy supporter. Lombardi even supported unions—except the football players' union, but even in that case he wasn't fully on the side of the football team owners. Lombardi also supported equality among blacks and whites, and—amazing for his time—had not discriminated against homosexual athletes on his teams. It was Lombardi's wife, Marie, who was the blue-blood Republican. "The wrong Lombardi was a Republican," said Nixon in an interview years after the election.

Daley squelched the idea of Lombardi as vice president before any calls to the coach were made. "Look," said Daley, "dere are dose of us in da city [meaning Chicago] who aren't too crazy about Lombardi an' hate his Packers ta death—an' I don' want no nut in Wisconsin goin' after my Bobby just 'cause he wants ta see his team's football coach as president! That's a no-go—*an' I mean it!*" Because this was a time when celebrities in politics were not commonplace—people around the nation were still laughing at California with its movie star senator, George Murphy, and governor, Ronald Reagan—the Draft Lombardi for Vice President movement died before it was born.

Some black and student activist delegates floated the name of a young black Southern activist, Julian Bond, and momentum was beginning to gather. Larry O'Brien, Steve Smith, and Walter Reuther screamed that this would be a disaster. "We need to hold the white working-class vote here, Bob! This will kill us!"

Kennedy refused to intervene but let it be known that perhaps Mr. Bond's bid was premature. He asked the young firebrand Reverend Jesse Jackson and the Reverend Andrew Young, two African American leaders close to the late Dr. Martin Luther King Jr., "How do you fellows think a Kennedy-Bond ticket would do in Texas or Virginia, at least one of which we need to win? Can it bring out enough blacks in Virginia, or blacks and Spanish Americans in Texas, to overcome Wallace and Nixon?" Bobby, who had learned how to massage the egos of Southern governors while leading the attorney general's office under his brother Jack, knew that Young and Jackson themselves wanted to be considered vice presidential timber one day. Bond was a bit of an upstart to them. Bond hadn't been with Martin at the Lorraine Motel in Memphis on April 4, 1968, had he? Bond wasn't there when Martin was shot down, was he? Young and Jackson saw the tumblers of telling the truth and their own career advancement fall perfectly into place. They both told the presidential nominee-to-be that they would work to quash the Bond bandwagon, and that was all it took.

Kennedy, sitting in his hotel suite, despaired to Allard Lowenstein. "Al, can't you and your allies accept *any* Southerner? We gotta have one. How about George Smathers from Florida? Florida's got a lot of ex-New Yorkers and such, right? Florida's a southern state we could easily win if we had a Florida senator on the ticket!"

Lowenstein snorted his disapproval.

"Al, Smathers is a good, decent guy! Really! He's not as bad as Senator Eastland, 'Mississippi's finest' . . . " Kennedy was trying a humorous approach now. Humor wasn't working either. Lowenstein refused to respond with any words. Instead, he arched his bushy eyebrows.

Kennedy stood up, trying to show some authority, even though he was clearly doubting himself and what he was trying to say. "I was thinking," he said, "about this young fellow who was recently appointed to the senate seat from South Carolina, Ernie Hollings, but he's running for reelection for his first full term. The only other fairly, well, civilized southern senators who would join with me—Sam Ervin of North Carolina, Herman Talmadge of Georgia—they're both running for reelection, too." He began to drift, walking toward the kitchen area of the suite.

Lowenstein stood up, trying to create his own show of authority. "Look, Senator. You know and I know you're gonna have a hard time in any southern state this year. There's hardly anyone who'd run with you for fear of getting hit with a race-baiting primary in the next election cycle. I don't see why you can't go with George McGovern, who is a great Midwesterner— South Dakota's still Midwest on the map, right?—or Vance Hartke of Indiana. He's good, too. Very good. And so is Al Gore of Tennessee.[4] Heck, I think you can get away with Adlai III . . . "

"Adlai Stevenson? Are you crazy? The son of a two-time loser? Come on! Stevenson probably wouldn't want to run with me anyway, what with our history with his dad. Remember, Jack turned down the vice presidency in Stevenson's dad's run in '56 . . . Well, maybe it wasn't quite that way . . . . And Gore, not a bad choice, but he's losing his southern accent, if you know what I mean—"

Lowenstein looked sharply at the senator.

Kennedy continued. "Well, that's what I hear from some of my brother's old supporters down there. You think I haven't thought of that angle? Plus, Tennessee's not deep enough in the South. So goes Tennessee, so goes . . . what? Nothing! And what's it got? A few electoral votes? Same thing, geography-wise, with Indiana. I like Senator Hartke . . . a lot! If it makes you feel any better, I'm definitely leaning toward him. But Larry O'Brien says Indiana thinks like a southern state and won't influence enough other Midwestern states. Vance Hartke is a longtime supporter of my brother and me, though . . . Either way, I still may ask him." He walked up to Lowenstein, close now.

Lowenstein started to sweat a little as Kennedy put his arm around him. Bobby Kennedy meant more to Lowenstein than anyone else ever did or would. Each time Lowenstein looked at the senator, post-Los Angeles, he thought he was looking at Moses, if not Jesus. Sometimes Lowenstein couldn't even look him directly in the eyes, and instead looked downward.

"You know, Al, I already approached Vance, but two liberals on the tic—why are you looking down, Al? That's better. I like Vance, don't get me wrong. But can't you give me a break with a more conservative guy? I mean, really! FDR had John Nance Garner for vice president and that didn't upset anybody, right? And didn't Garner get shot when that gunman went after FDR?"

"No, Senator, that was the mayor of Chicago, I think." Lowenstein wasn't laughing at Kennedy's joke. He hated it when Kennedy made even an indirect reference to what happened in Los Angeles. Lowenstein composed himself enough to say, "Senator, you think this year is like 1932—"

"It's a crisis year, that's for sure, Al."

"Yeah, it's a crisis all right. But it isn't the same kind of crisis. We got race riots and a divisive war on our hands, Senator, not an economic depression that can make people more united in their thinking. We may be closer to 1860 than 1932, if I may be blunt."

"You always can, Al, even when I don't want 'blunt.' My ears still ring with your telling me off last year for not running for president then." Kennedy smiled at Lowenstein. He genuinely liked Allard Lowenstein, much to the consternation of other Kennedy loyalists. "Al, this could get embarrassing if we don't get this wrapped up today. I need a Southerner or a Midwesterner now!"

"Okay, okay! I'm just thinking here. How about Texas Senator Ralph Yarborough? He endorsed you late last month . . . "

"He did? Yarborough? When? I mean . . . Why . . . did he endorse me, I mean?"

"You were just leaving for Moscow, I think—but I can't say why, other than he agrees with most of your policy positions. It didn't make a big splash, or really any splash. He never called anyone in the national media, as far as I know, which I understand is kind of typical for Yarborough. He's not a joiner outside of Texas circles."

Kennedy was almost laughing at the suggestion. "Yarborough's a prairie liberal! How's he gonna help us get Wallace voters to vote for me?"

"Well, I . . . uh . . . w—why don't we ask him? He's from Texas, a state worth five Southern states in electoral votes, and with influence . . . It's worth a shot—oops . . . uh . . . "

Kennedy laughed this time. "Al, it's okay. I still say 'It's worth a shot.' It's no big deal." Geez, he thought to himself. Even my own people can't rid themselves of the feeling that another nut . . . Kennedy paused in his thoughts, then quickly defaulted back to Yarborough. "Al, let's talk to Ralph. He's here, right? Good. At least I can thank Ralph for his endorsement and support. Guess he must be falling out with Lyndon to endorse me!"

"Who knows?" said Lowenstein. "I don't understand Texans any better than you, and they don't understand me. Let's ask Walt Reuther what he thinks, though, before we go further with this idea of mine. He's worked with Senator Yarborough."

Kennedy immediately called Walter Reuther to his suite. When Reuther heard Yarborough mentioned as a possible vice presidential candidate, he enthusiastically explained to Kennedy how Yarborough would help. "Senator, I think Yarborough's a great choice! He's as pro-labor as anyone— and talks about civil rights in a way that enough white folks can get it through their heads that the boss likes racial divisiveness in order to keep down wages. Ever hear Ralph's stump speech about helping the little fellow get to the 'jam on the shelf?' Brilliant! You can send Ralph Yarborough any-where in the South and he'll keep Wallace support down to a workable level. He'd also help you take Texas and he'd help in Indiana, southern Illinois, and Iowa. And you know what? I almost forgot, since some of our union rank-and-file who hunt don't like this much. Ol' Ralph is pushing for protecting forests and little critters—species to you, dinner to me—who are almost extinct. You know, kinda like the bald eagle, although I wouldn't eat that! I'd be a little worried if Ralph started telling automakers how to make nice-smelling cars, but . . . God! Yarborough's a natural, Bob, a natural! You could even send him to Oregon! I love it!"

Kennedy wasn't loving it yet. "But why did Yarborough endorse me? Isn't he still on good terms with Lyndon?"

"Well, theirs is an interesting relationship," said Reuther. "Johnson, as you might know, is friendly with Yarborough, but Johnson's always been more friendly with John Connally, who was admittedly close to ol' Coke Stevenson—no relation to Adlai, at least as far as anyone knows—and the segregation crowd that still runs Texas. Johnson's a crafty old politician. Yarborough's presence kept a lid on attacks on Johnson from the Connally side of the Democratic political machine. He could always play moderate between Connally and Yarborough. But now Johnson's time is over, and Ralph did come out against the war a while ago. And Ralph, well, he's always been a bit of a gadfly in Texas politics, but that doesn't mean he isn't sharp and strategic-minded. And here's something else to think about: Did you know that he was supposed to be sitting in that limo with your brother in Dallas, not Connally? Connally pushed Ralph out, even though Ralph had been U.S. senator longer than Connally had been governor at the time. Ralph was a big deal in Texas at that point—"

Kennedy snapped his head upright. "You're kidding me! Yarborough was supposed to be in that car?" Reuther started to speak again, but Kennedy held up his hand as if to say, Not yet. Shaking his head sadly, he thought about his brother again. "This is getting weird, Walt, real weird."

Reuther sighed and started again. "Well, I was about to say, Ralph may well have been thinking strategic when he endorsed you. I haven't spoken to him since he arrived here at the convention, but Ralph must think he's gonna face a tough reelection campaign in 1970 if Johnson isn't going to help him next time. Plus, Connally's been pushing this young millionaire, Benson, or something or other, I think his name is to run against Ralph in the primary. This Benson . . . nah, that's not it . . . " He hemmed and "ummm'd" and then said, "I got it! Bentsen, Lloyd Bentsen. That's it! Anyway, this Bentsen guy is no friend of labor. I was just hearing about it from one of the oil worker union reps down there. That Texas Senate primary in '70 is gonna be a helluva fight, I think."

"Hmmmm. I know Yarborough has been pretty strong against the war . . . And you like him, right Walter?" Reuther nodded in agreement as Kennedy continued. "And kids will like him since he's against the war. Yeah, a prairie guy who wants to save endangered animals, not just eat them . . . "

"Bob, there's one more thing you should also know." He paused for a second or two before continuing. "Yarborough was originally, but not vocally, backing Gene McCarthy up till June. He—"

"I can understand it if he endorsed McCarthy earlier. Big deal. Lots of good people did," nodding in the direction of Lowenstein. "What I don't get is why didn't Ralph call me, Walter, if he was going to endorse me like he did?"

"Well, Bob, maybe that's just it."

"What's 'it'?"

"Maybe all he was doing in his little press release—it wasn't a press conference, when he endorsed you—was telling Lyndon Johnson he was endorsing you. He was telling Johnson, 'I know you're not gonna support me, so why should I support you?' Texas politics has its own rhythms, as you know from dealing with Johnson and Connally. This may be Ralph's way of saying, 'I need help nationwide in '70 from kids, environmentalists, and union guys.' One thing about Ralph, he works to make his politics fall in place with his principles, not the other way around."

Kennedy had been smiling as he mulled the idea of Yarborough as a vice presidential nominee. He was beginning to like this idea, but his smile receded as he realized he hadn't received Ralph's endorsement after all. He may have been nothing more than a vehicle to allow one Texan to piss on another. Still, he thought to himself, let's not be too hasty in rejecting the guy. "Okay, Walt. Now the tough question: Is Ralph interested?"

"Well," Reuther began, "I'm not sure. He may not want to go that far out on a limb. Maybe I'd better check, if that's okay—"

"Walt, we're running out of time. We blew it big-time not thinking about vice-presidential candidates sooner. I always thought Humphrey was interested—and I figured if I stood up there with Humphrey the first night of the convention, the crowd would go wild for both of us. But Humphrey still wasn't interested and the antiwar delegates . . . Anyway, I didn't take that 'I'm going back to the Senate' line all that seriously—and I was wrong. When Humphrey bowed out, Ted Van Dyk, Humphrey's top guy, gave us a good

hint he'd run with me, and we figured that was basically it. After I got back
to the States, I called Hubert and couldn't believe he wasn't interested. He
said he really wanted out of politics for a while and then wanted to go back
to the Senate. He hated being VP because, he said, 'Even when you think
you're friends with the president, you're dirt compared to some assistant secretary of the interior, not to mention someone like the secretary of defense or
state.' I offered him the job as HEW secretary. No bite at all. After I calmed
down, I couldn't say I blamed him, you know? Lyndon treated him as bad as
we treated . . . well, maybe worse than we treated Lyndon. I just wish I'd
thought more about choosing a VP—and sooner."

Reuther went to see Yarborough. Kennedy asked Lowenstein and Ted
Sorensen to join Reuther. When the three men arrived at the hotel room
where Yarborough was staying, they found Yarborough alone. Yarborough
said to the trio when they arrived, "Why, hello fellas! Good to see y'all. Mah
wife, Opal, will be raht back. She's downstairs gettin' some postcards. You
know, it's very important to have a wife who helps with the human touch.
Why don't you boys—and Walter—come in and set a while?"

The trio entered the hotel room, reintroduced themselves, with each
telling him how pleased they were that Ralph had endorsed Kennedy. Ted
Sorensen began to circle in on the topic of the vice presidency as he said to
Yarborough, "We could have helped you get some good publicity for that,
and on a national level. You didn't call, however. We'd like to help you more,
though, and we were wondering if you'd like to set up a time to talk about
something rather important, if this isn't convenient for you right now."

Yarborough was very blunt, but smiling his usual bright and cheery smile.
"Fellas, I feel like a rabbit in a dog hunt with you boys hoverin' over me. Let's
get to it. What do you fah-n gentl'men wish to discuss? Notice Ah'm bein'
polite in askin', too."

The offer was presented, and Senator Yarborough sat for a moment. It
was one thing to think of someone offering the vice presidency, but hearing
it said with seriousness hit him squarely in the gut. He told the group he was
surprised to be considered. He had spoken jokingly to Opal about how he'd
be interested in the VP position, but he remembered how badly "ol' Lyndon"
was treated by those "rich Yankees," the Kennedys.

Yarborough, more as a defensive mechanism with these Yankees, decided to
throw some extra "corn pone" into his already deep drawl: "Gentlemen, Ah
hope Ah'm not too tough'n here, bee-cause Ah am honored. But Ah thought . .
. well . . . you know . . . Ah thought Kennedys didn't take to Texans all that
well." He then reminded Ted Sorensen that nobody had called him either when
he endorsed Kennedy, and that Kennedy didn't ever say much to him when they
were in the Senate together, even though they were "natural" allies. "Man's
gotta respect his subordinate, gentlemen, if the subordinate's gonna be able to

do his job, know what Ah mean? Not to say Ah think Senator Kennedy doesn't lahk me or mah fellow Texans. Ah know since his tahm in the Senate, he's spoken up to help the reg'lar folks, and especially p'or folks, and Ah admire that in a rich man. That's why Ah endorsed him. He's become a great man, overcomin' a lot of bad influences in his life. Plus, he was respectful, if not overly friendly to me when we did talk from time to time in the Senate. Ah'd be willing, Ah say, if he would like to discuss things personally with me. Then we'll see where things go."

That was enough for the trio. "He's interested," said Sorensen afterward to Kennedy. "He just wants to know you won't treat him the way Jack treated Lyndon." Ted Sorensen was diplomatic in not mentioning that Bob, not Jack Kennedy, had been roughest on Johnson when Johnson was vice president under Jack.

Reuther wasn't sure his friend Ralph was interested, but he now saw the urgency in making a choice sooner than later. In a guilty moment of gallows thinking, he thought to himself: "President Yarborough" sounds pretty damned good in case another nut is out there. That ought to be insurance enough to keep big-business right-wingers from going after his friend Bob Kennedy, or even whipping up the kind of hatred that had been brewing in Texas as Jack Kennedy traveled to Dallas in '63.

Yarborough and Kennedy met late in the evening just after that conversation with Sorensen. Within ten minutes, Kennedy was gushing with enthusiasm over Yarborough's salt-of-the-earth language and his desires for the country. Yarborough, in turn, was impressed and flattered, within fifteen minutes, by the man he always had been a bit wary of as being too "above it all" compared to old-style politicians of his kind. Yarborough asked for some time to think about it some more.

Kennedy responded, "Senator Yarborough—I should say Ralph—I admit I didn't plan this too well. I haven't got much time. I need an answer within an hour. I hate to be hard here, but time is very sensitive, as you know. We have to announce a choice tomorrow."

Yarborough called Reuther to his hotel room a half-hour after the meeting. He said to Reuther, "Bob has changed, Walt. He seems, well, grounded in humanity and even has some humility. A rare trait for a Kennedy, wouldn't you say?"

They laughed.

Reuther answered, "Ralph, it's now or never. You need to say the word." Yarborough nodded yes, and Reuther picked up the phone to Kennedy's suite.

Reuther said into the phone to Kennedy, right in front of Senator Yarborough, "Senator Kennedy, I think we have a ticket."

Yarborough smiled at Reuther and said to the union leader, "Tell Senator Kennedy he's got his man."

Kennedy said, "Thanks, fellas," hung up the phone, stared down at his shoes, and thought, I hope we have a winning ticket. That seemed too damned easy. He thought, Could this be a plot by Johnson against me winning? Nah, I can't be that paranoid. He thought again, Can I be?

Yarborough was the choice, but O'Brien and Mankiewicz had to keep it under wraps until the morning. To throw people off who might have seen Yarborough come into Kennedy's suite for their talk, they floated rumors of Kennedy picking Senator Ed Muskie of Maine or Fred Harris of Oklahoma. Nobody bought the Muskie rumor, but some bought the Harris one. It actually hit some wire-service stories and sent Mayor Daley into a fit bordering on a heart attack. He called Kennedy at his suite in the early morning hours before dawn, waking him up. "Bobby, what da hell ya pickin' dat damned Indian for vice president for? What happened ta Yarborough!"

Kennedy, a bit groggy, said, "Who? What Indian?"

"Harris! From Oklahoma! I t'ought you're goin' wit' Yarborough!"

"Mr. Mayor, I'm sorry. I'm so sleepy this morning. Harris must be a rumor going around, I guess. Harris wasn't even on my short list, if I had one. Oklahoma's too small a state and Harris doesn't buy us any votes we don't already have."

"Dat's my Bobby! T'ank Mudda Mary herself! I t'ought my heart was gonna stop—maybe it did for a secon'."

"Mr. Mayor, I'll see you after Mass. Maybe I'll join you there tomorrow."

"Bobby, when was the last time ya went ta Mass? I'm strongly requestin' ya join me tomorra. I never miss a day! I don' like showin' disrespect ta da man upstairs."

"All right, Mr. Mayor. I'll be there. Let's talk later today, can we?"

"Any time. Take care, Bobby."

Mayor Daley and Tom Hayden, who in the first timeline sat crying in different parts of St. Patrick's Cathedral at Bobby's funeral, now had, in this timeline, the opportunity to bond. Hayden was respectful but blunt in his statements to the mayor that the city of Chicago needed better housing and schools for the children and families on the South Side, where the black population resided. "We must have integration, Mr. Mayor. That is the least we must do—at the very least to hold the Democrats together!"

Daley liked that last part. It showed the kid was trying to think strategically about the Democratic Party. Daley was also beginning to realize that a new era was dawning. He was deciding he could like this earnest kid, Hayden, who at least wasn't dressing "like a bum" anymore. "Let me tell ya som'pin', young man. People don' need ta live next ta each ot'er all da time ta get along. I t'ink we jus' need ta get some money over dere—kinda like what Senator Kennedy wants ta do with dat part o' New York like he says."

Hayden was not happy, but thought to himself, Well, it's a start.

Daley, ever the politician, asked Hayden to pose in photos with him—but only when Hayden put on a white shirt, black tie and black jacket. The two of them were photographed, smiling, on the dais on the first day of the convention.[5]

Meanwhile, joined by only a few hundred supporters from around the country and without any permits—except for the day of Kennedy's acceptance speech—the Yippie protest leaders Jerry Rubin and Abbie Hoffman found themselves easily subdued by the Chicago police. Their presence generated no press or media coverage to speak of.

Kennedy gave his carefully planned programmatic speech on the fourth and last night of the convention. Near the beginning of the speech, while the audience was still exuberant at the sight of him, Kennedy spoke of the importance of "America's businessmen" playing a role in ending poverty in distressed communities and of his reverence for the system of free enterprise. He did this to assuage Tom Watson, president and chairman of the board of IBM, one of his few corporate supporters. In the union-rich delegations, that line received only tepid applause. To make matters worse, a few television cameras showed confusion and disappointment among some of the union delegates.

Kennedy then mentioned the subject of the Vietnam War. Rather than demand that America immediately halt its bombing of Vietnam, which was what antiwar protesters were adamant about, Kennedy merely pledged an "honorable and just peace." He said that everyone in the nuclear age must recognize that one must speak with one's enemies, however untrustworthy they may be. That was all he said directly about the war in Vietnam. He then said that raising taxes would not be necessary once the war was brought to an "honorable end." Further, he said, "We must be vigilant in making sure inflation doesn't bite away at both paychecks and profits."

A couple of antiwar activists tried to interrupt Kennedy's speech by shouting, "Stop the bombing" and "Johnson is a murderer." Daley's security quickly intervened and led them out of the hall. Tom Hayden became enraged at Daley's guards, going so far as to call them "thugs" in an interview with Pacifica radio news. It took a full day of negotiations, with Daley's son William and Kenny O'Donnell as the mediators, to sort things out between Hayden and the mayor. O'Donnell and the young Daley persuaded Hayden to "capitulate" in order to unite for a successful election.

The rest of Kennedy's speech, however, had the delegates on their feet and filled with a fervor that was the personification of Walt Whitman's "body electric." Kennedy called for renewed public transportation programs for metropolitan areas to create jobs for black and white workers. He called for a national health insurance program, "a program our party has proudly advocated since the time of Harry Truman!" He promised to spend more money on poverty programs but would "make them accountable to local government," which was a bow to Daley and other big-city mayors that most delegates and Americans didn't quite understand. Tom Hayden understood it, however, and wasn't sure he liked it. Kennedy also called for the repeal of restrictive labor laws, more water and road projects for the South and the West, and, potentially contradictory, new environmental laws to help "restore the natural wonder and beauty inside America."

After the speech, and still hot over the lack of specificity with regard to the Vietnam War, Hayden confronted Kennedy. "We have some very disappointed delegates, sir. There was no mention of a bombing halt or negotiations. A 'just and honorable peace' is . . . well . . . I have to say it: Nixon's kind of talk."

Kennedy struck back, sharp and sarcastic. "And Tom, you think while the Russians are mopping up in Czechoslovakia with real people's blood, that I ought to start calling Johnson a murderer? You think I didn't hear those radical slogans out there when I was speaking?"

Hayden wasn't backing down. "All you needed to say, Senator, was we should stop the bombing."

A younger Bobby would have banished Hayden from the campaign right there. However, he had learned from his dealings with Lowenstein that killing a young person's idealism was worse than winning a debating point. He spoke softly and put his arm around Hayden. "Look, Tom, I couldn't say that, not with Nixon running around saying he won't criticize the president or telling us what he'd do because it could supposedly stiffen the resolve of the North Vietnamese—"

Rennie Davis interrupted as he came running over. "There's a problem in the Michigan, Minnesota, and California delegations. They want you to reiterate on the record that you support a bombing halt and recognition of the National Liberation Front at the peace talks."

Al Lowenstein ran over as well. So did reporter Dan Rather from CBS Television, along with some cameramen, cameras that were "live" and looking for dissension in the Democratic Party between "America's youth and our national leaders." Rather asked, "Senator, can you talk about the comments I'm hearing from some of the younger delegates about your acceptance speech and the war in Vietnam?"

Kennedy smiled confidently into the camera and said, "Yes, I would be very pleased to answer your question right now, but I would like to verify if there is anything to this. I do not think it appropriate to respond to off-the-cuff remarks made in haste by individual delegates, if they were made, and I'd like to get back to you. I can assure you we stand united as a party and will unite the nation in this election. Thank you."

Kennedy grabbed Lowenstein, who nodded to Hayden to join them in a small meeting room just off the convention floor.

Kennedy lost his earlier control and went into a frenzy against Hayden. "What the hell do you think you and your friends are doing out there? Are you and those delegates out of your freakin' minds? Why don't you call Nixon and Wallace and tell them you're willing to work for them, because you can't do any better than saying that shit to the press and television people!"

Hayden started to squirm, then thought to himself, Here comes the liberal let-down.

"Tom, I've already said I think there should be a bombing halt. And after I said it, the bombing continued and got worse! If you don't know by now, Lyndon Johnson hates my guts more than Nixon! And more than that friggin' nut with the goddamned gun in L.A.! If I say 'black,' Johnson says 'white'! And he's got a whole network of powerful people out there to tell people black *is* white. Did you know that Nixon and Johnson met at the goddamned White House last month? You didn't? Well, you think they just met for tea and crumpets? Get real, Tom! I'm ending the freakin' war as soon as I get in! Can't you and your young friends take yes for an answer? Must I meet some rhetorical litmus test every time I open my mouth on the subject? The war isn't *everything*, you know! It's a lot, damn it, but it isn't everything!"

Hayden sat back, slightly more convinced Kennedy wasn't backing down from his commitment. That didn't stop him from speaking in a still frustrated voice. "Thank you, Senator. I just got one problem. How do I convince them downstairs?"

Lowenstein was testy now. "Shit, Tom! That's *our* problem, not his! We're gonna go downstairs, you and me—and get Rennie in this, too! We're just gonna say what the senator said, almost. And we're gonna tell them if they talk to any reporter about what the senator just said here, they're out of the campaign and there's no job waiting for them in Washington. Got it?"

Tom was going to respond that most of them were thinking of joining communes in Oregon and Idaho, not working in Washington, D.C., but thought better of it.

Lowenstein had the credentials and the drive to start calming down the delegates in private meetings. Tom proved to be a great closer, saying, "We're just over three months away from overthrowing Lyndon Johnson and defeating Richard Nixon. You can't expect Bobby to get us out of the war before the final election round begins—especially after the Russians just invaded another country. Remember, he talked of peace, not continued war!"

One radical delegate wondered if Russia was right to have invaded Czechoslovakia. The other delegates groaned at that remark.

Kennedy eventually told the CBS reporter Dan Rather that he had spoken with the delegates to reaffirm there was no change in his position. "There was at worst a misunderstanding among a couple of delegates, that's all." He then begged off answering any other questions "for now" and walked away.

The question some pundits asked was, "What is Bobby Kennedy's precise position beyond a bombing halt?" Did it include recognition of the South Vietnamese guerillas known as the Viet Cong? That was anyone's guess since Kennedy had been all over the place on that one.

Rather, more interested in the personalities than such highbrow questions, tried to get a scoop on the discussion from some of the delegates, but the word was out and it worked. Most delegates sang the praises of the nominee and his "healing" speech. One young delegate, smiling ear to ear at being interviewed on national television, said, "Bobby Kennedy is going to lead America to the promised land."

The night before Kennedy's failed attempt at an unexciting but programmatic speech, Ralph Webster Yarborough, son of Texas, had delivered what proved to be the best speech of the convention, even if it ruffled a few more feathers on Wall Street and in corporate boardrooms across the nation. Yarborough delivered a new version of his usual stump speech in prime time to those union and nonunion working-class voters who were hearing the racist and antigovernment siren call of Alabama's George Wallace. Yarborough was warmly introduced by Mayor Daley and then by Senator Vance Hartke.

Yarborough walked up to the podium. He smiled in his typical way, living up to his nickname, "Smilin' Ralph." The nickname sounded more appropriate for an aluminum siding salesman, but it was actually a testament to his being honest and caring about regular folks. Beaming into the audience and into the television camera lenses, Yarborough began to speak to twenty-two million Americans:

> Folks, with all this war stuff goin' on, and people yellin' at each other, you wouldn't know we were in the greatest economic expansion this nation—and the world—has ever seen. You wouldn't know that more people are able to buy a house than ever before, that more people who earn the minimum wage have better buyin' power than ever before. Heck, with a minimum-wage job these days, you can afford to provide for your family, live in a decent place, and even buy a couple o' cars—on installment time, of course, with the banker man!

Yarborough paused for a little giggle from the audience.

> But there's still some work to do, ladies and gentlemen. We Democrats have been doin' a good job o' cuttin' poverty. A few bizness folks are steppin' up, too, provin' that a few of 'em know a healthy economy and money in people's pockets means more customers for them.
>
> Just a few years ago, back when the Republicans last ran things, poverty was almost 30 percent. Now, Ah'm not talkin' 'bout Herbert Hoover and the Crash of 1929, heah. Ah'm talkin' just 'bout the

1950s when we had three—that's raht, three!—ree-cessions. With the start of the boomin' economy in 1963, the yeah Jack Kennedy gave his life for this country, the poverty rate had already dropped down to 20 percent. It never got much below that in any previous boom time, no matter how much the economy expanded. That's why President Johnson started the Great Society programs. Sure, there's been lots o' hemmin' and hawin', but in just three and a half years, we've cut that 20 percent in half, down to almost a 10 percent poverty rate. That's the lowest rate we have ever seen!

But 10 percent of people livin' in rural and urban slums, some of them on welfare, that's still a lot o' po' folks for the wealthiest country in the world. And Ah know we're great enough to do better—for ev'r'one, white, black, yellow, brown, or what have ya! We're all in this great land ta-geth-a!

The delegates, who had been interrupting nearly every sentence of the speech with whoops and hollers and applause, more mechanical after a while, now exploded with hollers and yelps almost to the level of joyous tears. The applause lasted a good three or four minutes before Yarborough could continue. Yarborough was rolling, and now he put up his hands to quiet down the audience. They ain't heard nothin' yet, he thought to himself.

Ladies and gentlemen, there are enough of us out there who remember the Great Depression, who remember how that Republican President Hoover, who promised us a chicken in every pot, and then, when the tough times hit, wouldn't even help us get the pot, let alone the chicken—

Laughter from the delegates was louder than Ralph thought it should be. He then remembered that "pot" now had a new secondary meaning—and a *primary* meaning to certain youth in the society. He cut that thought out and returned to the dangers of modern Republicans.

And those Republicans. Don't they say you have to feed the richest folks first so more crumbs fall off the table for the rest of us? That's what they call their 'trickle-down' eeee-con-omics, I think.

Whoops and hollers galore on that one in the union-dominated audience.

Yeah, Ah know you heard that one plenty o' times, that trickle down eeee-*con*-omics. Well, folks. Ah think there's still some folks left who haven't been gettin' much tricklin,' or even crumbs these days, and Ah am not just talkin' 'bout the poor who can't get jobs.

Ah'm talkin' 'bout folks who work forty, fifty hours a week in rural areas where the laws of minimum wage still aren't bein' enforced, and where people don't have any health care for their ailments which they got on the job in the first place. Our rural, hard-workin' folks in the mines of West Virginia and elsewhere, our textile workers in North Carolina, South Carolina, and Alabama, and mah oil field workers and sharecroppers in north and east and south and west Texas—gotta say all that when you're talkin' 'bout Texas, you know—and the hard-workin' grape and lettuce pickers in the fields of California, they ain't been allowed to organize themselves the way our daddies organized themselves thirty years ago in the auto factories, the steel factories, and lahk there. The textile workers, the fruit pickers, the oil workers, and the sharecroppers deserve the same rights lahk the rest o' the country, don't they?

And what about the folks who are jus' makin' it in the nonunion factories, the secretary jobs, the city-fied jobs where they see poor people's programs? They ask, 'Do Ah gotta get poor to get any help?' Well, help is on the way. Every citizen ought to get a basic benefit in health care, and more help makin' that mortgage payment to get into a house or just get to keep it!

A storm of applause, foot stomping, and even a spontaneous round of "There is power in a union!" popped out of a few state delegations. Yarborough quieted things down again with a wave of his massive arms.

We're gonna repeal that bad ol' Taft-Hartley Act, that's what we're gonna do.

Screams of applause from labor delegates jumped out on that one.

Some folks here know what Ah'm talkin' 'bout, but maybe some o' the rest o' you don't. That's the law that the mean ol' Congress twenty years ago passed over Harry Truman's veto to say that a union ain't got the freedom o' speech and right to support other unions when they're strikin' for decent wages and benefits. That law isn't American, when you think about it. How can a union man get put in jail in America if he, as say an autoworker, can't say to his boss, Ah'm gonna support the steelworkers in their strike in the same town? Now Ah can imagine that in Russia, or one o' them comm'nist places, but not in the good ol' USA.

And why does it gotta be so comp-li-cated just to get a vote for a union in the fu'st place? Raht now we gotta deal with all these darned rules and stuff. Why not just have a vote, a private ballot, and if the union wins, that's it. No recertification process, with a bunch o' lawyers, bless their hearts, and none o' that other stuff. We don't do no certification process when we vote for senators and congressmen! Why do we have to do a certification process after a union election? Lahk Ah said, this ain't Russia!

There were roars of applause and stomping of feet. Whoops and wails against those businessmen and commie bastards keeping down unions! Reuther, listening in the back of the convention hall, smiled and thought to himself, Classic Yarborough! Just classic!

Now, Ah think it's time to build on the good things President Johnson has done and improve the things that just haven't worked out that well. And Ah'm not just talkin' 'bout that war in that God-forsaken place halfway 'round the world as far as you can get. Ah'm talkin' 'bout some o' the things we've learned as we help other folks get more opportunity in our great land. Ah know that Senator Kennedy's gonna make the greatest president for workin' folks all over this country, and for those who aren't workin' but wanna work. Work is what makes a man, and workin' men are what makes a country succeed. It seems simple, and the more you learn about how things work, the more obvious that becomes. You know Ah always lahk ta say, 'You got to put the jam on the lower shelf so that the little people can reach it, too.' There's plenty o' jam we've made over the years, and we all know it. And you know, there's plenty enough jam to go around, too. All we gotta do is jus' work together to keep producin' that jam, and put that jam on the lower shelf, shall we?

Four minutes of wild delegates screaming with joy, laughter, hope, and faith—and the confidence that this was the greatest ticket in American political history. Ralph Yarborough managed to get back control of the crowd and end his speech:

In closin', ladies and gentlemen, Ah want to say that Ah am honored to be the vice presidential candidate for our next president, Robert Kennedy.

Two more minutes of applause followed. Yarborough continued toward his close:

You and Ah know how important Robert Kennedy's brother, President John Kennedy, was to each and every one of us, and how deep has been our loss since November 1963. Ah know we can restore the kind of government that all Americans can believe in. Ah know we can rally and unite people to treat each other with respect and provide opportunity for all. Ah am deeply honored to serve Robert Kennedy because Ah admire men who have the drive to win, and to win for the American way. Ah was privileged to serve under General George S. Patton, a California boy who led us to victory, along with that other great general, General and former President Eisenhower, back in the Big War. Robert Kennedy has the experience and has been there to fight the tough battles against poverty, against racism, and against injustice at home and around this world of ours.

We have a lot of good still left in each of us to show each other right here in the good old USA. Ah know we can do good things together and bring us close again as a nation. Senator Kennedy and Ah are gonna work hard for you, and we know you'll work hard to help build an America that is strong, united, and prosperous. An America that leads the world toward peace, in freedom and with prosperity for *everyone!* Thank you, and God bless all o' you out there in America. And let's hear it for the next president o' the United States, Robert F. Kennedy!

Before Yarborough's speech, Kennedy had been concerned about its antibusiness tone. But Larry O'Brien convinced him that Yarborough's speech would "throw the red meat to the delegates—and that sends them home ready to work for us through election day."

After hearing and watching the speech, Kennedy realized that Yarborough had, in the parlance of the time, "hit a home run."

He and Ethel had come down from the hotel to the convention hall to watch Yarborough's speech on the closed circuit television away from the delegates. He wanted to get a closer, if not firsthand sense of the reaction of the audience and reporters. Against the advice of O'Brien, Kennedy wanted to be on-hand to tell reporters that he was still very pro-business as well as pro-labor to blunt any overly pro-union message of Yarborough.

Ethel Kennedy was impressed with Yarborough, as was her husband. "Bob," she said, "that man knows how to speak in a way that makes us feel like we're all together as Americans—even if I'm one of those 'rich' people!"

Bobby nodded in agreement and, surprising Ethel, said to her, "Let's go."

With that, Bobby and Ethel Kennedy entered the stage of the convention hall as the delegates continued their applause for Yarborough. The delegates exploded in screams and more applause when they saw Bobby and Ethel, surrounded by Secret Service agents, stride up the aisle and up on the platform toward Ralph and Opal Yarborough. After greeting and hugging each other, the four of them did an early version of the now mandatory eight-arms-held-high convention salute.

Kennedy, smiling, began to shift his mind to political strategy. Good choice, Bob, good choice. This guy Yarborough can probably get a lot of Wallace votes—and we're definitely going to win Texas! We're going to plant this guy in the South for the next two or three months and he's gonna win us a couple of states there. He's a liberal all right, but he makes it sound like he's at a square dance or with the Lawrence Welk crowd, people I've been slowly losing. He's definitely "down home." I may have to calm him down a bit because Tom Watson of IBM isn't going to like that union stuff. And that stuff against the rich—gotta be careful there, too. I can't send him to any big fundraisers, or anywhere in New York or the West Coast, that's for sure— well, maybe a union hall. But, man, I'm gonna need him in a lotta places when things tighten up and with Lyndon gunnin' for me with Nixon. And Wallace out there lurkin' like a snake in the grass—this drawl is mighty contagious, I gotta admit!

As the soon-to-be-nominated Bobby Kennedy stood there with Ethel, and Ralph and Opal Yarborough, the newspaper photographers and television cameras caught him in a broad smile. But no camera or other recording device caught his calculating thoughts about his new running mate and the 1968 presidential election.

Chapter 7

NIXON VS. KENNEDY, THE SEQUEL

The Nixon campaign had reason to be glad that the Democratic convention still showed some signs of disunity, but its more seasoned advisers knew that Kennedy and Yarborough were going to be a formidable pair as they toured the nation. It was that insight that led Nixon and his advisers into what became a simmering strategy feud throughout the rest of the campaign. The strategy feud boiled down to one question: Should Nixon debate Kennedy or not? The debate over whether to debate lasted well past Labor Day, when the final campaign began.

Ailes wanted Nixon to debate Kennedy, the sooner the better—and maybe even two or three times. However, he knew there was no consensus among the more senior advisers on the issue, so he stuck to the negative ads he and Treleaven had created. The ads started running the week of the Democratic convention. Even his Democratic Party counterparts admitted the ads were "state of the art." They took the emotional negatives about Kennedy—his divisiveness, his intensity bordering on recklessness in a world full of nuclear weapons, his flip-flops on the war and on welfare programs—and had people "on the street" say, in general tones, that they did not like those traits in a leader. In the punch line of each commercial, the people said how much they admired Richard Nixon's steadiness, his earnestness and knowledge of foreign affairs, his experience, and especially his caution against economic experiments that cost average taxpayers more and more money.

Nixon's corporate supporters, not the campaign, paid directly for the ads. At the end of each ad, the tag was always "Paid for by Citizens for Good Government," or "Democrats for Nixon," or something similar. Despite Yarborough's strong populist speech, Kennedy's numbers started to go down after the convention. Pundits noted the decline and cited as a cause not only Nixon's ads, but also Kennedy's lackluster nomination speech and the rumors about "the simmering disunity" remaining within the Democratic Party. The one positive thing for Kennedy was that his support among union voters was holding strong and steady.

Nixon, however, was restless in mid-September 1968 as he entered the back room of the campaign headquarters for a special meeting with his top aides. In that room were the following people: attorneys John Mitchell and Leonard Garment; John Ehrlichman, a trusted aide who had been with

Nixon not only in 1960, but also during 1962's ignominious defeat at the hands of California Governor Pat Brown; Roger Ailes; Frank Shakespeare; Harry Treleaven; Richard Allen, a foreign policy expert and political operative who had been instrumental in keeping Rockefeller in line after the convention; and campaign speechwriters William Gavin, Patrick Buchanan, and Ray Price.

John Mitchell spoke for the candidate: "That Commie Yarborough's going around the South making county fair speeches that are just killing us, and more to the point, are taking back votes from Wallace—votes we should be getting. What are we doing about that, gentlemen?"

Ailes couldn't believe it. That was no way to start a strategy meeting! Bobby's numbers are going down. That's a *good* thing. You don't start the meeting with a bummer, he thought to himself. Ailes was now seething at this old man's cluelessness. Nevertheless, he knew from dealing with movie and television stars not to pounce. Instead, he smiled at Mitchell and said, "Yarborough's getting one-tenth of the audiences we get in a single night of television ads. Television is the precinct leader now. Look at the polling numbers we've been getting from Kevin Phillips on our staff. We've cut Bobby below 50 percent in three weeks of ads after his nomination. We didn't get a post-nomination bounce, but they got a reverse bounce from our ads."

"Maybe Bobby's just coming back to earth for the moment," said a still stern-faced Mitchell. "He did before. And then a couple of speeches in Europe and the reporters just swooned—"

"Eastern liberal reporters, Jew editors," mumbled Nixon. Len Garment heard this and shook his head, thinking, outside of the *New York Times,* most editors were anything but Jewish. Why does he say that kind of stuff? thought Garment, who respected Nixon as much as, if not more than, anyone in the room.

Ailes was undeterred, but willing to be respectful. "Mr. Mitchell, I understand your point that we have to hit the traditional ground level out there. We can do a train whistle-stop. We can have Mr. Nixon make some speeches to various war veteran groups or other safe places where hecklers are limited. But you can't deny that television has been Mr. Nixon's friend this time around."

Nixon cleared his throat and said, "John, Roger's right on that. I am very pleased with the newest polls. We need, I think, however, to shore up our right flank because Yarborough is using that Commie-union crap that is confusing voters who are divided between us and Wallace. I can't stay any longer. I just want you people to work this out. Mr. Mitchell will let me know all the details for my final approval. Thank you, gentlemen."

With that, Nixon left the room. Too many people, he thought to himself.

And then the fight over whether or not to debate reached its fever pitch among the assembled. Ailes, Shakespeare, and Buchanan were adamant that Nixon should debate, while Price, Mitchell, Erlichman, and Gavin thought he should avoid any debate. Treleaven and Garment were in the middle but found the middle ground to be quicksand. You had to get to one side or the other—and quick.

"Harry, there is no middle ground here!" Buchanan shouted at Treleaven. "Nixon either debates like a man or cowers behind a television commercial or a phony kaffee klatsch! Kennedy is still ahead, and Yarborough's taking more votes from Wallace than we are! I don't care that Bobby's down to 48 percent. The problem is *we've* hardly moved. That's the story right there!"

Ray Price, who hated the bullying posturing of Buchanan, said in measured tones, "We can't get lost in tough-guy posturing. We're talking Richard Nixon here, gentlemen. A brilliant man, but not someone who easily handles live television in an uncontrolled environment. You can put makeup on him, but you can't change the fact that he isn't a natural actor like the Kennedys."

Ailes started to speak, but Frank Shakespeare beat him to it. "Look, Ray, I was against this debating at first, too. But the Lasky book and my conversations with Roger made me realize we've got to debate, not play it too safe. If this was Humphrey running, and if the college kids acted out more this year against the Democrats, maybe have a riot, I'd say 'Hold tight and keep Nixon under wraps,' for goodness' sake. But we're running against the Kennedy myth here—with 'myth' being the key word! A myth that can be broken, too! Remember, we're running against ruthless, sputtering Bobby Kennedy, not smooth-talking Jack. For chrissakes, Bobby's just as liable to crack under the cameras as Nixon. I saw the tapes of him and Gene McCarthy from late spring. He looked scared, damn it! Scared! He isn't his brother, that's for sure. The commercials we did have now overcome, at least with our supporters, the Kennedy inevitability that seems to shroud everything we do here. We now have to take the second and most important step—and that's to start chasing Bobby Kennedy around the country calling him a coward for not debating. That's going to help, too."

John Ehrlichman spoke, after getting the go-ahead from Mitchell. "Gentlemen, I have had the opportunity to see Yarborough in action throughout the South, starting in Texas. I've also seen Wallace quite a few times. All of you are forgetting two things that people such as Mr. Mitchell, Mr. Price, and I know full well. One, Richard Nixon is a deeply private man who hates confrontation and personal contact. I wouldn't say this to anyone other than this group—and even this group is too large—but let me give you some background to make this first point clear. Every Christmas and New Year's, I prepare for Mr. Nixon a list of personal information on each of his 'friends.'" Ehrlichman made the quotes sign with his fingers. "When he calls them, I have written on a sheet of paper the friend's wife's name, the kids' names, if they just had an anniversary, birthday, graduation, or some big event we can find out about, and it's totally scripted. A couple of times I've sat with him in case someone says something unexpected, like 'My wife has cancer' or just died—whatever! Then Mr. Nixon writes down 'cancer' or 'wife sick' and I write back what he should say. You think he's going to be able to handle something in the middle of a national debate we haven't thought of, no matter how careful we are?"

"Whose side are you on, John? Don't you believe in Mr. Nixon?" demanded Buchanan.

Ehrlichman stopped and glared at Buchanan. Mitchell put his hand on Ehrlichman's shoulders and said, "That's okay, John. Make your other point." That was a signal to everyone, including Buchanan, that Ehrlichman was speaking with full authority of the candidate.

Ehrlichman, calmed by Mitchell's hand on his shoulder, continued. "Thank you, sir. Gentlemen, all this talk about debates has assumed it's only Kennedy versus Nixon, Part II. Yes, I—I mean *we* think that Bobby is a much weaker debater, and if it were just these two, I'd be saying let's go to a debate by all means. Go for the win, not the tie. But, gentlemen, I've seen Wallace, and he could, in a three-way debate, smoke these two guys, and that spells big trouble for the country. You let that crazy redneck get too popular and even in a position to win the ball game . . . "

He hesitated, and Buchanan broke in. "So we should lose because we're afraid Wallace could win? I don't believe it! What's the big deal even if Wallace won? He'd do a lot of good in getting things back under control for Middle America, wouldn't he?"

Leonard Garment shuddered at Buchanan's comment. Ailes, however, was struck silent by Ehrlichman's point. He hadn't quite seen the danger of a Wallace plurality victory. He also noticed that Nixon's top man, John Mitchell, nodded gravely in support of Ehrlichman. This was no time to go out on a limb with Buchanan.

Frank Shakespeare put up his hand and, ignoring Buchanan, said, "John, let me think about what you said for a moment . . . or perhaps a day or two." Brilliant, thought Ailes. Shakespeare was making a short-term retreat with dignity. There had to be another way, Ailes thought. There had to be.

Treleaven, showing respect, raised his hand to John Mitchell to be allowed to speak. Mitchell recognized Treleaven and Treleaven said, "Mr. Mitchell, why don't Mr. Ehrlichman, Mr. Garment, Mr. Price, Frank, and I talk about this tomorrow? Is that appropriate, or should you or someone else perhaps be included?"

John Mitchell said, "No, Mr. Treleaven. Mr. Ehrlichman is more than capable of leading this discussion further." With that, Mitchell mumbled that the meeting had come to an end and left the room.

The next day the participants continued arguing back and forth about whether to debate Bobby. Without reaching a conclusion, they decided to watch Kevin Phillips' tracking polls for another ten days. Maybe Nixon would start to pick up steam finally, and they wouldn't need to decide to debate. Ailes, still of the opinion that Nixon should debate, didn't want to be the only one siding with Buchanan. He therefore agreed with his elders, Shakespeare and Treleaven, to watch and wait.

The Johnson White House was carefully watching the election, too. President Johnson, speaking to Secretary of Defense Clark Clifford, said, "You see those ads Nixon's running against Bobby? They're damned effective. You know, Clark, if Pontius Pilate had the ability to run attack ads on television against Jesus Christ, we'd all be prayin' to Zeus or whoever!"

Clifford said, "Mr. President, surely you aren't comparing Senator Kennedy to—"

"Come on, Clark! Ah know that little shit has more faults than Rockefeller has money! But damn it, Clark. It's just that, magnified on the TV, Ah'm startin' to wonder whether *anyone* can be made to look bad. Even Jesus!" Even me, thought Johnson, glad to be getting out now. "Clark, you know what the biggest problem is with this TV stuff goin' all over the place? Pretty soon you won't be able to tell different things to different people in different parts of the country anymore—and then where the hell will ya be?"

Kennedy's camp was deeply worried about the drift below 50 percent in the polls. O'Brien told a friend, who told a reporter, that things were in a panic. Kennedy began wondering whether he should replace the whole damned staff, or maybe ask Tom Watson to manage his campaign if things didn't improve. Yarborough, testing his level of access to Kennedy, asked for a private meeting with the senator, who readily agreed. Might as well hear from Yarborough, Kennedy thought to himself.

"Senator Kennedy—"

"Just call me Bob, uh, sir."

"Sir? Now, Bob, Ah may be older than you—Ah just turned sixty-five this year, but Ah can outrun any forty-five-year-old, that's for sure! But please! Call me Ralph! We gotta make sure we're informal with each other if we're gonna heah each other."

"Okay, Ralph," said a slightly more relaxed Kennedy. "What's on your mind?"

"Bob, Ah'm watchin' the polls, too, and Ah know you're concerned. Ah've also seen a few of them commercials on the tella-vision. Ah think, if ya don't mah-nd me sayin' so, we gotta shake things up against Nixon. Get people thinkin' about Nixon. Right now those ads make 'em think 'bout you too much—and not in a way you want. You know and Ah know that those commercials are all bein' done by Nixon. They talk about Communist fronts? Well, these are Republican fronts—there isn't any 'new' Nixon, and we know it. Now, the way Ah see it, mah hunch is that Nixon doesn't want to debate—"

"Yes, Ralph, that's my hunch, too. But how do we *know* that and, more important, how does debating help *our* side?"

"If Ah may say so . . . first, we know that Nixon doesn't want to debate for one simple reason: We aren't hearin' a damned word out of their camp to debate—at all! That's how we know! If they had the slightest bit of interest, we'd hear about it. You know, 'sources within the Nixon campaign' in the papers and all that. But there's nothin' but crickets out there chirpin' on the near side prairie. Nothin' 'bout any ol' dee-bate!"

"You know, Ralph, when Johnson used to talk like that, I'd be embarrassed. With you, I think it's quite . . . terrific." Kennedy paused again, and then said, "Now tell me how that helps me—I mean, us . . . "

"Thanks, Bob. Now here's the plan. We've been too quiet the last few weeks. Playin' possum, ridin' on high polls and such. Ah know you said off the record that you'd love to debate old Tricky Dick. Ah have my sources, too, in the press. Been enjoyin' talkin' to the boys on the bus. Anyways, Ah think you ought to go public with that 'off the record' comment and—"

"I can't, Ralph, and you should know why . . . " He was now slightly agitated. "Don't you?"

"Try me."

"Wallace. He's a great debater, and he's got 12 percent in the polls—and he may be rising. We look bad, all of us, if Nixon and I keep him out. I—"

"S'cuse me, Bob, but that's what Ah'm trying to say here. Nixon is *completely* afraid of Wallace. After the first few votes, more starts comin' outta Nixon's behind than our . . . uh . . . side. We keep pushin' Nixon to have a debate and demand he include Wallace. The Wallace voters see you actin' *lahk a man.* They lahk that—Ah know ah do, too! And Nixon's havin' to say nothin', or say he won't, or can't say yet, and . . . Ha! There's no way that dog's gonna hunt for nothin'! While he's fumblin' around looking weak—and lookin' weak in this world of nuke-u-lar weapons isn't very presidential—we get our investigators out there and find out how 'Democrats for Nixon' is tied into Nixon and—"

"Got that going already, Ralph."

"Gotta keep me in the loop if we're gonna make this work, Senator Kennedy." He was showing formality to make a point about trusting him.

"You're right, Ralph, and I apologize. You know, I like your idea. I was afraid of including Wallace. If I get you right, you're saying my fear is really Nixon's fear, right?"

"You got it, pardner! One thing Ah've learned in mah life, Bob, is this. Usually your biggest fear is inside you—and more times than not, if you face your fear in a campaign, it becomes the other fella's fear, not yours."

"You know something, Ralph? You're right. It's kind of what Emerson said: 'Always do what you're afraid to do.'"

"Damn straight, Senator Kennedy! *Damned* straight! And make the *other* feller scared!"

Kennedy smiled as he said, "Ralph, I think you're gonna be one of my closest advisers." Then he became very serious. "But what happens if Nixon accepts?"

"Bob, if Nixon accepts, that's *really* his problem! Remember! Put the fear into the other fella. You're a better debater than you think. It all depends on who you're debatin'. I heard you were a little stiff against Gene McCarthy. That's 'cause you guys didn't have anything to argue about. How do you debate someone you basically agree with? Here you'd be debatin' Nixon and Wallace—the Bobbsey twins preachin' hate out there! You can't get all passionate and excited for that? Come on, Bob, even Ah know you better than that! But don't worry. Ol' Tricky Dick ain't gonna ever put himself in a deebate with Wallace and you! No way!"

"Let's try this out on the other guys, shall we, Ralph? You know, I *am* relieved. Like a big rock lifted off my chest. You'd make a great shrink, Ralph. A great one."

"Ah hope that was a compliment, Bob." Ralph smiled as he said that.

Kennedy's lead staff wholeheartedly accepted the strategy proposed by Yarborough. In addition, Kennedy made another strategic decision that went against his core advisers, including Yarborough and especially Mayor Daley. Kennedy was going into the crowds, come what may. He was tired of speaking behind bulletproof glass in large auditoriums, where people spent hours waiting because everyone had to be searched as they came through the doors. He also made clear that he hated being surrounded by Secret Service agents as if he was a touring display of the Queen's Royal Jewels.

"I'm going out there, and you can come along or stay behind," Kennedy told his assembled group. Because there was no choice, the staff went out "there" with him, eyes always casting about for anyone who looked suspicious—which included lots of otherwise normal-looking people.

Johnson, who had authorized wiretaps on both Nixon's and Kennedy's campaigns, soon found out about Yarborough's idea. "Sumbitch, that Yarborough!" laughed Johnson slapping his knees. "That's just good ol' Texas wisdom—that's what that is. Go at your fears and make 'em the other fella's fears." Then he remembered how mad he was at Ralph for going over to Kennedy. "Damn!"

Nixon met privately with Ehrlichman, Mitchell, Ailes, and Treleaven. Nixon spoke this time. "Gentlemen, our boy wonder of pollsters, young Mr. Phillips, has decided that Yarborough's 'cornpone' is keeping enough Wallace voters in the Kennedy-Yarborough camp in Texas, Tennessee, and maybe Indiana. Wallace is still strong in Mississippi, Alabama, Georgia, and South Carolina, but in North Carolina and Virginia, Kennedy-Yarborough is gaining momentum. One thing is clear to me: Debating with Wallace only legitimizes Wallace. And that bastard Kennedy is running around baiting me to debate. He's rebuffing our efforts to do two debates: one without Wallace and one with Wallace. I thought they'd go for it since Wallace takes away some Democratic support in Michigan, Ohio, and even New Jersey, where we stand a good chance to win, if . . . " His voice trailed.

Mitchell broke in. "Gentlemen, what Mr. Nixon wants to tell you is that we must step up the attack ads. We cannot debate since debating only legitimizes Wallace. I've been in touch with Victor Lasky, the fellow who wrote that book on Kennedy, and he has some interesting information about the senator and Marilyn Monroe as well as trysts he had with other starlets and various women during his primary campaign. He learned about this from various sources after his book was published."

To get any red-blooded American male's attention in 1968, or even 1998, all you had to do was utter two words: "Marilyn Monroe."

It worked here as well. All of them leaned forward in their chairs, many shifting something inside their own pants. Now it was Ehrlichman's turn to speak. "Here's the scoop . . . " said Ehrlichman, and he revealed what Lasky had learned about Bobby's affair with Marilyn, with corroboration from Peter Lawford (through a female Nixon spy) and even Lawford's mother— although her knowledge of her son's activities was strictly hearsay, and her claim of friendship with Monroe was weak. A source in the FBI was helpful, with phone logs showing calls going from Monroe to the Justice Department when Kennedy was attorney general serving his brother. Monroe made the calls in the weeks and months up until the day before her death. And there was evidence, said the FBI source, that Bobby had been at Monroe's house within the last twenty-four hours of her life. Joe DiMaggio, the famous baseball player and Monroe's ex-husband, who was supporting Nixon, spoke one evening with a friend, who relayed it to Victor Lasky, that Bobby was there just before Monroe died. DiMaggio was ready to go public if Nixon asked— if only to "get" Bobby Kennedy.

Ailes was deeply disappointed about there not being any debates, but this information about the late movie star was fantastic. He muttered a couple of times while listening, "This is unbelievable! Amazing!" But, he thought to himself, Who was going to run this ad? "Maybe we should just leak it," he said aloud.

Nixon flashed with anger. "You think those reporters and editors don't know this? Come on, Roger! They know it and knew it at the time. Damn it! I heard about it before Jack was killed! First, it was Jack having his way with her and then it was Bobby! Disgusting!"

The other men nodded, but they weren't sure it was disgusting. A couple of them were already visualizing themselves in the Kennedy brothers' position. As sexual fantasies descended upon the males—except Nixon—in the room, Nixon was suddenly aware that their minds were losing focus.

"Gentlemen," Nixon said, banging on the table, "Dick Nixon is not going to sit by and let another pervert enter the White House!" Nixon knew Johnson was a womanizer of the first order, too, but figured it was just a legacy of Southern wildness and incivility. And Ike's mistress was, well, one of those things gentlemen don't talk about. In Nixon's view, Kennedy, however, was a serial sexual addict.

After making his point, Nixon left the room. John Mitchell now spoke—and it was clear to everyone in the room he was speaking for the candidate. "Roger, are you up to organizing a series of ads in this regard? I need someone who can be trusted to put this together in secrecy, and without our being seen as connected to it in any way. It is also important that we only state that there is evidence of this relationship, but that further investigation by the Congress or the newspapers is necessary. That will tie things up for our opponent . . . " He almost smiled.

Roger said, "Yes, sir. I can make it happen, sir." Unlike the prudish Nixon, Ailes was fairly comfortable with the '60s' changes in matters of sex. He really didn't mind the youth culture of the '60s all that much, except when it came to the hippies moralizing about trees and singing "Kumbaya." Ailes said to the remaining assemblage, "I think it's an excellent idea, sir. Sex sells, and sex scandals really sell!"

"For the good of the nation," said Mitchell, "we can rid ourselves of these perverts. Television and radio can be cleaned up *after* Mr. Nixon is elected." Everyone harrumphed in high moral splendor and righteousness at what they were about to do. Yes, for the good of the nation, this information must be exposed to the public.

Meanwhile, the "debate" debate continued to rage within the Nixon camp. There was seemingly no end in sight as Nixon himself began vacillating on the subject—knowing full well he didn't want to debate, but thinking he might have to debate.

Frank Shakespeare secured Nixon's approval to run some Red-baiting ads in the South directly against Yarborough. "Sir, we tried to get some flip-flop stuff on issues, but Ralph's pretty consistent. And while it's easy to line up his liberal views with Communists and such, truth is, he stays pretty well clear of Commies—plus, in Texas there aren't a lot of Commies to begin with!"

Nixon was focused in his response. "Run 'em, Frank. Run 'em. Helen Gahagan Douglas, my Senate opponent in 1950, didn't know Vito Marcantonio—he was a Commie congressman from New York—from a hole in the ground. But we ran advertisements showing how they voted the same way on issues we researched. The point is do their records line up? That's the *only* point. Yarborough's been getting a free ride from us because we're all looking at Kennedy. Even me."

The ads ran. Ralph was flattered at the special attention at first, but then realized he needed to strike back. He called Kennedy and said, "Bob, while it's nice to know the opposition thinks the vice presidency is so important these days, it does bother me that they're callin' me a mean ol' Red in these ads. Ah'd like to do a commercial right back at 'em, if that's okay with you."

"Ralph," said a smiling Bobby, "they beating up on you now, too? Go get 'em, tiger! Talk to one of our West Coast commercial guys. How 'bout that guy who did the ad with the little girl picking flowers and the nuclear mushroom cloud at the end? The one that knocked out Goldwater for good—even if Johnson's campaign took some heat. Get that political commercial guy! Spend what you want!"

"Nah," Ralph said, then stopped, realizing he'd been too quick to disagree with his boss. "Bob, if you don't mind, Ah'd like to just do it straight up and at 'em. Just talk into the light of the camera. Did it before. Worked fine in my Texas Senate campaign in '64. It'll work again. They're late in gettin' to me. Ah've been runnin' all over—word's got out. Just gotta reinforce who Ah am."

And that's just what Yarborough did. He smiled into the camera and told those Southern white working class folks, and the black folks, that some "Yankees" were trying to "call me a Comm'nist . . . " Then he spent fifty-five seconds talking about his time with "General Patton in Dubya Dubya Two," his family, and his love for "the greatest nation known to mankind." He had his counter-ad splashed in between Lawrence Welk's "white swing/polka" music and the local news shows. Yarborough had most of his wavering supporters firmly back within the Democratic Party fold within a few days.

It was now the first week of October 1968. LBJ was endlessly arguing with himself, and from time to time, Clark Clifford and Doris Kearns, about whether to stop all bombing and "sue for peace" before the election. He kept wanting to hurt Bobby but held back because he couldn't tell how it was going to affect the Democratic Party across the nation. Would the Republicans start asking, "Who lost Vietnam?" Worse, would the Republicans be able to convince people that peace or more bombing was a political ploy, in which case Democrats across the country would be at risk? And worst of all, would undermining Bobby strengthen Wallace on a national, not just a regional, basis?

Johnson was awfully worried about George Wallace's third-party candidacy. Wallace, despite Ralph Yarborough's barnstorming through the South, was still running at 10 percent in the polls in late September 1968. Wallace's momentum had definitely slipped, and he was on his way down—but not fast enough. Wallace was still winning in the Deep South and could turn an election to the Republicans in any number of Northern states, such as New Jersey, Michigan, Ohio—and Midwestern states such as Indiana. Johnson kept demanding of everyone who would listen, "Does Wallace have coattails that make for Republicans in Congress? And if you don't know, then damn it, find out!"

Every time Johnson thought he'd decided to act against Bobby and tilt to Nixon, Johnson's civil rights platform came into view. Nixon was doing nothing to ease Johnson's concerns there. If anything, it seemed that Nixon was sending out his vice presidential running mate, Spiro Agnew, and other surrogates to wink and nod to the racially minded white folks that they would get more under Nixon than Wallace. This was a carefully orchestrated strategy coordinated by Kevin Phillips, supported by Frank Shakespeare, and approved by John Mitchell and Nixon himself. The wiretaps were clear on that, too, and a few copies of Phillips' memos, at least, had "floated" into the Kennedy camp and the Johnson White House.

In early October, the polls showed that Kennedy was back over 50 percent. The calls to debate had made him look tough in a positive way. And being out with the crowds again, in state after state, had energized him and his campaign. He found it easier to talk about other things than the war; people seemed weary of war talk *and* antiwar talk, too. Kennedy went to white, working-class neighborhoods in cities and in the countryside, making sure they understood that he was on their side—but without any calls against welfare cheats, or for shooting rioters, or any of the things coming out of the Nixon camp. Instead he talked about making sure the police were protected when they did their jobs, and about restoring neighborhood policing to bring people together with law enforcement, protecting workers from workplace hazards, and fighting for better wages. He talked about bringing jobs back to the inner cities for white and black workers. He talked about the need for national health care, rebuilding old roads, and introducing, when possible, public transportation—and rebuilding the major cities so that "everyone can feel safe again."

In black and Latino neighborhoods, he spoke of the same things, but always added how Martin Luther King would want people to not lose hope in themselves—and to not lose hope in America. He went to Latinos with Cesar Chavez of the United Farm Workers union in tow and didn't really have to say a word. Chavez's presence said it all, loud and clear.

Yarborough, meanwhile, continued his barnstorming marathon, going into the border states, a few close-call Southern states, and the Midwest. He hit hard on populist themes going back to William Jennings Bryan, and even Huey Long, when necessary. Yarborough was trying to make sure people thought of class issues as much as they could—anything to put a lid on thoughts about race. Some might have thought the schedule grueling, especially for a sixty-five-year-old man, but Yarborough came from strong blood and kept pace better than most of the Kennedy aides, and sometimes even Kennedy.[1]

Yarborough and Kennedy kept in touch with each other by phone, going over speeches together. Johnson kept tabs on both through wiretaps.

Kennedy, to his credit, ran some respectable television and radio ads. They were fairly innocent. He kept from going negative against Nixon—Nixon's negatives were always at least 30 percent when a Kennedy was running, so there wasn't a need for negative ads. The ads concentrated on making sure people knew prosperity would continue or expand only under a Robert Kennedy administration. He made sure the ads were program based with jobs, jobs, and more jobs being the mantra. In New York and California, Kennedy's speeches touted his past support for civil rights, but not future proposals. Even in the North, talk about civil rights was becoming somewhat dicey. In the Midwest and the South, Kennedy never appeared without Yarborough, whether live or in advertisements on television and radio. In the ads, Yarborough would often have the voice-over, with Yarborough and Kennedy smiling in the visuals.

Wallace had dropped down to 8 percent in less than a week. Wallace's running mate, retired General Curtis LeMay, had gotten some bad press for saying the United States should "nuke Vietnam." This particularly hurt Wallace in the industrial states of the Northeast and in Michigan and Ohio. Wallace, however, was still leading in at least three or four Southern states.

Texas was looking more and more like a lock for Kennedy because of Yarborough. While some insiders noted that Yarborough was not the most popular politician in Texas and had plenty of enemies, he'd been looking great on the stump—and Texans were proud of their home-state candidate. Indiana, Michigan, and Ohio were opening up for the Democrats, including the Kennedy-Yarborough ticket. In California, some Nixon votes were going to Wallace. This allowed Kennedy to build a small lead of five points there. (In the first timeline of 1968, despite Nixon being a Californian, Humphrey lost there by only a few percentage points.)

Kennedy was pleased with the latest polling. He thought to himself, Just another few weeks and we're in. Then he heard the news. Despite Roger Ailes' best efforts, the Marilyn Monroe ads were too salacious to remain a secret. Kennedy's camp found out about the ads—and the candidate went into an immediate and deep depression.

In that depression, he kept repeating over and over: I've been faithful to Ethel since I promised her I wouldn't fool around on her. If this ad runs, I'm through—and worse, some gal will come out of the woodwork to say I . . . and then Ethel will believe her, not me! My credibility will be shit with everyone by then! Ethel might divorce me if this all came out. Nah, she wouldn't! But I'm history as far as this campaign is concerned . . . Rockefeller was attacked just for being divorced. Then again, maybe divorce would look good rather than having to face Ethel and the kids after the Kennedy name is splattered with mud—of my own making.

Kennedy mused about another irony, which was that his relationship with Monroe had been just a quickie—two or three meetings at the most. The reason people got wind of anything at all was her big mouth, he recalled. And she wouldn't stop calling him at the Justice Department. He hadn't even expected to go to bed with her at first. His original intent was simply to help Jack end his relationship with her. Jackie had gotten so angry about it that she threatened to move out of the White House if Jack didn't stop seeing Marilyn.

Who could say no to Marilyn Monroe, Kennedy thought? Nobody *I'd* respect, he answered himself. Maybe some beard or Allard Lowenstein, but not me. I do respect Allard, though. The problems Marilyn had . . . But, Christ, it wasn't worth even *that* to lose now. THIS CAN'T GET OUT . . . CAN IT?

The Democratic presidential nominee was not going to sleep well for a while.

Chapter 8

CHECKMATE

People in the know didn't call Clark Clifford "the fixer" for nothing. Clifford, Secretary of Defense under Lyndon Johnson, was a Washington, D.C., lawyer who first came to prominence in the Truman administration at the beginning of the Cold War. He was urbane in public but a bully in private—when he needed to be one. He had, by 1968, become one of the "wise men" deep inside the Democratic Party and the bipartisan Cold War establishment who would be called on to advise politicians to make tough, fundamental decisions concerning the American empire.

When McNamara "blinked" over the Vietnam War, LBJ essentially fired him as secretary of defense and replaced him with Clifford, who was seen as a war hawk. Clifford was expected to give LBJ the go-ahead to continue to prosecute the war. Instead, Clifford, who always maintained the closest connections to the Fortune 500 corporate leadership, particularly board directors, major stockholders, and the financial community in general, stunned Johnson when he said the United States needed to find a way out of the mess in Southeast Asia.

Clifford, a prodigious reader, had also taken the time to read the top secret and classified Defense Department study on American military and political involvement in Vietnam (which later, in the first timeline, became known as "The Pentagon Papers"). The Defense Dapartment, then under McNamara, had commissioned the government-connected Rand Corporation to review and analyze official memoranda and documents to determine how and why the United States became involved in a land war in southeast Asia. The documents went back to the 1940s and up to 1967, mostly dealing with policy issues as opposed, for example, to troop movements or other direct national security concerns. After reviewing this study, Clark believed the study was correct in its assessment that the war was no longer necessary for national security, assuming it had ever been.[1]

Clifford was not entirely happy with Bobby Kennedy's metamorphosis into a populist and antiwar politician. However, he knew the Kennedy family well and respected their allegiance to the Democratic Party and to the Cold War establishment. While remaining close to Johnson, Clifford began to feed helpful information to Larry O'Brien in the Kennedy campaign. Clifford believed that it was wiser to stay ahead of history, particularly since Johnson was going home to Texas, and Kennedy was still leading in the polls.

Despite Lyndon Johnson's order of neutrality—to the point where Kennedy concluded, "The son of a bitch is helping Nixon!"—Clark Clifford, who also heard about the impending Nixon ads, called up Larry O'Brien and said, "Larry, how would you like to come over to my house and have a little talk? I have some interesting information concerning Mr. Nixon that might be of interest to you."

O'Brien obediently went to Clifford's home late on a weekday evening. After initial pleasantries and getting comfortable in the secretary of defense's living room, Clifford told O'Brien that a fellow named Richard Allen, who was a Nixon aide and former member of the Council on Foreign Affairs, had a friend named Claire Chennault, who was a walking personification of the military-industrial complex. A former general who became head of a corporation called The Flying Tigers, Chennault was married to a Taiwanese woman named Anna. Anna Chennault was an extreme anti-Communist who, with Allen's support, was lobbying—and now convincing—President Thieu, the dictatorial leader of America's ally, South Vietnam, not to agree to any peace before the U.S. presidential election in November.

Thieu had previously thought only LBJ could save him, and he was concerned that even Nixon was a "peace" candidate. For Thieu, peace meant death because he recognized there was little support for his regime outside of Saigon and a couple of other cities or towns. With Nixon's overtures through Chennault, Thieu was becoming convinced it was worth it to wait out the election before hastily agreeing to any "peace." Thieu then told the Johnson administration that he refused to attend any peace talks. This stymied those in the Johnson Adminstration who had begun to convince Johnson of the need for peace talks.

"How do you know this Chennault lady did this? Can we prove Nixon's staff, or better yet, Nixon approved this?!" O'Brien was amazed and, while wanting to believe, was incredulous.

"Of course we can," Clifford said in his most assuring voice. "I'll tell you what—we've got John Mitchell, Nixon's top lawyer and aide, on the record for this. Now, Larry, I must say the evidence is, shall we say, less than admissible in a court of law. However, the content of the information is not something Mr. Nixon would wish to see in, say, a newspaper account, if you know what I mean." Clifford was serene to the point of smugness.

There was strong reason to believe, Clifford continued, that Nixon approved this through John Mitchell. Nixon and Mitchell were known to be gravely concerned, said Clifford, about an "October surprise," and Nixon had been quoted saying as much. After noting some confusion on O'Brien's face, Clifford explained.

"What I mean by 'October surprise' is simple, really. I mean that Nixon is afraid President Johnson will end the war with Vietnam just before the election, or take significant steps toward ending the war, to help Democrats in tough races throughout the country. Nixon knows that LBJ hates Bobby, but he knows LBJ is also thinking about the prospects of the Democratic Party nationally to save at least the civil rights platform. Now, Larry, this part can't leave this room, okay?"

O'Brien nodded.

Clifford lowered his voice and said, "Good. You need to know this, Larry. Nixon is more right than he could ever know about the president's hatred of Senator Kennedy. The president is vacillating against the senator and leaning toward Nixon. Truth is, the president has thought more about the war in the last two years than civil rights. I wouldn't let the senator know about that since, as you know, the senator is already pretty emotional about the president. But President Johnson's going back to Texas, and the Democrats need to win next month. Remember, a presidential election is not about one man. It's about thousands of executive branch employment positions for party regulars, loyalists, and the occasional expert or adviser. And no matter how President Johnson feels at any given moment, we know Senator Kennedy is meaning to unify the Democrats again so we don't hand over the country to the Republicans, who, frankly, don't know how to govern. But that's a whole other topic altogether."

Clifford stood up and concluded, "Now, Larry, I happen to have a very nicely written report for you on the subject of Mrs. Chennault, Mr. Allen, and Mr. Mitchell. Please use it as you see fit, as I know you will." He went to his bedroom, came back with the report, and handed it to O'Brien. "If you need anything else, and you know I never give *everything* away unless I have to, just let me know."

O'Brien was speechless as he accepted the report. He finally said, "Why, sir, are you doing this?"

Clifford smiled a little, then became more grave. "Larry, I heard about the advertisement Nixon is producing regarding the senator and the movie actress. It isn't good for the country to publicize things like that—and, frankly, it reaffirms my distaste for Mr. Nixon. This report I've provided should help persuade Mr. Nixon to rethink whether he wishes to run such an advertisement. President Johnson may not be happy about what I'm doing, but this is about more than the president right now."

When O'Brien asked how Clifford learned about the ads about Marilyn Monroe, Clifford replied, "What do you think that dragon lady was telling Thieu as to why he shouldn't make any deals with Johnson?"

O'Brien took the report home and kept it under his pillow the entire night.

The next morning, Kennedy called in O'Brien to figure out what to do about the Nixon ads. Kennedy had even thought of resigning, but realized he couldn't—more for family pride than anything else.

O'Brien laid the report on Kennedy's desk to let him glance at it. Kennedy, after reading some of it, looked up and said, "Larry, this is too good to be true. *Too* good. Know what I mean? Are you sure of this? Nixon wouldn't be that stupid, would he?" He pushed the report back to O'Brien across the desk, suddenly angry. "I think it's a trap, Larry, a Lyndon Johnson trap. The coincidence is too much! How can we suddenly be handed this report when I'm sure they know about the . . . the . . . the ad?"

"They *do* know about the ad already, Bob. But Clark Clifford wants to help you—or at least the Democratic Party, and this is on the level. He's going against Lyndon Johnson on this, from the way he described it." *I hope it's not a trap,* O'Brien said to himself.

The senator sighed now, anger receding into despair. "Oh, hell. Who cares? We're going down when that ad hits. I just feel it. Do what you want." He waved O'Brien off, but O'Brien decided he needed to speak frankly with the clearly depressed candidate.

"Bob, I know I may be out of line here, but we have heard the rumors about you, President Kennedy, and Miss Monroe for the past couple of years at least. We can continue to deny the reports. The press boys may be pissed that Nixon went around them by going through a political advertisement. They know, too, that lots of guys would have wanted to go to bed with Marilyn Monroe. And lots of guys in high places do stuff like this all the time. Every convention of every business group has prostitutes galore! I just think—"

Kennedy stood up and pounded his fist on the desk. "Larry, this is *different* this time. I'm supposed to be *'pure'* to a lot of people! And nobody in the hinterlands has heard *any* of this shit! They think we're monks in politics when it comes to this stuff. Money scandals, no big surprise. We can deny and weather that. I can't lie about this stuff as easily. Ethel never spoke up before, and right after the—the—you know, L.A.—she did. If she spoke up and said she wouldn't take it anymore, how do we know lots of other women voters won't say the same thing?"

"Bob, I think we gotta use this report. It shows Nixon's people, probably even Nixon—who we know runs a tight campaign!—committed treason, Bob. Treason!"

"Okay, Larry." Kennedy spoke as he fell back into his chair. He then waved *his* "Bobby" off for a second and final time. "You know what we need, right? You need to call the Nixon camp and arrange—"

"I'm on it, Bob."

The candidate sank back further in his chair, put his hand on his forehead, and shielded his eyes from the room's natural sunlight. O'Brien thought he saw a tear running down his boss' face and quickly left the room. There was work to be done.

O'Brien, acting on Kennedy's orders—and, of course, ready to go to jail to deny receiving those orders—called Roger Ailes and asked for a meeting. Ailes, getting his orders from Nixon campaign attorneys Leonard Garment and John Mitchell, suggested the silk-stocking law office of Sullivan and Cromwell for a chat. Knowing this was the former firm of the infamous Dulles brothers, O'Brien balked. He suggested Leon Jaworski's office in Washington, D.C. Jaworski had a pro-Democratic reputation but was fairly conservative. And this was, after all, the D.C. office, not the firm's home office in Texas. If Nixon won, the Jaworski firm didn't want to be completely frozen out. Jaworski himself readily agreed to provide the "neutral" meeting place. Ailes, after checking with Nixon through John Mitchell, agreed.

Ailes prepared for the meeting with Garment, Mitchell, Shakespeare, and Treleaven, each speculating that O'Brien was going to whine about the impending negative ads concerning Bobby's sex life. They figured O'Brien would try to say that he could get the *New York Times* and perhaps some other highbrow papers not to cover such an undignified story. That, thought Ailes, showed why these guys were on the way out. Television is the name of the game, and salaciousness is what defines the game, not some backroom, backslapping hypocrisy from good ol' boy newspapermen.

But instead of looking worried, O'Brien arrived the next day for the meeting with Ailes looking very confident, almost happy. He sat down and invited Ailes to sit, too. He then looked straight at Ailes and said, "Well, Master Ailes—" O'Brien was referring sarcastically to the fact that Ailes was still under thirty years old—"I want you to look at this report, straight from an impeccable source, on the conduct of one Richard Allen of Mr. Nixon's campaign, and his discussions with a Mrs. Anna Chennault, and her discussions, in turn, with President Thieu of South Vietnam. It looks like Mr. Nixon's secret plan was to undermine potential peace talks and manipulate foreign affairs just before an election." He pushed the envelope and report over to Ailes.

Ailes read some of the report and looked up. He thought he'd heard something about this stuff but couldn't be sure. In any event, he told himself, he wasn't going to be leaned on by some old-guard operative.

Ailes looked right back at O'Brien and said, "So? A bunch of hearsay and bullshit. And even if this outrageous accusation has a shred of truth, how you gonna tie Nixon in? You think anyone will believe the hearsay that Nixon approved what you say Allen and Mr. Mitchell supposedly did? Maybe this lady simply misunderstood Allen in the first place?"

Ailes thought to himself, If I bluff, they might not have the goods.

O'Brien smiled, smelling that Ailes was bluffing. He talked even more boldly to Ailes, "You really want to test this, knowing that what I'm saying is true and knowing how tight your campaign has been wrapped? You think people are really gonna believe Nixon and John Mitchell were not involved on this one? Don't worry, Roger. I got more than enough 'hearsay,' as you call it, to wrap a rope around your bosses' necks—" He paused to utter an obscene pun regarding the Republican candidate's nickname. "Or shall we say, dicks?"

O'Brien had played some bluff poker in his time, too. On the other hand, since both men knew Nixon was a detail man on all campaign moves, and probably approved this operation all the way, this really wasn't bluff poker after all.

Chennault, unfortunately for the Nixon campaign, was so proud of her "patriotic" work she had already been telling various people about her own activities and the support she received from John Mitchell and Nixon himself.

"Oh," continued O'Brien, almost nonchalantly, "and, Master Ailes, we also have it on good authority that the Greek military has been sending money to the Nixon campaign, presumably because they are so glad a Greek American, Mr. Agnew, is the vice presidential candidate for Mr. Nixon. I've even got my own confirmation from a Greek source on that one. It was beautiful how that one worked. The American taxpayers pay their taxes that go to the CIA. The CIA pays the Greek military, and then the military, through Greek American businessmen, funnel the money back into Nixon's campaign coffers. Now, that wouldn't be a nice thing for the American people to learn—that Nixon treats his own country like a banana republic? Not even Checkers would approve of that," said O'Brien, referring to Nixon's dog.[2]

O'Brien had spontaneously thrown in "the Greek connection" even though he didn't have Clifford's support in talking about that. Nobody in Kennedy's camp, including the candidate, knew about the Greek connection. O'Brien did, however, have a Greek dissident journalist friend who had sources deep inside the Greek military junta that had taken over Greece in a 1967 coup. O'Brien was concerned about the extent of Ailes' bluffing, however, and wanted to make sure he got Ailes' attention.

This Greek connection revelation was too preposterous *not* to be true, thought Ailes. He therefore yelled, "That is preposterous! Is that fantasy the best you got, O'Brien?"

O'Brien nodded his head and said, "Just try me, Roger . . . "

Ailes finally cracked. He said to O'Brien, "Look, I can't believe this shit you're throwing around here. But tell you what, asshole. I'll take it back to my people, and we'll get back to you. I won't run the ads until I get word from my people. *My* people, not your people! Okay?"

O'Brien came back strong and hard. "What we want are those sex ads recalled and burned, got it? We're ready to go public on this one involving the dragon lady doing Dick Nixon's bidding to prolong the war. The press will take this one and run. We don't need no stinkin' ads! They won't be telling jokes about this in Johnny Carson's late-night monologue, either. You're talking treason, son, the kind that your boss knows about from his days hounding Alger Hiss."[3]

Ailes smiled back and said menacingly to O'Brien, "And what makes you think we're gonna let you blackmail us, O'Brien? What makes you think people are going to vote for Kennedy if we decide to let it *all* hang out? Bobby's gotta face the public immediately—it's him, and only him, screwing these broads! Meanwhile Nixon can say he didn't know anything, fire Allen—and maybe Mitchell, too—and buy two or three weeks more through election day."

O'Brien was impressed. He smiled back at Ailes with the same menacing grin. "So, Roger, you really think it will be that easy for Nixon? You think Dick Allen would fall on his sword for something that he could go to jail for—and possibly die for? This isn't any campaign finance scandal, Master Ailes, and you know it. And let's say you're right about the public. What do you think some of those Wallace voters will think once it 'all hangs out' as you so eloquently put it? You want to take the risk that Wallace wins this goddamned race—or, if you're lucky, a plurality—and the election goes to the House of Representatives for a tie-breaker? You want to take the whole country into a freakin' civil war? Because that's what happens when you 'let it all hang out.' I don't know if you realize this yet, but an election isn't some afternoon television talk show. This is real life, with real consequences, with real blood flowing if you—that's right, you, too—let things get out of hand. Nixon isn't going to play hari-kari on this one, even if you give him your grand strategy. You want to run ads like the ones you've already got out there about Bobby's flip-flops, his actions as attorney general? Go ahead! You want to keep your bullshit going by playing to the racism in Wallace's supporters, like your other boy genius, Kevin Phillips, says? Fine. I got hold of Phillips' memo where he said something like 'The essence of politics is to know who hates who.' That's cute. And it's good—" Ailes went white on finding out that O'Brien had that memo.

"Don't worry, sonny," said O'Brien, "I'm sure we haven't got all your spies who've infiltrated *our* campaign either. Now where was I? Oh yeah—the reason I'm laying this out for you is to make sure Nixon gets the right advice, and quick! It comes down to this: Drop the sex ads! Now! And we stay quiet over Nixon acting against his own government in a time of war. Got it?"

Ailes was silent.

O'Brien stood up, leaned over the conference room table, and almost shouted at Ailes, "Got it, sonny?"

Ailes tried his best to smile, but it came out a smirk. "I'll get back to you this afternoon, O'Brien."

O'Brien wasn't sure if he had won, but he figured Nixon would know what to do. O'Brien's last comment to Ailes was: "And don't be late. You know how to reach me."

Ailes met with John Mitchell and Nixon only. Nixon, after Ailes relayed the information, was excused. Nixon immediately had John Mitchell call Henry Kissinger, who had been parlaying and speaking with both the Kennedy camp and the Nixon camp. Kissinger had been useful, in the previous weeks, in feeding Nixon information from his White House sources as to the potential of peace negotiations with the North Vietnamese Communists. Kissinger called Nixon back and confirmed that the Johnson administration knew of the Nixon campaign's activities, even the Greek connection. They said Johnson didn't want the Greek connection coming out, but who could predict what would happen if things started leaking to sympathetic reporters? The irony, said Kissinger, was that LBJ had attempted to keep a lid on the information and away from Bobby's campaign. Kissinger also confirmed that Johnson was still toying with the idea of a bombing halt before the election but was also still pursuing the "bomb first, then talk" approach.

Nixon wanted better information than Kissinger was giving. Talking with Mitchell, he exclaimed, "Someone's got to know for *certain* over there if there's going to be a bombing halt before the election!" He called in Richard Allen, who had connections throughout the largely bipartisan Council on Foreign Relations. Allen said, "Dr. Kissinger is right, sir. Nobody knows what Johnson's going to do. He could stop the bombing at any time. But I must say, from what I hear, Johnson isn't interested in anything except to figure out a way to defeat Bobby Kennedy without hurting the Democratic Party. He really hates Bobby Kennedy. And, sir, I want to apologize. I never said anything to anyone about Mrs. Chennault and President Thieu."

"I know you didn't. The broad couldn't keep her mouth shut."[4]

Nixon smiled a bit—for Nixon. He then said to Allen, "The information on LBJ and the bombing halt. That's good to know, but it's still not enough. I must get more. You lie low for a while. Do, however, say hello to Dr. Kissinger for me next time you talk." Allen left the room, and Mitchell followed shortly afterward. Nixon brooded alone, wishing he had a piano to play at the headquarters.

Needless to say, the ads never ran. Nixon ordered everything connected with the ads destroyed. To those in the know, Nixon let the word get out that the ads were dropped because he found them "distasteful" and against "fair play."

Johnson, though he continued to vacillate, never did stop the bombing before the election. He decided, in the last few days before the election, to *increase* the bombing to get the Vietnamese "so pissed off" that Kennedy "wouldn't be able to just give it all away. It might even keep him from pursuin' any quick pullout of troops there." At least that's how he explained it to Doris Kearns.

Johnson watched Nixon move closer to the Wallace vote, and it bothered him that Nixon couldn't see the importance of civil rights anymore. "When Nixon was vice president, and Ah was in the Senate," he told Doris Kearns in that same conversation, "Nixon was pretty interested in civil rights in a positive way, even before he ran for president in 1960. He was better than Jack Kennedy, and certainly Bobby Kennedy, on that issue then, let me tell you. The damned Kennedy ass-kissers won't hear it, though, and they write the history books, don't they? . . . Ah mean, for the most part," as he gestured toward Kearns. "Nixon could have been takin' a political opportunity, but there were never any votes for civil rights for a Republican at that point. Ah just don't know where Nixon really stands on civil rights anymore . . . Doris, you think Bobby really wrote that new book of his on the Cuban missile crisis? It doesn't read like a diary, and you know, Ah could tell you somethin' about how the deal was reached with Khrushchev that doesn't quite add up to what the so-called 'brave' and 'wise' senator has written."

Kearns asked what it was. Johnson waved her off. "It's not the time. That man could be our next president. Probably will be." Johnson was more depressed about himself and the nation than ever.

As it turned out, Johnson's last bombing rampage against the Vietnamese people helped Kennedy at the end. People were outraged by the increased bombings, the effects of which were shown in gruesome detail on television news. Nixon raged that it was an October surprise in reverse, to no avail.

On the last day of October 1968, Yarborough made a special speech before the Veterans of Foreign Wars after pulling a few strings with some old military pals. In his speech, which received prominent coverage, Yarborough told the assembled veterans, "Ah fought, as did many of you, in the big one, Dubya Dubya Two. Ah know when there's a time to fight and a time to talk. We've bombed these people in Vietnam enough, and Ah think it's time to talk. You don't have to lose by talkin', you know. And Ah saw my share of what happens when a body gets in the way of even a grenade, let alone one o' our big bombs fallin' out of a B-52. It isn't lahk they show in the movies. We know what it really looks like, don't we?"

Some in the crowd grumbled, but many others muttered they sure did know. "I still have dreams of my pals," one man said at a table near the platform where Yarborough was speaking.

Yarborough said, "Ah hear you, sir. Ah have those dreams about dead buddies, too." He then put his notes back into his jacket and resumed. "Ah have a strong belief raht now that Senator Kennedy and Ah can end this war. Honorably. The first thing we gotta do is stop droppin' them bombs. You wouldn't want to talk with someone who was bombin' you, right? And nobody's doin' much talkin' now. So let's just stop for a bit and let's see where that goes. Ah ain't sayin' this off the cuff, either. Ah don't need any notes to say it, Ah know it so well. Ah thought about it a long time, even talked with Senator Kennedy yesterday about what Ah'm sayin' here. And when we're elected, Ah'm gonna be there, right up front—representin' you! That's raht! Someone who was there with many o' you in the big one. We're gonna do raht by you, by your sons and nephews who have risked—and some who lost—their lives over there. And by God, we're gonna do raht for this great nation o' ours!" Nearly every time he said the word "you," he thrust his right index finger toward the center of the auditorium. And when he said, "this great nation o' ours," he pounded his chest with pride. Pure Yarborough all the way.

As his speech ended, the veterans jumped out of their seats and wildly applauded one of their own. That's all they wanted to hear, some veterans told the reporters afterward: that someone understood their feelings on patriotism and fighting wars, and was on their side. Not some kid with long hair calling their nephews and sons "baby killers."

Meanwhile, Kennedy spoke in California about nutrition programs and said, when asked about Johnson's military action, "My record is clear on this subject. We need to get beyond where we continue to be," which, of course, was anything but clear. And then he turned to the schoolchildren and said, "How are you? What are you doing in school these days? How many in your family?" This had been Bobby's personal strategy for the last two weeks: schools, factories, auditoriums filled with regular folks, train stops—the way Truman traveled in 1948. Not much policy talk.

Nixon's camp was frustrated. Many on the Nixon staff were outraged that Nixon had suddenly pulled the Marilyn Monroe ads. Buchanan in particular was fuming. He tried, without success, to get the information leaked—even tried the *National Enquirer.* They were interested, but Kennedy's camp promised a post-election interview with the *Enquirer* if the information was suppressed. The *Enquirer* relented and didn't run the information, at least for the time. The *Manchester Union Leader* in New Hampshire was going to run the ads in print, but Nixon personally called the publisher, William Loeb, and told him he would hurt the conservative cause more than help it. Loeb, out of respect for Nixon's record against Communism, reluctantly relented.

Nixon himself saw he was going to lose and believed he needed to do something. He finally agreed to debate Kennedy, along with Wallace. Larry O'Brien, standing next to Jack Newfield, said at a press conference, "We'd love to debate, but we believe Mr. Nixon's call has come too late. There is not enough time to set up a debate. Our schedule's all filled."

The press bought it, even though one could always fill a slot in the schedule somewhere. The proposal died on the vine. Nixon knew the more he asked for debates at this point, the more the Kennedy camp would say, "Why didn't you want to debate all those weeks before? Where were you when it counted?"

Nixon redoubled his efforts in the closing days of the election on what his aide Kevin Phillips called the "Southern strategy." The Southern strategy was to carefully use "coded," racially charged phrases designed to appeal to white people who no longer wanted to be seen as overtly racist. Nixon continued making speeches sprinkled with words and phrases such as "I know we should do something about civil rights, but let's start with some law and order!" "We need responsibility, not welfare!" "Our greatest social need is not throwing money at problems, it's getting the white and black youth to mind their manners and know their place in society."

Nixon's campaign seemed to be picking up support, more in the South than anywhere else. In the last days of the campaign, Nixon was in Florida, before a white audience, talking about "the need for our minorities to avoid seeking special privileges" and the need for "judges to respect states rights" and "not be super-legislatures." That speech made the evening news, and Nixon's campaign hoped it would create a storm among those whom Nixon called "New York Jews and liberals," which it did. His speech solidified votes in some Southern states, as well as in Arizona, Utah, Idaho, and Montana, over the last weekend before the election. Some polls showed Nixon moving to within five points in New Jersey and within two points in Ohio and Indiana. The Southern strategy seemed to be working, as the votes came almost all at the expense of Wallace.

Nixon might have had a chance to win, wrote some pundits in postmortems, but he ran out of time. That's what they say in most elections, however.

The final election results of 1968 showed Senator Robert Francis Kennedy of New York (and some would say, Massachusetts) with 50.6 percent of the popular vote. Nixon received 43 percent of the vote, with Wallace winning 6.3 percent. A few radicals voted for various other radicals for the remaining 0.1 percent. In the electoral college, however, Nixon's defeat—and Kennedy's victory—was more dramatic. Kennedy had more than 340 electoral votes. He had defeated Nixon in the larger population states, including California, Illinois, Ohio, Michigan, Wisconsin, Minnesota, and most important, Texas. Kennedy barely won in New Jersey and barely lost in New Hampshire, but handily won the rest of the Northeast, including Pennsylvania, Connecticut, and New York.

Kennedy lost Indiana, but it was very close. Kennedy won Tennessee by a razor's edge, thanks especially to Yarborough. Yarborough was the key to Kennedy's victory in Texas and in a couple of other Midwestern or near-Southern states, and for that, Kennedy would owe a lot to Ralph Yarborough's folksy, Southern populist charm.

The ticket, united in its pro-labor stance, made a strong showing in labor union households, which were the key to the victories in New York, California, and the other industrialized states. More than 85 percent of union households voted the Kennedy-Yarborough ticket.

There was a lot of rejoicing in many households that had been divided by the war, including those that split along Nixon-Kennedy vote lines. There was joy in and around the universities. Even business executives who had not voted for the winning ticket began to find reasons to be glad Kennedy had won. They decided it was time to get past the war. It was time to continue with civil rights reform because it increased their customer base. They didn't like that they would have to deal with a White House beholden to labor unions, but they figured they simply had to increase their contributions to key representatives in Congress to bottle up any new pro-labor legislation.

Roger Ailes didn't need to be told Nixon had lost. He had left for Los Angeles the day before the election to be with some West Coast Republicans who had movie and television connections. On election night, Ailes found himself at a Republican Party function in Los Angeles. There he was introduced to a drugstore magnate named Justin Dart. Ailes told Dart about his frustration with Nixon for not debating. He railed at Nixon's inability to project a natural image off the cuff.

Justin Dart listened quietly, but with interest, to Ailes' tale. When Ailes took a breath and a sip of his drink, Dart smiled and said, "Roger, why don't the two of us have lunch next week with Nancy Reagan? I'd like you two to get acquainted."

Ailes was a bit surprised. "You—you mean . . . Governor Reagan? You mean his . . . wife?"

"Yes, Roger. Ronald Wilson Reagan is your candidate for 1972. He'll debate Bobby Kennedy, not like Nixon, who was wound more tightly than a Swiss clock. Roger, Ronald Reagan's a pro from the word 'go'! He can disarm anyone. He and Nancy are close personal friends of mine—and my wife, too. But you've got to understand one thing before I set you up here. You gotta believe in one thing, which I'm about to tell you, because it's true and most people don't get it." He leaned into Ailes, with just a little alcohol lingering on his breath.

"The key to working with and understanding Ronald Reagan," said Dart, "is that he is always underrated. People think he's dumb. He isn't. He simply keeps to what he does best: delivering speeches someone else writes, hitting his 'spots' for the best lighting, and making the right quip in the right situation. He knows more about issues than people give him credit for, even if sometimes some of his advisers have to check his sources. Bobby Kennedy's never gonna live up to people's expectations because nobody can, and certainly not him. Tonight's election is only one round in a much longer fight to get rid of these damned liberals, labor unions, and all their fellow vermin," said Dart, who was smiling from ear to ear as he reached his last sentence.

Ailes said, "But why Nancy Reagan and not—"

Dart was sharp, but still smiling. "Because you don't go *anywhere* with the governor without Nancy. Nancy is the strategist. The real brains. And she knows what she wants for her Ronnie." Dart stood up, shook Ailes' hand, and said, "We'll talk."

Ailes leaned back in the plush hotel chair and sighed with the first relief he'd felt in a long time. Behind every cloud, he thought, there is a *golden,* not just silver, lining.

Back in Washington, D.C., President-elect Robert Francis Kennedy wasn't rejoicing or even smiling. He was moody, somber. He wouldn't come down to accept his victory until very late in the night. He remembered the cliffhanger in 1960, and while this wasn't as much of a cliffhanger as far as the electoral college was concerned, it didn't matter to him. It was always going to be close, he had said over and over. "I'm not going to be Tom Dewey," he kept saying to his friend Kenny O'Donnell.[5]

Kennedy waited until well after most people in the East and even some in the West had gone to bed to publicly accept his victory. In a short speech, the new president-to-be thanked everyone he could think of, this time starting his list with Ethel. Ethel was by his side, beaming brighter than a spotlight. Kennedy ended his acceptance speech by saying, "I am humbled beyond all words and pledge tonight to do my utmost to reunite this great nation."

He and Ethel then returned to the hotel suite upstairs. After a few minutes, he suddenly ordered everyone to leave the suite. He told Ethel to go to bed to rest. Their new baby was due next month, and as Ethel headed toward the bedroom, he told her, "Honey, I'm sorry I put you through this during your pregnancy."

Kennedy sat alone at 2:30 A.M. on a barstool in the kitchen area of the suite. The Secret Service men stood guard, inside and outside the room. Despite saying, "I wanna be alone for a while," Kennedy knew he wasn't going to be alone, either tonight or for at least four more years.

He held the election return reports in his hands—hands still callused from handshaking and being grabbed and squeezed. He carefully studied some pages of the election reports, but skimmed others. He read all the Southern states' returns, which showed a South deeply hostile to him. The Southern reports reminded him that, although he had won the national vote, 49.4 percent of voters had voted against him, more than a few with raging hate. And then there was the Congress, with its Rules Committees and entrenched Southern Democrats who were in office when he was in kneepads.

He dropped the papers to the floor, looked up at the ceiling and beyond with his mind's eye. He looked in vain for his slain brother Jack and his older brother Joe, who had been killed in World War II. Then he realized he was now going to be the president. He alone. Not Jack. Not Joe Junior . . . And, thankfully, he thought to himself, not his father.

He then stared straight through the window of his hotel suite and into the Washington, D.C., skyline. He was more saddened with victory, he thought, than if he had lost. He asked himself, Is this how Lincoln felt after he won in 1860?

Part II:

PRESIDENT BOB

Chapter 9

RESTORATION

Lyndon Johnson awoke the next morning feeling a great weight off his neck and shoulders. He had slept through the night, a rarity for him these days. He got dressed and walked into the Oval Office, and ordered one of his several assistants to summon Clark Clifford. When Clifford entered, Johnson didn't wait for him to sit down.

"Clark, Ah want to announce a bombing halt. Today."

Clifford said, as if at attention, "I will alert the press and order preparations for your announcement. Is there anything else, sir? Do you have a prepared text? Have we spoken to any congressmen—committee chairmen? I mean . . . I did *not* mean to ask so many questions at once, Mr. President."

Johnson smiled. "Thas' all right, Clark. Ah feel fahn today. Ya know, Ah realized this mornin' Ah let Senator Kennedy keep me preoccupied with politics when Ah meant to get away from politics when Ah said Ah wouldn't seek reelection. Ah don't want us leaving these people in Vietnam behind, but our involvement there's gonna end anyway—or somehow. Heck, even the Wallace voters are tired of this damned thing!" He sighed and then said, "The public has spoken, and Ah know you'll still be here after Ah'm gone, regardless of whether he keeps you on—"

"I have no intention of staying on, sir. I plan to return to an informal advisory capacity, if you don't mind my saying so . . . I didn't mean to interrupt—"

"No offense taken, Clark. Ah know you've been talkin' to Bobby's campaign for quite some time, and Ah understood—although Ah did wanna yell at ya some days . . . "

A flustered Clifford stammered, "I-I-I only—I mean, Mr. President, I—"

Johnson waved at Clifford and started to laugh at the sight of the smooth insider suddenly ruffled. "Clark, Clark. It's all past now. Ah'm past, too. The country will survive Bobby Kennedy, Ah'm sure of it. They would have survived Nixon. And hell, maybe even Wallace! Well, maybe not. Eithah way, Ah've got no text for mah announcement yet, but it's gonna be simple. Now, go and call Senator Kennedy and tell him he can coordinate the next moves with you and State—well, maybe Rusk is not too happy with the results yesterday—to see if we can be on our way to a final peace over there—at least as far as we're concerned—before inauguration day."

Johnson was true to his word. At the press conference he announced that he was calling a halt to the bombing of both South and North Vietnam. He also said that he was going to seek immediate coordination with Senator Kennedy's foreign policy team to allow for a smooth transition between the two administrations. And that was the end of the press conference.

It was strange, Johnson thought to himself as he left the pressroom at the White House. It was almost as if, on Vietnam at least, a different political party was taking over.

In a way, it was a different political party. Kennedy loyalists were calling it a Restoration. Others, mostly wags and humorous commentators such as Art Buchwald, were calling it Kennedy II—in a play on the famous Vatican II, at which Pope John XXIII instituted liberal reforms in the Catholic Church.

Kennedy II

It was a Restoration in some ways, but not in others. Bob Kennedy—he made clear to his staff that nobody was to call him "Bobby" anymore—was replacing his brother's and Johnson's secretary of state, Dean Rusk, with Chester Bowles. Paul Warnke, a so-called dove on arms control but a disciple of the original Cold Warrior, George Kennan, was tapped to be secretary of defense. Health, Education, and Welfare was slated to Sargent Shriver, a Kennedy brother-in-law who had run the Peace Corps in the early '60s and later oversaw the initial Great Society programs under Johnson.

There was some surprise when the president-elect offered the secretary of labor post to Walter Reuther. Although it was true that Reuther had enjoyed a close relationship with Johnson up to the California primary, seasoned observers knew that Kennedy's relationship with Reuther went back to the late 1950s, when Kennedy, as attorney for the Democrats on the Labor Racketeering Congressional Committee, protected Reuther from charges that Reuther was a Communist. The real surprise was that Reuther accepted the post and gave up his power as head of the United Auto Workers union. Labor insiders, however, knew better as they saw Reuther having a hard time dealing with insurgencies by black workers, who demanded more than what they called "lip service" in what was a somewhat progressive but white-led union. Reuther, for his part, wanted something else that he could not get with his position as UAW leader—and that was to become, through the labor secretary position, the one true national labor leader. Now, he thought to himself, AFL-CIO President George Meany will have to deal with me.

Kennedy, happy to have Reuther, immediately turned to finding a business leader or two to show the business community that corporate friends would also be rewarded. Toward that end, Kennedy met personally with Tom Watson of IBM to ask him to become the secretary of commerce. Watson respectfully declined. He did, however, suggest IBM's president, T. Vincent Learson, for the post. Learson was in his mid-fifties, and, per IBM policy at the time, he could not serve IBM after age sixty. This did not leave Learson much time to take over IBM from Watson, which caused Learson more than a little dissatisfaction.

The age limitation applied, in theory, to Watson himself, who was a year or two older than Learson. But unlike Learson, who was simply an executive at the mammoth corporation, Watson was the son of the founder of the company and was the CEO and chairman of the board. Watson told his friend, the president-elect, that he wanted control over his company's direction and needed to stay with IBM at "this critical time." Watson, in proposing Learson, cited Learson's exceptional skills in guiding the development of computer technologies, and the company overall, through the 1960s.

To convince Learson to accept the post, Watson told Learson that he needed to have him inside the new administration because of rumblings of antitrust suits.[1] Learson initially thought he'd decline the Commerce Department post. However, he quickly realized, with Watson's prodding and the politics at IBM, that it might be personally profitable for him to take this "government sabbatical." He thought to himself, Watson doesn't see the need to produce smaller and smaller computers for consumers and businesses to use. What could be better than to lead the U.S. government into funding further development of small computers out of, say, NASA or . . . the Department of Commerce? Then when I return to the private sector, I might be able to interest Xerox or that West Coast nuisance—otherwise known as Hewlett-Packard—unless I go back to a hero's welcome at IBM. Let the government pay and do the heavy lifting first.

Learson was ready to accept the position, he later told an official biographer, by the time he flew to Washington to meet Robert F. Kennedy, but he was worried about Kennedy's harsh views regarding corporate leaders. At their meeting, however, the president-elect treated Learson like royalty and Learson, at the end of the meeting, readily and gladly accepted the position. What Learson didn't learn until much later was that Bob Kennedy was beaming at his luck of landing a leading business executive on his administration team to counter all the "beards" and "liberals."

There were more slots for Kennedy to fill as he assembled his team. One of his more interesting administrative choices was tapping former CBS news executive Blair Clark to lead the U.S. Information Agency. Clark, a manager in Gene McCarthy's campaign the previous spring and an antiwar activist in his own right, caused some grumbling among the more reactionary members of the Senate. The more moderately conservative observers humorously rationalized away their fears: How much, after all, could anyone do in what was essentially a "low-frequency" post?

Kennedy's riskiest administrative choice came when he personally asked Jack Newfield to become his press secretary. Newfield, an iconoclastic, left wing journalist and a Jew, was not someone the white bread, mainstream, and usually passive, press corps ever envisioned for such a prestigious position.

"What? And I suppose Izzy Stone wasn't available!" cracked a sarcastic Helen Thomas of UPI to *Washington Post* reporter Meg Greenfield at the National Press Club luncheon following the announcement.

Many shared Helen Thomas' feelings on the matter.

Kennedy, for his part, made it clear he wanted Newfield. He argued over his choice with his new presidential chief of staff, Kenny O'Donnell, and with Larry O'Brien, his chief of domestic policy—essentially an assistant to the chief of staff. The "O Boys," as Yarborough promptly named them, adamantly opposed naming Newfield as press secretary.

O'Donnell said, "Bob, there was an obvious choice here instead of Newfield—and you know who I mean!"

"Yes," added O'Brien, "John Seigenthaler! A respected *Southern* journalist, editor, and—as we all know—someone with government experience!"

O'Donnell said, exasperation in his voice, "Why not Mankiewicz if you're going to be different or daring?"

"I talked with Seigenthaler, guys," replied Kennedy, "and he's the one who led me to Jack Newfield. Seigenthaler is returning to the South as editor of the most respected newspaper in Tennessee. He told me, 'You don't need me for press secretary. You need another southern newspaper telling your side of things, besides what folks might read in Hodding Carter and Harry Golden columns!'"

"But what about Mankiewicz?" demanded O'Donnell.

Kennedy didn't want to say so, but he had asked Mankiewicz, too. But Mankiewicz, for his part, had been receiving too many financially lucrative offers from lobbying companies such as Brown and Williamson. He rejected Kennedy's offer as politely as he could. He told Kennedy, "I'm just too exhausted right now to deal with a whiny group of Washington reporters. I'm sorry, Bob."

Kennedy offered the O Boys his version of his conversation with Mankiewicz saying, "Frank's not enough of a newsman, he told me. He doesn't think he's right for the job."

O'Brien said, "I can't believe he could be worse than Newfield with the Washington press corps!"

Kennedy took the high road as to why he wanted Jack Newfield. "Guys, I don't want someone like John or Frank, who would be so smooth when it came to tough policy issues that reporters wouldn't trust him. I want someone who speaks his mind. Someone who'll be honest with reporters—perhaps to a fault. I want someone who I'm gonna have more trouble with than the reporters are."

To which O'Brien sharply answered, "And why the hell do we want that? Are we *asking* for trouble? You think it's going to be a cakewalk with Congress just because the Democrats are in the majority? Remember, I was the liaison to Congress under your brother. The southern Dems are in lockstep with the most conservative Republicans. Southern Democrats like Senator Eastland voted for Wallace, if not for Nixon, for chrissakes! When you add them together, we don't have a majority on *key issues* starting with labor reform, and we might have a problem getting a Vietnam peace treaty through. And speaking of shit, the Washington press corps are just courtiers who want to be flattered more than informed! When did they ever break any story that wasn't a controlled leak?

Bob, I think this is a *big* mistake. Really big! Major! I hate to say all this, but I must! And I say it even though I *like* Jack Newfield!"

Kennedy held up his hand. "Larry, Ken, you gotta trust me on this. Jack Newfield is a great Jew. He wants a moral universe, like other great Jews. That's what he and I talked about a month or two ago while we were out campaigning. Can you believe it? He actually asked me to change the national anthem to 'This Land Is Your Land'! That's Jack right there! But Jack's a reporter, too, and he was very effective with the press guys on the road. He's full of pep and makes even the most mundane things sound important. He and Yarborough taught me a lot, I have to admit. They're very different, but very similar in lots of ways. Jack'll massage and persuade those boys—and Helen Thomas of UPI. None of them want to lose access to us, as you say, Larry, and that's why they'll try to like him. And they'll be impressed with his candor soon enough—and they'll learn to keep quiet again when we want them to be—at least most of the time. And if Jack resigns after a couple of years, and we're not too badly burned, then we'll have done a lot to restore some confidence around here, won't we? The key point is restoring the confidence of the press corps. The war undermined that confidence, that's for sure. I talked late one night with Ward Just, the war reporter for the *Post*. He said he didn't think he could ever trust any politician again after 'the five o'clock follies' as he called the press conferences in Saigon. That's big—major— as you say. The press corps may not want to roll over if anything happens on our watch. I don't know. But I do know this: I want Jack Newfield."

There were counterpoints to that analysis and assumptions to challenge. But that was it. Jack Newfield was in as press secretary. O'Brien, however, still thought he might have a shot if he spoke with Mankiewicz. When O'Brien called Mankiewicz the next morning, Mankiewicz surprised him by saying, "Larry, I'll lay it on the line for you. Although I told Bob I was too impatient to deal with sniveling whiners like the Washington press corps, that's not the real reason I didn't want that job. You see, when I grow up, I don't want to be president. I want to be Clark Clifford. And Clark Clifford would never be *anyone's* press secretary!"[2]

O'Brien shook his head. He thought to himself, We're gonna have our hands full with Newfield. He sighed and hoped Bob Kennedy didn't have any other "interesting" choices.

Kennedy did, in fact, make a somewhat politically safe choice for Treasury Secretary. He chose a "nobody" in Washington, D.C., circles, but a favorite of certain Southern Democratic senators—a young and rising banker from Georgia by the name of Bert Lance. Kennedy had met him once, in a post-election meeting with Ralph Yarborough. He saw that Lance wasn't an "old Southern gentleman," both literally and in terms of personality, but he said to himself at the time, I doubt I'll ever listen to that fellow on anything—ever. Kennedy was surprised when Yarborough said, "You know, Bob, that Lance fella's not too bad. I think we can work with him."

Kennedy said, "Okay, maybe . . . " but thought, Probably not. Anyone the southern senators like can't be very good . . .

Kennedy was, however, thinking more seriously about money and the economy, beyond the Treasury Department. He had, by this time, become concerned about the power of the quasi-governmental federal agency known as the Federal Reserve Board, or as it was called by bankers and other insiders, the "Fed." The more he and John Kenneth Galbraith discussed the "Fed" and how he needed to work with that agency, the more Kennedy realized this was not something technical or divorced from political issues and his own power as president.

During the fall election, he had begun with simple questions such as, "How does it really work and why should I care?" He graduated to more complicated questions such as, "What's M-1?" or "Why can the Fed, not the president, decide to raise interest rates?" He then began to realize that the Fed was something *beyond* his power in large part—unless he undertook some subtle actions and strategies. Galbraith had to admit that, until Kennedy started asking so many questions, he hadn't thought much about the institution either.

By mid-November 1968, Kennedy had learned that the current chairman, William McChesney Martin Jr., was a fixture at the Fed. He also learned that some considered Martin to be possibly past his "prime rate," to quote Galbraith's rather lame pun. Galbraith said Kennedy should consider a replacement for Martin when Martin's term ended in early 1970. Kennedy responded, "Well, let's see if Martin plays ball with us. We may not have to replace him."

Galbraith nodded but knew better.

Kennedy, after the election, asked Galbraith to join the Fed board at the next vacancy and smilingly said, "Maybe I'll replace Martin with you."

Galbraith demurred, saying there were "younger fellows" who would be more appropriate, including James Tobin and Kenneth Arrow, who had been lower-level economic advisers in Jack Kennedy's administration but who now had the maturity to lead the Federal Reserve Board.

"Well, let's give this Martin fellow a chance," said Kennedy, deciding there were enough "younger" people to choose for other positions.

Kennedy initially wanted to replace all current Lyndon Johnson cabinet level holders, including Attorney General Ramsey Clark. However, at Sargent Shriver's and Larry O'Brien's insistence, he met with Attorney General Clark, who had been fairly isolated from Johnson in the last year of Johnson's administration. Clark was so isolated that he was writing a book to be entitled *Crime in America*. Clark talked with Kennedy about lessening crime in poorer areas with community policing and direct government programs designed to help the areas become viable for private investment. This was right up Kennedy's alley for development of poorer areas, as exemplified by his famed Bedford-Stuyvesant plan, named after a particularly poor area in New York City populated largely by blacks, with a sprinkling of Puerto Ricans and a few left-over Jewish and Italian Americans.

Clark said that crime in the corporate arena, from bribes to pollution, was a major cause of problems besetting the United States—costing taxpayers and our society far more than the street crime menacing Americans who lived inside or closest to the largest five or six cities.

Kennedy came back from his meeting with Clark feeling horrible. He had always figured he would name his friend Joe Dolan as attorney general, considering Dolan's long government experience, his understanding of government and business—particularly antitrust matters—and strong political savvy. It was clear, however, that Clark was a "Bob Kennedy" type of administrator. He was principled and came from a long line of federal government cabinet members, advisers, and Supreme Court justices. Like Dolan, Clark was an expert in antitrust law. But unlike Dolan, Clark was also very adept at enforcing civil rights laws. Kennedy at that moment knew he needed to place Dolan somewhere else, perhaps on the Supreme Court of the United States. Clark was going to stay as attorney general.

Stewart Udall, a favorite of Jack Kennedy's but not quite a favorite of Johnson's, was asked to return to the government as secretary of interior. Udall had become a major player in the growing movement to protect the environment after his first tenure in the Interior Department ended the first time in the mid-1960s. Udall gladly and eagerly accepted a return to the interior department with the hope of shaping a pro-environmental agenda.

Haggling with Hoover and the CIA

The big question on everyone's mind, including Bob Kennedy's, was whether the president-elect was going to ask J. Edgar Hoover to resign. Hoover, according to protocol and the law at the time, was supposed to have retired a couple of years before. Yet Johnson kept him on, not wishing to rock any boats. The two became allies when Johnson had learned to hate student radicals and black nationalists as much as Hoover did. Johnson was also a big proponent of wiretapping, and Hoover obliged because he was already wiretapping various black leaders and student radicals. Johnson's and Hoover's relationship reached an epiphany with the wiretaps on the three main candidates in the 1968 presidential election.

Unlike his relationship with Johnson, Hoover saw no hope of ever aligning himself with Robert Kennedy. If anything, Kennedy's relationship with Hoover turned even more sour as the 1960s wore on. In 1967, for example, Kennedy, as a senator, endorsed the antiwiretapping bill that Hoover saw as a direct challenge to his authority as FBI director. Hoover, using some well-timed leaks to favored reporters, let it be known that Kennedy, while attorney general, had ordered a wiretap on Martin Luther King Jr. Kennedy played into Hoover's trap by initially denying this allegation. Hoover then reenforced his attack by providing documentation to these same reporters that proved Kennedy's denial was, to put it delicately, not quite correct.

Kennedy, forced to admit the truth, then let friends know the wiretaps were approved because of Hoover's pressure and Hoover's paranoiac hatred of King. Kennedy knew he could not directly respond this way because it undermined his image of being "tough." For people would likely ask, how could a tough Kennedy be pressured into wiretapping someone who had subsequently become a martyr? Worse, the question might arise, what else could Kennedy be afraid of?

Kennedy was absolutely afraid of that last question because the answer was not merely his dalliance with Marilyn Monroe or other women. There was also the first Kennedy administration's Operation Mongoose, also known as the hot little war against Castro and Cuba, which involved the CIA and the Mob. Hoover knew a lot of other secrets, and the question was whether he was more dangerous inside or outside the Kennedy tent.

Kennedy was, therefore, both angered and frustrated by Hoover's continued presence. More than anything else, Kennedy wanted Hoover out. At first, he thought he could force Hoover's retirement. Hoover was now approaching seventy years of age, which could only be seen as "young" if he were compared to Senator John Stennis of Mississippi, Senator Strom Thurmond of South Carolina, or Supreme Court Justice Hugo Black. But Hoover had already received, from President Johnson, a waiver from the federal law at the time that required retirement before age seventy for appointed federal executive or administrative positions.

Kennedy, again following Yarborough's advice of facing your fear and making it the "other fella's" fear, decided he needed a face to face meeting with Hoover—alone. Just before Thanksgiving 1968, a lengthy meeting occurred between President-elect Kennedy and Mr. Hoover at Kennedy's home in Hickory Hill. There is still no reliable record of what each said, though each man leaked different things at different times, which only means any historian must be cautious in determining what was supposedly said.

A week following that meeting, a member of Kennedy's staff leaked to reporters that Hoover was going to continue as FBI director in the administration. Predictably, the liberals, the student Left, black activists, and the nascent feminists screamed with rage. Nobody wanted to hear about the fact that Kennedy secured a signed agreement from Hoover promising to step down no later than December 1, 1972. One of the first leaks, which came through Rennie Davis by way of Al Lowenstein by way of Sargent Shriver and originating with Kenny O'Donnell, indicated that Kennedy secured that promise because he claimed to have something on Hoover, that guardian of guardians, of a compromising nature. It was said, in various retellings, that the compromising information centered on two particular items long discussed among certain inhabitants of the Washington, D.C., "village," though never in the press or other media.

The first was that Hoover was "on the take" from the Mob. This item stayed afloat because Hoover kept testifying at congressional committees year after year that there was no such thing as any "significant organized crime" threatening the United States. Adding to the speculation was the fact that Hoover's home and other possessions reflected greater wealth than his public servant's salary could probably afford, no matter whether people knew his actual net worth or not.

The second item was that Hoover had a more than normally friendly relationship with his office confidante Clyde Tolson. They were a constant item together, as noted by many of the rich and powerful, and it didn't help quell the rumors when both Hoover and Tolson frequented nightclubs and bars together—and retreats in a homosexual hangout near Del Mar, California. This rumor seemed easy to prove but was not. And, again, Hoover had files on "everyone"—and "everyone" had something to hide, especially the Kennedys. Kennedy insiders *claimed* that Kennedy told Hoover, "If I go down, you go down. It's like nuclear war and mutually agreed upon destruction."

Kennedy, believing his deal with Hoover was the best he could get, was not in a conciliatory mood when he heard the outcry from "movement" people at the reappointment of Hoover. Kennedy screamed at Al Lowenstein, "You and your friggin' bearded liberal friends better keep their goddamned eye on the goddamned ball! Ending the war isn't gonna be easy, you know. I'm already betting I'm a one-term president before I start! That's how I scared Hoover, if you really wanna know. I told him, if I go down, so will he! And forget Vietnam for a moment—for once! Do you think it's gonna be easy to get money to rebuild the damned ghettos? Do you? Christ! Tell those 'movement' assholes to lay off!"

Lowenstein got out the word as best he could. There was a big gulp in the white student movement, and especially among some black radicals who were already aware of the FBI program COINTELPRO ("Counter-intelligence Program"), which consisted of wiretapping, harassing, and engaging in violent police actions against black radicals around the country.

The president-elect realized he had better take all his lumps now by filling the CIA role. He lamented to O'Donnell, "Kenny, I can't take this shit and it's just starting. Lowenstein and his friends want me to *abolish* the CIA, not just put someone they like in. I can't do either, and Lowenstein, of all people, should know that. Wasn't he just identified by some radicals as having had ties with one of those CIA-funded 'cultural' or student organizations? He, of all people, should understand the situation. Damn! I'm gonna have more problems with the libs, I bet, than some of these right-wingers on the Hill."

O'Donnell said, "That's because we haven't talked to the right-wingers yet, Bob. This job is gonna be one day at a time. The vision part was the campaign. Now it's getting done what we can. That's what I learned from the last time around with Jack and you. Let the historians put it together after we're done.

That's *their* job. Your job is to get us out of Vietnam—which you and I knew was trouble back in '63, when Senate Majority Leader Mansfield told Jack to get out. Your job is to start rebuilding the cities, get black people integrated into society without too much bloodshed, and maybe help Walt Reuther organize the South so we can get some support there in '72." O'Donnell smiled, knowing he'd made a great adviser's speech.

Kennedy's tenseness subsided a bit. He then said, "Okay, Kenny, bring on the CIA director candidates." He paused before adding, "I'm ready."

But there were hardly any candidates so far. The O Boys, desperate for someone palatable, called in Ted Sorensen to interview for the CIA position. Sorensen was Jack Kennedy's White House counsel and a former Wall Street lawyer who knew something about the world of skullduggery. He had been a participant in key national security meetings from the Bay of Pigs fiasco in 1961 through the Cuban missile crisis of 1962 and was, on rare occasions, useful as a liaison with the intelligence "community" as the CIA was often called.

Bob Kennedy rejected Sorensen, however. He thought it better to have a CIA insider at the top, someone who could—just maybe—also be trusted to listen to the president of the United States.

"Great!" said Larry O'Brien. "Where the hell is that unicorn?"

"Yeah," said a sardonic O'Donnell, "you're looking for a dreamboat, Bob."

Kennedy said, "Gentlemen, you know my motto from George Bernard Shaw, 'There are those who see things as they are and ask why, and those who see things that never were and say, why not?' Find me someone else."

O'Donnell and O'Brien could have recited the Shaw quote with him, since Kennedy had often used that quote while a senator. But when they heard it this time, they just moaned.

"Okay," said O'Brien, "we'll ask around—again."

O'Brien, feeling like he had no choice, asked Allard Lowenstein to suggest someone to head the CIA. Lowenstein, realizing he and his friends were not going to get any support from Kennedy to abolish the agency, said he'd check around. Lowenstein called some alumni from the National Student Association and eventually spoke to the prominent feminist, Gloria Steinem. Ironically, Steinem had also been exposed for having been active a few years before in what was being called a "CIA front." When Lowenstein asked her who she thought should run the CIA, she immediately suggested Cord Meyer Jr. "He's one of the few men in public power I have had consistent respect for," said the woman who most men, and not a few women, thought was simply a "man-hater."

Meyer was brought in to meet Kennedy. Kennedy liked Meyer, but said afterward to O'Donnell, "Al Lowenstein says Meyer's a liberal, but I'm not so sure. He's been handling the CIA's 'dirty tricks' department under Lyndon. Plus, that scandal about recruiting radicals, including Lowenstein and that feminist lady, doesn't help me in most liberal circles anyway. I told Meyer he could stay in the 'dirty tricks' department, and he was fine with that. I asked Meyer if there was a 'can do' guy in the agency who he thought was considered a more moderate-to-conservative type, not an extremist—and someone who didn't have a blind ideological block to a more liberal administration, starting with Vietnam. He suggested a fellow named David Henry Blee. Let's find this Blee fellow and see if he's interested."

The O Boys shrugged their shoulders, but hustled to find Blee. After they located him in South Asia, Blee was immediately flown in to Washington D.C. to meet the president-elect. Blee was fifty-one years old in 1968. He had achieved some notoriety among insiders when he was CIA chief in India for helping Joseph Stalin's daughter safely defect to the West. When Kennedy checked out the story with Chet Bowles, who confirmed it, he was very interested. "Can do" guys were always Bob Kennedy favorites, especially when they acted to help individuals in need.[3]

Blee, however, initially hesitated in accepting an interview with this "far-out liberal" Kennedy. When he finally sat down with the president-elect at Kennedy's home for the interview, Blee spoke bluntly, if not coldly. Blee said he was unsure if he wanted to work for someone who, as "my friends" put it, was "chickening out" of Vietnam. He wanted to see Kennedy's reaction.

Kennedy said, "I understand those feelings and have them sometimes myself." Kennedy stood up, walked to the front of his desk, and leaned against it. "But I think you will agree, Mr. Blee, on one thing. Our country has spent a lot of years there, with almost as many losses as in Korea, and several different governments in Saigon. Yet we still don't see a government there that can stand on its own without doing a lot of damage to a lot of the people we're supposed to be saving. If *you*, sir, think I'm chickening out, you should say so. I am not interested in what others think, but what *you* think. I've thought a lot about our presence in Vietnam and so have many others with even better pedigrees in fighting Communism than I have. And those others see it just the way I do, by the way."

Blee started to sit back in his chair. Then, realizing Kennedy's body-language power play, sat up and said, "I respect that response, Senator Kennedy. I think I even agree with your sense of what has gone on in Southeast Asia, at least sometimes. In my career, I've seen too many things I don't like, but I also remind myself why I'm doing what I'm doing. The world is more gray than people on the outside know or think up there on Capitol Hill or even in the White House. I'm willing to support a man who will do his best for this country. But I want to know, sir, with all due respect, are we supposed to just walk out of there—out of Vietnam, I mean?"

Kennedy stared straight at Blee and said, "No, unless you want to stay on the sidelines and leave me with the antiwar protesters who think that's what we should do. There is a way out with dignity and honor, at least I hope there is. But we'll also need a commitment to try to help the Vietnamese rebuild their nation in a way that's more effective and more akin to our best traditions than what we've given them."

Blee thought a moment and said, "Well, sir, listening to you, I don't think you'll just walk from Vietnam. You've been through other crises before, that's for sure. It's not like you're some governor out there who never had to deal with a foreign crisis."

Kennedy liked that response. He went back around his desk and sat down. He said, "That's fine, Mr. Blee. I don't want a yes man in this position. I want someone who's gonna give me facts, not ideological bullshit. I also need to have someone as head of the CIA who knows the difference between a foreign leader who merely disagrees with us as opposed to someone who's an enemy. If you think the people who fall into one of those two categories are even mostly the same, then you're not the man for the job. I need reliable information, not like the shit my brother got before the Bay of Pigs and not the shit we got from even our own military about the coup in Saigon back in 1963 . . . you know what I mean?" He paused and saw that Blee was thinking. He decided to soften things a bit. "You know, Mr. Blee, I thought you did great with Stalin's daughter. I respect smart and quick action in a crisis situation. That is *key* in my book."

Blee smiled and then began thinking it might be worth the risk to take this position. He, too, wanted to keep the CIA's focus on objective intelligence gathering, with covert operations as only a last resort, if at all. In speaking with various personnel at the CIA headquarters in Langley, Virginia, Blee had learned about CIA reports of North Vietnamese infiltration in Saigon in 1967 that were ignored by General Westmoreland and President Johnson—reports which, if heeded, would have alerted the U.S. military to the early 1968 Communist military strikes known as the Tet Offensive. Blee thought if he provided Kennedy with reliable information, he could become an important adviser to the new president and maybe displace some of those radicals in the administration the CIA was warning him about.

Blee stood up and shook Kennedy's hand. He liked Kennedy's handshake, which sealed the deal completely in his mind. Kennedy, for his part, said to himself, This is the guy, even though he'll be a double agent for the CIA. But at least he's better than Hoover. He's as close to a "unicorn" as I could expect.

As Blee drove away from Hickory Hill after accepting the job, he thought to himself, Kennedy isn't quite what I have heard, which I know I shouldn't be surprised about. Better for me to be here than someone else who isn't from the agency. The Soviets and Red Chinese are pretty dangerous, more than Kennedy or these other civilians know. My goal has got to be to get the CIA back into the good graces of the executive branch again.

That night Kennedy said, while getting into bed with Ethel, "Well, Ethel, I just completed filling the two most important positions in the military-industrial complex, to quote an ex-president. The FBI and the CIA."

He laughed, but Ethel just gave a worried smile. She was more afraid of those agencies than comforted by them. Kennedy spoke again. "Now I have to deal with the radical students, and—oh, Christ!"

"What?" Ethel was startled.

"I . . . I forgot to put a Negro, er, black in the damned cabinet!"

The next morning, Kennedy called the O Boys and asked them to start mending fences with the civil rights leadership. He rationalized his error by telling himself that he had not heard from them since the election, either. The civil rights leadership had, during the campaign, assumed a black would be asked to head a cabinet post. They never pushed it, however, and found out too late that it was not going to happen. They were seething by the time the president and the O Boys began their calls of apology.

Kennedy explained his failure to choose a black for a "first-level cabinet position" on the ground that he needed some time to massage the white vote in the South with a strong labor campaign—and break the back of the Wallace constituency throughout the country. Kennedy was not sure this was the truth, but Yarborough told him it would be effective. Kennedy, continuing to make it up as he went along, also told several civil rights leaders that his plan was to give blacks prominent roles in subcabinet positions.

For example, Andrew Young was asked to be the United States ambassador to the United Nations. O'Brien, for his part, received the president's approval to appoint Julian Bond to lead the Housing and Urban Development Division in the Health, Education, and Welfare Department. Kennedy himself personally asked Charles Smith to take the top assistant's spot under Ramsey Clark. Smith, a "Negro"—to use the parlance fast fading at the time—had been a highly respected U.S. attorney under Kennedy, when Kennedy was attorney general. Ramsey Clark was very pleased to support Smith for the position, telling Kennedy, "Charles is one of the best young lawyers in the country, sir."

Roger Wilkins, an assistant attorney general under Lyndon Johnson and nephew of NAACP chairman Roy Wilkins, was approached to become the solicitor general. The solicitor general position was, next to the attorney general, the most prestigious position for any lawyer in the Justice Department. The role of the solicitor general is largely to file legal briefs and argue cases on behalf of the government in matters of constitutional import. Wilkins, however, would not be the first black solicitor general. The first black solicitor general was also the first black Supreme Court Justice, Thurgood Marshall. Johnson had appointed Marshall to both positions during his four-year term as president. Marshall was, by far, the most respected civil rights trial lawyer in America at the time he was appointed solicitor general. Wilkins would have very large shoes to fill, at least in the eyes of the black community.

Kennedy, working overtime to mend fences with the civil rights movement, also spoke to his senate aide, Peter Edelman. Edelman, who was white and Jewish, was married to a black attorney, Marian Wright Edelman. Kennedy asked Peter Edelman if his wife would be interested in becoming the assistant secretary of education in the Health, Education, and Welfare

Department. There, Marian Edelman would be charged with developing and supporting school programs for inner-city and rural-area children as well as national education policy making. Peter Edelman was, in the same conversation, offered the position of general counsel to the HEW. When Peter wondered aloud whether it was appropriate, considering his wife was likely to agree to be the assistant secretary of education, Kennedy responded, "If I could report to my brother as attorney general, you can be general counsel in your wife's department, right?"

"Right" was all Edelman could say.

The soon-to-be former UN ambassador and past Supreme Court justice, Arthur Goldberg, said to the respected black leader Ralph Abernathy at a cocktail party at Hickory Hill, "Remember Reverend, in FDR's day, some folks said the Jews were running FDR—yet FDR had no Jewish cabinet appointees until his last two administrations. But we were in the background, as perhaps you and your activists will be. This is only the start. You'll see. The various subcabinet positions are clearly a positive."

Abernathy wearily smiled in agreement. He thought to himself, Progress is progress, no matter if it's a little slower than you want.

The Young appointment to the UN made headlines for five or six days, with speculation from the Cold Warriors that Young would seek the immediate removal of South Africa and Rhodesia from the United Nations over their apartheid, or racially segregationist, policies. People put two and two together from the appointment and Bob Kennedy's 1966 speech denouncing apartheid in Soweto, South Africa.

The response of some ethnic whites in the industrialized North and Midwest was that "blacks were taking over in Washington and the United Nations." This was enough to convince civil rights leaders that white liberals, not blacks, needed to be out front in the first days of the administration, as Kennedy had said.

The ethnic whites and Cold Warriors, of course, had no need to worry, for, as usual, two plus two did not equal four in politics. Kennedy was simply engaging in handing out the spoils of election, trying to balance factional politics. The president-elect was also more interested in ending the Vietnam War than starting a war against South Africa or Rhodesia, especially when he knew that the white-controlled African governments had powerful supporters among the elite in Washington, D.C. In a hastily called second press conference, Young was forced to say that he would "constructively engage" the South African and Rhodesian governments, not seek their expulsion from the United Nations. But, he said to himself, Not yet, anyway.

As fences with the civil rights community were being mended, Kennedy called Lowenstein and asked him to come to Hickory Hill to talk about a position in the administration. When Lowenstein arrived, Kennedy led him to the kitchen where they sat down. Kennedy, with no formalities besides a smile and grunt, immediately asked Lowenstein to consider leading the Peace Corps. Lowenstein surprised him, saying he wanted to lead the domestic version of the corps, known as VISTA. Lowenstein said, "I speak better Southern than Swahili, Senator—I mean . . . "

Kennedy was used to this by now. "Al, you can call me Bob, Senator, Mr. President, or even what you called me in late '67—" He laughed. "Uh, no, not that—at least not before we start governing."

Lowenstein smiled wide. "Thank you, um, Mr. President. It's not that I don't want the Peace Corps post. It's just that I'd like to organize the kids in this country, our own country, to get people working together to help the poor and neglected—again, right here at home. VISTA isn't high profile, but I'll make it high profile." The deal was done on that, thought Kennedy. Better a high profile of college kids helping people instead of screaming epithets and burning draft cards.

When Kennedy told O'Donnell and O'Brien what Lowenstein had said, O'Donnell sighed. "Bob, let's give Lowenstein the Peace Corps job anyway and pack him off on a one-way trip to India."

O'Brien added, "Better yet, put Lowenstein in charge of NASA and send him to freakin' Mars! High profile? You wanna let Lowenstein go high profile on anything? You're outta your mind if you let him have the VISTA job or any position like that!"

Kennedy just laughed. "Guess you'll have to keep a better eye on me, fellas. I thought I did well there! Lowenstein's in. Oh well. That's that."

The sound of "ughs" and sighs permeated the room—though none came from the president-elect.

Later that day, Tuesday, November 19, 1968, Kennedy called from home to ask O'Donnell to track down Tom Hayden. He wouldn't tell O'Donnell why, but O'Donnell knew Hayden was going to be asked to head the Peace Corps now that Lowenstein had turned down the post. When O'Donnell located Hayden in Chicago, he asked Hayden if he was interested in "something like" the Peace Corps. Hayden shocked O'Donnell with his answer: "The Peace Corps? Wow, that's a great honor, Mr. O'Donnell. But, um, it's . . . it's . . . it's just that I realized, with this election and my time in major cities during the riots in L.A. and especially Newark, New Jersey . . . I guess I mean to say . . . the cities are where it's at today. The cities are where we have to begin to rebuild our country, know what I mean? Ya know, I'm starting to feel comfortable with Mayor Daley—and there's this great Catholic Cardinal Bernardin, too, who is really into what he calls the social gospel. I think my best place is to stay here in Chicago. I think I can make a difference here—and anyway, the Peace Corps will take me out of America and you know what, I really don't feel like leaving. It's been a couple of years since I've felt that."

Kennedy tried to work up a smile when O'Donnell told him about Hayden. Then, he told O'Donnell, "Hey? What about the other radical, that Davis kid?

He was real helpful, had connections with the students and his father I think worked for Truman, if I recall. Nice kid, well groomed, too. Let's track down Rennie Davis."

O'Donnell, grumbling because he was now approaching yet another radical, dutifully tracked down Rennie Davis. Davis, unlike Hayden and Lowenstein, immediately accepted the post of Peace Corps director. To assist him, he brought in Sam Brown, a rising antiwar student leader and a Peace Corps veteran.[4]

Davis introduced Brown to O'Donnell and said, "Sam and I are going to make the Peace Corps high profile—a profile of peace, community assistance and love. Love, not war."

Brown smiled and added, "You said it, man!"

O'Donnell smiled wanly and thought to himself, Oh boy. We're in for it now—and so are they.

Hunting for Peace in Vietnam

Throughout November, Kennedy maintained a more frenetic pace than he had even during the last week of the election. The fast pace began the morning after the election, when he received Clark Clifford's telephone call telling him that Johnson had ordered a bombing halt in Vietnam.

Clifford, speaking in a manner combining fatherly advice and his insider wisdom, told Kennedy, "I believe we Democrats will only be able to govern effectively if we use the opportunity between now and your inaugural to enter into a peace treaty with the North Vietnamese. Based upon my experience, Bob, if you don't mind my saying, you—and we Democrats—may not have the usual luxury of a slow-moving transition."

Kennedy, chastened by Clifford's words and remembering his sense of somberness at the task ahead in uniting the nation, sprung into action. After speaking with Clifford, he called upon Chet Bowles, Ken O'Donnell, and Larry O'Brien to assemble a team of advisers. The first task was to build up a National Security Council with experienced, but forward looking diplomats or analysts.

Henry Kissinger had been lobbying O'Donnell and O'Brien for the position of head of the National Security Council through a variety of sources over the last weeks of the campaign. Kennedy met Kissinger at Hickory Hill four days after the election, but afterwards told O'Donnell he was not impressed.

Kennedy tried to be witty, though serious about his rejection of Kissinger. He said, "Sitting with Dr. Kess—inger—is that his name?—I kept thinking about Dr. Strangelove, with that heavy accent of his. I didn't like his talk about the constant need for secrecy in policy, not just during negotiations. I told him we had too many secrets in foreign matters when my brother was president. And secrets always get out when you least want it, and that damned Hoover uses it to squeeze people anyway—I didn't tell him that last part, though . . . "

O'Donnell nodded, but wondered how one could do without secrets in Washington, D.C. Secrets were the currency of choice in the nation's capital.

The other two finalists for NSC adviser were Stanley Hoffman and Daniel Ellsberg. Kennedy thought to himself, three Jews, including "Kessinger." These are my choices? What bothered Kennedy even more was that, at one time or another, each had taught at Harvard. This is all so insular, he thought to himself. But he owed it to each of them to see what they had to say.

Kennedy interviewed Stanley Hoffman just after Kissinger. Kennedy liked Hoffman's understated style, his fluent French, his scholarly ability to see the world in grays, and, most importantly, to see real faces in third world leaders and peasants. However, he felt "something missing" in his interview. He was, said Kennedy, just a bit "too reserved and . . . well, French . . . if I don't sound too crass. Let's talk to Dan Ellsberg," he told O'Brien. Of the three candidates for the NSC, Kennedy knew Ellsberg the best. Ellsberg, unlike so many Democratic Party advisers and policy insiders, had openly supported Kennedy back in March and April—back when most people "in the know" were backing McCarthy or Humphrey. Ellsberg also offered the campaign detailed foreign policy advice—and a government memo or two. Kennedy recalled how helpful Ellsberg had been in explaining the latest inside information concerning Johnson's prosecution of the war.

Ellsberg had also been a primary author, through the Rand Corporation, of the Pentagon study on the Vietnam War, which report Kennedy and Bowles had skimmed through—well, really they had read little beyond the special "executive report" Clifford asked Ellsberg and the other Rand Corporation employees to prepare.

Ellsberg's interview left Kennedy dazzled and excited. Ellsberg's knowledge of the history of the Vietnam war came alive off the written pages of the Pentagon study. What sealed it for Kennedy was learning that, like himself, Ellsberg had been a strong supporter of the war in the early '60s and, again like Kennedy, eventually saw the war's futility.[5]

Near the end of the interview where Ellsberg had already discussed other issues besides Vietnam, including other southeast Asian nations, Red China, and Soviet Russia, and international negotiations for arms control, Kennedy decided to play with Ellsberg a bit. He said, "Now, Dan, when I was a senator, I was glad to have some of the inside dope and even some documents from the Johnson administration."

Ellsberg brightened and said, "Oh yes, sir. I appreciated your confidence in me. I believed it was important that you knew—"

Kennedy surprised Ellsberg by suddenly turning dark for a moment. He leaned over toward Ellsberg and said, "That's just it, Dan. I can't have you leaking anything out of my administration just because you and I happen to have a disagreement. Okay?"

Ellsberg shrank back and his face flushed. "Sir," he said, "I didn't do that with just anyone, and I don't plan on doing it now. I went to you with that small but significant bit of information because you were, in my mind, not simply a senator but . . . What I mean is . . . um . . . if that's not—"

"Dan, I understand," interrupted Kennedy, smiling this time to give the flustered Ellsberg a chance to breathe again. Kennedy continued, "My hope is that we can be far more open to analysis and debate in my administration. I also hope to be more straightforward with the American people. But no more leaks, okay, Mr. National Security Chairman?"

Ellsberg let out a deep sigh and said, "Mr. President, I am honored to serve as your national security chairman. Thank you, sir." With that, he and Kennedy stood up and shook hands, formally consummating their agreement.

Kennedy, however, knew he wasn't done. He also wanted a military person among his advisers in ending the war, but not necessarily someone like his and his brother's favorite military leader, General Maxwell Taylor. Max Taylor may be great on most issues, Kennedy said to Chet Bowles, but he already had someone else in mind. On the campaign trail he had read a book, or at least a good part of it, called *The Betrayal*, by a Colonel William Corson. He had received the book from *Washington Post* reporter Ward Just shortly before the Chicago convention.

Corson was in hot water because he had published the book in 1967 without prior military approval, which only increased Kennedy's interest in him. The book stated that the corrupt South Vietnamese government was beyond help. Corson criticized the American military strategy as being overly brutal in propping up that regime, which resulted in peasants joining the Communist-backed Viet Cong, or staying neutral, which was practically the same thing to the Johnson administration and the South Vietnamese government. Kennedy met with Corson in mid-September 1968, and both knew they had found a kindred spirit.

Corson spoke with Kennedy after the election to warn him that he had heard that General Earle Wheeler, the Chairman of the Joint Chiefs of Staff at the Pentagon since 1964, would oppose anything other than renewing a military commitment in Vietnam. Corson said, "Wheeler thinks the war in South Vietnam is winnable and doesn't want to change—unless it means more bombing, more troops, or at least more training of South Vietnamese troops, and chasing the Reds into Cambodia. The same thing holds for Ambassador Ellsworth Bunker and General Creighton Abrams. You might have to replace them all if you want to find your way toward—"

Kennedy said, "Wait a minute! Johnson replaced General William Westmoreland with Abrams in Southeast Asia just a few months ago. Isn't that good? Wasn't Westy pushing for more American troops? I've heard Abrams isn't asking for more troops and wants to send some home. He should be on our side, right?"

Corson laughed. "Uh, sir, one question at a time. Westmoreland's problem was that he was a politician. He did what Lyndon and the other civies wanted. He told them what he thought they wanted to hear and eventually believed it himself. We didn't do so bad at the time of the Tet Offensive this year, but it looked bad because Westy ignored reports from the CIA that the

Commies were gearing up, and worse, the Commies hit us right in Saigon. The reporters were talking on deep background with those in the military, and in the administration, who hung Westy out to dry. That's why things looked so bad to the public.

"Your second question, I think, concerns Abrams, but it's really Abrams, Ellsworth Bunker, the U.S. Ambassador in Saigon, and especially General Wheeler. All three are serious about winning the war, as if it can be won without a lot more dead Vietnamese—and American soldiers. Their plan, from what I've heard, is to bomb more in North Vietnam and in the Cambodian sanctuaries. They also think they can train more South Vietnamese soldiers not to run to the other side five minutes after the fighting starts. And then after that, they think it would be a good idea to mine the Haiphong harbor in North Vietnam, as if killin' a few hundred thousand Vietnamese with flooding will win over their 'hearts and minds' or somethin' like that. It might work—I won't say it can't. But what's the point of all this when the South Vietnamese government has never had hardly any support outside of Saigon in the first place? That's all I'm saying, sir."

Kennedy nodded then thought to himself, I like this guy, although I see why he's on the outs with the military. He asked Corson, "Who else is there at the Joint Chiefs who sees what you and I see?"

Corson replied, "Hard to say. Remember you got to deal with Wheeler till 1970 when his term is up at the Joint Chiefs—I checked that out already. You'll have to find out who's a likely candidate in the Joint Chiefs some other way—I wish I could help there, but I can't. All I know is that Abrams is with Wheeler, but Abrams may not be as blind a follower as anyone might think. Abrams has at least been trying to listen to his men out in the jungles, including battalion leaders, and getting their feedback, even if he doesn't like what he hears."

"Meaning?" said a very attentive president-elect.

"Well, meaning there was one battalion leader, I think his name is Hackworth, who said pretty much what I'm saying. Hackworth was pretty blunt—and Abrams didn't like it. But Hackworth's got a great rep. Likes to be out there in the jungles and Abrams respected that. Look, Mr. President . . . I mean . . . whatever I should call you right now. I am sick of this war and what it's doing to our military—to the marines I love! Just before I got out of the jungle, with shells going off all around, I held a young marine soldier in my arms just before he died—and you . . . know . . . what . . . "

The colonel fought back tears for a few moments before continuing. "An' you know what that dyin' boy said to me? He said, 'Colonel, doesn't anybody care?' I . . . told him they . . . they did care . . . even though I didn't believe that myself . . . anymore . . . maybe he knew it, too." Gaining some anger at the expense of his tears, Corson then said, "He asked me, 'Then why isn't anyone tellin' people the *truth* about this war?' I said I would. And he grabbed me by the arm and said, 'Colonel, do it!' Then he died. Right there in my arms, sir."

Corson sat back with tears in his eyes for a few seconds, as Kennedy realized the man was crying. Kennedy was fighting tears himself. He knew the pain of losing someone you were supposed to watch out for.

Corson then spoke again, now with anger, "And you think I was gonna let some bureaucrat in the military threaten me with in a court-martial without a fight—all for writin' what I think was the truth? No freakin' way, pal! No freakin' way!"

Kennedy was stunned. He never thought the military could be a stumbling block in trying to end the war. Didn't they just follow orders from civilian leaders? General Taylor never challenged his brother's authority, had he? Kennedy learned one important thing from this meeting with Corson: He'd better keep an eye on Wheeler, Abrams, and the Joint Chiefs. And he'd sure as hell better replace Ellsworth Bunker, the U.S. ambassador in Saigon.

Aftter talking with Corson, Kennedy asked Ralph Yarborough to search around the Joint Chiefs for a suitable leader who understood that a negotiated peace was a more preferable option than what sounded like a possible expansion of the war into the Cambodian sanctuaries with further bombing and mayhem. After investigating, Yarborough reported back that Admiral Thomas H. Moorer might be the best candidate to replace Wheeler as head of the Joint Chiefs of Staff in 1970. There was a hitch, however, said Yarborough. Wheeler had been chief of staff for several years and was very popular with Congress at the moment. For now, Kennedy might have to deal with Wheeler and try to make him an ally, or at least not so complete an enemy.

Kennedy said to Yarborough, "Let's set up lunch with Moorer, since Wheeler happens to be in Vietnam and is probably very busy right now."

Yarborough smiled and said, "Now that's a good plan. Ah wish Ah'd thought of it." As he later told Opal, he *had* thought of it, but he didn't want to be seen as pushy. "Had to measure the man again. Sometimes winning makes a fella run scared tryin' to make friends with his enemies."

Just before Thanksgiving 1968, Kennedy called Clark Clifford and told him his team was in place and ready to meet at the White House to receive a briefing and status report on the military effort in Vietnam. Clifford happily obliged and said he was ready the next day.

Clifford, the next afternoon, gave a three hour presentation at the White House to president-elect Kennedy, Chester Bowles, Paul Warnke, Ralph Yarborough, U.N. Ambassador-designate Andrew Young, CIA-designate David Blee, new Kennedy military adviser William Corson, and Dan Ellsberg.

Kennedy had asked Galbraith to join them for the meeting at the White House, but Galbraith suggested inviting George Kennan instead. Kennan, a legendary State Department foreign policy expert, now in his sixties, was the author of the policy known as "the anti-Communist containment doctrine" dating back to the beginning of the Cold War. Every post-war U.S. administration followed this policy in word and deed, if not always in the same subtlety that Kennan intended. Kennan, ever the diplomat, agreed to attend after speaking with Clifford, who was pleased to know the incoming administration had invited Kennan. Kennedy had originally been reticent to invite Kennan, thinking he was "old school." But Galbraith responded that Kennan had become something of a "dove" on the subject of Vietnam, just as Kennedy had. As early as 1966, Kennan had spoken of a six-month organized withdrawal from Vietnam as part of a negotiated settlement with the Viet Cong and the Communists in the North. Kennedy had attended part of those hearings as a senator, but frankly forgot that Kennan had stated that in his testimony.

Kennedy also wanted to "back door" his good friend Bob McNamara into this meeting, but Mac vehemently refused. "I had my time, Bob. I've already made more than enough enemies, and I've frankly had enough of that part of my life. Just hear me out from time to time when I call from the World Bank. Lyndon put me here as president of the World Bank and I'm staying for awhile, at least to do some penance around this planet of ours."

Clifford began his presentation with a brief survey of the situation in Vietnam. "As we have announced a couple of weeks or so ago that we have halted our bombing campaign, the North Vietnamese Communist government has agreed to talk about specific proposals for peace. The North, in fact, has privately offered the following peace proposal: Immediately create a coalition government in South Vietnam with the Viet Cong as part of the coalition. Free elections in South Vietnam in six months' time, with the Viet Cong participating, of course. Any and all North Vietnamese troops who are currently in South Vietnam are to remain in South Vietnam. Our troops, however, must begin to leave immediately. In return for our beginning to leave, the North promises to halt further troop infiltration into South Vietnam. They will also respect the results of any election; at least that's what they are saying now. They also, however, expect new elections for unification with the North to be held in the year after the initial elections. This means they expect the Viet Cong, or something akin to the Viet Cong, to win the immediate elections. They are emphatic that the Geneva Accords of 1954, which were the peace accords agreed to after the French war in Vietnam, and which the Eisenhower administration frankly undermined, be followed completely. Finally, the North believes that the devastation to both North and South—by American bombing, by use of defoliants such as our Agent Orange, as well as napalm, and the general destruction attendant to any war—requires us to provide at least some economic and development aid. I find this last proposal ridiculous in its implications, if not its overall policy—I hope you don't mind that editorial comment, gentlemen."

Clifford then looked at Kennedy and said, "Mr. President, you should know that President Johnson is emphatic in not giving—I wish to quote him exactly here—a 'thin dime to those murderin' Viet Cong.' President Johnson also rejects, strongly I might add, involving the Viet Cong in any coalition government. He wants the Viet Cong to drop their weapons and submit to an open election. If I may comment again, I should say I have, over time, said to President Johnson that we cannot move forward by ignoring the Viet Cong—or bombing the countryside outside Saigon, I might add."

Kennedy, less than happy at the continued stalemate and Johnson's refusal to look for alternatives to get to peace, spoke first to immediately show he was in charge of his own advisers. "Gentlemen, I want to first thank Secretary Clifford for all his efforts over the past year and over the years for his service to our great nation. I would like, however, before we speak further, to ask Secretary Clifford what our response has been to the North Vietnamese offer, which off was made when?"

Clifford replied, "The North Vietnamese offer was made within forty-eight hours of the bombing halt. We had heard this was going to be their position for quite some time before, Mr. President. It is, in all candor, not too different from what we've heard over the last two years."[6]

"But, Mr. Secretary," said Kennedy, "what has been *our* response to this offer?"

Clifford replied, "We have told the North Vietnamese, particularly Mr. Le Duc Tho, their chief negotiator in Paris, where the talks are scheduled to begin again, that we cannot respond until we speak with you and your incoming administration. I told Mr. Le that he can expect a response around Christmas, if not before. I hope I was not too presumptive, but I did not wish to have them think our administration was unduly delaying matters—or that we were pushing too hard to give an answer."

Kennedy smiled and said, "Clark, why don't you stay on and finish this thing? You know where we're at in this room. We've got Mr. Bowles, Mr. Kennan, Mr. Ellsberg, who you know, among others. I believe—"

"Mr. President," interrupted Clifford, "I must interrupt, with all respect to you, and decline your generous offer. This has been very trying, and I simply believe it is better that I hand the baton, as it were, to you and your fine advisory staff."

Kennedy nodded, saying, "No offense taken, Mr. Secretary."

Kennan, getting too old to simply watch the dance, spoke up. "Gentlemen, I think this offer from the Communists is genuine and is a good start." At the word "genuine," Clifford and most of the others raised their eyebrows, except Bowles, who knew that in Kennan's world of international diplomacy, the word "genuine" didn't mean much.

Ellsberg spoke next. "I am all for a Marshall Plan for Southeast Asia, if I may say so, Secretary Clifford. General Landsdale and I have long argued for this, I should add. However, we need to press the North to take most of its troops out of South Vietnam and from their so-called sanctuaries in

Cambodia. We'll never get all the troops out, but we should try to get most out. I think, if I may, Mr. President, that we must take an initial hard line for at least domestic purposes, and to show the North that we are not simply walking away."

Ellsberg was shocked to hear himself sounding like a "hawk" again, knowing that he was considered a "hawk" who became a "dove." But his Harvard theories about hard-nosed diplomacy gushed out of him like a pent-up geyser. He was an insider again, and he saw himself falling back into that mode.

Kennedy was about to ask Chet Bowles' opinion when Ellsberg interrupted, "Mr. President, sir! Um, may I also say just one more thing? I don't mean to contradict myself, but I do believe we can make a firm counteroffer and also make clear our intentions for peace . . . by agreeing in principle to certain principles such as the economic aid—or something. . . . We can, I think, talk specifics later today." Ellsberg, seeing Kennedy's perplexed but less than enthusiastic facial expression, knew he should have stayed quiet. Ellsberg sat back, angry at himself.

Kennedy was gracious in his words, but Ellsberg heard a slight condescension in his tone. "Agreed, Dan. We ought to think over our strategy. I'm not sure, though, we should agree to anything until we have *all* the points established." He turned from Ellsberg to Bowles, saying, "Now, Chet, what are your thoughts?"

Bowles, recognizing Ellsberg's predicament in trying to be a "tough dove," said, "I think Mr. Kennan and Mr. Clifford are correct in regard to each of their statements. We must immediately tell the Vietnamese we are going to consider the offer carefully and with timely diligence. We know there are aspects we are not likely to accept, such as North Vietnamese troops staying in the South—at least most should go, as Dan says.

"I have read," said Bowles, now looking at Ellsberg, "the Pentagon's Vietnam report prepared by Dan and others at the Rand Corporation. I found it not only fascinating but, frankly, sad in the fact that successive presidents, starting with President Truman, have missed opportunities for peace and development in this area. In speaking with Mr. Kennan, I think we are all in agreement that we must insist that the Viet Cong in the South conduct themselves peaceably in an atmosphere of ballots and elections, as opposed to bullets and terror, before we consider allowing them into any South Vietnamese government coalition. I have read Mr. Kennan's testimony to Congress from a year and a half ago. I asked him, before this meeting, if that is still his position today—and he assured me it is. We need, as Mr. Kennan has testified in Congress, a decent interval of six months for withdrawal in order to give meaning to Dan's point about firmness. Over that time, elections can be held in which we must, again, insist on openness to all sides in South Vietnam."

Warnke nodded strongly in approval, while Corson raised his hand to the president-elect. "May I say something?" he asked. Seeing Kennedy's signal to proceed, Corson began, "I hope you don't mind my saying, gentlemen, but this is not gonna be a quick or easy agreement to execute in the jungles and hamlets. Not because of the Viet Cong, but because we gotta watch our backs right here in our own military and with our 'allies' in the South Vietnamese government. I'm not paranoid, but even paranoids got enemies. There's a whole bunch of people in the brass, in Langley—sorry, Mr., Mr.—"

Corson pointed to Blee, who responded in a less than friendly tone, "Blee!"

Corson smiled humbly, and then said, "Yes, thank you, sir. Mr. Blee. Um, anyway, I'm sorry to say, there's a lot of folks in the CIA, and maybe in Congress, who think that whatever deal we make that allows the Viet Cong to participate even in a South Vietnamese election—forget any coalition before the election—I mean, man! You guys are the political experts and stuff, but I think we're playing with fire here and we better . . . whaddyacallit . . . 'analyze' the situation before we start shootin' here." He looked around, saw some discomfort on most faces, including his boss', and said, "Sorry, sir. I just . . . thought . . . I'd . . . well, say what I think . . . in the spirit of getting to our goal . . . sir."

Kennedy stood up, went over to Corson, and put his hand on his shoulder. "Colonel Corson, I am glad to have you here among all us 'civies!' You're right." He turned to the others and said, "Can you believe it? The military guy has to remind us of the politics of this whole damned thing!" The room filled with nervous laughter.

Blee now spoke, shaking his head at what he was about to say. "Yes, Colonel Corson is . . . correct, um, in part, at least. I too have read portions of the Pentagon report on Vietnam—thank you, Secretary Clifford, by the way—and I know I can speak persuasively to many of my friends in the military, as well as my close friends in the agency, about the need for a bipartisan resolution of this matter. I would suggest that, if at all possible, if we worked with real live Nazis and Fascists right after World War II in setting up West Germany—in fact, in most of post-war Europe—and we seem to be working well with a very rough individual, General Suharto in Indonesia[7]—I think we ought to gauge the Viet Cong in Vietnam to see if they are willing to work with us as they worked with our OSS in World War II. I'm not a politician—though the agency does have its politics and bureaucracy like any organization—but I know strange things can happen when peace breaks out, just like we became friends with our enemies in Germany and Japan after World War II. There is no way anyone in the intelligence and military communities will support the Viet Cong in any coalition government. They might take a chance if there was an election as Mr. Kennan states. But if this fails, and I must emphasize this, we could be in a real shooting war again."

Clifford was pleased and smiled at Kennan. "Gentlemen, I am very interested to hear more from you after you have had a chance to digest the report my staff prepared regarding peace negotiations between President Johnson's negotiators and the North Vietnamese over the past eighteen months. It should bring you up to speed and hopefully point you all in the right direction—if I may say so—to a successful and possibly early resolution to this terrible conflict."

Kennedy said, "Gentlemen, I think I'd like to confer further with each of you in smaller groups, review Secretary Clifford's reports, talk with each of you for more insight, and then move forward with a counteroffer to the Vietnamese Communists. In closing, what I am about to say may sound naïve, but *please*! No leaks! Please, *no leaks!* As Colonel Corson has reminded us, or at least me, the politics of this peaceful resolution may be as important as what we finally agree to in content with the Communists! I say that not because it is the thing that drives us. I am, however, saying that we must consider it if our course of action—our policy—is to be successful. Thank you for coming today, and I would like to thank Secretary Clifford and President Johnson, who I gather was unavailable today, for their professional courtesy and cooperation."

As they were leaving, Kennedy stopped Clifford in the hall. "Clark, can we talk in private?"

Clifford said, "Of course."

They went over to an open office and closed the door.

"Clark, I haven't heard from President Johnson since the week of the election. I have been tempted to call, but I frankly don't know how to talk to him. I heard he's angry at my victory, more so each day. He really regrets his decision in March not to run and—well, I need to know. Is this true? I already know. I just want to hear it from you so you don't think I'm crazy—"

"It's true, I'm sorry to say." Clifford let that sink in before continuing. "But, Mr. President—"

"Please call me Bob, sir."

"Then Bob it is, Mr. President . . . Bob. In any event, sir, President Johnson will be *very* pleased with my report from today's meeting. He will see you are not taking any different tack than what I have proposed for so long. He doesn't like my approach either, but he has generally assumed you are—I wish to be candid here—going to just walk away from South Vietnam. I think . . . I think President Johnson needs to read my report before we all meet together. Afterwards, allow me to call you to set an appointment for the three of us. If you don't mind, you may wish to bring Senator Yarborough along. I assume you know, but Ralph sent President Johnson a very nice letter two days after the election, thanking him for all the great work he did for the working poor, and especially for Negro Americans. He wrote that Lyndon was one of the finest presidents the country ever saw and that he knew he—meaning Ralph—could never say he'd have done anything different if he was sitting in Lyndon's chair when it came to the war. I saw the letter. It was beautifully written. Lyndon called him the same day he got it. They had a 'good old time' on the phone I hear."

Kennedy was caught completely off guard and was simmering as Clifford spoke. He said, almost yelling, "Ralph never said a word to me! And President Johnson didn't return my call to the White House the day after the election either."

Clifford did his best not to appear flustered. "You know, um, President Johnson, well . . . He . . . He's a proud man, Mr. President. He just thought you two would end up screaming at each other—or really, him screaming at you over walking away from the South Vietnamese. I think he's mellowing, and Ralph helped. Let's talk after Thanksgiving Day, maybe as early as Friday afternoon, about setting up a meeting. After the first meeting with President Johnson, we should, I think, bring in some Republicans. Rockefeller could be one. I also think we can talk with a couple of senators, maybe Ev Dirksen for starters. We need bipartisanship here, Mr. President, even though I sense we won't get it down the road no matter what the solution is—because, I must say, the South Vietnamese government leaders will not go quietly into retirement. And, as I hope you know, they have their supporters in Saigon and here in Washington."

Kennedy smiled wanly—again. He was already tired of not speaking his mind lest people say "ruthless Bobby" was back. He said to Clifford, "I know. Corson's told me and so has Blee. He and Blee may be my best clutch-hitters in dealing with this situation."

Clifford smiled the smile of a father to a son. "You'll be fine, Mr. President. I am sure of it. Your brother was a great leader, and I know you were his rock." He patted Kennedy's shoulder and walked him out of the office. They shook hands warmly, and, as Kennedy began to walk away, he felt at least a little better about possibly leading the nation to peace. He laughed to himself, thinking, I better enjoy this moment while it lasts.

When he looked up, he saw the limousine driver waiting to take him back to Hickory Hill. He focused now on his wife and children—all ten of them, and soon to be eleven. For he knew they were dealing with more local issues of sibling rivalry and housecleaning—or, in Ethel's case, the lack of house-cleaning, despite maid after maid. Ethel, he knew, was allergic to tidiness. The White House, he laughed to himself, is going to be a noisy, messy place when our brood moves in.

Chapter 10

THE POLITICS OF PEACE

"Ralph, I've got a bone to pick with you," began Kennedy to his vice president–elect, whom he summoned to Hickory Hill immediately after
leaving Clifford. "You tell me how I've got to keep you up to speed on
everything. Now I learn from Clark Clifford that you've been talking with
Johnson when you know I can't even get him to return my call!"

"Ah humbly apologize, Mr. President," answered a crimson-faced
Yarborough. "Ah sent a li'l note to Lyndon, and he called me out o' the blue the
day he got it. He asked me not to talk to you about our conversation. Ah told
him he needed to give you a chance, considering you're gonna be president in a
couple o' months. Ah said Ah'd be the intermediary, but he waved me off. He
said he just needed ta-hm and he would lahk to make the first call on this. He's
pretty depressed, if Ah may say so, in the two or three calls Ah've had with him,
despite his outward appear—"

"Two or three calls you've . . . " Now it was Kennedy's face that was crimson—from anger, not embarrassment. "Ralph, if I hadn't gone through the
election with you, I'd . . . I'd . . . Ralph, I'm really . . . How . . . How could you
talk to that . . . *bastard?* He almost ruined the goddamned election for us and
would've screwed over his own civil rights policies for Nixon—the mother—"

"Now, Mr. President, Ah deserve to be in your doghouse, but Ah had to
give Lyndon time. Clark Clifford called me and warned me you were gonna
call—didn't think you'd call so quick, though. He tells me Lyndon's ready to
talk now in a way that's gonna . . . that could get enough of this rancor and
recrimination out o' the damned way! Mah loyalty to you through this campaign was *total*—and unwavering! Even when Ah found out about strategies
and commercials from O'Brien as an afterthought, Ah didn't complain. Ah
wasn't consulted in several o' the cabinet choices—Ah didn't even meet Blee
until after you announced him as headin' the CIA—and all along, Ah haven't
said a word! Now here Ah'm trying to get you and ol' Lyndon together, and
you start runnin' in yo'r bare feet down a bad road filled with broken glass,
rattlers, and scorpions."

Kennedy laughed at that last bit of corn pone. He said, "Ralph! Ralph!
I'm sorry. Really!" He patted Ralph's arm. "You're right, Ralph. I've been
running in different directions all at once—and I didn't keep you in my sights
much, either. Maybe the Massachusetts Irish and the Texas good ol' boys

don't communicate very well, do we? I mean it. I'm sorry. My tone implied more frustration at you than 'ol' Lyndon,' as you call him. Maybe I need to turn some political swords into ploughshares, don't I?"

"Yes, Mr. President. Ah told Lyndon that he can't change the past, but he can set the stage for a better future for him, for you, and the country. You may not believe this, but he could be a good source—if we'd let him be one—when we twist some arms on this Vietnam thing, and maybe some more domestic matters."

"Well, Clark Clifford says Johnson's going to like the report Clifford's preparing about our meeting this morning." Seeing Yarborough's face, he realized he should have invited his vice president-elect to that meeting, too. "Sorry, Ralph. I'm starting to see what you mean . . . "

"Well, that's real good then. Now Ah don't guarantee that ol' dog Lyndon won't pee on our legs when we get talkin' with him, but Ah been thinkin' we ought to be able to talk at least as friendly with him as we plan to talk with the Vietnamese . . . "

Kennedy nodded and smiled. "I guess it's better we had this conversation now, isn't it?"

Yarborough smiled back and said, "Bettah now than nevah. Now you follow up with Clifford and let's meet with him and Lyndon—the sooner, the better." Seeing Kennedy was fine now, Yarborough took a big risk and asked, "By the way, how many tahms you call Lyndon?"

Kennedy, reddening slightly from embarrassment, said, "Well, just once, personally, if that's what you mean."

Yarborough patted the president-elect on the shoulder and said, "Hmmm . . . You two got some real issues to work out now, don't ya?"

"Yeah, I guess we do. Kinda like the country."

"You got that raht, pardner." Yarborough smiled as he said that. And Kennedy smiled back.

Kennedy and Yarborough met for lunch with Clark Clifford and President Johnson on Sunday, December 1. Johnson made the first move by getting up from behind his desk and walking over to the new president- and vice-president-to-be. Johnson grabbed Kennedy's hand with a warm handshake and said, "Ah'm very impressed with you and your team's approach to the Vietnamese, *Mis-ter* President—yeah-up, might as well get used to hearin' yaself called that now." He smiled in what Kennedy perceived to be a genuine manner, which made Kennedy feel relaxed in a way he'd never experienced with Johnson before.

Johnson then grabbed Yarborough's shoulder with one hand and, with his other hand, shook Yarborough's hand so much it almost loosened Yarborough's teeth. "Great to see you, Ralph! Couldn't be happier for you!

Gentlemen, please! Sit down and let's talk! Ah hope mah staff is cooperatin' at every level and makin' this the best transition anyone's ever seen. If you don't mind, Ah'd like to talk about Clark's report, fu'st off. Ah read Clark's report and, while Ah can't agree with every li'l detail, as you and Clark know, Ah think a majority of the public has spoken pretty clear. The question is how you gonna sell the Republicans and conservatives and make sure we don't have riots and protests over peace like we did with the . . . the . . . " He didn't like to say "war" any longer. " . . . um . . . situation in Vietnahm."

Clark Clifford spoke first to make sure Kennedy would see this was not a time to disagree with the president. "Yes, Mr. President, I think we are all in general agreement that the peace must be bipartisan and broad in its support." He looked at Kennedy, who got the cue.

Kennedy jumped in, feeling the time was right for magnanimity, not rancor. "Mr. President, I am deeply honored to be here with you and greatly appreciate your comments regarding my team and me. You accomplished more than most any other president, including FDR, to bring people's attention to the plight of the poor. You did more than Lincoln for black Americans. And I know we agreed on the war at one time—I . . . I know . . . I know we've had our differences which I . . . which I know go back to . . . well . . . Well sir, I don't—I can't change what went on and—" Kennedy stood up, reached across the desk with his right hand outstretched. He said to Johnson, in a voice filled with emotion and humility, "Mr. President, I want to do my best for the country, and if there's one thing I've got to do, it's to reunite the country on some basic issues. If I don't start making amends with people with whom I've crossed swords, then I'm not . . . I'm not 'walking the walk,' as some of the civil rights marchers say. Mr. Johnson, I want to apologize for how I conducted myself with you over the years. I know I haven't been the easiest person to get along with sometimes. It's just—-nah, no excuses now, sir. I'm sorry."

Johnson hesitated more from shock than anything else. He was the one who usually was dramatic in a given situation. He knew, from his experience with Bob Kennedy, that this wasn't easy for him, nor would it be for any Kennedy. It proved, once and for all to Lyndon, that Ralph, Clark, Larry O'Brien, and those others might be right. There was a change in Robert Kennedy, first with his brother's martyrdom and now with his own just-missed martyrdom.

Johnson stood up, grasped Kennedy's hand, and said, "Son, Ah mean, Mr. President, it takes a brave man to say what you just said. Ah've not been too good to you mahself—as Ah know *you* know!—and we gotta get along more than ever 'cause we'll be one of the few who've been or will be presidents, and there aren't too many of us around at any one given time. Ah know Ah'd have liked to talk more with Ike or Truman, but neither of 'em have been much good for bouncin' things off of, if you wanna know the truth. Ah'd like to be of help to you since we've had a hell of a decade to be president in, unlike Ike at least."

Kennedy said, "I'd like that sir," and surprised himself because he really meant it—for the moment at least. He then sat down.

Johnson kept standing though, and kept talking. "Now, gentlemen, Ah hear you need some bipartisan support on this peace deal, am Ah raht?"

Yarborough, deciding to speak before Johnson or Kennedy made a misstep and blew it all again, broke in. "Yes, Mr. President. This one could be like a goose where it looks real quiet and easy to catch, but then starts honkin' and runnin' all over the farm—" He turned to Kennedy, saying, "if you know what Ah mean . . . "

Johnson didn't think to look at Kennedy as he responded, "Ralph, Ah know it all too well. Ah called Governor Rockefeller in New York and invited him to come down this week to meet me. Ah sent him a copy of that Pentagon report and Clark's report, too. Ah told him he's gotta help you fellas get a peace agreement where we avoid any o' this bull over 'Who lost Vietnam.' The governor, as you know, had set forth a similar plan as you to end the war, if Ah recall, this past Ju-ly. Funny how ev'ryone sees things so clear when they're not in this seat. Ah remember me and Senator Russell talkin' 'bout this problem back in '64— before Ah was really used to this seat, Ah must say. We thought a president would be impeached if he tried to get outta Vietnam too quickly or without a clear victory. Anyways, the country can't handle any more division, and the South Vietnamese leaders gotta understand that. They've had more than enough time and help from us in firepower, God knows."

Kennedy was shocked. *How dare Johnson pull strings without asking me? He thinks he's gonna run things like I'm some kid? A handshake and he thinks he's gonna screw me with kindness? I know he wanted Rockefeller for president more than anyone this year, but this is ridiculous!*

Kennedy's face was flushing again, and fortunately Yarborough saw it before Johnson, who was too intoxicated with his skills of diplomacy and political strategy right then.

Yarborough said loudly to get Johnson's attention, "Bob and Ah thank you for your willingness to assist here. Ah think, however, and with all due respect, Mr. President, that Bob and Ah should discuss strategies and details with Governor Rockefeller when he gets here so he can hear our thoughts directly. He's here when, sir? Thursday, you say?"

That meant Rocky's coming here tomorrow, thought Yarborough. *Better get on it today.*

Yarborough continued. "Mr. President, the president-elect and Ah will be glad to call Governor Rockefeller when he gets here"—*we're calling today,* he thought to himself—"and Ah know," now almost pleading with Kennedy to keep in line—"the president-elect and Ah will keep our eyes on the ball game, which is getting the best peace, and one we sorely need as soon as possible. And if some don't like it 'cause they'll *never* like it, then we just gotta play that much harder to win." He turned to Kennedy and said, "Right, sir?"

Kennedy wanted to glare at Yarborough, but he knew Ralph was right to stay cool. "Right, Ralph. I—Ralph and I are the ones who need to keep our eyes on the ball, Mr. President. I also meant to say earlier that Ethel had a rough night last night—the baby's due in just a few weeks and Ethel's confined to her bed, as you may know—and I promised I'd be more attentive to her needs now that the election's over. I hope you don't mind if we cut out a bit early today. I know I'd like to speak more with you about the transition and particularly this peace issue. Can we set up another time after today?"

Johnson was suspicious, but who can argue with a husband who has a sickly pregnant wife? "I understan', Mr. President. It's important for you to take care of that little lady. A fahn woman, Ethel." They all stood.

Johnson waited for Kennedy to reach out again with a handshake, but the wait appeared to be in vain. Kennedy began walking out of the room when Yarborough tripped into him with a grunt that said, "Think, stupid!"

Kennedy stopped. He saw Johnson standing at his desk. Again, he buried his ego for Johnson and walked back, saying, "Mr. President! I am so worried about this one—number eleven, you know—I know I shouldn't, it's just strange . . . I . . . " He put out his hand to shake Johnson's hand, and, despite using Ethel's poor condition as an excuse, his anger somewhat dissipated with thoughts about his new child. Johnson took his hand warmly, thinking, Poor devil. Got to be president now, and he's gotta worry about babies and a pregnant wife. Maybe Ah should give him another chance, God knows.

Kennedy's anger returned the farther he got from Johnson's office, but he did not want to show it while at the White House. Yarborough knew he didn't have much time before Kennedy exploded, so he focused on strategy, not emotions. Yarborough said, "Bob, if you called Rocky in New York, would he open up to you?"

Kennedy, not quite ready to explode, breathed deeply and replied, "I can't say we're close, but we're close enough, I guess. I mean, we weren't close, but I did help him in 1965 in getting him on the commission looking into poverty in rural areas. We got some areas of New York State included. I can make some calls—since Rocky's coming in Thursday—"

Yarborough decided at that moment that if he yelled first, maybe he could keep Kennedy from exploding. With both of them now safely inside Kennedy's limousine, Yarborough almost shouted, "Bullshit, Bob! Rockefella's coming in tomorrow or maybe tonight. Ah didn't miss ol' Lyndon in there, and Ah didn't miss your reaction either! Get to Rockefella today and tell him that he needs to talk *now* as to whether he's on board and that bein' on board means we gotta be open with each other. You got as much a mandate for a quick peace as anything in an election lahk we went through. Ah'll call Dirksen's office with Clifford and O'Brien and get goin' on that front."

Kennedy grabbed Yarborough's arm, more in frustration than anger. "Damn him, Ralph! It's *my* turn now! Johnson's turn is over. *Over!* I prostrated myself to that . . . that . . . son of a bitch and he pulls this stunt—bringing in Rockefeller before we even thought it through!"

"Bob, with all due respect, let's just take it that he greased the skids for us. This is no tahm for anythin' except makin' lemonade outta all the lemons that get thrown in our way. Ah would, if ya don't mahnd, humbly suggest ya get home to your wife and tell her to let it get 'round she had a *real* rough night las' naht. You know Lyndon's gonna check up—and even if he doesn't, you're covered. Now, let's talk later today and compare notes, okay?"

Kennedy nodded. "Ralph, I didn't think I needed a Texan on my side like I've needed you. You Texans are a different breed, and I'm not sure I like it one darn bit!"

Yarborough smiled wide on that and thought to himself, Different breed? He don't know the *half* of it, the poor Yankee.

Kennedy went home and talked with Ethel, who dutifully launched the rumor about her bad night. Meanwhile, Kennedy called around to get to Rockefeller. Rocky was definitely a peace supporter but had problems with letting the Viet Cong take part in elections. "They're Communist guerrillas, Bob, worse than Black Panthers! We can't let them walk in and take part in elections like they were Democrats or Republicans."

Kennedy replied, "But Governor, the point of the Pentagon report—yes, Governor, I'm glad President Johnson sent the summary to you the other day—the clear import from that report is that the people in Vietnam, particularly South Vietnam, seem to believe in the Viet Cong and are often willing to die for them. If we get the guerrillas out in the open, there could be schisms between the Viet Cong and the people there, and among the Viet Cong, according to George Kennan. Let's argue it out with my team and bring in someone who you want for an adviser."

Rockefeller immediately suggested Henry Kissinger. Kennedy winced at his end of the phone line. Rocky caught the delayed response, interpreting it correctly. "I know you didn't much like Dr. Kissinger, Mr. President, but he's very knowledgeable about international diplomacy in our nuclear age. He speaks highly of you and knows—and respects—the members of your team."

Kennedy knew he needed to cajole Rocky, not debate him. "Governor, Dr. Kissinger is an excellent choice. Bring him along. You have any ideas, by the way, for who in Congress we could call on for bipartisan support from the Republican Party?"

"Let me think about it, Bob. But Ev Dirksen would be nice, wouldn't he?"

"He would be great to have aboard, Governor, you're right. We're working on that, I believe, for a few days now," making this up to show he was strategizing. "Any help in that regard is more than welcome, though I would request we coordinate so we may all be most effective together."

"I suppose," replied the governor, with all the savvy of a patrician grandson of an oil robber baron.

While Kennedy was making it up, O'Brien met with Ralph Yarborough. Instinctively understanding they needed Republican Senator Everett Dirksen on their side, they drove over to see Dirksen, who had stayed in D.C. instead of going back to Illinois, his home state. Dirksen was feeling a little more tired lately. This winter he was slow in getting packed and saying farewell to his staff after the Senate adjourned until January.

O'Brien had an extra copy of the Pentagon report and a copy of Clifford's report, which Clifford had personally sent him. They brought the documents over to Dirksen. Though they had no appointment, Dirksen agreed to speak with them at his D.C.–area home.

"Well, gentlemen, please allow my staff and me to review this report and this memorandum," Dirksen said in his slow, gravelly voice. "I will, thereafter, be glad to call upon Mr. Kennedy to discuss with him the issues surrounding the status of the negotiations with the Communist enemy. Our country, if I may say, does perhaps need closure on this important issue. While I do not believe we should simply walk away from a commitment, we must review each situation on its own merits. We must . . . " Dirksen went on for about ten minutes, with Ralph thinking, Mah head's gonna fall off mah neck if he don't stop this pontificatin' like he's doin' his usual filibuster.

O'Brien, more patient with Dirksen's lengthy speeches, stood in the doorway with awe as he realized the senator did this in his "off hours" as well as at the Senate. O'Brien concluded it was a politician's gift to say a lot of words in a high-sounding way without committing to a position. It ought to be real interesting to hear Dirksen's further response, thought O'Brien, after he and his staff review this stuff.

Dirksen was impressed with the Pentagon report and Clifford's report. Hearing from constituents at home all year in a way that suggested a growing hostility for the war, Dirksen decided that perhaps it was time to see if a resolution could be had. He agreed to a meeting with Rockefeller, Kissinger, Kennedy, and Kennedy's advisers on Tuesday, December 8.

Kennedy, Bowles, Blee, Corson, and Yarborough met two days before at Hickory Hill to talk over the peace strategy. The men knew pretty quickly what they were going to agree to with the Vietnamese. The key, they realized, was how to get the two Republicans to agree and then go in tow with Bowles and Blee to the Senate and House Foreign Affairs Committees. The tentative counteroffer most likely would be leaked by a Republican staffer after they spoke to the congressional committees, but they figured the momentum of bipartisanship would derail the far-right elements in the Republican Party.

"I don't want to be the Woodrow Wilson of my time and lose the peace," said the president-elect. "I need to neutralize any Henry Cabot Lodges out there. Dirksen is important, but we gotta get those committee guys on board!"

Before anyone else could speak, a plea for help came from Ethel from Kennedy's bedroom at the family mansion. Kennedy sighed aloud and said, "Geez, how am I going to get any work done in the White House with eleven kids, including a new baby? Even with the nanny, Ethel still screams for me. She wants me 'involved,' she says. Like I have all the time in the world!" He then looked out the door of their meeting room and sighed before speaking again. "Larry, I haven't got time for this right now. We need Dirksen and Rockefeller on this Vietnam thing or we're in for some fierce fighting here at home, let alone in Vietnam! Meet somewhere else with these fellas. You and Chet make the judgment calls. We can't lose momentum!"

"Right, sir," and O'Brien got up to leave. The others followed him as if in a line. They met at O'Brien's place and finished their strategy discussion for the meeting with the two leading Republicans, Rockefeller and Dirksen.

The December 8 meeting with Dirksen, Rockefeller, and Kissinger was held at the Pentagon with the acquiescence of Defense Secretary Clifford. The meeting did not start off well, however, when Dirksen revealed he was less impressed than Rockefeller about a Marshall Plan for Southeast Asia. "Do you think it is wise to spend all this money in an area that is not as strategically important as Europe? Must we always spend money on problems, instead of letting people take care of themselves? I can think of several arguments in favor of and against my proposition, but I do not mean to filibuster here, gentlemen," said a smiling, yet serious, Dirksen.

Henry Kissinger, who was sitting so close to Rockefeller that they appeared to merge, spoke in his deep, grave, German, accent, "Senator Dirksen, I, too, qu-ves-chon such a commitment. However, ve haf made a deep *military and political* commitment for almost five years, perhaps longer, beyond even de length of our involvement in World Var II. Ve cannot trust the Communists, but ve cannot defeat dem right at dis moment either. If dey violate any accords, I am sure de United States vould appropriately respond . . . " He turned to Rockefeller, who nodded.

Kennedy realized right there that this was the *real* Lyndon Johnson plan, even if it wasn't. He thought, There will always be some violation by either or both sides of some part of any peace accords—what with President Thieu of South Vietnam itching for a fight to get us back into war there. I can't let these bastards suck me back in before I take the oath of office! Never!

He spoke cooly, though. "Very interesting position, Dr. Kissinger. We cannot trust the Communists, but we have not been able to trust our ally in South Vietnam to make the necessary reforms to improve their standing with the people there—and fight this battle themselves. Right, Colonel Corson?"

Corson interpreted Kennedy's comment to mean he could speak pretty bluntly to these civvies, which wasn't quite Kennedy's intention. "Yes, thank you, Mr. President. Now, Senator Dirksen, Dr. Kess-inger, and Governor, I was out in those jungles for a few years. I saw quite a bit on the ground, too.

We can talk about commitments all we want from those Reds, but they made things happen to get people on their side—and we didn't. And we don't need to fight for another four years to know that we won't be likely to change that equation. God knows there've been enough generals running various South Vietnamese governments. And people in our country won't stand another four years of boys comin' home in body bags when they don't understand why we're there. With all respect, Senator Dirksen, if we made such a deep military commitment, the least we can do is help clean up the mess like we did for the Europeans and even the Japanese after Dubya Dubya Two. I fought in that one, too, when I was just a kid, and I saw how quickly most of us accepted the fact that it was time to rebuild our enemy's country."

Kennedy glanced at Corson to indicate that he had given them enough—respectfully, he hoped.

Dirksen was moved. "Colonel, I never argue with those who do our fighting with the strength of mind and body as you have. I, too, am tired of a no-win situation and more and more mothers and fathers in my great state of Illinois crying over lost boys. I am merely concerned that if we are perceived to have lost this war, unlike World War II, then people might not be so forgiving with the Vietnamese as we were with the Germans and Japanese."

Kissinger, however, was after larger game, and that was influence with this new administration by whatever means necessary. He looked directly at Kennedy and said, "Mr. President, I know I may be zpeaking out of turn on behalf of Governor Rockefeller, but I be-lief de Pentagon study or report is ezzentially correct and ve must act upon it by purzuing peace." He glanced at Rockefeller, who gave him the green light to continue, and said, "Ve vould propose dat da Viet Cong not be made part of any coalition. Dey must declare der villingness to diz-arm and renounze violenze if dey vish to take part in any elections. Dey must respect zee outcome of any election as vell—although ve may not haf to."

Chet Bowles said, "Dr. Kissinger, I believe you are correct in some of your comments. However, I do not think it is likely they will fully disarm, nor do I think that it is wise to insist on that as a deal-breaking point—although it is certainly one we will consider at the outset. President Thieu is not likely to agree to any elections that are truly free, and I would expect, based upon conversations I've had with my staff—and Dan Ellsberg—that we can expect violence by some elements on both sides. We had this after World War II, particularly in Germany, much more than in Japan, I must say. There were the German 'werewolves' and other pro-Nazi groups blowing up trains, some buildings, and succeeding in some assassinations. We didn't go back to war with the Germans, did we? Plus, from what I've seen from reports, our government has killed quite a number of Vietnamese civilians over the past few years—so it's not a question of not caring about casualties in implementing the peace. Do we say we will never fight again? No, but we have to be careful not to be led back into what we don't want by those who have no motive other than to continue the fighting."

"That sounds defeatist to me, Mr. Bowles," said a suddenly testy Rockefeller. "We must have peace, not defeat."

Bowles, who never liked the New York governor's swagger, had vowed that he'd fight anyone this time around who dared challenge his "toughness." He eyed Rockefeller and said, "I'm not talking about defeat, Governor. I'm talking peace with elections. You want to talk about defeat? Someone with your presidential primary history ought not to be talking about defeat—"

Rockefeller jumped up, jabbed his finger at Bowles, and exclaimed, "Bowles, are you calling me a loser?"

Bowles stood up to meet Rockefeller almost nose to nose. He was uncharacteristically seething with anger. "No, Governor. Unless you're calling me a coward! And if you want—"

Neither had seen Corson and Kennedy jump up. The two men separated Rockefeller and Bowles, who retreated to corners of the room.

Corson broke the awkward silence, mistakenly thinking he had the same opportunity for bluntness as before. "Gentlemen, let's keep our heads here. If our goal was to make South Vietnam a bastion of democracy, we haven't done very well, have we?" He looked over at Rockefeller, then Kissinger, as he spoke. "But we now have a chance to dictate some important points for peace, including an election that might make a difference to the people there. I mean, I thought fighting for freedom was what we went over there for. And if it wasn't for our boys fightin' their hearts out, the South Vietnamese woulda lost to the Reds a long time ago. But I know one damned thing: *More* of our boys dyin' isn't gonna change a thing out there! What I think we can all agree upon is that our boys will stay on to keep peace the best they can during the election process—and they'll do a great job, particularly my marines, sir," he said, nodding toward Kennedy. "Makin' peace gives us a chance to see the Viet Cong out in the open for the first time. That's not defeat in my book. No, sir! That's gonna make it easier for us to know what's goin' on. Open fields, not jungles all the time with no end. If there are snipers, we gotta make it so that we have a pipeline directly to the snipers' superiors, so *they*, not we, enforce discipline. I see it as kind of like a labor war in the fields, like back when I worked with migrant farmers as a kid before 'the big one.'" Everyone understood Corson's reference to World War II but not the one referring to migrant workers. "The leaders on each side have gotta enforce the discipline to make peace after a long battle. We'll know if the Reds are keeping the bargain—although my hunch is the toughest job's gonna be with the South Vietnamese guys from Thieu on down, pardon me for saying so. But it's the truth!"

Kennedy wanted to laugh, but he knew Corson was right. It was amazing to him that Corson could make a better appeal than a dozen "beards" ever could. Blee, however, stayed quiet.

Dirksen, thinking again about the innumerable constituents, including World War II veterans who had, over the past two years, lost their sons and questioned the war's conduct and aims, pondered Corson's blunt observations. He then spoke, looking at Corson the whole time. "Mr. President, Governor Rockefeller, and each of you gentlemen, including especially Colonel Corson. I thank you, Colonel, for your assessment. I believe this could be a tougher peace than it was a war, which was itself difficult, if we don't act in a bipartisan manner. All this reminds me of when I met President DeGaulle a few years ago." He didn't want to say it was at Jack Kennedy's funeral.

Continuing, Dirksen said, "I asked him about this Vietnam mess—that was back when the escalation was starting strong—" Dirksen couldn't resist that dig into Kennedy—"and DeGaulle said we're making a terrible mistake. I then asked him what he would do. He said we needed to set up elections, make sure they're relatively clean, and let the chips fall where they will. If it's their mess, meaning the Vietnamese, they'll work harder to clean it up. If we keep trying to manage the details, we just keep creating more Viet Cong." He turned now, looking at Rockefeller. "At the time, I thought that was defeatist, I must say, but I thought DeGaulle, who was a leader of the French Resistance, was one of the bravest and bluntest people I've ever met. Colonel Corson, you remind me of him today, which I hope you don't take in the wrong way—"

Corson gave a half-smile, almost but not quite sure of Dirksen's meaning. "Senator Dirksen, I know as a proud marine I would have told DeGaulle then that the French didn't know what they were doin', but that we did. I was part of a winning team in the big one and won my share of battles in Korea. That oughta tell you somethin' about why I feel so strong today about what we need to do now. We won battles here in Vietnam, lots of 'em. But we gotta help their people have an election they can believe in, where they make the choice. That's worth fightin' for most in my book."

That was the hook that got Rockefeller and Dirksen aboard.

Dirksen made sure, as the meeting broke up, that Rockefeller and Bowles shook hands. The two men did so but eyed one another with less than respect. Dirksen, letting the others get ahead of him, stopped Kennedy to say, "I like that Colonel Corson! He's a real closer. You'll need him on the Hill, too. And I have to say I'm impressed with the tenacity of your new secretary of state, Mr. President. Frankly, having seen him speak a few years ago on Capitol Hill, I thought he didn't have it in him!" He slapped Kennedy on the back, while Kennedy thought to himself, I didn't think he had it in him either.

After the meeting, Rockefeller told Kissinger, "I would have walked out of that meeting after that bullshit from Bowles. But my brother David told me that he and his banker friends want out of Vietnam—now. They've had it with the stalemate and don't think any more war will do anything for American interests in Europe and elsewhere." At the time of Rockefeller's comments, his brother, David, headed up Chase Manhattan Bank, one of the largest banks in the world.

The next morning, at Kennedy's home in Hickory Hill, Kennedy met with Bowles, Corson, Yarborough, Blee, and O'Brien to plan how to win over the Senate and House Foreign Affairs Committees, particularly the Democratic majority chairs and the Republican House and Senate leaders. Kennedy said to Blee and O'Brien, "Fellas, Senator Fulbright's no problem. He's ready for peace at all costs. He's tired of NATO, I think, too, from the way he talks."

Blee grunted in agreement, but he wasn't smiling at Kennedy's joke about Fulbright and NATO.

"But," said Kennedy, "damn it, it's Hickenlooper, the old codger, I'm worried about. The bastard's been a senator from Iowa for years—Christ!—must be since the 1800s he's been there. I think he fought against the League of Nations—maybe Indians, too . . . "

O'Brien said, "I meant to tell you, Mr. President. The word is out that George Aiken, the liberal Republican—from Vermont, Mr. Blee—is taking over as minority chair of the committee. Hickenlooper is retiring, and he's out in a few weeks. Already packing his coffin, if you know what I mean."

Kennedy was elated. "What? Retired? Great! I like George Aiken. The Senate's an easy sell—"

O'Brien was sharp. "Bullshit! I mean, sorry, uh . . . sir. Aiken buys us next to nothing. He hardly gets along with any Republicans except for Clifford Case from Jersey, who might as well be a Democrat, too. You *like* them and the Republicans *hate* them for the same reason. Aiken's only getting the post because of seniority. We need a couple of hard-assed Republicans on board, not just Aiken."

Kennedy was grating as he said, "Then, Larry, you better get on it. It wasn't like I was so loved in that gallery either."

"I'm on it already, sir."

"Okay, what about the House?"

O'Brien explained that Thomas Morgan of Pennsylvania was still the Democratic chair of the House committee, but no clear name had surfaced yet on the Republican side. The outgoing Republican committee leader, Francis Bolton, had no successor yet.

"What do we know about this Morgan fellow? What's his leadership ability?" asked Blee.

"Not worth a shit," came O'Brien's quick response. "Morgan's a follower, not a leader. If this gets too controversial, I doubt he's worth much." Yarborough nodded in agreement, wondering if he could even remember what Morgan looked like.

Suddenly, Ethel, confined to her bed on her doctor's orders, cried out in pain from the master bedroom of the house.

Kennedy immediately left the meeting and went to his wife. After several minutes, he returned and said, "Um, gentlemen, we have to call the doctor right away. This could be serious this time." Obviously distracted, Kennedy said, "I don't know how I'm going to get anything done here! Eleven children, a wife, the screaming kids—Larry, Chet, you guys huddle and quarterback this thing—again. Sorry. I mean you know what to do to get the leaders in Congress to back this, Larry. The more we deal with this, the more we need to make peace with the Vientamese *before* my inauguration. So let's keep this moving no matter what, okay?"

"Yes, sir," O'Brien said, quickly gathering his coat and walking toward the door. The others just as quickly followed.

Bob and Ethel Kennedy's eleventh child was born after a Cesarean delivery on December 12, 1968. The proud parents decided to name the baby in honor of the Kennedy matriarch, Rose Fitzgerald Kennedy. While the matriarch herself was not initially happy about the new proposed name, Bob did not like Ethel's alternative name, "Rory," either.[1]

Speaking with his mother, Kennedy said, "Mother, we have a child named for Dad. It's about time we named a child after you, at least with a *first* name of 'Rose,' don't you think?"

Rose caved in with that question. For with the newborn baby, she remembered how good it was that her "Bobby" was still among the living. And whatever her boy wanted, well . . . it was all right with her.

A couple of days after the birth of baby Rose, O'Brien came back to Hickory Hill with an update on the politics of bringing peace. He told Kennedy he had talked with Rockefeller and Dirksen about bringing on more Republicans for bipartisan support. He also said, "Mr. President, we may have a youngish Republican, a new senator named Bob Dole, who'll possibly support the peace effort. He's been a congressman for a few years and has some influence. He's in with the agricultural company, Archer Daniels Midland—he's their man—and they like peace because they have lots of wheat to sell. He's a World War II vet, busted arm from the war, pretty far right, though. He seemed noncommittal to the point of grease. He respects Dirksen, though, and says he may go with us—"

"Yeah, I've seen him around when he was a congressman. Nebraska or somewhere—"

"Kansas, Bob. The heart of America."

"That's a start, at least. You got anyone else?"

"The usual liberal Republicans—Case, Aiken—but not much else from Republicans in the way of commitment or support. They're reading tea leaves, these guys, I hate to say." He stammered, more than paused, before continuing. " . . . I was thinking . . . don't laugh, but . . . you know, Barry Goldwater just got reelected in Arizona. Maybe we can ask—"

Bob practically guffawed. "You're kidding, Larry! Are you out of your mind? That's the funniest thing I'm gonna hear all day long! All *year* long! 'Bomb 'em Barry' gonna go dovish with *me?*"

"Sir, I thought about it yesterday and tried it out on Dirksen. He laughed at first, but then started to like the idea. Dirksen's gotta cover his right flank as much if not more than we do. Dirksen, who didn't want to seem interested but was, told me that if we go through any of Goldwater's aides, it's a no-go. But how about you invite him here and let him see that Pentagon study beforehand? I didn't say this to Dirksen, but my theory about Goldwater is that he's just not informed on a lot of things. I've watched him for years. When he's informed, he's pretty good, almost a liberal even—well, I guess I'm pushing that. My reason for thinking this is that he's a great defender of the Indians on the Indian Affairs Committee. Knows a lot of Indian history and culture. And something else. When he was running this year, he said he was sorry for his vote against the '64 Civil Rights Act. He thinks it's a good thing it passed. And you know Barry just doesn't say things to get elected. Maybe he's ready for another change of heart."

Kennedy nodded. "Jack liked him personally. I thought he was a patsy for '64, and he was. I dunno. What's the harm in giving him the Pentagon study? Made a believer outta Blee, who's very smart and had set views, it seems, before he read it. But that assumes Goldwater reads and understands the damned thing."

"Why don't you call him yourself, Bob? You know, both Ronald Reagan and Goldwater think your talk of local control and support in poor places like Bedford-Stuyvesant is like the states' rights they talk about—"

"If that's true, then they're outta *their* minds!" Kennedy said with even more emphasis this time. "But Barry is so righteous, unlike Reagan, from the couple of times I've met Reagan. If we get Barry, though . . . Okay, it's worth a try. It looks like you and Dirksen think we're not getting enough Republican support yet. I mean, what's Barry gonna do if I let him in on things? Leak the report or something? I'll talk to Barry. Get me his number."

Within two hours of speaking with O'Brien, Kennedy spoke by telephone with Goldwater, who was back in Arizona and packing for Washington, D.C., after a four-year hiatus. Goldwater read portions of the Pentagon study, not much more than the executive summary, after it was sent to him the next morning by military plane. Goldwater placed a call to Dirksen to determine if this report was on the level and came away a possible convert. After Goldwater arrived in Washington two days later, he was driven to Hickory Hill.

After the usual pleasantries, including cooing at the new baby, Goldwater sat down with Kennedy to talk. Goldwater said, with his usual bluntness, "Why all the lying by every damned president, Bob? That's the thing that truly *bothers* me reading that report and looking at some of the documents! I can understand Truman not wanting to deal with Ho Chi Minh if the little Commie was bein' hostile, but the man was writing Truman, after all, looking for a way out, maybe, from the Russians. Who knows? Truman passed the buck—*again*—the way I see it. And Ike, too, undermining those Geneva Accords calling for free elections in the 1950s, when he made public statements that he supported those accords. I hate lying like that—and you and your brother don't look too good either. And Lyndon! I can't believe that Fulbright was right when he said we were duped into supporting the Gulf of Tonkin Resolution—that supplemental portion of the report about the North Vietnamese maybe not attacking our navy boats in '64, my God, man! I talked about this to a navy pal, way up there brass-wise, and he confirmed it, too. But, Bob, I started thinking as I read this—well, not every word of it, of course. I thought if we mined that harbor in Haiphong, bombed the sanctuaries in . . . what's that place next to South Vietnam, with the playboy king that plays along with the damned Chi-com . . . ? No matter. But that's what I was thinking. And then I spoke with Ev Dirksen. Ev said to me, 'Barry, to what end? Who are we bombing, and who gets the brunt of the massive floods when we mine those Haiphong dikes? That's gonna make them love America?' I said, 'Ev, I don't want them to love America. I want those Reds to give up and leave those people in South Vietnam alone.' And Ev, bless him, said, 'Barry, we think they're ready to make peace, and if we don't, they'll just keep on fighting us to the last peasant.' Gave me a pause, Bob, right then and there. Started thinking of the last Indians fighting it out against us decades ago. We don't need to do that again. I even had an aide get me that book by Colonel Corson, who you said was your inside adviser on Vietnam. Read a little of Corson's book on the plane ride here. Quite a bit, in fact. Tough fella. Don't blame him a bit, even though military men should follow our leaders' orders, even if they're wrong. We're not Nazis, you know."[2]

Goldwater stopped himself from going off on a tangent and then continued. "Anyhow, Bob, we shoulda hit that Viet Cong harder and earlier—but I see it's different now, after all this fighting. If we're gonna have people over there support us, we gotta have an election that's genuine. Even my kids tell me that the elections in South Vietnam are as rigged as a Commie election, for the most part. And Commies take part in European elections—though maybe that's different— but we oughta take a chance on that here, too, I guess. That Pentagon study is something, but if it got out, folks'd be going after Ike's head as well as Truman's, Lyndon's, and maybe your brother's, too—and that means you. Your brother and I had our disagreements, but I always respected the man. And the country is right to respect his memory . . . "

Kennedy said, with as much sincerity as he could muster, "Senator, Jack and I were just learning the first time, a few years ago, I have to say. We respected President Eisenhower's—Ike's—policies, too, as you know. We got burned in Cuba at the start, but sometimes being too tough can be very dangerous, as we learned in '62 in that crisis over Cuba and the missiles. I learned a lot myself with Jack. Barry, you'll be impressed with Colonel Corson and Mr. Blee, my nominee for the CIA. Let's have dinner here this evening, and you can speak with them directly."

When Goldwater met with Blee and Corson, it was Blee's hook—"We're fighting for a free election"—that reminded Goldwater of his conversation with Dirksen. Goldwater was on board the only way he knew how: with conviction, right or wrong.

The next afternoon, Dirksen, Kennan, Ellsberg, Goldwater, Blee, and Corson briefed the joint Foreign Affairs Committee chairs and minority chairs by telephone, as most were now home for the holidays. And when they were done, Kennedy had his bipartisan support. From the Right, how could you get any better than Dirksen and Goldwater? And the Left, well . . . Kennedy decided it was better to keep them in the background. Deep in the background, at least for now.

The counteroffer the incoming administration was going to make was as follows: The North was to remove its troops from South Vietnam over a nine month interval, with most leaving after free and open elections. The United States was going to demand the South Vietnamese government agree to free and open elections, with Japanese, American, and European (mostly French) observers. If the South Vietnamese government proved to be the sticking point, Goldwater, Kennedy, and Blee agreed—with Clark Clifford's approval via President Johnson—that the United States should start to pull out a few troops to show South Vietnamese President Thieu that the United States meant business. If the North refused to agree to elections in the South, then the bipartisan coalition was probably doomed.

Goldwater almost broke himself from the group when he seriously, but innocently, asked, "Why aren't we calling for free elections in the North? Why do the Communists get to have it both ways?"

Kennedy didn't like the question, but it was a good one, he thought. Kennan, who happened to be present, responded, after looking to Kennedy for the go-ahead. "Senator Goldwater, we are here to provide the Vietnamese in the South the opportunity for freedom. The North Vietnamese people have not shown their willingness to revolt at this time. Perhaps they will be inspired by the example of the South."

Goldwater smiled. "I like that, Mr. Kennan. That sounds like a plan."

Kennan nodded, wisely letting the subject drop. Kennedy thought to himself, I should have thought of that. Thank God for Kennan!

The American counterproposal also included a proposal to create a joint commission of leaders from the United States, South Vietnam, and North Vietnam—but no Viet Cong were to be included. The U.S. position was that it didn't want the commission to look like a coalition government. The commission was merely to monitor violations of the electoral process and to investigate crimes committed during the process. The elections would take place no later than May 1969; assuming accords could be signed before January 20, 1969, Kennedy's inauguration day. A separate unification election or referendum would be held a year later.

It was becoming clear to all in the incoming administration that the hardest sell was going to be to the South Vietnamese leaders, starting with President Nguyen Thieu. Kennedy knew that General Abrams and Joint Chiefs of Staff Chairman General Wheeler would most likely side with Thieu to keep up the fighting. Corson's initial analysis to Kennedy had proven right from various sources Bowles and Defense Secretary designate Warnke had checked with at the Pentagon.

The new peace talks between North Vietnam, the United States, and South Vietnam began in Paris, at Kennedy's insistence, the day after Christmas. Thieu gave grudging approval to negotiations, believing there were plenty of domestic U.S. roadblocks to stop any true peace. The North Vietnamese rejected the American counteroffer just as Thieu acidly told Bowles, but did indicate they would come back with a modified offer in seventy-two hours. The North Vietnamese said the likely deal-breakers were the U.S. refusal to seat the Viet Cong in the South Vietnamese government or the commission, and more important, the U.S. demand that the North Vietnamese remove their troops from the South.

This set the stage for one week and one day of intense negotiations, punctuated by daily break-offs and threats to resume the war—with the American negotiators following Ellsberg's advice to a reluctant Kennedy to threaten that the collapse of the American bipartisan coalition would mean a resumption of bombing. When the Vietnamese leaked this information to the European press, who in turn leaked it to American dissidents and antiwar protestors, the left flank of Kennedy's coalition began to crack.

Allard Lowenstein told Kennedy at that point, "The SDS is already making signs that say, 'Hey, Hey, RFK, How Many More Will Be Killed Today?'"

Kennedy exploded. "What kind of bullshit is that! Nobody's getting killed—hardly. There's no bombing, some sporadic fighting, mostly snipers against our GIs for chrissakes, and these SDSers are gonna start comparing me to Lyndon Freaking Johnson while we're trying to make peace? If I didn't want peace so bad, I'd have walked away from this whole damned negotiation and started bombing already! Let them know *that,* Al! I dare 'em to see what'll happen if I start to bomb again! I'll get more support from the American people, and there'll be calls for jailing your buddies like you never heard!"

Al was shocked. He thought, but didn't dare say until many years later, that Bob Kennedy seemed to be on the verge of becoming Lyndon Johnson. He started to speak, but Kennedy was not yet done with his harangue.

"And, Al, let your friends think about this. Those poor guys on the USS *Pueblo*[3] just came home after almost a year's confinement in Communist North Korea. Thank God there wasn't a lot of press play on this, or else we'd be having a hard time talking to *any* Communists anywhere, especially in Vietnam. Damn it, Al! Are your friends that isolated they don't see we have to be at least a *little* cautious here? Think, man! We've got Dirksen and Goldwater agreeing to let us talk with the North Vietnamese about peace! Chet Bowles tells me we're making tremendous progress. The European leaders, starting with Wily Brandt in West Germany, are telling the Vietnamese to trust my people and make peace while we all can. Can't you tell your friends to give me a break for a few weeks— or at least till I'm inaugurated? Jesus!"

Lowenstein thought about yelling back but instead said, "I understand, sir. I appreciate your efforts to get to peace this quickly."

Kennedy, realizing he'd probably gone too far, went over to Lowenstein, put his hand on Lowenstein's shoulder, and said, "Al, like I said, we're not even inaugurated yet. Just give me a break, okay? My goal is to get this settled by inauguration day so we can talk about fixing up the cities, move toward economic civil rights for blacks, and start cleaning up polluted lakes and rivers. Doesn't anyone in the student movement think about anything besides the damned war?"

Lowenstein said softly, "I do, sir. A lot of us do." He then mumbled a good night. He was still a bit angry, but also humbled by Kennedy's words. There would be a lot of important domestic issues to fight about if America's military involvement in Vietnam could possibly be ended. But he immediately realized there would be an even bigger fight inside the United States if the war did not end. He shuddered at the thought of what that meant in terms of student and other youth unrest.

As it turned out, Lowenstein's fears went unrealized. On January 7, 1969, a tentative agreement was reached with the North Vietnamese that one-quarter of their troops would stay in the South for "a decent interval," but that the North would begin an immediate demobilization coinciding with the start of an American troop withdrawal. The key for the negotiators was to require the Americans and the North Vietnamese to show each other a step-by-step good faith effort.

The North was very wary of complete demobilization before any elections in the South. It made clear during the negotiations that it remembered well the betrayal by President Eisenhower and Secretary of State John Foster Dulles after signing the 1954 Geneva Accords, when the Vietnamese troops were moved out of the southern region in order to allow a similar interval for the French troops to leave. The accords made it clear these were regions, not separate nations. The accords also called for complete demobilization first and then having nationwide elections in 1956. That interval instead allowed the United States to bring in Ngo Diem, create South Vietnam, and refuse any unifying elections; at least that's how the North Vietnamese saw it.

At one point during the negotiations, Chet Bowles met face-to-face with Le Duc Tho in a private room. As Bowles recounted many years later, he told the North Vietnamese premier that Bob Kennedy was under great pressure from political and military elements in the U.S. government to have the negotiations fail and to resume bombing. He explained in detail the significance of having Goldwater and Rockefeller on the side of peace, but that both Republican leaders were also itching for more bombing at the slightest sign of failure. "We are in a precarious moment, Mr. Premier, and Bob Kennedy is willing to risk being a one-term president to create the basis for a lasting peace. Please, Mr. Premier, you can help us help you if we can just agree to a significant demobilization and keep the Viet Cong out of any commission or coalition government until after the elections in South Vietnam later this year."

Le, the next day, agreed to the 75 percent demobilization. He said, however, that the North was not willing to compromise on the question of the Viet Cong's participation in the commission. The Viet Cong must be included, said Le. "They earned that participation with their blood, Mr. Bowles. I cannot consent to their exclusion."

The North finally agreed on the issue when Bowles suggested that the commission not contain Viet Cong *as* Viet Cong. Instead, Bowles suggested a couple of Viet Cong could be on the commission as part of North Vietnam's delegation. Le made a call to Hanoi to see if this was appropriate. Le later told a historian that he spoke personally to North Vietnamese President Ho Chi Minh and Communist Party leader Le Duan. Le Duc Tho related that Le Duan was not willing to make any further compromises, unlike Ho.

Le Duc Tho told the two men that he would put his position as a high level Communist officer on the line to back up his belief that the American leadership under Bob Kennedy and Chet Bowles was sincere in its desire to bring peace. He also told them that Bowles' reputation among United Nations delegates was very positive with regard to the concerns of third world nations.

Le Duan remained skeptical, however. He believed there could be a coup in the United States, based upon spy reports out of Saigon from sources close to the American military there. What was the point of making peace with a less-than-one-term president such as Kennedy, who had already been shot at, like his brother?

Le Duc Tho said to Le Duan, "With all respect to my most respected comrade, we have the opportunity to create a strong basis for peace. The Americans are tired of the war, but we do not dare insult the giant into taking up his mighty armaments again."

Ho, who had been silent, finally said, "A little more sniffing of imperialist dung may perhaps be worth it in order to smell the flowers of Saigon. Comrade Le, I believe this represents the best method of reuniting ourselves. I am an old man, as you well know. Before I die, I would like to see Saigon as part of our one great nation."

Le Duan grunted, but said, "It is done. Tell the Americans . . . it is agreed."

Under the peace accord, the South Vietnamese government was to hold open elections on May 7, 1969, with the full participation of the Viet Cong as candidates only. The Viet Cong would not be part of any coalition governement unless it first earned it with votes in the elections. On May 6, 1970, a year later, there would be unification elections for all of Vietnam, all consistent with the original Geneva Accords of 1954.

The South Vietnamese delegation, however, refused to sign the accord, saying that while they "tentatively agreed, but with reservations," they needed to confer with President Thieu in person. Kennedy raised the temperature on Thieu by saying publicly that an agreement had been "essentially" reached and all that was needed was a "final confirmation from the South Vietnamese government over the next few days or maybe a week."

With the announcement from Paris, there was joy in the streets of that city, in Hanoi, and in Washington, D.C. From Saigon, however, there was merely an eerie silence. Some said there was even shock that peace might be "at hand" this quickly.

Chapter 11

PLAN B IN SAIGON

Believing they could overcome South Vietnamese President Thieu's objections to the peace accords, Corson, Bowles, and Blee immediately set off for Saigon on the afternoon of January 7, 1969. Less than twenty-four hours later, the men arrived in Saigon where they had a short meeting with the U.S. ambassador to South Vietnam, Ellsworth Bunker.

Kennedy wanted to remove Bunker as ambassador back in mid-November 1968 after learning that Bunker wanted victory, not peace in Vietnam. Bunker remained, however, because Kennedy decided, after consulting with Bowles, that Bunker would be more trouble if he came back to the United States with things not yet settled. But now, with the agreement with the North worked out and Bunker cabling opposition to it, the trio arrived in Saigon and politely explained to the ambassador that his "resignation was accepted." Bunker dutifully packed his belongings but was outraged at being "dumped by these cowards who want to turn Vietnam over to the Reds," as he said to friends when he returned to the United States.

The trio then anointed Colonel John Paul Vann as the new ambassador-designate, subject to almost certain confirmation by the Senate. Vann was a well-known and respected warrior who had been assisting Bunker. But Vann, who was always a bit of a maverick, had developed significant differences with Bunker as to how the Americans could turn the tide in their favor once and for all. Vann believed that the South Vietnamese government must earn the respect of the people in the villages and hamlets with significant land reform and open elections. He was a favorite of such diverse persons as Major General Edward Lansdale, new NSC chairman Daniel Ellsberg, and various non-Communist reformers in and out of the Thieu government.

With Bunker out of the way, there remained other American opponents of peace, namely the American generals, Wheeler and Abrams. The idea was to cajole them into supporting the peace plan, but Corson believed more was needed. Corson, who had conferred on a "Plan B" with Bowles in case Thieu decided to fight rather than accept the peace agreement, joked about his own plan, which he called "Plan H" for "Help!" Corson knew Abrams and Wheeler were never going to pressure Thieu to sign the accords, as Kennedy and his other advisers hoped. Acting independently, Corson secured, through his sources, a copy of Colonel David Hackworth's battalion commander report to Abrams—the report that had caused Abrams such grief when he first read it. Corson then confirmed that Hackworth had essentially taken the same position as Corson did two years earlier, expressing similar impatience with the bureaucratic games being played by the military in dealing with the politicians in Washington, D.C. Hackworth was also concerned that the South Vietnamese government was not meeting the needs of the people outside of Saigon.

Corson, through John Paul Vann, contacted Hackworth and asked Hackworth to meet him at the U.S. embassy in Saigon. Hackworth told Corson he would first have to speak with his commanding officer, General Abrams. Corson gulped, but told Hackworth he would do the same if the positions were reversed. Hackworth told Abrams about the meeting and said, "I won't go if you tell me not to."

"No," said Abrams, "I won't stop Corson from seeing you. Just tell me what's said—all of it."

Hackworth, with suspicion and some trepidation, met Corson at the embassy. When Corson told him there might be problems with Thieu accepting any peace agreement and asked what was going on in the jungles these days, Hackworth replied, "Colonel Corson, I'd rather not be here, let alone tell you what's going on in terms of our military operations. You're a civilian now, but I will always call you 'Colonel' out of respect for a fellow officer. The way I see it, it took a presidential action to keep your ass out of a military prison just for telling the truth about the shit our military's fooling with in this damned place. Why should I risk my career when your commander in chief flavor of the month"—meaning Bob Kennedy—"could get his head blown off, with no misses this time, and then another Texan starts the fighting again?"

Corson said, "Colonel Hackworth, I appreciate your concerns. I already know your feelings on the conduct of the war. Your reaction also tells me you understand where things could be heading. But I wouldn't make the assumption that Bob Kennedy automatically gets 'blown away.' I guess I have less to lose by being blunt at this point. If you think Ralph Yarborough is just another Texan, then you haven't met Ralph Yarborough. He's not Lyndon Johnson by any means. In many ways, he's more dangerous to the status quo than Bobby Kennedy is. Yarborough's a working-class fella from the heartland who knows the score and means to change things. I haven't seen a fella like that since I was pickin' crops during the '30s and worked with some union organizers. They'd need a military coup to get both of them out, and that wouldn't be easy either."

"And that's supposed to convince me? Like there wouldn't ever be a coup? I have doubts, like lotsa folks, about how the first President Kennedy got killed, don't you?"

"Colonel Hackworth, I was going to beat around the bush, but I see that's impossible. I am asking you, as a fellow soldier, to consider taking a risk in your career. But it's not as big a risk as you think. All I want to know is whether you are going to follow Wheeler and Abrams and tell the soldiers under your command that it's better to go back into the jungles or tell them to support your new commander in chief and make peace work through the elections that are part of this agreement we—the United States—agreed to, and that we're going to get approval from the South Vietnamese government, come hell or high water. I am not interested in debating 'what ifs' in history. I think you're gonna find that we are going to prevail in making peace that will be good enough to allow us to get out of this mess and give the South Vietnamese people a chance to choose their leaders, whoever they may be. And if we have to come back here with any military force, at least it will be clearer than it has been so far. And let me say this. Yes, my career in the military is over. Very much so. But Abrams and Wheeler are making a career mistake if they think the civilians are going to roll over and slip back into four more years of bombing, or expand this war into Cambodia and Laos. In fact, you may be making a great career move in the military by getting on board with the new president. You aren't naïve enough to think, Colonel, that making general is about winning military battles. You think MacArthur and Westmoreland were military heroes who just happened to be crowned? Come on, Colonel. I know you—without knowing you—better than that."

Hackworth smiled slightly. "You think I care about bein' any ass-sittin' general? You betcha I hate that careerist crap. We're no better than the civilians in our back yard, and maybe worse." He paused a few seconds before speaking again. "You're right about this war, Colonel Corson. Maybe I would wind up screwing myself sooner than later since Abrams thinks he can win by just bombing more with less American troops—and with no real pressure on the South Vietnamese government to get their act together with the people here. General Abrams' plan ain't gonna work much better, is my gut feel on things. Abrams is a great general, though, and miles ahead of Westmoreland. I just don't want to go sideways with him. What do you want from me? I mean, I just don't get why we're talking here."

"Colonel Hackworth—may I call you David? Thanks. David, this war is not going to be fought like Abrams wants, so he could be out like Westmoreland, too. Again, we have a chance to give the boys who died here a reason for their deaths. The point of the peace accords is to have a free election, with as little bullshit as possible. If the Commies win, then we won't be surprised, considering what we both have seen in the jungles. I have a hunch, though I can't prove it, that we'll win more hearts and minds, even from some of those Reds, if we get 'em out in the open. My concern, though, is the assassinations Thieu and the Reds will commit against each other as we get to the elections later this spring. It won't be pretty for a few months till the elections, you and I both know. We can win and still lose—or seem to lose and then turn the tide. It all depends upon American soldiers like *you*. The president needs you. The country needs you.

And what we need is for you to say you'll support making this peace process work. You have great respect out there among your battalion and other soldiers—and you gotta make that clear to those troops so they can make this work out right. For the country we're sittin' in and our country back home."

"Aw, cut the shit, Colonel! The country? I'm tired of that. My boys? Yes, that's a damned good reason. But I still don't get it. What am I supposed to be doin'?"

"You're gonna run the field operation for the U.S. government—you and the American troops—and try to keep a lid on the Viet Cong and Thieu's friends killing each other off while the election campaigns are going on."

"What? If that's the case, they'll be shooting at us from both sides!"

"Aren't they already, David?"

"I never can tell, really, when you get right down to it. But you make your point, though. And for one reason. I can't justify much more why I should send the boys in my battalion to die for the bureaucrats in our military—and the civilian government especially! I think you make the best case that the reason we fight for the next few months is a free election—or the best we can get under the circumstances, what with the killings that will happen—where all the people, including those Reds, get to have a vote. Maybe that's better than this bombin' and shootin' we've been doin', and what the boys with birds on their vests wanna keep doin'."

"Thanks, David. You're right. That's what sent me over into this strange position with this new President Kennedy. I never thought I'd be in any administration with a bunch of hippies and civvies."

The two men, realizing they were kindred spirits, shook hands warmly.

Hackworth said, "Colonel, I must say something or else you might think badly of me if you found out later. I only went to this meeting upon approval, such as it was, from General Abrams. He wants me—it's hard to say it was an order, even if it was—to tell him everything that was said here. I'm gonna have to do that; not every word, but enough. I respect my commanding officer and that's that."

Corson did his best to smile. He then slightly nodded his head, pursed his lips, and thought a moment before speaking. "Colonel Hackworth, you are a brave man, braver than anyone I've seen in a long while. You didn't have to tell me that, but you did. You know what? I'm not afraid of Abrams, or Wheeler either. I wouldn't have wanted you to tell them anything, but if that's the way it's gonna be, so be it. Tell him what we discussed. I know you'll be fair. I'm sorry that you're going to be in for a rough forty-eight hours, and your career may well hang in the balance. The old preachers who say the 'truth shall set you free' don't know the half of it, do they?"

Hackworth laughed darkly. "You got that right, pal. The truth is downright dangerous, particularly in war."

As he left the meeting, Hackworth realized that his career was already over if Abrams or Wheeler weren't forced out. Entering Abrams' office, he briefed the general regarding his meeting with Corson. He told Abrams that he would fight the war however the generals or the commander in chief wanted. He said he'd consider resigning, if that were the thing to do. But he quickly added that he didn't think he'd be resigning just yet. Hackworth went on to say he believed he could carry out his duties for more war, for preserving the peace during elections, or "whatever comes down the pike next."

Hackwood also told Abrams that he had told Corson he'd be reporting on his meeting with Abrams. Abrams winced at that one but knew Hackworth was in a tight spot. Hackworth had conflicting orders from above and was only respecting each person's office and authority the best he could. As Abrams said to Wheeler that evening, "Hackworth's too good a man to lose. But one thing is clear, Earle. We have got to stop the South Vietnamese government from signing this peace agreement, or it's over."

Wheeler nodded at Abrams' remarks, not sure what to think any longer.

The South Vietnamese leader, Thieu, formally balked at the agreement the next day, as Corson expected and Bowles feared. Corson, Bowles, and Blee spent the next twenty-four hours pleading with Thieu to sign the agreement—at least that's what the public understood was the case.

Generals Abrams and Wheeler, when finally meeting with Blee, Corson, and Bowles, said they were nominally in favor of the peace proposal for reasons of respect for their civilian superiors, but reiterated they would not "pressure" Thieu to sign the agreement. Blee and Corson, both experienced in the military, decided they needed to have a "one on one"—or really "two on two"—private discussion with Abrams and Wheeler. The discussion occurred while Bowles and Colonel Vann met again with Thieu to convince him to sign the peace agreement.

Corson started the meeting by talking about the Pentagon report on Vietnam. Wheeler harshly dismissed the Pentagon study, which he had been provided with months before, as "civilian chicken shit."

Abrams, who hadn't read it but had heard enough about it, called it "diplomatic, long-haired treason-talk." Abrams also took the opportunity to slam Corson. Said Abrams, "That Pentagon civilian-initiated report is a report for losers, Colonel Corson. I can't believe you, as a marine, could fall for that crap! But you like to write books, too, I guess. War is hell, soldier. That's something you seem to have forgotten when you put on your civilian suit. And, soldier, we've got to *win* this thing for the boys who already gave their lives, not spit on their graves by letting the Commies take part in any election. Elections are bullshit anyway!"

Corson looked like he was going to strangle Abrams when Blee put his hand on Corson's shoulder to calm him.

Blee then said to Abrams, "You know, General, we don't need a lecture on war from anyone, including you. Your own battalion commanders know this war isn't worth fighting for any longer, and every kid who dies from now on out there is dying because you and a few others can't face the facts on the ground. It isn't just civvies and us who see it as we do. It's what Lansdale and what Colonel Vann say, and even Hackworth, your best battalion commander, probably thinks. What are you going to tell the mothers and fathers of those boys who come home in the body bags next year? Just what you said now? The elections, General, are gonna determine whether these people in Saigon want to defend themselves. And if you think elections are 'bullshit,' then maybe *you* are the one who's a loser! Got that?" Blee leaned in, daring Abrams to punch him, which forced Wheeler to step in between them because Abrams was ready to do just that.

Wheeler said calmly but firmly, "And who is going to sign this so-called peace agreement on behalf of our allies here in Saigon? You know damned well Thieu isn't signing."

Corson, who still wanted to wring some fat generals' necks, simply said, "I've had enough of this bullshit. He'll sign. You watch. Let's go, Mr. Blee. The fighting's gotta be in rounds? Fine."

Corson and Blee left the room, with Corson walking directly to ambassador-designate Vann's office. He told Vann, "Find me Colonel Hackworth—fast." Vann complied, and Hackworth, who had been on patrol, came in and met with Blee and Corson.

The two men praised Hackworth and told him what had happened. Blee said, "Colonel Hackworth, hold tight. There's gonna be peace, and while Wheeler and Abrams don't get it, they will. Your commander in chief is going to probably be putting you in charge of this peace process till the election, and you may get a bird on your vest before long."

Bowles, later informed about what had happened, shook his head. "You military guys are making me very nervous. Very nervous. Who is this Hackworth fellow? You know we have no authority to put this guy in charge of anything! I'm very worried our bipartisan coalition is going to break down if we don't get a South Vietnamese leader to sign this—*now!*" He paused, thinking about how developing nations have had bloody coups over fights smaller than this.

After a pause, Bowles spoke again. "It's time for Plan B, isn't it, gentlemen?"

Plan B was the plan decided upon back in Washington, D.C., with approval by not only Kennedy and his "Vietnam" advisors, but also Rockefeller and Dirksen. Goldwater had not been involved, and was specifically left out of the discussion because he was not seen as someone who could keep a secret of this nature. Plan B was to convince the South Vietnamese military leaders to back the peace and then, if Thieu resigned, someone from the military would take Thieu's place and sign the agreement.

George Kennan explained it this way: "It doesn't have to be a coup, Mr. President, or at least a bloody one. It's just another way of persuading President Thieu—or someone with the authority for the government—to sign."

The American trio of Bowles, Blee, and Corson set up a meeting with Lieutenant General Duong Van Minh before speaking again with Thieu. Minh was a highly regarded general in the South Vietnamese army. Unlike Thieu, Minh was known to believe the Viet Cong should be respected as fellow Vietnamese, not alien Communists. Minh immediately said he enthusiastically supported the peace agreement. When told of the situation with President Thieu, he beat them to the punch. "Someone must sign the agreement. There will be someone to sign if the president does not." Nobody dared go further in that meeting, but the message was clear enough.

People in and around the South Vietnamese government knew that any number of generals would step forward when the United States thought a coup would be in order. That had been the case at least twice before in South Vietnam's brief history.

When Thieu learned that Minh essentially said he would sign the agreement, Thieu knew he was being boxed in. Thieu decided, under the circumstances, to resign. He also pressured his vice president to resign, telling him, "It might be more dangerous for you to disagree than agree with me at this time."

Then, on January 14, 1969, Secretary of State designate Chester Bowles publicly announced from Saigon that General Minh was stepping in "during this time of crisis for the South Vietnamese government." Bowles then announced that General Minh had signed the peace accords "on behalf of his nation and his people."

Thieu himself called a separate press conference and said he would not sign "South Vietnam's death certificate." He also said he would "not rule out" his running for the presidency in the elections set for May 1969 to secure the "mandate" he needed to "finish the battle we are leading against international Communism."

Minh himself, before agreeing with the Americans, took his own poll among the regular army staff. Most of the staff affirmed their support for Minh and were willing to trust anything that might lead to peace without a complete defeat. Minh also went to Wheeler and Abrams and said, "My most honored guests, I must do what is right for our people. Our people are confused about whom to support, with many believing the Viet Cong are their saviors. We cannot keep killing them for that belief. An election will more effectively resolve this issue among my countrymen. Please respect this decision."

Abrams was unmoved, but he respected Minh at least somewhat. Wheeler found himself persuaded by the politics, not the facts, of the situation. He knew now that he was risking his own standing among the Joint Chiefs of Staff back home if he persisted in trying to stop what at this point looked unstoppable. An aide called from Hawaii to say there was talk at the

Pentagon that fellow Joint Chiefs of Staff member Admiral Thomas Moorer had had another pleasant lunch with the president-elect.

The elections in Vietnam should be interesting, Wheeler thought to himself.

Abrams was not as politically minded at that point. He attended the press conference with Minh, standing on the platform with Wheeler, Corson, Blee, Bowles, and Vann. However, unlike Wheeler, Abrams also stuck around for Thieu's conference and sat in the front row to make sure people noticed he was there. Abrams then submitted his resignation to Bowles, who in turn told Kennedy he was glad to accept it.

Wheeler, unlike Abrams, was staying on. This was, he thought to himself, simply one battle in a much larger war—a war with larger consequences than the one being fought in Vietnam. For Wheeler was not only angling to maintain his position at the Joint Chiefs; he was worried about a continuing investigation regarding an alleged massacre in a small village called My Lai about ten months before. Wheeler thought to himself, If the full story gets leaked at this point, that hippie-Commie crowd coming into the White House could exploit it as an excuse to leave immediately without any interval for elections—and just hand everything over to the Reds! Heck, My Lai was nothing compared to what we just did in Kien Hoa, which was one of our most successful "pacification" operations![1] Those Kennedy doves might even stop our Phoenix anti–Viet Cong pacification program just because there are some collateral civilian casualties, as if that was something we can stop in a war. That program had successfully killed a lot of Viet Cong, thought Wheeler.[2]

Wheeler sighed. He realized he would miss at least one civilian who had resigned from the government after the 1968 American presidential election. That civilian was Robert Komer, who had helped initiate the Phoenix military program in Vietnam. Komer had once told Wheeler, "You know, General, the Chinese Commies used to say the guerrillas swim in the sea of the people. What we have to do—and I've heard this from others higher up than me—is *drain the sea.*" Shit! At least Komer understood we're fighting international Communism here, not serving tea and crumpets!

The general and countless other military and political leaders were fond of using the phrase "international Communism" when justifying their bombing and other hard-line policies. It became, during the Cold War, a talismanic phrase designed to overcome any qualms about killing peasants and their children, pounding the soil, and destroying the foliage of a once-peaceful countryside. The phrase helped overcome any rational thought about who those peasants would turn to in response to such U.S. actions—unless of course the bombing and killing were so relentless that perhaps the peasants would tire of the continued trauma and "give in." That was the hope of many U.S. leaders in Vietnam as evidenced in the various memos revealed in the Pentagon study and in oral histories.

Lost in that "analysis," of course, was that a policy of terrorizing civilians, when applied to certain German Nazi officers and Japanese warlords after World War II, was a working definition of a "war crime."

Wheeler wanted to stop what he saw as a "surrender" to the Communists. However, he realized if he openly fought Kennedy and the doves, he'd likely be replaced as head of the Joint Chiefs. Moorer, he noted, was already kissing Kennedy's ass. Wheeler muttered aloud, "These people aren't *ready* for elections, probably never will be." Two months from now, maybe three months, he thought to himself, when this election nonsense is battered with bullets from the lying, conniving Viet Cong, Kennedy would be forced to listen to cooler heads.

After Abrams announced his resignation, Wheeler called in Hackworth to let him know that he, Wheeler, was "on board." Wheeler told Hackworth, "Colonel, I won't mince words here. You know that General Abrams and I were not initially on board with the incoming administration's proposed agreement with the Communists."

"Yes, sir."

"I think you have handled yourself well in making decisions as you have." The words were laced with malice, but not enough so it could be proven.

Hackworth was cool. This wasn't the precise moment to end his career by speaking freely. The political situation was still fluid, both in and out of the military. He realized he needed to say something, however. He finally spoke. "General, my views on how to win this war were known to General Abrams when he asked for my report from the field. I have fought harder than life for the people of South Vietnam and especially for the soldiers who serve under my command. General Abrams didn't like my report, but he knew I continued to be loyal to his commands. Later I received what was essentially an order from the commander in chief—at least in a week or so he will be—that, not to mince words, either, we should go a different way to the same goal, one hopes."

"You never called General Abrams about the second meeting with those men."

"I told him about the first meeting, not the second. And I was wrong not to do so, sir. I apologize for that. I could come up with excuses, but I won't."

"Colonel, you are a credit to the military, that much must be said. You're getting a bird right away from what I hear. And you will be running this operation for the new elections, God help you. It isn't going to be easy, because if you think this war was politically charged before, well . . . you just watch. You didn't have to side with those new Washington fellows when you did, but you did, and you have handled yourself as best as any one of us could have under those circumstances. I asked you here because I agree with you that it is important that the military not lose sight of the fact that we report to the political leaders who are chosen by our fellow citizens back home. I simply need to know one thing, and you are, if I must say, ordered to speak freely. How high a price do you think Colonel Corson, Mr. Bowles . . . and *Senator* Kennedy are willing to pay for this peace they are proposing?"

The room fell silent. Hackworth finally took a breath and said to himself, There's nothing to lose anymore. I'm probably cooked already. "General, I will speak freely under your order as stated. General, I think we could still possibly win this war with more killing—lots more killing—but at some point, we're still more likely looking at talking with the enemy and making the sort of concessions we are making now. South Vietnam has had several governments in the past few years, and we're still no closer to support in the jungles out there for any of those governments. Our South Vietnamese allies fight hard, but our enemies fight harder. That's it. The enemy continues to lose individual battles, but they win because we're fighting on their land. I don't know Bowles or this new Kennedy from a hole in the ground—'cept for one call when this new President Kennedy, when he was attorney general, told me off for not being respectful—I was part of the troops leading protections of Negroes in the South during their protests at that time."

Wheeler piped up on that one. "You worked with Bobby Kennedy before?"

"No, sir. Not at all. It was one phone call. I didn't know it was Bobby Kennedy—or anyone important—at the time. I called in to Washington to give my daily report from Alabama during the civil rights problems there. Some guy comes on the line to bitch about missing one vehicle out of the hundreds we had down there. I gave him a wise-ass answer 'cause who gives a shit about one vehicle, especially when it's probably out there and some accounting clerk missed it? I thought it was some accounting clerk who was doin' the bitchin'. Instead, this guy goes, 'Let me speak to your commanding general!' And I say, 'Well, who are you?' And then he says, 'I am Robert F. Kennedy. I'm attorney general. I'm *commanding* your organization.'"

Wheeler slammed his hands hard on his desk, laughing. He choked out his words through his laughter. "Son of a bitch, Hackworth! That's a good one! You know, I think I heard about that from General Cassidy. Those civvies are such a pain—" He cleared his throat and said, "Go on, Colonel. I didn't mean to interrupt."

"Well, sir, I was surprised I wasn't replaced right then and there—and I kinda think it's interesting that he would want to have me around at all. Guess the new president doesn't know or forgot. Anyway, that's all I can say."

"Thank you, Colonel," said Wheeler, still smiling. "I think you've reaffirmed to me what I need to know to support this process. Dismissed."

Bob Kennedy sat in Hickory Hill watching the daily television news reports regarding the peace process, but getting the latest inside information from Bowles and Corson by government encrypted cable. Kennedy was elated when Wheeler capitulated, particularly after he had heard from Corson about the previous argument with Abrams and Wheeler. He agreed with Bowles that Abrams would have been a disaster if he led the troops during the election phase.

After much prodding, Clark Clifford and Ralph Yarborough convinced Johnson he couldn't be the "star" at the stateside press conference announcing Minh's signing the peace accords. Johnson had to let the president-elect announce that the agreement had been signed and answer questions. Johnson stood just behind Kennedy, along with Ev Dirksen and the chairs and minority chairs of the Senate and House Foreign Relations Committees. Barry Goldwater was there after some prodding by Dirksen, Corson, and the newest senator from Kansas, Bob Dole, himself a war veteran. Goldwater said he didn't like coups, "peaceful or otherwise, even if they led to free elections." He nonetheless relented since the transition in South Vietnam was peaceful, not like with Diem back in '63.

At the press conference, in addition to reiterating the terms of the peace, Kennedy emphasized that the peace accords stated that the return of all prisoners of war would begin immediately. "I expect many, if not all of our prisoners of war will be home by January 20, 1969, with the rest by the end of the month," Kennedy said solemnly.

Meanwhile, the O Boys, who had orchestrated the P.O.W. homecoming for maximum public relations purposes, smiled deep in the background of people standing on the press conference room platform.[3]

The press conference was like a mini-inaugural. Kennedy was glad that he wouldn't have to concentrate on Vietnam in his inaugural address, however. But it would still loom large. Everything was connected, he thought to himself, but not by much more than a thread that could break at the slightest wrong pull.

In turn, this reminded Kennedy he still had no inaugural speech completed yet. Kennedy had given up writing his own speech after tearing up his eighth "final" draft. He had wanted to prove he could write his own inaugural address the way Teddy Roosevelt and Woodrow Wilson had done, but he was giving up. The Vietnam negotiations, his new baby girl, and his refusal to rest after the election had caught up with him.

Kennedy spoke with Yarborough at his home in Hickory Hill later that night, feeling like he was already losing control, though he hadn't taken office yet. "Ralph, remember what Lyndon said about impeaching a president who walked out of Vietnam? I'm starting to feel we're in for some backlash even with Goldwater, Rockefeller, and Dirksen on our side. It's gonna be 'who lost Vietnam' more than likely if the Communists win the election, isn't it? I hate saying this, but I'll say it again. It looks like I'll be a one-termer, and the Republicans will win big in the midterm elections."

Yarborough smiled. "Yes, Mr. President, there could be a backlash. But why assume you lose before the game begins? Ah've had mah share o' impossible scraps, and yeah, we could lose, and so what? Bob, you know you have to do what we're doin' here. Let's jus' see how this plays out. Ah think you also made a good choice in puttin' Colonel Corson on that commission with Ted Sorensen—and makin' that Colonel Hackworth a general after you take over so he can command respect when he runs that holdin' operation while elections get held. That General Abrams needed to come home, and that was a good move, even if he runs for office. We'll know our political strategy well before mid-term elections next year. We'll know by how the Vietnamese elections go in May."

Kennedy didn't want to let go of the subject despite Yarborough's attempts to put it off for a few months. "You heard what Reagan said yesterday, Ralph, didn't you? Listen to this quote in the *Washington Post*—the *Post* printed this guy. I can't believe it! Reagan said yesterday that he wished the South Vietnamese hadn't signed the peace accord. And this really riled me. He said, 'We didn't fight this war the way we fought the Germans. We played around with these Communists, made them see we were too weak to bomb them into submission. There was no need for negotiations, in my opinion. What was needed, and is still needed, is a whisper into Ho Chi Minh's ear that we're prepared to use nuclear force if he doesn't stay the heck out of South Vietnam with his puppets the Viet Cong.' Geez, Ralph! Reagan and Abrams are gonna be a tag team on this, I bet. What really gets me is, how come, when Reagan attacks our nation's foreign policy, nobody calls him a traitor?"

"Simple, Bob. And you know what Ah mean here. If you're on the side o' power, and power hates anyone who challenges why big business makes so much at ev'ryone else's expense, then you can say anything you damn please. No 'un-American activities' committee up there in Congress to talk 'bout his comments against the president, no suh! The thing that bothers *me*, Bob, is that two-bit movie actor never seen anythin' on a man other than ketchup. He wouldn't know a nuclear bomb from a fart. That's why he likes to talk about war all the time. He or Abrams might be trouble for us, Ah'll admit that. But Abrams isn't MacArthur. Ah served under MacArthur in early post-war Japan. Mac had political ambitions, sure. But he liked bein' king, not president. Abrams is just too angry to be more than a nuisance, though that's enough trouble as it is."

"I agree, Ralph. Tom Watson says the businessmen he's talked with are tired of the war. And yet, I think they'll go for Reagan, and maybe Abrams, if either runs a national campaign in '72."

"You're right, Mr. President. Businessmen may be tired o' this war, but it don't mean that they're tired o' fightin' Commies, and they hate unions more than they hate Commies, Ah'll tell you that much. That's why we gotta come out strong in supportin' union organizin' in the South, for starters, and gotta get some pro-union legislation passed, startin' with repealin' that Taft-Hartley law that's been on the books since Truman's time. By the time there's midterm elections, we gotta have our organization in place, get out the vote, and box their ears—or they'll box ours. The businessmen will come around—but only if we win. Otherwise, they'll pick us apart like vultures pick apart a carcass—we bein' the carcass."

"Ralph, I hear you. The thing that concerns me is . . . well, I didn't fight in World War II like you and the other guys did. I tried to enlist at seventeen, but couldn't get in. I did some time in the ROTC, and at the end of the war, had some boring duty in the navy. Reagan just made war movies, I know, but Reagan's not a bad fellow. He's even—I hate to admit—a nice guy. Not a war monger when you meet him. Does go off the wall sometimes—he's all for sending in the police to bash heads and even shoot student radicals. Hasn't said the last part publicly, but Jess Unruh in California heard him say he wouldn't mind a bloodbath on one campus just to make the kids stop protesting against their country."[4]

Yarborough said, "See what Ah mean? Now, Ah'd *never* say that even though some o' them kids might just need a spankin'. A bloodbath? He's a damned fool, if Ah may say."

"I'm sorry I sidetracked us, Ralph. What do you think about public support for the peace accords we just got through?"

"Mr. President, we know the public's supportin' these peace accords. The public lahks the way we pulled together with President Johnson just as we said we would. And the unity with leadin' Republicans was very important. Things are pretty quiet now on campuses, and not jus' 'cause they're just back from the holiday. As for detractors, there's always a third out there who hate you—and me, too. We've already won somethin' important and won it in a way Ah didn't believe we'd get: Goldwater, Rockefeller, and Dirksen are on *our* side, not Reagan's. He's lookin' real lonely out there, and that's why the *Washington Post* had to go to California to get a word against us. The conservatives are divided, and Ah think that's permanent on this issue no matter if the Viet Cong win big in May. That's weakness, son, not strength Reagan's showing out there. Let's just see how this puppy plays out.

"Now, if you don't mind, what are you gonna say to America on January 20? That's the thing to keep our eye on raht now! And if you want to win a second term, Ah'll say it again: We gotta organize the South for unions and get some good reform Democrats lahk us elected to Congress in '70—or make prairie populists out o' some of our Southern Democratic allies. Ah don't think people will be thinkin' 'bout Southeast Asia when there's some real live labor unions fightin' for representation against the bosses in the textile plants, the mines, the grocery stores lahk Wal-Mart—"

"And that's supposed to make me feel better, Ralph?"

"Bob, nothin' brings a community closer than a good ol' general strike!" Ralph slapped his knee, laughing a hearty one. "Bob, I'm just pullin' yo'r leg there! Now, let's get talkin' 'bout that big ol' speech o' yours. People gonna be watchin' that one on their TVs and listenin' on the radio all 'round the world. Let's bring 'em into *our* world and *our* view of things."

"Ralph, I haven't got a speech yet. I've got what they call writer's block, I think."

"Damn, son—Ah mean—"

"Ralph, you can say 'son.' You earned it."

"Not respectful, sir. Gotta get it raht. Now, whaddya mean, haven't got your speech ready? Get that history professor you and your brother had around—Ah've seen him around your campaign, too—forget his name right now . . . "

"Arthur Schlesinger?"

"Yeah, that's him. And get those kid speechifiers o' yours together with him. Ah lahk their spirit! That speech is gonna determine how long a honeymoon we're gonna have with Congress—and the country."

"You're right, Ralph. It's just—"

Suddenly, Ethel was yelling at the kids, the baby started crying, and Kennedy, looking helpless, got up and walked briskly to help calm the baby down. "Sorry, Ralph. I . . . I . . . Can you wait, or should I walk—"

Yarborough laughed. "Ah know mah way out, Mr. President. You all's got your hands full. Ah had mah share o' family man duties. Just call me later if the speechifiers haven't got what ya need."

Chapter 12

THE THREADS OF HISTORY

On the morning of January 15, just five days before his inauguration as the thirty-seventh president of the United States, Kennedy met in his home office with his two young campaign speechwriters, Jeff Greenfield and Adam Walinsky, and the Kennedy family's favorite historian, Arthur Schlesinger Jr. There they discussed Kennedy's writer's block and his thoughts on what he wanted to say to the American people on January 20.

Kennedy said, "Last month, just before Christmas, Tom Hayden sent me a printed copy of a sermon of Chicago's Cardinal Bernardin. Bernadin talked about the church's consistent opposition to the killing of life. That's why we Catholics oppose the death penalty, oppose some of those new state laws on abortion, and why our church talks of ministering to the poor and even supporting government programs for the poor. He called this respect for life the church's 'seamless garment,' kind of what he said Jesus wore when he was crucified. I thought . . . isn't that a beautiful and unifying idea to think about? A seamless garment. The seams that bind the garment together. Well, what do you think?"

Schlesinger was somewhat sharp, though still courtier-respectful. "Sir, you aren't looking to make a religious speech, are you? The public might fall back on some of that anti-Catholic sentiment—"

"Arthur, come on! I know that—and that's not what I'm saying. I was thinking about 'seamless garments' in American life, in American politics. I started thinking about Jefferson, Madison, Washington, Hamilton, Adams—father and son—Henry Clay, Lincoln, the Roosevelts . . . what are the seams . . . or threads that hold their visions together that make America what it is when it's at its best? Threads of history—*that's* what I mean! I kept thinking about seams and that's—Arthur . . . and you guys, too . . . what are the threads of history that we want to hold together and improve upon for the next few years? Can you guys see clear from there? I want people to see that if we do new things, there's a past thread that it relates to . . . I just don't know enough American history to say so, to prove so. My speech must be about the different generations understanding that nobody is inventing the wheel in the arguments we have. That's what I want, and I need it in two days so I can practice saying the darned thing!"

Schlesinger and the two young speechwriters went to work. The "two kid speechifiers," as Yarborough called them, wrote separately from Schlesinger, who wanted to write his own version of "the threads of history." Walinsky did some research at the Library of Congress and nearby university libraries, while Greenfield called up some professors of history. Two drafts crossed Kennedy's desk at Hickory Hill on January 18, just two days before the inaugural. Kennedy edited, rewrote, moved sentences and paragraphs, deleted entire sections, and changed words—and changed, moved, and brought some back again. He went to his own works on Emerson, Thoreau—no Greeks or Romans this time . . . Well, maybe, he thought to himself.

Ethel had also been busy with what one could also term domestic political matters during the presidential transition. She had contacted Lady Bird, President Johnson's wife, to go over what Johnson called "the wifely things," such as linens, who should be in what bedroom, moving in and moving out furniture, where painting and touch-ups needed to be done, and what the maids and chefs were like. The two women had been friendly when they first met in the late '50s, but had hardly spoken in the past several years as the relationship between their husbands had swelled into contempt and bitter hatred.

The women found, however, a common bond with little Rose cooing and crying in front of them as they discussed how a family functions in the White House—a home that is also an office and a tourists' museum. Ethel made sure she listened more than spoke because she wanted a positive report to go back to Johnson. Bob might need the soon-to-be-former president at some point early in the administration, she figured, whether it was over the war, the civil rights movement, the poverty programs, or something.

Lady Bird, for her part, was surprised that Ethel was so respectful and didn't act with any of the false airs of a Kennedy. Ethel's horse riding and tomboy personality had always intrigued Lady Bird. Plus, Ethel didn't have to go far to win Lady Bird's gratitude, since Jackie Kennedy more than once had treated Lady Bird the way a society lady treats a trailer park widow.

Lady Bird reported to her husband the "very kind and considerate" treatment she received from Ethel, and President Johnson was more than pleased. "Nice to see these people growin' up," Johnson told his wife.

After a night during which Robert Kennedy tossed and turned, saying his speech over and over in his head, his inauguration day finally arrived. January 20, 1969 was not the coldest day for an inauguration, but it was still more than cold enough to see your breath as you spoke.

And on this particular January 20, 1969, with Robert Kennedy set to assume the presidency, many American soldiers in Vietnam would have a much better day than they had in the first timeline when Richard Nixon was inaugurated.

Soldiers who didn't die on January 20 or January 21, 1969, under President Robert F. Kennedy included Paul Allen Ballard of Columbus, Ohio;

Miguel Heredia of Bakersfield, California; Roy Franklin Phillips of Sarasota, Florida; Terry Lynn of Milwaukee, Wisconsin; Johnny Lomas of Kansas City, Missouri; and Donald John Turner of South Boston, Massachusetts. In addition to these men, about fifteen to twenty others survived those two relatively quiet days. Their families were spared the grief and anger that came with their sons, brothers, or fathers dying for the vanity of politicians—and military leaders who acted no differently than politicians. Under President Robert Kennedy, there would not be full fields of crosses added to military cemeteries across the nation marking the graves of Vietnam War casualties, at least, one hoped.[1]

President-elect Kennedy, the thirty-seventh president of the United States, took the oath of office from Chief Justice Earl Warren. Ethel was nervous as she was now at every outdoor event. Secret Service men surrounded them, and there were more agents scattered in the crowd than at any previous inauguration—for obvious reasons.

After the oath, Kennedy hugged his wife and then warmly and respectfully shook hands with Lyndon Johnson. He walked a few steps over to the Plexiglass-shielded podium and spoke to the nation and the world:

Mr. Chief Justice Warren, President and Mrs. Johnson, Vice President and Mrs. Humphrey, Vice President and Mrs. Yarborough, Mr. Speaker, distinguished guests and friends, and all our fellow Americans here at home and around the world. For too long, and far too often, we think with regret and frustration of the trying times we live in. We think about the wars going on around the planet. We think about famine, civil strife, and neighbor distrusting neighbor—and often with prejudice based upon skin color, upon religion, upon whether we are men or women instead of human beings equal in the eyes of our creator. We know we live in troubled times every time we breathe in polluted air. And we find ourselves resigned to polluted rivers and soils as if they were somehow the price of "civilization." When we think of all of this today, we often say, "Times have never been worse!"

But we must ask ourselves, Are today's times worse than in 1860 when President Lincoln was desperately trying to hold the nation together on the eve of a bloody and protracted civil war? When President Lincoln had to enter Washington in secret out of concern for his life?

A gasp went up among the crowd at the assassination image. Ethel shuddered to herself, That line was not in the speech he read to me!

Are today's times worse than in 1941 when our nation was still working its way out of the Great Depression, when Hitler was on the march, and the world grew dark?

For almost two hundred years, our nation has not only survived, but grown stronger and stronger as we met the challenges that faced us. Despite the setback of a civil war, our nation endured and grew prosperous after rejecting the sin of slavery. Our nation endured and grew as we extended the right of women to vote and participate in government. Our nation, through the policies of presidents from Franklin Roosevelt through President Johnson, has created a middle class with wealth and luxuries that are the envy of the world. And after more struggle and debate, we have now rejected the scourge of Jim Crow segregation. And again, we are enduring—and growing. We have cut poverty in half over the past seven years, and we have made strides for racial equality under the law that many would have thought impossible just a decade ago. And I would be remiss, and it would be wrong, not to give great credit and thanks to President Lyndon Johnson for leading the effort for civil rights and equality, and for fighting poverty, and, my fellow Americans, for guiding our nation through much of this difficult decade.

Kennedy stepped back, went over to Lyndon Johnson, and shook Johnson's hand. The crowd of two hundred thousand, shivering in the cold, wildly applauded, with tears streaming down many faces, including Lady Bird's. Lady Bird, in turn, rose from her seat and went over to Ethel Kennedy and gave her a hug and whispered, "Thank you."

Kennedy returned to the podium, and Lady Bird went back to her seat. Johnson, shivering with amazement as much as the cold, was photographed at that moment, smiling and tenderly holding his wife's hand. Kennedy spoke again.

Throughout human history, there has been strife and disagreement at one level or another. There was, for example, almost a civil war between labor and business in our nation in 1877, when federal troops had to be called forth in at least half of our major cities. Before that, there were draft riots during the Civil War, and coal mine wars on and off for forty or fifty years from the 1870s through the 1920s in rural areas from Kentucky to West Virginia and beyond.

But we must always remember that there have also been times of peace and times of cooperation throughout human history where public policy was promoted for the sake of the most vulnerable and for the best ideals of our community. Take the case of child labor in America. Child labor in our country was commonplace in our parents' lifetimes.

Some businessmen of the day said child labor was necessary and could not be changed because it was the natural state of things as they are. Women's groups, labor groups, and independent citizens, including many businessmen, said that regardless of whether someone thought child labor was "natural," it was wrong, morally wrong. Weaving together a coalition, these groups worked to pass laws abolishing child labor, just as we did with slavery. The businessmen not only adapted but flourished—and profited—in a new "natural" order where children could go to school instead of into a dark, sulfur-laden coal mine.

Now let us consider today the deep divisions over public policy that exist in our country. Does anyone think that today, unlike the good old days, we have too many factions in our society? James Madison and our nations' founders knew that "factions" would be immutable and ever present. Madison, in Federalist Paper Number 10, said that there exist, at *all* times, what he called the monied interests, landed interests, mercantile interests, financial and other interests. Madison said that it is the role of a "modern" government to "regulate" these various interests. It almost sounds as if Mr. Madison was anticipating the consumer advocates and other agitators of our own "modern" life.

Yet, our founding fathers were also enlightened and visionary businessmen, from Benjamin Franklin, James Madison, and Alexander Hamilton to Thomas Jefferson and George Washington. For example, Alexander Hamilton proposed, and Congress created, a national bank owned and operated by the government. Yes, you heard me correctly when I said there were, at our nation's founding, government-owned banks in America. If someone called for government-owned banks today, people would say such an individual was a socialist radical. Certainly, in their day, and even by many of today's standards, our founders were, indeed, radicals. But our founding fathers saw the need for nation building and nation sustaining, as have all our best Americans at all times in our nation's history. The founders saw government-owned banks as a way to create wealth out of poverty, as a way to develop business and creative pursuits. And when private enterprise developed, we found that we no longer needed government-owned banks.

Senator Henry Clay of Kentucky, and before him, Albert Gallatin, secretary of the treasury under President Jefferson, wrote and, yes, agitated about the need for "internal improvements." Just as we are on the verge of putting a man on the moon with cooperation between NASA and private industry, so, too, did these nineteenth-century visionaries see the benefits of partnership between private enterprise and government in developing canals along rivers, railroads across the land, roads for carriages—and later motor carriages to ride across, through, and around a growing nation.

It wasn't called "big government" and "pointy-headed bureaucracy" when our forebears called for these things—and certainly not "socialism." Why then, should today's calls for internal improvements in recreating wealth in our inner cities and in rural areas be labeled with such terms? Yes, plans for internal improvements were controversial in their day and were often rejected in name, though not in deed. Just as certain, these ideas were accepted over time, and we are all the better for it.

Abraham Lincoln, the first Republican president, saw the need for a government that enriched the community and not merely the business world. He supported wholeheartedly the building of the transcontinental railroad, just as we have in our time supported the development of modern superhighways. Lincoln, however, like the Democratic president Franklin Roosevelt after him, recognized that business is not the only interest or faction we must concern ourselves with as a nation. Lincoln said, in a speech to workers in 1864, that "Capital is only the fruit of labor, and could never have existed if labor had not first existed. Labor is the superior of capital and deserves *much the higher consideration.*"

Lincoln and Roosevelt were great presidents because each saw the need for balance and for expanding the power of people in a just society, as we must do in our lifetime. And in our lifetime, we must reform our labor laws to bring them up-to-date and to allow free working men and women to organize and have representation at their place of work in every region of the country.

Alexis de Tocqueville, the French aristocrat who studied America up close in the 1830s, saw that one of America's greatest strengths was its equality among men in terms of the distribution of wealth. He noted that if cities became too populated in the East, people could move west to enjoy a chance at creating wealth; de Tocqueville also saw, however, the makings of an aristocracy in industry. He specifically warned us that our equality is imperiled when those of us in factories work on the same item day in and day out, every year, with no time to see our families or to develop our minds as free Americans—while others grow rich from paper investments.

With the loss of the frontier in America, and the space frontier still not quite upon us, it is important to reflect upon our industry, the wealth of the few, the anxiety of the middle class, and the 10 percent still in dire poverty in rural and urban areas of our nation.

Our founding fathers spoke of governments passing laws for both our general welfare and our common defense. They were, as usual, very wise in speaking of the nation's welfare as well as its defense. For it is fundamental to a just society that our nation's welfare be continually promoted, particularly in our time where most of us no longer till our own land for food, nor shear sheep for clothes.

We also face a side effect of success in a modern, industrial society that our founders may not have seen, but that their children and their children's children saw clearly enough. And that is pollution. Over one hundred years ago, Thoreau and Emerson wrote about the health problems that result from factories befouling the air and water. John Muir, in the last years of the nineteenth century and the beginning of our century, wrote of similar concerns, adding that we might lose the "sanctity of life" in the modern world if we became too focused on accumulating material things. In our own day, our children warn us about the state of our land, water, and air. We call the new "back-to-nature" people radical, but are they "radical" or even "new"? Or are they possibly "conservative" when one compares them to others in our history?

Perhaps the new mall developers are "radical" because they are making something new and different to our eyes and experience—or is a mall simply a new version of the public square of old? Perhaps the recent war protestors are "conservative" because they are in the tradition of those who opposed the Mexican American War of the 1840s—a group that included Abraham Lincoln—and those who opposed World War I, a group that included people such as Helen Keller and Eugene Debs, the famous labor leader.

Lincoln was certainly a radical in his day, but we see his desire for "malice toward none" and "charity for all" as conservative, traditional values that we admire and wish for ourselves today. When Lincoln talked of the need to love our neighbor as ourselves, was he a radical, much like an earlier and radical prophet almost two thousand years ago? Or were Lincoln and Jesus reminding us of something that must continue throughout our own days and beyond? "With malice toward none, and with charity for all . . . " is something we should well recall and act upon in our time—today.

When we look at the problems of today, whether they be a troubled war, race relations, the continued presence of poverty amidst plenty, the generation gap between young and old, we must, my fellow Americans, see past the agitation. We must not label people we don't like as "radical" or "reactionary," "imperialist" or "hippie." We must see past the generations, and generation gaps, people incessantly speak of.

We must, instead, look deep into our history and our heritage. We must, in short, *reconnect* with each other. Parents to children, children to parents, neighbor to neighbor, stranger to stranger, nation to nation.

So many times our parents or grandparents have told us, "There is nothing new under the sun." Well, I am here to say to my fellow citizens, there is nothing new in the arguments we have with each other. We may have fast cars and planes. We may have rockets and bombs. We may have washing machines and televisions. We may have medical science that is the stuff of science fiction—with the ability to transplant the heart of one person into another. But our disagreements with each other still concern, as Emerson wrote over 100 years ago, the continuing argument between "patrician and plebian, of parent-state and colony, of old usage and accommodation to new facts, of the rich and the poor."

My fellow Americans, if we are to heal those divisions, if we are to see each other as Americans, first and foremost, if we are to live in peace, and to develop our nation and our world, then we must see that we are but part of *the threads of the garment that is our history.*

Every one of us wears the garment of our forebears, of our nation, and of our humanity. We wear a garment of history that contains *many* threads. There is the thread of our boasting of the greatness of our nation. That thread is woven into the thread that includes a vigorous dissent against certain policies in our history that we have pursued against various peoples and individuals, and that our nation now sees as misguided.

We wear a garment that contains a thread that weaves together slavery and the Declaration of Independence's promise of equality. That thread is woven into the threads of the Reconstruction period following the Civil War, the institution of segregation, our movement toward *integration,* and, most of all, our tolerance and respect for one another as human beings. There is the thread of the preservation of nature, of fields, trees, and mountains, all woven into the development of nature into real estate and buildings. There is the thread that contains labor and capital, the rich and the poor. There is the thread of technology and nature, science and religion. We think these threads are separate, but in fact they are part of the same garment that makes us the greatest nation on earth.

The thread that led to the creation of a government-owned banking system and the building of canals and roads leads today to increasing credit opportunities for the poor in our cities and rural towns, and to developing public transportation. The thread that says we must be wary of foreign entanglements runs from President

George Washington's Farewell Address almost two hundred years ago through some of our children's concerns about the nature of our recent entanglement in Southeast Asia.

The garment each of us wears contains the threads that include homestead laws to build the West and policies to restore power to local people to rebuild their economically and socially depressed communities.

The threads of the Shakers, the Oneida, and other communal settlements in the nineteenth century run through youthful experiments with communes today—although Ethel and I hope our oldest children are immune to communes, I must say!

My fellow Americans, let us not judge each other by some of the harsh words or actions of a few, and only a few of those with whom we disagree. To our children who are students at colleges and on the streets today, it is time to remember that your parents are not oppressors. They are your fathers and mothers trying to do their best for your future and to take care of your needs today.

To my fellow parents out there, we must not see our children as traitors when they challenge the status quo and the way things are. They are, in the end, our children, whom we love, whom we want to see grow and have children of their own, and whom we want to be able to live in peace, prosperity, and brotherhood. Their concerns and our concerns should be complementary, not adversarial. We as parents must make the first move toward that understanding. For it is our world now, in business, in government, and in the academies, no matter how much we complain about "the kids."

A famous historian once said, "Loyalty . . . is a realization that America was born of revolt, flourished in dissent, and became great through experimentation . . . " He also said we miss the point of America's promise if we "celebrate the rebels of the past . . . while we silence the rebels of the present."

We do not—WE DO NOT—exalt *all* rebels. And we know that the only and best way to challenge lawful and decent authority is through lawful and decent methods. All of us, from rebel to patriot, from businessman to laborer, from student to senior citizen, must recognize that the threads of history intertwine us all. If we pull too harshly on a thread that is loose or bothersome, we may weaken or, worse, unwind the very thread that holds our garment together.

When we work together, without recrimination, we will find we will be a warmer nation of peace against the cold winds of war. When we work together, without discrimination, our garment will shine in its many colors and will be stronger and brighter than ever before. And when we work together, as Americans all, we will be able to reweave those threads that are worn, and strengthen those threads that are weakened by cold, by sorrow, by impoverishment.

The garment is our planet. The garment is America. The garment is our family. Our parents and our children. The garment is our past, our present, and our future. The garment is life in all of its facets, struggles, and glory. We must, and we will, protect this garment and nurture it.

I ask all Americans to join me in this endeavor. We have all got some weaving, cleaning, and shaping to do. Ours is a precious and seamless garment. One that stands for all our loving faiths and our best creeds. Our nation, our society, is a garment created in liberty, with the wisdom of equality and the freedoms guaranteed by our Constitution.

As I said to Chief Justice Warren in taking the oath of office, I *will* work to serve the people of this nation and the Constitution for which it stands. Thank you, and may God bless America and our world.

The nation reacted to Robert Kennedy's address with even more emotion and pride than they had expressed in response to John F. Kennedy's address eight years earlier. "Kennedy spinners" from Hugh Sidey at *Time* magazine and Ben Bradlee at the *Washington Post,* to Walter Cronkite and Chet Huntley on the television networks, spoke in near-religious tones about the beauty and grandeur of the address as it reinforced their belief in the majestic image of the Kennedys. While they all said, perfunctorily, that there was no single great quotation in the address, such as "Ask not what your country can do for you . . . " as John F. Kennedy stated in his inaugural speech, they all agreed that "the threads of history" was as "vital" a phrase as any "statesman" had ever uttered, and that all political discussions and policies should be conducted with that in mind.

Chet Huntley said to his news-reading partner, David Brinkley, on the air following the address: "Parents and children who follow the threads of history may find peace with each other, and that is the best thing that can happen for this nation right now."

David Brinkley, the more acerbic and pro-business of the two, replied, "Chet, I should point out that just a year or so ago, the former senator, now President Robert Kennedy, wrote alone, or with others perhaps, a book called *To Seek a Newer World.* Yet, in today's speech, he said, 'There's nothing new under the sun.' Both times he appeared to mean what he said. In fairness, President and former Senator Kennedy could be right both times—and that is often the mark of a great leader."

Critics, outnumbered, remarked that the speech was devoid of specifics. Others said it was ahistorical because there were no big government social programs in 1789 or 1899, for example. For many critics who were already opposing any new policies being proposed by Kennedy and the Democrats, the interpretation of history offered by the new president was nothing short of blasphemy against "free enterprise"—or capitalism, to use a less propagandistic term. However, many historians, including Samuel Eliot Morison, who was anything but a modern liberal, said that the new president had "rendered an important public service" in offering "a reasonable interpretation of American history that is often neglected in many historians' discussions."

Some Cold Warriors, such as Walter Lippmann and Joseph Alsop, complained about the reference to Washington's Farewell Address and its mention of no "foreign entanglements." Lippmann wrote an essay for *U.S. News and World Report* that read in part: "We have a duty to the world that was most recently and eloquently expressed by John Kennedy, the new president's very wise and older brother, who said we must not shrink from 'meeting any burden' or 'fighting any foe' in order to avoid larger and more deadly struggles. One hopes the new president is not sounding a clarion call to retreat from our moral imperative to promote freedom in world affairs."

Critics from the Left did their own carping at the inauguration speech. David Horowitz, one of the editors at *Ramparts*, the radical magazine of the student Left, said, "Yes, Mr. President, we know all about threads in American history. We know about the thread that began with slavery, expanded through the genocide of the Indians, and passed directly to mass murder with the latest technology in Southeast Asia and South America—and the one continuing thread of white patriarchy oppressing and killing black Americans. No matter how much the sycophants of this new President Kennedy applaud, we know that no American who aspires to the presidency will ever acknowledge the fundamental malice behind American policies against the third world, our own nation's poor, the blacks, and the youth." Apparently, there were still those who were not quite ready to make peace among the generations or within the nation.[2]

Chapter 13

LABOR PAINS

T he newspapers and morning television and radio news programs reported that the new president and his wife left the inaugural ball as soon as the curtain came down at the end of the various musical performances. Kennedy, said reporters, had pointedly refused to stay to chat with Hollywood stars and singers such as Paul Newman, Martin Sheen, Warren Beatty, Tony Bennett, Rosemary Clooney, or even his best Hollywood friend, Bobby Darin. The new president especially stayed away from the rock bands brought in by Jeff Greenfield and Jack Newfield—and by the new president's oldest son, Joe. Newfield, upsetting the O Boys, had brought in the radical folksinger Phil Ochs for the ball's final act, to sing Woody Guthrie's "This Land Is Your Land." The entire audience, including the president and his family, gave Ochs a standing ovation.

O'Brien said to Newfield afterward, "Okay, Jack, the song went over great. But don't think we'll even consider messing with 'The Star Spangled Banner'! Either way, an anthem is just a damned song!"

Newfield answered, "An anthem is what you sing with pride while you're doing something for your country, Larry."

O'Brien snorted and snickered. "Aw, come on, Jack! We both got work to do tomorrow!"

Kennedy was glad to read the press stories because he was making a conscious statement by not staying late after the inaugural ball. He wanted the world to see him as serious about peace, prosperity, equality, and justice— mainly because, apart from ending the war in Vietnam, he hadn't thought much since the election about how he was going to pass legislation in the areas of labor reform, public transportation, poverty, and race relations.

The new President Kennedy also wanted to make a statement to the residents of the village known as Washington, D.C., that he was not going to be having sex with starlets or other women as had his brother Jack. Kennedy had instead become a convert to the cause of marital fidelity. And as recent converts make it a point to demand that everyone else immediately repent, Kennedy called his youngest and only remaining brother, Ted, to the White House in the afternoon between the inauguration and the celebration later that evening. There, the two brothers had a heart-to-heart talk—Larry O'Brien called it a "Come to Jesus" meeting—in which the new president told Ted that the latter's skirt-chasing would no longer be tolerated.

Kennedy said, "You remember what Nixon tried to do to me during the campaign, Ted? Well, Hoover won't hesitate if he makes up his mind that he can get away with attacking me—or attacking *you* in order to get to me. That's why you have to stop all the skirt-chasing and . . . well, adulterous behavior."

"Bob, you can't be serious! I mean, you kept that out of the press—don't forget that, and nobody wanted to write about it even after they learned about it. And the press will never cover that sort of thing, even for Hoover."

The President shook his head and said, "Ted, you're not getting me. It's over. Times have changed."

"You mean . . . all of them? But what about—"

"Yes, Teddy, all of them. Including that gal in Florida with the shell shop—"

"Helga? Bob, she is *very* discreet—and I *need* to talk with her from time to time. She's much more level-headed than my wife mostly is—"

"Ted, let me put it to you straight! I can't have any sex scandals around me—*at all!* I'm asking you as your older brother to stop cheating on Joan. We have to protect each other, our family and, just as importantly, this administration. You are going to be targeted just as much as I am—and I am not waiting to be proven right. The attack at the Ambassador Hotel, the campaign attack from Nixon—all that made me think about Ethel and my relationship with her." He paused, trying a softer tack. "You know, maybe we don't give our wives enough credit. Ethel has said some politically astute things since I've begun to listen more to her. Mayor Daley says he listens to his own wife a lot, and he's damned successful! It's not as if I'm asking you to drop Jack Gargan—a *real* adviser!—and make Joan your new political adviser. Just . . . just . . . Why don't you start seeing what you can do about Joan's drinking, at least? Maybe if you were home more . . . Joan is a very pretty woman, Ted. And Ethel says she's very bright . . . "

Ethel had said no such thing—and Bob didn't know one way or another—but he did everything he could in that conversation to find some way to make his brother understand.

The words stung the younger brother, but in the end, he realized that Bob Kennedy was the undisputed leader of the Kennedy clan—and also the leader of what the political commentators and clergy liked to call the "free world," with all the moral authority accompanying that phrase at that time.

Kennedy was up early the next morning, his first full day as president, and had more on his mind than his discussion with Ted. He met first with Yarborough, the O Boys, and his cabinet in order to make sure everyone had met each other and were ready to begin doing right by the nation.

At the meeting, they discussed labor reform, strategies for environmental legislation, the public transportation bill, and Commerce Secretary Learson's and Defense Secretary Warnke's ideas for joint research on civilian applications for computer technologies created during the space program. Kennedy then held a separate meeting with Yarborough, Reuther, and the O Boys to specifically discuss the mechanics of labor reform.

Yarborough spoke first, with some hesitation in his voice. "This morning, Mr. President, at the cabinet meeting, Ah detected an element o' concern in your comments about movin' forward on labor reform. Your statement about 'not wantin' to start a civil war here when we're just gettin' out o' a war in Southeast Asia,' was . . . well, humorous, but a bit disconcerting, if Ah may say."

The president responded with a very serious tone. "I *am* concerned, Ralph. First off, I remember leaks from the last time I was in the executive branch. Remember, you have Learson of IBM in the room. You think I want to let him tell his friends at the Business Roundtable to prepare for the great labor assault?"

"It's out there already, Mr. President," said a starting-to-get-suspicious Walter Reuther. "There's no secret—"

"There's a difference between talk and action, Walter, and I want them to think we're just talking for now, at least for a few weeks. Have you got enough support in Congress to overcome a filibuster from Dirksen, for example?"

O'Brien stepped in. "Yes, sir. We know, back in '65, how Dirksen filibustered away the last labor reform bill. The three of us—Walter, Ralph, and I—have been preparing our assault on Congress. We've been talking with the AFL-CIO about coordinating strategies to organize the largest Southern employers in textiles, oil and gas, and retail—specifically this new conglomerate grocery store, Wal-Mart. We're working as hard on this as you and Chet Bowles worked on the Vietnam agreement."

Indeed, O'Brien, Yarborough, and Reuther had been busy. Reuther started immediately after the election in his own backyard with the UAW. First, he maneuvered to install Doug Fraser as his successor as soon as Kennedy asked him to join the cabinet as secretary of labor.[1] Fraser, in turn, immediately called friends at the AFL-CIO to begin the process of bringing the UAW back to the larger group of national and international unions, where, said Fraser, "we belong!"

Help in returning to the AFL-CIO came from the American Federation of State, County and Municipal Employees (AFSCME) and, somewhat surprisingly, the Communication Workers of America (CWA). The head of the CWA was a close Meany associate and was hostile to Reuther, but he liked Fraser. With the help of these two unions, Fraser had negotiated the return of the UAW into the AFL-CIO just before Inauguration Day.

Meany acted magnanimously in inviting Fraser and the UAW back into the "bosom of the union family." Privately, he was concerned that with

Reuther as Secretary of Labor, the UAW under Fraser could wind up leading all unions into a new association, leaving him and his carpenter's union alone in the AFL-CIO.

Reuther, for his part, was surprised, and concerned at Fraser's quick moves back to the AFL-CIO. Fraser answered Reuther with an equally surprising candor, "Walt, we must unite with the larger part of labor if we're going to help you—and organize the South. Meany is reconciled to the fact that the war in Vietnam is coming to an end. He doesn't see me as the threat to his leadership that you were." Fraser hoped that last remark sounded sincere, since Fraser was thinking about announcing a challenge to Meany at the next September meeting of the AFL-CIO if the Southern organizing campaign was going well. "And," Fraser continued, "Meany knows damned well—his assistant Lane Kirkland said this on the record to me—that you may be the best appointment organized labor will ever have in *any* administration."

With the war probably winding down, and to avoid any challenge to his leadership, Meany decided to ride out this "fad," as he saw it, of Southern organizing. Meany believed the labor law reform bill was likely to be filibustered to death as it had been the last time it was tried in the mid-1960s. Another defeat of labor law reform in Congress, he believed, would likely cause most labor leaders to question the efficacy of trying to organize the South. At that point, he would reiterate his belief that organizing the South was a waste of time and precious union resources. For Meany, the culture of the South was too virulently antiunion—even more than it was racist.

Nonetheless, Meany and Fraser became cochairmen of the AFL-CIO's Southern Organizing Committee (SOC). The SOC vice chairs were Leonard Woodcock, the one-time heir apparent in the UAW, David Dubinsky of the textile workers union, and Mike Hamlin, a leading black militant union worker also in the UAW. On the committee's board were Herbert Hill, of the labor section of the National Association for the Advancement of Colored People (NAACP); Arthur Goldberg, a leading labor lawyer and former UN ambassador and U.S. Supreme Court justice; Jerry Wurf of AFSME; Lane Kirkland, a leading Meany aide; and a surprise—a young steelworker and new lawyer named Rich Trumka, who came highly recommended by reform elements in the United Mine Workers union.

When Reuther and Yarborough told Kennedy of the SOC and passing labor law reform before summer, Kennedy smiled as he said with sarcasm, "I gotta hear this, guys! How you gonna get past Southern Democrats, or Dirksen—who filibustered you guys before—or the newly returning Barry Goldwater? Give me a break!"

Turning serious, Kennedy then asked, "And how much are you going to mess up my Vietnam peace agreement to fail at this? Unless I hear something even remotely convincing, I'd rather wait till next year, an election year, when we turn up the heat on these guys and get our rank-and-file-members out there . . . " He trailed off, having convinced himself to stop this dream before it turned into a political nightmare that unraveled the bipartisan Vietnam peace accords.

Reuther, at that moment, realized he needed to resell his boss on the immediate need for labor reform. Reuther began, "As we know, Mr. President, we in this administration owe much of our victory last November to the union households. The one important policy all the workers, at least in the Northeast, Upper Midwest, and West, agree on is the repeal of antilabor legislation passed in 1947 and 1959. I speak, respectively, of the Taft-Hartley Act and the Landrum-Griffin Act. I know that it would be too much to ask to repeal both of these laws in their entirety at this time. I would suggest, however, that we at least repeal those portions of the Taft-Hartley law so that labor organizers going into North Carolina and points south can count on unions throughout the country to back them up with sympathy strikes. And once we get those union elections won, there's got to be a union shop and no more state right-to-starve or freeload laws!"

"Huh?" said the look on President Kennedy's face.

O'Brien jumped in. "Mr. President, Walt's talking about right-to-work laws. A number of states, mostly in the South and Lower Midwest, passed laws saying that, even if the union wins, any individual worker doesn't have to join a union."

"I know you're gonna kill me, Walter, but why does a worker have to join a union against his—"

"Because!" said a flaring Reuther. Yarborough, sitting next to Reuther, put his large hand on Reuther's shoulder to calm him down. Reuther began again, saying, "Bee-cause, Mr. President, without a union shop, the employer is able to start a rear-guard action of picking off the union membership one by one. First the boss gives extra benefits to the freeloaders who don't want to pay dues but still like the benefits of the union. Then he gets a couple of other workers to think they can get a better deal for themselves if they break from the union—there's no initial risk because they still get the benefits of the union's collective bargaining agreement, plus the boss' payoff. The first workers who defect do well, of course, but eventually the union is weakened. And then the boss, after weakening the union, can push for cutbacks, and sooner than later, the boss holds all the cards again. The right-to-starve laws undermine solidarity, and that's why unions, to the extent they exist in those right-to-starve states, are not as strong as they can be—or should be. In a real union state, if a worker doesn't like his local union in a union shop, he can run for a union office, alone or with a slate, and turn out the incumbents, at least as well as in any democracy. He can also go work for nonunion shops—and make less money, of course!"

A firm but smooth-voiced Ralph Yarborough broke in. "There's a larger political issue, Mr. President, as to why we need to help labor unions. If we merely fight for racial justice—or for the poor who don't have jobs—without a broader economic justice program, the white workers, who are in unions, will be votin' Republican if we hit a recession and they get laid off. They'll blame us—and the blacks and the poor. If there's a strike by industrial white workers without labor law reform, those whites also know that employers use blacks as strikebreakers. Ah've talked with enough white workers in Texas to know they often see liberal northerners' concerns for blacks as just one more way to kick out white folks from their jobs. Ah'm not defendin' the racism, but that jobs part can't be criticized or ignored. And that's why Walter and Ah believe the commitment for civil rahts and workers' rahts go hand in hand—they must! Can't get one without the other because white worker against black worker equals a Republican South! Lyndon always believed that was his biggest risk in signin' the civil rights laws, but he did what was raht anyway. Ah was talkin' 'bout this with Senator Russell just the other day—well, maybe we're gettin' ahead o' ourselves."

O'Brien, who didn't want to take another chance with Reuther's temper, spoke before Reuther could start again. "No, Ralph, you're right on time to talk about the meetings in Congress."

The president, slightly chastened, said, "I think I'm beginning to understand, but I still need more than rhetoric. I already understand it's all connected—" The president thought to himself, Christ! There's labor reform, organizing the South, Vietnam, race relations, the environment. These are too many things crashing into each other.

With O'Brien's opening, and Reuther still looking angry, Vice President Yarborough continued. "Last month, Mr. O'Brien and Ah called a meetin' with various senators in the Democratic Party's Southern wing, at one o' the Capitol meetin' rooms. Larry was a good organizer, Ah must say, as was Mr. O'Donnell heah. Ah introduced the senators to the new secretary o' labor, but admittedly, Ah did most o' the talkin'. Talked with young 'uns, lahk Senator Hollings o' South Carolina, and middle-aged ones, lahk Herman Talmadge, senator from Georgia; John Sparkman and Jim Allen o' Alabama; Al Gore, Tennessee; and some older ones—Russell o' Georgia, Sam Ervin o' North Carolina, and ol' Spessard Holland in Florida, who may not run next year for reelection and is feelin' a bit, shall we say, interested in how he'll look in history. Also, we had a separate, more private meeting—just me and Larry O here—with Congressman Wilbur Mills o' Arkansas at Ways and Means and Wayne Hays of Ohio from the House Government Administration Committee. Wanted to make sure those boys weren't gonna derail nothin' there in the House. The message was the same: 'If you boys don't help unions organize the South, white folks are gonna desert the Democratic Party when Republicans play the race issue to the hilt. And we'll all wind up a loser 'cause, as Harry Truman told me, 'If you're a Democrat runnin' as a Republican, an' you go up against the

Republican, the Republican will win every time.' Plus, if you switch to the Republicans like ol' Strom Thurmond, you may be fannin' the flames o' civil war more than if you stay and fight for the right thing. 'Cause unions are gonna start risin' in the South one way or the other. And if we win, we're all gonna be in power a long, long time, boys."

"Strom Thurmond? That's a good one!" President Kennedy said with a chuckle. "Strom Thurmond's *really* ancient! How long's he got to live anyway? A few years?"

"With all respect, you never know how long an old pole cat lahk him can hold on—hear he's on the lookout for a new young wife, and he's got that gleam in his eye lahk he wants to make his own gran'kids! Anyways, them Congress boys know they ain't Strom Thurmond, and Ah think they understand real well which way things are headin'. All o' 'em—ev'ry one, was sayin' to me, 'Is the president fully supportive heah?' and we said—"

Kennedy interrupted, "Gentlemen, if you recall, the South was not my strongest region—it might be better if I came out *against* labor reform, saying labor law reform would help white workers in the South too much! That'll knee-jerk people into supporting it . . . " He was being sarcastic, of course, but he was also somewhat serious against moving too fast on labor issues. He didn't want to lose Dirksen's support on Vietnam, or else he'd be a less-than-one-term president. Damned Southeast Asia has always been a sideshow for domestic politics, he thought to himself.

Yarborough spoke again. "Mr. President, Ah believe that if Ah went South, made the speeches, while Larry O'Brien, you, and Walter twist arms up here, and maybe a visit by Secretary o' State Bowles goin' up to the Hill to talk 'bout it in national security terms—somethin' lahk, 'Fightin' for labor rights at home will show we mean it when we say we'ah for labor rights around the world, unlike the Communists, who are only for themselves and their party.' Ah won't promise, but we may beat down that filibuster before it starts."

Reuther broke in. "Mr. President, I don't know if you know this, but I have been quite friendly with Secretary Bowles for over ten years. When he was ambassador to India, I visited him there and spoke on behalf of India's right to be independent—something that did not go over well with George Meany at the time. Secretary Bowles told me that if you are supportive, he will personally meet with individual congressmen on the Foreign Affairs and Military Armament Committees."

The president looked around the room, smiling. "When were you fellas going to let me in on all this activity?"

"We did, sir, but you were busy with Vietnam, moving in, and all those other things. We just didn't talk about the details till we thought it necessary," said a smiling O'Brien, with a wink to O'Donnell, who had been involved in each move. O'Donnell had the same concerns as Kennedy, but was slowly convinced this was the way to hold down any losses in the midterm elections. O'Donnell was not focused on anything ideological, just short-term politics for his best friend, Robert Kennedy.

Reuther said, "Mr. President, Ralph and Larry O'Brien deserve much of the credit for making inroads in Congress. We'd like you to meet with Democratic congressional leaders, state your support of the legislation, and then assist with some of the Southern members of Congress who have had problems in the past with this. It will mean some pork for their districts—they understand that very well—but it will be worth the money."

O'Brien, sensing the president was on board, stepped in to say, "Jim Wright, the congressman from Texas, wants to spearhead things in the House. He and Tip O'Neill have dreams about being speaker after John McCormack passes on. Remember, in '65, the bill we're basically talking about did pass the House. It died in the Senate. But now, Senators Talmadge, Holland, and the new guy, Hollings, are willing to be 'ambassadors' to the Senate cause, as it were. Sam Ervin is with us on the sly, but admits he is very close to Roger Milliken, the textile mill king of South Carolina, not to mention J. P. Stevens in North Carolina—both of those textile guys hate unions more than they hate you, which means they hate them a whole helluva lot! We also have some Republican senators we can already count on to defect to the cause of labor—Clifford Case from New Jersey, the new guy, Charles Goodell, from your state, New York—"

"Goodell's more liberal than me!" said Kennedy. "Hell, you fellas might just pull this off!"

"—and, of course, Aiken of Vermont," said O'Brien, completing his thought. "We might even get Stennis or Eastland if it looks close because they don't want a messy primary fight from a white populist with black support in the next primary. We don't need their support. We just need 'em to vote to end the filibuster if Dirksen tries that again."

Reuther, having regained his confidence in the president, said, "Mr. President, we have worked hard for this moment, and we really need your leadership here. This has to be the top priority now that we are moving toward peace—we hope—in Southeast Asia. The AFL-CIO is firmly moving into the South, with money, bodies, minds, and hearts. Doug Fraser told me that Frank Fitzsimmons of the Teamsters is ready to commit to some reforms and unite with the rest of labor, starting with this bill and the organizing efforts—"

Kennedy was sharp. "What's Fitzsimmons want? That son of a bitch—"

"Nothin'," came the quick response of Yarborough. "He wants nothin' at all, sir. We made that clear to dem fellas. Larry and Ah attended a very productive meetin' last week with Mr. Fitzsimmons. Ah can assure you, sir, there will be no deals." O'Brien shook his head up and down with vigor so his boss would know Yarborough was telling the truth. Yarborough continued, "Ah think, with all respect, the Teamsters just want to make sure they aren't unnecessarily attacked under our administration—"

Kennedy, still angry, said, "That's easy. Tell them to clean their noses at least once in a while and stop sleeping with the God-damned Mob! Man, I think we need to let Justice know they have free rein against the Teamsters! We don't need to go after the Mob first off, though, because we have too many other—"[2]

Kenny O'Donnell, the president's chief of staff, raised his arm in front of Kennedy, but with a gentle voice said, "Mr. President, may I suggest we visit those points, however much I agree with you, another time? The war, organizing labor unions in the South, the environment, public transportation—that's enough for one day, or year, I think—and we haven't even met the Joint Chiefs yet today." He voice was calming, caring. O'Donnell, and everyone else in that room, realized there was one rift—the one between the Teamsters and Robert F. Kennedy—that wasn't going to be healed with rhetoric about coming together to sew the threads of history.

Kennedy softened, saying, "Fellas, I think your plan is excellent, and your execution so far is well . . . nothing short of miraculous! But, let's be careful. We may have a downturn in the next year as we end the war and send troops home. We need solidarity from workers, both from a policy standpoint and a Democratic Party standpoint, if we are to survive past the midterm elections. I see now the sooner we get laws that help with labor organizing, the better. Just let me know what I can do, since it appears we all agree I could be a liability or at least a burden on this one, considering my standing in the South—unless I throw in some pork-barrel projects. And I don't want to piss off Dirksen. Really!"

With that, the meeting ended, and Kennedy, O'Donnell, and O'Brien went on to formally meet the Joint Chiefs of Staff. There, with Defense Secretary Warnke, they talked over the status of the implementation of the Vietnam peace accords. The meeting was more cordial than one might have imagined a few weeks before. General Wheeler had all the enthusiasm of a convert, which relieved the president.

Admiral Moorer saw through Wheeler's obsequiousness, however, and began his own back channel to Vietnam with General Alex Harkins, who was, in turn, in contact with Colonel Hackworth. Moorer wanted to make sure the elections in Vietnam were a political success so the United States didn't get dragged into another military buildup in Vietnam or, God help us, he thought to himself, bombing sanctuaries in Cambodia or Laos. Moorer knew better than to believe that Wheeler had given up his idea of trying to "win" in Vietnam.

Secretary of Defense Paul Warnke announced a Pentagon study to modernize military procurement procedures. He also spoke of "productive" meetings with Commerce Secretary Learson about working jointly with private industry to develop computers for home and business use. Warnke tentatively proposed that military contractors would manufacture minicomputers for civilian use, with that technology having a military application as a side benefit. The Joint Chiefs knew that Warnke, one of the better-known doves in the Johnson administration, was a major proponent of "military conversion" for the post-Vietnam period. The Chiefs assigned Admiral Moorer to be their representative on the study panel, concluding Moorer's growing friendship with Kennedy would be useful in making sure the results of the study would not hurt the interests, financial and otherwise, of the Pentagon and its allies in the military contracting industry.[3]

Warnke, later in this meeting, outlined goals of nuclear arms control with the Soviets, and eventually the Chinese. This was met with polite, tepid nods and "Yes, agreed," around the table, even on the need for an antiballistic missile treaty. The Joint Chiefs knew that there was no reason to believe the Russians had any technology capable of striking down missiles, and neither did American scientists. Jaws dropped around the table, however, when Warnke said, "I also believe we need to stop production on MIRVs as part of our arms control program." MIRVs were "multiple independent reentry vehicles" attached to nuclear warheads, precisely what Brezhnev in the Soviet Union had warned Kennedy about the previous summer. MIRVs allowed a single nuclear warhead to divide into different warheads and strike separate targets.

The Joint Chiefs, led by Wheeler, were shocked to hear Warnke say this because, unlike the antiballistic missile defense idea, MIRVs were already developed and tested, and were shown to work. And besides, ran the military's argument, if the United States didn't go ahead with MIRVs, the Soviets would—and they may already have started MIRVing their land-based missiles.[4]

The president, hearing these concerns, said he would like to hear more from Secretary Warnke as to how the United States could verify if the Soviets were not already engaging in MIRV development. The Joint Chiefs, happily realized Warnke's position was doomed because verification was a question of degree that one could always argue was not enough.

At the end of the day, after meeting with other cabinet members, including Ramsey Clark at Justice, President Kennedy had a private conference with O'Brien and O'Donnell to discuss the openings for justices to the U.S. Supreme Court.

There were two openings on the court now, ironically because of a political maneuver of Lyndon Johnson's that had backfired. Johnson had tried to take advantage of Earl Warren announcing his retirement from the court two days after the 1968 election. Johnson, who wanted to do one last favor for a friend, nominated Supreme Court Associate Justice Abe Fortas to replace Warren as chief justice. Fortas had been on the Supreme Court for three years, having been nominated by Johnson and approved by the Senate in 1965.

Kennedy was initially angry at Johnson's move because Kennedy reasonably thought he should be able to nominate the next chief justice. However, the O Boys had convinced Kennedy not to make a "big deal" out of this situation because Fortas was already on the Court and Kennedy still had the opportunity to replace the retiring Warren. This was simply a technical designation for Fortas to go from associate justice to chief justice. Besides, they said, there were several justices of "retirement" age already, and they expected at least two justices to retire in the next two or three years.

What the O Boys did not know was that Strom Thurmond and some other Republican senators had decided to fight the Fortas' nomination as a way to let the Democrats know that they would not rubber stamp Supreme Court nominations. Thurmond's staff dug into Fortas' financial and legal dealings and found some financial irregularities and some questionable ethical lapses—although, at that time, one could have identified such ethical lapses in plenty of judges Thurmond previously approved. Regardless, there was now a growing sense in the Senate that Fortas was not chief justice material—or perhaps any justice material. A convergence of ethics-minded liberals and political-warfare-minded Republicans doomed the Fortas' nomination by mid-December 1969.

Fortas, under fire now from Democratic Party allies as well as Republican foes, withdrew his nomination. Then he stunned Democrats—and President Johnson—by announcing his retirement from the Supreme Court. This was how two vacancies opened on the Supreme Court for the incoming president to fill.

Kennedy now said to the O Boys, "As I said two months ago, I thought I was owed the right to choose the next chief justice. We already know we're putting in Archie Cox[5] for one of the slots, maybe even chief justice. I figured the other slot would be for Joe Dolan. You can't possibly have anyone else in mind, right?"

"Well, um," said O'Donnell, slightly hesitating, "with our bipartisan peace accords to protect, the coming battle for labor reform, not to mention other proposals such as public transportation development, Larry and I thought we could use a compromise candidate for the Senate to confirm who doesn't create the kind of controversy Johnson had with Fortas."

Kennedy, sensing O'Donnell's hesitation, asked with more concern in his voice, "What's goin' on, guys? You've spoken to Archie and Joe, right? They're my guys for the two open Supreme Court seats! I don't have any time or patience left today—and I've heard enough of the kids in the hall to know I have to talk with Ethel tonight. And don't think I'm looking forward to that, either."

"Well . . . well, we . . . um," stammered O'Donnell, " . . . Mr. President, we have no problem with Professor Cox, but the thing is . . . the Fortas' nomination was filled with an underlying anger among Democrats and Republicans about cronyism, and . . . "

"What's that got to do with *Professor* Cox, as you now suddenly call him?" said an angry Kennedy. "I've had *no* financial deals with Archie Cox, and Archie is cleaner than anyone, especially someone like Fortas! And you know it! And Joe Dolan is no more a 'crony'—damn it!—than you are, Kenny! You're a *real* crony, if someone wants to be rough—and I would never let anyone tell me that I can't have you right next to me! Jesus! I have all but promised Cox and definitely Dolan a seat on the Court. Cox is probably the finest legal mind in the country—"

O'Brien jumped in, saying, "We have no problem with Archie Cox, Bob. He's definitely getting one of the slots. But to have both Cox and Dolan . . . well . . . It may be too much too soon . . . I have to take the fall on this, not Kenny. My concern was to avoid appointing too many of 'us' from the first time around . . . and with the Vietnam thing, the economy, the labor union fights we expect, not to mention the nature-lover stuff, we thought . . . Please, Bob, hear me out. We talked this over with Joe Dolan, and he's fine with what we're proposing here."

Kennedy asked with resignation, "So what are 'we' proposing 'here,' if you don't mind filling me in for once?"

O'Brien gulped and said, "Well, we're putting up Cox for the nomination for one of the Supreme Court seats. For the other seat, there's a fellow named Frank Wheat; he's been chairman of the Securities and Exchange Commission—and he's a top lawyer, big nature-loving fellow like Justice Bill Douglas, fairly liberal. But he also has great corporate credentials to boot—big silk-stocking firm—and he ran the SEC well, we hear from all quarters. And—sir, I must be blunt. We thought the best plan was to have a quick hearing for the Senate to choose Cox and Wheat and then have current Justice William Brennan succeed Earl Warren as chief justice. Brennan's popular within the Court—the whispers around Capitol Hill say this is a great choice—Brennan's a good consensus builder there. And Frank Wheat's a lawyer's lawyer, Protestant, and *not* controversial. He's clean, and Thurmond and *his* cronies can't lay a glove on him—and won't. I also checked around: Justices Hugo Black and Bill Douglas are comfortable stepping down during your first term, perhaps as early as next year. We can get two at that time: Joe Dolan and maybe refill the traditional 'Jewish' seat—"

"Fine," said a terse and still displeased Kennedy, who was beginning to realize certain limits of presidential power in his first day on the job. "Gentlemen, I am not happy—but what are we doing for Dolan? Can't we do something for him?"

O'Donnell nodded, and then said, "Mr. President, there's a slot opening on the Ninth Federal Circuit Court of Appeals and we've already offered it to Joe. Thurmond is going to be a prick on Supreme Court nominees no matter what, but not on appeals court nominees, at least at—"

"My concern," Kennedy shot back, "is that this might be the *best* time for Joe to go on the Supreme Court, especially if the economy gets in trouble, or the war doesn't end right for us—geez, guys! I hope you know what you're doin' on this. If we don't get Joe in by next year, he may never get in—and I think the country will be the worse for it—and that isn't *cronyism*." Kennedy's icy tone showed how bad it was for the O Boys to even hint at a comparison between the relationships Kennedy had with Cox or Dolan and the one Johnson had with Fortas.

After a pause, Kennedy said, "Is that it, guys? Look. I don't want to be bothered with Supreme Court nominee decisions, other than making sure the people we choose are concerned with civil rights for minorities and won't be overturning labor law reforms and other federal programs we have in mind. I don't want them going too far out one way or another. That's it. But I want one thing clear: Joe Dolan is the one for the next Supreme Court opening unless I say otherwise—*clearly* say otherwise! Got that?"

The O Boys nodded.

"Anything more?" Kennedy said, trying to smile away his tiredness and frustration.

The O Boys looked at each other and shook their heads.

"Fine," said Kennedy. "We're done. Don't call me unless it's necessary. And don't get me wrong. I'm glad we're here and not Nixon, and I am glad *I'm* still here to be having *angst,* as the German philosophers say." He put his arm around O'Brien and playfully punched O'Donnell with his other hand. "Thank you, guys, for being there."

And with that, the public portion of the first presidential day was over.

Kennedy went upstairs to the White House private quarters—"home"— to Ethel, who was just putting down the baby for an evening nap—she never slept more than a few hours at a time. The new president watched Ethel and the baby and wondered how anything other than politics might ever get his attention. "Ethel, I think I am beginning to understand how a president gets isolated, and it's only my first day."

Ethel said, "Well, maybe this isn't the time to say that the kids have petitioned me—really, a *written* petition—saying they want to go back to Hickory Hill with a few servants and let us stay here with the baby. I don't know, I—"

"You don't *know?*" Kennedy exploded, as husbands usually do after being nice to people at work all day. "Out of the question! Out! Out! Out of the question! That was the *right* answer to that pe-petition! The *only* answer, in case you're wondering, Ethel!" He punched the air with a fist and started pacing around the room screaming at his wife for not managing the family in any organized manner.

He looked over at Ethel and saw she was about ready to cry. He stopped pacing, breathed deeply, and spoke calmly. "Ethel," he sighed again, "please tell me. What's the problem with the kids?"

Ethel took in a deep breath as well and spoke slowly, but firmly. "It's not just the kids' problem, Bob, it's *ours*. This White House is too cramped with all the offices, Secret Service people, tourists—the place feels like a fishbowl, not a home! And with the baby and all . . . Why can't we stay at Hickory Hill—at least for a few months? There! I said it! I-I-I don't mean to! I mean it! Yes! NO!" She started to sob while saying, "Bob, I'm not ready for this! Little Rose's colic won't go away. The older kids don't want to watch the younger ones anymore. And even when you're here, I can't call on you—I don't want to interrupt—and now I'm supposed to have a 'cause,' according to both Kenny and Larry—like being a mother to eleven children isn't enough of a cause for anyone? I don't know *anything* anymore!" She let out a big sob with that exclamation.

Bob walked over to Ethel and hugged her. He kissed her hair and cheek, then her lips. "I love you, darling. I really do. Don't even think about a cause right now except you and the children. It's only the first day. That's what I've said to myself *all day*. I can't solve the world's problems in one day, and you can't solve all the children's problems and homesickness all at once either. Call a family meeting for an early breakfast tomorrow. I'll speak with all of them."

He then kissed her lovingly on her lips. The two of them stood there a few moments, holding each other. Ethel brightened a little, then a lot, knowing her Bob was still with her.[6]

Chapter 14

SAILING INTO THE STORM

The Wheat and Cox nominations, along with Brennan's nomination to be chief justice of the Supreme Court, were announced later in the week. Wheat sailed through—although Thurmond tried to stir things up with questions about Wheat defending, among many other corporate clients, *Playboy* magnate Hugh Hefner. When Thurmond asked about it, Wheat smiled and said, "Senator, I assure you I only read the *articles* in *Playboy* magazine, as I am sure many of the senators here do as well!" That broke everyone up, and Thurmond, who didn't want to have anyone question whether he read only the articles in *Playboy* magazine, shortly thereafter ended his inquiry about Mr. Hefner and Mr. Wheat's representation.

Thurmond voted against Wheat, just for sport, but only John Stennis, a Southern Democrat, and a couple of other Republicans joined Thurmond. Wheat won approval from the Senate with ninety-five votes out of one hundred.

William Brennan was approved as chief justice on a slightly more partisan vote—though the hearings were rather dull and without controversy—with ninety votes for and ten against. Brennan made clear that he could not ethically discuss pending cases or most past cases because "issues continue to come up that explore the contours of those cases. I do not want to be seen as potentially prejudging cases before I hear them." This impressed most of the senators, who were looking for a reason not to have any contentious hearings with regard to his nomination as chief justice.

Kennedy wanted to take no chances with Archibald Cox. He worked with Democratic senators on the Judiciary Committee to call a variety of legal experts, both liberal and especially conservative, on behalf of Cox. The experts spoke of Cox's integrity, his rigorous legal mind, and his devotion to the Constitution of the United States. Thurmond countered with a few witnesses who testified about Cox's "extremely liberal tendencies" and his support of decisions that amounted to "judicial legislation," but these witnesses tended to oppose most civil rights rulings of the Court for the past fifty years. This did not help Thurmond's cause in stopping Cox, and in the end, only eleven senators voted against Cox's appointment to the court. Nine of the eleven were Republican. The other two no votes were from the "twin devils from Mississippi," as Ralph Yarborough called them: longtime Democratic senators James Eastland and John Stennis. Still, eighty-six senators voted to confirm Cox, with three senators, all from the South, absent for the vote.

As for Dolan, Kennedy immediately nominated him for the first open position on the Ninth Circuit Federal Court of Appeals, which covered the western region of the United States. It was an appropriate slot, Kennedy believed, since Dolan originally hailed from Colorado. Thurmond and the Republicans seemed to care less about judicial positions below the U.S. Supreme Court, and so Dolan sailed through without a dissenting vote. Kennedy, after congratulating Dolan, told the newest federal appellate justice that the next Supreme Court opening would go his way. Then Kennedy whispered to his longtime advisor, "Joe, just keep your nose clean! Don't do anything that I keep doing—like making myself look like some radical!"

Appellate Justice Dolan replied, "Don't worry about me, Bob. It's *you* who needs to keep on being who you are—or else I'll stop keeping my nose clean and go marching with the kids outside the White House!"

At the second weekly cabinet meeting, Secretary of Interior Stewart Udall presented plans for federal programs to clean the air and waterways in nearly every American city. "It will be a mini–Marshall Plan," he said to his open-mouthed fellow cabinet members and presidential advisers, "except this time, we help Mother Nature in our own backyard." Udall detailed how he had been in touch with the then radical group, the Sierra Club, as well as the Wilderness Society, the National Geographic Society, the Audobon Society, and particular senators and members of Congress about "restoring lost natural beauty, cleaning lakes and streams, and improving air quality."

To promote the environment, Udall and Senators Gaylord Nelson, a Democrat from Wisconsin, and Mark Hatfield, a Republican from Oregon, among others, were already planning a nationwide pro-environmental rally on April 21, 1969, which would have been the 131st birthday of naturalist John Muir. The idea was to celebrate something they would call "Earth Day."

President Kennedy said, "Hold it, Stewart. How can we possibly get anything done so quickly—and push for new laws on something we haven't had much legislation on so far? I don't want a repeat of the Poor People's March of last year, for heaven's sake! Remember, we have the continuing situation in Vietnam that can still fall apart with a murder of anyone by any side. There have already been some killings of pro–Viet Cong and pro-Thieu mayors in some villages— and Bill Buckley and Ronald Reagan are already saying we gave away the store to the Communists! As we just announced this morning, we have to do our best to support the right of people to organize unions in the South and get labor reform through Congress—which isn't going to be easy, to say the least! And this? Now?"

Udall started to speak, but Kennedy cut him off. "Stew, this is not like repealing a couple of sections of already existing laws and putting in a few lines here or there—that's what the labor reform bill is all about. What you're proposing is writing whole new laws like we haven't done before! How far are we with legislation? Which department, or departments, will enforce the legislation? Where's our budget for it? How much support is there on Capitol Hill? I can't take a loss now on anything until at least after the May elections in Vietnam and the labor reform battle. I remember the Endangered Species Act that was passed last year—or maybe two years ago—but this is a different animal altogether, if you don't mind my little pun. Why don't you ask your friends to plan a big event for *next* year? Whether Muir would be 131 or 132 is not a big deal, is it? Let's get the legislation written, with labor's input—Walter can tell you we've got to be really careful here! So let's get this done right the first time with a wide coalition, especially with labor. The Hollywood liberals in California will love it, this year or next, but the votes are going to depend upon regular lunch-bucket folks' reactions—"

"Mr. President—" Udall knew he had to break in or lose everything. "Sir, working people are worried about their drinking water, the quality of the air they breathe, for their children—"

Reuther broke in, "Yes, Mr. Udall, I agree. However, I also know how workers can be scared about losing their jobs if you shut down smoke stacks, not only in the auto industry, but in textiles, lumber, and in the chemical and oil fields."

Kennedy nodded to Udall and said, "Stewart, as you know, Walter is wise enough to support nature protections, and yet he knows the dangers we're facing if we do not gear up a bit better on this. I read where Franklin Roosevelt once had some labor folks in his office ask for his support out front on an issue—I can't recall what it was. The point is, Roosevelt said, 'Get out there and agitate. Put my feet to the fire! Call me a son of a bitch for not moving fast enough!' That's what I'd tell your nature friends out there. Say I am against it or don't care enough. That will test whether you're right that the nation is ready for this—and I will publicly support your legislation when the time comes."

Udall, turning red as much from being dressed down as from anger, kept his cool enough to say, "There's a fellow, Brower, I believe, he's on the Sierra Club's board—he's a longtime nature activist—he said he had no faith in you or any administration to solve this problem. He's already saying what you say you want us to say, but I can't believe we want that kind of criticism. I hate to think—"

Kennedy laughed sarcastically. "So, this Brower fellow wants to play Malcolm X to others' Martin King—and I get to be Lyndon Johnson on this? Fine! I love this! Let Brower rail! If he does his job right, it'll make your job easier to convince Congress to support these laws—and even make Reuther's job organizing workers easier." The president sat back, put his hands behind his head, and said, "Blessed are the radicals, for they make the rest of us look reasonable!"

The gathering laughed at the quip. Udall, having been shot down and essentially humiliated, forced his laugh. It hurt more because a newly elected

Bob Kennedy, in November 1968, had told Udall that if he returned to Washington, D.C., to become interior secretary, Udall could rewrite environmental policy "to your heart's desire."

"A fickle heart beats in the new president, I guess," said Stewart Udall to his brother Morris, a congressman from New Mexico, later that day at lunch. And that was the kindest thing he said about the president during that lunch.

Secretary of Labor Reuther, meanwhile, was feeling half his nearly sixty-two years after hearing Kennedy say labor reform was the top domestic priority. After the meeting he called two of his former lieutenants in the UAW, Leonard Woodcock and Irving Bluestone, to come east for a special meeting. "Bring Leslie," "Bring Barry," Reuther said separately to each man, referring to their children, Leslie Woodcock and Barry Bluestone. "I need the kids' help with something their radical friends can really sink their teeth into!"

Leonard Woodcock, still smarting a bit at Reuther's betrayal in supporting Doug Fraser as Reuther's successor at the UAW, knew this was not a time for recrimination. Woodcock never said so, but he largely blamed his daughter, Leslie, for his failure to succeed Reuther. For it was Leslie Woodcock, as a student protester in 1967, who challenged Reuther over the Vietnam War one evening during a family holiday dinner among the Reuthers, Bluestones, and Woodcocks. She demanded to know why Walter Reuther refused to speak out against the war in Vietnam. Reuther replied that he could not oppose Johnson's military actions in Vietnam at that point because there were important collective bargaining negotiations coming up between the auto workers union and the auto companies. Reuther said he needed Johnson's support for those negotiations.

Leslie screamed at Reuther, "You've said it! You've finally said it!"

When Reuther asked what she meant by "it," she told him, "For fifty cents an hour extra in the pay envelope, you'll let thousands of Vietnamese and Americans die in the war."

Reuther denied he meant anything of the sort. An awkward silence followed and dinner ended shortly thereafter. [1]

Confrontations like these had raged across America during many family dinners in 1967 and 1968, particularly in families in which the parents had supported labor, the New Deal, and the war in Vietnam, while the children opposed the war, were impatient with labor, and were now supporting outright socialism—or something close to it. The entire New Deal coalition of labor and the civil rights movement was in danger of collapse in the last year or so of the Johnson administration, but there was another chance to save that coalition.

From Leonard Woodcock's personal perspective, however, the Bobby Kennedy era had not started well. In mid-November 1968, when Leonard Woodcock learned that Reuther had endorsed Fraser to succeed him at the UAW, Woodcock recalled that holiday family dinner at Irving Bluestone's house in 1967. Father never said anything to daughter, but daughter knew, too. She sat next to her parents during Kennedy's speech at the inauguration and wished she could make it up to her father somehow, now that the nation—or at least labor union members and student radicals—might no longer be so sharply divided.

Answering Reuther's call, the Woodcocks and the Bluestones arrived in Washington, D.C., on a particularly blustery February morning. Reuther was at the airport to greet them. Reuther warmly shook Barry Bluestone's hand, then hugged Leslie Woodcock and said, "No hard feelings, I hope." Leslie wanted to cry, not quite because she felt remorse over the truth of her statements almost two years before—she thought to herself, I was right, wasn't I?—but because she knew now if she had just stayed quiet at one dinner gathering, her father might have become the head of the UAW. She choked up and shook her head before sputtering out, "No, sir." Reuther thought she was simply shivering in the cold and wind of the day, but Woodcock and his daughter knew better.

Reuther hugged her again and said, "Leslie," and then he put his arm around the younger Bluestone, "and Barry, I've got something exciting for you both—and for as many of your friends as you can ask! Let me open the car and get the heat on!"

Driving to his new home in Chevy Chase, Maryland, Reuther explained the president's wholehearted support for the union organizing campaign in the South. He talked about Congress passing strong labor reform legislation, probably later in the spring, and the national labor board already preparing regulations to streamline union contests. He turned back to look at Leslie and Barry and said, "This is really going to be the next level of the civil rights movement."

The two student radicals were still too cold to roll their eyes, but were nonplussed to hear Reuther's comment. They considered Reuther better than most labor leaders but still rather tepid on civil rights for minorities. Reuther kept looking forward as he drove through the ice and snow but now and again darted his eyes to look at them in the rearview mirror. "I know you may not see it, perhaps especially coming from me, but please think about what I'm saying! The unions that do exist in the South are horribly racist. The carpenters union, well, I guess most of the building trades down there, supported Wallace from the get-go, and while they made positive noises once Yarborough was chosen as vice president by Bob—I mean the president— their hearts, and some ballots, I bet, were still with Wallace.

"If," he continued, "we are going south, we have to do *double* organizing. We can't organize only white workers. We have to organize black and white workers—*together!* Otherwise, we can't reform the Democratic Party leadership down south. The president knows that, and you two definitely know that. The war in Vietnam will end, or at least our military involvement will end. We heard you! We heard you! We now need to work *together*—I mean this—on improving life for workers, white and especially black in the South. There will be vote drives for political voter registration, not just vote drives for union representation. There will be federal troops down there early, I suspect, and it could be dangerous—the president didn't talk about this, and we didn't talk about it with him, either, 'cause he's focused on the fight in Congress for labor law reform."

He kept talking about racial equality, about Martin Luther King's Poor People's March and how union organizing was "the real McCoy." He spoke of how King would have supported this organizing drive and how he and Yarborough had already lined up the support of the civil rights leadership, starting with the NAACP's Herbert Hill, A. Phillip Randolph, Ralph Abernathy, the young but self-centered (according to Abernathy and Randolph) firebrand Jesse Jackson, and even Mike Hamlin, one of the black (and, according to Reuther, militant) union leaders inside the UAW.

Reuther pulled up to his home and said, "I was going to wait to talk about this until we got you to our new home—I figured we'd talk about the weather and family in the car—but I just couldn't wait. I need to know now! Are you interested?"

Barry and Leslie both started to say yes, but Barry was more assertive than Leslie for once. Barry said, "Yes, sir! This is my dream come true, Mr. Reuther. I have been talking about this for the last year with Todd Gitlin, who was running the SDS. The black sanitation workers' strike in Memphis last spring got me thinking about it as a real possibility . . . "

Leslie broke in. "You didn't have to convince me either, sir. With Dad on the SOC, I had already asked him about it. I just needed to hear about your commitment to equality and jobs for black workers. And you know there are a lot of women in those textile and farming jobs, right? Not just the men." There was a small dare in her voice.

Reuther said, "Yes, sir—I mean—ma'am, Leslie. There is power for *every-one* in a union—black, white, men, women, you name it. That's what this is all about."

Fathers and children smiled and hugged as they left the Reuther-mobile. "It might as well have been Los Angeles in July," Leslie recalled years later. "That's how warm our bodies, hearts, and minds felt walking up the steps to the Reuther home that day."

Later, over cocoa, Reuther gave his one cautionary note: "There's one thing I ask. If Sam Ervin or one of those senators says an awkward thing on race, remember! They all understand the message that they need to move toward integration and labor rights. They may slip up from time to time, particularly Sam, who once went to the U.S. Supreme Court holding a Bible to fight for that son of a—pardon me, Leslie, well, you know, Roger Milliken and his textile companies. We can't punish those senators or other politicians for any misstep while we stand on 'purity.' We have to keep our eyes on the prize, as

Phil Randolph told me years ago. They appear, so far, to be with us. If they stop being with us, we'll all know, and we'll evaluate our next strategy. The first test is if the labor reform bill doesn't pass by May of this year," meaning 1969.

Leslie looked mildly cool at this but said, "That's fine, sir. We want to win this time—together." Inside she added, Leslie, don't hurt Dad again. Who would have thought a year and a half ago we'd be here talking about labor reform and racial integration of workers in the South—and peace accords already signed in Vietnam?

Walter Reuther's eyes welled up with tears as he sipped the hot cocoa his wife, May, had prepared. He thought to himself, I've had more second chances than any man deserves. May came in from the kitchen and asked, "Seconds, anyone?" It might as well have been a Norman Rockwell painting at that moment, but reality does, in fact, mirror the most hopeful and romantic art more than the sophisticated cynics can ever understand.

In early March 1969, the Southern Organizing Committee began to send its scouts to get jobs in the textile mills, the cotton fields, the southern factories of northern businesses, the power companies, and other places ripe for union organizing. Local 1199, a militant hospital workers' union in New York City, was already in contact with hospital workers in North Carolina who had been trying to organize a union there since 1968.

The SOC set up organizing seminars and meetings to train organizers and to teach tactics for staff in handling labor organizing drives. In the South, there were internal union meetings where the word was clear: "If you want to strengthen your union, then you have to integrate the Negroes, not let the boss use them as strikebreakers."

To make sure this would be the reality, the civil rights leadership had met with the SOC already and sent word out that unions in the North would pay blacks *not* to take jobs during strikes—as long as they helped in the organizing drives. A few black preachers were invited to the union meetings to make clear that white union men and women could count on solidarity from "your Negro neighbors"—none dared to say "brothers and sisters," having been warned by labor organizers against saying that phrase for now.

In the North and West, there were organization meetings for the less radical elements in the SDS, led by Todd Gitlin as well as student antiwar groups and leaders who were looking for a new "political kick" after returning to school from winter break—only to find America's war in Vietnam nearly over. Included in the meetings, at the demand of the student groups, were members from black and Latino liberation groups, and women's liberation student groups, which were just forming. The latter proved the most contentious during the meetings. ("We are not making coffee, damn it!" screamed a young Barbara Ehrenreich at a union leader who asked her, politely, he thought. "And don't call me a 'little girl,' either!" she said when he tried to apologize as if he was talking to his own daughter, who at home was starting to scream at him as well. As Ehrenreich later said, "All we wanted was some respect as fellow workers and organizers—and it took a martyr or two to get that respect, I hate to say.")

The SOC leadership, headed by a reinvigorated Leonard Woodcock, was in no mood to make enemies with the "kids" this time around. At his first meeting with the student organizers, Woodcock said he was very heartened to see the "commitment of youth to economic justice for all." And in one meeting, Woodcock and Hamlin made the coffee, with some help from other mostly older male labor leaders—and daughter Leslie, too. That broke, and began to melt, the ice between generations and the sexes—at that meeting at least.

Woodcock, with the advice of AFL-CIO Vice President Lane Kirkland and Michael Harrington, a socialist intellectual and activist close to labor, tried to keep Communist Party members from attending the training sessions, however. Woodcock demanded that each student specifically sign a statement saying he or she had never been a member of the Communist Party or any group advocating violence and had no intention of joining such an organization.

This almost caused a breakdown of relations between the students and the unions. Mediators were brought in to hold the student-labor coalition together, including Robert Hall, Molly Yard, and Joseph Lash, former student radicals from the '30s who had led "Union Rides" to organize mine workers in the South during that decade, as well as Mike Hamlin and Jesse Jackson.

The uneasy solution, first offered by Robert Hall, was that the students who were Communists or Black Panthers or such specifically resign from those organizations, cut their hair, and avoid any clothes or insignia bearing any "scent of Communism or radicalism." Hall, a native of Mississippi and a former Communist accused of heresy against the Communist Party in the mid-1940s, said quite bluntly at one point, "This is no different than the '30s, Ah hate to tell y'all. The same 'cafeteria Communist' debatin' societies, the same rhetoric Ah hear in this room. Kids, Ah hear it and feel what you say. It's just this, though: These workin' people down there are just gonna be turned off—is that how the young'uns say it?—turned off by all this rhetoric! And how do Ah—and Joe and Molly and others from our era—know that? Because we got whooped in our rears by the sheriffs *and* the workers—white workers mostly—when we were students tryin' to organize workers down South! And Ah was a good ol' Southern boy, too, from Missasippah! It's already bad enough you're mostly Yankees, with New York accents, some o' ya's!

"Unless ya wanna get killed—and it won't be just one o' ya, it'll be others too, so don't get all martyred now either—we have to talk about how we com-mun-i-cate with noncollege working people who stay behind after our little tour and who have, in the past, seen organized labor—I hate to say this, fellas," he turned briefly to the union leaders, "—fail miserably down there!" Turning back to the students, he concluded: "Times are changin', though, and we expect to win this time—but we can't repeat our mistakes that make it easy for people to stay away from us like we was lepers! And, hate to say it, but bein' in the Communist Party is a big red flag that says, 'Stay away from me, you workers, if ya know what's good for ya!'"

An SDSer and Communist Party organizer for the left-leaning United Electrical, Radio, and Machine Workers union—known by most as the U.E.— spoke up. "Mr. Hall, my family's from Tennessee, sir, and I understand what you're saying. I hope Al Lannon—he's a peach! You'd love him, Mr. Hall, you really would—I hope Lannon forgives me, but I'll quit the party—I haven't been a member long anyway. People down there need unions as much as they need the air to breathe—and if you notice, I already cut my hair, too!"

The crowd of labor leaders and students wildly applauded, but later that night, doubts remained on both sides. Can we trust Commie kids? Can we trust these old, white, labor guys not to sell us out? Such were the questions on both sides.

The first Union Freedom Rides began in late April 1969. The male students, with short hair (some with crewcuts!), put on button-down-shirts and slacks. The women wore flowery dresses. All made sure they were scrubbed clean. The union leaders told them if they blended in, it would be harder to shoot them in broad daylight. "Is it my neighbors' kids or them Commie kids?" they'll ask themselves, said Rich Trumka, the young lawyer and firebrand from the United Mine Workers. Trumka added, "And make damned sure the suits and dresses are old and used. New suits and dresses will make ya stick out like you were wearin' nothin'!"

Northern labor union leaders had long private talks with racist Southern union leaders and told them, "Get with the program or you're out!" Some got out, while those who stayed remained a greater worry for the SOC, since one never knew if they were feeding information to the Ku Klux Klan, the local police (sometimes rampant with Klan members), or the employers in a show of "regional solidarity."

Longtime "liberal" Southern newspaper editors, Harry Golden and Hodding Carter, among others, opened their homes to the students. Golden said to Reuther, however, "It may take a Goodman-Cheney-Schwerner incident, God forbid!"[2]

Hodding Carter—a very distant relative of then Georgia state legislator Jimmy Carter, added gravely, "You realize, Walter, these kids are cannon fodder for the *real* union and civil rights organizers, don't you?"

Reuther never directly responded, but nodded his head and then shrugged his shoulders. He said finally, "We will protect these union riders with federal troops if we have to. This is war, after all, and we are going to win—we *better* win!"

Chapter 15

SAIGON BYE-GONE,
HELLO VIET CONG

Meanwhile, there were still American troops in Vietnam, though less and less every week. In the several months leading to the May 1969 elections, the U.S. troops under General David Hackworth suffered just over twenty-five casualties. Each of these deaths was given banner headlines in the American press, which initially undercut support for President Kennedy's policies.

Evans and Novak, William Buckley, and other extreme anti-Communist political pundits were demanding "massive retaliation" to avenge the "Red murderers," even though more than half of the troops killed turned out to have been killed by right-wing "death squads" organized, some thought, by former President Thieu and his immediate allies.

Thieu and other former South Vietnamese high officials knew that there was still a strong constituency in the American military and political corridors to come back and finish the fight against the Viet Cong and the North Vietnamese. Convincing Americans that the Commies were the ones killing U.S. soldiers was seen as the best way to inflame American anger and overturn the 1969 Paris Peace Accords. They were shocked that the Pentagon investigated the murders deeply enough to uncover the Thieu-supporting death squads, considering the incident at My Lai was still not disclosed to the American public.

Thieu and his supporters recognized that support for them in the South Vietnamese villages was always lacking. They reasoned the "death squad" strategy made more sense because inducing fear in the villages was better than suddenly trying to promise the peasants that everything would be great if the peasants freely elected them to office.

While the American press focused more on American casualties, the death squads had a great deal of success in assassinating Viet Cong supporters and sympathizers in small towns and villages. The most prominent murdered Viet Cong was Tran Van Giau, who was murdered in an open square by an ex–Viet Cong—and current Thieu supporter—who said Tran had killed his brother during Viet Cong purges in the early 1950s.

The Viet Cong were under strict orders from presidential candidate and Viet Cong Justice Minister Truong Nhu Tang[1]—backed reluctantly by the North Vietnamese—not to fight back. "We must avoid inflaming American war sentiment. Two or three more months adding martyrs to our cause is not a great sacrifice, including my own martyrdom, if necessary," said Truong. Still, some Viet Cong fought back, and not only did they kill pro-Thieu forces, they also killed a few Americans who were seen as more likely backing Thieu—or General Minh, who, having earlier replaced Thieu as president, was running in the elections under strong pressure from President Kennedy.

President Minh publicly and privately demanded that the electoral monitoring commission fully investigate the various killings of Vietnamese and Americans. "Only truth will suffice," he said simply. The commission members, prepared for this contingency in advance, had agreed among themselves that "paths should follow to wherever the truth is located," according to Ted Sorensen in his later memoirs.

Sorensen and Corson, the two Americans on the commission, were pleasantly surprised at the honesty shown by the North Vietnamese commissioners, who included Truong Chinh—a leading military theorist on "people's war"—in denouncing Communist-inspired murders.

The irony of so many male Viet Cong being assassinated in various villages and towns in the three or four months before the election was that various women—wives, sisters, and in some cases, mothers—came forward as Viet Cong candidates. This put a lid on death squad activities—killing unarmed women was much more difficult for the death squads.

The turning point in solidifying American public opinion in favor of maintaining the election course came when the first woman Viet Cong candidate, Ngo Thi Tuyen, was murdered at a political rally in Saigon on April 19, 1969. Ngo had announced her candidacy for mayor of a small town outside of Saigon two weeks before. She had said, in announcing her candidacy, "At no other time in Vietnam's history has the will of the people become more necessary for national survival. When even the gentlest woman I once was, and long to become again, could be inspired to enter the male world of politics, and yes, face the potential of death by violence—which violence we must all now renounce!—it is clear that ending this war must become a reality."

Lost in most of the American reporting was that Ngo had been a seasoned Viet Cong soldier, attacking U.S. planes and supplying Communist-backed Vietnamese defenses on a key point along the famous "Highway 1" road and bridge artery that ran through North and South Vietnam. She was not a woman who had recently entered the "male" political scene.

American reporters were often ignorant of the names of most Viet Cong and often retained certain assumptions about "subordinated peasant women." This led them to continue to picture Ngo as a simple woman running for office for reasons of "civic duty" to her country, to use a typical phrase from American reporters.

This ignorance, and leaping assumptions, sensationalized the story. Even conservative pundits from Bill Buckley to radio and television host Joe Pyne shared in the ignorance and assumptions, talking about "Tuyen" as "caught in the cross-fire" and how "Tuyen paid an awful price for being an ignorant dupe of the Viet Cong." California Governor Ronald Reagan, hoping more than knowing, suggested that the Viet Cong had killed Tuyen in order to make Thieu's forces "look bad."[2]

The commission's formal finding, released on April 26, 1969, that Ngo was killed by the death squads associated with Thieu, was a fatal blow to Thieu's campaign. It also increased sympathy and support among the peasants for the Viet Cong.

The election results, as certified by official European and American observers, were as follows: the National Liberation Front (NLF, or Viet Cong), 48 percent; General Minh and his Unity Party, 35 percent; and President Thieu's National Party, 9 percent; with a small Buddhist party receiving much of the remaining 8 percent.[3]

South Vietnam had, nominally, a parliamentary system in place. Therefore, the NLF needed to enter into a coalition in order to govern. President-elect Truong's first victory statement included an offer to General Minh to form a coalition government including the NLF and the Unity Party. "It is clear that our countrymen are still divided," said Truong, "and that even some of our supporters believe reunification cannot be immediate. While we reaffirm our commitment to our brothers and sisters in the North, who have supported us so gallantly during the struggle, that reunification is coming, we must reunify ourselves first in the southern portion of our nation at this difficult, but hopeful, moment."

Officials and courtiers in Washington and Hanoi were in shock, but for different reasons. In Hanoi, North Vietnamese General Giap was outraged that Truong had not sought "permission" from the North to speak so boldly. He exclaimed at a Communist Politburo meeting in Hanoi, "How dare Truong act as a Western bourgeois politician and not submit to the collective will of the people?"—by which he meant, "the party." Giap then said, "It is bad enough to have submitted the struggle to a bourgeois vote when the only true path is the armed struggle."

General Tran Van Tra, who was expected to take over the military forces of the South Vietnamese army—and the NLF itself—after the election of the NLF,[4] said, "The NLF has always had an independent influence and bourgeois tendency, and it must be removed as one removes a wart from our bodies!"

Yet another Politburo member said, "Perhaps the Americans should have continued bombing the South!" A gasp went up at that remark, but the member continued, "Comrades! Do you not see what I mean? The so-called glorious Tet Offensive last year was a failure in terms of strategy for our southern comrades. We now have more of *our* Democratic Republic of

Vietnam forces down south—as replenishment troops—than we had before the Offensive because the Americans killed so many southern comrades and civilians. If the Americans had kept up its attacks on the South, as some Americans still propose, the South would need more of our troops. And then the people would have only one choice: us or the Americans!"

Ho Chi Minh listened but said nothing. Ho knew he was dying, but fought with his body to live to see the reunification of his nation. Ho allowed the denunciation of Truong and the NLF to continue, but then put up his hand and said, "Comrades, comrades. We must not flail over what has been done. Truong spoke as the leader of the victors, and in this victory, we must look to share power, at least for now. We are, alas, playing in the fields of bourgeois elections, which tend to give succor to the forces of reaction and war. We must ride this bourgeois tiger for a short time more while Comrade Truong goes about the task of reunifying the South. Many there have forgotten they are missing half their body by remaining separate from their Northern brothers and sisters. And to my comrade who says it is better the Americans keep bombing, does that comrade think the Americans who want to bomb are happy with these bourgeois election results? Time, comrades, time is on our side." As he said this, Ho thought to himself, Time is on our side, but will there be time for *me* to see reunification?

Ho guessed correctly about the American reaction to the elections. The victory of the Viet Cong landed like napalm among American foreign policy circles, American media commentators, and the Oval Office. How, Americans wondered, could so many people—almost half!—have voted for blood-thirsty Communist killers? Is this what almost 24,000 American soldiers had died for, to see so many South Vietnamese support Communists?

War hawk columnist Robert Novak's prose in the *Washington Star* was frothing from the page: "This election had to be a fraud, and sources inside the government of South Vietnam and the United States confirm that the Reds committed massive election fraud. The Kennedy administration is not happy at the result either, having supported the hapless General Minh. However, as with his entirely weak and pitiful approach to world affairs, particularly in Vietnam, Robert Kennedy—who once boasted that he would have been a revolutionary if he were poor, heaven help us!—will no doubt endorse this Viet Cong 'victory' at the ballot box."

Walter Lippmann, an elitist courtier who wore the crown of "dean of journalists," wrote in the *Washington Post* that, "Kennedy naively thought he could secure victory through elections in South Vietnam. Instead, he is on the verge of a slow-burning Bay of Pigs. Unlike his brother, who consistently showed the proper level of concern regarding the threat of Communism, the world will see whether Robert Kennedy has the ability to understand the threat to freedom arising from the Viet Cong victory in Vietnam following these so-called elections."

President Kennedy was indeed shaking his head with deep concern, as much on the domestic political fallout as the foreign policy implications. He always thought General Minh would win the plurality, despite CIA estimates that the Viet Cong were ahead.[5] Sorensen and Corson, who had recently returned to Washington with their final pre-election report, had shocked Kennedy with their assessment that the Viet Cong would win a majority of the vote. They also noted, within the commission, that the Viet Cong were developing a sense of independence and resentment against the North. "It was clear from day one who were Viet Cong and who were North Vietnamese representatives," said Corson.

Kennedy called a meeting with Corson, Bowles, the O Boys, Jack Newfield, and Ted Sorensen. The purpose was to prepare for a press confer-ence to discuss the results of the election in Vietnam. After reading the transcript of Truong's statement, Kennedy turned to Corson and asked, "You don't think we can really work with the Viet Cong, do you? Do you really believe the Viet Cong are independent from Hanoi?"

Corson said, "Sir, I can't say anything for certain with these people. I do know this, though. General Hackworth told me the Viet Cong were easier to deal with and were more cordial than Thieu's folks, and sometimes Minh's supporters in the last couple of months. The Viet Cong sent flowers and a note of apology when their loonies killed the first couple of American sol-diers—they didn't send one *every* time, I should say. The local Viet Cong–led villages cooperated overall with our boys. Again, there were definitely excep-tions—but better than the Thieu bunch, I can tell you that much, again from Hackworth, at least. We had a defector from the death squads tell our com-mission the death squads were completely orchestrated by Thieu and Marshal Ky—we couldn't confirm enough of it to go public, though. Some leaks did appear in the international press, but luckily our reporters didn't cover it—on Mr. Sorensen's request, I might add. I hate the press myself—always in the damned way, and they never get it right even when you spoon-feed them! We won't know the whole story for a while yet—but my hunch is that this Truong fellow may really be seein' the light and wants to tread real careful with the Reds up north—I don't know, though . . . "

Bowles quickly doused a small smile of agreement and solemnly said to the president, "Mr. President, we do have more than a hunch that President-elect Truong means what he says. I spoke with an aide to General Minh, who you know had to be talked into running for office—the general didn't want to lose his neutrality for the elections, but we didn't have anyone else with his stature to run against the Viet Cong, or NLF, as we better start calling them in public. Sir, the aide said that President-elect Truong is known as a man of his word and says Truong comes from a family that has supported the South Vietnamese government, not the Viet Cong, over the years. There is precedent, we know from the Rand report, for reconciliation between the warring factions. I recall reading where Diem was thinking of starting talks with the North before he was . . . well . . . overthrown in that coup . . . " Bowles forgot, in his desire to provide information, that he was talking with a president who, as attorney general, had endorsed that overthrow of Diem, perhaps just for that reason.

Kennedy stiffened, hating to be reminded of the coup that had occurred so close in time to his brother's slaying. "I honestly can't recall anything other than Diem wasn't winning this thing for us, and we believed the generals in South Vietnam knew better for their countrymen. . . . " He then shook his head and looked down at the floor, not wanting to discuss the past.

Bowles noticed this and returned to the immediate political and diplomatic issue. "Sir, the immediate question is, what are we going to say in response to this election result and President-elect Truong's statement? We have to say something. Reporters are calling me to respond to those who are already saying that we lost Vietnam—"

"What?" Newfield shouted. "By letting people choose their own destiny? Elections are the *first* freedom, damn it! If people choose differently than we do, or if they are divided—hell, we've had elections in our history where presidents didn't win more than 50 percent, haven't we? And we had elections here in America where only white property owners voted, for chrissakes! Who are they to lecture—"

"Jack, Jack," Kennedy said in a calming voice, surprising himself. He was set to blow up at Bowles' last statement, too, but Newfield's outburst helped him keep his cool. "Don't get too concerned—yet. I'll make a statement that will be clear and firm tomorrow morning."

And he did. Kennedy called a press conference for the next morning. There, the president admitted the United States was not pleased with the results of the election because, he said, "no party won a majority, nor was the neutral unity candidate, General Minh, the winner of the plurality." However, contrary to "rumors" published in the United States, there was "no evidence of any significant irregularities in the electoral process, according to our own observers, the French observers, and our intelligence analysts. This is the first election in South Vietnamese history where there can be no reasonable quarrel with the process."

President-elect Truong, said President Kennedy, was to "be congratulated for his moderate stance toward potential unification with the North Vietnamese, and we expect him to make good on his promise to preserve and promote free institutions in South Vietnam. We also note our pleasure at seeing the Viet—I mean, the National Liberation Front—offer a ruling coalition with General Minh and the Unity Party. At this time, it is up to the people of South Vietnam and North Vietnam to make good on the promise of peace after this election. I am not able, however, to answer questions at this time."

To buttress the position of the fairness of the elections in Vietnam, Kennedy sent Chester Bowles to Capitol Hill for a private national security briefing on intelligence data showing a higher percentage of support, and sympathy, for the Viet Cong throughout South Vietnam and Saigon than had showed up in the election results. Corson and Sorensen spoke of potential rifts between the Viet Cong and the North Vietnamese leadership, as they had with the president.

Senator Barry Goldwater, unlike other conservatives, refused to denounce the election results as a fraud. However, he continued to express surprise that essentially half the South Vietnamese people would choose Communism. He said to Ev Dirksen, loudly enough to be heard by others, "I'm glad we didn't keep fighting there, Ev, if at least half the people—probably some of those General Minh supporters were leaning Red—didn't want us there. We need to do a better job next time with these sorts of people, that's all I have to say!"

After the private session with Bowles, Corson, and Sorensen, Goldwater decided he had more to say to reporters waiting outside. Goldwater denounced "those who criticize our nation's president and our nation's foreign policy based upon innuendo and petty politics. We have secret information—I'm sad to say that it must be kept secret to protect our sources—that shows the Viet Cong have legitimacy regarding the extent of their votes, however odious their Communist beliefs. It is up to us as Americans, to work with moderate forces—if we can find any—to make sure freedom prevails in South Vietnam. The point of our efforts there was a full and free election, and we appear to have succeeded, at least so far, by most reputable accounts."

Then Goldwater, as he often did in his career, went that one step beyond diplomacy and tact. "And let me say one thing to my Senate colleagues and to those conservative friends who tell me I have left my senses: I hope to God the Viet Cong never unify with those darned Communists! I get the feeling Mr. Truong is starting to learn the truth about Communists and Communism!"

Bowles and Kennedy, as well as Ev Dirksen, heaved a collective "What?!" in total disbelief when reporters informed them of Goldwater's remarks. Kennedy said to Bowles afterwards, "Damn! Damn it to *hell!* Why did Barry say that!? That may f—up this whole thing! Now Truong is *really* gonna feel the pressure from the North—who still have troops down south—and those Viet Cong to the left of Truong! Whose side is Barry on?!"

Bowles said softly, "He would have been a terrible president, that much is clear." Then he mumbled, "Too honest in his feelings."

"I heard that, Chet," said a perturbed President Kennedy. "I'm honest about *my* feelings, too—I just don't go off spouting them in broad daylight in front of a worldwide audience when important diplomatic issues hang in the balance! Well, the only good thing that happened today is our labor bill passed. Maybe that will blow away coverage of Barry's statement." He thought to himself, Maybe? Better make that extremely doubtful.

Chapter 16

SOUTHERN DISCOMFORT

The labor reform bill did, indeed, pass on May 8, 1969. The president announced he would sign the law immediately, which he did the next day. The new law contained language mandating that nonunion members whose wages and hours were under a union collective bargaining agreement must join the union, even if such persons were themselves antiunion. This federal law overruled any state laws known as "right-to-work" laws.

"Equal dues and membership for all those who gain from wage increases and other benefits of union representation is the only fair thing," said the president as he signed the bill into law. "To allow any one worker a free ride on the backs of those supporting the union is, to my mind, not what the American way is all about." Reuther was standing behind the president, who was seated at his desk in the Oval Office as he signed the bill into law. Some saw tears in Reuther's eyes when the president said those words, but Reuther denied it for the rest of his life anytime someone mentioned it.

The new federal labor reform law allowed unions to engage in "secondary boycotts" (also known as "sympathy" strikes in support of other unions on strike). It also relieved unions from all antitrust laws. The law further reaffirmed that courts were barred from issuing injunctions in labor disputes, leaving this to the National Labor Relations Board.[1]

There were compromises, however, with antiunion forces in Washington and the business community across the nation. First, the new law, in an effort to democratize both the Teamsters and the United Mine Workers, among other unions, required that all labor leader elections be decided by popular vote of the members of the union. The law also authorized the National Labor Relations Board to take over, through receiverships, recalcitrant unions, or those with a clearly established history of criminal corruption, such as, again, the Teamsters and the United Mine Workers.

George Meany, head of the AFL-CIO, adamantly opposed that requirement but was forcefully told by Secretary Reuther that this was "the only way to get enough votes to make it easier for the Southern congressmen and senators to vote for the bill."

Another new aspect of the reform law, which Reuther himself did not want, was allowing workers to check off, on their yearly dues statements, whether unions could spend dues money for political action purposes.

Reuther took a deep breath on that one, saying to Doug Fraser of his old UAW, "We better do a good job communicating with our workers that the five dollars we spend of their dues each year for politicking go to causes that benefit all workers—or else, we may have defunded ourselves!"[2]

A final portion of the bill, which was added as a rider after a personal appeal by President Kennedy and Secretary Reuther, put farm workers under the protection of the National Labor Relations Board for the first time. The money influence of farmers and growers in the West that had succeeded in keeping farm workers from having labor law protection for many decades was finally defeated in this growing pro-union political environment.

Cesar Chavez of the United Farm Workers union was specially invited by the president to the ceremony to celebrate the signing of the labor reform bill into law. During the ceremony, President Kennedy brought out grapes and asked, "Now, Mr. Chavez, we can eat these again, can't we?" Everyone in the room, reporters, politicians, and union leaders alike, heartily laughed and "dug into the grapes," as Reuther later said. That day, Chavez formally ended his labor-consumer boycott of grapes grown and harvested with non-union-represented workers, for he now had Federal legal protection for his workers' labor strikes.

Flush with the victory of the labor reform bill, more young students and postgraduates headed to the South to organize black and white workers. The initial strategy was for the white students to meet at white Baptist and Methodist churches. These were the two largest religious denominations in most of the South, and each had clergy sympathetic to unions and, less so, integration. Then there were to be joint meetings with black Baptist and Methodist clergy. The thought was to use religion and morality as a backdrop to lessen racial tensions and promote labor unions as a moral imperative.

Having a religious base appealed to Kennedy and to Walter Reuther, but it did not appeal to certain liberal, secular elements in the North and on the West Coast. However, television personality and liberal activist Steve Allen responded to that secular criticism in an interview with late-night talk show host Dick Cavett. Allen said he fully supported the inclusion of clergy and churches in the efforts to promote integration and to improve working conditions for white and black workers. "I, as a nonbeliever, fully support the efforts of the students, the unions, and our government with nearly any clergy . . . . If there is a church group that believes pumpkins give divine guidance to people, but they work hard and in good faith to help people overcome racism and help improve working conditions, I would support that church group. Abe Lincoln is reported to have said in a related context—and whether he did or not may be less relevant—'I care not for any man's religion whose dog and cat are not the better for it.'"

The first union drives took place in three different locations. A hospital workers' drive in North Carolina was coordinated with the militant hospital workers Local 1199 from New York. The other drives, directly supported by the AFL-CIO, involved two J. P. Stevens' textile mills, one with a predominately black workforce in Statesboro, Georgia, and one with a predominately white workforce in Roanoke Rapids, North Carolina.

These three were chosen because the workers in each place had been organizing for at least a year before the students and the AFL-CIO arrived, so it was harder for corporate America to argue that "union agitators stirred these local folks up."

J. P. Stevens, like other Southern businesses including Wal-Mart and Milliken Mills, was notoriously antiunion. Stevens, in particular, compiled a long and horrible record of labor law violations concerning wages, safety, and the firing of workers suspected of favoring labor unions. Roger Milliken's textile companies were hardly any better and sometimes worse. For example, after a union won representation in the 1950s in Darlington, South Carolina, Milliken closed down the mill where the workers had prevailed. Wal-Mart, befitting its white-collar, retail profile, had perfected management techniques of weeding out labor organizers through psychological testing, peer pressure to be "associates," not "employees," and requiring new "associates" to watch anti-union films as part of "orientation."

As unionists and civil rights workers knew, Southern businesses could also count on the local police to be brutal in suppressing civil rights or union demonstrations or strikes. This included jailing of organizers, physical threats, and turning the other way when gunshots were fired into activist households, mysterious fires burned activists' homes, and, in the 1960s and before, committing outright murder. And, of course, there were the various "white citizens' councils" and their notorious complements in the Ku Klux Klan who could be counted on for anything not traceable to regular law enforcement.

Under President Bob Kennedy, the combining of the movements for labor and civil rights was in essence a declaration of war on the Southern white business elite. To preserve their power, white business owners would, as Robert Stevens of J. P. Stevens said in early April 1969, " . . . stop at nothing to preserve our traditional, Southern way of life"—in other words, to keep out unions and to keep blacks under the boot of the whites.

Years later, in an interview with a university professor, Stevens said, "If it was just on racial grounds, I mighta gone along with Bob Kennedy after a point, since we had some good nigra workers at our company. But them unionists— lots o' Northerners and comm'nists, you know, with Red labor money behin' 'em—they was after our biz-ness, and Ah regret nothin' we did personally to protect ah-selves. Ah'm not talkin' 'bout violence by othahs, of course."

It didn't take long for the first martyrs for the combined movements to appear. On Sunday, June 19, 1969, just before midnight, explosions ripped through a small United Methodist black church just outside Statesboro,

Georgia. Most of the churchgoers, union supporters, and civil rights workers had gone home after a long day that had included prayer, organizing meetings, and a rally in the early evening.

The FBI later reported that the explosions came from several pounds of dynamite that were planted under the wooden church. Inside the church were seven people. Three of the seven were killed, and the remaining four were badly injured. The three people killed were Barry Bluestone, Addie Jackson, and Maurine Hedgepeth.[3]

Barry Bluestone's death was a natural focus for television coverage because, despite his radical views and actions before 1968, he was basically a "good boy" who had given up the style of dress common among young radicals in the '60s. More important, his father, Irving Bluestone, was a top respected national union official at the UAW.

Addie Jackson was an African American mother of two children who had lost her job during the early part of the union struggle at the Statesboro J. P. Stevens plant. Because Addie Jackson was a pretty, lighter-skinned woman, and unmarried at the time, there was talk of a sexual relationship between her and Barry Bluestone in local papers in Georgia just after their murders, but the talk was quelled in the national reaction. Jackson was almost ten years older than Bluestone and, in the words of one friend, "married to the union and not to any man—evermore!" The photos of Jackson with her children gave her a sympathetic persona that would have, in an earlier era, been ignored by the white national media. If the young Bluestone and Addie Jackson weren't an "item" in life, they were the personification of the "marriage" of the civil rights and labor union movements.

Maurine Hedgepeth came from a pro-union family in Roanoke Rapids, North Carolina. In a show of union solidarity, she had traveled by bus to Georgia for the rally that weekend. A frumpy-looking white lady, lacking in both prestige and glamour, her martyred life was not as widely trumpeted in the national media as the other two individuals. Yet, after her murder, her picture adorned nearly every Southern union hall and many other union halls where women were a major presence. Local union organizers mentioned her at nearly every black and white worker meeting to highlight that "we're all in this together," as Herbert Hill constantly said from his position within the NAACP.

Walter Reuther was unavailable for comment and refused to leave his home for the first three days after learning of Barry's murder. He was in a deep depression over the murder of the son of his friend. "I killed Barry! I killed him!" He kept repeating those words in a nightmarish mantra, sitting for hours with the shades drawn. He tried several times to call Irving in Michigan but kept hanging up the phone. It was left to May Reuther to speak with the Bluestones and to apologize for her husband not calling. Irving said, "It's alright, May. After shiva,[4] I'm coming to see Walter. He must understand, it wasn't his fault." Irving began to cry, as did May.

May said between tears, "He might listen to you, Irving. He won't listen to the president for goodness sakes, or me or even Leslie Woodcock. You know, ever since that Passover dinner two years ago, he's used Barry and Leslie as his moral barometers. . . . He always says, 'If Leslie and Barry think it's wrong . . . '" May began crying harder. "Why Barry?" she wailed, and now it was Irving who had to calm May.

"May, crying won't bring Barry back. I know." He breathed a deep sigh to clear his tears. "May, I keep telling myself, Barry died for his country! I have friends whose sons were killed in Vietnam. My son was killed in a war, too. A different war. One we knew we would have to fight right here at home. Walter and I talked about this before any of the students went down there. We just . . . we just didn't . . . May, I gotta go. I'll . . . talk . . . " He hung up.

Two minutes later, Thelma Bluestone called to apologize for Irving's failure to say goodbye. The two women wept together before they said goodbye to each other.

Ralph Yarborough went personally to the Reuther house, at May's request, to try to get Reuther out of his depression. Yarborough found his longtime supporter was unmovable in his sorrow. May told Yarborough about how Irving Bluestone had compared his son's death to a death in a war. Yarborough said, "That's it! Damn it! Why didn't Ah think o' that? Good God!"

May said, "What, Ralph, what?" Then she saw a gleam in his eye, and she was horror-struck. "Ralph, please don't exploit young Barry's death! Don't!" She was flashing anger and tears at the vice president.

Yarborough looked at May with a firm, serious stare. "May Reuther, Ah would nevah exploit *anyone!* It's just that Ah realized that Barry Bluestone, Addie Jackson, and Mrs. Hedgepeth died in a *war!* We honor war dead when they fight in battles overseas or when there's a civil war at home. But we never do *anything* to honor people who give their lives in a battle to help people earn a decent wage, or help people overcome racial prejudice. All the people who fight those battles get grief, or they get called bad names—if they're lucky! When they're not lucky, they're put in jail or killed. May, you and me must get Walter outta this house. He's a general in this war, and Ah'm countin' on him to help us win. When Ah spoke with Irving Bluestone, he said the same thing as you did, and you know, Ah didn't think o' what Ah'm thinking o' now. Ah just kept thinkin' 'bout how, if it was mah kid, Ah'd be cryin', too. But Walter has got to see this!"

With May Reuther following, Yarborough marched right into the darkened living room of the Reuther home, turned on the light, and said, "Secretary of Labor Walter Reuther, this country needs your command and needs you raht now!" He then said what he had told May.

Reuther said, "Ralph, I've thought of that, too. I thought I was . . . well, it made me feel like I didn't care about Barry, or Irving and Thelma . . . I knew Barry when he was a little boy . . . I . . . I . . . " He tried to fight back his tears but lost.

Yarborough said, "Tomorra, Walter, you are goin' back on the job. We got a rally to plan. Ah got an idea that will make sure this doesn't happen to anyone else's sons or daughters—and if it does, damn it, it's gonna be one o' them racist bastards doin' the cryin'!"

The Reuthers' mouths dropped in unison and in shock.

"Sorry," said a red-faced Yarborough. "Ah was in Dubya Dubya Two and we didn't take it lyin' down when one o' ours was killed. Guess Ah had one o' them flashbacks they call it. Sorry, folks." He said a quick goodbye and marched out of the Reuther home.

And remembering his days as a soldier, Yarborough continued marching straight over to the White House—well, driving to the White House, anyway. Once inside the Oval Office, he told President Kennedy, "Ah want to set up a big ol' rally in front o' the Lincoln Memorial with you, Mr. President, me, Walter Reuther, and a general or Admiral Moorer to speak about how those three people that died should be seen as real honest-to-goodness freedom fighters no different than if they went off to Germany in World War II—"

"Whoa, there, pardner!" said Kennedy. "You mean we're gonna compare our own South to Nazi Germany? Great! That oughta get some people riled up to vote for us in '72! Come on, Ralph. I know Walter's depressed over his friend's son's death, and believe me, you may not remember how I was when my brother was killed . . . " Kennedy paused and took a deep breath before speaking again. "Go plan a rally, but I'm not going out front like that, and neither are the generals."

Yarborough hesitated. He realized he better retreat a little, even though he was determined to make sure there was a memorial rally for these war heroes, as he saw them. "Sorry, Mr. President. You're raht. Ah guess Ah got carried away thinkin' 'bout those young people just tryin' to do good. Ah'll be planning somethin' and Ah'll let you know beforehand. We'll take this to the South rather than here in the capital. Now Ah understan' we need to be politically careful not to fan flames, but Mr. President, we gotta make sure Hoover and those FBI boys find those murderin' bastards—pardon mah French, if ya please—and get them in front o' a federal court jury and hang 'em . . . well, at least put 'em in jail for a long, long time!"

"Ralph, I thought you opposed the death penalty."

"Ah did, and Ah will always oppose it. Just not today or at least this moment, Mr. President." He smiled that winning smile, and Kennedy could only smile back.

"Do what you're gonna do, Ralph, but let's not get carried away, okay? I've already sent some National Guardsmen down there, and we've just called up more troops to go to Statesboro, too. God, I hope this isn't gonna be like Little Rock under Ike or worse . . . Fort Sumter . . . "

"Not yet, Mr. President. Ah think we're gonna beat the Old South with the New South this time. That's mah strategy."

Yarborough agreed not to follow through with the Lincoln Memorial idea, but he came up with a more wide-ranging alternative. He and Reuther, with Senator Gore of Tennessee, got on the phone and called country and western entertainers such as Roy Clark, Glen Campbell, Roger Miller, Tammy Wynette, Charley Pride (who was one of the few black country and western stars), and comedienne Minnie Pearl, plus the usual Hollywood and New York celebrities, to perform at civil rights and union marches and rallies in Charlotte, North Carolina, Birmingham, Alabama, and other points in and around the South. Yarborough appeared at the first one in Charlotte, after getting a bunch of his Southern military buddies together to show up with him. All of them, including Yarborough, wore their World War II uniforms—some fitting better than others—and Ralph made a speech that made the evening news.

In his speech, Yarborough expanded upon what he had said to May Reuther—with his corn pone eloquence—about those who fought and gave their lives to make this nation a better one. He talked about abolitionists, the founding fathers, union strikers in the late nineteenth and early twentieth centuries, and civil rights workers. Then he said, "To-naht, ladies and gentlemen, Ah wear this uniform to honor all those people who fought the wars at home so we can be proud o' our country when we have to fight the wars we have to fight abroad. Let's bow our heads in prayer for Barry Bluestone, Addie Jackson, and Maurine Hedgepeth. May their lives give meanin' to us and to our nation. Help us, God, to help everyone in this great land to always live up to our best principles and ideals. Amen."

As he said those words, all the uniformed men behind him took off their military caps and bowed their heads in attentive silence. The crowd went silent, too. Even the rednecks who had come to heckle were shocked into silence by the power of Yarborough's call to God and country and the sight of those men in uniform on the stage.

Yarborough then said, "Now, ladies and gentlemen, some great folks have come here—free o' charge—to entertain us tonight for the cause o' good wages at our workplaces and treatin' everyone as God's chillun'. Y'all made a donation in comin' here, and their playin' and dancin' and jokin' is their donation to you and our great country. So, let's get this show movin' along!" When he and his uniformed friends clapped their hands, the spirit of life came back into the crowd as well.

At least one million Southerners saw the concerts and rallies in person, and tens of millions of others watched the clips on television or heard one or more of the concerts on the radio. The USIA, under Blair Clark, recorded and filmed the rallies and concerts, offering them free to the television and radio stations. Years later, people recalled seeing, at the various marches throughout the South, the rows and rows of whites and blacks marching together.

Clark's camera workers recorded at least one march for posterity that tended to be used by most documentarians and historians for their classes. It showed country singer Roy Clark and pop and jazz singer Tony Bennett arm in arm with United Mine Worker representative Rich Trumka and Coretta Scott King—wife of the slain Martin Luther King Jr.—marching over the Pettus Bridge in Atlanta, Georgia.

At one of the concerts recorded by the USIA, Maurine Hedgepeth's widowed husband gave a speech before the start of the music and dancing. He summed up the feeling of many white workers who were coming to grips with the effect of the "marriage" of the labor and civil rights struggles:

"Ah was raised in a place that hated nigras, an' Ah remember bad things done to 'em, 'specially when they was brought in to work when people was strikin'—an' sometimes folks did bad things to 'em jus' . . . well, jus' because. Ah learned from mah wife that we are all in this world to git along, an' we can't get nowhere unless we march together for better job pay, better protect'in at work, an' stuff. Ah ain't as brave as some them fellas an' gals, 'specially mah wife . . . but Ah know we gotta be strong now, an' we gotta stop hatin' each other now, an' . . . an' all we wan' from the bosses is jus' fair treatment an' fair wages like they get inna rest o' 'merica, ya know?"

Coretta King walked over to Hedgepeth, who was starting to cry thinking of his wife, and she hugged him. Two white workers jumped up on the stage and put their arms around Hedgepeth. One of the workers yelled, "This is America, man! We ain't lettin' this man down or this country down, alright?" The crowd of fifty thousand blacks and whites cheered wildly. Civil rights icon Ralph Abernathy said after that concert rally, in what Arthur Schlesinger Jr. later called a "lovely mixed metaphor," "Freedom was truly in the air and could be tasted like cool, clean, mountain spring water!"

The bosses and mill owners, however, had other ideas. Workers in various mills, stores, and factories were locked out immediately after every rally or march. Workers who hadn't been on strike were now affected by the employer lockouts that occurred—some said they were "coordinated" by— Wal-Mart, Duke Power, Milliken, and J. P. Stevens.

In earlier decades, such a move might have simply precipitated a few threats and an occasional killing of a (usually Communist) labor organizer, usually by Southern police or private detective or security agencies. And then the workers would drift back into work. This time, however, the AFL-CIO was ready with a rapid-response team, offering food and money to pay bills. The activists staged daily rallies in strategically chosen towns and other smaller venues—including places such as Gastonia, North Carolina, where some violence flared. The idea was to have local small town folks to meet the city folks and vice versa. At the first sign of violence from police agents in the movements or "vigilante citizens' councils," Secretary Reuther conferred with Attorney General Clark, Defense Secretary Warnke, and the president, among others, and more federal troops came out to protect union organizers, student radicals, and civil rights activists. "Having the federal government on our side was crucial," said Leonard Woodcock to labor historian Eric Foner in an oral history project on the rebirth of the labor movement in the late 1960s.

Union and civil rights organizers quickly made sure the troops were not only treated with respect but with home-cooked meals from women textile workers—black and white—and music from guitar-strumming students. President Kennedy placed several calls to Southern governors and senators, demanding they speak of peace and support lawful restraint—not action—by local authorities. In what some critics later called a "provocative, militaristic" tone that seemed to contradict that call for peace, the president went on television as he announced more troops going into the South three days after the Statesboro tragedy.

In his televised speech, the president said he supported the workers "in their efforts to go back to work. I must also say this to all my fellow Americans: It shouldn't be a crime to want to earn a decent wage that workers in other parts of our nation already earn. It shouldn't be controversial to protest against working in sweaty, unsafe conditions and without adequate medical benefits. As one of our greatest jurists, Oliver Wendell Holmes Jr., once said, 'I think the strike is a lawful instrument in the universal struggle for life.' I can only add that we can't send a message of hope to the world and to those suffering under tyranny without showing that we listen and respond to the despair of our own, even in this great country."

After that speech, Senator Ervin placed a private call to the South Carolina textile magnate Roger Milliken, whom he had been close to for many years. As an aide said to a reporter from the *Charlotte Observer*, Milliken told Senator Ervin that he was "no bettah than a damned Commie" for supporting the workers. Ervin later told Yarborough privately that "the ol' pole cat called me a Commie and then hung up on me. Ah cast my lot, haven't Ah?"

Yarborough said, "Welcome aboard the labor express, Sam."

Ervin smiled, but it wasn't one of his brightest.

Just after the rallies ended in late July, the FBI arrested two men in Georgia who they claimed were responsible for the bombing of the church near Statesboro. The two men were J. B. Stoner and Robert "Dynamite Bob" Chambliss, two white supremacists who were behind bombings against civil rights activists and churches in the early 1960s. Both men were turned in by either friends or family who were tired of the violence done in the name of "preserving the South" and "white rights." Stoner and Chambliss, in turn, named two accomplices in exchange for life sentences without parole. The two accomplices were arrested and quickly agreed to the same plea bargain.

Chapter 17

A SMALL STEP, A HOP, AND A LEAP

In the summer of 1969, the moon-landing mission of *Apollo 11* went forward, and on July 20, men walked for the first time on the moon's surface. The astronaut chosen to take the first step, Neil Armstrong, was given something to say that was supposed to be momentous for the occasion. President Kennedy, exercising his executive authority, had, early in the year, called upon the poet Archibald MacLeish to prepare that special statement for Armstrong. But when MacLeish unveiled his proposed "Moon Poem" to Kennedy, Kennedy believed it did not "ring right."

Talking to Ken Galbraith after MacLeish left the Oval Office, Kennedy said, "Archie is just being too . . . too . . . I can't find the word, Ken—"

"Pedantic?" said Galbraith.

"Well, I wasn't thinking of that word, but it'll do. I like the first part, you know, 'From here, we're just a small blue sphere . . . ' But I think it's a downer overall, and who knows if the astronaut is gonna get it right. Too many words. Geez! I've got better things to do, but the O Boys aren't thinking about posterity here. Ken, the guy who takes the first steps on the moon is speaking for all of us on this planet. I don't want to take this away from our poet laureate, but maybe we need some competition here. Something hopeful is what I'm looking for, you know?"

Galbraith said, "Let me think about who we can call on this, Mr. President."

Galbraith talked with some Harvard colleagues in the English and philosophy departments. He also, with some reluctance, decided to speak with his longtime right-wing friend, Bill Buckley. "Bill," asked Galbraith, "what do you think the man who takes the first steps on the moon ought to say? I don't think it should be a speech or a poem. It can simply be a phrase, and I am starting to wonder whether we ought to get a speechwriter to write this instead of asking long-winded poets or philosophers."

Buckley replied, "Well, how about something when he is actually stepping on the surface of the moon. Something such as 'A simple step for a man, but something momentous for mankind?' Or . . . perhaps . . . "

Galbraith was almost breathless. "Bill, that's it! You . . . you . . . wouldn't mind . . . I mean, you've been very critical of the president . . . I wouldn't want to—"

Buckley said, "Ken, I am not in love with what I just said. It needs refining. You are correct that I have no wish to help this administration do anything but lose in 1972, but this is an auspicious moment in the history of mankind. 'One small step, one large jump—leap' . . . Anyway, unlike some of your friends, I am loyal to my nation even when I strongly oppose our commander in chief. Let me think about this for a day or two. You are assuming, of course, that the president will respond with something other than reprobation when he learns the source."

"Let me take care of that, Bill. I'll give him your name *after* I read it to him!"

Galbraith called the president a few days later and premiered the statement he had secured from "a friend": "One small step for a man, one giant leap for mankind."

Kennedy almost yelled into the telephone: "That's brilliant! Ken, did you write that? Come on! Who wrote that? Whoever wrote that deserves a Medal of Honor!"

"Really, Mr. President? You mean that—sincerely?"

Kennedy was annoyed. "Of course I mean that! This is a very important moment for the nation and the world! I don't care if a Communist wrote it!"

"What about a Fascist?" said a now playful Galbraith.

"Who? Ezra Pound? Is he still alive?" asked Kennedy, still thinking about poets writing the statement.

"No, I'm joking, at least a bit. Brace yourself, Bob. You sure you want to know who—"

"Stop jerking with me, Ken. I haven't got time for bullshit!"

"Fine. You asked for it. Bill Buckley wrote it."

Silence. Galbraith thought the telephone line had gone dead. "Mr. President? Mr. President, are you there? Hello? Hel—"

"I'm here, Ken." More silence. Then a weak-voiced Kennedy said, "Call O'Brien. We'll use it." There was more silence before Kennedy said, "Do we have to give him a medal, Ken? You haven't said—"

"No, Mr. President. A simple thank you and perhaps an evening at the White House—I'll be there, of course—will more than do. Bill believes, and I think you will agree, that his authorship ought to remain quiet for perhaps domestic 'diplomatic' purposes—at least at this time."

"Agreed. Anything else?" asked the president, still shocked that the best line written for the moon landing had come from one of his harshest critics.

"No, Mr. President."

"Well, um, see ya, Ken. And tell Bill thanks from me personally . . . seriously. Thanks." Click.

Kennedy shook his head as he sat in the Oval Office. "What a strange world we live in!" he said as a smile returned to his face.[1]

Meanwhile, in more earthly areas, there continued to be violent confrontations between pro-union protesters and employer-sanctioned counterprotesters.

More people were killed and more names added to the pantheon of labor martyrs. The federal troops, including the National Guard, moved from city to city in the South.

Some commentators, including Walter Lippmann and David Broder, worried openly about civil war. President Kennedy personally went to several cities and met with business representatives and local labor leaders. He demanded and secured their agreement that they would make "joint statements for peace." In Greensboro, North Carolina, where eight workers were killed in a battle with security guards hired by Roger Milliken—Reuther called it a "massacre"—Kennedy sent in federal troops to "enforce the peace." He asked, in a behind-closed-doors meeting with business leaders—though Milliken refused to attend—"Gentlemen, do you realize that South Vietnam is more peaceful and in less danger of civil war than Greensboro? Let's show some perspective here. Lots of places in the United States have unions. If you want our administration's National Labor Relations Board to forget the violence engaged in by your private security companies as we sort through each side's claims of NLRB violations of collective bargaining, you'd better start full-scale negotiations with the union representatives—now."

Kennedy then went to the largest church in Greensboro, and in a packed auditorium implored working families to remember that "businessmen are human beings and have families, too. And it is high time for all sides to stop their rhetoric of hate. We must remember that ours is a peaceful nation, a nation dedicated to the principle that we are a nation of laws, not merely of people." He announced, even though he did not have an agreement yet from the businessmen, that the business interests of Greensboro, including Milliken, the other textile manufacturing executives, and the local hospital board "will begin negotiations with the labor representatives no later than tomorrow. Otherwise, I am authorizing the NLRB, under the new labor reform law, to recognize the union and hold the employers in contempt of the law."

The crowd's reaction was ecstatic. The hospital board and some textile mill owners, faced with Kennedy's fait accompli, began negotiations with the labor unions. Milliken closed down his second plant in less than three months. He was already looking to build textile mills abroad, preferably, he said, in Hong Kong or Brazil.

The AFL-CIO and the SDS, two organizations fast becoming the closest of friends, sponsored a special rock, folk, and country music benefit show for the martyrs of the labor and civil rights movements at Shea Stadium in New York City (while the baseball team the Metropolitans, popularly called "the Mets," were on the road). The "Concert for America's Dream" featured Phil Ochs, The Who, Joan Baez, Bob Dylan, Roy Clark, Glen Campbell, John Lennon and Yoko Ono, Traffic, Jimi Hendrix's Experience, and Jefferson Airplane. The show was nationally broadcast on the privately-held network television stations with commercials, while on public television, it was live without commercials.

Two other concerts were held, one in Chicago and one in Los Angeles, with different stars and rock bands, including The Doors in Los Angeles. These concerts had the effect of undermining the so-called "Woodstock" festival set for the middle of August 1969. The Woodstock festival, said its promoters, was going to be based upon "peace and love," something that seemed vague or even frivolous to many youth caught up in the wave of the civil rights and labor rights movements.

In the weeks leading up to the Woodstock festival, student movement leaders, including Todd Gitlin of the SDS, Tom Hayden, newly appointed alderman in Chicago, and Al Lowenstein, now running VISTA, criticized the "rich dilettantes" and "corporate promoters" of the Woodstock festival for trying to "exploit" the civil rights and labor movements.

The New York Times quoted the new SDS vice president, Bernadine Dohrn, who had rejoined the mainstream of the SDS, on the Woodstock festival: "Barry Bluestone and Addie Jackson didn't die for people to get high and [have sex] at a corporate-sponsored circus." That partially censored quote made Newsweek and Time, and the CBS Evening News with Walter Cronkite. The Woodstock promoters found that several of the biggest acts, including some that had played at Shea Stadium, canceled in the weeks before the concert.

Despite those criticisms, twenty thousand young people showed up for the Woodstock festival. The concertgoers who showed were unruly, and violence broke out when the rains came and the food and drink ran low.

During 1969, and particularly after the Statesboro bombing, there was strong public support for the union-organizing efforts in the South and for combining civil and economic rights for blacks. The new labor law allowing sympathy strikes empowered Northern unions to threaten strikes in sympathy with their Southern "brothers and sisters." With the rising militancy among workers across the nation, the corporate-owned media had a hard time making its case against strikes on behalf of "consumers." Most people knew family members involved in strikes and knew further that most people didn't go on strike unless, as one local union representative said, "you had a damned good reason!"

The immediate success of the labor reform law regarding sympathy strikes put tremendous pressure on Northern business leaders to call upon their commercial brethren in the South to acquiesce to the unions. At various national meetings of business interests, Northern businessmen would say to their Southern counterparts, "I don't want any trouble at my plants, so you better find a way to take care of your union problems."

Henry Ford II put it in a more friendly way to an agitated Roger Milliken when the two saw each other while in Washington for their own separate lobbying purposes. "You'll learn to live with unions, Mr. Milliken. You'll also find stability makes for more consistent profits."

Milliken snarled, "Ah make what Ah need without no unions tellin' me what ta do."

Ford shook his head and walked away, thinking to himself, The poor bastard. He'll learn . . .

Northern business owners who did not have worldwide businesses such as Ford also realized something else as the strikes continued: If the organizing down South was successful, they wouldn't have to face competition from Southern businesses with cheap Southern labor. This economic reason allowed them to sound downright "noble" in saying they didn't oppose the union organizing in the South. They could also wax morally on the importance of securing "equal rights for all in our great nation."

On the Southern side, however, Sam Walton of the grocery–general store chain known as Wal-Mart, said at the yearly convention of the national Chamber of Commerce, "Y'all oughta know better that this is only the *start* of our battle against unionism, Comm'nism, and lawlessness." Walton showed up to build support for his idea to take over the Republican Party as the "true" party of business and to "get a look" at Governor Ronald Reagan of California, who was the keynote speaker at the convention. In his speech, Governor Reagan spoke about the need to reduce and begin to eliminate government regulations, and to "restore the balance between worker and management as we had under the great Taft-Hartley law."

Walton said to one of his sons during Reagan's speech, "There's Dwayne Andreas over there. He's head of that big grain merchant company, Archer Daniels. He says he makes more money for his wheat business when he gives to the politicians in both parties. Well, that ain't my strategy. I'm giving to whoever is gonna back business and free enterprise a thousand percent, and I'm gonna give to whatever party is on the outs with unions. And Reagan looks like a good bet for starters."

Unlike the executives at the Chamber meeting, who found themselves on the defensive, the union leadership was ecstatic with the first months of the presidency of Robert Francis Kennedy. At the September 1969 AFL-CIO convention, a smiling and very confident Douglas Fraser was named to the presidency of the AFL-CIO. To avoid a bloody battle against some of the old guard, Fraser agreed to share power as a copresident with the incumbent president George Meany for one more two-year term. Most recognized there was only going to be one president, which was Fraser. The labor leaders, however, realized they needed to show unity, not dissension, during the Southern organizing drives.

Fraser stressed the theme of unity to Northern and Southern white union workers, some of whom, in both regions, were still unhappy with the "uppityness" of black union workers. "We'll have no racism here!" thundered Fraser during his inauguration speech as AFL-CIO leader. "We are moving forward together because that's what union solidarity is all about! To show the seriousness of what I am saying, I am going to make this commitment, since we may be in for some turbulence this year and the next while we make America stronger and more fair for all workers, union and nonunion alike: *There will be no raises for union local leaders and state leaders and a 10 percent cut in pay for national leaders starting with me!* The money saved will go toward our strike funds and our funds to organize! Our first concern is for the health and welfare of the working people of America! There is power in a union! Power in black and white workers working together for all of us! *Repeat after me! There is power in a union! Together as one!"*

The convention hall erupted with the chant.

People watching television across America saw the speech carried live by the networks. The mood of working people, as a result of that televised convention, shifted more strongly in favor of class solidarity than at any time since the middle of the New Deal. It was the first time a speech at a union convention was carried live or on tape by television.[2]

In November 1969, Kennedy, who had been lunching quarterly with Federal Reserve Board Chairman William McChesney Martin, told Martin he was not going to be reappointed as fed chairman in 1970. "I never felt the knife sliding into my back," said Martin to his colleagues in the banking industry. Martin knew, too, that with a pro-Kennedy Democratic Congress, there was no way he'd get the support he needed to stay.

Kennedy saw no subterfuge on his part. But CBS newsman Dan Rather, at the next press conference Kennedy held, questioned the president, saying he had spoken with bankers close to Martin who were upset by the decision to replace him. "In all candor, Mr. President, many leading bankers believe you built up a relationship with Mr. Martin in order to keep him from seeing that you were going to replace him."

"In all candor, Mr. Rather, I must say that's ridiculous," said the president, barely concealing his rage at what he believed was Rather's petulance. "I notice nobody said this to you on the record, and more importantly, it contradicts what Mr. Martin said to me, and what others have said. Presidents serve for a maximum of eight years, as you know. Surely, it cannot be wrong to seek a new Federal Reserve Board chairman after twenty years. Next question, gentlemen and ladies."

Like most stories related to finance, "this one just died on the vine," said Rather years later in an interview with historian Robert Dallek, who wrote extensively about the Robert Kennedy presidency. Rather added in his interview with the historian, "If I wanted to be rough on the president, I could have shot back that Hoover was still running the FBI after *forty* years! I might as well have asked it because I never got another story leaked from that White House. Of course, that only caused this ol' dog to hunt harder—and I did get a great story later on from sources *outside* the White House. But again, that particular source may not have liked that follow-up question!"[3]

Kennedy fumed after the press conference to press secretary Jack Newfield, "Who the hell is that Rather guy to talk to me like I was a god-damned losing candidate for city council?"

Newfield shook his head gingerly and said, "Mr. President, Dan Rather's a Texan, which means he's hard to control when he puts his mind to something. And he's not going away. He hides his accent pretty well and that's because he wants to sit in Walter Cronkite's chair some day, anchoring the *CBS Evening News*. He's decided hard questions to presidents and other politicians are the way to CBS chairman Bill Paley's heart. Paley doesn't like our FCC commissioners, I hear. He hates the new airwave access and license fees to fund the expansion of public television stations for Blair Clark and the USIA. Paley isn't about to tell Rather to cool it, either. Paley thinks he and the other network owners did more than enough for us by carrying, live and in prime viewing time, the AFL-CIO convention speeches of Reuther and Fraser."

Kennedy was still angry. "If Paley wants my opinion, and I know this is a free country with a free press and all that, tell him he'd do better to replace Dan Rather with Roger Mudd! Mudd's at least been neutral—not biased against us. Who did Rather vote for anyway? Nixon?"

Kennedy didn't want to admit to anyone that he felt guilty about replacing Martin. He had wanted to keep Martin, but saw from their lunch conversations that Martin would think of the financial community first in a recession. Martin, like many bankers, was more concerned about curbing inflation than about whether the unemployment rate went up as a result of curbing inflation.[4]

O'Donnell and Galbraith suggested Kenneth Arrow, the chairman of the Council of Economic Advisers, to replace Martin at the Federal Reserve Board. When Kennedy interviewed Arrow, Arrow told the president, "Mr. President, the nation is likely to get hit with inflation first, and then perhaps concurrently, recession when the troops finish coming home from most of Southeast Asia. By 1971 you could have inflation and a recession at the same time. Wage and price controls would alleviate the problem in my opinion, since unemployment is likely to be worse than inflation from most people's viewpoint in the short to middle run."

"Arrow's my guy!" said Kennedy to the O Boys, Galbraith, and Yarborough. "Arrow has a point of view that is independent of the bankers. He'll listen to us more in avoiding a situation where the Fed raises interest rates, cuts the money supply, or whatever it does—I still don't get this. And one more thing: The more I learn about the Federal Reserve Board, the more I don't like this idea of bankers running the economy! I'll ask it again: How does a single agency or board get to override Congress and the president?"

Yarborough said, "Let's just put this Arrow fella in and maybe, with this new Congress, we can start talkin' about reformin' this board o' bankers. But Ah say, from talkin' with Secretary Warnke and even Secretary Learson, they have ideas on how to avoid inflation or recession or both without messin' with the Fed through legislation. The two o' them are talkin' about makin' computers the big-ticket item for jobs with the war basically over, as part o' a larger program they call 'conversion of military programs into civilian technologies and products.' Got some professor named Melman—from Harvard or Columbia, maybe—who worked in the last administration. Melman's been doin' studies showin' how we can keep people employed without runnin' into a recession, and keepin' things movin' and in motion, so to speak. Might be some good factory work in makin' civilian products down South, too. It's also good for keeping Southern congressmen and senators on board for union and civil rights policies."

"Maybe," said a slightly worried Bob Kennedy. "I can't even remember my inaugural speech anymore, fellas. It is turning into a blur every day, like you said, Kenny. Too many things crashing into each other and being dependent upon each other. At least we've not had too much controversy—public wise—on foreign policy matters outside of Vietnam."

Chapter 18

BACKING INTO VIETNAM

Before and during the May 1969 elections—in which the NLF won a large plurality, just short of a majority—the Thieu forces had been particularly brutal in committing political murders and harassing opponents. While this had the effect of depriving the NLF, or Viet Cong, of a clear majority, it also devastated Thieu's election hopes. After the election, the more "moderate" Unity Party of General Minh, along with the Buddhists, formed a coalition with the NLF, as President Truong requested. As part of the coalition, and at General Mihh's request, Tran Ngoc Chau, a non-Communist opponent of former President Thieu, was named foreign minister.

Former President Thieu had imprisoned Tran for sedition, but he was immediately released after General Minh assumed control of the South Vietnamese government in January 1969. Tran had an excellent reputation among certain key American officials, including Daniel Ellsberg, Major General Edward Lansdale, and Colonel—now Ambassador—John Paul Vann. However, others in the U.S. military and intelligence hierarchy, who were supportive of Thieu, distrusted Tran as little better than the NLF.

Ellsberg and Ambassador Vann had suggested Tran as the presidential candidate for the Unity Party, but Kennedy had insisted on General Minh. "I hear Tran needs reigning in from time to time. I don't think we need that much excitement from our point of view," was Kennedy's ultimate view, after reading the conflicting reports on Tran.

The new coalition of the NLF, Unity, and Buddhist parties in South Vietnam proved a success because, for the first time, there were leaders who had genuine support among people in the villages and towns in, around and outside of Saigon. The new coalition partners, at the start of their administration, unveiled their most important public policy initiative for the people of South Vietnam: a wide ranging land reform for the peasants of the nation. This initiative, coupled with emptying the jails of remaining dissidents and commencing a local VISTA-type program to rebuild the nation after years of bombs and infantry warfare, heightened support among the population. As one elderly Vietnamese teacher said to CBS news reporter Morley Safer, it showed there was finally a possibility of "a third way" between capitalism and communism after so many years of war.

Rennie Davis, receiving praise in the U.S. press for his "practical idealism" as head of the Peace Corps, offered the South Vietnamese and North Vietnamese governments the "deployment of American youth" to come to Vietnam to replant and reirrigate fields, to carefully remove land mines, to clean up bombing debris, to bury the dead in proper funerals, and to assist in building a community infrastructure of hospitals, schools, and farming cooperatives. The South Vietnamese government heartily accepted, and the United States "invaded" the South with Peace Corps volunteers. The North Vietnamese, on the other hand, refused to acknowledge Davis' offer and then, after some time, rejected it.

Some Americans who were veterans of the Vietnam conflict, including a couple of former POWs, volunteered through the Peace Corps to come back to South Vietnam. They found the experience gave them an "overwhelming sense of serenity and closure," as W. D. Ehrhart, a soldier turned writer, wrote in an article in *Newsweek*. Ehrhart opened his article with a quote from one of the longest-held prisoners of war in the conflict; a man named Jim Thompson. Thompson told Ehrhart: "We thought we went over the first time to help these people. We realized we were only truly helping them the second time around."[1]

The American antiwar movement, meanwhile, disbanded with the return home of American military troops throughout 1969. Most of the antiwar activists moved on to domestic labor and civil rights activities. However, certain American intellectuals and activists who, before 1969, had been opposed to America's war in Vietnam, such as MIT linguistics professor Noam Chomsky and the Berrigan brothers (two radical Jesuit priests), remained very interested in the events unfolding in Southeast Asia. These intellectuals and activists respected President Truong from the beginning of his term as president. Truong's genuine pursuit of an open society, with significant land reform, only increased their admiration for him.

Chomsky, in particular, wrote in the September 11, 1969, edition of the *New York Review of Books,* that the "NLF may have the opportunity to show a true third way beyond the impulse of both Stalinism and American militarism." The events over the succeeding year would vindicate Chomsky's position.

President Kennedy, concerned over the North's rejection of Rennie Davis' Peace Corps volunteer offer, asked for a telephone conference with Ho Chi Minh. He was able to speak directly by telephone with the dying North Vietnamese Communist leader—but only after diplomatic red tape from the North Vietnamese side. Kennedy said to Ho that regardless of whether the North accepted Peace Corps assistance, the American government would send the $750 million promised to the North under the Peace Accords of 1969.

Kennedy then asked Ho directly if he would reconsider having American youth come in to help rebuild "all of Vietnam, as the U.S. did in Western Europe with the Marshall Plan and in keeping with your letters to President Truman twenty years ago." Ho enthusiastically told the president he would refer the request to the Politburo for "strong consideration." He also thanked the president for his "fealty to the negotiated agreements."

Unfortunately, Ho was already weakened physically and was unable to persuade a hardened North Vietnamese Politburo to trust the Americans. Ho, unbeknownst to most Americans, including the CIA, as well as most Vietnamese, had been reduced to a mere figurehead. Ho died a few weeks after his talk with President Kennedy, in September 1969, never again seeing Saigon, as he had long wished.

Upon Ho's death, the North became officially ruled by the Politburo in Hanoi. The Politburo was led by hard-line Soviet-aligned Communists such as Le Duan, and military men, including Generals Giap and Pham Van Dong. The Politburo, like most governments run by committee and in secrecy, moved slowly in response to events, which was to put Hanoi at a disadvantage when compared with the dynamic new coalition government to the South.

The South's negotiations with the North became more and more strained as the South began to prosper with American economic aid and the enthusiasm of the Peace Corps volunteers, who eventually included far more Vietnam War veterans than anti–Vietnam War protestors. After several months of discussions for reunification, which the North decided were not getting anywhere, Le Duan yelled at South Vietnamese President Truong that it was "time to give up this bourgeois charade, comrade. Simply announce the reunification! There is no need for elections. You have the power. Seize it! The Americans are tired of us—*all* of us!"

Truong shook his head and said, "That is not the way of our ancestors, and it will not be our way now." As with every nation's history and culture, dual forces were battling one another: warriors and peacemakers, elitists and populists, and those who seized power and those who governed with at least an informal consent of the governed. This was simply another moment in that historic battle.

North Vietnamese troops who remained in the South soon began to engage in military skirmishes with local villagers and South Vietnamese troops. This time, however, with the NLF and local villagers cooperating with General Minh and his South Vietnamese army, the Northern troops were quickly disarmed with few casualties.

The North Vietnamese Communists looked to the Soviet Union for approval to redeclare war against the South Vietnamese government but were told there would be no support forthcoming. "Finish the negotiations with the NLF," said Soviet Premier Kosygin to General Giap when the latter went to Moscow for consultations.

Some of the North Vietnamese troops, sensing that they might not be welcome any longer, began to return to their homes in North Vietnam. When word filtered south that those who returned were arrested and shot for "treason," North Vietnamese troops who were still in southern villages began turning in their weapons and uniforms. They announced they were remaining in the South, as one North Vietnamese veteran said, "to heal the wounds of our proud homeland." Stalinist-style purges can sometimes have a salutary effect on those lucky enough to be far away.

By the time of the Tet festival of 1970, South Vietnamese Foreign Minister Tran told President Truong, "We must inform the North Vietnamese leaders that we are not likely to complete the reunification in the time set by the Americans and the North. We must at least propose that the elections be postponed—otherwise, if there are elections, I will have to oppose any reunification. It has become clear to me that we are not ready for reunification, particularly with the attitude shown by our northern brothers. It may mean war, however. If there is war, Mr. President, I believe this time it will truly be North versus South, and not North versus South, and South versus South, and Americans versus everyone—as before."

Truong reluctantly agreed with Tran's assessment. Truong had fought most of his adult life against successive military governments in South Vietnam with the strong support of his Northern comrades. He fought for the Communist side even when his family had opposed the Communists. Now events and the arrogance of his northern comrades were forcing him to postpone the vote, or vote against immediate reunification of his nation.

Truong, on the advice of Ambassador Vann, had been reading a book about Lincoln's efforts to reunite the American nation. As he read, he became *more* internally divided because he realized Lincoln's demand for unification was a position almost as unyielding as his northern comrades' position—and that Lincoln was able to keep the nation whole only by soaking the land with blood. Vann had thought, ironically, that Truong would see Lincoln as more like himself, not his northern comrades, and that Truong would be unifying his nation for "freedom" against "Communist slavery."

Truong, on February 28, 1970, formally asked the North to postpone the May 1970 reunification elections. As Truong had anticipated with foreboding, this request infuriated the North. The North broke off discussions, saying this was a "second treason" by the "illegitimate Southern entity."[2]

Again, the Soviets refused to support any North Vietnamese action against the South. The Chinese, however, vacillated, with Defense Minister Lin Piao supporting a full frontal assault by the North against the South and Chou En-Lai in opposition. Mao broke this particular "tie" in favor of Chou En-Lai, who broke the news to Premier Van Dong by saying, "The NLF, while showing clear bourgeois intentions and actions, has been properly following the guerilla movement of two steps forward, one step back."

When Van Dong protested, Chou said, with a firmness that shocked Van Dong, "North Vietnam cannot expect the People's Republic of China to support any aggression by the North against South Vietnam at this time. We have heard from Communist comrades in other nations who are impressed with the new American administration, particularly with United Nations Ambassador Andrew Young. We know, perhaps better than North Vietnam, the price of isolation from the United Nations, and we are becoming hopeful the Americans will see the advantage of having all of China represented in the United Nations. We will be speaking with the Americans before long. There is no other choice, except war—and that is no choice. Almost thirty years ago, Chairman Mao would have entered into a coalition with Chiang Kai-Shek had Chiang not shown such hostility. Remember, comrade, when the sea of peasants is not providing enough protection for your guerilla fish, the guerilla fish must evolve."

The North Vietnamese diplomat Le Duc Tho also sought support from the Communist dictator in Cuba, Fidel Castro, for an invasion of the South. Castro told Le, "Comrade Le, now is not the time for your nation to invade the South. It will bring disrepute to the entire Communist world. While the Americans have not yet ended their imperialist embargo against our island nation, we have already had indirect discussions with prominent Americans—I cannot say who—that lead me to believe the Americans will end the embargo against us within the foreseeable future. Comrade, you must complete your negotiations with President Truong and his coalition government."

The North refused to return to the negotiations but decided not to invade—just yet.

Truong, despite his requests for a formal agreement to set a new date for reunification elections, heard nothing from the North. In mid-March 1970, Truong spoke to his fellow South Vietnamese, via radio and television, to announce that he was requesting North Vietnamese troops to lay down their weapons and "stay to rebuild our country or to leave and go back to the North until we are able to negotiate a truly lasting peace with our northern brothers and sisters." He also announced that he would urge the people of South and North Vietnam to oppose the reunification elections scheduled for two months later on the basis that they were "premature."

Within hours of the speech, most remaining North Vietnamese troops, surprising the Hanoi Politburo, immediately reported to the local South Vietnamese military and civilian leaders to turn in their arms. A few of the rest trickled out of villages and hamlets, quietly and with humility, to return to their "northern comrades." Hanoi, fearing a loss in the reunification vote would be worse than a postponement, agreed to postpone the elections for two more years and further agreed that the remaining troops were "welcome home" as "heroes." The Stalinist purges were "in error," and Le Duan was held responsible for the "unfortunate events." Le Duan resigned from the Politburo and all other positions of power he had held. He was then sent to a remote village in North Vietnam close to the Laotian border.

The reaction in official Washington, but outside the White House, was one of disbelief. Joe Alsop, writing from Washington for the *New York*

Herald Tribune, said, "A year ago, nay, six months ago, no one would have guessed that it would take the NLF to rid South Vietnam of Communist troops. The land reform proceeds apace, with some conservatives in the U.S. intelligence and military communities saying the land reform is so extensive, it may be little different than if the Communists had taken over South Vietnam. However, former United States Secretary of State Dean Acheson, the dean of American anti-Communism, said in a recent speech to the National Press Club that he found 'much to support in the Kennedy administration's handling of the situation.'"

Ronald Reagan, continuing to comment on national affairs as he prepared for the 1972 presidential election campaign against Kennedy, said, "This euphoria over events in Vietnam may well be short-lived. It is important to state that our own intelligence agents are saying that President Kennedy's actions, or should we say inaction, not only here, but in South America and Africa, are likely to embolden the Soviet Union and Communist China to consider overcoming their temporary differences."

"How the hell does he *know* that?!" yelled President Kennedy after reading Reagan's remarks. He immediately called a meeting with the O Boys, Secretary Bowles, and CIA Director Blee to find out where the leaks to Reagan and his other "enemies" were coming from. "Reagan had to have seen the information about China and Russia in this report you gave me two weeks ago, David," he said, turning to Blee. "There's been nothing in the press about the report, so it had to be a direct leak. Reagan's too dumb on policy to say anything like that unless he or his advisers read that report! And who the hell gave him that report? Well? Anyone?"

The assembled said nothing, but what could they say in any event? Blee knew there were still elements in the CIA, the military, and the State Department who hated Kennedy, hated the idea of peace in Vietnam, and hated anything that didn't result in more troops abroad and rattling the Soviets and the Chinese. In a luncheon conversation he'd had a few weeks before with Chet Bowles and George Kennan, the three men had concluded that to kick out those now-dissenting people could result in a new witch-hunt atmosphere.

As Kennan said at the time, "Removing people based upon 'loyalty' is akin to stepping into a house of mirrors. It will never be the ones you suspect. Worse, the ones you suspect are likely to have done something wrong, but not what you thought—or cared about. I often think the loss of the China hands, and experts in Southeast Asian affairs, during the period of the early 1950s, proved disastrous in terms of our nation losing a learned perspective for our nation's politicians."

Back at the meeting held in response to Reagan's comments, Kennedy slammed his hand on his desk as he spoke. "I want this leaking stopped (slam), and I want to track this one down (slam)! Who's feeding Reagan, damn it (slam)? I know we can't do wiretaps anymore without going to the judiciary, thanks to the Wisconsin boys—which law I gladly signed (slam), remember!"—referring to the tough antiwiretap law sponsored by two Wisconsin Democrats, Senator William Proxmire and Congressman Les Aspin—"But, gentlemen, this is as close to treason (slam) as I can think of right now (slam)!"

Chet Bowles took the risk that this was a momentary frustration. He looked carefully around the room and saw most heads were down. He audibly cleared his throat and said, "Mr. President, I fully agree that tracking this leak is appropriate. However, the *content* of the report is more important than what Reagan says or doesn't say. The report merely said there was some lower-level discussion among Soviet and Chinese diplomats, who our sources indicate are tentatively seeking a cease-fire in the Manchurian region, with only vague hopes for a closer relationship with each other. The border disputes, however, run deep, and actual military engagements between Chinese and Soviet troops at their common borders continue to occur, with the worst coming just in the past few weeks. Governor Reagan, or his people, obviously did not read that report very well."

"True, Chet, true," said Kennedy. Taking in a breath to calm himself, Kennedy continued, "Maybe we should have Soviet Ambassador Dobrynin over again. I think we need to make sure we move toward the Soviets before we move toward normalizing relations with the Chinese—who seem, I hate to use the cliché, more 'inscrutable' than ever. And, David, let's see what you can do about cutting Reagan off from at least *some* of the leaks. I know there are too many damned people at the CIA who want nothing better than to see us lose in a couple of years—and they better know—" He sighed. "We'll deal with them later."

Turning to the O Boys, Kennedy concluded, "I want the report we're discussing here leaked, in its entirety, to show the press Reagan doesn't know how to read what's leaked to him!"

O'Brien gasped. "Wait! You want us to leak the whole report!? But—"

"Look, Larry. We are leaking it for the same reason my brother disclosed the maps we had showing the Russian missiles in Cuba. If something's already out there, but isn't believed, like the missiles, or is wrong, like Reagan is, we gotta get the truth out or else our denials become confirmation of the falsehood—or what our opponents *say* the truth is. The White House press corps is a good place to start. Call Jack. Let him be the bearer of good tidings to some lucky reporter."

"But, Mr. President," said a concerned Blee, "if we set a precedent, we'll get more leaks since they know we might release—"

"I'm aware of that, Mr. Blee," said a slightly irritated president. "That's why I want the head of one of the suspected leakers, whether we have the full goods on him or not, to set an example." Blee shook his head, but then quickly nodded to show he agreed with the president.

Kennedy said tersely, "Gentlemen, dismissed. Thank you for coming on short notice."

The president was already angry that day because of the scandal regarding his brother, Senator Ted Kennedy, which had just hit the media. Refusing to heed his brother's warning, Ted continued his womanizing ways. In early July, a few Southern newspapers began writing about Ted Kennedy's various "girlfriends" and one "mistress" in particular in Florida by the name of Helga Wagner. *ABC News* picked up the story nationally on the day Kennedy demanded the head of whoever was leaking information to Reagan. It was bad timing all around for the president's younger brother. By the time Senator Ted came to the White House that evening to speak with President Bob, the latter was in a belligerent and vindictive mood.[3]

Ted, after he arrived, told his brother that the scandal "would blow over" because he was going to seek a divorce from his wife, Joan—and an annulment of his marriage in the church. Then he would marry Helga. "I think this is the most honorable thing to do, and I doubt Joan feels differently," said Ted, already practicing his speech to the press and public.

Bob Kennedy, head of the Kennedy clan, exploded. "You might as well resign from the senate right now, Ted, 'cause I'm not having my brother go through a divorce brought on by scandal at this critical juncture. It's simple. Either get out there, apologize to Joan in private and in public, and say you're gonna have marriage counseling or whatever people do these days—and get our priest and Joan next to you when you say it—or you're no longer a senator."

Ted couldn't believe his ears. He immediately reminded his brother that when Bob was the freshman senator from New York and Ted was the "veteran" senator from Massachusetts—with two and a half more years' experience—they would call each other "Robbie" and "Eddie." During senate proceedings, "Eddie" would tell "Robbie" when he was speaking too much, when to vote, and—in the early days—*how* to vote on particular bills. He then told his older brother, "Let's not go overboard, Bob. I've been in this town a long time and have been just as much in the public eye. I know what I'm doing here."

"Ted, you expect me to respect your wishes when you disobeyed mine? I'm only president for maybe two more years and six if I'm lucky—*very* lucky! And you couldn't keep to your own wife for that time? Christ, Ted! I . . . I . . . I can't believe you would do something like this when you know what happened to me when we were going against Nixon! I changed, damn it! I adapted! What the hell is wrong with you? I hear you and the young Dodd—it's Chris Dodd, isn't it?—can't keep yourselves from staying out half the night at the thousands of bars around here—chasing women and drinking yourselves into a stupor! I try to get Ethel to give Joan a pep talk once every few weeks, and all the while you kept this little tryst going—"

"Bob, that 'tryst,' as you call it, is what keeps me sane! Helga understands. She's not weak like Joan. She runs a business and is someone I can talk with about things without feeling like I'm boring her—and she doesn't say a word to the public about us—"

"Well, *someone* did say more than a word, Ted! And you don't seem to understand, do you? You're speaking with me *here*—at the White House! I'm the president twenty-four hours a day. I'm not just 'Bob' or 'Robbie' anymore. I'm President Kennedy, President *Bob* Kennedy! Or that ruthless son of a bitch! Just ask Ethel! She had to learn—and she did! I wouldn't wish this job on anyone, Ted, not even you, no matter how mad I am right now! I thought it was hard working with Jack, but I had no idea . . . " He waved his hand. "Ted, you make the call. But if you don't do what I say, you *will* resign. That's it. I can't have this country go into civil war—with this labor strife down South—and be worried about some sex scandal at the same time—"

"Fine. Done. I know how to take care of myself. I'm outta here!" And with that valedictory, the younger brother walked out, head high and ready to punch a wall, if not his older brother.

Despite his firm statement and exit that night, it was a reluctant Edward Moore Kennedy who announced his resignation in the Senate press gallery the next day. Massachusetts Congressman Edward Boland, known to the Kennedy political clan as "Eddie," and a friend of Kenny O'Donnell, was quickly appointed senator by the governor of Massachusetts. The governor, who had previously been elected three times as a liberal Republican, had switched to the Democratic Party in October 1969 rather than face a tough reelection bid in 1970.

Ted immediately moved to divorce Joan and annulled his marriage to her in the church. Joan accepted the end of the marriage with some sadness, but was more relieved than anything else. As she told nearly anyone who asked, she was always the odd woman out among the Kennedy wives and that whole "secretive clan" in general.

After the divorce was final, Ted immediately moved to Florida and married Helga in a small, private ceremony. He then became active in a local south Florida children's hospital, becoming the hospital director within two years. He served with distinction and later became a prime mover in developing children's hospitals throughout the Southeast. As Ted later recalled to one of his brother's biographers, he was, from the time his brother Bob announced for the presidency, "way down the line" after people such as the O Boys, Sorensen, and Yarborough. Said Ted, "My brother Bob idolized Yarborough for his cool, sharp mind and folksy and easy demeanor." On the subject of his resignation, he said, "I shouldn't have been surprised that he'd want me out and Eddie Boland in as senator. We were eventually reconciled after several years of barely talking. We were brothers, after all—Kennedy brothers through thick and thin."

Joan Kennedy, retaking her maiden name of Bennett, had often thought of playing piano professionally in an orchestra. As Joan Bennett, and with the

Kennedy family's backing—her relationship with Ted, through the children, was more stable after their divorce than it had been during their marriage—she eventually realized her dream. After becoming a fixture at the Boston Pops Orchestra, she married composer Marvin Hamlisch in 1980.

Chapter 19

MINDING THE WORLD'S BUSINESS

Before casting his brother Ted from the national political scene, President Robert Kennedy had entered the year 1970 with cautious optimism. He had reason to believe, as the Southern labor organizing movement was beginning to bear fruit, that he might hold down the number of seats the Republicans would be likely to win in Congress in the November midterm elections. Although he thought he was going to be able to concentrate on domestic political issues, he found himself dragged into worrying about world affairs, more so than he had in 1969.

First came events in South Asia, where a war "suddenly" broke out between Pakistan and a government created in eastern Pakistan, which now called itself the nation of Bangladesh. The military leader of Pakistan thought the United States was too concerned with domestic affairs and foreign matters in Vietnam, the Soviet Union, and China to care about what he thought was going to be a quick military action against the breakaway province.

To compound matters, a skirmish and then a short war broke out between India and Pakistan over India's Kashmir province. The province of Kashmir was largely Muslim, as was Pakistan, but it was ruled by a Hindu maharaja who was tied to India. There were many Muslims, therefore, in Kashmir who supported Pakistan and opposed the Indian government, which kept the province almost continually on the verge of war. Though the maharaja accepted India's assistance over the years, he nonetheless sought independence for his province, or at least autonomy, which the Indians consistently opposed.

Secretary of State Bowles had been inclined, during his tenure as U.S. ambassador to India, toward India's position on Kashmir and against control by the Pakistanis. Yet he handled the situation in a way that surprised the so-called experts, though it was consistent with his long-held views of self-determination. Bowles knew the history of the last fifty years in the region and recognized that both Bangladesh and Kashmir had several things in common. First, both had fairly strong elements who wanted autonomy or independence. Second, Pakistan and India recognized, at least through implication, that their respective regions were difficult to control. Third, Pakistan and India each feared losing its region to the other, and this, in turn, caused them to head toward war. As an important corollary, this lingering dispute caused both India and Pakistan to engage in an arms race that included the development of nuclear weapons.

Bowles decided, considering these factors, that the "obvious" solution was to allow Bangladesh and Kashmir to simultaneously become independent nations—or at least autonomous regions that would be considered independent, in fact, if not in form. To convince the Indians and Pakistanis to accept this solution, Bowles began what the U.S. and Western press later called "shuttle diplomacy." This involved his flying back and forth on *Air Force Two* for diplomatic meetings in India, Pakistan, Kashmir, and the self-proclaimed Bangladesh.

Bowles decided to use the United Nations General Assembly as a moral bully pulpit for his solution to the problem of both Bangladesh and Kashmir. He called upon American U.N. Ambassador Andrew Young to be his point man at the United Nations and in the international media. Young spoke to the General Assembly to support self-determination for the two breakaway provinces. Bowles had Young confer with the Soviet ambassador, who reluctantly agreed because, as Politburo member Mikhail Suslov said to President Kosygin, "We will look reactionary in the eyes of many third world peoples if we said 'nyet.'"

Bowles was confident this solution would work because he knew the Indian government already trusted him, and during his meetings with the Pakistani government, he had impressed them with his sympathetic view of their other disagreements with India. Pakistan also saw that world opinion was against them as the Bengalis refused to surrender after mass killings by Pakistani soldiers.

Andrew Young, in speeches at the UN, spoke of the need for peace and for the autonomy of both Bangladesh and the Kashmir region. The thunderous applause he received from the General Assembly was noticed by the U.S. media. Americans were heartened that the Kennedy administration was seeming to "finally convince the rest of the world that we are truly interested in peace and self-determination," said CBS television commentator Eric Severeid, during a news broadcast in August 1970.

Then, as the negotiations neared a successful conclusion, Young spoke with a reporter from Bombay, India. In the reporter's interview, he quoted Young as saying "The Western world is beginning to recognize that conquest and colonialism are no longer the answer for either the colonialists or the colonized." This proved too controversial to be ignored by the American press. Columnist Walter Lippmann, writing in the *Washington Post,* fumed, "Who is Ambassador Young referring to? For the sake of continued credibility of the Kennedy administration, he must affirm that he is not referring to the United States."

William F. Buckley Jr. wrote, in a widely disseminated article, "Surely Ambassador Young has more perspicacity than to think there is any truth to the canard that the United States is 'imperialist,' as is stated in standard Communist propaganda. As evidenced from Ambassador Young's foolish remarks, the Kennedy administration continues to pursue a foreign policy based upon a dangerous belief that the way to defeat the Communistic-atheistic empires of Russia and China is by supporting Communists in the third world who continue to take their orders from the aforementioned atheistic regimes. For example, President Kennedy believes, one hopes merely naïvely, that the NLF truly intends to pull South Vietnam from North Vietnam's Communist orbit . . . Seasoned diplomats in both political parties do not know what to expect next from this Kennedy administration. Will the president suddenly announce that Communist Cuba should become our fifty-first state, with Fidel Castro as governor? We steer our ship of state perilously toward Lotusland when a president refuses to express opprobrium against such reckless utterances from our United Nations ambassador."

After Bowles made a hasty return to the United States, the administration demanded that Young publicly state that he "was not referring to the United States as imperialist" and that he "did not mean to attack any particular nation existing today." Young complied, but not before almost quitting over the episode. Talking the night before his "act of contrition" with the other two leading blacks in the administration, Julian Bond and Roger Wilkins, Young said, "Of course our policies are to some extent, in some nations, a carryover of European colonialism! I've learned quite a bit from my discussions with UN ambassadors from South and Central America. You know, I'm starting to believe we have behaved no better toward the people in those regions than the Soviets have toward their Eastern European captive nations!"

Bond and Wilkins ignored Young's last remark. Bond coolly responded that this was not the time to quit because Young was needed to guide the "constructive engagement" with apartheid in southern Africa. Bond said, "Constructive engagement in South Africa and Rhodesia will mean doing nothing or *worse* if you aren't there!"

Wilkins quickly added, "Andy, we must move step by step here. Southern Asia is not worth losing the battle over southern Africa."

Young stayed—and apologized. Returning to New York and his office at the UN, Young was approached by an ambassador from a small third world nation. He said to Young, "I am glad, Mr. Ambassador, that you are still with us. We understand the pressures you are under and wish you well in your continued fight for people around the world." Young smiled as he realized he was not going to be seen as a hypocrite by most of his colleagues at the world organization.

Bowles returned immediately to the Asian subcontinent. When he arrived and saw that a peace agreement was still not quite within reach, he decided to call upon Ambassador Young, if for no other reason than because Young's stature in the world had grown, not contracted, as a result of his remarks. Young proved very effective in "closing the deal," as Bowles, the former businessman, said in a press conference announcing the agreement among the respective nations and regions. Under the agreement, India and Pakistan were to grant autonomy and ultimately independence to the Kashmir and Bengali regions, respectively. The two regions were to be demilitarized, much as Japan had been after World War II. Finally, the United States was to provide economic aid and Peace Corps volunteers to help build the two regions, which had experienced war and, in the case of the Bengalis, starvation.[1]

None of the participants was fully happy about this arrangement, whether Bengali, Indian, Kashmiri Muslim, or Pakistani. However, Bowles and Young were persuasive in their argument that more fighting would not be in anyone's interest. As Bowles remarked in front of a joint House-Senate Subcommittee for South Asian Affairs a few days after the agreement was signed, "Our experience in showing that peace and respect for self-determination were the answers to the war in Vietnam made a significant impact upon the various parties to these land and sovereignty disputes. Our Vietnam policy gave us credibility to convince the parties involved to come to the negotiation table and allow them to resolve their differences. I must also single out for praise the work of Ambassador Young. His knowledge and experience in practicing Gandhian nonviolence was impressive to all sides, including the Pakistanis." The House approved $650 million in additional foreign aid to the entire region, which, in those days and for that region, was an extraordinary amount.

Bowles, however, had little time to enjoy the prestige of settling a long-simmering international dispute. In September 1970, an openly Marxist candidate won the election for president in the Latin American nation of Chile with a plurality of 36 percent of the vote in a three-party race. Chile, at that time, was considered to have the most stable government, with the most developed democratic traditions, in all of Latin America. The Socialist party candidate, Salvador Allende, was a university economist. He spoke with a moderating tone but was adamant that foreign companies controlling the copper and telecommunications businesses in Chile should end their "plundering ways." Kennecott and Anaconda were the main foreign copper companies. The telecommunications company he was referring to was the powerful international conglomerate International Telephone and Telegraph (IT&T).

President-elect Allende, the morning after his victory, announced that he would like to meet with President Kennedy. Kennedy, following the advice of the O Boys and overruling Vice President Yarborough and Secretary Bowles, declined to meet with him. Kennedy, through Bowles, cabled the Chilean government that he would not be available but that Secretary Bowles might be available to briefly meet with the new Chilean president.

"Election politics ruled in this case," O'Brien said many years later. "I knew IT&T, Anaconda, and Kennecott had strong support on Capitol Hill and lots of money to throw around to politicians and the press. Plus, during that time, IT&T had a former CIA director, John McCone, as a member of its board of directors. Can you say the word 'connected'? We didn't want a fresh charge of being 'soft on Communism' that was sure to come our way if the president met with Allende immediately—particularly after we had tiptoed through the NLF winning in South Vietnam!"

Bowles, in an oral history interview released after his death, admitted O'Brien's election advice was probably correct. To combat the impression that Chile was "lost to Communism," however, Bowles charged ahead to learn more about how and why Allende had succeeded in the Chilean election. To begin his investigation, he called and spoke with Edward Korry, the U.S. ambassador in Chile since 1967. Bowles found Korry to be totally against Allende. Korry had coordinated the flow of millions of dollars through his office, from the CIA and the three U.S. companies, in a futile attempt to defeat Allende. Newspapers, businesspeople, the military, and politicians in Chile were on the U.S. payroll, courtesy of the CIA. Korry shocked Bowles when he admitted that he would rather see Allende be "taken out" than succeed.

When Bowles returned to Washington, he spoke with various persons within the State Department. He found a former marine and long-time State Department aide, Wayne S. Smith, to replace Korry as ambassador to Chile. Bowles went to President Kennedy and said, "Mr. President, we need to have a change of ambassadors in Chile. I have a strong candidate, Mr. Wayne Smith, an expert in Latin American affairs—and Soviet affairs, too—who will have credibility with both Latin American leaders and the Soviets. I believe he will help us constructively engage the situation we face in Chile. The current ambassador, Korry, stinks to high heaven with money from the copper interests and those in the CIA who generally oppose us politically."

Kennedy said, "Chet, it's your department. Go ahead."

Ambassador Korry was recalled within twenty-four hours of Bowles' meeting with Kennedy and replaced by Wayne Smith as interim ambassador. Kennedy quickly learned there might be a fight on Capitol Hill over replacing Korry and confirming Smith. In fact, it took less than twenty-four hours after Smith's appointment was announced for Kennedy to receive a call from Clark Clifford, who had been hired to represent the interests of IT&T in Chile.

Clifford said to Kennedy, "Now, Mr. President, I recognize Secretary Bowles has the right to conduct what some—not me—have called an 'idealistic' foreign policy, but we must recognize certain geopolitical principles, such as the right of American businesses to conduct themselves without interference from governments unfriendly to freedom. You are aware, I am sure, of Secretary Bowles' rather rash action in recalling Ed Korry from Chile. As you may already know, Ed has an excellent record of public and diplomatic service. He served, for you and President John Kennedy, as ambassador to Ethiopia in 1963—"

Kennedy said, "Clark, I think you believe I am more knowledgeable about this situation in Chile than I am. I recall going down there as a senator and finding the university students quite radical—although I also found the conditions in the copper mines to be absolutely disgraceful. This President Allende, according to Chet, is a reasonable fellow who may be able to take the wind out of those more radical sails."

"Mr. President, I would like to meet with you and CIA Director Blee—and I'd like to bring John McCone, who is now on the board of directors of IT&T. John, as you know, served our nation well as director of the CIA—"

"John's with IT&T now, Clark?"

"Well, IT&T is a very large company with relationships with many governments, including ours. As I said, let's meet to discuss some things that Secretary Bowles may not be aware of. I'm sure Mr. Blee can fill you in on how we need to meet this threat in Chile before it gets out of hand—"

"Well, I'd like to bring in Secretary Bowles and hear what the State Department has to say, Clark—"

"As you wish, Mr. President. How about tomorrow?" Clifford hoped to catch Bowles off guard with a quickly scheduled meeting.

"Sorry, Clark. Let's do it next week. I just don't see Chile ranking so high on my radar when we're looking at midterm elections in less than two months." Realizing that sounded more like a statement Lyndon Johnson would have made than the principled message he wanted to project to Clifford, he quickly added, "And, uh, we also have a continuing concern with labor issues down South, Vietnam, with the Middle East, and trying to get arms control talks started with the Soviets."

After ending his call with Clifford, Kennedy immediately called Bowles. Bowles barely hid his fury. "Mr. President, I have already ordered that a State Department white paper on the Chilean situation be prepared. I will have it on your desk before the meeting next week. From what I have heard thus far, Korry and his friends in the CIA have made matters worse in Chile during the past year as opposed to helping to avoid a radicalized situation there."

"Fine, Chet, fine. You know I believe in you, and that's why I demanded your presence at this meeting next week." He then added, laughing, "Plus, I don't recall IT&T being on our campaign donation list either!" Turning serious again, Kennedy said, "Look, Chet. You've been one of my best appointments, if not the best. If you didn't think Ed Korry was right for this assignment at this time, you had the right, as secretary of state, to replace him."

Bowles presented the white paper to Kennedy within five days of their conversation. It revealed that IT&T, and the two copper companies, had a cozy relationship with military dictators throughout Latin America, both historically and continuing through the time of the report. More ominously, the companies had cultivated an especially close relationship with certain military leaders in Chile.

The white paper also explained that, during the previous ten years, Peru and a couple of other nations had nationalized IT&T businesses without arousing much controversy in the United States "to speak of." In Chile, the previous Chilean president, Eduardo Frei, had already established an agreement with

IT&T some years before to allow Chile to purchase, over time, the assets of the Chilean-based IT&T businesses. Frei, a Christian Democrat who was anti-Communist, announced plans in 1968 to seek the "nationalization" of IT&T because IT&T had been dragging its feet in implementing the earlier agreement. Frei promised "reasonable compensation," but IT&T refused to discuss the matter further with the Chilean government. Ironically, Frei had been elected in 1964 with millions of dollars worth of support from the United States—and IT&T.

The white paper stressed that the IT&T communications system, while charging excessive prices to the people of Chile, was not performing well from a "consumer" standpoint. This, said the report, was not an anomaly limited to Chile. The IT&T systems in pre-Castro Cuba under Batista and in Peru were known to be corrupt in terms of widespread bribery and also provided inefficient and incompetent service. The copper companies, for their part, had horrible conditions and very low wages at their workplaces—something President Kennedy already knew from his trip to Chile in the mid-1960s.

Worse, said Bowles' study, other American companies, not only IT&T, had shown a willingness to allow military leaders in the nations they were in to use violence to stop union organizing and other activities that threatened their profitability. The copper industry, to the extent it shared ownership with wealthy Chileans, detested anything smelling of "public accountability," let alone "Communism," often confusing the two.

Bowles was glad that Kennedy read the report and very glad that he found it "fascinating." But Bowles knew the report would not be well received by Clark Clifford, CIA Director Blee, and especially John McCone. McCone was furious before he even finished reading it. He called the president directly and demanded to know how such "Commie propaganda" could come from the U.S. State Department.

Taken aback by McCone's anger, Kennedy said, "John, I'm sorry you feel that way. But I do not see why President Allende's request to continue discussions of nationalization begun under Chile's previous president—which previous president your company, and our CIA, spent a lot of money to help elect—is either surprising or, frankly, controversial. You know as well as I do that the ball to keep our eye on is with the Soviets and the Red Chinese. Chile is small potatoes in the grand scheme of things, John. President Allende has promised to work with us and promises to treat IT&T fairly, despite some of his campaign rhetoric about IT&T being a 'plundering' company, for example."

McCone was shocked. "Mr. President, I cannot believe I am hearing this kind of talk. Are we going to simply let this go along and do *nothing*? That is not what I recall from our times together with President John Kennedy—"

Kennedy was sharp, having heard indirectly that Rusk and some others, possibly McCone, were saying that Bob Kennedy was not showing the same level of "toughness" in the Oval Office as his brother had. "John, my brother learned things—as did I—the hard way. I am the president now, and my brother is not here. Do I need to remind you that you initially supported a general air strike at the beginning of the Cuban missile crisis and finally came around to our position—which, when implemented, averted a nuclear war and resulted in the removal of the Russian missiles from Cuba?"

The president knew McCone would not interrupt him as he continued. "With all due respect for your vast experience in government and in business, we are going to engage, constructively, President Allende and his new administration. We will be on your side if we believe that the Chilean government is not acting fairly in its negotiations with your company. However, we believe it is their right, as a sovereign nation, to negotiate for the purchase of the IT&T telephone holdings, as well as the copper holdings in Chile."

McCone was silent but burning with fury. He wanted to remind Kennedy that unlike him, McCone had *opposed* the coup overthrowing South Vietnamese President Diem in November 1963 and had spoken out about it before it occurred. McCone finally replied, with a tone barely concealing his disrespect for this "naïve" president. "Mr. President, I appreciate your candor and will inform my board of our discussion, if that is appropriate."

"It is," said Kennedy with lessened sharpness, but still wanting to show strength in his position.

McCone took a breath and stated in as friendly a tone as he could muster, "Thank you, sir. Regards to Mrs. Kennedy and your family. Oh, is there anything else you wish to say—I didn't mean to end—"

"No, John, I have stated my position on this matter at this time. Do you wish to still meet with us now that you've reviewed this report?"

"Mr. President, may I have twenty-four hours to consult with my board before I answer that question?"

"Yes, John, you may."

"Thank you, sir. Goodbye, Mr. President."

After McCone hung up, Kennedy rang up CIA Director Blee. "David, we have to talk about Chile and Allende. I'd like to see you first thing tomorrow." Blee complied, knowing already it had to be about McCone, IT&T, his department's activities in Chile, and the white paper. Blee, who agreed with McCone and IT&T in this matter, knew he was going to have more than simply a "turf war" with Bowles over Chile and its socialist president.

Bowles was also called in to this meeting. It was a stormy conversation that ensued, with Blee providing evidence, largely from the now former Ambassador Korry and a couple of Chilean CIA agents, of Allende's "Communist policies and support."

Bowles had heard such rhetorical "evidence" for years and now was in a position to challenge it. He said to Blee, "My God, David! Do we really have to go through this kind of argument again? How many times must we lose sight of the nationalist dynamics that make up the leaders of emerging nations? Ho Chi Minh wanted to deal with us originally, as we know from the Pentagon study. In the early 1950s, Arbenz in Guatemala was initially seeking a strong Washington connection—and all we see now in Guatemala after his overthrow are ruthless military dictators killing tens of thousands of peasants. We don't seem to mind dictators when they kill people by the score in Nicaragua, El Salvador, Brazil, the Dominican Republic, Ecuador—just as long as they call themselves 'anti-Communist!' Must we go on and on like this in our policies?"

"Arbenz was taking weapons from Czechoslovakia—"

"*After* we were going after him, David—'we' being the United States, the United Fruit Company, and its board member, Senator Henry Cabot Lodge! And what do you want to do, David, with this latest potential dictator, as you see Allende? Turn Allende into another Castro and try to overthrow him later—or kill him now? Instead of spouting rhetoric about Communism, let's see the CIA answer the points in our white paper! Don't give us Korry's nonsense about 'Communist' infiltration. As far as I'm concerned, Korry's acting no differently than a drunken cowboy looking for a gunfight!"

Kennedy jumped in. "Now, Chet. I think we have to maintain some decorum. I briefly knew Ed Korry and he's a bright guy—"

"Mr. President, he was running a money-laundering operation that would have made Jimmy Hoffa proud! Korry was dead serious when he said we ought to 'take out' Allende. He meant assassination—not take the guy to dinner and a movie! Is this what we want to do, after all the goodwill we have built up in Vietnam, in the Indian-Pakistani situation—and as we try to move toward arms control with the Soviets?"

Blee was seething. "Gentlemen! I hate to interrupt this Pollyanna tea party, but we have a serious problem in Chile that, yes, Mr. Bowles, could turn into another Cuba! They are talking expropriation of American business property for starters. Remember when Castro told us he wanted to be on our side, and how he wasn't a Communist? Well, where'd that get us? Well?"

Bowles was not backing down. "I'll tell you, Mr. Blee, because I was *there*. We were trying to overthrow Castro from the day he came into power when Eisenhower was still president. The Bay of Pigs was an Eisenhower operation that President John Kennedy inherited—and don't tell me that garbage that Jack should have provided air support to the rebels we trained to fight against Castro either. As I said, we deal with thugs all the time. We can deal with an economics professor in Chile who likes Marxism—as long as he wants to deal with us, damn it!"

Blee sat back, noting that Kennedy's body language was leaning clearly in the direction of Bowles. "Mr. President, there are many people in the community"—he meant the CIA—"who feel strongly about this situation. I see nothing but trouble if we let Allende think we're—"

Kennedy didn't even want to hear the word "weak" leave Blee's lips. "David," he said firmly, "Secretary Bowles is the only one meeting with this Allende fellow. We will make no commitments at the meeting, right Chet? I am not meeting with him because I do not wish to show that we are pleased with the results of the election there. President-elect Allende will have to show us more good faith than simply asking us to meet him."

Kennedy realized he was not ready to take on the CIA, Clark Clifford, John McCone, and the American business establishment in Latin America— the U.S. "sphere of influence," as Galbraith, Harriman, and Kennan loved to call it—over a sliver of land called Chile. There are military regimes we're close to in Brazil, Venezuela, Argentina, and a host of countries that might get worried if we made any move to support radical reformers, Kennedy thought to himself.

"David," Kennedy said in a sympathetic voice he hoped sounded sincere. "Let's not act hastily either way. If you'd like, you can meet President Allende with Chet and size him up. Remember, President Truong in South Vietnam is turning out to be a fairly reliable ally, even though he was Viet Cong. They don't *all* have to turn out to be Fidel Castro."

Blee had to agree with that last point. For it was a point he continually made to his friends at the CIA when the subject of Vietnam came up. He also knew that many of the facts in the State Department paper were true, including the fact that the previous President, Frei, was as likely to nationalize IT&T's holdings as Allende. Maybe his argument with Bowles was based upon his trying to placate some of his own friends in the CIA "community" who were angry with the leftward trend in foreign policy shown by this President Kennedy.

There were also internal CIA-turf issues to consider. Blee knew his assistant, Cord Meyer Jr., had interviewed for the CIA director position. He also knew Meyer was of the opinion that Allende should be given a chance to survive, at least for a while.[2] After the meeting with Kennedy and Bowles, Blee told his confidantes at CIA headquarters that they would have to swallow hard. As Blee also said in a telephone call with former CIA Chief Richard Helms, "If I resign over this, sir, you're looking at Cord Meyer being the new director of the CIA." Helms shuddered at the thought of Meyer working in tandem with Bowles and Kennedy.

If Allende's election, the continued uncertainty in Vietnam, and South Asian rivalries were not enough to distract the president from his domestic policy agenda, the year 1970 had also seen tension mounting in the Middle East. Israel was conducting raids into the border region of Jordan in what it called "retaliation" for the border raids conducted by the Palestine Liberation Organization (PLO) into Israel. The PLO had established camps within Jordan and was becoming a threat not only to Israel, but also to the Jordanian monarchy of King Hussein. Hussein was already fighting a local cold war with Syria, which included its own border skirmishes. Syria, in turn, was supporting the most radical elements of the PLO in an attempt to overthrow Hussein—and allow those Palestinians who were living in Syria and nearby Lebanon to return to their "rightful place" they called Palestine. And Palestine included what Syria and other Arab nations called "the Zionist entity," meaning Israel.

Some Israeli military leaders, notably Generals Ariel Sharon and Raphael Eitan, suggested the simplest solution to the problem of Palestinian refugees in the West Bank and Gaza regions of Israel would be to help them form their own state in the one country where Palestinians made up a majority of the population—namely, Jordan. The United States and the Israeli leadership, led by Prime Minister Golda Meir and Defense Minister Moshe Dayan, opposed this "solution," however. Meir, Dayan, and the Americans did not want the Soviet-supported PLO establishing a government in Jordan. As Israel's foreign minister, Abba Eban, explained to Secretary of State Bowles in early 1970, "The U.S. government has long maintained friendship with King Hussein. Also, we in Israel sense that the King is someone we can deal with on a diplomatic basis from time to time, if not eventually on a permanent basis."

The Jordanian king, fearing the PLO might overthrow him and his monarchy, finally took action against the PLO in the late summer of 1970. As a result of the fighting, which in the end involved the massacre of more than ten thousand Palestinians, the PLO was driven from Jordan into Lebanon, and parts of its leadership fled to Libya. The influx of Palestinian refugees into Lebanon merely added to the strain developing inside that small nation between Christian and Muslim Arabs. Lebanon was called, in foreign policy circles, a "buffer state" because it was between two nations hostile to one another—Israel and Syria. With the deterioration of Lebanon's central government, Israel and Syria each realized one or both of them were eventually going to carve up Lebanon.

Bowles was distressed by the events unfolding in the Middle East but was preoccupied with South Asia, Chile, and other continuing foreign matters at the time of King Hussein's massacre of the Palestinians in September 1970. Bowles turned to the State Department, which, with its long years of hostility toward Arab guerilla movements and cold attitudes toward Israel, concluded the actions of King Hussein were "an internal affair." Bowles, dissatisfied for once with his department's analysis, spoke with Israel's ambassador to the United States, Yitzhak Rabin, about the Palestinians and Hussein's actions. Rabin reiterated Foreign Minister Eban's belief that King

Hussein was the one potential Arab ally for Israel and, therefore, the massacre was an "internal affair" of Jordan.

"What a mess that area of the world is!" said Kennedy to Bowles on the evening of Bowles' discussion with the Israeli ambassador. "The only thing people seem to agree upon in that region is killing each other! It's like Northern Ireland, except there are additional factors of oil and East-West intrigue. If we can solve the Indian and Pakistani disputes and keep Chile from becoming a Cold War testing ground, I'd like to start to look for a comprehensive solution for the Middle East with the Soviets' help—assuming the Soviets want to talk with us about the Middle East—or anything!"

Kennedy was indeed having some problems setting the parameters for definitive arms control talks with the Soviet Union. The Soviets, for their part, were having disagreements within their Politburo over how to handle the growing respect the Americans were earning in the third world for their foreign policy endeavors, which ironically was delaying the start of negotiations, for the Soviets could not agree on a strategy in effectively dealing with this new President Kennedy.

President Alexei Kosygin was interested in pursuing significant arms control with the Americans and creating a thaw in the Cold War. However, Secretary Brezhnev was adamantly opposed because, as he said to Kosygin during a meeting of the Politburo, "Comrade Alexei Nickolayevich, remember what happened when the *other* President Kennedy agreed with us to limit above-ground nuclear testing, let alone arms control. He was killed, and the next president pursued new military weapons systems and expanded the war against Vietnam and invaded the Dominican Republic. Strength is what we must show the world, and to our allies, starting in Vietnam."[3]

Long-time Politburo member Mikhail Suslov, a hard-liner who was often a liaison to third world revolutionary guerilla movements, was still in Brezhnev's camp at this point in 1970, but he was beginning to doubt his usual hard-line position as he observed the United States' actions in South Vietnam and in the India-Pakistan disputes, and Secretary Bowles' arrangement of a friendly meeting with Allende. Suslov also was becoming concerned about Andrew Young's off-the-record discussions with various third world leaders who had been fully in line with the Soviets. He heard about Young's willingness to criticize South Africa and Rhodesia to the extent that Young promised "apartheid will end sooner rather than later." And, most importantly, Young was—well, he was black, a fact that gave him a considerable advantage not merely in Africa, but with South American and Asian diplomats.

Worse, Suslov heard from guerilla leaders from Rhodesia, Angola, Nicaragua, and Peru, who now openly praised the efforts of President Kennedy and Secretary of State Bowles. "When," asked Robert Mugabe of the antiapartheid Communist guerrillas in Rhodesia, "will the Soviet Union and America set aside their differences so that we can import food and farming tools, not military hardware?"

Suslov, in October 1970, spoke with his protégé, Yuri Andropov, at the former's dacha. Since 1967, Andropov had been the director of the KGB, which was the Soviet "CIA" and "FBI" combined, with nearly unlimited powers. Twenty-first century historians have been able to piece together the following conversation the two had in the fall of 1970:

Suslov spoke first. "Comrade Yuri Vladimirovich, I am concerned that our traditional strategy of supporting freedom-fighters against Western imperialism is beginning to show signs of strain. The Americans are becoming more and more willing to consider limiting or ending their support for reactionary elements in emerging nations. Is this how you see things from your position?"

Andropov, almost in a whisper, answered, "I am glad we are speaking outside instead of in our offices or homes, Comrade Mikhail Andreevich. I, too, am concerned. Our agents are saying that the American leadership under Kennedy is seriously considering support of the very people we have supported in the emerging nations. There is much anger within the CIA, and in the American military at the top levels, according to our sources. I cannot help but think there could be coup d'état or another assassination attempt against this President Kennedy, and more successful this time, like his brother's assassin. I, for one, am glad there is no Oswald right now—we never should have even let that anti-Soviet spy into the Soviet Union!"

"Agreed. We learned from that. Luckily the Americans did not try to publicly blame us. I had thought we were being set up when I read the initial report showing Oswald had lived here and had a Russian wife. What were we thinking to let in that American just after the U-2 spy-plane incident? In any event, comrade, President Kosygin has always been 'naive' to my way of thinking—and dangerously so, particularly in allowing capitalist encroachments into the Soviet Union and the Warsaw Pact nations. Secretary Brezhnev believes Kennedy's actions are a sign of weakness. He expects Kennedy to be either defeated in the next American presidential election or . . . well, as we said. He therefore believes it will only hurt the Soviet Union to discuss arms control at this time. He says the Americans may unilaterally denounce whatever agreement they reached if there is a change of government—just as they did on questions of Allied control of Germany after World War II when President Truman replaced President Roosevelt. If you recall, the setting up of NATO in Europe also violated the accords at Yalta. I, too, have found it hard to argue for a change of policy toward the Americans, but I am starting to wonder if perhaps we are not fighting the last war."

"Comrade Mikhail Andreevich," said Andropov, "you have always been someone I admire and respect. I cannot disagree with the positions you have expressed. We must recognize the possibility this President Kennedy may be successful in his foreign diplomacy. A bright young man who assists me—his name is Mikhail Gorbachev—has been in Western Europe—a lovely wife he has, comrade!—and he is convinced that this President Kennedy has strong support among European leaders and enough support to continue developing his power in the United States. The vice president, Yarborough, is considered a left-leaning bourgeois politician who speaks a common person's language, according to our sources. If anything, this appears to protect Kennedy against the reactionary ruling class, who consider Yarborough a 'Communist.' They expect Kennedy and Yarborough to win reelection because some business interests have been receiving bourgeois government subsidies. If Kennedy becomes a supporter of anticolonialist movements, the Soviet Union may have to compete for their support, and it may hurt our international credibility if we do not consider arms control, more economic assistance, and perhaps other reforms—"

"Precisely what I am thinking, Comrade Yuri Vladimirovich! I daresay it may force us to move in the direction of economic reforms along the lines of what President Kosygin has suggested. How can we compete economically with the Americans without improving our own economic condition? I am starting to long for the sureness of Stalin's time but recall all too well the personal uncertainty for those in our position when a single leader was able to act with such 'sureness.' Comrade, I believe we must begin the process of having you join the Politburo. We need new blood there. I will speak with perhaps one of our friendlier comrades about nominating you for a position. We will need your international perspective and swift analysis to respond to this situation as it unfolds. You and I may also find ourselves having to decide whether to join Kosygin or stay with Brezhnev—and how best to maintain our position, wherever that takes us . . . "

Suslov, later in the night after that conversation, realized he had told more than he wanted to tell his protégé. From his experience in the Politburo and in Soviet "politics," he did not like any specific discussion of a fundamental change in policy that was outside official channels. He was old enough to recall how easy it was for "Comrade" Stalin to have people "admit" to things they didn't know they were thinking of with reference to intrigue and treason, when all they may have voiced—if anything—was a mere concern over an individual policy, however trivial, at any given time.

Chapter 20

RISING WITH THE FALL

Fortunately and unfortunately, none of the foreign policy problems or successes merited much attention from the American electorate when compared with the union organizing and civil rights marches taking place in the South. The union organizing was proceeding apace in the southern states, with sporadic violence and the continued presence of federal troops in Alabama, Georgia, and North Carolina for weeks or months at a time.

Kennedy refused to hold troops in any given locale for more than six weeks. "I don't want this to look like Reconstruction, " he said to Secretary Reuther. It took more than two years for Americans to see that Kennedy had followed "the six weeks and out" pattern, even though, on occasion, troops stayed longer than six weeks in a few Southern cities.

Before noticing that Kennedy was presiding over a second Reconstruction, Americans noticed another pattern: When federal troops and national guardsmen were called out, it was the formerly "radical" students providing support to the troops and guardsmen—complete with songs, donations of food and clothing, cookies, and coffee. A couple of romances even blossomed between female "labor freedom riders" and troops or guardsmen.

What surprised the nation, and heartened Bob Kennedy in terms of his political fortunes, was that the *new* violent radicals were white, conservative fraternity students and some antiunion workers screaming epithets and getting into fights with the guards and troops. The national guardsmen at Louisiana State University, during one such conservative student demonstration against unions and civil rights, shot and killed three white students in April 1970. One of the students killed was a young Nazi follower named David Duke. The National Guard spokesman claimed Duke had a gun in his possession, although David's family denied the allegation. While the guardsmen were later cleared of any manslaughter charges, allegations continued in the conservative press that the investigation was a "cover-up" and that the troops were "itching for a fight" with the radical conservative students.

The mood of the nation, in the words of Secretary Reuther, remained strongly positive toward union organizers and the union movement as a result. The violence, if anything, put the conservative politicians and pundits on the defensive, forcing them to say they abhorred all violence and to defensively argue that "conservatism does not mean marching and fighting." The radical left-wing journalist Izzy Stone quipped in his *Weekly* newsletter, "It's about time the shoe was on the other foot—meaning the *right* foot!"

Stone, in a more reflective article a week after making that quip, reminded his readers about such thugs in the highly charged political atmosphere in America and Europe in the 1930s. "Each political viewpoint has its own dirty laundry, including those of us who have supported radical reform from a socialist or leftist perspective. We must break the cycle of demanding draconian responses against those with whom we disagree. Demonizing our enemies is bad for our political discourse and for our nation in the long run, if not sooner. If there are proven violent attacks against police or civilians, that is one thing. With the killings at LSU, there are still more questions than answers right now, and it would be better if the nation's liberals showed more compassion for the families of those students who were killed. One never knows where the next act of violence will come from and against whom it will be committed."

As a result of the violent right-wing and racist protests, southern politicians now found it easier to side with the union and civil rights movements, particularly with the clergy who supported the unions and the civil rights groups—and they were able to say, in patriotic tones, that they supported the president "in a time of crisis." The politicians now made inspirational speeches about the well-behaved VISTA and union freedom-rider volunteers who were helping to create better working conditions and to improve wages for all working people. More whites and blacks were being registered to vote at labor union halls and churches than ever before, a trend that boded very well for those politicians, as well as the president.

President Kennedy remained concerned, however, about inflation—despite the fact that it was held in check because business leaders were afraid that if they raised prices, the administration would clamp down with wage and price controls. Kennedy, recognizing that businesses would not hold down their prices for long, said on more than one occasion to his aides that this could be his Achille's heel, for if he instituted wage and price controls, he was not sure how the public would react.

Meanwhile, Kennedy had not said much about the environment. This, however, did not mean the issue was lying dormant. Interior Secretary Stewart Udall, after being stung by the treatment he had received in the early days of the Kennedy II administration, decided the way to pass environmental legislation was to immerse himself in the mechanics of writing laws and engaging in traditional coalition building outside and "under the White House's radar," as he put it to Senator Gaylord Nelson of Wisconsin.

The strategy first called for coordinating with environmental groups to lead town meetings with people around the country who were on the short end of the developers' and industry's stick, such as those who lived down-stream from plants spewing toxic waste and those in poor areas, north and south, who lived near waste "factories." This allowed Udall to counter the belief that the environment was an elitist or upper-class person's concern. These meetings also featured hunters (including a few from the National Rifle Association) and campers who were concerned about the loss of "natural wonder" and the need for a "balance of wildlife."

As Udall said to his brother Morris, "I taught middle-aged white gun owners and hunters—at least some of them—that 'balanced ecosystems' are good for maintaining hunting populations!"

In dealing with congressional representatives, the interior secretary proposed provisions in the environmental laws that detailed government subsidy programs for building "new technology recycling plants" in particular districts. "A little pork with the nature-lovers' salads," is how Udall put it in one meeting with his aides.

Even if Kennedy was largely ignoring the issue, the environment stayed on the public's television screens during 1969 and 1970. First, there was the spectacular but tragic fire in 1969 on Cleveland's toxin-laden Cuyahoga River. Later in the year, similar fires broke out along the Great Lakes, which were also full of industrial waste and sludge. The suffering of the American lakes and rivers was so great that it soon became fodder for jokes by late-night television talk show hosts. Deadpanned Johnny Carson, "It used to be a miracle if someone could walk on water. But I read yesterday a garbage man—sorry, a 'sanitation engineer'—practically ran a fifty-yard dash across Lake Michigan!"

Other rivers, including the Delaware River near Philadelphia, were rapidly losing their fish population, not to mention plant life around the river, from the discharge of polluting chemicals and sewage.

Stewart Udall made several public appearances and held conferences at each of these places identified in the news. He met with local, state, and federal officials, and with industry and labor leaders to get them to agree "that environmental concerns," as Udall said, "are not just for bird-watchers and nature-lovers. Such concerns are about preserving life itself on our planet for our children and our communities."

Secretary of Labor Reuther, in his address to the AFL-CIO in the fall of 1969, offered "solidarity" with Udall's concerns, saying to the labor convention, "Labor is in favor of doing everything we can to protect nature and our environment! Having clean air to breathe and safe water to drink is as important as having good working conditions and good wages at our jobs!" In the back rooms with Udall, however, Reuther was a formidable foe of placing environmental concerns above workers' concerns. He liked having environmental laws in theory, but not at the cost of union-scale factory jobs. This forced Udall to constantly develop cost-benefit analyses for Reuther showing new job creation resulting from the pursuit of environmental goals, something that was hard to do as it crossed into various industries—and various unions.

Udall had spent the better part of a year trying make the environmental movement as American as apple pie, baseball, and the flag. As part of that effort, he promoted the first Earth Day, which, after initially being pushed aside by Kennedy, was now set for April 21, 1970. Senators Mike Mansfield and Gaylord Nelson, in order to help Udall, appointed Nelson's young aide— Denis Hayes of Stanford University—to do the "leg work" and organize festivities around the nation for this new "holiday."

Earth Day events took place as planned on that date, which was John Muir's 132nd birthday. As part of the price of Udall's involvement, the main festivities were held in Chicago, Illinois. Udall wanted to highlight the horrible industrial pollution of the lakes surrounding Chicago. Mayor Daley did not like to call attention to such things, but the payoff was in the form of massive federal subsidies and government-paid jobs that Alderman Thomas Hayden—no longer "Tom"—demanded be spread throughout the city, particularly among the black population on the South Side of Chicago.

Udall, in his speech, presented the issue of environmental consciousness to America as part of "the seamless garment of life and the continuing thread of history, in the timeless words of our president." Chicago's Cardinal Bernardin gave the invocation on the moral imperative for people of all faiths to protect our planet. As Bernardin said, "God has given us this planet, and we are its shepherds and stewards. It is an awesome and abiding responsibility. As people of any religious faith know, it is a sin to shirk from this responsibility."

Others who spoke in Chicago that day included Vice President Yarborough, Alderman Hayden, Mayor Daley himself (who opened his very brief remarks by saying, "Now, I'm not one o' dem guys who eats Grapenuts, but . . . "), Denis Hayes, and the well-known television and radio personality Arthur Godfrey. The speakers spoke of the safety and health hazards of water and air pollution. They spoke of the disturbing new trend in the lumber industry to clear-cut entire old-growth forests, which, Udall said, "threatened to undermine the gains of conservation efforts adopted by *Republican* administrations in the 1920s!"

"And the *Socialist* forester, Robert Marshall, who worked for those Republicans!" shouted environmentalist activist David Brower from the front of the audience. The comment caused more than one nervous chuckle from the podium where the speakers sat.

The speakers also spoke of endangered species, including "that symbol of America, the bald eagle." They demanded that Americans recognize that "poor people and working people disproportionately bear the brunt of the toxic smell of our air, the sewage that turns our lakes into liquid asphalt, and the respiratory and pulmonary diseases that arise in distressed communities," in the words of Senator Nelson.

Denis Hayes made the evening television news with his quip: "If the environment is a fad, it could be our last fad."

Udall also chose Earth Day to announce his support, with Kennedy's "tacit" approval—given only after Reuther and Yarborough agreed—of the first Clean Air and Clean Water Acts then pending before Congress. To secure passage and funding, the bills were amended to include job-training programs for poor communities in recycling and other environmental-control businesses. Also included in the bills were retraining subsidies for textile workers in the South, lumber workers in the Northwest, and other factory and mine workers throughout the nation in case of job loss. The programs were to be administered out of the Department of Interior in cooperation with the Labor Department. Denis Hayes and Barry Commoner, a scientist and environmental activist who was teaching at a Midwest university, were asked to lead the environmental division of the Interior Department.

The bill also included programs for research and development of alternative fuels, with the Department of Commerce teaming up with National Institutes of Health and the National Academy of Sciences to oversee such endeavors.

Udall, through his congressman brother, Morris, and Senator Nelson, convinced various representatives and senators, including Democrat Wayne Hays of Ohio, Democrat Shirley Chisolm of New York (the first black woman elected to Congress in the twentieth century), and Republican Mark Hatfield of Oregon to cosponsor the first federal environmental laws. Their staffs worked with Ralph Nader's Public Citizen consumer organization, environmental groups such as the Sierra Club, and the AFL-CIO's hastily created "environmental working group," headed by Tony Mazzocchi of the Oil, Chemical, and Atomic Workers International Union, in crafting the first legislation. Mazzocchi proved to be an ironically strong choice for Udall's purposes as Mazzocchi had been championing the cause of safety at the workplace and had been at least privately sympathetic to environmental concerns.[1]

"We'll make a lot of jobs there," said Representative Wilbur Mills to Udall during one planning session, "and there's some good money from Uncle Sam for incentives to the right businesses who support us and who want to enter into these environmental enterprises." Mills had suddenly found "religion," said Udall, who noted the increased voter registration from the union and civil rights movements had added new voters to assuage in Mills' Arkansas district.

Kennedy had not attended any Earth Day events. He had followed the suggestion of the O Boys, who called Earth Day a "third rail" too dangerous to touch. Publicly, he claimed to be too tied up in foreign affairs matters in Vietnam and with the slow-moving arms control negotiations with the Soviets. But Kennedy recognized a bandwagon when he saw one. He therefore spoke about the environment in his next weekly radio broadcast after the success of the Earth Day festivities among the American people.

The Republicans also knew how to spot an issue to oppose the Kennedy administration. Congressman William Roth of Delaware, running for the Senate in 1970, said on the Sunday afternoon political talk show, *Issues and*

Answers, "All this environmental law-making sounds like New Deal–creep-ing socialism to me." Roth, a fast-rising star in an otherwise moribund Republican Party, also said on the interview program, "I think the govern-ment ought to assist business in developing new ways to help people and protecting against pollution, but I do not like this demonizing of our nation's chemical companies that we hear so often. And this talk in new laws about retraining workers—to do God knows what!—is more Washington hocus-pocus. Jobs are created by business, not government. I'm also worried about losing the budget surplus we started with when this particular President Kennedy took office."

Roth was, between the political commentary, worried about one particu-lar chemical company in his home state—the international conglomerate DuPont. Dupont produced many chemical products as well as industrial goods. DuPont was also, of course, a major backer of Roth in his upcoming campaign for the Senate.

Kennedy was glad the Republicans were forced to say "yes, but . . . " when it came to environmental protection. On the other hand, he was con-stantly thinking about the midterm elections set for November. At the cabinet meeting following the successful Earth Day, Kennedy complimented Udall for building a strong foundation with clergy, labor groups, and minorities, and not simply the usual "nature lovers, who tend to be well-off and likely to vote Republican. I never would have believed it, but our stance on the environ-ment may actually help us with swing voters in this midterm election year."

Yarborough added, "Ah am also pleased that we were able to rustle up some o' them NRA gun folks on protectin' our natural resources, Mr. Secretary. Been startin' to wonder where we stand with them folks since we're still goin' on 'bout gun control—not much talk, thank goodness!" Attorney General Ramsey Clark furrowed his brow, disappointed that gun control efforts had been stymied.

Yarborough, a former supporter of further regulation of the purchase or use of guns, had cooled on the subject as he became closer than ever to organ-ized labor, which had many rank-and-file members who were hunters. That some Republican pro-business interests began to be sympathetic to gun con-trol ultimately pushed Yarborough past the tipping point. He said to Kennedy after the cabinet meeting, "We can't afford to give Republicans any issue that is popular with our constituents—but Ah say let 'em have gun control, since our own people in the unions who own guns will really stick with us then. Ah'd like to limit handguns, at least, but we need to keep our eye on the economic issues we're fightin'. If Ah had to pick an issue to put on the back-burner, Mr. President, it would be this issue o' taking away people's guns."

Kennedy nodded and said, "If doing that keeps us from losing seats in the mid-term elections, then so be it. We have much bigger issues facing us right now. Too bad, though, Ralph, I have to say."

The Democrats were not alone in facing choices regarding issues to fight for and issues to back away from. The Republican Party was also facing an even more significant ideological split. Congressman Roth, coasting toward a senate seat in corporate friendly Delaware, began to speak in various places around the nation about *cutting* taxes instead of "taking more and more tax-payers' money to build socialist dream houses."

A reporter asked Roth if tax cuts could also undermine "traditional" Republican commitments to a balanced federal budget. Roth replied that it was better to "give money back to the people to spend where they'd like than have a bunch of bureaucrats spend the money." The reporter restated his question and Roth said, with some hesitation, "If there's a small deficit for a year or two, the economy will grow from all the investment with the money we gave back." Roth, in that second reply, had now dared to openly challenge the Republican's orthodoxy of staid, balanced budget talk that had characterized Republican platforms for almost 50 years.

The Republican siding economist Herbert Stein sensed the gravity of Roth's heresy and immediately penned a strong attack against both Republican Roth and the Kennedy Democrats in a *Time* magazine essay entitled "The Bi-Partisan Tax and Spend Program". Stein wrote, "Whether it's spending or cutting taxes, both the Democrats and a growing number of Republicans are intent on creating deficits in the annual federal budget that will, in later years, cause a terrible rise in our national debt. The result of this profligate policy is high levels of inflation, a prospect that should concern us all, not merely investors."

Stein cautioned whether electing Republicans was the answer. He wrote, "It might be worse if the Republicans won back Congress in 1970 because they might force the nation to endure tax cuts and then cave in to the Democrats for increased social spending, since, as Congressman Roth says, the economy will alledgedly 'grow' enough to cover the initial decline in revenues. The Republicans need to make up their minds: Do they wish to be 'me-too' spenders, or do they wish to balance the federal budget?"

Luckily for the Democrats, the in-fighting among Republicans on a fundamental ideological plank was proving to be a bigger problem for them than the gun control issue was for the Democrats.

Nonetheless, the Kennedy administration was concerned about running too high an annual federal deficit. Toward that end, the president had resisted any increase in military spending, though he partially relented in the face of the bipartisan congressional push for MIRVing nuclear warheads. The MIRV program was worth tens of thousands of jobs in ten different districts alone, according to Reuther.

Kennedy also went against the advice of both State Secretary Bowles and Defense Secretary Warnke by proposing to the military contractors that they consider selling more weapons to other countries. Warnke put his opposition most bluntly. "Mr. President, the very people who would want to buy our arms are the military dictators who will likely use them against their own populations, as opposed to any external threat."

Kennedy responded, "Paul, you think I don't know that risk is there? I have to balance that risk against the contractors firing people with union jobs, which will increase unemployment and other social remedial spending. There are less savings than we might think with some of these military cuts, if I understand Walt Reuther right. We also need to keep an eye on our right flank, not only in the South but also in what some of our beards around here call the Cold War establishment. Some of that constituency could desert us for the Republicans, who always drop their anti–federal government rhetoric when it comes to military spending. I think Jack Newfield is right when he calls the military the biggest socialist program of them all, but a fat lot of good that insight does for us."

Kennedy finished his meeting with Bowles and Warnke saying, "Gentlemen, let's get through the mid-term elections first, shall we? Then we can revisit this."

Warnke, still trying to convince the president to see his way to start work on government programs designed to wean military contractors off military products and into civilian ones, wearily went back to his new friend, Commerce Secretary Learson, and said, "Vince, we need to strategize together on this if we're going to get anywhere."

Kennedy, in mid-July 1970, signed into law several environmental bills that contained job programs; seed and research monies for recycling industries; and studies on solar and wind power, organic food, and other "green" reforms.

Kennedy also began to call on Congress to pass a national health insurance program and for increased support for public transportation, but those particular bills languished and failed to generate significant support. Elite media commentators and Republicans (and not a few Democrats in the South) called upon various economists, including not only Herbert Stein, but also a couple of somewhat liberal economists including Aaron Wildavsky, who claimed the health insurance and public transit expansion would cause deficits to balloon to "unprecedented levels." Such deficits, they claimed, "could choke most, if not all private investment."

Even without these programs, various economists signed a petition saying that the Kennedy administration would likely face a deficit of thirty billion dollars by the fall of 1971. It was this prediction, made most forcefully by Stein, that became the figure all Republican candidates bandied about during the fall 1970 midterm election campaigns—even as they continued to support spending on *other* spending projects or tax cuts for *their* constituents, which the purist Stein abhorred.

Roth, who scoffed that "old-guard" Republicans were not living in the real world of politics, actively pursued his new tax-cutting strategy as part of his larger strategy to rebuild the Republican Party in the suburbs of the coastal cities and in well-off enclaves in between the coasts. Roth's aides noted that these areas had voters who historically showed up in high numbers on Election Day, unlike many working class districts. It was a strategy many Republican insiders were seeing as a way to sound more exciting and vote-worthy than their traditional dour lectures on thrift and balanced budgets.

Roth's growing national presence as a mere Congressman running for a Senate seat also proved that the 1972 Republican presidential nomination race was wide open. The Republican Party was in transition, and Roth, noticing his growing national media time as a spokesperson for Republicans, and maintaining a comfortable lead in his senate race, began to wonder if he might be presidential material over the next two years.

With Richard Nixon off the national stage after two presidential election defeats, the three other leading contenders, *not* including Roth, appeared to be the perennial Republican presidential candidate, New York Governor Nelson Rockefeller, and two relatively new national figures, California Governor Ronald Reagan and General Creighton Abrams.

Making things more interesting for Roth's presidential musings, Nelson Rockefeller, a leader of the liberal wing of the Republican Party, was having a hard time in his campaign for reelection as New York's governor in 1970. Although organized labor was not displeased with Rockefeller, it was strongly backing the Democratic Party's gubernatorial candidate, Arthur Goldberg. Goldberg was a well-liked former labor lawyer, Supreme Court justice, and United Nations' ambassador. Said Secretary of Labor Reuther, "Organized labor is feeling its oats. We don't need to support liberal Republicans like Rockefeller, especially in union-friendly places such as New York!" It was going to be a rocky road for the incumbent governor known as "Rocky."

Compounding difficulties for Rockefeller was the fact that Roth was gaining more and more support among business leaders, a natural constituency for Rockefeller, as Roth continued to "do battle" in Congress against the Kennedy White House. Rockefeller, thinking beyond his own state, was forced to try and balance tax cutting, balancing the budget, and his fealty to working-class voters and their labor leaders who supported more government intervention and spending for workers and the poor. This was difficult to do, at best, with Robert Kennedy in the White House actively supporting pro-labor candidates.

Roth was also challenging Reagan's economically conservative base. For Roth was more consistent on the subject of taxes than Reagan had been. Reagan did not initially sense the direction of business supporters in the Republican Party when, in his first term as California governor, he had greatly *increased* corporate, income, and sales taxes.[2] To combat this image of being a "tax and spend" governor, Reagan, in his reelection campaign for governor in 1970, suddenly threw his support behind a previously moribund bill to cut personal income taxes.

Despite Reagan's raising of various taxes, however, he reminded national Republicans that California's economy was prospering under his administration. The success of the California economy, however, could be ironically credited to federal military spending programs, federal labor law reform (which scared many employers into providing wage increases to workers rather than face labor agitation), federal water projects, and federal farm subsidies. In other words, Reagon's success may have been due to various national "tax and spend" programs that Republicans said they opposed.

As Ralph Yarborough observed to Kennedy, who would often fret about Republican campaign slogans and strategies, "Ah find most corporate folks, when they are away from their country club meetin's and Rotary Club convention speechifyin', are happy to have federal subsidies and military 'make-work' programs. So let's remahnd people out there that Republicans are only for cuttin' government when it comes to the li'l guy, not them." Kennedy liked it when he heard Yarborough say it, but so far, he hadn't found a way to say it in any way that made him comfortable.

Another potential Republican presidential candidate also worried Kennedy, and that was General Abrams. The general had already wrapped up the vote of those Republicans who still lit candles to the "beloved" memory of the Red-baiting 1950s senator from Wisconsin, Joseph R. McCarthy. The number of such Republicans was small, but included many of the small town activists who mailed the mailers and went to local Republican Party committee meetings.

In speech after speech to Rotary Clubs, Kiwanis Clubs, Chambers of Commerce, and the Boy Scouts—and even once to the Girl Scouts, where he made clear that women ought not be forced or even allowed in the foxhole with dirty, dangerous men—Abrams talked about the Communist threat to the American way of life. He also did his best to line up as many business supporters as he could. What Kennedy worried about with Abrams was how good Abrams might look if the Communists overran Vietnam and America was unable to stop them. And that was a real worry, no matter what had happened so far.

Despite Kennedy's continued nervousness about likely Republican pick-ups in the 1970 congressional midterm elections, Kennedy had more and more cause for what he called "cautious optimism" as the year 1970 wore on. First, there were new reports from the Justice Department that showed the crime rate had decreased slightly for the year 1969, a trend that continued even more strongly into 1970. This was good news for Kennedy's domestic agenda, as it allowed him to connect increased anti-poverty spending with declining crime, something that was not happening in the mid-1960s.

When the latest crime rate figures were released, it convinced Kennedy that Yarborough and Reuther were right to "back-burner" gun control as an issue. This political decision shocked Kennedy's wife and many of his well-to-do supporters, but Kennedy followed his political nose, not his political heart.

Gun control advocates, stunned at first, began to confront Kennedy with what they called "details" from the good news in the drop in the crime rate. They correctly pointed out that the overall decrease in crime rates masked an *increase* in violent crime in the South and in some inner cities in the North and West.

Kennedy responded to gun control advocates by pointing to the success of the Bedford-Stuyvesant "experiment," his inner-city "baby." The Bedford-Stuyvesant project was designed to use federal sources to help inner city poverty-stricken areas help themselves, with job training, local business subsidies, and federally paid jobs. This would, said Kennedy, "reinvigorate a new culture of working and independence." Kennedy had an easier time with liberal congressmen, and even some liberal Republicans, than he did with some civil rights leaders who saw the program as diverting attention from racial integration in the cities and the suburbs. But Kennedy met privately with all leading civil rights leaders to assure them that integration in the form of anti-discrimination enforcement was his top judicial and law enforcement priority. Further, he said that rebuilding cities, which contained largely racial and ethnic minorities, was good for their community development and would allow those successful minorities to more easily transition to suburban environments if they wished.

Congress easily passed legislation promoting the Bed-Sty program for that particular area. New York Governor Rockefeller, hoping to keep some black voters from deserting him for the labor-endorsed Goldberg, added state monies for the program. However, as the state monies were supported by Democrats and Republicans, Rockefeller "got less mileage than he thought," according to one of his campaign aides at the time.

After a year of the program's existence, Kennedy proudly noted to gun control advocates that the crime rate in Bed-Sty had gone down by more than 38 percent between 1969 and 1970, according to Justice Department statistics. As Kennedy began to deliciously add, this was all done without any gun control legislation—and with already existing New York state gun control laws, which, gun control advocates admitted, had loopholes big enough to drive a big rig truck through.

The Bed-Sty project was also good for expanding union participation without undermining existing union workers' jobs. Under the legislation, the federal government paid union workers to train previously unemployed black workers for private sector jobs in Bed-Sty. "This is no different than federal farm subsidies going to big agriculture companies," said Reuther in a sometimes testy exchange with Republican Senator Dole on the subject. The legislation also provided that, if there were no immediate jobs for the trainees, the first "jobs" would be fixing up the Bed-Sty community—which, since the administration knew there were no jobs, was precisely the point.

To further placate skeptical civil rights leaders, Julian Bond came forward with a plan out of the Housing and Urban Development Department to integrate black youth into the building trades by requiring the government to accept only union labor for these jobs, and that the union labor be "local." Reuther loved the idea because it allowed white workers, who were not getting work in Bed-Sty anyway, to further help black workers take care of the blacks' neighborhoods and not feel any immediate competition. It also allowed black and white workers to be in the same unions, which meant more bi-racial solidarity, now in the North as well as the South.

Besides government subsidies helping rebuild Bed-Sty, there were volunteer workers and monetary grants from the unions and businesses (including the AFL-CIO, Ford Motor Company, Tom Watson's IBM, and the investment banking firm, Lazard Freres), and charity groups such as the Big Brother and Big Sister programs and the United Way. The key, said Bond, Reuther, and others, was to develop a sense of pride of ownership by having the people of the area involved, motivated and working.[3]

Kennedy knew, however, that in promoting the program, labor and black civil rights leaders' support was not enough. He needed to convince the great white majority in places where blacks were seldom seen or heard, and saw big cities as places where there raged all sorts of sin, that this was a good investment for America as a nation. In his nationwide speech announcing the experimental program, Kennedy said, "Our program is not some complicated, bureaucratic, red-tape-laden program. It is based upon common sense and what everyone, liberal or conservative, Democrat or Republican, can agree upon for any local community in distress: Fix the windows, remove lead paint and asbestos, repaint and reroof buildings with modern and safer materials, and clean the streets. By paying people to perform their own work, with workers from other areas providing assistance, we will restore a sense of pride in these troubled communities—and rebuild a trust that used to exist between one community and another. The property crime rates will fall as people see that things are better and can remain better with proper care and respect. Businesses will also feel more secure in coming back to a community where there is self-respect.

"Our new policy also encourages city police officers to work with churches and other community groups, and to get to know the people of the community on a personal basis. Most people in these areas want the best for their children and are afraid of criminal elements that prey upon them and their families. We will also take affirmative steps to recruit local young men into the ranks of the police so that at least some of the people serving the community live in the community." While this last policy would prove most difficult to enforce in practice, it was something Kennedy insisted upon with the support of Attorney General Ramsey Clark and Housing Secretary Bond.

The morning after Kennedy's speech, Allard Lowenstein announced that his VISTA "kids"—college students and young men and women in their twenties—would be "all over Bed-Sty." The VISTA volunteers immediately descended upon the area, first by going door-to-door and making telephone calls to promote the training programs. They also gave help to the overworked and frustrated teachers in the schools by tutoring the "slower" students before and after school, and mentoring "troubled" students. The volunteers supported social workers hired to work at individual "social crisis" centers and family counseling centers. Certain universities, including a few Ivy League schools, gave "credit" in the summer, and eventually during the year, to students who took part in VISTA programs. As the houses were being cleaned, and job training and education support arrived, prostitution and drug dealing rapidly declined.

As harbingers of a national cultural trend, the VISTA volunteers and labor freedom riders became more and more embarrassed by their own "recreational use" of marijuana and other drugs that had begun in the mid-1960s. Many of the young people in the VISTA program and labor freedom rides had been "clean" in the Eugene McCarthy and Bob Kennedy campaigns of 1968—meaning they had cut their hair, stopped taking drugs, and put on clean, conservative clothing of the time. Now they found their "cleanliness" was no longer a short-term strategic political maneuver but a completely new lifestyle, at least for them. The expanded VISTA programs and labor freedom aides, and the Kennedy administration's support, had begun to affect how young people saw themselves within the nation's larger culture. The generation gap was beginning to narrow as well, with older union workers working side by side with younger VISTA workers, and even younger union workers—all for the same goals of improving living and working conditions for black and white workers in America.

It also helped that the government-mandated minimum wages in 1969 were well *above* the poverty level, and municipal government jobs were paying the minimum wage as a starting rate for these largely black and Puerto Rican-born workers in Bedford-Stuyvesant. Unbeknownst to many voters, until Kennedy signed federal legislation on the subject in 1969, most municipal jobs had been exempt from the federal minimum wage requirements. The jobs also included federal employee medical benefits, which meant that poor inner-city parents who had young children quickly saw the upside of employment overall, especially following the job training.

Down came many of the liquor stores and up went restaurants catering first to the government workers and then to the newborn black entrepreneurs and white-collar (called "white-*colored*" by black nationalist detractors) workers from the new businesses springing up in town. The improved economic conditions increased the marriage rate among the community's inhabitants. The increased marriage rate consequently lowered the welfare rate by more than 40 percent in Bed-Sty from mid-1969 through mid-1970, according to a study from Sargent Shriver's Health, Education, and Welfare Department.

Bed-Sty also became a safer place for outside businesses to relocate than states in the South undergoing racial and union strife. As a concession to other industrial-area economies, no federal matching funds were allowed for businesses that relocated a plant from another region into Bed-Sty. The growth had to be from a new plant, said government officials.

Watson's IBM led the way in building a new plant in Bed-Sty, saying, "We were planning to build a new plant overseas, believe it or not. However, we decided that we should expand our domestic operations in Bedford-Stuyvesant as we now see an *increase* in our domestic consumer base. We will not, at least at this time, need to cut other labor costs to protect profits." Watson, of course, also liked the federal subsidies for the new plant.

Southern politicians began calling the Kennedy administration for seed monies for their inner cities and rural areas. Mayor Daley and Alderman Hayden also called seeking a "Bed-Sty" program for the South Side of Chicago. "A helluva program, Mr. President," said Daley. "This is as good as the Civilian Conservation Corps—somethin' you oughta consider revivin', too! Lots o' dese Negro kids still gettin' too much o' dat Black Panther stuff—need ta clear de'r heads in da countryside plantin' trees, ya know?"

Hayden, in a separate call later in the same day, said, "The mayor is right about the CCC, but wrong about the Panthers. I have completely won over Fred Hampton, the leading Panther here in Chicago. His breakfast and tutoring program, which he started in '68, is now receiving local city funds—and funds from a couple of the banks here, and even Sears. It's great publicity for them, and Sears is considering opening a store on the South Side based upon that subsidy program. It is not a relocation, but a new Sears store."[4]

Kennedy said, "No problem, Tom. You keep working with Mayor Daley. But one thing—"

Hayden gulped, not knowing what the president was asking.

"Are we getting these people registered to vote later this year?"

"Yes, sir!" laughed Hayden. "That's what it's all about, isn't it? That and getting them to the polls on election day!"

Kennedy laughed right back and said, "You know, Tom, you think you're influencing Mayor Daley, which you are. But he is sure influencing you. I bet you'd still be picketing in the streets if we weren't here!"

Hayden was laughing nervously now. "Well, um, I uh—"

Kennedy sensed he had gone too far. "Sorry, Tom. I shouldn't have said that. You've been very supportive, and I deeply respect what you have stood for these past years."

"Thank you, sir. That means a great deal to me."

"Fine. Let's see you next time I'm out Chicago way. Bye." Click.

The Bed-Sty program was popular with almost everyone, but not necessarily with J. Edgar Hoover over at the F.B.I. In late 1969, Attorney General Clark came to the president saying, "Mr. President, Mr. Hoover's FBI is becoming a problem again. They are engaging in some frankly nefarious conduct in this so-called COINTELPRO, which is the Counter-Intelligence Program started against Communists back in the '50s. He's continuing to use it against black groups, not just the Panthers, and worse, he's using it against what he calls 'Communist infiltration of the VISTA program.'"

Kennedy motioned Clark to sit down. "I know about the COINTEL program, Ramsey. You, Mr. Hoover, and I limited Mr. Hoover's activities by requiring him to go through you before any surveillance was placed upon any but the most violent elements of the Panthers. We recognized there was a schism in some Panther parties, with some very good members such as Fred Hampton in Chicago and that Bobby Seale fellow out in Oakland. I just got word from California Assembly Speaker Jess Unruh that Seale's gonna run for Assembly from Oakland—as a union-supporting Democrat!"

"Sir, I am aware of all that—except that last part. My concern is that Hoover is just going ahead without our approval, and most of it through agents not likely to tell us, either. I have managed, nonetheless, to obtain new information showing he is still sending agents into the Panthers and other black-oriented groups without our approval. He is creating phony documents designed to make people believe that most Panthers favor violence. There was even a flyer and pamphlet prepared by an agent, approved by high-ranking F.B.I. officials, that were meant to stir up black and Jewish hatred—the Jews are admittedly overrepresented in the VISTA programs. Frankly, this type of behavior is likely to bring about what Mr. Hoover claims he is trying to stop. And it's not simply black communities. Hoover has actually, if you can believe this, recruited, ahem . . . lesbians—" Clark shuddered with embarrassment—"to infiltrate women's consciousness-raising groups and women's rights groups in San Francisco, Manhattan, and Ann Arbor, Michigan."

"What does he want to do with the women's groups, do you suppose? Stop bra burning?" Kennedy laughed at his own joke.

Clark wasn't laughing, however. "Sir, Mr. Hoover and I have no love lost, as you know. I also know you have kept him on, and, no matter what he's said, he shows little sense that he's retiring at the end of your first term. I—"

"Ramsey, we may not love J. Edgar Hoover, but he is a fixture here with many powerful friends. You think you're alone in coming to me on this? Walt Reuther is very steamed about Hoover sending agents into the ranks of union organizers. Hoover says the unions are becoming 'hotbeds of Communism once again.' I remember in the 1950s, Hoover warned me, through associates of his, about Walter being a Red. Unbelievable. I wish he were even half as interested in organized crime as I was back in the—" Kennedy remembered he was supposed to be defending Hoover now. "All the same," Kennedy said, clearing his voice, "Mr. Hoover is not going away. I think the best thing is to have a meeting with him, confront him, and let him know that I will back you in making sure you, as attorney general of the United States, have full access to FBI policies and decision making in this particular regard. He already knows where I stand on the infiltration of the labor groups. The attorney general, not the FBI, since as far back as Truman, and maybe FDR, has always been in charge of determining whether a group is considered 'subversive' and the response thereto."

Kennedy had become legalistic in his speech as he desperately tried to defend the FBI director, whom he hated more than ever. But as long as Hoover held the secrets of the Kennedy family, and his brother's administration, it was difficult for Kennedy to counter him. Attorney General Clark said, "Mr. President, we'll need another meeting together, with you present, if I am going to be effective in controlling his . . . excesses—I hate using that word to describe someone who runs the FBI."

"After the start of the new year then," Kennedy said, more coldly than he intended.

"Yes, Mr. President," said a disappointed Clark, who knew that meant after the mid-term elections. "Is there anything else you wish to speak with me about at this time, sir?"

"Nothing, Ramsey, other than I am pleased with the crime reports showing the decline in various crimes where our programs are taking root. It shows the quality of your analysis of the causes of crime, I should note."

"Thank you, Mr. President. I'll speak to you when I present my next update."

After Clark left, Kennedy thought to himself, Hoover will never change, damn it. Even Wallace, that racist son of a bitch, is showing signs of moderation. But Hoover! Christ! He thinks he's above everyone! The president, Congress, the Supreme Court. Everyone! I can't wait until 1972 when he finally quits—if he sticks to his deal.

It was true, as Kennedy noticed, that George Wallace was "moderating" himself. Wallace was serving as governor of Alabama through his wife, who had been elected governor in order to defeat the intent of term limits in Alabama. In speeches Wallace made to various groups, he was starting to make noise that "he'd always been fair to the nigra," and "Ah think that fed'ral gum'mint money aw'ta help *all* our people, black an' white, get jobs here that pay good an' treat people good."[5]

But all was not perfect with the Bed-Sty program and urban renewal under President Robert Kennedy. The most controversial consequence of the Bed-Sty experiment was the fact that minority voters in these areas, more empowered than ever, were voting or pressuring out various white ethnic superintendents of schools, school boards, and district attorneys, most of whom were either Jewish or Italian. This was happening regardless of whether these ethnic whites were liberal or conservative on matters of race and economic issues. Jews and Italians left their employment in municipal departments of Bed-Sty in droves, which caused the community to become more racially segregated; meaning it was now more black and Puerto Rican than ever before. The good news of lower crime and more employment trumped the bad news since those on the losing end—the white ethnic groups—fled anonymously to jobs in the suburbs.[6]

Black (though for some reason not Puerto Rican) middle-class families became the staple of newspaper and television "success stories," which comforted most whites across America. This, ironically, further undermined pro-racial integrationists among the civil rights leadership, creating a schism between Bed-Sty supporters and those who supported integration first and foremost.

The most angry integrationists were those who had supported forced busing as an integration solution for American inner city and suburban schools. Using busing to achieve integration of the schools was proceeding apace in the South, where blacks and whites lived close together. In the North, however, the battle to bus white and black children over long distances was just starting through the judicial system. And Robert Kennedy wanted no part of that battle. In mid-1970, the Kennedy administration, through Solicitor General Roger Wilkins, argued in a government, friend-of-the-court, legal brief—*against* several of the school busing programs, beginning in Boston—where Kennedy administration officials heard loud grievances from both black and white parents. The whites had "the usual reasons" against busing their children to predominantly black schools, said Wilkins in a memo to the president. The surprise for Wilkins and other civil rights leaders was that blacks in the poorer sections of Boston objected, too. The reason, it turned out, was that blacks in the Roxbury district of Boston, and other poorer districts, had just begun to receive federal subsidies similar to those given out in Bed-Sty. They saw the importance of avoiding what a white radical activist, Barney Frank, called "the brain drain" of professional blacks leaving "home" for jobs in the still mostly white suburbs.

"These better educated and more achievement oriented blacks," Frank told Wilkins before the start of a town meeting on the subject of busing, "are the glue that holds this fragile community together. And their parents don't want their children to leave the community, especially when they see an opportunity to finally build up the community."

Solicitor General Wilkins, still under pressure to support integration from his uncle and some other nationally known civil rights leaders, announced his opposition to busing, but phrased his argument on the basis that the busing program was disruptive to local control of schools for blacks in the inner city. As Wilkins said to Harvard sociology professor Kenneth Clark, whose studies on the positive effects of integration had led to the unanimous Supreme Court decision against school segregation in the 1950s, "Dr. Clark, I, too, am concerned that not pursuing full integration could be detrimental to black children's self-esteem and grades. On the other hand, the Bed-Sty experience, plus my discussions with white activists and black parents, is beginning to convince me that rebuilding neighborhoods and allowing black parents to have more participation in their local schools should also improve self-esteem. My arguments to the Boston federal judge have merely asked for time to consider this experiment before mandating a busing solution that right now at least has slipping support in the black community and outright hostility from the white ethnics."

Dr. Clark, no relation to the Attorney General, was not happy, he told Wilkins, but was willing to give this another year or two. "Roger, our opportunity to complete integration could slip by us if the Republicans win the presidency in 1972. Please keep a close eye on this development. I have known you and your uncle too long—and your Uncle Roy, I know, agrees with my concerns—to believe that you will turn your back on the movement for equal rights under the law."

Wilkins' arguments had the effect of stopping most of the pro-busing rulings coming out of liberal judges' courtrooms. Courts were glad to put off a ruling on the grounds of it being "not ripe" for adjudication in light of other government initiatives. The Supreme Court rejected a hearing on such a ruling, even though some scholars, such as the young liberal professor Laurence Tribe, found the "ripeness" argument to be inapplicable to this situation. "The question, sixteen years after *Brown v. Board of Education,* which assured the right of blacks to attend integrated schools, is more than ripe. The fruit on this judicial branch is so 'ripe' it is starting to rot. If this position of the courts, backed improbably by the Kennedy administration, continues, it will most certainly rot and die on the branch of the mighty judicial tree."

Black radicals and bohemians had their own separate critique against the "black success" stories coming from what people in the media were now referring to as "Bed-*Stay*" programs. In the fall of 1970, Stanley Crouch, a young black writer for the bohemian New York weekly, the *Village Voice,* criticized the mainstream, white-dominated media for creating what he called the "Julia-ization" of black America. "Julia" was the name of a somewhat banal situation-comedy television show about a black nurse who worked for a cantankerous older white doctor. Said Crouch in his essay, "Julia, the light-skinned black nurse with European features, exhibits no knowledge of Langston Hughes, Paul Robeson, or Ethel Waters—I can't imagine she ever heard of Ben Davis or William Worthy! Julia has no memory of Emmitt Till or Medgar Evers, martyrs of the civil rights movement. Yes, she knows of Martin Luther King, but how could she not? She is virtually indistinguishable from a white suburban mother who has no husband—and that should be the greatest cause for alarm among those who care about the African-American experience in today's America. Where is the dark black father? In jail? On welfare? Still doing 'clean-up' in Vietnam?"

Although Crouch's analysis rang more true for certain blacks in New York, who hadn't dealt with—or had forgotten about—Southern and Midwestern racism, many blacks outside the major Northeast and West Coast cities clamored and prayed to be as "normal" as "Julia" and whites in general. Most blacks were not seeking to "raise their culturally radical 'consciousness'" said the now elderly black union leader A. Phillip Randolph in a reply letter to the *Voice*. "Contrary to Mr. Crouch, most blacks need jobs, stability, and safety in their lives first, not another course in bohemian and radical Negro history."

Julius Lester, in his radio program on New York's radical station WBAI, said in response to Randolph's letter, "Spoken like a true light-skinned, passing brother!" At the other end of the spectrum, however, right-wing black writer George Schuyler wrote in the *Manchester (New Hampshire) Union Leader*, "Mr. Randolph understands very well the corruption in the thinking of those who extol the myths of the so-called Harlem Renaissance of the 1920s. Now, if Mr. Randolph could only disabuse himself of his misplaced faith in unions and socialism. That, unfortunately, is too much to ask in light of 'Comrade' Randolph's career."

In the Kennedy II era, jobs were being created and welfare rolls were shrinking. No American workers' jobs were moving overseas, but they were expanding into American inner cities. The resulting tax revenues from inner-city workers' wages, the purchase of tools and materials for rebuilding neighborhoods, from the construction of recycling factories and laboratories for the study of alternative fuels, and from other new occupations, kept the deficit below seven billion dollars for the 1971 fiscal year budget. The budget for 1971 was set in October of the preceding year, as is customary. The fact that this was one month before the 1970 midterm election was a happy coincidence, said Ken Galbraith to President Kennedy. Galbraith also gloated, "I guess my friend Herbert Stein was a bit off in his doom-and-gloom."

Stein, for his part, wrote an article in the *Wall Street Journal* after the elections that said the seven-billion-dollar budget deficit was a sign of future inflation and worse deficits to come. The public, however, was uninterested in future predictions of this sort. The Republicans, including Stein, had overstated the budgeted fiscal 1971 deficit, which was itself merely a forecast set by the nominally objective Congressional Budget Office. Many Republican politicians, unlike Stein, also recognized—too late—the antideficit strategy was a loser with voters.[7]

In the midterm elections, California Governor Reagan, in his reelection campaign, barely squeaked past his Democratic opponent, Assembly Speaker Jess Unruh. Worse for the Republican Party's prestige, New York Governor Rockefeller lost, in a very close election, to Arthur Goldberg. Rocky, defying his advisers, had been outside the state "on the road" for a good part of the campaign trying to keep up with Abrams, and sometimes Roth, on the "rubber-chicken, business-club circuit." He refused to believe the polls showing a close race with Goldberg, telling his frustrated campaign manager, "All I have to keep saying is 'Hi-ya, fellas' when I'm with the little people. The ones who supported me before will vote for me again, I'm sure of it. The economy in New York's getting better, not worse, and people'll vote their pocketbooks. They won't vote for a New York City Jewish labor lawyer, especially Protestant and Catholic voters who are upstate."

But Rocky was wrong this time. Although Rockefeller won a small victory in many parts of rural New York, it was in the larger cities of Buffalo, Rochester, and, of course, New York City, and even in parts of Long Island, where Goldberg, seen as a scrappy, but thoughtful man, overwhelmed Rockefeller with white working class and minority support. Kennedy made three trips to New York in the last two months of the campaign, twice when Rockefeller was out of town. Kennedy never criticized Rockefeller, though, because of Rockefeller's support during the American military withdrawal from Vietnam. Instead, as he said in a speech in New York City, "Nelson Rockefeller is a great Republican—and I wish there were more like him—no booing now. This isn't a war; it's an election in a free country! As I say, Mr. Rockefeller is a very good person. *But,* candidates such as Arthur Goldberg come along only once in fifty years. No one, I repeat, no one, will fight and protect your interests as citizens, as working people, and as Americans better than Arthur Goldberg! He is the *best* choice for governor this November!"[8]

As Kennedy said to the O Boys the night of the election, "I can't stop thinking about whether Rockefeller would have been the easiest candidate to beat in '72, or the hardest."

O'Brien, who worried about Rockefeller every time he heard his name, said, "Who the hell cares? He's gone. Toast. Butter him and eat him."

In the rest of the nation, the results for Republicans were not anywhere near as bad as in 1964, but were still disappointing because the opposition party generally picked up seats in a midterm election. Walter Dean Burnham, a respected political scientist from the Massachusetts Institute of Technology, noted in his review of the elections that Republican incumbents couldn't help but take credit for the money that flowed into their districts from Uncle Sam. This, however, cut into Roth's and others' strategy calling for tax cutting and limiting government involvement in the economy. Further, voters watching or listening to television and radio political advertisements heard a Republican incumbent claiming credit for a rising economy, while the Republican challenger in the next district over said otherwise. Worse, Republicans relying on a strategy of claiming credit for government spending also made it more difficult for Republican challengers to attack Democratic incumbents as "the tax-and-spend party." The Democratic candidates, meanwhile, were more united in their focus on jobs and supporting the president.

In the elections for the United States House of Representatives, Democrats extended their lead over the Republicans in the House by nine seats, all due, said Reuther and Yarborough, to union organizing and the Bed-Sty programs. In the Senate, the Democrats gained one seat—this one in the state of Ohio, where Bob Taft Jr., running for his father's old seat, lost in a close race to Howard Metzenbaum.

In bad news for Reagan and Abrams, William Roth garnered national recognition as he easily won his Senate race in Delaware, although ABC television reporter Peter Jennings said Delaware was a state that was considered very pro-business from "top to bottom."

In Texas, a former aide to Vice President Yarborough, Jim Hightower, won a three-way race, saving Yarborough's seat for the Democrats. The Republican candidate, George Herbert Walker Bush, came in third behind Governor John Connally, who ran as an independent. Connally claimed he ran as an independent because the Democrats had "lost their traditional values"—to which the liberal-leaning New Republic magazine responded sarcastically, "Yes! The southern Democrats are losing their tradition of racism! What a shame for ol' John!"

Connally had originally hoped to divide the Democrats and let a "Mugwump Connecticut-Carpetbagger Republican," meaning Bush, win one term—"And then we'll knock out that little varmint next tahm!" But halfway through the campaign, with polls showing him running neck-and-neck with Bush for a not-so-distant second, Connally decided he might have a chance to become a senator without a Republican interlude.

Connally miscalculated that the more people saw him, the more likely he'd win. In the end, he wound up stealing more votes away from Bush than from the young firebrand Hightower. Hightower appealed to the working folks, black, white, and Latino, and benefited from Yarborough's active support and almost weekly appearances in Texas during the months of September and October 1970.

Yarborough said to Kennedy, "Jim's got a great heart an' a smart brain an' can make ya laugh an' cry in a five-minute speech—and get ya all riled up against the rich plutocrats!"

Kennedy smiled but wondered, Does that mean he's on our side or not?

In other midterm election results, the biggest—and happiest—surprise was that the southern Senate Democrats, moving left on labor and race issues, held on to beat the strongly business-backed Republicans running on "old" George Wallace– and Richard Nixon–inspired themes of being against "federal gum'mint meddlers an' comm'nist union agitators." While the Southern Democrats in the Senate did not win by much, they realized they had, as Sam Ervin said, "cast [their] lot with integrationists and labor unions, for better and hopefully not worse." Speaking with Southern newspaper editors Hodding Carter and John Seigenthaler at a White House fete in December 1970, Ervin explained, "Ah think we're raht though, especially since ol' George Wallace is startin' ta sound lahk he was for int'gration and them unions all along. An' ol' Strom Thurmond an' John Stennis are startin' ta look more ancient than their years, Ah must say."

Stennis, the longtime racist Democratic senator from Mississippi, switched to the Republican Party in early 1970 in order to avoid a tough primary challenge from a pro–civil rights and pro-labor candidate. The Republicans figured correctly that Stennis would win, even if it was close, and therefore increase their opportunities for more Republicans in the Senate. As it turned out, the race was extremely close, with Stennis winning just barely 51 percent of the vote. Blacks turned out in record numbers for the Democratic Party candidate, but the race was lost on "race," meaning that the white vote for Stennis was more than 70 percent, and upwards of 90 percent in rural white communities in that state. As Stennis' leading aide said after the election, "We'ah safe for anothah six-yeah term. Let Senator Eastland," Mississippi's other Senator, "worry 'bout the next couple yeahs!"

After the election, newly elected Senator Roth said to a small gathering of business lobbyists and Republican operatives, "When we run on our pork-barrel projects, we're running as Democrats—and that's why Democrats keep us on the defensive! Instead, we must set our position on cutting taxes clearly and consistently. And we must stop creeping socialism at home and our passiveness in the face of the Soviet and Red Chinese threat abroad!"

Roger Ailes, who was present for the speech, heard the room thunderously applaud. Ailes called Edwin Meese, legal counsel to Governor Reagan, after Roth's speech and said to Meese, "Roth's already running for president, and he hasn't even started his senate career! How can that bastard do that?"

Meese said in response, "That's not a surprise, Roger. Remember Jack Kennedy, with as little experience as Roth, was on the national scene in 1956 as a vice presidential candidate. But you're right. There's a vacuum with Nixon and now Rockefeller gone. We have to get moving—now—if we're going to take on Roth or General Abrams! Nineteen seventy-two is just around the corner, but there's plenty of time for Roth to cement his national reputation!"

As President Kennedy reviewed the results on the morning after the 1970 midterm elections, he said to his wife, who was with him in the presidential bedroom, that he was "the happiest man on earth." All along he had expected Republicans to gain seats in the House and Senate. He then quipped to Ethel, "If we can keep South Vietnam free, which I still doubt, and keep more people from getting killed as labor unions push through the South, keep from having a nuclear war with the Soviets or Chinese, and avoid too much inflation, or worse, a recession, I might win in '72!"

Ethel replied, "Well, you *should* win, Bob. But if you let that new federal bill get passed that make abortions legal, you won't get *my* vote!"

Kennedy, hoping not to look as shocked as he was, said, "Uh—Ethel, you . . . you . . . we . . . um . . . I don't think . . . that bill's outta . . . out of . . . committee, I think." Composing his thoughts, he said, "Don't worry, sweetheart. There are plenty of other bills that are trying to get across my desk. We've gone nowhere on a European-style health care system or a public transportation system, and that really concerns me. Ike got the highway legislation passed, why not public transportation? Ethel, don't worry. That abortion bill's going nowhere. Plus, we got welfare reform set again for next year. I'm starting to wonder whether the negative income tax for welfare recipients is not so bad an idea—" He stopped and realized, why worry about anything now? He really did have a good chance to win reelection in 1972.

Then the presidential husband smiled playfully at his wife. He tugged at her nightgown, saying, "How about an even dozen children—this morning?" He gave her a lusty growl. Ethel said, "No way, mister! Eleven is where it stops!" She kissed him, turned over in their bed, and said, "I'm a liberated woman now—and mister, I'm sleeping in this morning!"

Postscript: In late 1970, the world-famous rock and roll band, The Beatles, broke up. Whether Bobby Kennedy lived or not had nothing to do with the fact that John Lennon met Yoko Ono. And Kennedy had nothing to do with Paul McCartney and the other band members being upset at losing John to Yoko. However, unlike the Nixon administration, the Kennedy administration did not try to chase Lennon out of the United States. Lennon left on his own, however, in 1972. Why? Because he found that taxes were getting higher and higher for rich people in the United States. Announcing that he was tired of paying taxes and of the continuing union-led strikes in New York City, Lennon said, "If I want higher taxes and union strikes, I can move back to Liverpool!" Lennon moved, not to Liverpool, but to London.

When Lennon arrived in England, he told the press, "At least I understand their accents when they go on the dole and ask for more money from blokes like me."

Lennon lived in London until his untimely death in 1979, from injuries suffered when he was struck by a taxicab near his home. In the autopsy, there was a trace of heroin found in his bloodstream. The world mourned, but there was hardly any talk among the faithful as to Lennon's status as a political icon since Lennon never recorded any antiwar music, ironically owing to the early success of Robert Kennedy's first year in office in 1969. The 1972 hit song "Imagine" was slightly, but significantly, altered from a lyric standpoint as well.

It said in its last verse, "Imagine all the people never taxed again," instead of the first timeline last verse, "Imagine all the people living life in peace." Lennon also recorded, on the *Imagine* album, a new version of "Taxman," which he sang with George Harrison, changing the name of the British politicians to American leaders Kennedy and Reagan ("Taxman Mr. Reagan . . . Taxman Kennedy!").

Chapter 21

A STRIKE IN GDANSK

B ob Kennedy did not have much time to celebrate his midterm victories, nor did he have to wait very long for one of his deepest fears—nuclear confrontation with the Soviets—to again become at least a possibility.

Just two years after the Soviets crushed the Czech political and economic reform movements, Poland, long an unwilling vassal of the Soviet Union, suddenly became more restless than at any time since the early 1950s.

In December 1970, Polish Communist First Secretary—and undisputed leader—Wladyslaw Gomulka announced price increases on food, fuel, and other goods. He also canceled the annual Christmas bonus for Polish workers. Gomulka was, he said in an interview with newspaper reporters, "forced" into these measures because he wanted to reform the "inefficient" Polish economy and eliminate "government deficits in spending." An American comedian, George Carlin, noted that the Polish leader's words were, in this sense, not much different from those of U.S. Republican leaders. He then quipped, "Does that make newly elected Senator Roth a Communist or does it make Gomulka a Republican?"

Gomulka's "shock therapy," a phrase used by the U.S.-dominated International Monetary Fund (IMF), had unintended, though not unsurprising, effects on the Polish people. Polish workers immediately called for and held demonstrations. The largest demonstrations against the cuts began in the Lenin Shipyard in Gdansk, just off the shores of the Baltic Sea.

More surprising to Western leaders and commentators, the leader of the demonstrations in Gdansk was a crane operator at the Lenin Shipyard named Anna Walentynowicz. Anna W., as the Western press quickly called her, was fifty-one years old when she found herself in the international spotlight after toiling for many years in the shipyards as a loyal party member.

Strikes spread into other Polish towns and cities, including Gdynia, Szczecin, and even parts of Warsaw. Gomulka, not wanting to wait for Russian tanks to overrun Poland as they had in Czechoslovakia, immediately ordered military troops to suppress the strikers. In Szczecin, troops were told to shoot to kill the workers, with Gomulka's military leaders telling the troops that the workers were supporting an American and West German invasion of Poland. The result was that forty-five workers were killed in what was immediately decried as the "Szczecin massacre."

The Soviets then moved quickly to avoid having to repeat their actions in Czechoslovakia. The Soviet ambassador, acting, he said, on strict orders from Moscow, strongly advised Gomulka to resign immediately "for health reasons." The Soviets also "suggested" that Edward Gierek, a party leader in Poland's industrial belt of Silesia, replace Gomulka. Gierek assumed control, but he continued the policies of Gomulka regarding the price hikes. He nonetheless decried the use of force and, as a show of "good faith" to the people of Poland, he removed some troops from Szczecin and other cities.

As Gierek took these actions, however, a leading Catholic cardinal in Poland, Stefan Wyszynski, spoke at a well-attended church service in Warsaw. The cardinal called upon Gierek to rescind the Gomulka price hikes. He also defiantly called on the government to recognize freedom of speech and freedom of religious practice, which, he said, represented "Poland's true roots." For balance, he called upon all Poles to engage in the "hard work of life" and to return to "our jobs as our Father, Jesus, would want. We must, in Christ's name, forgive our fellow citizens in the military and in the government for their transgressions of recent weeks."

In Washington, Kennedy was receiving conflicting counsel as to how to react to the events in Poland. On the day of the Szczecin massacre, CIA Director Blee was counseling the president to take a hard line in rhetoric, but to do nothing to assist the Polish workers. "Mr. President, I personally wanted to see what we could do to help the workers in Poland, but the agency veterans here are certain, from their intelligence analysis, that the workers in Poland will not revolt if the Soviet Union sends in tanks and troops. If the strikes continue, the Soviets will certainly invade as they did recently in Czechoslovakia. No matter what our feelings are on this matter, we do not want to risk World War III over Poland!"

Blee was present in the Oval Office, along with Secretary of State Bowles, Vice President Yarborough, and George Kennan, who had been called personally by Kennedy into the meeting. Also present, at the request of Bowles, was Secretary of Labor Reuther. Bowles said, "I know it's unusual to involve the labor secretary, Mr. President, but the situation in Poland deals with labor issues, and Secretary Reuther has the most experience in what he calls 'wildcat strikes'—meaning spontaneous ones—and how things can escalate into violence in such situations." Kennedy replied that he was glad to have Reuther present, especially with Bowles' introduction.

Kennan spoke next, echoing Blee. "Mr. President, our dealings with the Soviets must always be analyzed in terms of preventing a nuclear confrontation. This also means accepting certain spheres of influence, particularly where Poland is concerned. Poland's borders with the Soviets make it a particularly delicate area where no previous American administration has dared to go beyond the usual diplomatic channels and sentiments."

Bowles, Yarborough, and Reuther, however, did not agree with the cautious assessment of Blee and Kennan. "Mr. President," said Bowles, "we have a great opportunity here to show the world that we support democracy and workers' rights *consistently*, unlike the Soviets—and unlike our own conservative elements who seem to only support labor unions behind the Iron Curtain, if I may be so blunt as to say so."

"Amen, brother," said a nodding Reuther.

"Um, thank you, Walter," said Bowles. "Mr. President, I do not believe we would be risking a nuclear exchange if you came out with a statement of this nature, except that last admittedly partisan jab at Republicans. Others will note that, I am sure, if we wanted it noted. We must immediately respond in word, and possibly in deed, to the actions taken by the Polish government, particularly in that one town in Poland today. . . . I'm not as sure of this as the vice president, for example, but I think—"

Yarborough jumped in, seeing that Bowles was wavering from what they had just discussed before the meeting. "Now, Mr. President, Ah am not counselin' us doin' a blockade lahk yo'r brother had to do in '62 in Cuba, but we oughta at least consider givin' some food supplies to these workin' folks in Poland as it is gettin' maht-y cold over thay-ah, just lahk heah. The way Walt, Chet, and Ah talked about it, is this. We call the French and German trade unions—maybe English ones, too—to send a convoy o' civilian trucks. And send some folks from the AFL-CIO while we're at it. And ya bring them trucks o' food raht up to the West German border with East Germany. Raht to Checkpoint Charlie! No airlift, lahk Berlin in '48, either. No guns, no bombs, no tanks. Nothin' but food on reg'lar trucks. Solidarity forever! That'll rattle some sense into those Politburo boys, get 'em good and embarrassed to maybe listen to their workin' folks in Poland—instead of talkin' about imperialism and all those high-brow things. We didn't pull a trigger in Cuba or Berlin either, if Ah recall, but usin' tanks and military planes was kinda risky there. In this plan, we know we don't have no triggers to pull."

Kennedy was shocked at what he was hearing. "I can't believe this, gentlemen. Director Blee of the CIA counsels caution, as does the 'father' of the Soviet containment policy, Mr. Kennan. I expected such caution, if you don't mind my saying, from Secretary Bowles. Yet Mr. Bowles tells me I need to make a tough statement and maybe consider some action to help the workers in Poland. And then Vice President Yarborough is telling me to go face-to-face against the Soviet military machine with food trucks—as if that isn't going to provoke World War III any differently than if we came in with bombs and tanks! If things keep going like this, I guess Walt Reuther here will tell me to start putting wiretaps on the AFL-CIO leaders to look for Communist subversion!"

Kennedy was too shocked to laugh at this joke. He threw his hands up in the air and said, "Gentlemen, we need to say something to the public. I don't know quite what. We need to avoid doing anything to make the Polish workers think the Eighty Second Airborne is coming over to rescue them from Communism, and I frankly don't know how the Soviet leadership is going to react to *anything* we say! We could end up in a situation as bad or worse than the Cuban situation back when my brother sat in this chair!" Kennedy then sat further back into the president's chair that was now his.

Bowles stood up to speak, not wanting to wait for Blee or Kennan to make a speech as to why Bowles and the others were risking war with "naïve idealism." "Mr. President, the first thing we should do is have you meet with Soviet Ambassador Dobrynin. He knows you very well from the Cuban crisis, and frankly, he may give us an insight as to our best strategy and response to the situation."

The president thought for a few moments. He looked at Blee and Kennan, who nodded in approval. Kennedy sighed and said to the assembled, "You're right, Chet. Gentlemen, our meeting here may be premature. Let's get the Soviet ambassador over *now*, Chet."

Kennedy thought again before adding, "Chet, you and I—alone—will meet with Ambassador Dobrynin. I will provide a summary of the meeting to this group tomorrow. At that time, we will discuss our strategy. Right now, I know there will be voices—" Kennedy was thinking of Reagan, Roth, and retired General Abrams—"who will be telling us we need to stand eyeball to eyeball— or some such nonsense. They'll call us weak unless we unleash all our nuclear weapons. We are not going down the road of the Cuban missile crisis, but we will not back down here either! We tested the fate of the world once before, and that was enough for all of us."

Kennedy thought to himself, If the Soviets could just calm down and let Eastern Europe develop more autonomy . . . at least a little bit.

Dobrynin spoke in a cool but uncertain voice when Bowles called him on the telephone from the Oval Office. He had not yet received any instructions from Moscow as to how to respond to questions regarding the events in Poland, particularly that day, the day of the Szczecin massacre. Through an interpreter, Dobrynin said to Bowles, "Why are you calling the Soviet ambassador in regard to the situation in Poland, Mr. Secretary? Did we call you when France's students went on strike, which, in the opinion of the French leaders, threatened significant institutions in France?"

Bowles decided he could not afford to upset the ambassador but also needed to break certain diplomatic protocol. "Mr. Ambassador, we are calling you because, as you have noted in our newspapers, there are many in the United States who are very sympathetic to the plight of the Polish workers, and based upon what happened today—which did not happen in France during the May 1968 student strike, at least to the same extent—we have concluded that the Soviet Union and the United States, the two most powerful nations on the planet, should at least discuss this situation. Smaller nations have, as we know, started a series of events in the past that swept up more than those small nations."

Dobrynin was silent with surprise. Bowles is very serious, he thought. I cannot fail to respond positively, even though I have no instructions on this matter. Perhaps Kennedy is losing control to more reactionary elements. "Mr. Bowles, please state the nature of your call, and if there is a request, please make that request for my consideration."

Bowles asked Dobrynin to come to the White House to meet with him and the president. No agreements needed be reached at the meeting. "Just an exchange of ideas and analysis."

Dobrynin, acting against implied instructions from his superiors in Moscow, agreed to come. "When do you wish we meet, Secretary Bowles?"

"Tonight, Mr. Ambassador. Please bring your interpreter and one other person so that you may confer with someone at the meeting if you wish."

Dobrynin was surprised at the urgency but did not wish to challenge Bowles any further. He simply said, "I will come with my interpreter only."

"That is perfectly agreeable, Mr. Ambassador. We will have our usual interpreter, Mr. William Krimer, whom you know."

The meeting was set for 8 P.M. at the White House. Dobrynin arrived promptly.

In the minutes before Dobrynin arrived, Kennedy and Bowles were still figuring out their strategy with the Soviet ambassador. They had no "game plan" as to what to say or not say to Dobrynin. They quickly realized that, in calling the meeting, they could not afford the luxury of listening. In fact, they had given Dobrynin the advantage of merely "listening."

"Mr. President," said Bowles, "we should simply ask the ambassador how he views the continuing strikes in Poland, the change in government there, and if the Soviets will be making any official statement regarding the events in that small Polish town today. We can also, diplomatically, let him know that the United States views the situation in Poland as significant and that we expect to comment favorably upon many of the demands of the workers in Poland. The Polish workers' demands are not unlike those made by labor in the American South, which we as an administration have supported in a very courageous way at home, I might add. This will show him that we take this matter seriously as an international issue and that the Soviets will need to confer with us on it."

"That's true. But Chet, we can't be risking World War III here. On the other hand, I think it's reasonable for the Soviets to see that we've accepted the Viet Cong in Vietnam and President Allende—a Marxist for chrissakes— in Chile. They ought to accept—or at least listen to their workers in Poland. That would immediately cool things down. If we accomplish just that, I will take whatever political heat there will be from Reagan and those others when we publicly applaud the Soviets' willingness to listen. Again, we ought to be keep in mind—" The phone rang. The ambassador was waiting. "Send him in. Thanks."

Kennedy shrugged his shoulders. "Here goes, Chet. I think I've got it. I mean *we've* got it. We've been through worse, Chet, and, in this case, I don't want to wait for things to get worse again." Within a few moments, Dobrynin walked into the Oval Office with his interpreter.

Kennedy called in Bill Krimer, the Americans' interpreter. Exchanging pleasantries, Kennedy decided he was going to lead into the discussion with at least semi-sincere flattery.

"Mr. Ambassador, you and I go back for almost a decade, and you know I have nothing but the greatest respect for you and your diplomatic efforts over the years." Dobrynin nodded without emotion. "And you know I definitely valued your insight and your wise assessment of events during the Cuban missile—I mean, the situation in Cuba some years ago." Dobrynin nodded again, but Kennedy sensed distrust emanating from him. Kennedy paused, wondering if he was making a mistake in meeting with Dobrynin at this time.

Dobrynin, for his part, immediately recognized he needed to respond with an equally favorable remark. He said, through the interpreter, "Mr. President, I, too, have always valued your sense of practicality and your respect for the people of the Soviet Union. As I said to Mr. Bowles, however, if this is about the situation in Poland, you should perhaps be speaking with the Polish ambassador. I doubt we in the Soviet Union have anything to say. We do not normally interfere with the internal issues of allies and merely respond to their requests if conditions require the avoiding of unnecessary bloodshed." Dobrynin said to himself as he spoke, Don't admit anything or say anything of substance, Anatoly. Listen to Kennedy, but don't react to him.

Kennedy paused a moment, and then said, "Mr. Ambassador, we know each other too long—including some circumstances none of us wish to repeat. I must now be blunt in what I have to say."

Bowles audibly cleared his throat, hoping to stop the president from speaking further.

Instead, Kennedy's voice grew stronger. "I asked you here, and I am most grateful that you agreed to come on such short notice, because I . . . I frankly think the resumption of arms control discussions between the Soviets and the Americans are long overdue. However, we will have even greater difficulty in starting these discussions if the situation in Poland further deteriorates. You have read, I am sure, what our administration's opponents are saying, yes?"

"Yes, Mr. President," said Dobrynin. "However, if I may also speak freely, I have read what some 'unnamed officials' of *your* administration are saying, and I am not sure there is much difference between many in your administration and your opponents on this particular issue. As for the content of your request, namely beginning arms control discussions, I do not fully understand, Mr. President. As I have said just in the past two weeks to Secretary Bowles, my government is interested in discussing arms control with the United States, but we believe the MIRVing of weapons your administration has undertaken also undermines the integrity of arms control discussions. The issue of MIRVing nuclear weapons, however, is a grave concern of the Soviets. It is one that causes us to be concerned about the degree of success of arms control agreements. As for the situation in Poland—I fail to see the relevance. The Soviet Union worked with President John Kennedy even as he was escalating the war in Vietnam. Arms control discussions occurred throughout President Johnson's administration—through the American invasion of the Dominican Republic and in Southeast Asia. The current situation in Poland is nothing like the situations in Vietnam or the Dominican Republic. It will pass, and therefore there is no need for further discussion of that subject."

"Well, maybe so, Mr. Ambassador. But I can't believe the position of the Soviets to not negotiate is based upon our MIRVing of warheads. The MIRVing project has been openly discussed since the time of my brother's presidency." The president could feel the discussion's temperature rising and didn't like it.

"Then," asked Dobrynin, "what about the American position on the development of antiballistic missiles? I have read a number of newspaper articles, including articles written by those close to your administration, who desire the development of these weapons that can only destabilize the world with their illusions of antinuclear missile 'protection.'"

"I am aware of this debate. In all frankness, Mr. Ambassador, I would like to discuss a treaty that would be comprehensive, including the prevention of the deployment of antiballistic missiles, if possible."

Bowles' face tightened as Kennedy spoke. Bowles had, with the support of CIA Director Blee, been asking senators to refrain from killing research on antiballistic missile defense for the rather *realpolitik* reason that antiballistic missile research could be used as a bargaining chip with the Soviets. However, Secretary of Defense Warnke openly opposed such research on the grounds that it was impractical. Warnke was completely outnumbered, even as he argued that he had other and more pressing research projects to spend dollars on in his department.[1]

Kennedy paused again before beginning. "Mr. Ambassador, I am going to be more blunt than I have ever been. I must say this squarely." He raised his hand to Bowles, who was starting to interrupt to request a break in the discussion to make sure Kennedy didn't say anything unrehearsed, which, of course, he was about to do.

"Mr. Ambassador, I would like to propose something. The United States, under my administration, has already accepted elections in Vietnam against the wishes of certain well-known elements in our country, and we are now speaking with and working with the National Liberation Front–led government in South Vietnam. We had, as you know, spent the better part of a decade fighting the National Liberation Front, who many here call the Viet Cong—or Communists."

Dobrynin began to say something, but Kennedy stopped him.

"Please, Mr. Ambassador. I need to say this clearly and without . . . well, clearly. We have met with President Allende of Chile, who is an avowed Marxist, and we have not attempted, at least since he's been elected, to stop his plan for nationalization of certain American business interests there. We have offered to start arms control negotiations with the Soviet Union on *all* issues other than MIRVing. You have discussed this already with Secretary Bowles and Secretary Warnke."

Kennedy paused for a split second, and feeling like he was arguing a case before a jury, took what he knew was a risky plunge.

"There is at least one thing I have learned from events over the past two full years as president—and my years in my brother's administration. And that is this: When we, the United States, have problems with certain nations with whom we've been friendly, we get much further in reaching our goal of peace by speaking to the reformers who appear to have the support of their people as opposed to allowing the government we have traditionally supported to silence the reformers. I have never said this to anyone, not even Secretary Bowles, but I've been thinking about this for some time. Why should either we or the Soviets have any nuclear weapons or troops in Europe at this point? After all is said and done, don't we worry about what will happen in Europe in large part *because* of all the nuclear weapons and American and Soviet troops poised on either side in Europe? Shouldn't we allow reformers to speak in Western and Eastern Europe without either or both sides worrying about nuclear war among the superpowers?"

Dobrynin's eyebrows rose perceptibly to all in the room. He stiffened, looking first at his interpreter, then at the American interpreter to make sure he had heard Kennedy correctly. Both interpreters looked at each other in surprise. Then both nodded to Dobrynin, in effect saying that Dobrynin had indeed heard correctly. Kennedy was calling for nuclear weapons and American and Soviet troops to be removed from Europe. He was essentially calling for the United States to leave N.A.T.O. and the Soviets to leave the Warsaw Pact.

Bowles gulped again, this time to the point where he felt compelled to say, "Mr. President, may I have a word alone with you, sir?" He got up as he said this, and Kennedy nudged him—then motioned him—to sit down.

"Secretary Bowles, I am aware of what I have said. I think I have made it clearer than I could ever make it to Ambassador Dobrynin as to what I have said. He will, I know, have to take the points raised in this discussion back to Moscow. If the Soviet Union wishes, I will say what I have said again. Publicly or privately. Heck, I may say it publicly whether the Soviets like it or not. Whatever way I say it, my goal is to move forward to more peace and trust among the leading nuclear powers and eventually the world."

Now Kennedy stood up and walked over to the globe near his desk. "You know, Mr. Ambassador, my brother never felt better about America, Russia, and the world than when he and Mr. Khrushchev signed the Nonproliferation Treaty in August 1963. I have thought of this from time to time but believed it was too idealistic or, frankly, naïve to think about taking the next step. But as president," he gently spun the globe as he spoke, "I realized I was being naïve in a *negative* way *not* to say what I have just said. We must be strong in our faith to resolve our differences, Mr. Ambassador, and I know and respect your judgment on the matter. We can always go the other way, and there are plenty of Americans who have been led to believe that other way is the only way."

Dobrynin smiled for the first time. He looked carefully at his interpreter and then straightened himself, almost at attention, and said, "Mr. President, I shall be honored to report your request to Moscow. I cannot say what will be the response, however." He suddenly sighed with no small fear about what would happen to him if he were too strong in pushing this idea once he returned to Moscow. He had heard rumors of various intrigues among the Politburo members, which seemed unending since the overthrow of Khrushchev in 1964. "Please, Mr. President, just one favor. We cannot let this discussion leave this room until I can confer with my superiors in Moscow. I think we must not let events get ahead of themselves as we almost did during the missile—the situation in Cuba."

Kennedy and Bowles smiled for different reasons. Kennedy smiled because he knew he had convinced Dobrynin. Bowles smiled because he saw the meeting was over. He was also glad Dobrynin recognized the political dynamite the president had just unloaded. Bowles thought to himself, I need time alone with the president . . . to ask him . . . what the *hell* he was thinking in making such a rash and dangerous gesture!

Dobrynin shook Kennedy's hand warmly and almost kissed his cheek, but thought better of it. The Soviet interpreter smiled broadly as he shook Kennedy's hand as well. The American interpreter, Krimer, was caught up in the moment. He was thinking, as he recorded in his diaries published in 2006, five years after his death, it will be winter in Moscow if we go for further talks there, but the Cold War may begin to thaw into a Moscow spring . . .

Kennedy smiled a smile of relief that lingered after the two Soviet officials left the Oval Office and were escorted out of the White House. Kennedy thought about his brother's wish for peace with freedom throughout the world, and seeing the Soviets reform their system into a more open and possibly democratic system.

"Well, Chet," Kennedy said, "I feel just great! Just great! Dobrynin understands! We can maybe end the Cold War in time—"

"Mr. President! Do you realize how easily this could leak to the public? It could come from the Soviet side through CIA moles—who would send it back here and leak it all over Washington! You have just proposed 'Finlandizing' Western Europe, in all candor—"[2]

Kennedy was sharp. "Jesus, Chet! You, of all people, should see that's bullshit! The Soviets can't control Eastern Europe without having troops there! How are they gonna invade and hold Western Europe? You know what Kennan said to me when I called him to come to the meeting we had earlier today? He said, 'Mr. President, the Soviets can barely hold Eastern Europe. Our containment policy is looking better all the time, and the Soviet leaders will have to see at some point they cannot continue to invade rebellious satellite states in the Eastern European region.' That's what *Kennan* said, Chet! Even if he wanted a more cautious approach right now. But either way, that really got me thinking about this."

Bowles was looking thoughtful as if considering the proposal, but wasn't fully buying the point yet. If Kennedy really was thinking along these lines, Bowles thought to himself, why didn't he speak about it with me—or anyone else for that matter?

"Okay, Chet," said Kennedy, sensing Bowles' skepticism, "look at it another way. France and Germany are not Czechoslovakia. You think DeGaulle, and now Pompidou, can't defend France? The French have the friggin' bomb, Chet, and seeing how in love they are with their bomb, they'd use it if they thought the Russians were going after them. You can't think the Russians really want to risk the French bombing Moscow! The French don't even worry about their Maginot Line anymore, or whatever that was back in the '30s. Jack knew more about European history than I do. The Germans are a lot more stable and united, in a good way, these days. Remember when Willy Brandt told us in 1968 that he thought the East and West were starting to see that a mixed economy—some socialism, some capitalism—makes the most sense, and that both sides do not, under any circumstances, want to risk nuclear war. The Europeans and Russians know—unlike many of us, I'm afraid—what it's like to look for loved ones in buildings reduced to rubble. Chet, I'm rambling. Don't you see it? Call Yarborough. He'll see it, I bet. Better yet, I'll call Yarborough."

Chet Bowles didn't know what to say. He was having his first deep dispute with Robert Kennedy, the same man who had called Bowles "soft" when Bowles doubted the Vietnam venture in 1962 and early 1963. Yet, now, in this dispute, it was Bowles who was essentially calling Kennedy "soft."

Bowles shook his head. "Mr. President, I can't disagree that at some point—who knows when—it could be decades and decades—the wall comes down, and we have independent nations in Eastern Europe, free of Cold War tensions. But a Soviet invasion of Poland is *imminent,* and they are still mopping up in Czechoslovakia—which occurred *after* Brandt's . . . um, optimistic comments. The Czech reform leader, Dubcek, was initially sent to Turkey as ambassador but has since been recalled to Czechoslovakia and relieved of all public duties there. Repression continues against Havel and the rock and roll musician we met, and others, of course. Kosygin can't even get the rest of the Soviet Politburo to meet with us to seriously discuss arms control—"

"Didn't you see Dobrynin? He believes in the proposal I made! He believes! It's a solution that gets to the heart of the matter."

"Yes," said Bowles, "and that's what worries me. How can someone as experienced in diplomatic affairs as Dobrynin believe in an all-at-once solution, particularly at this time? Mr. President, we need time to think this through. Please give this some thought—some long, *hard* thought, *please.*"

Kennedy was still smiling. "Don't worry, Chet." Then, with a slyness added to his already broad smile, Kennedy put his arm around Bowles and said, "Chet, you'll come to your senses. You're too pie-in-the-sky!"

Bowles shook his head, wondering at the continued lack of consistency in the thinking of Robert Francis Kennedy. Kennedy could go from hawk to dove to Wilsonian peacemaker in a New York minute, he thought to himself. After Bowles left Kennedy, he couldn't get the thought of Woodrow Wilson out of his mind. Kennedy's proposal to Dobrynin cannot stand, thought Bowles. The Soviets, if we're lucky, will just ignore it or at least say they'll need time to consider it to death. Otherwise . . . Bowles didn't want to even guess at what "otherwise" could mean.

Dobrynin immediately asked the Politburo for permission to return to Moscow. He said he had important information to relay from the White House that he did not wish to state over the telephone. He was given permission and landed in Moscow in just under one day to appear at an emergency meeting of the Politburo. At the meeting, Dobrynin told the assembled old men of the Soviet empire that the American president had proposed that the United States and the Soviet Union simultaneously remove their nuclear weapons and troops from Western and Eastern Europe.

Kosygin sat back in disbelief. Brezhnev yelled, "What?" and Konstantin Chernenko snarled, "It's an imperialist trick!" Suslov mumbled, "The military in America will kill him if he tries that. . . . It can't be true . . . " His voice trailed off, according to the transcripts of the meeting. Others at the meeting had essentially the same range of responses, with slight variations.

Dobrynin himself sat back and watched. He was not going to propose anything, he thought to himself. Then Kosygin asked, "How can we begin to trust the Americans on such a . . . a . . . Is there a *plan* for this proposal, Mr. Ambassador?"

Dobrynin said, "No, President Kosygin. I have to admit that Secretary of State Bowles seemed somewhat surprised, although Secretary Bowles, I'm sure—at least from his public statements over the years—would not be against such a proposal as made by President Kennedy. There was no plan offered. President Kennedy simply asked if the goal was the same from our point of view."

"Of course it is! But so what?" boomed Kosygin, who did not want to let Brezhnev be the one making this point. "The Americans have shown no interest in such a proposal before—they won't even renounce the first use of atomic weapons as we have!"

Suslov joined in. "And look what happened to the last President Kennedy, Mr. Ambassador. How can we respond with any assurance that the American government and the imperialist business elements will not sabotage any agreement we reach?"

Dobrynin decided that if he was going to lose his ambassadorship merely for relaying this information, he might as well go down with some dignity. "Honestly, Comrade Suslov, I cannot say with certainty how we may get from point A to point B. However, this President Kennedy has been fairly popular with a good deal of the public. He has a very reformist vice president whom business elements fear more than they do the president. The administration also has Secretary Bowles and United Nations Ambassador Young. Each are considered very progressive from an international point of view. This is very different from the first Kennedy administration. Also, during the Cuban situation, I dealt personally with this President Kennedy when he was the attorney general. As we all recall here, *Robert* Kennedy was the one who proposed the trade on missiles with Turkey and promised us the United States will no longer attempt to invade Cuba. He was a key participant in resolving that situation—and the Americans, even after his brother's untimely death, kept to that bargain."

Chernenko was not impressed. "This new president's CIA was still attempting to undermine the Chilean elections this past fall—without success, I may add. There is nothing new from the imperialists in Washington but this ridiculous proposal designed to confuse us and divide us!"

Kosygin had little respect for Chernenko and saw the latter as solidly in the Brezhnev camp. Kosygin said, with some acid in his voice, "And I may add, Comrade Konstantin Ustinovich Chernenko, that American Secretary of State Bowles met with the Socialist president, Allende, after the election in Chile. According to our sources, Allende was treated very well. Allende's nationalization plans for the cooper mines and the telecommunication system are expected to continue. And the CIA appears to have stopped most of its activities against the new Socialist government in Chile. That is *very* significant, I believe."

Suslov spoke. "Comrades, I have been reconsidering the entire matter of how we deal with this American administration. We keep waiting for it to fail, or for this president to be—I hate to say—neutralized by one of the reactionaries or imperialists, and yet he continues on. Our supporters in the developing nations who are fighting against Western imperialism and colonialism are finding the Americans more friendly and more willing to seek solutions that do not involve American troops, at least in the way the

Americans used to involve troops. Comrade Leonid Ilyich, what is your take on the American administration's proposal?"

Brezhnev eyed Suslov and then looked around the room. He could not tell whether Suslov was with him or leaning toward Kosygin—or worse, attempting to play one against the other to increase Suslov's own power. "Well, Comrade Mikhail Andreevich, I . . . um . . . we . . . uh . . . The American proposal is . . . may not be a true proposal since there is no plan. What troops leave first? Where do we begin such a withdrawal? What about weapons pointed at us by the Americans *and* the Europeans? Will the Europeans keep their nuclear arsenals?"

Suslov looked at Kosygin, who was listening but not responding. Brezhnev also looked at Kosygin but saw what he perceived as weakness in Kosygin's manner. Brezhnev continued, stronger now against the proposal. "There is no plan for peace. There is, on the other hand, a plan for war. The Americans continue to MIRV their nuclear weapons. *That* is the proposal and *that* is the plan, comrades. The Americans continue to arm their submarines and jets with more sophisticated nuclear weapons. We have relatively few jets and submarines with nuclear capabilities—even though, of course, we have many more land-based nuclear missiles than the Americans."

Kosygin spoke tentatively. "The Americans have asked to speak to us about many other issues relating to limiting nuclear weapons, Comrade Leonid Ilyich. Isn't that true, Mr. Ambassador?"

Dobrynin did not want to be seen agreeing with Kosygin at this point, but also wanted to honestly respond, hoping someone would back Kennedy's proposal. Suslov seemed close but still unlikely. Dobrynin said, "Comrade President, that is what Secretary Bowles has said over the past year, and President Kennedy said in the same meeting as he made his proposal."

Suslov spoke. "Mr. Ambassador, what do our sources in the CIA and FBI say at this time about this president?"

Dobrynin breathed deeply before beginning his answer. "The CIA is largely against the president, but the higher one goes in the hierarchy, such as with Director Blee and Assistant Director Cord Meyer, they seem to be backing him. Mr. Hoover in the FBI is largely opposed to the new president and appears to be hoping for a change, according to Washington newspapers. Our sources say the FBI director has not openly criticized the president in front of them, however."

"Our sources seem to know less than the newspapers!" grumbled Brezhnev. He wanted to end this discussion while the proposal seemed to be stillborn within the Politburo.

Suslov, however, was not ready to side with Brezhnev. He said, "Comrades, I would like to ask our newest member, KGB Director Andropov, about his sense of this proposal and if the American government is likely to follow through with this proposal. Comrade Yuri Vladimirovich?"

Andropov did not know what Suslov wanted him to say. Suslov seemed to believe the proposal had merit, otherwise he would have already agreed with Brezhnev. Andropov knew Suslov had had to pull strings to secure Andropov's place on the Politburo and that Brezhnev was very reluctant, if not opposed, to Andropov's appointment. What was Comrade Suslov up to, thought Andropov? Why is he doing this to me? He has jeopardized my advancement if I do not answer correctly.

Andropov finally decided it was easier to speak the truth. Shrugging his shoulders, but not obviously so, Andropov answered, "Comrades, our sources believe that the American administration is controversial but continuing to survive and develop. In the last congressional elections, the American administration strengthened its hand for bourgeois-limited, worker-oriented reforms. It is also true that American efforts to topple the newly elected Socialist president in Chile have been officially ended, although some elements in the CIA have remained in contact with American corporate business interests and military personnel in Chile." He was stalling, looking at Suslov, who sat stone-faced, looking ahead at no one in particular.

Andropov turned to Kosygin, who was nodding in agreement, and then toward Brezhnev, who seemed almost hostile. Andropov continued, "Comrades, may I have twenty-four hours to determine what, if anything, we are hearing regarding this proposal? We may better gauge our response, assuming one is necessary, with more intelligence information."

Suslov remained as he was. Kosygin looked disappointed. For his part, Brezhnev looked relieved but not happy. The others took their cues accordingly. Suslov, still maintaining his stony visage, said, "Then we will meet tomorrow evening to discuss this matter, unless Secretary Brezhnev decides otherwise . . . " He waited to see if Brezhnev, as general secretary, was going to say "nyet." Brezhnev nodded and said with his teeth almost crushing each other, "That is agreeable."

Andropov went to Suslov the next afternoon with the latest intelligence information. "Comrade Mikhail Andreevich, our sources say there is nothing coming out of the Americans with regard to this proposal. They do not even believe such a proposal is being made—"

"Then it is something the president has decided himself, Comrade Yuri Vladimirovich. This is very dangerous." He thought a moment. "Perhaps we should reject the offer . . . " He thought for another moment. "Let us take a walk, comrade."

The two men walked together through Suslov's garden. Suslov said with some endearment to Andropov, "Sasha, I believe it is safe to say here in my garden what I would not say in the house. What if we told the Americans that we would like to discuss this matter—and said this *publicly*? What do you think the reaction would be of the—"

"The Politburo would *never agree,* comrade! I must say, with all respect to you, why are we talking like this? Chernenko, Brezhnev—I have checked our sources within as well—"

"I have done my own investigation internally, and we do not need Brezhnev or Chernenko to prevail at the Politburo. Our own nation's military leadership doesn't want to invade Poland or any other Warsaw Pact nation, Sasha. I thought very much about the conversation you and I had just before the Polish strikes. I also thought about the advice Kosygin and even Brezhnev gave our comrades the North Vietnamese. They told the North Vietnamese to deal with the Americans, essentially. The North Vietnamese refused and what happened? They lost their ability to take control of events in the South. Dobrynin told me after the meeting he had with the president the other day— I asked him to speak privately with me—that the newspapers reported in Washington that someone in the administration called for a civilian truck convoy to go right to the Berlin border with food—not weapons. Just food. For the strikers. While this report generated much derision, it is something I would hate to see because of its ultimate propaganda value against us. There is something else that concerns me. The Chinese are apt to make friends with the Americans if we don't act first. That is what truly concerns me."

"I am glad you have brought up the Chinese, Comrade Mikhail Andreevich. We just learned this morning, but I still cannot verify it—Chinese Defense Minister Lin Piao may have been placed under house arrest this morning by his own government. I still have no confirmation—"

"What? Comrade Yuri, this is very dangerous news! What can this mean if this is true? Is Chou En-Lai behind this? Those skirmishes in the past year along our borders with China in Manchuria have been Chou's doing, I have long believed. Chou is also highly interested in entering the United Nations by making amends with the Americans. This could be part of Chou's signal to the Americans that China wishes to resume relations with the American government! We may not have the luxury of waiting for confirmation of the status of Lin Piao, who I have had my own misgivings about . . . The American proposal must be considered *immediately,* comrade."

"But, Comrade Mikhail Andreevich, you have never trusted the Americans. You have always told me the Americans—"

"I know what I have said, Comrade Yuri. As vice secretary, I have been in charge of overseeing international actions against the American imperialists. For two years now I have been hearing from our supporters—and again we have said the same to the Vietnamese, to the Indian and Pakistani Communists, to the Syrian Communists, and even in Chile—that the Americans may have changed some of their international positions. Their decision to MIRV their nuclear bombs, though, has remained a stumbling block to our moving forward in diplomatic relations. Dobrynin, who reads the American newspapers and receives a summary of the *Congressional*

Record of debates, says there is deep division in the United States Congress over the MIRVing of weapons. He says the administration gave in to the American military on this but has not given the military much else. I am a cautious man, as you know, with regard to capitalists, who are constantly breaking agreements. But . . . and I say this carefully, we may find our negotiating position with the Americans undermined if the Chinese get to the American administration before we do."

"You may be correct, Comrade Mikhail. However, the Americans could change administrations again, either through violence or . . . President Kennedy may simply lose in the 1972 elections. We don't know. I think, Comrade Mikhail, that we should perhaps take advantage of the opportunity to deal with the American administration now as opposed to—"

"Precisely, Comrade Yuri. Precisely what I am thinking. I was, as you know, very much opposed to the invasion of Czechoslovakia until I saw there was no choice. We did a grave disservice to our cause internationally when we invaded, although it was necessary at the time. And the new administration in America has done everything to exploit this against us with their subsequent actions. Labor Secretary Reuther said on American television the other day that the Americans 'support labor rights at home and abroad,' and that their support of Polish workers proves this—at least he says that is proof. This complicates our efforts in controlling Poland. Worse, our other allies in the Warsaw Pact are already calling on us to invade again—just as in Czechoslovakia. If we invade Poland, will the Polish army shoot back at our Soviet troops or at the Polish workers? And then what happens either way? If that American truck convoy full of food and blankets for workers goes into West Berlin, things could get out of hand. And then we'll look like . . . " He wanted to say "imperialists," but he would dare not use any such word in that context, even with a trusted protégé.

Andropov, for his part, understood what word was not being said. He replied, "We must engage the president of the United States on this proposal. Better to have the Eastern bloc leaders angry at us than the entire world, including people in our own country. Where does Foreign Minister Gromyko—"

"He agrees with Dobrynin that we must engage the Americans on this proposal," said Suslov, interrupting.

"And Kosygin is in favor of continuing the dialogue at least. He may even support a joint statement by him and President Kennedy . . . "

"Kosygin has his bloc of support, and together we will prevail. Gromyko spoke with Dobrynin before the meeting yesterday and was very interested in following up on the proposal. The military will definitely see the Chinese situation as a reason to support moving forward with the American proposal, I believe."

Andropov agreed. Suslov and Andropov went to Foreign Minister Gromyko, who had known of the situation in China before Andropov. Gromyko was already speaking with Military Minister Malinovsky, who agreed it was time to speak with the Americans.

"Gromyko must have sources in my head," Andropov said with a slight shudder afterward. The military did not relish the prospect of invading yet another Eastern bloc nation, Poland, particularly with the situation along the Chinese border becoming more tense. Rumors of Lin Piao's arrest sealed their decision.

That evening, the Politburo called itself to order. Suslov, who met briefly with Kosygin before the meeting, confirmed that Kosygin was in favor of pursuing the proposal from the American president. Kosygin was shocked, however, when Suslov said the Soviets might wish to consider a joint public announcement if the Americans asked for one. Kosygin saw, with that comment, that Suslov, the hard-liner, had made a switch to Kosygin's camp. Kosygin thereafter walked into the meeting with an assurance he had not had since the overthrow of Khrushchev in 1964.

Before calling the meeting to order, Brezhnev whispered to Chernenko, "Suslov has betrayed us. He has sided with Kosygin and Gromyko. The military is hesitant to fight anyone because of the situation in China. We must not let this American proposal move too quickly. We must gain time. I have already asked our sources to leak this absurd proposal to those CIA agents who are opposed to the American president. The opponents of President Kennedy may be our best—if unwitting—allies. We cannot act rashly simply because a friend in China, Lin Piao, may be no more." Chernenko, who was not known for either deep or independent thinking, nodded. He didn't trust Americans for any purpose, and he respected Brezhnev's political maneuvering.

The meeting was relatively short. Kosygin and Suslov made the Chinese issue their cornerstone in supporting the opening of a dialogue to remove troops from all of Europe. Suslov invoked Brezhnev's advice to North Vietnamese Communist General Giap as to why the "new" President Kennedy deserved a hearing on any issue dealing with peace. Suslov said, "Our world credibility depends upon who raises this proposal, and *how* it is raised. With the Polish situation and now the Chinese situation, we cannot afford to be opposed to increasing the prospects of world peace, particularly in Europe."

Harrumphs of agreement went around the table. Brezhnev could not believe how quickly his position had been undermined. Perhaps the Lin Piao story is a hoax from the KGB, he thought to himself. Brezhnev now feared for his position as general secretary. Better to go along at this point, he thought, and maintain my power base as general secretary.

Chernenko, meanwhile, whose thoughts tended to plod along at a slow pace, said with fury in his voice to the assembled Communist leaders, "We cannot trust *any* Americans! They have lied in the past and have changed their presidents—sometimes violently—when a president has tried to engage in nuclear arms limitations!" He went on in this way for almost five minutes. All Chernenko needed for his speech was one of Khrushchev's shoes to bang on the table.

Dobrynin, who was allowed to attend the meeting at the joint request of Kosygin, Suslov, and Brezhnev, was ecstatic as Chernenko stood alone. Dobrynin never showed any emotion during the meeting, however. In his diaries published after his death in the late 1990s, Dobrynin wrote that after that meeting he thought he could fly to Washington without a plane. Dobrynin left for Washington the night of the Politburo meeting. He sent word to President Kennedy requesting a meeting as soon as he landed.

In Gdansk, however, the situation turned more violent, as dock workers refused to leave the docks. They threatened to take over the docks in a "new soviet" or workers council. "A new Krondstat is coming," muttered Suslov, referring to a strike by sailors at a Russian port during the Russian civil war following the Bolshevik Revolution of 1917 (during which Trotsky and the Red Army mercilessly killed or imprisoned the striking workers). "But this time we cannot easily justify—if at all—why suppressing this deviation from socialism is necessary to preserve the Revolution."

Suslov, meeting with Kosygin, Gromyko, and Andropov, asked aloud, "How can we meet with the Americans and invade Poland as we did in Czechoslovakia? Yet if we don't meet with the Americans, we lose an opportunity that might not come again for a decade or more—and we could find ourselves in a nuclear confrontation with either the United States or, more likely, China by then."

Gromyko put up his hands. "Comrade Mikhail Andreevich, we have been through worse, as you well know. We defeated Hitler, and our ancestors defeated Napoleon, although I am sure you will say that the issues were clear in those instances—and they were. On the other hand, I will say that we can move forward with the Americans and suggest that the Polish military and party leaders simply handle the situation themselves, perhaps with some level of appropriate force. The Americans are not going to invade Poland to protect the counterrevolutionaries, either. And that so-called food truck convoy proposal is not likely to go anywhere—if we are talking to the Americans."

Suslov agreed, as did the others.

Kosygin said, "I leave for Washington tomorrow and will arrive on January 1, 1971. Ambassador Dobrynin tells us that the CIA is leaking the announcement around Washington, but he believes we can undermine the political strife President Kennedy will face from reactionaries if I come to Washington to formally announce the beginning of our negotiations. I am glad, Mr. Minister Gromyko, that you are coming with me to start what are surely historic negotiations."

Kosygin was correct that the proposal had been leaked to newspapers in the United States. The leaks came from within the bowels of the CIA directly from Brezhnev-led conservatives.

Ben Bradlee, the executive editor of the *Washington Post,* heard the information and called the president directly on the evening of December 30, 1970. "Mr. President, I have information from what I am told are reliable sources that the United States has proposed to the Russians, and the Russians are said to have tentatively accepted, the removal of all American and Russian troops and weapons from Western and Eastern Europe. Are we proposing to make Europe 'neutral,' sir? I am loathing to print this information if you believe publishing this will violate national security. But I must also say that a different source says CBS News is going ahead with this regardless, as is the *New York Times."*

Kennedy replied with anger, "Ben, you'd think people would be home with their families and getting ready for the new year instead of . . . Damn it, Ben! My brother once said he wanted to cut up the CIA into fifty pieces. Right now, I'd say he didn't go far enough. There is nobody except Chet Bowles and me who knew of this proposal—and I know Chet didn't leak this information. Chet was specifically concerned that the information would come through the CIA from the Soviets—and now—Christ! The *Times* and CBS are gonna publicize this without even seeking *our* comment? What's gotten into those guys? They working for Reagan?" Kennedy let loose with expletives and called Paley and Rather of CBS and Sulzberger of the *Times* "sons of bitches" and "worse than Communists!"

"Mr. President," said a now very careful Bradlee, "I share your sentiments and concerns regarding our competitors. May I gather from your comments that the reports are . . . well . . . somewhat true?"

Kennedy sighed deeply, and said, "Yes, Ben, we *are* making this proposal— and the Soviets are accepting! And it's not to 'Finlandize' Europe—I bet that's how the leakers are playing it, isn't it?"

"Well, sir, I used the word 'neutralize,' but the talk was . . . well, it was . . . "

"Then it's got to be coming from the CIA sources you newspapers and television reporters have! The bastards! Can't they see the problems the Soviets are having just trying to hold on to Poland? Christ, even Kennan sees this! And that dissident who was exiled here, Andrei Amalik.[3] Amalik met with Chet and me earlier this year and stated his reasons why the Soviets are in trouble. And he's no Soviet plant either! Ben, why didn't those news organizations call my office for confirmation? Jesus!"

Bradlee spoke softly. "Mr. President, the people I talked with at CBS said Director Blee was contacted and wouldn't comment, per the usual CIA policy. They tried to find Secretary Bowles, but he didn't answer their calls. The *Times* spoke again with their CIA sources, who confirmed the information. They, in turn, contacted CBS, and both compared notes from their sources in the intelligence agencies, not just the CIA—"

"Probably the National Security Agency! That's another lunatic asylum—they leak and it's called patriotism! Anyone else leaks and they scream 'Communist' and 'traitor!' Assholes!"

"Well, sir, based upon who they were hearing this from, the *Times* said it was going to get what it sees as the biggest scoop since . . . since I don't know when—"

"Well, they aren't getting much of a scoop, Ben. I'm going public on this, but I have to give Ambassador Dobrynin a call first. You just got the first confirmation from the president of the United States. God, I hope the Soviets don't back off this. If they do, you'll have a scoop and I'll be calling for investigations starting with CBS and the CIA, you mark my words. They could lead us to World War III if we don't—Dobrynin said the Politburo—Enough! Maybe some diplomatic talks should remain confidential—for once!"

"I understand, Mr. President," said Bradlee. "We'll wait for the announcement from Press Secretary Newfield. By the way, sir, if you don't mind my saying, Newfield's been a breath of fresh air around here. We all thought he was . . . well, you know . . . I mean, he wrote for the *Village Voice,* after all. But he has been fairly honest about when he had authority to speak and when he needed to be off the record. He's a good man—I told him at our office Christmas party the other day that he was welcome here after his stint in government—he could be our first 'radical Jew' columnist! Imagine that!"

Kennedy laughed hollowly. "So, you like Jack's leaks, eh, Ben? Oh well. Jack wasn't behind this one, I know that!"

Just after hanging up with Bradlee, Kennedy received a call from Bowles confirming that CBS had called earlier in the evening. Bowles had been out. Kennedy immediately called Yarborough, Dobrynin, and Newfield. It was close to midnight. Kennedy told Newfield to call CBS and the *Times* and then contact the usual sources to inform them that a press conference would be held at 8 A.M. on December 31. Because this was in the days before 24/7 news channels, the networks and the newspapers kept quiet. The *New York Times,* responding to a personal call from Kennedy, agreed to run a rare late edition rather than print their now confirmed story.

Dobrynin called Moscow for instructions from Foreign Minister Gromyko, who contacted Kosygin, Brezhnev, and Suslov. It was agreed that Dobrynin should be standing next to President Kennedy and that the announcement should be a "joint announcement," not an "American announcement."

Dobrynin called Kennedy to demand the "joint announcement" format, and Kennedy responded, "Of course, Mr. Ambassador." He said to Bowles, who had come to the Oval Office to begin to craft the statement, "The Russians are committed to this, Chet. More committed than I could have hoped."

Chet said, "Mr. President, I hope we know what we're unleashing here. I would rather the Soviets start with some arms limitation agreements." He shook his head. "Is Dobrynin coming over, sir?"

Kennedy nodded yes. "He'll be here within the hour. You know, I also spoke with CIA Director Blee. I just don't think we can trust him anymore. I was livid at his not calling me when CBS called him to confirm the proposal. He thought the information coming out of the Soviet Union was, as he put it, 'disinformation,' and didn't want to bother me, he said. That's bullshit!" Kennedy paused. "It's worse than that, really. The fact that he thought it was disinformation means he thinks I'd have to be crazy to accept that type of proposal, let alone propose it myself!"

Bowles nodded in agreement, but knew he couldn't blame Blee in the least. Bowles had also been thinking about the political fallout if anyone remembered that the Soviets had proposed something similar to what Kennedy was proposing now, when Khrushchev was in control of the Politburo in the late 1950s. Bowles wasn't ready to remind Kennedy of this just yet. He simply responded to Kennedy's emotional concerns, saying, "I can't believe we are being forced into announcing this so early—"

"Chet, we can't control everything, but ironically, the leak has only given the Soviets the backbone to go forward. There isn't even enough time for them or us to tell our allies—damn! Chet, you better alert President Pompidou of France, Chancellor Brandt, and Prime Minister Heath in England. I hope they see this proposal as positive—not like you and those diplomatic folks—and certainly not like the CIA!"

The president needn't have worried about the European leaders' reactions, which were completely positive.

In preparing the protocol for the joint announcement, President Kennedy asked Dobrynin if he, Kennedy, could speak first so the American people could hear the American president announce the proposal on American soil. "Plus, Mr. Ambassador, I outrank you!" Dobrynin agreed with a smile and a nod.

Kennedy began the press conference saying, "This morning I am here to announce that the United States of America and the Soviet Union are going to begin bilateral talks on significant nuclear arms control"—he and Dobyrnin took the opportunity to push for nuclear arms limitations, since that would occur anyway, they thought, with the removal of troops and weapons from Europe—"and more importantly, to begin discussions on the removal of American and Soviet troops and weapons from the soil of Eastern and Western Europe."

A hush fell over all the reporters, including CBS' Dan Rather, who had been planning to air his report later that morning with a twist against the "dangerous idealism" of the proposal. Watching the president, he realized now there was no way Walter Cronkite would allow any negative twist on the story.

Kennedy continued, "I recognize this is being carried throughout the United States and in many other areas of the world, including, I am told, the Soviet Union. President Alexei Kosygin, on behalf of the leadership of the Soviet government, has agreed in principle with my administration that the time has come to formally end the presence of foreign troops on European soil, whether in West Germany or East Germany, whether in France or Poland, whether in England or Czechoslovakia. Europe has had time to heal its wounds of two world wars, and we are proud of the role we have played in our Marshall Plan." Dobrynin winced a bit at that but knew the president was speaking to his American audience with that remark.

"The United States," Kennedy continued, "and the Soviet Union cannot, overnight, withdraw their troops and remove their weapons. The ambassador and I have tentatively agreed, however, to come to an immediate decision about where to begin the demilitarization of American and Russian troops. President Kosygin is on his way to the United States as we address our respective citizens and the world. Please know that the Soviet Union and the United States still maintain fundamental differences over the type of government, the type of economic structure, and the type of culture we believe is best for each of us, and our allies. However, we both agree that our allies deserve the opportunity to decide their own fates, and we are confident that Europe, as a whole, is ready to take on its own responsibility to pursue peace, economic stability, and political freedom. I now turn the microphone and podium over to someone for whom I have a great deal of personal and professional respect, the Soviet ambassador to the United States, Anatoly Dobrynin."

Dobrynin, speaking through an interpreter, said that the Soviet Union recognized the responsibility of great powers such as the Soviet Union and the United States to foster peace. From his observations, Europeans had grown weary of the shadow of the two superpowers and the threat of war that was often beyond the control of any single nation. He believed "the time has come" to allow the Europeans, who "have greatly rebuilt their economies, and who understand well that it is far more difficult to build than to destroy," a chance to "deal with each other in trade, in reuniting families, and promoting cross-cultural missions of peace."

These were unusual statements coming from a Soviet ambassador. Kennedy was going to express these ideas, but he wanted Dobrynin to say something hopeful and positive beyond mere diplomatic jargon. Dobrynin, who was caught up in the moment, threw aside his fears of upsetting whatever hard-liners remained in the Politburo and the military, and spoke with a moving sincerity that shocked many American viewers. He recorded, in his diaries, that "my utterance of these words and phrases produced the most liberating feeling I had felt in my heart since we first heard the news that Nazi Germany had surrendered to the Soviets and Americans."

Shortly before his death almost twenty-five years later, Dobrynin told historian Robert Dallek that he was prepared to follow President Kennedy's advice "even if it meant I had to defect! The sincerity of President Kennedy, his intense sense of purpose to the ends of justice and peace cannot be overstated."

Questions from the press followed. The first question came from Dan Rather. Kennedy thought to himself, Might as well get it over with and then said aloud, "Yes, Mr. Rather."

Rather asked, "Mr. President, there are those in and around the Pentagon, the Congress, and the like who see this proposal as no different than when President Khrushchev of the Soviet Union proposed a 'neutral' Europe in the late 1950s or early 1960s. How do you respond to those critics, sir?"

Kennedy smiled. "Mr. Rather, thank you for your question. The answer is clear that Western Europe was still rebuilding in the 1950s. There was also far more distrust among Soviet and American leaders going into the early 1960s as you may or may not recall. At the time, neither Presidents Eisenhower nor John Kennedy believed the time was right for such a proposal—and I agreed with their assessments. Now Western Europe has been rebuilt, the French and British both have significant militarily defensive capabilities, and the Germans are firmly dedicated to peace and to economic and political justice under Chancellor Wily Brandt. Brandt, in fact, was a freedom fighter against Nazi tyranny in World War II. Eastern Europe has begun to develop a stable economy—I am thinking more of Hungary than perhaps Poland at the moment. And, as Ambassador Dobrynin said moments ago, the Europeans will find more peace and stability helping each other than having to worry about a superpower confrontation simply because there is a strike in Poland, for example. Before our conference this morning, Secretary of State Bowles and I had personal talks with President Pompidou of France, Prime Minister Heath of Great Britain, and Chancellor Brandt of West Germany. All are enthusiastically endorsing this proposal. Next question."

Kennedy had accurately anticipated Rather's question, having brainstormed with Bowles, Dobrynin, and George Kennan, who, despite his age, had come to the White House at five o'clock that morning. Kennan, a former U.S. ambassador to Russia, immediately grasped what he called Kennedy's "root solution" to East-West distrust. Kennan, Bowles, and Dobrynin helped formulate the answer the president eventually gave to the CBS news reporter.

Dan Rather's question was tame compared to the outrage that spewed from the conservative pundits and their supporters throughout the nation. The conservative elements referred to Kennedy's proposal as the "surrender" of America's sphere of influence, leaving Western Europe unprotected from the threat of Communist aggression. Governor Reagan said, "Two years of appeasement have led to the surrender of Western Europe to the international, atheistic Communist regime in Moscow. We handed the South Vietnamese government to the Viet Cong, allowed a Marxist to gain power in Chile, and this is the result. We might as well invite Cuba's Communist dictator, Fidel Castro, to the White House Easter egg hunt next spring." The last remark was witty, but Reagan's tone made clear he was serious.

William F. Buckley wrote in the *Washington Star* the day after the press conference: "This reckless administration of Robert Kennedy's has continually rewarded the student radicals who attacked their own country with foul language and treasonous actions throughout most of the previous decade. These radicals did not merely oppose what they saw as a less than perfect government in South Vietnam. Instead, they, and now the administration, have eagerly supported a government led by the Communist Viet Cong. With this latest gambit, one must reluctantly conclude that we have a president who is in the midst of what psychologists may call, in another context, a 'midlife crisis.' President Kennedy believes words will create peace. We have not seen such hubris and benightedness since the Kellogg-Briand Treaty. In 1928, President Calvin Coolidge's secretary of state, Frank Kellogg, thought he could outlaw war with a treaty made only of words. Perhaps it is time for sober Americans, particularly our veterans' groups and people who know the horrors of Soviet tyranny, to use some of the same methods that have been so handsomely rewarded by the Kennedy White House. We cannot, and must not, allow an idealism based upon illusion, and delusion, to weaken our nation."

Buckley, in turn, was mild compared with other commentators such as Evans and Novak, Victor Reisel, and Joseph Alsop, who each called their NSA and CIA contacts to provide "evidence" of Soviet duplicity and intrigue, including an alleged military plan to reinvade Europe after U.S. troops were removed. Alsop charged that "President Kennedy acts as if he wants peace at any cost. Kennedy's pursuit of this scheme is undermining our military readiness as our citizens will undoubtedly begin to clamor for more social spending instead of the military apparatus required of a superpower on behalf of the Free World. Robert F. Kennedy, unlike his brother, appears to passively accept the threat of Khrushchev's shoe pounding on the United Nation's table. President Kennedy's scheme will most likely not bring about world peace. It will, instead, likely turn all of Western Europe, from England to Germany and beyond, into a neutered Finland, forever in fear of Soviet domination."

The conservatives in the Pentagon, the press, and Congress were given an initial boost for their positions when the Polish military arrested Anna W. and a young, brash Polish striker named Lech Walesa two days after the "joint announcement" in Washington. Polish President Gierek, pursuing a divide-and-conquer strategy, simultaneously revoked the food price increases and the wage freezes. The Soviet Union backed Gierek's strategy, as Kosygin's memoirs explained a couple of decades later when he wrote: "We believed the Polish situation had to abate in order to proceed with the proposal to remove American and Soviet weapons and troops from Western and Eastern Europe. We proposed to Poland's President Gierek that the Soviet Union would provide more economic aid to Poland if there were a revocation of the food price increases and the wage freezes. President Gierek and Polish General Jaruzelski demanded they be provided the right to arrest and jail or deport the two main labor leaders,

Anna Walentynowicz and Lech Walesa. The Politburo reluctantly approved that request, which, as things turned out, was a mistake."

Walesa was beaten in jail—he was, said the Polish military police, "resisting arrest"—fired from his job, and sentenced to internal exile in a small village near Lodz, Poland. Anna W. suffered a "mild" heart attack while in custody and was removed to a military hospital. She was subsequently released but not before it was "suggested" she leave the country. She refused, saying, "You might as well finish the job here and kill me."

Cardinal Stefan Wyszynski was threatened by the Polish secret police but neither imprisoned nor silenced, as the Polish government had done to him between 1953 and 1956. Unbowed, he rose the following Sunday at the main church of Warsaw to deliver a sermon. In the sermon, he praised the Polish government for its actions in sparing the people of Poland from the food price increases and the wage freezes. However, he denounced the government's actions against "our own flesh and blood, Anna and Lech, two lambs of God who stood up to the evil the government finally admitted it was committing against its own people!"

He then ended his sermon abruptly, saying, "This sermon is over, but our action is only beginning. We must show solidarity with these two courageous Catholic union members and march—not fight. Fighting is what the government wants. The government, as we all know, has all the guns and weapons of destruction and death. We have our feet, our canes for walking only—not fighting!—our hearts . . . *and our spirits.*" With that, the cardinal almost leaped from behind the pulpit and began to walk down the aisle of the massive church. People in the pews were stunned at first, with many admittedly frightened of the military stationed just outside and all around the church and the church district.

The cardinal was not to be deterred, however. He turned around in the middle of the center aisle and shouted, "Do we believe in a just God—or not? Is Jesus Christ our Lord and our Savior—or not? Do we want freedom for *all* Polish people—or not? I do not fear evil when God is with me!"

People began to follow the cardinal through the church doors and then into the streets of Warsaw. Soon half a million people were facing the main government building of Warsaw, with the cardinal demanding the release and return of the two leading union strikers. The Polish government called the Soviet ambassador for "advice," and he, in turn, called Foreign Minister Gromyko, who told the Polish leadership to allow Anna W. and Walesa to return to their employment at the docks. The crowds were ordered to disperse as the government told the cardinal they would agree to speak with him and another representative of his choosing—other than Anna W. and Walesa. The cardinal agreed, sending the people home.

He said to the crowd, "If anything happens to me, do not allow my death or injury to be an excuse for violence. You must march, like the American black people, like Gandhi, and like we have today. March home today and come march again to demand justice!"

President Kennedy called Ambassador Dobrynin when the news of this event came over the press wires. He said an American president must show his consistency in his pronouncements on labor issues, East and West. Dobrynin could say nothing, but asked the president to tone down his comments so as not to abort the U.S.-Soviet talks that were to begin a week later.

President Kennedy said in his comments to the press the Tuesday after the Sunday church march: "My fellow Americans, the story coming out of Poland should fill us all with hope that peace may yet prevail in its struggle against war, that freedom will prevail against tyranny, and that workers' rights are respected in America, in Europe, in Poland, and all throughout the world. We call upon the Polish government to return Anna W. and Lech Walesa to their employment in the Gdansk shipyards and for the government of Poland, in return for a promise from strike leaders to return to their jobs, to begin negotiations with the new unions there to improve working conditions. What is good for America—free, independent unions—is good for Poland and for the world."

Yarborough and Reuther wanted to include a promise of food and non-military aid to the Polish workers, but Kennedy thought he was "playing with enough fire, gentlemen."

The day after the president's speech, President Gierek announced that his government would allow Anna W. and Walesa to return to their jobs in the shipyards. Upon their return, the nascent trade unions in Poland demanded that economic reforms begin, which Gierek said he would agree to after the strikers returned to work. This took a few days, while industry after industry held "elections" to vote on the return to work. The proposition to return to work passed, which quelled the crisis. Gierek had told the Soviet ambassador to Poland that a no vote was likely to result in a Polish military coup. "We were essentially told by President Kosygin that the Russians would not invade and that we had to clean up this mess ourselves. Thank God," said the Communist-atheist president of Poland to a reporter a couple of years later, "the unions voted yes on the proposition to return to work and begin negotiations."

The new unions in the various industries created an umbrella group, patterned after the AFL-CIO, called "Solidarity." In an effort to create a broad coalition, the new umbrella group included young dissident intellectuals, including a Jew, Adam Michnik, and, of course, Cardinal Wyszynski.

President Kennedy said to Ethel in the last days of the Polish strike crisis, "Ethel, this is very different from what we faced in Cuba a few years ago. There, I always felt we might not be doing the right thing in the sense that I could never understand why the Cuban people did not simply rise up against Castro. Here, the people are rising up, and . . . " He shook his head and paused a moment. Then he said softly, " . . . I understand what's happening in Poland. I feel it in my bones, and I almost feel like it's worth going to war over. . . . The right wing in the military and the CIA, you know, in the papers, they scream we should take action, but privately they wish the Polish military would take over there. Yet Yarborough and Reuther, they see it as just another fight no different than labor against capital, and they want to directly help the workers, even if there's a world war . . . It's weird. . . . "

Ethel, sitting in bed with her husband, said simply, "I saw May Reuther yesterday. She stopped by after visiting Walt at his office. I asked her about this whole thing, and you know what she said? She said businessmen and military people hate labor unions everywhere. Businessmen here only root for labor in the Soviet Union and their satellites because they see them as disruptive of society. I had to say to May that unions do disrupt things. She just laughed and said, 'Walter says you can't achieve anything worthwhile without some agitation.' I wasn't laughing, but I did do my best to smile. Was that okay, honey? I . . . I just . . . I haven't kept up all that much—the kids are constantly in need of my attention—there's nowhere for them to go without the Secret Service—they just stay in the house or have friends over—"

"Honey, I know. The kids are more often interrupting meetings during the day than not, although I manage to keep them out of the foreign policy meetings—with armed guards! We set a record for children in the White House that I doubt will be repeated by anyone!" He looked at her with sympathy more than love at the moment. He kissed her forehead. "Ethel, I apologize for not being there enough for you and the kids. This situation in Poland is, like I said, tougher than Cuba, I think, because we can't afford to miss this opportunity to truly reduce the possibility of nuclear war in Europe. The Soviets really want to talk here. I can feel it." Seeing her disappointment at the continued political pillow talk, he smiled and said, "You know, Ethel, I sometimes think about *other* things. Why, just the other day I thought, Why don't we have the Secret Service get us that Swedish movie, *I Am Curious (But) Yellow*—I think I can snag a copy myself from the Supreme Court chambers! Or how about something *really* dirty!"

Ethel pushed him hard, laughing, "You devil, Robert Kennedy! What would your mother say?"

Kennedy said, "My mother would say, 'Is your woman treating you right?' That's what she'd say!" And then he ducked under the covers as she grabbed a pillow to hit him.

"You come out here, Mis-ter President, and face your lawfully wedded wife! Otherwise, I'll call Mr. Buckley to say he's right—you are surrendering!" His head moved—no, jerked—under the covers as he grunted. "You think I don't have time to read any newspapers, do you?" She was laughing, playfully taunting him now.

"I'm only coming out on advice of counsel, Mrs. Kennedy."

"Well, I have some counsel here for you if you come out now," she purred—as best as an Ethel Kennedy could.

Kennedy stuck his head out from under the covers, and Ethel kissed him with the sort of passion long-married couples don't achieve very often with children in the house. It was a confident passion, unlike the passion brought on by fear the two of them had felt the day after the assassination attempt in June 1968. And with that confident kiss, the president and first lady engaged in something that almost resulted in their twelfth child. Almost. As Ethel said many years later to her daughter Kathleen, long after the latter's marriage and at least one child, "The rhythm method of birth control is ineffective most of the time, but that's part of the fun!"

The concerns of East versus West, the Cold War, labor strife, environmental destruction, national politics, and eleven particular children were thus forgotten in the presidential bed for at least part of one night.

Chapter 22

THE HITS KEEP COMING

In the week after the November 1970 elections, which by February 1971 seemed ages ago, Kennedy had discussed with select members of his staff and cabinet the strategy designed to take his administration into the presidential election year of 1972. The likely opponents in the Republican Party had narrowed down to the trio of California Governor Ronald Reagan, retired General Creighton W. Abrams Jr. and possibly the just elected senator from Delaware, William Roth.

Kennedy convened the strategy meeting with the O Boys, Secretary of Commerce Learson (it was one of the few strategy sessions Learson had been invited to), Secretary of Labor Reuther, and Vice President Yarborough. Kennedy said to the gathering, "Gentlemen, I expect, after this year of dealing more with foreign policy, that 1971 will be the year of domestic policy issues for us."

Kennedy continued, "We need a tax-cutting strategy of some sort to counter Roth and possibly Reagan, who is moving toward Roth on this issue. It's not to say foreign policy is not on our agenda though, because we have to find a way to speak with the Soviets and the Red Chinese, or at least the Soviets, if we are going to challenge the conservatives' attacks on our administration. The one argument they have is that our foreign policy of cooperating with the Viet Cong and not trying to overthrow Allende in Chile and such hasn't yielded any movement with the Soviets or the Red Chinese."

"That steams this ol' boy, I gotta tell ya, Mr. President," said Yarborough. "I didn't think we should MIRV our nuclear weapons—making each one o' 'em into four or five weapons. Yet everything I hear says it's because of them MIRVs that the Soviets won't talk! It's the conservatives' hard line, not our reasonable line—what the hell do we need to MIRV anyway?—that's stoppin' us raht in our tracks for gettin' arms reductions!"

Reuther nodded in agreement and said, "The Republicans are also hitting us hard on government spending on recycling plants and the retraining of workers in the lumber industry as we begin to cut back on the clear-cutting of forests. And I don't have to tell anyone here the Republicans are getting lots of money from Southern businesses as our union efforts succeed. So far, they have the money—but we have the power of the votes. The union organizing down South helped us in the midterm elections. We gathered more voters—white and especially black—than we could have ever hoped. The union victories in the hospital sector in North Carolina, Georgia, and Alabama, and the Statesboro textile plant of J. P. Stevens—that was a big win!—were definitely key factors in helping convince people to stick together as workers. Sam Walton closed down one of his Wal-Mart stores in North Carolina rather than let it go union. I called the head of another chain, Kmart, and told him if he let a union in from the get-go, I could help arrange a less-than-union-prevailing wage for the short run from the AFL-CIO. He went for it, saying he'd like to take on Walton in his backyard of the Southeast. The union reluctantly agreed, but only after seeing how they didn't have to charge much for dues or strike funds in the early stages." Reuther then added, while playfully pounding his knee, "Well, Mr. President, we're gonna be in good shape if we can just keep from letting the environment and that OSHA bill get too far ahead of us."

Reuther was referring to the fact that unions had joined with business in fighting the Occupational Safety and Health bill sponsored by Democratic Senator Harrison Williams of New Jersey. Williams assumed the unions would endorse the bill but found Reuther did not like the idea of the government replacing labor unions in fighting for worker safety. "I have to agree with the manufacturers," Reuther told Williams at a meeting in the Oval Office with President Kennedy in late 1969. "You will never get enough OSHA inspectors out there, and having OSHA may undermine what a union is supposed to stand for. I don't want bosses ever figuring they can tell workers during a planned union drive, 'Don't bother with the unions, boys! The government already gives you a decent minimum wage and an inspector for working conditions.'"

Williams, somewhat elitist in temperament, though a deeply humane, decent person, said to Reuther, "I don't see you coming out against the minimum wage, Mr. Secretary. In fact, you're always for an increase in the minimum wage. Why oppose my bill when the government and the unions can work hand in hand to bring safety to workplaces?" Williams also pointedly reminded Reuther of the high rate of injuries at plants and that a federal program to teach—and enforce—safety was needed.

Reuther answered, "We push for increases in the minimum wage because it helps us to keep pushing for even higher wages for union workers, Senator. This safety bill, so-called, on the other hand, threatens to get the government involved in day-to-day activities in the factory. The older I get, the more I understand John L. Lewis and the early CIO unions. If you get a Republican administration after you pass this law, it could wind up becoming a substitute for labor unions in a way that would not be good for the worker at all. As for safety records, my old union, the UAW, has the best safety record of nearly any union or industry. I'm sorry, Senator. You know I stand with you on nearly every issue we can name. But I can't go for this one in its current form."

Kennedy eventually secured a compromise, which was suggested to him by Vice President Yarborough. Senator Williams amended the OSHA bill in mid-1970 to include a carrot-and-stick approach: If a company had a union recognized as independent by the National Labor Relations Board—not a company-sponsored union—and had won an election with the workers, the company was exempt from the OSHA requirements. The only exception was if, after an OSHA investigation due to complaints from five or more workers, OSHA found a company-sponsored safety program was not being followed "with due vigor," the government could step in and subject the company to an inspection program. Again, however, the company could regain the exemption if the independent union was willing to become financially responsible with the company to meet the OSHA inspectors' recommendations.

Reuther was still worried about what a Republican administration would do but he would not openly oppose the bill. As he complained to Senator Alan Cranston, Democrat of California, who had been supportive of the Williams' bill, "They might make up a boss (dominated) union—and a boss union, like every dog, can have its day in an election." Ironically, a filibuster threat by Senator Thurmond, most Republicans, and some Southern Democratic senators fighting for what they told Kennedy and Reuther were their lives, kept the bill from being passed in 1970. Reuther breathed a small sigh of relief at the good fortune of having such unlikely political allies.

At the post-election strategy meeting, Kennedy said to Reuther, "Now, Walter, you need to let that revised OSHA bill pass this coming year. Senator Williams has reasonably compromised on its scope. In fact, I need to sign that bill before next spring," in 1971, "so we don't make it into an election year issue. The Southern Democrats are now ready to vote for it, or so they say."

Reuther nodded in resigned agreement. There are other fights, he thought to himself.

Then, turning to Yarborough, Kennedy said, "Ralph, I also think we may need to give something to the Republicans on this guaranteed minimum income issue. I have always wondered about whether a guaranteed income is a good idea, as some of you know. I think, from talking with Ken Galbraith, as well as our chair of the Council of Economic Advisers, Bob Lekachman, that we might be able to live with a negative income tax—"

"Ah'm real wary o' that one, Mr. President," said Yarborough. "Ah've been talkin' with some ee-conomists, too, but Ah'd like us to be real sure we don't wind up with too small a' benefit for people to survive on when they don't have a job. Or when a momma is home alone with the kids and no husband 'round to take care o' her. Ah mean to say that—"

Kennedy held up his hand to stop Ralph Yarborough from what Ralph called "speechifyin'." "Ralph, I share your concerns, but the Family Assistance Program proposed by Senator McGovern in 1969—almost two years ago!—has gone through hearings, with the welfare rights people saying we need a guaranteed income *above the minimum wage,* when you add in Medicaid and housing subsidies! I mean, why work at all if we're gonna do that?—and we have Abrams, Reagan, and Roth going on about the easy way to solve the welfare problem is with a negative income tax, end welfare, and *lowering* the minimum wage so businesses can hire more people—"[1]

Yarborough was not backing down. "But, Mr. President, the Republicans only want to spend a thousand a year on each welfare recipient, which isn't nearly enough. And may Ah re-iterate Walter's general concern he had with that OSHA bill? What if the Republicans get into power? What happens to poor people on a negative income tax then? They won't ever get a raise in their poverty transfer payment, assumin' the Republicans don't repeal the negative income tax—with no welfare to back it up, like Reagan or Roth sometimes get excited about in their speeches to the manufacturers' associations!"

Kennedy was looking for someone else to speak on the best strategy to follow here. He looked to Larry O'Brien, his longtime political strategist. When O'Brien spoke, however, he did not make the president happy.

O'Brien said, "Mr. President, I recognize your concern from the Right, but we have the Left to think about, too. Senator McGovern told me last month that we could face a possible Left flank challenge in 1972 from George Wiley, the National Welfare Rights Organization president, if we go with a negative income tax. He said the same thing last week. In talking with Senator McGovern about an idea we have from—"

Kennedy jumped out of his chair, slamming his hands on the Oval Office desk, and shouted, "What did you say? George . . . fff . . . fff—" He wanted to say a word that started with *f.* "George . . . Wiley . . . wants to . . . run against *me* in '72 . . . *over this one . . . God-damned issue?* Is he out of his ever-living *skull?*"

Next to Kenny O'Donnell, O'Brien knew Bob Kennedy the best of the assembled. He knew if he spoke directly and firmly, Kennedy would hear him. "Mr. President, Wiley isn't saying he's going to run. He knows better than that." O'Brien was saying to himself, *I hope.* "Wiley is very concerned that welfare people will lose out in any 'reform,' which is frankly what drives the Republicans to push for the negative income tax. The Republicans know that a minimum income, either directly or in a negative tax, replaces basic welfare payments. From there they hope to abolish the newer Medicaid coverage signed by President Johnson, and limit Julian Bond's house building, one step at a time."

Seeing Kennedy was still seething at the thought of Wiley running in a Democratic Party primary against him, O'Brien cleared his throat and continued firmly, and a bit louder than before. "Mr. President, as I started to say before, we have a way to get around Wiley *and* the Republicans and get a bill passed that won't hurt most welfare recipients, which will keep Wiley from doing something stupid . . . which he won't anyway!"

Kennedy was still angry but said, "Okay, Larry, what's the plan? I'm listening. It's good, right?"

"Well, it's good, and it's still a negative income tax. The way we push the bill through is this way. We propose a negative income tax that is 70 percent of the current minimum wage, excluding housing subsidies and Medicaid, which more and more poor folks are getting, thanks to the Democratic majority in Congress and some liberal Republicans in the Northeast and Northwest. This brings the payment up to the current minimum wage. That placates Wiley. Then, at the same time, we pass an increase in the minimum wage to cover the difference between the minimum wage and welfare payments in some states, like Connecticut, where people can make more on welfare right now than they would if they worked for minimum wage! We may not completely placate Wiley or the conservatives, but it sets us up as brokering the compromise and making the failure *their* fault if we don't secure passage of a bill."

Kennedy thought to himself, Wiley's got a good racket going for himself, doesn't he? To those present, Kennedy merely nodded.

O'Brien continued. "To prevent the working folks who make just above the minimum wage stop from feeling like they get the shaft for having a low-paying job instead of being on welfare—and those folks hate welfare recipients more than rich people, according to the Bell Commission testimonies taken from working people at that income level—we also increase eligibility for Medicaid and the housing subsidies to 150 percent *above* the minimum wage.[2] We haven't got the votes for a full-scale national government based health care program coverage for every American—at least not yet. This moves us much closer to that, though, and gives the working folks at the bottom of the wage scale sufficient incentive to keep working and feel better about their predicament. According to the Bell Commission, which is where I'm getting this from—the study's out later this week, held off till after the midterm elections on my advice to Professor Bell—we can buy off most of the combatants on the issue."

Yarborough and Reuther looked at each other warily and nodded.

O'Donnell, who hadn't said a word, now said, "A lawyer couldn't have crafted that any better, Larry. It buys off everyone—the Republicans on the negative income tax, the Wiley group with a welfare payment at the current minimum wage; plus, you increase the minimum wage to keep the lower, mostly white, working class from falling for Republicans saying 'the poor get more than you do.' We can hold everyone's feet to the fire, I think, with this one, can't we, Larry?"

"That's the idea, Kenny, just as I told McGovern today. McGovern is fairly close to Wiley and is ready to go for it, as I started to say before." O'Brien kept his eye on the president, who was warming up to the idea.

Kennedy said, "Ken Galbraith said to me last year that just about the only thing he and the conservative economist Milton Friedman, out of Chicago, ever agreed upon was the negative income tax. It stops the cost of worrying about whether the husband is there or not, and limits the cost of having a separate bureaucracy constantly having to find out if you're poor enough to receive welfare. If you report no income at all or income below the poverty line, you receive the negative income tax, which is a cash payment. Ken recognizes there will always be fraud, but that can be taken care of by the Internal Revenue Service. Some of the bureaucracy savings on welfare can be easily transferred to the IRS enforcement budget, he said, and I agree. I just can't understand why people think there's that much difference between a negative income tax and the guaranteed income."

"But what about those who can't read or can't fill out a tax form? And how do we stop the Republicans from undermining the income of poor folks down the road?" asked Yarborough, who remained leery of the negative income tax and the Republicans getting power at some point.

O'Brien said, "You'll see when you read the Bell Commission report. I'll get it for you. Bell had that Swedish economist Gunnar Myrdal on the commission—his daughter is married to a Harvard administrator, I believe. Myrdal said, to answer your second question first, that you tie the negative income tax to the Consumer Price Index so the poor are protected already. As for your first question, the unions could offer services to the poor—or the government could do the same in some places—and help people fill out the forms. Unions could get into places they never would have thought—"

"I love that idea!" shouted Reuther. "That's what we've been finding already in the South. The illiteracy in some parts—not just black areas—is unbelievable! Just to get the union cards filled out, we had to bring in student interns and some of our teachers from the teachers unions up north. Len Woodcock's SOC group has sponsored a couple of literacy programs, which, with Allard Lowenstein's VISTA kids, have been starting to show some improvement there. We can help poor people make money with the negative income tax and create some good feeling for our organizers."

"But where are the jobs coming from, gentlemen?" said Secretary of Commerce Learson, who by now had tired of being reticent around these "politicos," especially after he had been known to speak loud and often as an IBM executive. "I hate to spoil this strategy party, but we, in all candor, can't keep focusing on what some poor people's advocates are saying. We need jobs for the troops who are almost all home from Vietnam, and some of those who have returned from other areas of Southeast Asia, just for starters. As we are more successful in foreign diplomacy, we lose some of the need for aerospace and other contracts, according to the rather dark humor of my good friend, Defense Secretary Warnke. And you know, Secretary Reuther, that is where the best-paying union jobs, with overtime, are—and in Los Angeles, Atlanta, and other areas, you can't find any better-paying jobs for unskilled workers than defense jobs—at least not yet! The recycling plants are few and far between compared to those defense jobs. I hope I am not bursting anyone's bubble here."

Learson had resolved, in coming to the meeting, to speak his mind. He'd heard much criticism over the past eighteen months from businessmen on the occasional golf course outing about his working with "Commie Bobby" and his "radical administration." He would answer them by talking about creating a "small home computer industry" and the need for a civilian conversion program. The businessmen would roll their eyes and say, "You IBM guys are too much!" What they meant, Learson wasn't sure. He knew he was right, and besides, he was going to be on the ground floor of this when he returned to the private sector.

Still, by November 1970, Learson was wondering if his conversion project with the Defense Department would ever get out from under wraps. He didn't want to spend much more time in government without any advance in the small home computer project. While he had long decided against going back to IBM, he'd seen enough of the military contract industry to know they would need to change their slow and bureaucratic ways—"They're worse than the government! The surprising thing to me is that I find a lot of hardworking people inside the government, much better than the private defense contractors, for example. The government workers, though, make a helluva lot less, and without some of the perquisites we have in the business world," he'd tell astonished business colleagues.[3]

Learson saw President Kennedy was looking shocked by the harsh economic reality he had painted. He continued, more confident now, "Mr. President, Secretary Warnke and I, as part of our 'military conversion to civilian products' project with Professor Melman at Columbia, have come up with an idea to develop a domestic business and home computer industry. We also propose the government provide a large but appropriate investment for research and funding for the development of the wireless transfer of data, voice, and even visuals for civilian use, not simply military. I'll be the first to admit that IBM, both now and when I was there, hasn't been interested enough in this, largely because IBM's money has been traditionally made with large businesses and government. The research is still ongoing in the private sector and in the public sector through the Pentagon, with APRANET on the West Coast. I recently spoke with one of the top men over there, he's at UCLA, and he says they are already on the verge of a breakthrough, so I'm told, with electronic communication. The way I see it, gentlemen, our government went to the moon in about ten years. We made the leap into the nuclear age in less than four years following government-sponsored research of less than a decade. We can, I believe, do the same for civilian computers and wireless transmissions in five to ten years—if the government steps up its efforts here."

Learson concluded, saying, "Vice President Yarborough and I have also spoken about this, as I have on a couple of occasions with Secretary Reuther." Kennedy looked at Reuther and Yarborough, who both smiled in support of what Learson was saying.

Kennedy was especially intrigued. He had talked with Learson before, at Yarborough's request, but didn't take his talk about computers all that seriously. The Vietnam vets coming home were being integrated into jobs well enough at the time. Plus, every time Kennedy mentioned it to Tom Watson, who was still running IBM, Watson would say he didn't think personal computers were "practical." Now, however, Kennedy was starting to think about finding jobs in the South for union-minded workers and how to use a conversion program as a way to avoid a downturn in the economy and therefore defeat the Republicans in 1972. Since Truman's time, the great fear among the elite in America was that, without a military "pump primer," America could fall into a deep recession, or perhaps a depression as great as in the 1930s.

Kennedy couldn't recall Learson's first name, which was not surprising since Learson usually signed his name "T. Vincent"—preferring his middle name to his first given name. Kennedy said, "Secretary Learson, let's hear first about some of these conversion ideas from you, Mr. Warnke, and Professor . . . "

"Melman, sir. Professor Seymour Melman. As I said, Professor Melman is from Columbia. He is highly respected, and frankly, very practical once you get to speak with him. Professor Melman has done extensive analyses showing, for example, that we could build a subway system in Washington, D.C., for the cost of *one*—just one!—nuclear aircraft carrier, which includes the aircraft, the guided missiles, frigates, and other support costs, but does *not* include the personnel costs. When one thinks about the continuing jobs with that subway and the continued usage it could have, as opposed to having one more nuclear aircraft carrier, we can see the advantages. We could also build such a subway with a mechanism that would go through routes with sensors and the like, which might cost a few longer-term jobs, but the whole thing would run more efficiently. Another example of conversion: We can build over sixty-five low-cost two-bedroom homes for the cost of *one* of our Huey-brand helicopters. If Secretary Udall were here, he might find it interesting to know that our government could fund his entire clean-up program of our nation's main waterways just by cutting the anticipated cost *overruns, not the cost itself*—this is based upon historical data Professor Melman has utilized—on forty different proposed weapon systems."

What made Learson impressive is that he didn't have any report or notes in front of him. He had committed to memory and analysis the various studies he'd been reading.

The men in the Oval Office were silent now, hanging on Learson's every word. Learson continued, "Mr. President, you know that child nutrition proposal from Senator Clark of Iowa? We could fund that program *this year* with no tax or spending increases simply by not building just two DE-1052 destroyer escorts. One 'Main' battle tank would pay for the whole country's Special Milk program from the Department of Agriculture! Another example: Secretary Warnke has been trying to convince Congress to stop this new B-1 bomber program. He thinks it's a waste and has several fatal flaws I can't recall here and now—"

"One of our best senators, Alan Cranston of California, loves that program," whispered O'Brien to Kennedy, loud enough for Learson to hear. Learson charged on, seeing O'Brien was in no position to stop him at this point. "Mr. O'Brien, stopping the B-1 bomber would not affect our readiness in any way—and there are other programs we can send to California to replace the B-1. Our B-52s are still the best around. Yet, stopping the B-1 program, already in overruns, and redirecting the cost savings on overruns, allows us to fund, to take one example, the Federal Child Care bill that's working its way out of committee. That bill provides nutrition programs, health programs, and day care on a nationwide basis for all mothers—rich and poor—requesting it. Heck, just stop the B-1 and you can have back the two new DE-1052 escorts right away—and then some!"[4]

Seeing Kennedy's continued hesitation on the B-1 example, Learson said, "The overall point is more important than any particular example, Mr. President. I hope I am not speaking out of turn here, as I know I have spoken a while now."

"No, Mr. Secretary," said Kennedy, who was frankly shocked to hear such information and a rather radical point of view from a businessman. "Why don't you tell me a bit more about the small computer program for home use? I just haven't been able to see my way through this from a practical standpoint. A lot of people don't even need typewriters. Why would they need computers?"

Learson, taking a deep breath, admitted the program would not produce small computers "for practical use" for a few years, maybe several. "We're talking about a process. In speaking with some researchers at UCLA, as I said before, they are on the verge of something they call 'electronic communication' that could eventually replace or at least limit the need to write letters on paper— and that is a big use of the smaller computers for the typical consumer."

"Don't tell that to Moe Biller! " said Larry O'Brien. Learson did his best to look perplexed rather than angry at the interruption. O'Brien, realizing that he shouldn't interrupt a former high-level executive who was, he admitted to himself, making an excellent presentation, said a bit meekly, "Moe Biller's the head of the postal workers' union, Mr. Secretary."

Learson smiled a half-smile at O'Brien—he didn't want O'Brien to think he was angry with him either. He remembered the adage from the world of corporate politics about "planting seeds to build trees," which meant one must seek allies—not punish heretics—to win policy victories. Learson continued, "Well, gentlemen, just as we have smaller and smaller radios and televisions, we can have smaller computers, now that we have unlocked the first secrets of semiconductors and integrated circuits. I don't think you know Victor Grinich, who founded Fairchild Semiconductor, or Robert Noyce, who is one of the bright young minds at this new company Intel—they receive government funding already from the Defense Department, and public universities on the West Coast such as UCLA and Livermore in Berkeley—I'm sorry, I'm wandering and probably boring you all . . . "

In truth, he had impressed them already with phrases such as "integrated circuits," "semiconductors," and especially "communication through electricity." Reuther was wondering to himself, Is electronic communication done with lights like Morse code running through some small computer? Kennedy suddenly found himself interested in a way he wasn't before. He began to salivate the way he did over any "can-do" guy with a "gee-whiz" gadget or program—even if he didn't understand much about it himself. And who's this "Grinch" fella, Kennedy thought? Yarborough, who had spent some time with Warnke and Learson, decided to break in.

"Ah'm glad Vince is here to talk about these new-fangled things, Mr. President! Ah love this ee-lectronic stuff. Vince even showed me what they're talkin' 'bout. Ah thought the ee-lectronic stuff had to do with code, but—well, it does in a way—but it's really 'bout typin' words that go through telephone cables an' space an' stuff, Ah think." He looked at Learson, who smiled and nodded to keep going, even if he wasn't quite scientific in his explanation.

Yarborough continued, "Mr. President, this ee-lectronic mail could, if we can do it with the government, really challenge ol' Mama Telephone Bell— the Bell Labs been studyin' it, too, let me tell y'all! If the gum'mint gets started in the 'computers for the people' business—that's what Ah'd call it!— we can really get people talkin' to each other through their computers, and there's all sorts of things you can do with computers—calculatin' things, keepin' records, act lahk a typewriter—and Vince here says it could be lahk a TV one day with the circuits gettin' smaller and the power gettin' . . . well, more powerful . . . an' . . . now how's that again, Vince?"

Learson smiled, saying, "The circuits get smaller, but more powerful is correct, Mr. Vice President. They're faster and can store and move more information—not just data or words, but also voice and pictures. Bob Noyce tells me that every six months, they have cut down the size of the circuits, yet doubled the amount one can store on a circuit—I think that's what he said. And one can move the electronic information through telephone lines, but there may be a different kind of wire needed. They're still looking at that. But that's what's really interesting—the combining of telephones, computers, and maybe even television and radio. Gentlemen, I know this is a strategy meeting, but I only came to say we should consider the development of this program, which I have been working on with Secretary Warnke—and the conversion program fits right in with this for defense engineers going into this sort of research and testing."

Kennedy was hooked. He liked electronic communication and computers that could be like televisions—video telephones like the ones at the World's Fair in New York in 1964. Kennedy said, "Secretary Learson, I'd like to see you and Secretary Warnke next week to talk in detail about this program. Let's have Ralph here join us, too, and maybe someone in the Senate who's interested in this as a proposal."

Yarborough said, "Mr. President, Ah am sure glad you're interested in this. Already been speakin' with several senators, including Cranston, but also Al Gore o' Tennessee. His son was with him when Ah spoke 'bout this idea, and the son is very interested in helpin'—guess he's not too happy bein' a reporter in Tennessee these days. Seems lahk a nice fella—bit reserved, but earnest. Also, ya got Hollings o' South Carolina real interested. He says he needs any sorta industry down the'ah—and quick."

Kennedy abruptly ended the meeting. Because he was so taken with Learson's proposals and presentation, he forgot all about tax cutting. He did, however, finally have a negative income tax plan that could help end most of the welfare program, if not replace it entirely, and still help welfare recipients. Plus, he finally had a clear understanding of how a real conversion program could work. He especially liked the idea that public transportation, at least with regard to a possible Washington subway, was somewhat cheap to build.

After the meeting, Kennedy met with the O Boys. Kennedy kept coming back to the Learson presentation on conversion and computers in general. He told the O Boys he thought Learson's ideas were "like a political and economic MIRV! His ideas hit multiple subjects and work to defeat our Republican opposition in Congress!"

O'Brien was not convinced. He said, "With all respect, Mr. President, this home computer stuff sounds off the wall. People won't buy little computers to talk with each other 'ee-lectronically,' like Ralph says. It's a fad—and then what? We're hit by a Reagan or a Roth with the government wasting precious resources no better than ditch digging! Mr. President, we never discussed *any* strategy on fighting the tax-cutting proposals the Republicans are brewing up because we got sidetracked with this conversion scheme!"

Kennedy said to O'Brien, "Oh my God, you're right, Larry!" Then, like a child ignoring the spilled milk on the kitchen floor, he brightened and said, "But let's talk about the Learson and Warnke proposals a little more, at least for a moment. I have to admit, Larry, you sound like Tom Watson at IBM. I didn't give Learson a good listen to either when I first heard about these ideas last year—because IBM isn't interested in small computers. But I'm starting to believe we have to think further into the future than next year. Wasn't that interesting when Vice President Yarborough said AT&T—Ma Bell—is studying this? Well, that *was* interesting, don't you think? Who loves the phone company?

Not even the telephone union workers, I bet. Our attorney general, who was thinking about antitrust actions against IBM—I told him it may not be wise at this time—is thinking about an antitrust action against AT&T. This could really open things up—with the small computer program. We can use a carrot and stick approach with AT&T, with antitrust being the stick."

Kennedy then slapped his knee and began rocking in his chair as if it were a bronco. "I know what you were mad about when Vince was talking, Larry!"—Kennedy wasn't going to forget Learson's "first" name anymore!—"Vince said people could communicate with 'electric' communications instead of writing and mailing letters! You're just mad because you were postmaster general under Lyndon! You think this'll put the Post Office out of business!"

O'Brien shook his head in disgust. "I wasn't even thinking of that, Bob, and you know it! " He forgot to say "Mr. President," and Kennedy, enjoying his Freudian joke on O'Brien, said, "Don't worry, Larry. I bet Learson and Warnke will let the Post Office get in on some of that action. Maybe!"

Turning serious, Kennedy said, "Larry, Kenny, we need to give all of this some thought. If this was just Paul Warnke, who's talked conversion for years, I could say, well, it's not something we want to dive into heads first without a commission at least. But this is a top corporate executive, with great skill at analyzing information, great decision-making skills. Wait a minute! That's it! A commission! Let's make it a commission—and get this discussed with a bunch of businessmen who will see the profit potential for their various businesses! That Bell Commission on welfare sure was a neat idea. We get Melman to put some sympathetic people on, get a couple of Republicans . . . I hate to say so, boys, but we're going in for this! This will be better than the space program. Frankly, now that we know for sure that the moon is essentially uninhabitable, I think we need to work on more down-to-earth things. While this computer program seems a little pie in the sky, too, it's got some functionality that will improve our military capabilities—or at least as much as the highway program did when Congress said we needed to build highways for 'national security'!"

A few months later, in February 1971, Kennedy was far away from talk about elections, taxes, or welfare—although the conversion program loomed larger than ever if a million American soldiers were coming home from Europe. Kennedy was, by this point, euphoric about the Russians tentatively agreeing to a mutual withdrawal of superpower troops and weapons from Eastern and Western Europe.

Kennedy expected some static from the Joint Chiefs of Staff on the NATO troop and weapon removal, but surprisingly the chiefs expressed little concern. Admiral Moorer of the Joint Chiefs said that, with the nuclear weapons aboard the Strategic Air Command jets and the submarines in the navy, the United States could always maintain a credible first-strike capability against the Russians—who, said Moorer, did have more land-based missiles. The chairman of the Joint Chiefs, General Earle Wheeler, an army man, was less sure about being able to defend Europe if the Soviet Union ever sent troops in, but he did not want to resign just yet and join General Abrams on what he called "the rubber-chicken politics" circuit. When he saw Moorer and the others were in favor of the proposal, he decided to go along and let Moorer have the spotlight, thinking, Let Moorer deal with the political consequences if this deal falls apart.

On February 17, President Kennedy appeared at the National Press Club in downtown Washington to make a major address. Kennedy wanted to outline how the talks with the Russians were going to progress and give the press an understanding of the still tentative timetable being discussed with the Russians. He also wanted to announce the formation of the commission to study the conversion of military businesses into civilian businesses so that, as he planned to say, "down the road, we will be as prepared for peace as we have been, and continue to be, for war."

At the luncheon, Kennedy was enjoying himself at the dais—he almost forgot about the Secret Service agent standing just to his right behind him. Kennedy listened to the light banter of respected *New York Times* editor John Oakes, who had been asked by the Press Club to introduce the president. Oakes, in a friendly jest, asked as part of his introduction, "And what other surprises besides the impending withdrawal of troops from Europe does the president have in store for us? Is he going to begin selling moon cheese to the third world?" This example of the usual Establishment "humor" sent the largely fawning reporters into hysterics. Kennedy nodded with pursed lips, evoking, for the reporters' sake, a mixture of sarcasm and humility.

Kennedy stood after Oakes intoned, "And now, ladies and gentlemen, it is my greatest honor to introduce the President of the United States." Kennedy then began to step behind the Plexiglas platform to begin his speech.

Suddenly, a man stood up at a nearby table. Pulling a gun from his suit pocket, he shouted, "For the fatherland!" He fired three shots at Kennedy. The Secret Service agent standing behind the president, new to this particular detail, had seen the man pull out the weapon and pushed Kennedy to the floor, reinjuring Kennedy's ankle. The shots missed Kennedy because of the agent's quick action, but the agent was shot twice. One bullet hit him in the shoulder and another grazed his scalp. The third bullet missed both the agent and Kennedy altogether, striking the Plexiglas in front of the podium. The people in the audience seemed to choke on their screams, many ducking under their chairs. The thump of the third bullet, when it hit the Plexiglas, could be heard throughout the room because of the stunned, scared silence following the initial screams.

One of the other three Secret Service agents stationed near the back of the room began running toward the dais as the assassin stood and shouted. The agent pulled out his gun, and, when he reached a point about fifteen feet away from the would-be assassin, shot him in the back of the head, killing him instantly. A gasp went up through the room at the sound of the agent's gunshot hitting the would-be assassin, who was identified a few minutes later as Ivan Gavenenko, a former Nazi S.S. officer from Lithuania who had been recruited into the CIA in 1948. Gavenenko was of Lithuanian-Russian ancestry. Like many former Nazis, he entered the United States around 1950 without having to submit to anti-Nazi laws. This was a fairly common practice for the Truman administration, working in bipartisan cooperation with Republicans, such as Senator Arthur Vandenberg of Michigan, Allen Dulles, and John Foster Dulles, who would become, respectively, the head of the CIA and secretary of state in subsequent administrations.

By the mid-1950s Gavenenko had become an organization leader in the Republican Party caucus known as the Captive Nations caucus. The phrase "Captive Nations" denoted the Eastern European and Baltic-region nations under Soviet occupation.[5] The Captive Nations group was known to be full of Nazis and Nazi-sympathizers, yet Republicans and conservatives were rarely criticized for supporting the group or for appearing at parades or other activities with them.

Gavenenko, seeing himself as a martyr to the cause of Eastern Europeans long under the boot of Soviet tyranny, had written a suicide note, anticipating he was not likely to survive. In the note, he claimed Kennedy was "selling out Europe to the Communists" and that Kennedy was planning to "convert the United States into a Communist nation." After the attempted assassination, the discussion among opinion makers naturally turned to the Captive Nations' caucus and its membership, and the Republicans' and conservatives' endorsement of this group. It was a rare case in which questions of loyalty to one's government were directed at Republicans and conservatives instead of at Democrats and liberals.

Internally, the only issues being revisited were why Kennedy's request for only one Secret Service agent at the dais had been granted and why the Press Club appearance had been treated differently than if he was in a public auditorium.

Making sure nobody thought they were in any way behind this assassination attempt, the Russians and the Chinese—and even Cuba's Communist dictator, Fidel Castro—issued strong statements condemning the attempted assassination. The Chinese complained that "Fascists and Nazis have grown up like weeds in America." Soviet Ambassador Dobrynin made a heartfelt house call to the president and, surprising Kennedy, praised God for allowing Kennedy to live.

President Georges Pompidou of France made a speech in which he called upon all of Europe to cooperate in the "lessening of tensions that cause criminal minds to believe that killing one individual leader can somehow undermine our progress toward peace and freedom."

When Kennedy read Pompidou's statement on the second morning after the failed assassination attempt, he said to Kenny O'Donnell, "Is that the French government's way of saying I'm not that important?" He smiled at his own joke, but O'Donnell wasn't laughing.

"Mr. President," said O'Donnell, in a grave, measured tone. "I need to speak frankly with you, if I may. Bob, I am very concerned about this attack."

Kennedy shrugged his shoulders.

At that shrug, O'Donnell became agitated and emotional. "Bob, this attack occurred in the goddamned *Press Club,* for chrissakes! It wasn't outside along a Dallas parade route!" He paused, realizing he had used the word "Dallas" in Kennedy's presence. He breathed deeply and said, his voice starting to shake, "I . . . I . . . drank myself to sleep last night—and the night before. I haven't done that since . . . since your brother . . . well . . . "

Kennedy, sitting back in his chair with his bandaged ankle up on the presidential desk, said, "Kenny, don't worry. That was one nut from the Captive Nations group. The press is on the story now—I had no idea there were so many Nazi types in that group. My father liked some of those fellows, too. . . . Anyway, we're up in the polls, the Russians are behaving—heck, even the Red Chinese sent condolences, sort of, which we might turn into a way to start speaking with them—"

O'Donnell, who normally was reserved, but who could become menacing and physical when angered—particularly after a night of drinking—slammed his right fist hard onto the presidential desk. This caused Kennedy to wince in pain, grabbing his sprained ankle that bounced up and down after O'Donnell struck the desk.

"Bob, your brother died because of *me,* damn it! I'm not—" O'Donnell's eyes welled up with tears. He paused, then spoke again. "Bob, it's *my* fault what happened to Jack. I told him to go to Dallas. You're my friend, Bob, not just my boss! I won't let anyone hurt you—ever! No way, no how! Not if I can help it!" O'Donnell put his hands over his face as he tried to hold back the tears of regret and anger at himself for what had happened to Jack.

Kennedy gulped a bit, then spoke softly. "It wasn't your fault, Kenny. Really! Now cut that shit. You didn't tell my brother to drive in an open limo through Dallas, did you?"

O'Donnell shook his head.

"I didn't think so, Ken. And even if you did, if anyone was to blame for what happened to my brother, it was me." Kennedy didn't elaborate. "Now, Kenny, you're not going to tell me not to run next year—or worse, quit now—are you? That's Ethel's pitch—not to quit, but to announce I won't run next year. 'Let Ralph take the job,' she said—"

"I was thinking you ought to consider—" O'Donnell was stopped in his tracks when Kennedy hit his own fist on the table's edge, again wincing in pain from his sore ankle.

"No! No friggin' way, Ken! And you know *why* better than Ethel! I have got to finish what my brother started! We've gotten the country out of Vietnam, at least I think we're out of the military part. We're on the verge of realizing my brother's dream—that wall in Berlin—which went up when he was president—is gonna come down sooner or later, and I'd like to see it come down sooner! And I'm gonna make sure we get people out of poverty and make this country a place where they have economic security . . . " He was lapsing into campaign rhetoric now, so he stopped. "Look at me, Kenny! I'm not going anywhere, you hear me? I told this to Ethel last night—she's still under sedation—not strong, but enough. She's taken this whole thing worse than anyone, at least until you started in on this. Kenny, I love you like a brother. Heck, I'm closer to you now than Teddy—we'll be all right again, Ted and me, I guess. But you see, don't you? I *can't* quit! The bastards are runnin' for cover! I hate to say it, but the Nazi bastard did us all a friggin' favor, that's what he did! I'm tellin' you! Geez, if we let Ralph get to be president while we try to step out of Europe—he'd be mandating unions everywhere and passing more socialist legislation! Heck! All hell could break loose! Some businessman will really gun for him—" He stopped, realizing he might be overstating his point.

"Kenny," he concluded, "don't worry. I mean that. You need to know something. You didn't cause Jack to get killed, and you won't be causing that with me, either. I make my own decisions on whether I run again—and I *am* running for reelection. I am not running away! Got that? I'll stay out of trouble, you'll see."

O'Donnell, who had time to pull himself together listening to his friend and president, said softly, "OK, Bob." He sighed and said, "Bob, I know I can't always stand next to you—I'll take a bullet for you any day—*you know that!*" Realizing he was yelling that last part, he said softly, "Bob, you're everything to me, and to this crazy country of ours. I hate the bastards who hate you." That set him off again. He yelled, *"I'd like to kill 'em all—"*

Kennedy said sternly, "Kenny, let's remember our roots—well, at least our religious ones, not the Irish ones!" Smiling now, he said to O'Donnell, "We have to turn at least *some* of our swords into plowshares, and if our enemies hate us, we'll have to learn to love them—or at least be careful around them. And I promise you—and Ethel—both of you—that. Now get out of here and find out how we're doing around the country. We have to make sure this deal with Russia keeps moving forward—and with some support out there!"

Chapter 23

THE COLD WAR TWISTS IN THE WIND

The newspapers and television networks in the United States continued to debate the policy Kennedy was pursuing with the Russians, but the attempted assassination muted the opposition. Polls showed strong support for the removal of U.S. troops from Europe. There was surprising bipartisan support including not only "liberals," but also what the reporters called "old-style conservatives" or "paleo-conservatives," who had tended to support isolationist ideas in the past.

This group included Senator Bob Dole of Kansas, a state where leftover isolationism was common among the populace. Dole said on the Senate floor, "The Europeans seem to want us out, and they claim they can handle things themselves. Let's load 'em up and head 'em back home is what I say. I just wish the Frogs—I mean the French—would let us keep some extra missiles there. The Russians know, though, that our Strategic Air Command and our nuclear powered subs are always hovering around them. And to maintain a credible deterrent against the Russians attacking Europe, we must continue to strengthen our nuclear naval and air defenses—assuming the Kennedy administration doesn't go in for converting our navy into the pool equipment business!"

Within a few weeks, the American elite became used to the idea of peace with the Russians in Europe. From the other side of the globe, however, came reports that Lin Piao had escaped detention, and that there was fighting between the Chinese military, known as the People's Liberation Army (PLA), and Red Guards in various provinces—and within the Chinese military itself. Mao had ironically created the Red Guard, a largely youth-oriented military brigade, during the so-called Chinese Cultural Revolution to support the PLA. Increasingly, however, the Guard became a threat to the PLA and a threat to nearly everyone, including Chinese Communist commissars and any peasants not deemed sufficiently "anti-Western."

The Cultural Revolution had begun in 1966 under Chairman Mao's direction in order to rekindle what Mao had recalled as a spirit of togetherness in the early days of the Chinese Revolution. Instead, the Cultural Revolution ushered in a period of treachery, betrayal, and death that permeated through Chinese society within two or three years thereafter. Compounding matters was a famine that had begun in China in early 1969. This famine was the worst China had seen in at least ten years—if not the worst since the 1930s, when the Communists, ironically, were gaining support among the Chinese peasants. As with most modern era natural disasters, one can trace their origins in the human politics of the areas in which such disasters strike.

The official newspapers or television in China refused to acknowledge that there was either a famine or that there were mutinies and fighting among the PLA and the Red Guard. Chinese officials, including diplomats abroad, denied any problem in the Chinese countryside. All of them refused to admit whether Lin Piao had ever been arrested, let alone had escaped from arrest. The Chinese government's official position was that "Lin Piao is resting in the countryside at this time."

However, as learned years later from a review of records of the Chinese military, Lin Piao was in rural China secretly rallying various military personnel and the young people who made up the Red Guard. It was a strange turn for Lin Piao, who, in the mid-1960s, had been chosen as Mao's successor by Mao himself. Lin Piao was now forcing the issue of succession and rallying against the PLA he had helped create and sustain, and against what he called the "illegitimate government of Chou En-Lai in Peking." Because the Red Guard had been openly opposing senior military leaders since early 1968 and claiming the PLA was betraying the "revolutionary spirit of Mao Tse-Tung," Lin Piao and the Red Guards were fast becoming a team.

Lin told prospective followers that Mao was being held "prisoner" by Foreign Minister Chou En-Lai. Mao, said Lin, was "lacking full capacity" as a result of a stroke he had suffered in December 1970—the first of several. Chou never acknowledged this "ridiculous" contention, and, as if to prove Lin wrong, Mao was often seen waving to crowds from up high on Tiananmen Square, with Chou standing next to him as a "proud son of the Revolution," according to the official Chinese media.

The fighting among what were seen as Lin and Chou forces began to intensify as winter turned to spring in 1971 in southern and western China. In the major cities, Chou acted to shore up his power and consolidate control. He began pursuing a rhetoric that seemed to be more nationalistic than Communistic and included a reassertion of Chinese supremacy at the Russian-Chinese borders. As a result, the Soviet leadership decided it was important to speed up their withdrawal from Eastern Europe in order to fortify their borders with China.

As defense minister, Lin Piao had tilted toward the Russians against the bourgeois, imperialist West, particularly the United States. Because, however, he was now dealing with hungry, xenophobic peasants, and the highly nationalistic Red Guard, who hated anything "Western," including the Soviet Union, Lin, too, adopted a more nationalistic—and anti-Russian—tone.

Lin spurned Russian military aid, which was offered secretly through an intermediary of Konstantin Chernenko, with, said certain former KGB agents, the ultimate backing of Party Secretary Brezhnev. Lin said, "Even if I wanted this aid, it would make me look like a traitor to these peasants here. I could, however, use some rice to feed people, and perhaps that might help win more of them over to our side . . . " The Russians did eventually send some rice and grain, but because they were also suffering from shortages in these foodstuffs, very little arrived despite the promises to Lin.

With the confusion in China resulting from the effects of the Cultural Revolution (which Chou called a "self-inflicted anarchy" in his most private conversations), Chou was now more worried about holding China together than trying to establish better relations with the Americans or the Russians. He especially viewed the Russian buildup at China's borders as a threat to the nation, a not unreasonable view according to scholars Stephen Cohen and John K. Fairbank.[1] Chou also worried about what former Chinese Nationalist leader Chiang Kai-Shek would do in the event of continued infighting among the Communists. Former Generalissimo Chiang had been sitting for twenty years on the island of Taiwan, with his Nationalist Party's five hundred thousand troops, waiting for the revolution in China to fail.

While Chiang, indeed, had been monitoring events in mainland China, he was also having his own problems with the native Taiwanese. Rising consciousness among the Taiwanese "natives," Chiang believed with more than enough justification, was caused by the "meddling, radical American administration of President Kennedy and Secretary Bowles," according to his longtime friend Clare Booth Luce. Mrs. Luce was the widow of Chiang's oldest American friend, the larger than life Time-Life publisher Henry Luce.

Secretary of State Bowles had been prodding Chiang for over a year to allow the ethnic Taiwanese to have more freedom within Taiwan. Chiang and two million other Chinese had fled to Taiwan after escaping mainland China in 1949, after losing the civil war to Mao and the Communists. When the mainland Chinese arrived, many of the six million Taiwanese were decidedly unhappy to see them. Chiang did not help his cause among native Taiwanese when he immediately declared martial law, nationalized land—like a Communist!—and banned Taiwanese participation in "national" elections—although the "natives" could participate in local elections. His policies made clear that the natives were second-class citizens.

The only thing Generalissimo Chiang and Communist Chairman Mao agreed upon was that Taiwan was "historically" part of China and there was only "one China." Secretary of State Bowles, a believer in self-determination and democratic values, told Chiang, in a stopover he made to Taiwan in mid-1969, that the Taiwanese deserved full rights as citizens. He said Chiang was, after twenty years of exile, unlikely to regain hold of mainland China.

"General Chiang," said Bowles, "the United States would be in a better position to support Taiwan—and you—if you were to allow political reform *inside* Taiwan and begin to treat Taiwan as an entity deserving full, independent sovereignty from China. The Communist government in China is already recognized by nearly every important nation in the world—except the United States. While the Communist government is not currently ready to publicly speak with us, this could happen in the next few years, regardless of whether the president is Democratic or Republican. Even your friend Richard Nixon, in a very interesting article in *Foreign Affairs* in 1967, I believe, suggested this possibility. Whether he would have engaged the Communists may seem unlikely, but then again, I knew Mr. Nixon well enough to know that he recognized global realities."

"Mr. Secretary," said an irritated general, "do you speak for yourself or the administration in your musings?"

Bowles, now equally irritated, said, "To put it bluntly, the president of the United States agrees that Taiwan is better served if it begins to act as a sovereign nation separate from the nation of China. He does not, however, wish to force Taiwan, nor you, to do something you do not want to do . . . at this time."

"When you say the United States desires Taiwan to have self-determination and independence, do you mean the way the Philippines are separate from the United States?" asked Chiang caustically.

Bowles wanted to tell the general where to go—and it wasn't China—but kept his diplomatic face. He thought to himself, at least Generalissimo Chiang merely compared his situation to the Philippines and not American relations with the Native American tribes in the Dakotas, who, Bowles had learned from Senator George McGovern, were becoming "restless again"—for the first time since 1890.

After Bowles left for the United States, Chiang immediately called upon sympathetic senators, congressional representatives, media publishers and editors, and others who were known in elite circles as the "China lobby"—which didn't mean Chairman Mao. Soon, bills for increased military aid to Taiwan appeared in Congress, as did calls for a more aggressive policy against the Red Chinese. What that meant, short of nuclear war, was not made clear. News articles and opinion pieces also appeared along these lines. Former Secretary of State Dean Rusk, no fan of Robert Kennedy, wrote in an editorial in the *Washington Post* that the United States must support Chiang in his effort to "unify" China if the mainland "descends into chaos."

Bowles, for his part, was not about to give in without a fight against the pro-Chiang China lobby. On his next trip to South Asia, Bowles made it a point to again visit Taiwan. This time he met with Chiang and then met separately with a longtime Taiwanese dissident, Professor P'eng Ming-min. P'eng had been briefly imprisoned by Chiang in the mid-1960s. The professor was wrongly called a Communist by the China lobby, but Bowles prepared for that by having American reporters present with him while he spoke with P'eng. The reporters came away impressed with P'eng's knowledge and his honesty in discussing the situation, including the dangers of "too much freedom."

Wrote *New York Times'* reporter William Beecher: "P'eng is a Taiwanese citizen who demands freedom. He sincerely denies being a Communist or in any way being connected to the Communist Party." As Beecher recalled years later, in a second timeline oral history program at Hofstra University in New York, "I had to fight the editors tooth and nail to get those two simple sentences into my story. And I stand behind that judgment to this day. That man was not a Communist."

Luckily for the Kennedy administration, the China lobby failed to convince enough editors, let alone reporters, to make Taiwan a major, continuing story. There were too many other things going on, and neither Bowles nor Kennedy was making any moves toward opening relations with Red China. The administration continued to speak in terms of protecting Taiwan from Red China, which undermined the cries of the China lobby. The administration also continued to embarrass Chiang into calling for elections in which the Taiwanese could vote on their own future, a policy argument that constantly put the China lobby on the defensive.

President Kennedy remained firm on the subject through early 1971. In a private conversation at the White House with *Washington Post* editor Ben Bradlee the day before the second attempt on his life, Kennedy said, "Ben, the Red Chinese are beginning to make noise that they want to speak with us. We will protect Taiwan, but we can't expect to support Chiang Kai-Shek's dream of invading mainland China. The Reds have nuclear bombs now, as we both know, which changes things dramatically from when my brother was president. Chet Bowles' department just completed a white paper on Red China and Taiwan so that we are prepared to deal effectively with Red China if they are interested. I read the report, Ben. And I can tell you that I found it interesting that Chou En-Lai, who is still Mao's foreign minister, said in the mid-1950s, and most recently a few months ago, that the Red Chinese, as a condition for entering the United Nations, will agree to let the United Nations settle the issue of whether Taiwan should be part of China or not. The way things are going for us, I think we could get the United Nations General Assembly, and even the Russians, to agree to a plebiscite by the Taiwanese as part of that determination. And neither Chiang nor Chou En-Lai will be happy with the results of that plebiscite, according to Secretary Bowles. We have strong reason to believe the Taiwanese want to be a separate nation—and China isn't going to risk nuclear war, or anything like that under their current circumstances, if they can secure admission to the United Nations."

Bradlee said, "Mr. President, you don't mean to say you trust Chou En-Lai to give up Taiwan? I mean—"

"Ben, I mean that if the United States shows its resolve to defend Taiwan, with military fleets in the area, and there's a UN vote to allow the Taiwanese, including the natives there—not just Chiang's people—to have a plebiscite, the Chinese will not want to risk a military confrontation and world condemnation over Taiwan. According to that State Department report—Chet has really brought out the best in the State Department in these reports he's had prepared since we started—the Japanese held Taiwan for almost a century and up through World War II. The islands there often had autonomy approaching independence before that. It's not like there was total Chinese control all the way through."

Bradlee, an old newspaper hand and professional cynic, smiled and said, "You've made your point, counsel. So, how are you gonna get past the China lobby of Chiang Kai-Shek and his newspaper, government, and business minions? My publisher is pretty close to those folks as well, at least sometimes."

"I honestly don't know," said Kennedy. "I think we have to work first with the Russians, and maybe help them and the Chinese deal with their border disputes—assuming Chou En-Lai can stop the fighting in the rural provinces of China."

"It almost sounds like you're rooting for a Communist to win in China, Mr. President." Bradlee had had a few drinks and decided to bait the president a bit. Luckily for Bradlee, the president was in a contemplative mood.

"Well, Ben, it's Communist versus Communist *inside* China. And I'm old enough to know that Chiang Kai-Shek hasn't got a chance to take over mainland China, but he has the opportunity to lead an independent Taiwan—unless we want to risk nuclear war with China by supporting Chiang's dream of taking over China again. And not even Barry Goldwater wants to risk nuclear war for that—I don't think!"

Chapter 24

MORE TWISTING AND TURNING
AROUND THE GLOBE

Wheat Ties: the Policy of Champions

The negotiations with the Soviet Union proceeded more quickly than the Americans had anticipated, though not without some minor setbacks. Initially, Defense Secretary Warnke proposed that the Russians remove its troops from East Germany, with the United States removing the troops it had stationed in West Germany. The Russian negotiators appeared to support the plan, but rejected it less than forty-eight hours later. The East German Communist dictatorship, under the leadership of an aging Walter Ulbricht, was dead set against removal of Soviet troops. Ulbricht apparently feared his harsh regime would quickly unravel without the presence of the Soviet troops and weapons.

The Russians immediately offered a compromise of first removing their troops and weapons from Hungary, with the Americans removing missiles and troops from England. This was not what Warnke wanted because, as he said to President Kennedy, "Hungary's right in the middle. The Russians can invade with their troops from east, north, west, or maybe even south." Kennedy, however, was calm about it. "It's a start, Paul, it's a start—even if the conservatives in America say the same thing, which they will anyway." And they did.

Kennedy, for his part, responded to such conservative complaints at a White House press conference in March 1971. Kennedy told reporters at the time, "The Russians are removing their troops and weapons from Hungary. These troops have been there since they crushed the uprising in Budapest in 1956 during President Eisenhower's administration. I consider the Russians' removal of those troops to be a strong showing of good faith on their part. For our part, we are going to begin removing our troops and weapons from Great Britain. British Prime Minister Edward Heath has just this morning given his approval to do so, according to Secretary Bowles and our ambassador to Great Britain, Harris Wofford."

The Russians removed their troops and weapons from Hungary by May 16, 1971, and the Americans completed their removal of troops and weapons from England by June 1, 1971. By then, the Americans and the Russians had reached further agreements on the reductions of troops and weaponry in Western and Eastern Europe. The Soviets' next removal of troops and weapons was to take place in Poland, where the Russian leadership believed the local military was more ready to protect the Communist regime than nearly anywhere else. The Americans happily agreed to leave France—with many French people saying the feeling was mutual.

In September 1971, the Russians agreed to begin a slower removal of troops and weapons from Czechoslovakia and Bulgaria, and then East Germany would see the Russians begin to leave by March 1972, with the rest of the Soviet Warsaw Pact troops and weapons leaving by that summer. For their part, the Americans would remove their troops and weapons from Belgium, the Netherlands, Scandinavia, and Greenland. The last two nations to have American troops and weapons were military dictatorships, Greece, and Spain—with the elderly, and now ailing, Fascist president, Francisco Franco, very unhappy with these developments. The United States would leave these nations at the same time the Russians left the rest of the Warsaw Pact.

Kennedy insisted that the Russians and the Americans complete the removal of troops and weapons by August 1972 so that, at the time of the Republican and Democratic Party national conventions, the threat of Russian domination over Europe could be banished as an issue from American electoral politics. Kennedy publicly denied the motivation of this timing, of course, but O'Donnell, in his memoirs, admitted this was the political strategy.

While the Kennedy administration thought it was being "firm," the Russians had readily agreed to the timetable because they were more and more concerned about the possibility of a border war with China. As 1971 wore on, the Russians became eager to move troops eastward to the Manchurian border and other border areas with China for what they consistently called "defensive purposes." If the Soviet Politburo had any offensive purpose for stationing troops in the southern regions of their empire, it was to control the increasingly restless and anti-Soviet Muslim populations in places called Chechnya, Azerbaijan, and Siberia, among other long-held "Soviet nations."

Kennedy, regardless of Soviet motives, was also becoming more and more alarmed about the growing unrest in Communist China. He heard more about the situation through Ambassador Dobrynin, who was a biweekly dinner guest at the White House during 1971 and 1972, than he did from the CIA, which still had few agents inside Communist China.

To diffuse the accusation that he was spending too much time with a Communist ambassador, Kennedy often invited prominent business leaders to meet with Dobrynin. Business leaders were always eager to see if business could be conducted in the Soviet Union, though Russian "red tape" often scared them away after their initial interest.

Dobrynin nonetheless did his part to facilitate such business contacts. First, he pleaded with American agribusiness to sell grain to the Soviet Union to compensate for the almost annual poor harvests in the Soviet Union. To those who blamed Soviet wheat or grain failures on "socialist farming," Kennedy's Secretary of Agriculture Robert "Bob" Bergland reminded such critics that American farming was fairly "socialist" itself with subsidies and economic assistance galore. "The key is whether there's a dictatorship, not whether there's government support," Bergland told a skeptical Congressman Robert Michel of Illinois in testimony on Capitol Hill when the subject of poor harvests in the Soviet Union was raised.

The American grain companies were nonetheless convinced to sell grain to the Soviet Union, but only after the U.S. government agreed to guarantee the payments in case the Soviets failed to pay. The Russians, at Bowles' insistence, paid the agribusiness companies in gold, which the American companies then exchanged with the U.S. government for paper currency. Treasury Secretary Lance had previously told Bowles that U.S. gold reserves were starting to fall because European and other foreign banks were buying up U.S. Treasury bonds that, under U.S. rules stemming from the Bretton Woods agreement of 1944, needed to be redeemed with gold. With American businesses receiving tens of millions of dollars in Russian gold, the United States was able to replenish much of its gold reserves. Bowles was impressed with Lance's input, though again, Kennedy seemed less than interested in Lance for reasons nobody around Kennedy could ever understand.[1]

Within the Kennedy administration, Agriculture Secretary Bergland was a surprising dissenter to the Soviet grain sales. He was outraged at the policy of allowing the largest agribusinesses to sell grain to the Soviets with payments guaranteed by the federal government. Bergland, a Minnesotan recommended for the position by Hubert Humprhey, had been appointed to his position shortly after losing a close congressional election in 1968. He had been a quiet but effective player in the administration until he dissented after Kennedy announced the first grain deal to the Soviets in the late summer of 1971.

Bergland began "pestering" Secretary Bowles, as one of Bowles' aides put it, that it was better for the United States to allow smaller American farmers to begin growing grain instead of letting their land lie fallow. Bergland was concerned that simply allowing the largest agribusinesses to unload the wheat, especially in the face of an already developing worldwide drought, would unduly cause prices to rise to a level that would be inflationary overall, with little benefit to the small farmers who had problems competing with the agribusinesses in good times and bad.

Bergland also had an answer to the question of a decline in prices if small farmers suddenly started growing wheat they had previously been paid *not* to grow. To avoid depressing the price of grain for the American market, the United States would insist that the grain produced by the small farmers be sold abroad, starting in places such as the Soviet Union, and also would freely give the grain to poor countries—all backed by guarantees or subsidies, if necessary, from the United States. Said Bergland, "It's better to pay the small farmers to grow food for Russia and poor nations that can't afford to buy grain than not growing food at all—and better than letting Cargill or Archer Daniels reap larger profits in foreign sales while small farmers remain small and get even smaller."

Bergland, when finally granted an audience with Bowles and Kennedy, said, "Mr. Secretary, Mr. President. Cargill and Archer Daniels get more than enough help from the government just for being large agribusinesses. The last thing they need is yet another government handout!"

Bergland, a farmer with strong humanitarian, not corporate, instincts, was working with environmentalists and small farmers to create strategies for bio-sustainability while protecting the interests of small American farmers. Growing grain for export instead of paying people to do "nothing" was part of the strategy, as was using what Bergland called "organic" methods of production. The organic methods were cheaper, so far, in that they avoided costly chemicals. The methods also allowed for more creative ways to grow food, such as using various insects as helpers against other insects that would destroy crops. Although organic farming cut chemical costs for farmers, it admittedly required more acres to produce the same amount of crops. This required, in turn, that farmers be allowed to till more of their land.

Bergland also supported farmer-controlled cooperatives to promote "direct to market" distribution, which increased the margin of profit for small farmers, allowing them to handle demands for increased farm worker wages while cutting out various financial and distribution middlemen.

Secretary of Labor Reuther provided backup to Bergland with regard to the UFW and the fight for workers' rights in the fields. Reuther acted as a mediator between the UFW and the Teamsters over who would represent the farm field workers. The UFW won most of the contests in 1969 and 1970, and the Teamsters were looking for a way to salvage their losses in the fields. Reuther "persuaded" Bergland that because the Teamsters Union included many truckers, they would be "perfect" for hauling the goods from the new cooperative farms to the market. Most of the farmers, realizing that unions were here to stay, decided to cast their lot by hiring union truck drivers through the cooperatives than paying the middlemen to do it.

Bowles was convinced by the overall Bergland strategy as it spilled into foreign policy, but the president was not. Kennedy was hearing from the large agribusinesses that the "no grow" subsidies were good for the environment. The subsidies, they claimed, kept land from being "overused." Dwayne Andreas, president of the Archer Daniels grain company, told Kennedy and Bergland in a meeting at the White House, that the "most successful" agribusinesses were strongly opposed to reducing reliance on chemicals— "Chemicals are what we're made of, Mr. President!"

Bergland undiplomatically replied to Andreas, "But Mr. Andreas, the chemicals in our bodies are natural, while many of the chemicals you're talking about, starting with DDT, are not. And that's what's killing birds and may eventually kill people, if it isn't already!"

Kennedy was ready to side with Bergland by the end of 1971, but this came in response to the deepening economic effect of the worldwide drought from earlier in the year. The drought, combined with the millions of domestic bushels of grain sold abroad, mostly to the Soviets, created a "sudden" shortage of grain in November of that year. Grain prices escalated sharply, which led to an increase in wholesale food prices just before Thanksgiving and threatened inflationary rises throughout the American economy.

As the first reports of inflation began to hit the mainstream media news in mid-November 1971, Kennedy was fearful of giving Republicans a "free shot"—he used that phrase over O'Donnell's objection at a cabinet meeting—to attack his administration. "I don't want the Republicans to say we fed the Russians and caused inflation at home! We have to cut food prices, and we need to start with grain. If the Soviets need more grain, then we'll start to pay our smaller farmers to grow that grain, with a guaranteed minimum price if they produce too much and cause a severe drop in prices going the other way. We must *stabilize* prices even if it means we, as a government, end up more involved in the grain business!"

Kennedy immediately ordered the unleashing of the grain reserves to stabilize the price of grain and cap the inflation rate for the rest of the year. The Republican presidential trio of Reagan, Roth, and Abrams initially found receptive audiences in the Midwest on the subject of agricultural policies and inflation. But Bergland's strong stance for family farmers—and the ability of his department to hand out "goodies" and provide administrative protection for those farmers—nullified most of the political impact even in that area of the nation.

The Council of Economic Advisers in June 1972 issued a report that concluded the Bergland plan was anti-inflationary because it kept shortages from developing. Also, the government's ability to store the grain in air-conditioned silos for up to six months, if the price went too low, was a helpful "stabilizer." Overall, said the council, the Bergland plan increased productivity and, to the extent the plan allowed for grain sales abroad, lowered government subsidies to small farmers. It also increased both the viability of small farmers and farm labor employment at a time when both had been in a decades-long decline.[2]

Kennedy was glad to see the council's report but was happier still that he didn't need to impose wage and price controls during late 1971 through mid-1972. The stabilizing and even slight lowering of grain prices in 1972 kept meat prices from rising significantly. What did grain prices have to do with meat prices? It was, and remains, a fact among cattle farmers that cattle, particularly those on "factory farms," eat more grain than people do. Environmentalists would soon notice the "pollution" from the methane gas produced by factory farm animals, but agitation against meat and factory farms did not begin until later in the decade.

"Agriculture is one more thing to add to the other policies we have to balance," said Kennedy to the O Boys on April 24, 1972, according to O'Donnell's diary. "I *never* in a million years would have thought that!"

While the Russians were interested in American grain, America and Europe developed a special interest in Russian oil deposits. Discussions between Western oil companies, who generally acted in concert, and the Soviets began in November 1971 and continued into the winter of 1971–72. The oil companies, however, in the summer of 1972, on the eve of signing their first joint agreement with the Soviets, decided to put off purchasing oil, saying that the "oil glut" of 1972 made it too expensive to drill inside the Soviet Union. The Kennedy administration, which was quite busy with other matters at the time, was disappointed, but reluctantly agreed with the economic reasoning of the oil companies. Dobrynin and the Russians were even more disappointed because they had hoped to make some money selling those oil deposits for more gold and American dollars.

Kennedy, for his part, remained concerned with his own nation's economic future, particularly with American troops coming home from Europe. During weeks when Dobrynin was not coming to dinner at the White House, Kennedy would allow Defense Secretary Warnke or Commerce Secretary Learson to entertain business leaders there as a way of increasing business support for the administration. The two secretaries would attempt to interest American (and sometimes European) businesspersons in conversion projects and particularly the promise of the home computer business. Though Kennedy's conversion commission had begun its investigation of the conversion program (approved by Congress in late March 1971), so far only IBM, Intel, Hewlett-Packard, and Ross Perot's EDS were supporting the conversion and computer plans. The only "smokestack" industry to show any significant interest was Ford Motor Company, and then only because Ford Chairman Henry Ford II said he was "willing to listen" to a proposal to provide subsidies to car companies to develop an electric-powered car. The rest of Ford's management remained far more interested in gas-powered vehicles, particularly with the continuing oil glut.

Despite Kennedy's initial belief, after the mid-term elections in 1970, that 1971 was going to be a time to focus on domestic, economic issues, other foreign crises in 1971 continued to need his attention.

Southern Africa Turns Upside Down

The first of these foreign crises concerned South Africa. In early April 1971, a young group of black South African revolutionaries, who broke away from the African National Congress (ANC), almost succeeded in their plot to free the revered black South African leader, Nelson Mandela, from a South African prison. Mandela was a lawyer who had been sentenced to life in prison for his role in the early 1960s antiapartheid demonstrations against white-ruled South Africa. Because the escape plan was not approved by or even known to the ANC, Mandela was as surprised by the escape attempt as anyone else.

The young revolutionaries, who called themselves the African Liberation Front (ALF), fought their way inside the prison and eventually found Mandela to "free" him and take him to the African nation of Mozambique. Upon seeing them, however, Mandela became angry and told them, "You foolish children! Go home to your mothers and fathers!" The revolutionaries were stunned at Mandela's anger, for they had killed several guards to get to him, wounded the warden and tied him up, and overall had executed their plan almost to perfection.[3]

Mandela, sensing a trap, immediately asked to meet with the prison warden, who was still in his office. The revolutionaries thought Mandela was planning to kill the warden. They eagerly went with Mandela and awaited what they presumed would be Mandela's order to execute the warden. When they arrived, Mandela again surprised the revolutionaries and untied the warden. Mandela then switched on the prison's internal public address system and spoke throughout the prison. He called upon the guards *and* the revolutionaries to "lay down" their arms. "This is Nelson Mandela. I am *not* leaving this prison, and I am certainly not leaving this *country,*" he said. "I will only leave this prison when the South African government manifests its intent to begin to dismantle the apartheid system of discrimination against black Africans. *Not a minute before!* These brave but confused young men are to leave this prison immediately, and I order that immediate medical aid be provided to the warden and any other persons injured as a result of this childish but deadly prank."

The revolutionaries sheepishly left the prison, with two of them escaping into Mozambique. However, most were quickly caught by the South African military police not far from the prison gates. The international outcry that followed this failed rescue attempt kept the South African government from executing the apprehended revolutionaries. Mandela's stature, even among many white South Africans, significantly rose after this episode—and in the United States, many white Americans finally heard the name "Nelson Mandela."

United Nations Ambassador Andrew Young used the international outcry, and Mandela's extraordinary defiance of the revolutionaries, to pressure

President Kennedy to support a boycott of South Africa if it refused to end discrimination against blacks and racially mixed "coloreds." Young told the president, in the presence of Secretary Bowles and Secretary Reuther, that he would resign if the United States did not threaten the South African government with an immediate boycott. Young said the United States must demand the immediate release of Mandela—without conditions—and that the South African government must negotiate with Mandela and the ANC to have free elections within six months in which blacks and whites would be allowed to vote.

Kennedy strongly supported the idea in theory but was worried about domestic political concerns. Faced with Young's threatened resignation, however, he reluctantly agreed to something close to what Young was calling for. Kennedy agreed that, as a condition of the United States' consideration of any boycott against the South African government, the ANC or other black guerrilla groups must renounce all violence and agree to turn in their weapons within thirty days of the South African government agreeing to full and free elections. Kennedy realized that the entire subject was still "ahead of the curve for the American electorate," and that this was an issue likely to rise up in 1972 "if we're not careful here," as he said to Young. Now that Kennedy agreed somewhat, Young found himself wondering if he should continue to stay on board.

Luckily for Young, many Democrats in the Congress were not as reluctant as the president to challenge the apartheid system in southern Africa. Democratic Representatives Don Edwards of California and Shirley Chisholm of New York introduced a bill exactly along the lines of Young's proposal in the House, with support from Democratic Senator Edward Boland of Massachusetts and Republican Senator Mark Hatfield of Oregon. A tumultuous debate followed in Congress, with mostly conservative supporters of the South African government put on the defensive regarding their "hypocrisy" for supporting an embargo or boycott against Cuba but not South Africa. Although a powerful constituency in Congress, the media, and the U.S. military favored white-ruled South Africa, the events and structure of the debate favored those seeking the boycott.

The apartheid supporters could not kill the "boycott bill," as it was called. They merely succeeded in a compromise that gave the president the discretion to institute a boycott if the South African and Rhodesian governments failed to engage in meaningful negotiations to dismantle their apartheid policies. On the *Issues and Answers* television show on Sunday afternoon, May 2, 1971, the following exchange was recorded between Senator Robert Dole, who opposed the boycott bill, and Ed Boland, one of the boycott bill sponsors:

DOLE: "South Africa is a great friend of the United States, and it is ridiculous to compare it with the Communist dictatorship in Cuba."

BOLAND: "Senator Dole, for South African blacks, the government of South Africa is a prison no different than what Castro has in Cuba. This cannot be denied."

DOLE: "I find Senator Boland's statement to be very interesting, since just six months ago, he called for easing the embargo against Cuba because the embargo wasn't working. Now he says we must enact an embargo against South Africa. The only difference I can see is that Senator Boland seems somewhat enamored with Communist Cuba and angry with our traditional ally, the South African government."

BOLAND: "This sort of Red-baiting is beneath Senator Dole, I must say. The fact is that our embargo against Cuba is not working because most of the world trades with Cuba, including our European allies such as France, Britain, and West Germany, and the last time I checked, England and France weren't Communist countries, Senator. Second, South Africa and Rhodesia are already isolated from the world community, except for a couple of small nations and the United States. With reference to Cuba, I merely support opening simple diplomatic relations in order to reunite families who have been separated from their loved ones for over ten years now. I would also remind Senator Dole that there is no requirement in the South Africa and Rhodesia bill that a boycott or an embargo be instituted. The bill merely allows the president flexibility in continuing constructive engagement with the governments of Rhodesia and South Africa, with boycotting only being a last resort. This bill, when enacted, will work to allow the vast majority of the people in southern Africa to have self-determination, which is a democratic concept, Senator, not a Communistic one."

Dole, after the program, said to Boland, "Well, Senator, you may win this battle, but at the cost of making it more difficult for your liberal allies and the Kennedy administration to open up relations with Communist Cuba."

Boland, who did not appreciate Dole's Red-baiting, recognized that Dole had little to go on but that sort of attack. He knew Dole was a decent fellow on other issues, especially food stamps for the poor—even if his support for food stamps coincidentally benefited Dole's Kansas constituent, Archer Daniels, a major agribusiness. Boland did not respond to Dole's remark other than to nod, smile, and slightly grunt, "We'll see, Bob. We'll see."

The Congress passed the Southern Africa Engagement Authorization bill, and the president signed it on June 1, 1971; but Kennedy did nothing at first to use the powers granted to him. South African Prime Minister Voerster, seeing the handwriting on the wall, made things easier for the United States when told by his fellow ministers that South Africa "cannot afford to have the American government authorize a boycott" or an embargo. On May 31, 1971, Voerster agreed to free Mandela without restrictions or conditions. He also said he would begin discussions with the ANC for full and free elections in 1972. In a memorable phrase, he said, "Only the South Africans, not foreigners, can authorize 'negotiations' with blacks in our country." In fairness to Voerster, it must be recalled that in 1970, before the boycott bill even surfaced, he had eased a few apartheid laws by allowing blacks to commute from their villages into the cities and towns for factory and mining work.

Rhodesia's leader, Ian Smith, proved more intractable than Voerster, rudely telling the American ambassador in a public statement that Rhodesia would never bow to "American hy-plomacy," a turn of phrase combining "hypocrisy" and "diplomacy." Kennedy, by the end of July 1971, reluctantly authorized a boycott of military and economic aid against Rhodesia even though neither of the guerilla groups opposed to Rhodesia's apartheid system had anyone similar to Nelson Mandela in their top leadership. As Kennedy said in making his announcement, the United Nations had already instituted a boycott against Smith's government and Rhodesia beginning in 1968. "Mr. Smith of Rhodesia has therefore had years of warning from other nations, not a couple of months."

Three weeks after Kennedy's announcement, the Smith government, after consultation with the South African government, announced it would speak with a black Methodist Bishop, Abel Muzorewa, as a potential leader for the blacks inside Rhodesia. The United Nations General Assembly denounced this as a "sham," because Muzorewa had no organized constituency, unlike the often-dueling revolutionary black leaders Joshua Nkomo and Robert Mugabe, whose organizations were based in large part on the two main black ethnic groups in Rhodesia, the Ndebele and the Shona.

Muzorewa withdrew as a "representative of the black people" a week later after seeing that he would never be able to command a majority of blacks. He also wished to avoid an internal black civil war. Secretary Bowles, in a move that angered U.N. Ambassador Young, tried in vain to convince Muzorewa to change his mind. However, the bishop steadfastly refused to reenter the political arena.

The bishop did not merely disappear from the political scene within Rhodesia. In an effort to prevent civil war among the competing black revolutionaries of Rhodesia, Muzorewa called upon a prominent Episcopalian minister in South Africa, Desmond Tutu, to ask Nelson Mandela to assist in easing the tensions between Mugabe and Nkomo. Mandela, after receiving assurance from both South Africa and the United States that he was free to leave—and most important, return to—South Africa, traveled to Mozambique for a meeting with the two Rhodesian guerilla leaders. There, Mandela spoke with Nkomo and Mugabe and told them how important it was for Africans to set aside outmoded ethnic differences within the Western-drawn boundaries of Africa. Mandela proposed, and the two guerrilla leaders accepted, that the rival groups form a coalition to negotiate with the Smith government for a transition to a multiracial democracy and that Mugabe and Nkomo jointly lead a majority party.

"And remember," said Mandela, "we in the ANC have had white friends throughout our struggle, including people such as Joe Servo, the leader of the South African Communist Party. Do not forsake white allies, even those who come from the side of apartheid. Embrace them as you would a black ally.

We must struggle beyond recrimination, or else we will be forever fighting each other—and the result will be famine, poverty, disease, and death."

Mandela's stock in the eyes of the world and within South Africa rose to heights unimaginable just months before. In a sense, the "misguided" African Liberation Front revolutionaries succeeded in a way none would have previously thought possible. By September 1972, both South Africa and Rhodesia, the latter nation renamed Zimbabwe, had black African leaders, and the systems of apartheid were broken. Mandela was elected as leader of South Africa, and Mugabe and Nkomo became prime minister and president, respectively, of Zimbabwe.

In a bow to white fears, both nations used a system of cumulative voting that allowed the minority whites to vote as a block. The purpose of this style of voting was to force black leaders to listen to the interests of white voters, or else the white voters would vote "as a block for white candidates." Antiapartheid activists in the United States, mostly liberals and leftists, were against this electoral law, which they called preposterous, and worse, racist. American conservative and Republican supporters, however, replied that most American corporations allowed cumulative voting, and hence the idea was consistent with "democratic values."[4]

Secretary of State Bowles was present for the respective inaugurals of the new black leaders in southern Africa. While there, he heard the fears white business and political leaders raised about "black retribution." In a private meeting with Mandela, he was pleased to hear that Mandela, together with Nkomo and Mugabe, had called for a Truth Commission that would offer amnesty to white apartheid-era leaders if they spoke truthfully about their conduct to the commission. The three African leaders also signed legislation that ended the death penalties in their respective nations.

Bowles, recognizing that the problem of revenge and violence were likely to come from the local level despite the intention of the national leaders, unilaterally increased quotas for immigration by whites to the United States. Kennedy, in the midst of his presidential reelection campaign, absent-mindedly agreed, for he forgot such persons were unlikely to support the Democrats as new citizens, at least for a while. Luckily, relatively few such refugees fled to the United States, and, of those who did, most settled in the Southwest, where black-white tension seemed less apparent.

The Middle East Turns Upside Down, Too

Events also began to heat up during 1971 in the Middle East, though at first there seemed a real possibility for peace, not a war or crisis. The administration had not really paid attention to the region until King Hussein's massacre of Palestinians in September 1970. After the dust settled from that event, the administration went back to worrying about other things, seeing

Middle East political strife as intractable. Another reason to put the area on the back burner was the fact that if the administration made any comments that implied Israel should speak with its Arab neighbors, it was considered politically dangerous because of the growing strength of the so-called "Israel lobby."

"When the Arabs come to their senses," Kennedy told Chet Bowles, "then we'll worry about the Middle East. Meanwhile, we must let Israel keep building up its weapons and whatever else it needs to do to survive."

The Kennedy administration, therefore, was caught completely off guard when, on February 6, 1971, Egyptian President Anwar Sadat proposed a "plan for peace" with Israel. Sadat, a longtime top aide of famed Egyptian nationalist leader Gamal Abdul Nasser, had become president after Nasser's death the previous September. In Sadat's "peace proposal" speech he said he would abide by UN Resolution 242, which was more commonly known as the "land for peace" resolution. Sadat subsequently said Egypt would accept a peace with Israel even if only parts, but not all, of the Sinai Peninsula were returned to Egypt. Egypt had lost the Sinai to Israel in the 1967 war between Israel and Egypt.[5]

Chet Bowles called the Israeli ambassador to the United States, Yitzhak Rabin, for his take on Sadat's offer. Rabin admitted to Bowles that it was a "genuine peace offer." With Kennedy's approval, Bowles immediately traveled to Israel to speak with Prime Minister Golda Meir and a few members of her cabinet, including Defense Minister Moshe Dayan. Bowles wanted to go to Egypt first, but Kennedy, thinking about the Jewish vote in 1972, refused this request.

Bowles was in Israel when the second assassination attempt on Kennedy occurred. When he returned from Israel, he was glad to see the president alive. However, Bowles remained shaken by what the Israeli political and military leaders had said to him. In a private meeting with Kennedy, Bowles told the president that "the Israeli government and its military recognize the import of Sadat's proposal, but they . . . well, Mr. President, I must say, rather bluntly, that the Israelis are intransigent. They do not desire peace—well, they do, but really they don't, at least in my—"

Kennedy's eyes almost jumped out of their sockets. "Chet! Are you really saying the Jews—I mean the Israelis—don't want peace with the Arabs? Come on, Chet! You can't be serious!" He began to laugh, thinking Bowles was exaggerating. "Chet, all I hear from prominent Jews in this country—and I know this myself, with Nasser and the radical Arab world, particularly—is that the Arabs want to drive Israel into the sea. Abba Eban, one of the most astute diplomats I've ever met, told me a year ago the Israelis would love nothing better than peace with the Arabs. He says the Arabs—how'd he put it?—I think he said the Arabs 'never fail to miss an opportunity to *miss* an opportunity . . . for peace.' And now, here's this new guy in Egypt—what's his name?"

"Sadat."

"Sadat? Okay, this Sadat fella says he wants to make peace. That should be a no-brainer for the Israelis, shouldn't it? I mean, really, Chet, how can you say the Israelis don't want peace with Egypt, for goodness sake! Sadat said in that speech of his that he'll follow that UN Resolution Arthur Goldberg helped write after the '67 war with the Arabs. What more can the Israelis want? You know, I've heard the State Department—definitely not you, Chet—hasn't been very well disposed toward Israel or Jews, even during World War II . . .. Who did I hear that from? Maybe Jack Newfield . . . "

Kennedy leaned back in his chair. "Go on, Chet, I gotta hear how you reached this conclusion of yours. I gotta tell ya, I find your statement hard to believe. In fact, I'm shocked to hear you talk this way!"

Bowles, anticipating much of Kennedy's response since he himself had been shocked, pulled out his notes of his conversations with the Israelis. "Mr. President, hardly any of the players supported Sadat's proposal. That's the first thing. But it's what they said and how they talked about things that, frankly, floored me. For example, I asked Moshe Dayan about the Palestinian refugees in the Gaza Strip and the West Bank. I asked how we could approach the situation in that particular area. He said, 'We have already made clear our position toward these refugees, Mr. Secretary. We told their leaders that those peasants there can continue to live'—and this is his statement, sir, not mine—'like dogs, and whoever wants to can leave these areas, which they, like other Arab peasants, will. And that is the end of the refugee problem!' Dayan told me that already some one hundred thousand Arabs in the territories have left for other parts of the Arab world, and Jewish—I mean Israeli—settlements continue to be built in the 'occupied territories' night and day. One of the Israelis I spoke with called the settlements the 'facts on the ground.'"[6]

"Pretty strong stuff, I must say," said a now-interested Kennedy.

"The irony, Mr. President, is that Dayan is considered a *moderate* on Israeli-Arab relations."

Hearing that, Kennedy winced in some surprise.

Bowles was undeterred, however, and continued. "General Peres, who is considered a hard-liner, said that 'Israel's new map will be determined by its policies of settlement and new land development,' which means developing land in the existing territories now occupied by Israeli forces as a result of the 1967 war. I learned from news reporters there that the Israelis are already expelling Arab Bedouins by the thousands, destroying—I hate to sound too hard here, but this is true—graveyards, mosques, and homes in the Sinai and the Gaza–West Bank territories."

Kennedy was now stunned. He said, "Wait, Chet, wait! I can't believe Mrs. Meir's government itself endorsed such a strong stand as that general said. But if those actions are happening, the government must be behind this as well. It's too small a country and with modern communications—what does Golda Meir say about all this? I haven't spoken to her much beyond the normal courtesies—"

"Prime Minister Meir was blunt, Mr. President. She told me 'the borders are determined by where Jews live, not where there is a line on a map.' She also quoted, she said, Israel's founding father, David Ben-Gurion, who said in the 1950s, the Arabs who are displaced can go to places 'such as Iraq,' just as, she said, 'Israel has taken in those Jews chased out of Arab nations.' Her quoting Ben-Gurion surprised me since Ben-Gurion, according to our ambassador there, had recently said Israel should stop building settlements in the territories and go back to its pre-1967 borders."

"What did Mrs. Meir say to that? Assuming you brought that up . . . Did you?" asked Kennedy, feeling as if he were back at school learning calculus.

"She . . . " Bowles hesitated. "Well, sir, she was quite cold about it. She said, 'Ben-Gurion's no longer in power and doesn't understand the new realities.' I asked what were the 'new realities,' and she said, 'We have what we want, and we will keep what we have.' It reminded me of what Dayan said about the settlements being 'permanent' and . . . goodness, Dayan sounded almost like George Wallace when he said, 'The settlements are permanent, the settlements are forever, and the future borders will include these settlements as part of Israel.'"

"Wow," muttered Kennedy. "I think we better call Governor Goldberg in New York. See if he's in Albany this week for the legislative sessions. You know, I was meaning to put him back on the Supreme Court. There's two vacancies opening up—Douglas and Black are going to announce their retirement, and Harlan's giving indications he'd like to retire soon. First slot's going to Joe Dolan, though—nobody else. But Chet, what are we going to do about this if American Jews support that stance—I mean, we can't accept the Israelis flouting UN Resolution 242 when the most important—at least I think it is—Arab nation, Egypt, is publicly agreeing to abide by the Resolution and—didn't Sadat say he didn't want all the land back, just a good chunk of it?"

"Yes, sir. That's what I thought was most mystifying. He's recognizing the Israelis' security needs, and yet the Israelis are actively building settlements to make this difficult—and they're building settlements along the West Bank where Jordan borders Israel. It was Jordan's land, as you know, before the 1967 war."

"Well, the Arabs shouldn't have invaded Israel in 1967, though, right Chet?"

"Mr. President, if you recall from our discussions with Secretary of State Rusk from the last administration, the Israelis attacked Egypt first—though Nasser had been making many threatening statements and closed down one of the ports the Israelis used along the border with Egypt. The Russians convinced

Nasser to back down, but the Israelis defied President Johnson and attacked. There was also that incident during that war with the Israelis bombing one of our battleships, the USS *Liberty*. The State Department concluded it was accidental, which I think was giving the Israelis the benefit of the doubt. The Jordanians, who had a treaty with Egypt, did try to go to Egypt's rescue—"

"I remember now, Chet, but damned if the Jewish organizations don't see it as little David being threatened by a whole bunch of Arab Goliaths—and I agree with that position. Why should Israel have to give back most or all of its land? On the other hand, we know the Jordanians would probably agree to peace if the Egyptians would, and their armies are worthless anyway—except they mowed down those antigovernment guerillas in their camps a few months ago. The Syrians are a problem, and Lebanon, I don't know what's happening there—"

"Always a bit unstable and becoming more so. The Israelis are shelling the Lebanese border looking for terrorists, while the Syrians are looking for an excuse to take over Lebanon themselves. And Mr. President, the religious disputes—especially on top of border disputes—may be deeper and more intractable in this region of the world than the political ones like we have in Russia . . ."

"Chet, I better start feeling out the American Jewish groups on this. But we have got to help the Israelis see that a peace agreement with the Egyptians now is better for them than fighting these refugees who may or may not leave so fast, what with that . . . I mean, those terrorists . . . ?"

"Yes, sir, the so-called Palestine Liberation Organization," replied Bowles. "Sir, I'll get in touch with Governor Goldberg. He ought to be a great help here."

With that, the meeting ended, but discussions on the subject were just beginning. As it turned out, the American Jewish organization leaders almost unanimously supported whatever the Israeli government said. Polling requested by Kennedy, however, showed "rank-and-file" Jews in the United States to be far more supportive of Sadat's peace offering than American Jewish leaders.

Kennedy, to his great disappointment, and then anger, found that Governor Goldberg refused to support the Kennedy administration in asking the Israelis to pursue Sadat's offer. Kennedy had assumed Goldberg would be supportive of the administration because, before speaking with Goldberg, Kennedy had Chet Bowles review the historic internal record of events leading to the promulgation of Resolution 242. It showed, to Kennedy's satisfaction that then UN Ambassador Goldberg and then Secretary of State Dean Rusk understood Resolution 242 to mean that Israel would give up most (though clearly not all) of the land it won in the 1967 war in order to secure recognition by, and peace with, the Arab nations.

Consequently, when two vacancies came up on the Supreme Court in mid-1971—Douglas and Black jointly announced their retirement on July 21,

1971—Kennedy decided not to offer Goldberg a chance to return to his seat on the Supreme Court. Goldberg had hinted to Kennedy, right after he was elected governor of New York, that he would like Kennedy to hold "the Supreme Court 'Jewish' seat open," at least until after Goldberg's first term.

Kennedy, upset at Goldberg's refusal to support a peace strategy for the Middle East, let it be known that he had considered Goldberg but rejected him. Kennedy, to add a touch of finality to Goldberg's chances, picked, as his next Supreme Court nominee, UCLA law professor Harold Horowitz. Horowitz was one of the few prominent Jewish lawyers who supported Kennedy's current Middle East policies, unlike Goldberg and the respected judge Abner Mikva, who many observers also thought was on the Supreme Court nomination "short list." Horowitz had been the general counsel for President John Kennedy's Health, Education, and Welfare Department and was a noted expert in a variety of areas of constitutional law. In choosing Horowitz for "the Jewish seat," Kennedy essentially cut off his personal friendship with Goldberg. Horowitz was easily confirmed despite the usual challenges from Senator Thurmond.

The other nominee to the highest court was, of course, Joe Dolan. Court observers had found, as did the senators, that Dolan had shown a surprisingly moderate tendency while on the bench at the Ninth Circuit Court of Appeals. Dolan, therefore, overcame even Thurmond's initial knee-jerk opposition. Both Dolan and Horowitz were confirmed by a vote of ninety-nine to zero, with Thurmond failing to appear for the votes.

Bowles, meanwhile, had been dispatched to Egypt in mid-May 1971, amid statements from Jewish organization leaders who criticized the Kennedy administration for talking "first" with the Arabs. The organizations, beginning to play rough with Kennedy, "forgot" that Bowles had ignored Egypt and its president, Anwar Sadat, on the trip to Israel just after Sadat's February 6 peace offer. Bowles arrived in Egypt and, once there, found himself charmed by Sadat. The Egyptian leader told the American secretary of state that he was interested in closer relations with the United States and that even a "separate Egyptian peace," as opposed to a regional Arab peace with Israel, was preferable to another war between Israel and Egypt.

Sadat publicly reiterated his desire to have peace with Israel as long as Israel gave back 70 percent of the Sinai. The Egyptian president said, "I am, Mr. Secretary, glad to go to Tel Aviv," the capital of Israel, "to make my offer of peace." Bowles, however, believed that was premature, more for domestic political reasons than diplomatic reasons. Sadat, in what he termed a show of "good faith," offered to allow Bowles to go directly from Cairo, Egypt, to the Tel Aviv airport in Israel, something no Arab nation in the area had allowed.

The Israelis publicly agreed that Sadat's trip was indeed premature, but they reluctantly had to accept his offer of allowing Bowles to travel directly from Egypt to Israel. The Israeli leadership was secretly furious at the "naïve imprudence" of Bowles, but the Israeli public, and particularly the Israeli liberal elite press, led by *Ha'aretz* and the *Jerusalem Post,* called upon Golda Meir to begin immediate negotiations with Egyptian President Sadat. Ben-Gurion publicly said, "It is time to talk peace with Egypt."

Israeli Prime Minister Golda Meir met with Bowles on May 23, 1971. Earlier in the year, the prime minister had told Bowles she would not meet with President Sadat "until Egypt denounces Arab terrorists who continue to attack Israel."

Sadat, in response to Bowles' suggestion, now told a worldwide press conference as Bowles left for Israel, "Egypt renounces violence by all sides, whether against Israelis or against Palestinians. Peace is multilateral, if I may sound like a European diplomat for a moment!"

Meir responded to Sadat's statement when she met with Bowles later that day. She said, "Mr. Sadat has refused to accept my offer of peace. His renouncing of terrorism is conditional, not absolute. And he has the audacity to equate our protecting ourselves with the actions of the PLO terrorists! I have no interest in speaking with him."

Bowles shook his head sadly. He said, "Mrs. Meir, I regret to say that the United States is very disappointed in legalistic hair-splitting from a highly valued ally." It was a short meeting. Bowles immediately headed back to Washington, wondering why the Israelis were refusing to negotiate with Sadat.

The press in the United States, including the *New York Times,* the *New York Post,* the *Washington Post,* the *St. Louis Post-Dispatch,* and others (with the exception of the *Los Angeles Times* and the *Boston Globe*) greatly upset Kennedy on the day Bowles returned to Washington by publishing editorials siding with the Israeli government.

Kennedy called Ben Bradlee, the editor of the *Washington Post.* "Ben," said an exasperated Kennedy, "I guess one should expect the *Times* and the *New York Post* to be pro-Israel in the face of a genuine peace offer from what had been the most militantly anti-Israeli country in the Middle East. But how could you and Kay Graham . . . " He anger was now affecting him as he spoke. "Ben, I can't . . . Ben . . . Here we are on the verge of peace in Europe with the Russians, and now we get this peace offering from Sadat . . . What do you and Kay *want,* damn it—a goddamned *war* in the Middle East?"

Bradlee was cool over the telephone. He knew the editorial the *Post* had printed on Bowles' "misguided trust" in Sadat had been strong. He had disagreed with publishing it, but his disagreement was more on the margins than on the main point of siding with Israel. He told Kennedy, "Mr. President, you can call Mrs. Graham yourself. I don't need to tell you that, of course. I have my views, but Mrs. Graham feels Mr. Sadat is not to be trusted. Our military and intelligence sources in your administration, I hate to tell you, say that Egypt is still arming itself—with Russian arms, I might add. The *Los Angeles*

Times, which is in a rare mood of supporting your administration on this, also admitted that point. Sadat won't renounce terrorism—"

Kennedy jumped on that word, "Come on, Ben, the Israeli ambassador, Rabin, thought originally—before he got the 'party' line—that Sadat's offer was genuine. Geez! The Israelis are building settlements night and day in the Sinai and the other territories they won in the '67 war. Sadat's been open about getting arms, but he says he'll stop arming if the Israelis take up his peace offer. That's as straight as any leader I've heard—ever! The Israelis are the ones who are moving the goalposts, not the Egyptians. One of my White House aides, Pete Edelman, who is Jewish and has been with me for years, says he doesn't see anything sinister in Sadat's offer—and frankly, he is very disappointed with the Israelis. Jack Newfield agrees, and he told me this morning that Izzy Stone and Noam Chomsky—two Jews who usually tell us how 'conservative' we have been on many things—those two are now cheering Chet's statements and criticizing the Israelis—their own people!"

"Stone? Chomsky? Two Jewish radicals we'd never even think of publishing here? If I may say so, Mr. President, those are some strange people to be quoting to me—I can't even imagine Mrs. Graham . . . Well, Mr. President, there are plenty of *other* Jewish-Americans who are outraged over Secretary Bowles' insistence that Israel enter into peace negotiations to give back land, and they are already saying they'll remember this next year at election time. That's why Mrs. Graham published the editorial today by Amos Perlmutter. He's with the Jewish Anti-Defamation League, which is very moderate compared to some other Jewish organizations."

Perlmutter, in his column, had written that there was a "dangerous and misguided idealism on the part of Chester Bowles and the Kennedy administration."

"That bastard, Perlmutter, called me naïve!" yelled Kennedy into the phone. "He had the audacity to say that I'd desert Israel the way I somehow deserted Thieu in South Vietnam! Perlmutter, in order to criticize me over Israel, is standing with Reagan, retired General Abrams, and the John Birch Society over what you, Kay, and *everyone else* have said is a *successful* Vietnam policy!"

Bradlee was silent, wondering if he could respond by saying that maybe Perlmutter had a point about comparing Israel to the now-deposed President Thieu, although the comparison was a double-edged sword. Kennedy caught that silence and said, "Ben, you going sideways on me? I can't believe after all these years—you know me better than guys like Perlmutter! I have no use for people like Perlmutter—extreme nationalists, that's what they remind me of. They wake up every morning, open the window—I see this in some Irish Americans who obsess with me about Northern Ireland!—and no matter what the weather is, they sniff the air and ask, 'Is it good for the Jews?' I see this everywhere—Irish, Jewish, Italian, labor unions, environmentalists, Rotary Clubs, corporate executives! It's the same bullshit—but it really irks me to see this coming from the Jews—of all people! They should know better about the downside of any excessive nationalism, including their own!"

"Careful, Mr. President. Somebody might say you're saying the American Jewish leadership is a 'fifth column'—dual loyalty!"

"Ben—*God damn it! What the hell is wrong with you?*" Kennedy went from a yell to a scream into the receiver. *"I'm talking about a few assholes here!* Most Jews in America agree with me! They support Sadat's offer!" He sighed, calming himself. "God, Ben, your *own* polling showed that yesterday. That's why I couldn't believe that editorial today."

Bradlee didn't want to "go sideways" with President Kennedy. He had told colleagues at the *Post* that he disliked Reagan for being a "stupid movie star" and didn't like Abrams, whom he called "a little MacArthur." Roth, he thought, was "okay," but Bradlee still saw Roth as a "stuffed shirt who made Tom Dewey look as charismatic as . . . a Kennedy."

Now it was Bradlee's turn to sigh. Then he said, "Mr. President, it's *one* editorial! We had to print it! Mrs. Graham was getting pressure like mad from the Jewish community because we printed George Ball's column last week saying that the Israelis needed to respond positively to Sadat or risk isolation from the world like South Africa and Rhodesia. That was pretty damned strong, if you ask me." He sighed again. "Tell you what, Mr. President. We'll give you space to present your case. You might want to get a Jewish member of the administration, maybe Ellsberg from the National Security Council, to make the case. If Chet Bowles can get somewhere with the Israelis, well . . . well, I can't speak for Mrs. Graham." He quickly added, "You should, as I said before, Mr. President, speak with her, too. She just feels all these initiatives—Europe, South Africa and Rhodesia, Taiwan, Russia, China, and now the whole Middle East—and that's just foreign policy! We haven't even talked about the union radicals, calling strikes in major cities, the southern union organizing, the negative income tax—well, anyway, she sees all this as just *too much* . . . too much, too soon."

Kennedy shook his head at his end of the telephone line. "All right, Ben. I'll speak with Kay—and I'll call Ellsberg tomorrow morning. He'll have something to you in twenty-four hours—even if I have to write it for him!"

Ellsberg, as Kennedy knew, had been enthusiastically supportive of Sadat's offer and Bowles' efforts to persuade the Israelis to speak with Sadat. Kennedy had grown to like Ellsberg but still thought him a bit of an "egghead." Ellsberg, upon Kennedy's request, quickly wrote a strong article about the need for peace in the Middle East. Ellsberg quoted, with Kennedy's approval, the memos showing Resolution 242's original intent as he and the Kennedy administration saw it.

Ellsberg, before the piece ran in the *Washington Post,* received telephone calls, some of them threatening, from Jewish organization leaders. One leader yelled at him before hanging up, "How can you stab your own people in the back?"

Ellsberg went to Kennedy the morning the article appeared. He told the president, "What angers me, Mr. President, is that I was 'the anointed one' when we listened to the pleas of the organized Jewish leadership, their lobbyists—who sure throw their money and weight around—about the treatment of Jews in the Soviet Union! I am not religious, but being the closest thing to a Jewish secretary of state, well, the Jewish organization leaders treated me like royalty. And suddenly, I'm *trayf!* That's 'nonkosher,' but literally, it means 'bad' or 'unclean!' Ironically, I was, at that time, privately telling Chet I thought it was too risky to bring up the mistreatment of Jews in the Soviet Union when he was negotiating with Foreign Minister Gromyko over the withdrawal of troops from Europe. Yet Chet brought it up with the Soviets. And I couldn't believe the Soviets agreed last month to let 250,000 Jews leave the Soviet Union, with more promised this fall! It was amazing to me—Chet was right when he sensed the Soviets were relieved to make friends with us."

Kennedy nodded his head in agreement before speaking. "I don't get the Jewish organization leaders either, Dan. Peace in the Middle East is becoming more complicated than our dealings with Russia. The thing that pisses me off—sorry to say it that way—but it really bothers me that many of those Jews who are leaving the Soviet Union—they want to come *here,* not Israel. But the Jewish leaders screamed at Chet from the day the Soviets said the Jews could leave that these refugees must go to Israel and nowhere else—not even the United States. I was glad, I have to say, from a political point of view to let them go to Israel—can you imagine if those refugees wanted to settle in our Midwest—as opposed to the Middle East—I mean in Israel? That was a pun, wasn't it? . . . " He smiled for just a second, and then became gravely serious. "I thought that 'freedom' means you go where you want to go . . . At least I thought it did—that's what those 'Free Soviet Jews' protests were about, weren't they?"

Ellsberg nodded back, saying, "It all strikes me as very disconcerting, to say the least."[7]

"Dan, I'm starting to think we ought to hold back on this whole Middle East peace effort . . . I don't know . . . I mean, what if all the Jewish leaders and the others are right on this one? How can one really trust the Arabs? It's not like any of those countries, even Egypt, are a democracy—Sadat was more an heir of Nasser than an independent candidate for office, right?"

Ellsberg replied, "I don't know, Mr. President. Our nation has had no problem supporting dictators in Latin America, in Africa, and in places like Indonesia. I've thought a lot about this, trying to be objective, and not to look at it from the viewpoint of being Jewish. While the refugees in the West Bank and Gaza regions can't vote, Israel does allow the Arabs who live in the regular part of Israel—behind the 'green line,' as the UN calls it—to vote. The

Arabs even have representatives in the Israeli parliament. Yet, most Jews were expelled from most of the Arab countries over the years . . . including Egypt. But on the other hand—"

Kennedy jumped in before Ellsberg could identify what was "on the other hand." He said, "That's just it, Dan. Things can turn on a dime—and what if Israel makes peace and the Egyptian military or some radical group overthrows Sadat? There are radical elements left over from Nasser, you know. There's that Palestinian terrorist group, the PLO, and the Syrians are pretty hard-line . . . I don't know if we can risk upsetting the Soviets over this, but the Russians may ultimately understand . . . "

Ellsberg suddenly worried that the president was headed toward calling off Bowles and letting the Sadat peace offer fall into history's "black hole." Kennedy, however, arguing like a lawyer analyzing his case, pulled himself back toward the "peace" policy. He gave his own "other hand" to Ellsberg:

"But on the other hand, Dan, the rank-and-file American Jews are *for* Sadat's proposal, and they tend to be pretty independent on most things. . . . And Sadat seems genuine, at least according to Bowles. Bowles wanted to bring Sadat here—I said no way . . . Hmmm . . . if we can just get the Israelis to talk with Sadat, then King Hussein of Jordan would probably come out of the closet—could be a juggernaut, kind of like what happened when the Soviets realized we weren't going to renege on them and they could worry more about . . . Jesus! I keep forgetting about China! That's where I really see us having to watch out for a nuclear war—especially along the Manchurian border. Dan, what's the latest on that? I've been thinking about my reelection campaign next year; met with Chuck Goodell, he's gone Democrat—left the Republicans in New York. His fellow Republican New York senator, Javits, might jump, too! Well, he's Jewish, though. . . . He might stick with Reagan or someone. . . . Wonder what Reagan thinks of this—meaning what do his advisers think . . . "

Ellsberg finally broke through these rambling thoughts. "Mr. President, let's see what Secretary Bowles has to say after he has further discussions with the Israelis. He did make some headway with Dayan, if not Meir. Dayan, though, thinks Sadat can help force the Palestinian refugees in the territories near Jordan and in the Gaza Strip to leave. Dayan said something about sending them to Lebanon and letting them buffer the Syrians. Something like that."

The Ellsberg piece ran in the *Washington Post* on June 6, 1971. Two days later, a story broke in the *New York Times*: "Ellsberg Treated by Psychiatrist for Two Years." It was a true story, and probably "newsworthy." But the timing told more of a story than the story itself—which was not atypical in the world of the elite media and Washington politics.

Ellsberg had seen a psychiatrist in 1967 and 1968 for depression over a failing marriage and a distant, troubled relationship with his son. Once he became NSC chairman, however, his depression lifted, for the most part. He had seen the psychiatrist two or three times in the past two years—though that wasn't in any of the articles or television reports, for some reason. When Ellsberg told Paul Warnke at the Pentagon what the newspapers and television had missed, Warnke said, "Don't assume they missed that, Dan. They could be holding it back in case you fight this." He paused before asking, "Whatcha gonna do, Dan?"

Ellsberg said, "I thought about quitting. I went to the president to offer my resignation. He surprised me though. He's really starting to get angry with the press, especially after the *Washington Post* ran with the *Times* story on me. He called, I guess, Mrs. Graham and accused her of running a 'tabloid.' He had Jack Newfield and Ralph Yarborough call the *Times* because he hates the *Times* so much he'd probably 'cut their heads off,' as he told me. Pretty harsh stuff to say—I couldn't believe he wants me to stay on. And you know what else he said to me, Paul?"

Warnke shrugged as Ellsberg continued, "He said, 'I wish I had the courage to go to a shrink," Ellsberg laughed. "The president did correct himself, saying the right word. But then he said, 'I wouldn't have been in such a funk, Dan, for a couple of years—even now—if I could have talked to someone who might have been able to help me explain how I felt—why I felt what I felt about my brother, about my family, my place in the world.' I think I'm quoting him exactly right, Paul, 'cause it was amazing for him to say that. I couldn't believe it! I can't believe how much he's changed from when his brother was president." Ellsberg sighed as he shook his head.[8]

At a press conference Kennedy gave the next day, the president was questioned about Bowles' trip to Egypt and Israel, and the Ellsberg revelation. He answered a question from Sander Vanocur, a television reporter. "I would like to answer your question, Mr. Vanocur, starting with a global view of things. I think, no, I *know* the American people agree with me that our policy of tough trust with the Soviet Union is working and is lessening East-West tensions in Europe. And now, whites and blacks in southern Africa are learning to trust each other to pursue peace, and the peace process is going to begin any day in that region of the world. And yet, for over four months, the president of a leading Arabic nation, Egypt, the cradle of civilization, has been publicly calling for peace with its mortal enemy, Israel. President Sadat has consistently stated his willingness to abide by United Nations Resolution 242, which the United States strongly supported from the beginning. This administration will take a back seat to nobody in terms of supporting Israel's right to secure borders. But what does President Sadat get in response to his first offer of peace? All he gets is some people in our media and some in certain groups who claim—wrongly—to speak for others, shouting at this Arab leader, 'Liar!' And to compound things, these opponents of peace attack the privacy of anyone, Jewish or not, who dares to say we should explore our options for peace—" Kennedy paused, and then, stepping almost to the side of the press conference podium, continued, "in an area of the world where, frankly, God must cry every night at the killing that has gone on in his name over the years!"

Kennedy was not the author of that last line. Speechwriters Walinsky and Greenfield, both Jewish, had suggested that line for a speech on the Middle East that was, along with the rest of the speech, rejected by the O Boys. Kennedy, who read the speech and agreed with the O Boys, suddenly said the key line during the question-and-answer period, and . . . it seemed to work! Kennedy said it as if he was just making it up on the spot. Walinsky and Greenfield, standing at the back of the room, looked at each other with shocked expressions that said, Did we write that after all?

Answering a follow-up question regarding Ellsberg, Kennedy said, "Daniel Ellsberg has been a cool, steady person leading the National Security Council. I fully support him and expect him to continue serving the nation. He is among the most sane and knowledgeable men in the entire country. As the newspaper articles have admitted, he saw a psychiatrist for personal issues a couple of years ago, before joining the administration. There is no evidence—even if he saw a psychiatrist since that time—that it has affected either his work or his judgment." And that was the end of that "scandal" in the minds of most reporters and editors. The Jewish organizations, which had their share of professional psychiatrists as members, were in no position to complain about psychiatrists and gingerly backed off.

The response by the American Jewish leadership in Washington and New York City to the president's remarks on Israel, however, was entirely another matter. Hyman Bookbinder, a renowned leader of the American Jewish Committee and often quoted by mainstream media, wrote in an editorial in the *New York Times* two days later:

"How can the president trust the leader of a regime in Egypt who has publicly stated his continued support for that nation's former radical dictator, Nasser? It is easy to forget that Nasser died vowing to drive Jews into the sea, a view that put him in league with the Nazis. Simply because Sadat suddenly called for peace this year, the president and his advisers treat Israel, the best ally of the United States and the only democracy in the Middle East region, as a pariah state. Where was this President Sadat on the question of peace when Nasser was alive? Sadat has consistently spouted hateful words about Jews and about Israel in many other public statements over the years. In 1953, well after Hitler's crimes were proven to the entire world, Sadat wrote a 'eulogy' for Adolf Hitler saying Hitler was 'an immortal leader of Germany.' This same man also allows anti-Semitic books to be freely published in his country, even as he censors anything he claims opposes him or what he believes are 'Egyptian interests.' Many Jews were expelled from Egypt, starting in the 1950s and continuing up to the last couple of years. Why should anyone believe Sadat now, least of all the tiny nation of Israel, especially when Sadat continues to gather military weapons made by Communist Russia and Communist China?"

Powerful stuff, thought Larry O'Brien when he read the article. He went directly to the president with the article the morning it appeared, but Kennedy had already read it. O'Brien said, "Bob, we gotta talk. If you lose the Jewish vote, you will probably lose New York and California, which— California, I mean—is already gonna be a tough state if Governor Reagan is the Republican presidential nominee next year, no matter how close his reelection victory was last November. And without California and New York, you could lose the ball game! The Israelis aren't budging, and they keep building their settlements. Sadat just said he won't make peace if the Jews keep building housing settlements in the lands Israel won from the Arabs in the 1967 war. He said he'll consider a separate peace without other Arab nations, but only if the Israelis give back a big chunk of the Sinai *and* stop building settlements in the other disputed territories for at least one year following the agreement. Ambassador Rabin told Chet Bowles this morning that's a nonstarter. And the Jews here at home? Well, Bookbinder's a liberal, and he's starting to sound like Cardinal Spellman talking about the atheistic Communist menace!"

Kennedy rubbed his forehead, saying, "I'd rather fight Reagan, bearded radicals, and Strom Thurmond in one coalition than fight the Jews, Larry. But damn it, Sadat's saying exactly what the Israelis claimed they wanted to hear almost four years ago when the UN passed Resolution 242! As I keep saying to everyone I talk with, the Israeli leaders are moving the goalposts on us—and yet the press publishers, most of them non-Jews, are going along. I mean, Kay Graham is the furthest thing from a Jew I've ever met. I don't get it. I just don't!"

O'Brien stood up after starting to sit. He said, "Well, actually, her father was Jewish, but her mother wasn't—and she married a non-Jew—"

"She sure doesn't *act* Jewish, damn it! She carries on like a Boston brahmin Protestant—except on *this!*"

"Mr. President, forget Katherine Graham—at least for now! The polls show the rank-and-file Jews are becoming divided on this, even though a large majority was initially supportive of our position. Support for Sadat among Jews began slipping on overnight polls after Sadat made that crack that the Israelis shouldn't build any more settlements. I'm concerned where this will end up with the Jewish voters next year."

Kennedy said, "I'm starting to hate polls, Larry! I know they're useful, and I read 'em every day—it seems like that's all I'm going to read through the next election. But do we have to follow the polls or *lead* the polls—I mean, the nation? That's it in a nutshell, Larry. The country, not polls. We either lead or . . . or . . . I don't know. They'll all have to beat me! Reagan, Abrams, Roth, the Jews—the leaders I mean, maybe the Jews too . . . "

He trailed off, looking out the window at the morning protesters starting to gather. Protests over what, he thought? He couldn't tell anymore.[9]

Bowles went back to the Middle East in mid-June and stayed for almost two weeks before going on to South Africa. *Time* and *Newsweek,* two weeklies that were in sync with their worldviews and their stories more than they admitted, both published articles about Bowles' "shuttle diplomacy," commenting on the fact that Bowles had almost been living on *Air Force 2.* It was the kind of "contentless" story the news media loved to discuss for weeks. It "humanized" the political leaders for the masses, they told themselves. In reality, the masses could care less—they wanted to know if there was going to be peace in the world or if their sons were going to fight and die in another war.

In Israel, Bowles met with whomever he could find in the military and the government who was willing to pursue Sadat's peace initiative. Mrs. Meir almost refused to accept Bowles' latest mission but did not want to risk alienating American Jewish support by snubbing the American secretary of state. She did say, however, that she would "find time" to meet him during his "stay" in Israel.

Bowles took the comment in stride, saying to reporters, "I come to a land of freedom to take the opportunity to hear from leading Israeli citizens." The first person to befriend Bowles on this trip was Nahum Goldmann, the former president of the World Zionist Organization. Goldmann, an Israeli citizen since 1962, divided his time between Israel and Geneva, Switzerland. Goldmann told Bowles he had met with Sadat in Geneva and was an enthusiastic supporter of Sadat's efforts. Goldmann, in his meeting with the Egyptian leader, convinced Sadat to free from jail the respected Egyptian Jewish, but Communist leader, Shehata Haroun. Sadat, after meeting Haroun, found him to be a strong supporter of the Egyptian president's peace proposal. Haroun said publicly, "I am an Egyptian first and always. But as a Jew, I have a duty to Egypt to help make peace with my Jewish relatives in Israel."

Bowles brought Goldmann to the meeting he had set with Deputy Prime Minister Yigal Allon. Meir was outraged at Allon for meeting Bowles without her approval, she told Dayan at the time. Bowles found that Allon believed Sadat's offer was genuine. After meeting with Bowles and Goldmann, Allon, a former military leader, opened the way for Bowles to meet with sympathetic military leaders who, said Allon, wanted peace with Egypt "more than life itself."

One of them was the chief of military intelligence, General Yehoshafat Harkabi, a one-time extreme hawk who had begun having doubts about Dayan's and others' aggressive settlement policies. The more information Harkabi received from the Arab side, the more he believed, as he told Allon and Bowles, "that time will harden, not soften, Arab attitudes." He was particularly concerned with the unleashing of religious fundamentalism among the Arab population, he told Bowles. "You cannot talk peace with religious fanatics who want to die in a holy war. If such fanatics take over the Palestinian nationalist movement, we may have no choice but to defend ourselves to the fullest extent, and with a fury that Jews cannot afford to openly undertake with the eyes of the non-Jewish world looking on."

What Harkabi didn't dare tell Bowles was that the Israeli intelligence units were already funding Muslim fanatics as a way to split the Arab movement, which had been, until this point, led by secularists. The secular-oriented PLO used the rhetoric of "communist-nationalist" movements, not religion, to receive money from Red China, and especially Soviet Russia. (In the first timeline, Israeli government funding of certain Islamic fundamentalists subsequently backfired because the latter became more violent and more opposed to Israel than the secular leaders of the PLO.)[10]

Harkabi was, ironically, among the initiators of this "divide and conquer" plan, but intelligence reports caused him to reconsider his position, especially since the United States' embrace of Sadat's peace offer. Harkabi wrote a formal memo to the prime minister herself, not long after his meeting with Bowles, that said that "unleashing fundamentalist political movements" could unravel any long-term comprehensive solution and would "likely damage relations with the United States, our most valued protector and ally." Harkabi thought about quitting the government but decided to remain in order to support Allon.

Meir had been openly whispering to others that Allon was becoming a political "liability" before Allon met with Bowles. Allon heard the whispers, which was why he brazenly met with Bowles and Goldmann. Now Meir was "stuck" with Allon because firing him would create a political firestorm, at home and especially in Washington. As she said to General Shlomo Gazit, who was fast becoming a close adviser in her desire to derail the Sadat plan, "Time is on our side, General Gazit. Allon has no power in or out of our government. We must have secure borders, not trust, not peace, not anything else right now. Whatever it takes to delay diplomatic solutions, divide our enemies, and build permanent settlements is the policy every Israeli government must pursue."

Gazit nodded in approval, while wondering whether Harkabi, who had replaced him as military intelligence chief, was also becoming a "liability" to "greater Israel." Gazit knew Harkabi had agreed to meet with Allon and Bowles. It was a very small country after all.

Bowles returned empty-handed in the sense that Prime Minister Meir refused to meet with Sadat. The "good news," Bowles told the president, was that the deputy prime minister, Allon, and the military intelligence chief, Harkabi, were former hawks who were now becoming positively dovish. Bowles took the risk of saying to the president, "They remind me of you and Dan Ellsberg over the course of the Vietnam War."

Kennedy smiled, saying, "Then there's hope, isn't there, Chet?"

Bowles, more confident now, continued, "Mr. President, I believe that we cannot miss this opportunity to create peace between Israel and Egypt. I spoke with Sadat by telephone when I stopped in Paris on the way back here. He says we are running out of time. The new radical leader of Libya, Qaddafi, is calling for an international Arab summit to strategize against the West and against Israel. Qaddafi is telling Sadat not to waste his time with either the Soviets or the Americans, and to support a final holy war against Israel."

"What? Who the hell does this puny son-of-a-bitch nutcase from . . . where? Libya? Who cares, Chet, about god-damned *Libya?*"

"Well, sir, they have a lot of oil, and this Libyan leader, Qaddafi, is a military dictator who has our oil executives very nervous, according to Interior Secretary Udall and Defense Secretary Warnke. Qaddafi is working with Western oil companies for now, but I have to say that even the oil executives are wanting Sadat to have more influence on Qaddafi than the other way around—"

"Why would Sadat suddenly go in with this Daffy guy, who sounds like a nut—"

"Sir, Qaddafi is . . . a nut—when you hear the statements he makes. But he's not dumb. I think he's riling Arabs, and maybe northern Africans, up for a war, which will, he believes, increase his power. Sadat told me—point blank—that Israel cannot hold onto the Sinai forever. It is a matter of national pride to him—"

It was Kennedy's turn to interrupt, "Jesus! National pride? Sadat said *that?* Were the Jews right that Sadat will go from peace to war like . . . like . . . like turning a light switch on and off?"

"No, sir," said a grimacing Bowles, sorry for falling into a logical trap so easily. "Not at all! He said this because he doesn't want to lose control of his own people, who he says are still smarting over the defeat in '67 and feel betrayed by the Russians and the Americans, who, to them, are all 'the West.' Peace is the only way to lessen the tensions, and stopping the settlements— and returning just a good chunk of the Sinai—will create a momentum toward a larger, comprehensive peace. The Russian ambassador to France, and Dobrynin here at home, are both enthusiastic about a joint Soviet-American-Egyptian-Israeli peace conference. They want us to overcome the current Israeli intransigence, as they see it. There is a risk for us not doing what they ask. Dobrynin says Suslov and Andropov at the KGB, who he says were the key to our new Soviet-European policy, are very unhappy with us for not prodding Israel to speak with Sadat."

Kennedy went to the globe near his desk just to make sure he knew where Libya was located. "My God, Chet! Libya's right next to Egypt! I kept separating the Middle East from Russia and everything else . . . Hmmm . . . " He sighed. "Maybe Sadat has to watch it. Damn it, Chet!" Then, he grunted. "You know, I *hate* the Middle East . . . "

Kennedy vacillated between completely dropping or moving forward with Middle East peace efforts. He was able to be ambivalent because the American news media, outside of an occasional editorial in the elite newspapers, did not show a sustained interest in the Middle East. Oil was flowing as it never had before, and, luckily for Kennedy, the world was more interested at that point in the Soviet troop withdrawals, the historic peace process in southern Africa—in which the British and Russians were involved, along with the United States—and the labor strikes inside the United States, which were more numerous than at any time since the period just after World War II.

Even as Kennedy was "keeping a lid on the Middle East," as Larry O'Brien put it, Kennedy continued his discussions on the subject with Bowles. Kennedy eventually decided he needed to take the issue head-on if he wanted to keep the Jewish vote in his re-election campaign planned for 1972.

In August 1971, Kennedy finally met "alone"—meaning without Chet Bowles—with Larry O'Brien and Kenny O'Donnell to discuss Israel, Egypt, and peace—in the context of American domestic politics. He opened the discussion by saying, "Guys, I have a strategic foreign policy decision to make on the Middle East this coming month, but I have a political decision to make here at home, too."

O'Brien laughed a bit, saying, "So what else is new?"

"Yes, I'm aware of that Larry, but this one, if not handled right, could unravel my entire reelection campaign—as *you* keep telling me! Chet Bowles and Dan Ellsberg are making a strong case that we should force the issue with the Israelis to get them to the table with Sadat. There's a strongman in Libya, Qaddafi, who's stirring up things with the Syrians, with Arab religious fanatics throughout the . . . uh . . . Moslem world . . . and I have become convinced Sadat holds a large—maybe *the*—key to peace in that region."

By the summer of 1971, O'Brien hated "the Middle East" more than the president did. Nearly every time he'd been to Capitol Hill in the past few months, O'Brien had been hearing from Washington Senator Henry "Scoop" Jackson, a big supporter of Israel, as well as Jackson's aides, who sounded more like Abrams—or Reagan—supporters than Democrats.

O'Brien told Kennedy, "Scoop Jackson's on the warpath, as you know, and he's gonna take our heads off if we do anything to make Israel do something it doesn't want to do. He's gotten a truckload of money from the Jewish groups, even though there's not a Jew for miles in Oregon—I mean, Washington—well, both places really. Why are we wasting time on this when we have the European success with the Soviets—which we are not getting enough credit for? You know, you ought to talk with Reuther about telling the labor unions to cool their jets after this month! And the situation in China isn't going to be low on our priority list these next few months, am I right?"

O'Donnell, who was hearing more from wealthy constituents coming to Washington complaining about strikes by "uppity workers," chimed in at this point. "Bob, Larry's right on that last part. I can't recall the last time we were able to talk about *domestic* policy issues. And that's what elections ought to turn on! Let's remember one thing: Churchill won World War II and was kicked out of office right after! We have had more labor union strikes this year than in any year since Truman, according to the National Association of Manufacturers—which Reuther admits is true. Except Reuther—and Yarborough—they love it! Ken Galbraith told me to brace for some significant inflation. Yet Yarborough just says, 'Better than unemployment going up,' as if this was 1935. Well, maybe it is better than 1935, but it could be inflation that's the problem this time. The Republicans, from what I'm hearing, are getting their act together. They have a lot of natural support from white, upper-middle-class, middle-management types in suburb after suburb who hate seeing picket signs in train stations, in stores, and even at the Post Office—I mean, luckily we got that injunction at the NLRB against Moe Biller's postal union—I thought we'd go nuts here without mail service!"

Kennedy and O'Brien looked at each other with their mouths open, stunned into domestic political realities. O'Donnell was supporting O'Brien's position, not Kennedy's, as to why the Middle East was no place to be for someone running for reelection in the United States the following year.

Kennedy said, "I hear all that, Kenny, but I have spoken with Yarborough and Reuther about the level of strikes, particularly the sympathy strikes under the law we passed two years ago—and which the unions are really running with, too hard, even for me sometimes. It isn't *all* foreign affairs in the Oval Office, even if it feels like it. There's good news inside what you're saying, Kenny, beyond the middle management voters—who we didn't get much support from last time anyway. Yarborough, who I trust on this type of issue more than anyone, says workers are getting real solid in their voting rights now, more than at any time since the '30s. That means they're voting Democratic, they say, like when FDR crushed Alf Landon in 1936. Our party even won a special congressional election this year, guys! The unions get people out to vote—even when there isn't a regular election going on! That's unheard of—at least in our lifetimes—since special elections historically favor Republicans. We picked up one seat in Congress and scared the Republicans in another that they thought was safe. I am, though, worried about the Jewish vote. That's why I don't think I can wait for a war in the Middle East to break out next year and have people think we let it happen. Jews vote—more than just about anyone else. But I can't tell whether a war between Israel and Egypt would be good or bad for the Jewish people in America. If a war is bad for them, though, it's bad for the country and the world. The Israelis are divided at the top as we keep pushing this, but Meir is in charge and she's blocking our peace efforts there."

"You talk like that with anyone but us," said O'Brien, shaking his head, "and you can kiss the Jewish vote goodbye *yesterday.*" O'Donnell nodded in agreement.

Kennedy was ready for that. He said, "That's what I think most of the time. And then I think of what happens if I let Sadat keep building up his military weaponry—which I can't stop unless he gets friendly with us and we join him in pushing for peace. Foreign Minister Gromyko tells Chet Bowles they will support Sadat if we can't get a handle on the Israelis. Gromyko says if we don't get peace, there'll be war, and Sadat could join with Libya sooner than later. We need to stop Sadat from thinking he has to ally himself with this Qaddafi guy. The success of our global foreign policy is possibly going to turn on the Middle East region. Lucky for us, the oil industry has a glut of oil on the market. The Arabs, I'm told, don't have any wherewithal to withhold oil from us or Europe, according to Stew Udall at Interior. He says the U.S. oil companies, not the Arabs, control refining and distribution. Thank God for small favors ... "

O'Brien saw the point but still saw the immediate fallout. "How you going to get the Israelis to the table? I don't see it without a lot of blood— our reelection blood!—on the floor. Reagan, Roth, and the Republicans—and Scoop Jackson would probably turn Republican if the Jews wanted him to—they'll all get money from the Jewish groups, who give the most of any ethnic or religious group—and let's not debate whether Jews are ethnic like Poles or religious like Catholics!"

O'Donnell said defensively, "I was just wonderin' the other day, that's all! You know, I keep saying to myself, Why doesn't anyone fight about Northern Ireland in this country like we do about Israel?"

Kennedy, surprising O'Brien, answered O'Donnell. "I was wondering that, too, especially after the 'bloody Sunday' in Belfast a few months ago. Jack Newfield had the best answer, though. He says Irish Americans have intermarried with too many non-Irish, and their ties to the homeland, except for a minority, have long since frayed. More important, there wasn't any mass genocide of the Irish by the British or anyone in this century, as happened to the Jews. Jews are just more touchy about it, says Newfield. And, gentlemen," he said shaking his head sadly, "they will be for quite some time."

O'Donnell responded, "Yes, but I heard an earful from Perlmutter—I know you hate him, Mr. President, but here's his pitch: He said, 'Why are you guys pickin' on Israel when I don't see your administration pressuring the British to deal with the Irish Republican Army?' I found I couldn't quite—"

"Whadaya mean you couldn't answer that asshole!?" Kennedy turned beet red just thinking of Perlmutter. "Jesus, you think I haven't thought of that—and answered it? Perlmutter's got the wrong analogy, Kenny! All I'm asking Israel to do is engage in a peace dialogue with Sadat, who has made clear his willingness to talk peace. Sadat is not a terrorist killing civilians the way the IRA does. He is clearly calling for not only a cease-fire, but real peace! That's the difference, damn it!"

Kennedy held up his hand as O'Brien tried to speak. "Larry, Kenny. Let me get to my point now. The fact is . . . " He lowered his voice, still mustering his courage to say what he was about to say. "I think . . . I think I have to refuse the latest military weapons request the Israelis have before Congress—"

The O Boys screamed "What?" in perfect-pitch unison. Less coordinated, they said, "You're outta your mind!" "You're crazy!" "You'll bust up the city votes in the big states!"

Kennedy, who had expected this reaction, now raised his voice. "Yes, O Boys, I thought about that—*don't think I didn't!* I may be president, but I'm not stupid! The way I'm starting to figure it—I mean, the way we look at it is this. Assume the worst. Say we lose the Jewish vote, which I don't think we will from the polling—at least we won't lose more than half. We still have a whole bunch of support in places where the Jewish vote isn't significant, and that includes some urban black neighborhoods, and working class white Catholic and Christian ones, too. There's a cultural shift going on down South. The unions are growing down South and even some other places in an integrated fashion, and that's good news for us as Democrats. The Northeast and major cities in other areas are more segregated than the South—imagine that, guys!—maybe due to our Bed-Sty programs. The blacks in those northern inner cities, though, are being strengthened as they act on their own—with federal and state help. The crime rates are down, and there's some intermarrying among white VISTA workers and local blacks, which makes things interesting, according to Shriver at HEW. And what do all these people have in common? *None* of them want another Arab-Israeli war, especially one that might affect East-West relations and our other relations in the Middle East. And as I said, I think most rank-and-file Jews, not the organization leaders, want peace, too. There! I've said it! Am I anti-Semitic? If I am, someone tell that bastard Sirhan Sirhan! There! I said *that* too!"

The O Boys froze on those last words.

Finally, after a long silence, O'Brien said, "You really want to do this, don't you?" Kennedy nodded in response.

"Then," said O'Brien, "do it *right*. Johnson did refuse to ship some extra military parts bound for Israel after Israel attacked Egypt in the '67 war, especially after that incident with our navy ship. And Ike did withhold military aid to Israel *before and after* the '56 war when Israel, along with England and France, attacked Egypt after Nasser closed down the Suez Canal to all commercial traffic. Ike said he thought Israel was being too aggressive in invading."

"I think I remember the fight between Ike and Israel after the Suez War, but *before*, too?" asked Kennedy, not quite believing what he heard.

"Yes. I heard all this from Ellsberg, who was talking to me a few weeks ago about us possibly threatening to cut back on a limited amount of military aid to Israel. I thought he was crazy then, and you're crazy now. I admit the Israelis did capitulate to Eisenhower in the end—and gave back the Suez Canal and the Sinai after the '56 War against Egypt—just like we want them to do for Sadat this time. But why do we want to risk the vote of—"

Kennedy interrupted, "But we're on stronger ground than Eisenhower. Unlike Nasser, Sadat is seeking peace—out in the open and clear—"

O'Brien, sensing that his boss was looking at this like an academic problem, interrupted, saying, "Mr. President, what Ike or even LBJ did is no precedent for us—unless you like the sound of 'one term clapping,' if I can get Zen Buddhist here. My kid told me about 'one hand clapping' or some horseshit like that. Look, if we decide to do this, we'd need Ellsberg, that Goldmann guy—definitely Goldmann—and we'll need Senator Ribicoff from Connecticut and Senator Metzenbaum from Ohio all standing around us when we drop this political stink bomb! We better have a whole *bunch* of Jews around us—including Sammy Davis Jr., too! *I mean it!* And those Jews are gonna have to have a lot of balls—tons of balls—to take the heat *they're* gonna get!"[11]

O'Donnell said, surprising himself, "Well, at least American Jews don't have guns . . . Do they?"

Kennedy and O'Brien laughed darkly. O'Donnell wasn't laughing at all.

In September 1971, President Kennedy met with Senators Ribicoff and Metzenbaum, Chester Bowles and Dan Ellsberg. The two senators, as independent of mind and spirit as they could be, immediately grasped the need for Israel to accept Sadat's peace offer. They said they would wholeheartedly support the administration. Immediately thereafter, Bowles told Congressional Foreign Affairs Committee members that the administration would not support any new military weaponry for Israel for "at least" the next six months "unless there is a change in attitude in the Israeli government regarding certain international developments."

The Cold War establishment, which disliked much of the Kennedy-Bowles foreign policy, and the military contractors lobby, which thrived on military exports and wars in proxy states, immediately sprang into action. This time the Jewish organizations, which had tended toward the liberal, dovish wing of the Democratic Party, joined that coalition. Together they demanded that President Kennedy "speak openly on the subject, with no behind-the-scenes advisers," in the words of Amos Perlmutter of the Anti-Defamation League. Kennedy was almost giddy at the response by these groups because it was just what O'Brien had predicted. "Let 'em at me," he told O'Brien, while wondering to himself, Am I asking for more trouble than I realize here?

Within forty-eight hours of the outraged responses of the Cold Warriors, military contractors, and Israeli lobbyists, the president appeared on television and radio before a nationwide audience with the two most prominent Jewish and Democratic United States senators, as well as Nahum Goldmann and Daniel Ellsberg. Kennedy said that the administration's decision to withhold new military weapons from Israel, but not spare parts for weapons sold previously to that country, was reached "after careful thought." Israel, said Kennedy, was currently able to defend itself "more than sufficiently."

Kennedy further said, "Our commitment to Israel remains as strong as it ever was, and we will continue to support Israel in the United Nations General Assembly, in the United Nations Security Council, and throughout the world. Let me also say, however, that our nation has a duty and an obligation to promote peace in the world. This is especially true where the belligerents are already well armed, and where our continued military support would likely undermine legitimate peace efforts being made by one of the belligerents."

The Soviet Union, after informing Sadat of the impending American policy announcement, announced earlier in the day that it was halting shipment of new weapons to Egypt. Sadat issued a statement saying he accepted the Russian position as being consistent with the "cause for peace." Kennedy, in his speech, noted these developments.

American Jewish opinion following the press conference was divided in every temple, in every organization, and within every family. Family arguments reached a fever pitch on the autumn Jewish holiday of Yom Kippur, the holiest day of the year for Jews around the world.

During these arguments, Jews who supported Israel's position against the president called those who supported the president "worse than Nazis." In reply, those who saw the need for peace with Egypt and also opposed the building of settlements on Arab lands said, "We don't believe in Israel doing to the Arabs what Hitler did to the Jews!"

On Yom Kippur evening, October 10, 1971, Rabbi Avraham Hecht, an Orthodox Rabbi in New York, cited the thirteenth-century rabbi, Maimonides in a public sermon. Hecht said, quoting Maimonides, that anyone who takes "any life or property of the Jewish people," or who "conspires" in this regard to take Jewish life or property, was "worthy of death." Maimonides, said Hecht, also noted that whoever murders such persons is "worthy of praise by the Lord our God."

Hecht's remarks were printed in the Jewish daily newspaper in New York, the *Forward*, the following week. When asked by the reporter if his sermon applied to the president of the United States, Rabbi Hecht replied, "There's an old saying, 'If the shoe fits . . . '"[12] A complaint was made to the FBI by one of the *Forward*'s many readers, and the FBI, led by J. Edgar Hoover himself, swooped down on the rabbi and arrested him for threatening the life of the president of the United States.

Immediately, First Amendment attorneys, some of them Jewish yet supportive of President Kennedy and bitterly opposed to Rabbi Hecht, came to Hecht's rescue and secured his release. The rabbi's constitutional rights may have been vindicated, but many non-Jews in mostly Christian America, particularly Catholic Americans who revered Robert Kennedy as a living saint, were apoplectic over Rabbi Hecht's statement. Catholic priests and Protestant ministers had to deal with anti-Semitic statements from parishioners across the country: "The Jews killed Christ! Now they want to kill our president!" became a growing and familiar refrain.

Many Christian clergy sought out those rabbis who had joined them on multireligious councils and groups. They stood alongside those rabbis as the latter denounced Hecht. Most of these rabbis were Conservative and Reform rabbis. Most Orthodox rabbis refused to publicly attack Hecht. Nonetheless, a large majority of the Orthodox recognized that President Kennedy, by setting forth a mere temporary policy, should not have necessarily qualified as someone in the category Maimonides described.

The American Israeli Political Action Committee, a lobbying arm of the Israeli government, joined the Anti-Defamation League and the American Jewish Committee, among other Jewish groups, in immediately denouncing Hecht. To its dismay, the ADL learned from their FBI sources that there were plenty of other death threats against Kennedy uttered by Christian business leaders on country club golf courses, black Muslim groups in the inner cities, and the like. Yet, unlike the FBI's response to Rabbi Hecht, who was not known to use a gun or be personally violent in any way, Hoover had made no "public relations arrests" of those other persons for uttering threats against President Kennedy.

A young executive with the ADL, Abraham Foxman, wrote about Hoover's selective security concerns in the *New York Times,* but it failed to generate any sympathy. If anything, it only served, as the *Washington Post's* moderate columnist David Broder wrote, "to fan more flames of anti-Semitism among our less educated citizens."

O'Brien read Foxman's article and ran down the hall to show it to Kennedy. O'Brien said, "You know, don't you, that Hoover went after that rabbi to keep screwing us up with the Jews. That's what Foxman might really be saying here. Foxman's a liberal guy, Bob. I've met him a few times here in town."

Kennedy said, "I know. Hoover's a bastard, pure and simple. God, I hope I can really get rid of him after the election next year—that is, if I win, which I'm starting to doubt."

The American Jewish organizations, after seeing Foxman's article generate more anger than sympathy, realized that Hecht had unwittingly unleashed a new strain of anti-Semitism in the United States that could permeate into the elite opinion in the power corridors of Washington and New York. Hecht's comments and the reaction to them raised once again the ominous question American Jewry had just put to rest after the Red Scare of the 1950s: whether Jewish Americans had a "dual loyalty," and perhaps *no* loyalty to the United States under particular circumstances. The American Jewish leadership, through their usual back-door channels to Israel, finally began to call upon Prime Minister Golda Meir and her government to immediately respond to Sadat's peace offer and the demands of President Kennedy's administration.

Hyman Bookbinder of the American Jewish Committee, who had been deeply critical of Kennedy's policy concerning Israel, suddenly changed his tune as only political pundits and lobbyists do—by ignoring what they had said before, or twisting it in a way that allowed them to say they now had "more facts," even if those facts were previously known. Bookbinder, writing again in the *New York Times* and speaking on NBC's *Meet the Press*, suddenly called on Israel to "begin the peace process that has eluded Israel all along," as if Sadat had not been standing there with his hand outstretched since February.

Ambassador Rabin spoke at length with Secretary Bowles in Washington and, after agreeing to recommend peace talks with Sadat, was ushered into the Oval Office to speak with President Kennedy. Kennedy called Prime Minister Golda Meir on the telephone to confirm that Israel was now in agreement with the administration. Kennedy said he hoped Mrs. Meir would make a public statement the next day to this effect. "Mrs. Meir, the United States and the Soviet Union are expecting to take an active role in these negotiations. I have received assurances from Ambassador Dobrynin, on behalf of the Soviet government, that the Soviets will join the United States in stating that Israel needs strong, secure borders and full diplomatic and cultural rights as a sovereign nation."

Meir was prepared for the call, as the Israelis had already instructed Rabin to support the peace efforts. Nonetheless, she wanted to make the Kennedy administration "beg for it," as Dayan said years later. Meir, in a tone that bordered on condescension, said she would respond "happily to our longtime and the most important ally, the United States of America. But how, Mr. President, will the Soviet Union say what you believe they will say if they do not recognize us as anything other than the 'Zionist' entity?"

The words shocked Kennedy. He looked at Chet Bowles and asked to "hold on, if you would, Mrs. Meir." Bowles asked Kennedy to step outside the room for a moment, leaving Rabin alone in the Oval Office. Bowles told Kennedy that the Soviets were set to announce, at the onset of the peace talks, that as a gesture of good faith, they would formally re-recognize the State of Israel. He also reminded Kennedy that the Soviets had kept this under wraps, sharing the information with only Bowles and Kennedy.

Kennedy and Bowles quickly returned to the Oval Office. Kennedy picked up the telephone and said to Prime Minister Meir, "Mrs. Meir, you have my word that when the negotiations begin, you will be very *pleasantly* surprised by how the Soviet Union will be treating the State of Israel. I just wish I could remember what I was told by Ambassador Dobrynin right now."

Unbeknownst to Kennedy and Bowles, the Israelis, whose agents had penetrated deep into official Washington and the foreign embassies, already knew the answer. The only question Meir had was whether to leak the information in the hope of derailing the process and embarrassing the Soviets in front of their Arab allies. This was quickly rejected, however. As Minister Dayan said, "Mrs. Meir, the more I have thought about peace with Egypt, the more I believe it can become part of our overall strategy concerning settlement building in the other territories and the dispersal of the Palestinians."

Mrs. Meir smiled as she listened to Dayan's new strategy: Israel must start building dozens of settlements in the West Bank and Gaza areas before the talks begin and then agree to "freeze" the building of "new" settlements, while demanding that the ones already started continue to be built. She knew there was more than one way to pursue her pet policy, which she believed vital for the survival of Israel. The bulldozers went out that very night into forty different areas that would later become "permanent" settlements in the West Bank and Gaza regions, which would continue to be "occupied" by the Israelis.

On Sunday, October 24, 1971, the Americans and the Russians jointly announced that the Israelis and Egyptians would enter into negotiations with each other and that the Soviet Union would recognize the State of Israel for the first time in many years. October 24 was chosen by the two superpowers because it also commemorated the day of the founding of the United Nations. Larry O'Brien thought this was a "nice touch for gearing up the 1972 campaign for reelection."

Bowles and Kennedy wanted King Hussein to join the peace talks, but the Jordanian king refused before the Israelis had a chance to reject the more comprehensive peace negotiations. King Hussein, according to his biographer, Edmund Morris, was starting to wonder whether having the West Bank back in Jordanian hands, particularly with a growing militant Palestinian organization in its midst, was worth the risk to his kingdom. Meanwhile, Syria, Libya, as well as other more Western-friendly Arab nations—including Saudi Arabia and Iran—voiced outrage at Sadat's "capitulation to the Zionist entity."

Thus, peace talks were conducted only between Israel and Egypt, as the Israelis and the Americans refused to give the Palestine Liberation Organization or the Palestinian people any voice in the matter. After months of often heated and painstaking negotiations in Geneva, Switzerland, a peace treaty was reached between Israel and Egypt on February 23, 1972. In the treaty, the Israelis gave back 68 percent of the Sinai and promised to freeze further new settlement building for at least one year—with the proviso that more settlements would be built in the West Bank and Gaza Strip if other Arab nations did not come to the peace table.

The final peace accords included nothing regarding the Palestinians. Despite the fact that Bowles was starting to side with Sadat on the issue of the Palestinians having a right to their own separate state outside of Jordan, the Israelis—and, most important, Kennedy, who was acting on advice from Larry O'Brien—refused to agree to such a provision. As Meir said to Secretary of State Bowles, "Let the Arab refugee problem be solved by Jordan. And Egypt and Syria can help them if they wish. For almost twenty years, the Jordanians had control of the West Bank and Gaza, or as we Israelis call those lands, Judea and Samaria. Yet, they did nothing for these refugees. Why should we suddenly do something for them—especially when Israel took in Jews from all the *other* Arab lands and nations for the past twenty-five years?"

Bowles responded that the Israelis had conquered Gaza and the West Bank, and that the Palestinians were now Israel's problem unless they gave back the land to Jordan under Resolution 242. However, since Jordan had not yet made peace with Israel, Bowles knew his argument would not be persuasive. He was, he told Kennedy, happy just to "put a lid" on the Middle East through the 1972 presidential election—or at least he hoped he had. Bowles comforted himself with his failure to include the Palestinians by saying to himself, Who says I can't be a hard-nosed realist like George Ball or Dean Acheson by considering domestic politics in my decision making?

As things turned out, the Middle East was relatively quiet for the rest of 1972 as the Russians told the Palestinians to halt terrorist activities and wait out the results of the American election. While Yasser Arafat and George Habash, two rival leaders among the Palestinians, listened to this advice, Abu Nidal, another Palestinian leader, broke from the Palestine Liberation Organization. Nidal said to the Palestinian secular leadership, "The Palestinians have waited long enough! This peace treaty with Egypt is a hoax designed to deprive us of our land! There can be no peace with Israel! The Russians are Western imperialists no different than the Americans!"

Abu Nidal, backed by Libyan funds, immediately organized a new terrorist group known as the Black September group, in honor of those killed by King Hussein in September 1970. One would think with that name his group was planning to attack King Hussein. Instead, in September 1972, Nidal and his terrorist organization kidnapped and killed Israeli athletes during the Summer Olympics held in Munich, Germany. As Bowles said to Kennedy, "Those murderers just made it more difficult for us to pressure the Israelis—at least for a while. And what's worse is they call themselves Black September because of what Hussein did to them, but then they kill *Israelis*. The Arabs . . . I don't know what to do with them . . . "

"I don't get it either, Chet," said the president. Kennedy shook his head, wondering how anyone with an ounce of political savvy could think a massacre of civilian athletes could possibly help the cause of an oppressed people. "I think, Chet, we've pushed the Israelis far enough for the time being. I wish I could better understand Arabs. The only ones I really like are Sadat and King Hussein, who I sometimes wish would just make peace with *his* Palestinians and allow the ones in the West Bank, and maybe Gaza, to move across the Jordan River. But he's got his hands full trying to look tough against Israel for the Syrians and the Palestinian guerillas who won't back down—at least until Israel recognizes the Palestinians as a nationality. And the Israelis obviously don't want the Palestinians to overthrow Hussein either. Although I remember you telling me a couple of Israeli generals have thought about it . . . " His voice trailed as he sighed. "I've said it before and I'll say it again. What a web of hatred and recrimination!"

Bowles pursed his lips and nodded in agreement. He then said, "Mr. President, I never knew what we were setting in motion when we set up those elections in Vietnam. I sometimes wonder if it's all related . . . I can't help but think it may all be . . . related. The thing that concerns me is where this all leads. The Greek military regime was just overthrown, and the usual Cold War crowd wanted us to support a countercoup. We refused, and now the Turks are considering invading the island of Cyprus. We sent our navy out to the area, and that stopped that. But we're still in a mess in Cyprus, even with the new Greek civilian government—who are Socialists, at least in name."

The president said, "I agree, Chet, and it seems almost like Cyprus is another Northern Ireland or Arab-Israeli situation. But there's some chance with that Archbishop Makarios fellow—maybe."

"But it's not just there, Mr. President. It's like we're dealing with a different set of dominoes—if I can use President Eisenhower's metaphor for a moment. I mean, even as the Russians and the Chinese are retrenching or having major internal problems, Latin America is brewing with revolutionary activity—and yet the Russians are doing little or nothing to support them. The guerillas steal more of the American-made arms from the military regimes we support than what the Russians could sell or give them. Our 'self-determination' philosophy is being ingested nearly everywhere. What truly worries me is that our pursuit of 'self-determination' is being ingested by our own Native Americans in the Dakotas, especially South Dakota. Some people in Congress, including Senator Melcher in Montana, are starting to support radical Indian demands for reparations and land to honor the treaties our country broke almost a hundred years ago. There are leftists in Europe who say we acted toward Indians no differently than Chiang Kai-Shek acts with native Taiwanese, or the South Africans with the apartheid system, or even Israelis with the Palestinians if we don't—"

"Yeah, I read some of that crap, too, Chet. Let's just make it clear starting between us, okay? The United States will *not* give land back to Indians in South Dakota or anywhere! That's like saying a state can secede from the Union! Joe Melcher's an eccentric, Chet, kind of a Gene McCarthy. Senator McGovern—he's from South Dakota, as you know full well—he laps up the Indians' votes, and even *he* doesn't buy that radical Indian garbage! The Puerto Ricans just voted down statehood for Puerto Rico—*again!* And we're supposed to hand over South Dakota to the Indians like we were South Africa? Bull! The Indians are getting plenty of funding for the reservations— Ramsey Clark says he's going after the South Dakota state government for discrimination against Indians, and he's keeping a very tight rein on the FBI to stay the hell out of that state! Hoover's a different problem. He acts like the militant Indians are as bad as Communists. Maybe they're worse, maybe not. But the last thing I want is a confrontation between the FBI and the police on one side and militant Indians—with guns—on the other! McGovern gave me the whole story a few weeks ago after I read that article on Indian 'reparations'—where was it? The *Nation* magazine?"

"Yes, it was in that magazine, Mr. President. I don't want to belabor the point, but I do know from Attorney General Clark that the American Indian Movement—that's kind of their Black Panthers—are divided as to whether to work with our administration for antidiscrimination protections and development of the reservations. We've got Secretary of Commerce Learson investing government funds for circuit board manufacturing on a couple of reservations—with unions and good wages. But again, there are those who want no part of us 'European white race men.'"

"Wonderful, Chet, wonderful," said the president sarcastically. "Is there no group out there with legitimate concerns and needs who doesn't have some nut-case element who wants to fight or kill in the name of their so-called 'justice'? I am getting mighty tired of this continued rationalization of violence—especially after this latest peace treaty with the Egyptians and Israelis! The peace money we bribed the Israelis and Egyptians with—it was just over one billion dollars, which is almost all of our foreign aid last year!—was the clincher on that treaty getting signed. We can't afford to keep bribing people with money to do the right thing!"

Kennedy thought to himself, Can we?

Bowles thought a moment as well. Then he recalled what Defense Secretary Warnke had said when Senator Dole cornered Warnke the day the Egyptian-Israeli peace treaty was signed. Dole made the same criticism about "bribery for peace." Warnke replied, "We spend an awful lot on weapons and war, Senator. Why not spend some of that money on peace?"

When Bowles told that story to Kennedy, Kennedy smiled. "You know, Chet, Paul's right. Why *not* spend some of that money on peace for a change? I just hope enough people buy that argument this November when we're up for reelection. Otherwise I'll be quoting George Bernard Shaw about asking 'Why not?' in some Midwestern law school. I bet Ethel would be happier, though . . . "

Chapter 25

RUSSIAN SUMMER AND CHINESE FALL

The fall of 1971 brought the first nuclear peace treaty in almost a decade. In Geneva, Switzerland, the Soviets and the Americans agreed to an Antiballistic Missile Treaty that formally prohibited American and Russian research into missile defense systems. Each side, in pursuing the treaty, believed the "stability of nuclear terror" would be endangered if a nation's nuclear missiles could be blown out of the sky by another nation's "antimissile" weaponry. The technology, agreed the negotiators, was less than perfect and would still result in some nuclear bombs getting through with significant nuclear destruction. Thus, the terror remained even if the new military technology worked. The most compelling reason for each government to enter into the treaty was that the technology seemed terribly far off and therefore pursuit was not considered economically sound.

Kennedy was proud of concluding the treaty, but at that point, he was already focusing on other foreign policy matters. In mid-September 1971, Kennedy called a special meeting of Secretaries Bowles and Warnke, the O Boys, NSC Director Ellsberg, UN Ambassador Young, and CIA Director Blee to discuss what Kennedy saw as his next important initiative. Kennedy had not originally thought of inviting Ambassador Young, but Bowles specifically asked the president to include the ambassador.

Bowles said, "Mr. President, Ambassador Young is highly regarded in the UN, as you know. As many other UN Ambassadors seek his advice or bounce ideas off him, he has told us more 'secrets' about many nations than most CIA spies learn in ten years."

Despite the implication of Bowles' crack about the CIA, CIA Director Blee had become, during the year, a highly regarded adviser to both Kennedy and Bowles. After deciding not to resign over the Allende episode almost a year before, Blee had thrown in his lot with Kennedy's "Commie-loving" administration, as some of his agency friends continued to call it. It was, he wrote in his diary (released after his death in the year 2000), a decision he first made with anger, as in "I'm staying in to keep an eye on these guys." Then, as he saw the Russians leaving Eastern Europe, he decided that Bowles and the president were not only *not* naïve, as some of his Cold Warrior friends continued to say, but more effective in undermining the threat of dictatorial systems such as Communism than earlier administrations had been.

With the zeal of a convert, Blee began to fire or remove old-guard CIA agents from nations such as Chile, where nationalization of IT&T and the copper holdings proceeded apace, and where Allende kept his promise about not nationalizing other American businesses. Allende, however, insisted on supporting unions for workers in a variety of foreign and domestic businesses in order to increase workers' purchasing power. With the rise in wages, Chileans began to demand consumer goods, which caused American businesses, from soft drink makers to jeans manufacturers, to begin to build factories in Chile to meet that rising demand. Bowles, by 1974, would begin talks with Allende about involving Chile in an experiment of creating a "free trade" zone between America and Chile now that the latter had a strong economic basis in which to develop further.

But in September 1971, the issue on the foreign-policy-strategy-meeting table was not Chile or even the growing diplomatic rift between Israel and the United States. It was China and Russia . . . and the potential for war between those two Communist behemoths.

Kennedy opened his remarks at this meeting by saying, "Gentlemen, I have brought you here this morning to talk about China, a subject we have been speaking of more and more about in recent weeks. The border dispute between the Russians and the Chinese has gone beyond so-called 'incidents.' Two thousand troops are estimated to have died last week in fighting along the Manchurian border, according to Ambassador Dobrynin. CIA Director Blee has confirmed this figure with his sources as well."

Blee slowly nodded in agreement at the remark. Kennedy then asked Blee to expand upon this information, whereupon Blee told the gathered foreign policy and political advisers that China was splitting into two factions: One led by Chou En-Lai and the other by Lin Piao. To secure the support of xenophobic and hungry peasants, the competing Chinese leaders had recently made bellicose statements regarding the Soviets, with both hinting that nuclear weapons could be used if casualties and border fighting escalated. However, both the Russians and American intelligence believed that Chou was more likely to deal with the West, including Russia, and was less likely to resort to nuclear weapons.

Kennedy added that Ambassador Dobrynin informed him there were still those in the Russian Politburo who would rather take advantage of China's precarious internal situation for military gain, particularly after the hostilities that left so many Russians dead the week before, than find a way to resolve the border issues.

The reason for the meeting was twofold: Whether to recognize China now, and if so, what should the United States be trying to accomplish? There were also political layers below these questions such as whether the U.S. government's recognition of China meant that the U.S. no longer recognized Chiang Kai-Shek's claim over China from his fortress in Taiwan. Further, could the United States recognize both China and Taiwan as independent nations? What would conservatives and Republicans in Congress say or do in response? On the other hand, if there really was the potential for a nuclear confrontation between China and Russia, could the administration afford to wait much longer as the situation along the Russian-Chinese border deteriorated?

After much argument among the participants over whether to recognize Communist China unilaterally or bilaterally, act as a peacemaker with the Russians and Chinese, send the Seventh Fleet to help Chiang liberate China from Taiwan, or push for free elections in Taiwan for both Taiwanese native groups and Chiang's Chinese minority, Kennedy ended the meeting feeling he had "more confusion than solutions here."

After the meeting, Kennedy asked Bowles to stay and talk. Bowles was glad to stay because he wanted to discuss a possible scenario to get around what Kennedy kept calling the "politics of recognition."

"Well, sir," Bowles began with some unusual hesitancy, "the idea is more George Kennan's than mine. It goes against my better nature, but I . . . well . . . Mr. Kennan told me a story at lunch yesterday when I was discussing our dilemma and—"

Kennedy, frustrated at not yet having a strategy he believed in, said sharply, "Chet, cut the diplomatic pleasantries. Just tell me. What's Kennan's political strategy?"

"Well, sir, it seems that in early 1946 or so, Truman was wondering how to convince the American people that the Russians weren't trustworthy—at a time when many Americans were just wanting to have all our troops come home from Europe and Japan and not bother with international affairs. It seems that, at one point in a discussion Truman was having with the Republican Senator Arthur Vandenberg, Vandenberg told Truman he would have to 'scare the hell out of the American people' to secure sufficient funding for a military buildup against the Russians. There's even a memo I found afterwards in our State Department files that shows Vandenberg put this in writing."

"I'm not sure of Kennan's point, though, Chet," said Kennedy impatiently.

Bowles quickly added, "This is why I'm not sure I want to even offer this advice." Taking a deep breath, Bowles said, "The point is to scare the American people into believing the threat of nuclear war between Russia and China is even more imminent than we currently think it is. Our goal would be to speed up the process, for domestic political purposes, to reach our policy goal—and our policy goal is to recognize China and be in a position to mediate between the two Communist nations to avoid the real nuclear threat that's coming down the pike. With the threat of nuclear war, our domestic opponents will have a harder time justifying their opposition on the usual anti-Communist grounds. There. I said it."

Kennedy was struck dumb. This strategy went against his newer, more liberated nature as well. After some moments of silence he said to Bowles, "But suppose someone says, 'Who cares if two Communist nations blow themselves up? Now what?'"

Bowles breathed deeply—again. "Nuclear winds blow from the Far East and through America, Mr. President. Nuclear fallout knows no ideologies or languages or national boundaries. Kennan's point is that the threat of nuclear fallout is strong enough that most John Birch Society members in Orange County, California, would support mediating between Russia and China. I should say, though, there is also a potential political fallout: As Kennan told me, Truman was unable to control the anti-Communist rhetoric he set in motion. His setting up loyalty oaths and blacklists became grist for extreme anti-Communists and, eventually, his political opponents, who could not tell the difference between a real Communist and a strong New Deal liberal— meaning, the things we have come to associate with what we call 'McCarthyism.' The foreign policy scare tactics also undermined many of Truman's domestic proposals, although Kennan said he thought Truman never believed much in national health care or, for that matter, most of FDR's New Deal. In thinking about this strategy, however, I have not been able to figure out what we're ushering in by going in this direction."

Kennedy, speechless at what Bowles was proposing, but finding it could be the strategic solution he had been searching for, told Bowles he needed to sleep on this strategy and think about it. Bowles replied that he, too, needed to sleep in order to hopefully reject such a strategy. Said Bowles, "Mr. President, this sort of fear mongering is what got this nation into trouble in Vietnam. It created a hysteria that neither Truman, Acheson, or anyone except a military man, Eisenhower, could possibly control. On the other hand, history will not be kind to us if there's a nuclear confrontation—and the evidence which we see as tentative and remote would be read to be a stronger warning than we presently know. I guess that's the politics behind even this strategy, isn't it?"

The next morning, Kennedy woke up knowing this was the strategy to pursue, despite the risks Bowles outlined. Kennedy, however, realized he needed to run this scenario by Ambassador Dobrynin in order to see if the Russians were interested in the United States mediating the dispute and if the Russians would stay silent on the subject of nuclear confrontation for a few weeks while his administration announced its intention to recognize Communist China.

The Russian Ambassador surprised and alarmed Kennedy by saying he was less sure that Kennedy was misleading anyone if he told the American people that a nuclear confrontation between the Soviets and the People's Republic of China could occur. Dobrynin then immediately set off to Moscow to consult with Foreign Minister Gromyko and the Politburo over Kennedy's proposal and request. A week later, Dobrynin came back with word that the Soivet Union would welcome the United States mediating

Soviet claims with China after the United States recognized the mainland Chinese government. Soviet approval, said Dobrynin, was not as easy to secure as he thought it would be, but he would not elaborate.

Dobyrnin also said, however, that Foreign Minister Gromyko strongly insisted a top American representative travel in secret to China in order to give Chou En-Lai an opportunity to strategize for Chou's even more complicated domestic purposes. Gromyko suggested that the American representative travel through Albania, an Eastern European nation that was now closer to China than Russia, but one in which Russia still had their "assets"—meaning spies.

Bowles and Kennedy decided that Dan Ellsberg should make the trip. Before Ellsberg left on his secret mission at the end of October, he called upon some old State Department "China hands" who had been "retired" since the Red Scare of the 1950s. These former State Department advisors, including John Carter Vincent and John Stewart Service, had been kicked out of the State Department for being too prescient with regard to the Chinese Revolution during the 1940s, which in the parlance of the immediate post-World War II period, made them "Communists" or "fellow travelers of Communists." Each of the China hands told Ellsberg they were "honored" to assist their country once again.

As Ellsberg told Bowles the day before his trip to China, "They gave me quite a bit of insight, which allowed me to read between the lines, as it were, from our latest intelligence reports. We lost some good people during the Red Scare, Mr. Secretary."

"It was not a pleasant time for career diplomats," said Bowles vaguely.

Ellsberg traveled to Albania and eventually to Peking (as Beijing was called at the time). Once in Peking, he met and spoke with Chou En-Lai and stayed in Peking for two days. He learned that Chou had just escaped a second assassination attempt in less than one year. Ellsberg was the first American to confirm the information about the assassination attempts on Chou. Ellsberg also confirmed Dobrynin's parting information that China was in an escalating civil war. In speaking to refugees huddled in Peking, through an interpreter Ellsberg brought along, Ellsberg concluded that as many as two million Chinese may have died as a result of fighting and famine in the central, western, and southern sections of China.

Kennedy, sitting in his office with Bowles and Ellsberg listening to Ellsberg's report, murmured in response, "Killing one man is murder, yet killing millions is often merely a statistic."

Ellsberg heard that murmured sentence and answered, "That 'statistic,' as we could call it, sir, might be even higher, though Minister Chou told me a figure that was one-tenth of that, which is still not a small number. Worse, when I initially made clear that the United States was ready to recognize the People's Republic of China, the Minister wondered aloud whether our recognition would come too late. When I asked what he meant by 'too late,' he walked over to a globe in his office, pointed to northern Manchuria near the Soviet border, and said, 'Here . . . is what I mean by too late.' He then moved his hands and arms in the motion most people used to create a mushroom cloud."

Ellsberg admitted he forgot his diplomatic face and gasped—as did Kennedy and Bowles upon hearing it.

Ellsberg, seeing the reactions of his respective bosses, immediately continued. "Chou said to me, 'No, Mr. Ellsberg, this would not be *our* doing. What I mean is that Lin Piao has access, we fear, to a nuclear device—and shows little fear that he would use such a device. We are also concerned that one of the Russian generals in charge of the Russian side of the Manchurian border, seems to have, per our . . . sources . . . perhaps speculation . . . some interest in, shall we say, making history.' Chou also made clear he did not wish to test Chairman Mao's unfortunate remark some years ago to the French ambassador that a nuclear war would not mean the end of China, even if it meant the end of smaller nations such as France."

Seeing that Kennedy and Bowles were still hardly breathing, Ellsberg said, "But Mr. President, Mr. Secretary, there is good news here. Really. Minister Chou told me that he and Chairman Mao are prepared to accept American recognition and opening of diplomatic relations—and to have our country mediate the border dispute between the Soviet Union and the People's Republic of China. Even better, I asked Chou if he would hold to his public statements, going back to the 1950s, that China would be willing to submit the issue of Taiwan's sovereignty to the United Nations as a condition for China's entering that body as a member nation. He said he would"

Kennedy and Bowles almost leaped from their chairs, with Kennedy saying, "Then it's settled! So, why all the worry, Dan?"

Ellsberg replied, "Well, um, while I got this commitment from Minister Chou, I didn't get hardly anything from Chairman Mao. Mao is clearly incapacitated. He appears to have had a stroke earlier in the year. He can speak, but he slurs his words in either Chinese or his very limited English. If Chou is in charge and Mao is merely an old and infirm figurehead, then we have now laid the groundwork for recognition and mediation. Chou did introduce me to Liu Shao Chi and Deng Shao Ping, two Communist officials who barely survived the early days of the Cultural Revolution. If Chou fails to rally the people, or if Mao decides to change back to Lin Piao if he doesn't like what's going on—Lin was Mao's first choice to succeed him just a couple of years ago or so—then, this could all come to naught . . . or worse."

Kennedy said, "Dan, it's worth that risk. I'm now more worried about the immediate political reaction from the Republicans and those who are part of Chiang Kai-Shek's Taiwan lobby. If I were a Republican operative, I'd be accusing us of not only being soft on Communism, but actually helping Communist adversaries become friends again. That is as pro-Communist as one could get in American politics. I'm glad, though, that I can now focus on something I understand—like American politics."

Bowles and Ellsberg, less absorbed with domestic political concerns than the president, began, after the meeting, to put together a detailed plan of Red China recognition and logistics for a summit to head off a potential nuclear confrontation between China and Russia. Bowles dreamt of having Kennedy reprise the role Teddy Roosevelt was said to have played in resolving the Russian-Japanese War of 1904.

Then, suddenly everything went awry. Just after Thanksgiving, the CIA learned through its agents in Thailand that Chairman Mao, on November 16, 1971, suffered a massive stroke. It was Mao's second stroke in less than a year. As a result, Mao became completely incapacitated and would remain so for more than two months. According to Andrew Young's sources at the UN, there was much speculation in and around China that Mao was likely to die before the end of the year.

Inside China, Lin Piao was already acting in response to the rumors that Mao was dying. He now intensified his battle against what he publicly called "the impostor leadership of Chou En-Lai and his gang of counter-revolutionaries." He also leaked to conservative American sources, via "refugees" in Thailand, that Ellsberg had visited Chou. His goal was to split American opinion to stop any Russian-American coalition likely to back Chou.

The president refused to make a public comment in response to this leak, but press secretary Jack Newfield asked reporters, "Who you gonna believe? Us or Lin Piao?" The mainstream media suppressed the story, which kept most of the American public in the dark.[1]

The next day, from a province deep inside western China, Lin Piao announced over shortwave radio that he was the "undisputed" heir to Mao. He also said that he had control of "many weapons," including "one of the most powerful weapons known to mankind." He said he would never use such "force in the first instance. However, I am warning all those who attempt to defeat our movement for justice and freedom that we will stop at nothing to defeat the white-devil-led impostors who have overthrown our beloved leader, Chairman Mao, and installed their puppet regime—a regime acting on orders from the Americans and Generalissimo Chiang in Taiwan. The running dog Americans have become wedded to the running dog Soviets—and we must never forget that the Soviets, under Stalin and his successors, continually betrayed China and our beloved Chairman Mao before and after our revolution!"

The Soviet Union immediately went on nuclear alert in response to Lin's statement. Kennedy, upon receiving word of this from Director Blee, personally placed a call to President Kosygin to request that the Soviets "stand down." When Kosygin asked—almost demanded—why the Americans had not yet announced the recognition of China, meaning Chou's China, Kennedy apologized to Kosygin and promised the Soviet leader it was coming "within days." He also promised the Soviets that the United States would come to the Soviet's aid if Lin Piao attacked the Russians with any nuclear or other significant weapons.

Kosygin said, "I'm glad to hear that, but it does not give me much comfort, Mr. President. What we need more than ever is an American announcement on China. I will speak with the members of the central committee regarding your request that we stand down from nuclear alert."

A long twelve hours later, the Russians went off nuclear alert. Kennedy then asked Bowles to brief leading members of Congress on the situation in China and the need for recognizing Chou's leadership in Communist China in order for the United States to act as a peace broker between the Chinese and the Russians. At his briefing, Bowles emphasized the need to prevent nuclear devastation in the Far East and in southern Russia and repeated his line to Kennedy about nuclear winds blowing toward the United States. As Bowles told Kennedy afterwards, there was now little need for any Vandenberg- or Truman-style exaggeration or war scaring in light of Lin's statement and Mao's second stroke.

While Bowles spoke with Congress members, Kennan, Ellsberg, and Galbraith worked with Kennedy to prepare the president's speech announcing diplomatic recognition of China, which speech was to be delivered the next morning.

In his speech to the nation, Kennedy told his fellow Americans and the world that relations between Russia and China had deteriorated to the point where the Russians had recently gone on—and then off—nuclear alert (Kennan had secured Russian permission, through Dobrynin to allow the Americans to announce this). Kennedy then stated that, as part of securing Russia's pledge to stand down—he purposefully avoided using the name "Soviet Union" to soften the Communist angle—

> . . . it is now necessary for the United States to play a role similar to that played by President Theodore Roosevelt between Japan and Russia in 1904. And that is to bring peace to two nations who have found themselves in a spiral of recrimination and belligerence. I therefore declare that, in order for the United States to fulfill its historic mission of being a world peacemaker, that we must officially recognize the People's Republic of China as a nation with standing in world affairs. We take this very important, if not drastic step, not only for the Chinese and Russian peoples, but to avoid a potential nuclear confrontation between those two nations—a confrontation that would have catastrophic consequences not only for the people of those lands, but throughout the entire planet.
>
> In recognizing the People's Republic of China, I must reiterate that the United States does not in any way diminish its support for the people of Taiwan and the leadership of Taiwan. Both President Chiang Kai-Shek, residing in Taiwan, and Chairman Mao currently

agree that there is only "one China." But we must all discuss, at the United Nations Assembly and Security Council, soon, though not at present, whether Taiwan is part of that "one" China or whether it should be its own sovereign nation.

The American people, who had not been previously informed of the Soviet nuclear alert or any of these other matters, were shocked at the president's words. The fact that Russia and China were on the brink of nuclear war, as Kennedy hoped, made the issue of recognizing Communist China or whether China included Taiwan seem very small.

General Abrams, running hard on his anti-Communist philosophy, did his best to be skeptical, but he finally realized what some former Nixon aides now working for him long knew: that Kennedy had again managed to combine hawkish and dovish sentiments in a way that was difficult to directly criticize. At his own press conference, Abrams had challenged the president with a rhetorical question: "How do we know this administration, which continues to take a dangerously soft approach in dealing with the Communist threat, isn't overreacting to a somewhat tense though not necessarily dire situation between two Communist nations? If we wish to become involved in this alleged dispute, perhaps we should be asking President Chiang Kai-Shek, the true ruler of *all* China, to also participate in these discussions that concern *all* of the Chinese people."

Reagan, not about to be outdone by Abrams, said that according to his "sources," the people of China were "ready to reembrace Chiang Kai-Shek and reject the Communist-atheistic propaganda that has led to so much death and destruction in China." When White House reporters asked Newfield for a response, he said he would only reply "as a senior Kennedy administration official," which meant off-the-record. He then quipped, "Who are Governor Reagan's sources? *Reader's Digest* magazine? *Arizona Trailways*? The John Birch Society's *American Opinion* magazine?" Newfield then sent the reporters to a CIA representative who said, again off-the-record, that the CIA had not found any support for Chiang on the mainland. In their stories, the reporters noted that Reagan had not provided any sources for his statement, nor did sources within the CIA agree with Governor Reagan's comments.

Roth, who had recently announced his presidential candidacy, responded a day later. Roth's advisers convinced him to strike a more moderate tone than Reagan and Abrams, particularly after their review of initial polling that showed strong support for the president. Roth said in his first public statement on the subject, "While we must back our president in a time of crisis, we must also be diligent and careful as we navigate any course we pursue." As usual, "moderate" in this type of situation meant being vague.

Back in China, Chou En-Lai hoped the American announcement of recognition would unite the military in support of his leadership in Peking. But recognition had the opposite effect, at least at first. Upon hearing the news, the

People's Liberation Army suffered two significant defections among its generals. One of those generals, Li Peng, said, "The last time America tried to 'help' China, it was back in the late nineteenth century—and they merely exploited us further."

Later that same day, Madame Mao, herself an increasingly significant rival to Chou, said, "The Japanese defeated the Russians in their war at the beginning of our century. But the Americans, under the guise of neutrality, took away most of Japan's victory. Americans are westerners first—and always will be."

The government in Peking became very unsteady as a result of the president's announcement, and China's civil war entered an intense and bloody period as the winter storms descended. Civil war raged deep inside the countryside but also spilled into the streets of Shanghai and, for two days, into Peking. Mao's wife, sensing a "change in the political wind," as one biographer wrote, attempted to join the Lin Piao faction with the two defecting generals. However, all three were killed when air force pilots loyal to Chou shot down their plane over eastern Chinese airspace. It was reported as an accident in the Chinese newspapers, and western intelligence had no evidence at the time to rebut that claim.

Chou secured most of the military's support as he convinced most soldiers that money and food would flow from America if Lin Piao were subdued. By the time Mao regained consciousness in January 1972, Chou and his forces had already secured China's main cities. The hardest battles continued in the countryside, but Chou's forces moved decisively and with swift, deadly force against anyone standing in their way. Unfortunately, this included many young people who were members of the Red Guard or sympathetic to the Guard. China was, as the radical Australian journalist Wilfred Burchett said, "killing its own children to stay alive."

To further assist Chou in his drive to hold China together during this precarious moment, Mao agreed to speak to the nation. The speech was carried by Chinese television and radio and printed in newspapers. Mao, slurring his words due to the effects from the stroke, told the Chinese people that Chou was the rightful heir to his leadership and "is now the true leader of our fair but bloodied land." As for Chou's rival, Lin Piao, Mao said, "Lin Piao has lost his sense of China as a nation, as a fair maiden to be cherished and loved. Lin, in his individualist thirst for power, has rent China asunder by chaos, war, and dissension." Whether from ignorance, stoicism or self-denial, Mao never mentioned his now deceased wife or how the Cultural Revolution he had instituted in the late 1960s had figured in all this chaos, famine, war, and dissension.

Mao went on to say that securing peace must be the paramount and only goal for the Chinese people. "Peace," he said, "requires a strong and deep sacrifice. It is a sacrifice that is perhaps greater than the sacrifice one must make in a time of war."

He then read from the last stanza of one of the earliest poems he had written in the 1930s during the Chinese Civil War against Chiang Kai-Shek and

Chiang's so-called Nationalist Party. The poem was entitled, "Kunlun Mountain (The Abode of the Blessed)":

I say to the high mountains:
'Why so high? Why so much snow?'
Could I but lean on heaven and draw my precious sword,
And cut you in three pieces,
I would send one to Europe,
The second I would give to America,
The third I would keep for China.
So there would be a great peace on earth,
For all the world would share in your
Warmth and cold.

Then, in a strong, but plaintive tone, he said, "Comrades! What, after all, is a mere set of mountains in the vastness—and immortal history—of China? My children, we must have peace, not war. And we must respect and follow the leadership shown by Chou En-Lai in this precious moment. Lin Piao must stop this madness—or we must stop him, together. China must be ready to take her place again in the world. She cannot do this if she cannot have peace within herself. We must rescue our fair land from Lin Piao and those who would destroy us as a nation. I wish you all health, strength, and peace. Good night, my children."

Decades afterward, people in China remembered where they were when Mao spoke or when they first read what he said. The Chinese people were largely against this civil war as it only worsened the latest famine. The Cultural Revolution, with its excessive political rhetoric regarding proletarians, imperialists, workers, and dialectical materialism, had also left most Chinese mentally, physically, and morally exhausted.

Mao's speech convinced most people in rural China that it was necessary to take sides once and for all—and to take action against Lin Piao. Best estimates indicated that up to 70 percent of the peasantry and rank-and-file soldiers believed in Mao much as their forebears had revered the "holy emperors" of ancient China. If the emperor said, "Black is white," then black would become white. Once Chairman Mao said Chou, not Lin Piao, was the true leader who had "inherited" Maoist values, that was enough. And because those "values" had become based more upon worship than reason, Mao's words unleashed powerful emotions in the peasants and soldiers that were more hateful than loving and more vengeful than forgiving. The tide of the civil war over the next weeks turned in Chou En-Lai's favor and against Lin Piao, as Chou, the United States, and the Soviet Union had hoped. But the result was another nineteen million Chinese killed, mostly in the countryside.

On February 27, 1972, Lin Piao was killed while on his way to an airport in Lanzhou, deep within central China. Lin had planned to escape to the mountains of Afghanistan, but his own troops, who felt betrayed at Lin's "cowardice," killed him and his entourage.[2]

In the United States, meanwhile, there was an initial curiosity about the small, sympathetic figure of Mao reading poetry, talking of peace, and giving, in literary terms, a famous Chinese mountain to the Americans. Assorted leftists and certain Hollywood stars such as Shirley MacLaine, who wrongly thought Mao's Cultural Revolution was something akin to a garden party of creativity and a celebration of freedom, initially convinced some Americans that a poetry-reading leader could not be a mass murderer.

The backlash in the United States against "Chinese agrarian reformers and poets" began a short time later, however, as reports filtered in regarding Chou's consolidation of control in China. As with other civil wars in peasant societies, "consolidation" meant the continued killing, with peasants using pitchforks and pickaxes, of collaborators of Lin Piao, and government bureaucrats and related busybodies carrying out political retribution against enemies, political and personal. It would take decades, despite American recognition and foreign aid, for China to begin to rebuild itself as a stable nation.

As the young Chinese writer Chen Jo-his wrote in her memoir of these events, *China Fires*, the reprisals and killing ironically intensified after the defeat of Lin Piao, for the hatred among those siding with Chou and those siding with Lin Piao had become a personal matter. As a result, wrote Chen, "many noncombatants were thrown into the hot, warring caldron and renamed 'collaborators' to justify their murder. Both sides contained many who enjoyed this spectacle as there was no longer any right or wrong, but merely the will to gain or regain power—or exact revenge. The fight between Lin Piao and Chou En-Lai over the future of China let loose the rage burning inside a hungry people who were frustrated, angry, and betrayed by the twentieth-century promises of utopia, independence, and liberation."[3]

The "consolidation" also provided the pretext for American conservatives,[4] as part of their overall dissatisfaction with the "leftist-unionist" Kennedy administration, to begin to ask, "Why didn't the United States back Chiang Kai-Shek in his quest to restore his leadership over mainland China?" In some ways, at least to later generations' ears, this aspect of the debate over the situation in China was a farcical reenactment of the debate that had followed Mao's ascendancy in 1949 of "Who [in America] lost China?"—as if China was "ours" to lose.

It did not take long for the China lobby friends of Generalissimo Chiang to tell their version of recent history. The story of the United States' refusal to support Chiang Kai-Shek was initially leaked to the *Washington Star,* the *Manchester* (New Hampshire) *Union Leader,* the *Indianapolis Star,* and other "friendly" newspapers. While the facts are largely undisputed, the interpretation of the events continued to be debated for years.

On December 1, 1971, Chiang Kai-Shek decided that he must act to retake China, especially as he heard the same rumors that Lin Piao had heard regarding Mao's imminent death. Chiang began to amass his half-million troops for an amphibious assault on Shanghai and Peking, which also included air support. His plan was to secure a position on the mainland and then move westward against the various pro-Chou and pro-Lin troops, who, he believed, would continue fighting each other the way anarchists and Communists in Spain had fought against each other instead of against Fascist General Franco during the 1930s.

Chiang and his military advisers assumed the "silent majority" of peasants would herald his "triumphant return, just as they cheered on the Americans against the Japanese invaders in World War II," he wrote in a letter to his friend, Claire Booth Luce.[5]

Kennedy immediately learned of Chiang's plans from CIA Director Blee. After reviewing CIA reports of the situation in China, and Chiang's prospects if he went through with his plans to return to China, Kennedy personally called Chiang on the White House hot line. He demanded that Chiang pull back his forces. He also told Chiang that the United States would most likely block any attempt by Chiang to invade. "There is no intelligence—and believe me, I've *checked*—that says the Chinese people are waiting with open arms for you, General. Far from it! Those people are past their revolution, but they are not ready for you and your political party again either. I'll stake my entire administration and our nation's future on this, General, if I have to. There is no way we are going to risk nuclear war here, especially when our intelligence estimates tell us Chou En-Lai is likely to defeat Lin Piao, despite what this latest round of battles is telling us."

Blee had been gathering intelligence along China's borders with Vietnam, Bruma, Pakistan, and Thailand, mostly from refugees. He was also cooperating with the Russian KGB in gathering intelligence information. Blee thought to himself, I never thought this would happen—Russian and American intelligence agents cooperating on anything! Blee's intelligence coincided with what the Russians concluded: People still remembered that during the 1930s, Chiang's policies had brought China to its knees with famine, his dictatorial ways, and what they saw as his "weakness" in the face of Japanese military aggression. Hardly any of the refugees thought Chiang could be trusted, nor did any of them see Chiang as a savior in this situation.

Many of the refugees still believed in Chairman Mao, whether they sided with Lin Piao or Chou En-Lai. Many interviewed also believed the revolution must not "go backwards with Chiang Kai-Shek"—although most stated the revolution must be "reformed." Most deplored the killing, with many saying China had seen enough killing. This was not the view of all Chinese refugees, however. Blee heard from his station chief in Thialand that, during interviews with Chinese refugees, one elderly peasant, who had sat with his head down listening to others speak, suddenly lifted his head and said slowly, without emotion, "We have still not killed enough traitors in our midst." The

American intelligence officer preparing the report wrote: "None of us asked him who he meant by 'traitors.'"

Conservative journalist, Brian Crozier, disagreed with the actions taken by the Kennedy administration. In an article for the *National Review*, and later in a book on Chiang, he wrote that "with air support, the Americans could have neutralized Peking and provided backing for Chiang's assault on the mainland." Crozier further wrote that the Soviets were unlikely to object. He noted that Soviet Premier Stalin, during the 1930s and 1940s, maintained warm relations with Chiang, despite the Soviet Union's rhetorical support for Communists inside China—a fact Mao, Chou, and older Chinese veterans of the Long March and the Revolution never forgot. From his interviews with Russian defectors, Crozier learned that some of the Russian leadership warmly remembered Chiang's son, who graduated in 1937 from the University of Moscow with strong Communist beliefs.

More mainstream historians, from Douglas Brinkley to Robert Dallek and Arthur Schlesinger Jr., disputed Crozier's theory. They claimed Crozier and other critics underestimated the danger of not only nuclear war between the Soviet Union and China, but also the danger that the Chinese would unite against a "foreign invader," meaning Chiang and the United States. Contrary to the impression presented by Crozier, who believed Kennedy supported "Communists" more than "anti-Communists," Kennedy had briefly considered supporting Chiang's assault plan during the crisis. However, after reviewing the intelligence from Blee and discussing the matter with Chet Bowles and Harvard expert John Fairbank, Kennedy made his final judgment call that supporting Chiang created a greater risk that Chou would use nuclear weapons against Taiwan—and create an opportunity for Lin to use nuclear weapons against the Soviet Union or against the eastern coast of mainland China.

Internal U.S. government documents released in 1999 also revealed that Kennedy hardened his position against Chiang after receipt of a frantic cable from the United States Embassy in Japan that said Chou En-Lai was planning to drop a "tactical" nuclear weapon over Taiwan to stop Chiang's invasion. In response, Kennedy immediately called a meeting with Bowles, Warnke, Blee, and the Joint Chiefs. After a relatively brief discussion, none of the Joint Chiefs thought it wise to tempt the "Chinese dragon," as Admiral Moorer put it, perhaps indelicately.

Kennedy alerted Ambassador Dobrynin about the cable from the American Embassy in Japan—and told Dobrynin that he intended to blockade Taiwan. Kennedy then immediately cabled Chou in Peking, saying, "The United States is taking steps to stop any and all adverse actions by the forces of Chiang Kai-Shek against the People's Republic of China. The United States wishes to avoid all acts of belligerence against the PRC. In fact, the steps the United States is taking are a sign of the determination of the United States to enter into peaceful relations with your government."

Chou sent a cable directly to the United States Embassy in Japan, which was relayed directly by telephone to Washington, that his government would accept the American blockade against Taiwan "for now." Lin Piao, by this point, was not in a position to strike Taiwan and had already decided, based upon the information from his science adviser, not to use nuclear weapons from where he was stationed for fear of a wind-caused "blowback."

Kennedy then ordered the U.S. navy and air force into action against Chiang's forces in Taiwan. The navy and air force blockaded Taiwan's fleet in its harbors and issued a warning to Chiang Kai-Shek that the United States would shoot down any military planes and torpedo any ships heading out of Taiwan.

While Kennedy hoped to keep his actions from the public, Chiang's friends leaked the information. Kennedy responded to the leaks by going public with the information about the blockade and the reason for the decision. When the information was made public, the American people overwhelmingly supported Kennedy's action. They did not want to risk a nuclear confrontation that would incinerate Taiwan and probably result in a wider nuclear war among the U.S., the Soviet Union, and China.

Larry O'Brien always denied that he told the president that going public was a good political maneuver designed to rally Americans behind the president during a crisis—and the start of the president's reelection campaign. On the other hand, there is reason to believe that election-year politics played some role in this decision, according to historian Robert Dallek, based upon his review of internal memoranda of the White House counsel and Kenny O'Donnell's diary.[6]

As a result of the blockade, of course, Chiang backed down. Chiang was bitter, however, at the United States for "its final betrayal of China." He and his supporters never wavered from the belief that this was Chiang's and America's last chance to "save" China from Communism. Falling into ill health, he turned over power in Taiwan to his son, Chiang Ching-kuo, less than one year later. Chiang Ching-kuo, openly defying his father's wishes, petitioned the United Nations to allow for an election in Taiwan that included the right of native Taiwanese to vote as to whether Taiwan should be an independent sovereign nation. China itself did not contest the UN-sponsored referendum because this was the condition upon which it became a member of the United Nations.

Not too surprisingly, the people of Taiwan overwhelmingly voted to establish their own independent nation. Chiang Ching-kuo, hoping that his magnanimity in allowing the independence vote would sweep him to personal victory, promptly scheduled an election to formally elect a president. Most of his advisers objected to calling for elections so fast, but he stubbornly went forward. His opponent in the election was the longtime dissident P'eng Ming-min. The election, which occurred three months later, was closer than most observers thought it would be, but the result was what most expected: P'eng Ming-min was elected president.

Most of the world, including the United States, immediately recognized the new independent Taiwanese government. Despite a brief attempt at a coup by members of the pro-Chiang forces—quickly subdued by the Taiwanese and many Chinese nationals who were glad they would never have to return to China—the new government survived and even flourished economically. P'eng's government was very pro-American and pro-business. In fact, P'eng's administration was so pro-business that Taiwan eventually challenged Hong Kong as a haven for business development and manufacturing. Those American analysts who thought P'eng was a "Communist" were happily surprised that he favored a mixed economic system and an open government.[7]

As the dust of peace settled over Taiwan, and China, from a distant and global perspective, was merely smoldering, Kennedy told CIA Director Blee that he was very pleased with the work of the CIA in preparing analyses during the crisis. Kennedy said, "I have never been more proud of our intelligence units, David. You and the agency are to be commended for your efforts in terms of overall efficiency, speed, and timeliness in gathering and reporting intelligence."

"May I quote you on that to the agency, sir?"

"Yes, David. By all means!"

Blee immediately broadcast that oral commendation throughout the agency, which not only swelled pride among the agents, but also drew most of them closer to the administration—and away from their now former allies in the Cold War establishment outside the walls of the CIA building in Langley, Virginia.

Kennedy, for his part, breathed a sigh of relief as winter was ending in the nation's capital. He hoped, at least for the moment, that he could finally return to thinking about his reelection campaign. The New Hampshire presidential primary had occurred in late February while China seethed with internal strife, the Soviet Union continued its withdrawal—almost desertion by now—of Eastern Europe, and the Middle East peace accords were being signed in Geneva. And luckily for Kennedy, the number of labor strikes in America had declined as had the inflation of the previous autumn.

Kennedy had only visited New Hampshire twice in the preceding five months but won more than 90 percent of the vote in the Democratic Party's primary. No "name" Democratic candidate dared to file against him, other than the usual eccentric individuals who never received any coverage from most media outlets. Blair Clark at PBS, however, angered Kennedy with what became an Emmy-winning news report on the "no-name" Democratic and Republican candidates, candidates who naïvely thought "anyone" could run for president.

Because the program generated low ratings, Kennedy never said a word of anger to Clark, who heard only indirectly about Kennedy's reaction to the documentary. Clark, proving his own eccentricity, reveled at the thought of acting independently against a president he so strongly supported.

On the night of the New Hampshire primary, Larry O'Brien greeted the president with the sarcastic remark that Kennedy had won with "only" 91 percent of the vote. Kennedy was anything but pleased, however. "Look, Larry, I had no opposition to speak of—unless you really want to count Blair Clark's 'no-name' candidates. The Democratic turnout was also low because the real action is in the Republican camp—and New Hampshire's a state that hates unions, hates me for supporting unions, and, by the fall, won't care that we may have saved the world from nuclear war. It's Reagan and Abrams—and Roth, possibly—I am concerned with. And you, my political adviser, should be even more concerned than I am. That's your full-time job right now. I need a 'Bobby' again, Larry, and this time, I can't be checking up on every little thing, since this time, I'm running the country!"

Kennedy smiled as he said this last part, but he was very, very serious.

Larry O'Brien left the Oval Office wondering, if not muttering, Why isn't Kenny O'Donnell his "Bobby"?

As he walked down the hall away from the Oval Office, O'Brien thought about a recent offer he had received to become the commissioner of major league baseball. The owners were desperately seeking a new commissioner who had political savvy, knew how to deal with "uppity" workers, and had executive experience. This offer came just after former—and now reinstated—baseball player Curt Flood prevailed in the U.S. Supreme Court in a case where the Court ruled the owners' power to keep players under essentially "lifetime" contracts, with little or no negotiation, was a violation of the 13th Amendment to the Constitution. In the decision, Justice Cox called the owners' contracts with players little more than a modern form of indentured servitude.

O'Brien seemed to fit the owners' needs because he had run the heavily unionized Post Office for Lyndon Johnson and was admired for his work as the president's co–chief of staff. But O'Brien, after some reflection, decided to decline the commissioner position. He reasoned that the commissioner's job would be boring compared with all the excitement of a presidential reelection campaign, particularly with an incumbent president such as Robert Kennedy, who seemed to have more lives than an alley cat. And besides, with all the Kennedy children and animals roaming around that epicenter of world power known as the White House, his current job continued to be a lot more fun—and meaningful— than arguing over baseball batting and pitching averages, and television advertising revenue.

Chapter 26

REELECTION, PART 1

Supreme Politics

For the Republicans, the presidential reelection campaign had begun the day after the 1970 midterm elections. Abrams, Reagan, and Roth immediately began to raise funds and secure commitments from their closest supporters. Meanwhile, in Congress, the most conservative Republicans in the Senate filibustered on a variety of issues in order to undermine Kennedy's agenda. But the Republicans lost most of the time as northeastern and northwestern Republican senators, from Javits in New York to Hatfield and Packwood in Oregon and Washington, respectively, broke ranks to join with the Democrats to break the filibusters.

On the plus side for Republicans, some important filibusters worked. Casualties of successful filibusters included public transportation—except for the government's bailout of New York's Penn Central Railroad in 1971—and, as Republican Senator Strom Thurmond put it, "socialized Comm'nist medicine!"

Thurmond, not content with filibustering on policy issues, continued to try to make the Supreme Court a political issue for national elections. His questioning of judicial nominees was generally combative. A typical example was his questioning of Joe Dolan during Dolan's confirmation hearings: "Are you, Mr. Dolan, concerned about the loss of respect for our Constitution by liberal, activist judges appointed by an administration—yes, this White House under President Bobby Kennedy—that is causin' a radical transformation of our great nation and turnin' it into a slothful, lazy, socialistic, parasitic shell?"

Dolan, for his part, shook his head in sadness and replied, "Senator, if that is what you see, then I guess we don't live in the same country. I see no laws being overturned by this Court in the past two years at least, and I see more people working than ever before. I'm here to seek the consent of the Senate for a judicial position to uphold our Constitution. I'm not running for the legislature—and the last thing I want to do is interfere with the legislature's powers. I respect the separation of powers."

Even Republicans on the Senate committee were embarrassed for Thurmond after that exchange.

At the end of December 1971, Supreme Court Justice John Marshall Harlan II died after a short illness. Thurmond, still believing in what he called "the Lost Cause of State's Rights," was ready again to challenge whomever Kennedy nominated to replace Harlan. Thurmond was "keyed up," he told his aides, because Harlan, unlike Justices Douglas and Black, was a relatively conservative member of the Court. As Thurmond thundered to his chief of staff, "We ain't replacin' a moderate fella with one o' em Harvard radicals or some othah Kennedy cronies! No way in tar-nation! No, suh!"

Harlan was a legend not only for his own jurisprudence but also because his father had been a revered Supreme Court justice. Harlan's father had written the famous dissenting opinion opposing segregation in *Plessy v. Ferguson* 163 US 537 (1896). While Thurmond may not have supported "Harlan I" at that time for writing that famous dissent against racial segregation, "Harlan II" appealed to Thurmond because Harlan II stood for "the poh-lice and the honest-to-God fearin' American citizens—and not crim'nals." In other words, Harlan II dissented from some of the Warren Court decisions regarding the Constitution and criminal law.

Thurmond, Dole, and other hard-core Republicans also appreciated Harlan II's dissenting opinions in the "one person, one vote" legislative reapportionment cases. The majority opinions in those cases had paved the way judicially for the pro–civil rights Voting Rights Act of 1965, something only Thurmond and a couple of other senators continued to oppose. There was, however, one "mistake" that Thurmond was willing to overlook in regard to Harlan II's record as a Supreme Court justice. Harlan II was a key supporter of the "right to privacy" cases that were decided during the 1960s. It was the "right to privacy" doctrine that allowed married couples the right to buy contraceptives without fear of criminal prosecution and upheld the right of black and white lovers to get married.

In the midst of the various foreign policy concerns, not to mention the ongoing labor organizing in the South, President Kennedy, against the advice of the O Boys and others, decided in late January 1972, to nominate Solicitor General Roger Wilkins to replace Harlan II.

Many civil rights "conservatives" on Capitol Hill immediately and publicly denounced the nomination of such a "young man"—in private, a "colored boy." The three ancient racist Southern senators, Thurmond, Stennis, and Eastland, voiced open outrage at the nomination. Kennedy said to the O Boys, "Well, maybe this nomination will get foreign affairs and nuclear war off the front page for a few days!"

O'Brien shook his head at Kennedy's nomination strategy. "Boss, you're a regular genius at stirring things up. I'm thinking I can maybe resign and do something easy for once—like skydiving without a parachute!"

Kenny O'Donnell was similarly "impressed" with the president. "What's next, Mr. President? The Reverend Jesse Jackson replacing Chet Bowles?" O'Donnell was referring to the fact that Jackson had recently announced that he would be willing to be part of the United States delegation to mediate the Russian-Chinese border dispute. Jackson had gone to South Africa during the debate over the South Africa boycott bill and met with Nelson Mandela in a highly publicized meeting of what American media called "an American civil rights leader meeting a rising African leader."

Kennedy shrugged his shoulders at O'Donnell's remark and replied, "I am the president, after all, gentlemen. And if you remember, I ran my brother Jack's campaigns pretty damned well. Let's see what happens here. I'm so damned tired of the press telling us we're gonna die in a nuclear war, which I guess I should have anticipated. And when they're not saying that, they say there's going to be one big nationwide strike by the labor unions this summer that will somehow cripple the nation!"

Some longtime Kennedy observers, including current Supreme Court Justices Cox and Dolan, were surprised by the nomination of Wilkins on a different level. The word throughout the Washington, D.C. "village" was that Kennedy, if he picked a darker-skinned American for the Supreme Court, was going to pick Charles E. Smith, assistant attorney general under Ramsey Clark, and a former U.S. attorney in the Northwest under then Attorney General Robert Kennedy. Longtime Hickory Hill neighbor and friend Warren Rogers said to Ethel the day after the nomination of Wilkins, "I'd have bet dollars to donuts that Smith would have gotten the nod if the pick was going to be a black man."

Kennedy, while highly respectful of Smith, became more impressed with young Wilkins' performance as solicitor general. As Kennedy explained to his longtime friend, and now Justice, Joe Dolan, "Roger took on an important responsibility at a young age—kind of like me—and he did better than I did. At Justice Black's retirement party, Black told me that Wilkins' arguments to the Supreme Court as solicitor general were persuasive and moderate, and were argued in a mature and professional manner."

What Kennedy didn't say, but O'Brien later claimed to know better, was that Wilkins' uncle "just happened to be the head of the National Association for the Advancement of Colored People (NAACP)"—and Wilkins' nomination was, after all, coming at the beginning of the president's reelection year.

To allay any negative thoughts from Smith and his supporters, Smith was nominated for a position with the Ninth Circuit Court of Appeals headquartered in San Francisco. The Ninth Circuit was the most respected circuit court outside of the D.C. Circuit Court and was rarely overruled by the Supreme Court, now commonly called "the Brennan Court."

When the Wilkins' nomination was announced, but before Wilkins appeared before the Senate, Senator Thurmond, along with Senator Stennis, led a filibuster against even hearing the nomination. Kennedy became concerned when a cloture vote to defeat the filibuster in the Senate failed on the first day. On the second day, after Kennedy stayed up all night making phone calls to wavering senators, the Senate voted 61–39 to end the filibuster. Kennedy personally intervened with Senator Goldwater and Senator Roth. He argued that Wilkins deserved a fair chance to explain his positions before the Senate Judiciary Committee. "You don't have to vote for him," he told the senators, "but you ought to let the young man speak."

Wilkins duly appeared before the Senate Judiciary Committee the next week. There, he talked about his growing respect, while solicitor general, for the judicial philosophy of the late Justice Felix Frankfurter. Frankfurter was a political liberal whose judicial philosophy favoring a strong deference to the legislature turned him into a fairly consistent conservative justice on the Supreme Court. Wilkins also said that he was not going to be a "rubber stamp" for any administration. He rejected the view that "my skin color will be the basis or reason for my decisions. On the other hand, I must say, as the late Justice Harlan and his equally famous father said, 'Race is often a key consideration in American history,' which includes American jurisprudence."

The Senate voted 73–27 to confirm Wilkins as Harlan's successor. After the vote, Kennedy said to his White House counsel, Ted Sorensen, "Ted, the Supreme Court nominations are becoming way too political. Did you hear Roger testify? He sounded more like he was running for election than seeking an appointment. This keeps getting worse and worse, and I can't understand it."

"I agree, sir. But, the Court might still become an issue for the Republicans with some voters this year, although I doubt it right now. The Republicans are looking for any issue they can—and, I guess from a political standpoint, one can't really blame them."

"Ted, all I can say is the Republicans better not be right that Supreme Court nominees are a legitimate issue for presidential elections. I can't imagine our politics would be so devoid of important policy debates that an election would turn on something so technical as whom a president nominates for the Court. You'll see. Wilkins will be an excellent appointment. I really think he'll be a surprise to people. You know, Wilkins told me that he agreed with Justice Potter Stewart's opinion that the Sierra Club could not sue developers on behalf of the 'trees.' That was a close case, closer than it should have been. Thank goodness Wilkins isn't a radical environmentalist like Justice Wheat and Justice Douglas."

Sorensen smiled a bit, saying, "As you know, Mr. President, I didn't want to choose Wilkins until the next vacancy. But I think this was done early enough in the year that it shouldn't be a big deal even if he turns out to be a Bill Douglas liberal . . . At least, I hope."

"Well, if you think you're worried now, I guess I might as well tell you something, Ted. I just heard back from Marian Wright Edelman. I'm nominating her to replace Wilkins as solicitor general. What do you think of that? A black woman filing and arguing government briefs before the U.S. Supreme Court."

Sorensen sat back in his chair, shaking his head. "You're the boss, boss." To himself, Sorensen said, He's got a death wish. That's all it is. A death wish.[1]

Spring Training, Election Style

In early March 1972, Kennedy, relieved that the world might not end in a nuclear holocaust, called the O Boys, Yarborough, and Reuther into his office to discuss how to position his reelection campaign for the fall. "Taxes, gentlemen. That's what'll be on everyone's minds this fall. I know it and we better start preparing right now. Watching the first Republican presidential primary, I've concluded we need a separate federal tax *cut* this year for the median family wage earner. Some union workers are making enough money to start voting for Republicans, at least that's what I read in David Broder's column in the *Post* this morning!"

O'Brien spoke first. "Well, Mr. President, our proposed legislation on how states can combine to create a common corporate income tax has a lot of governors' support, including Republican governors. Under this plan, the federal government would pay for funding a computer system that allows states that don't have a corporate income tax to create one in conjunction with the other states. By having the various state corporate taxes collected nationally, but still going directly to each state, it lessens a corporation's ability to play one state off against the other. Because most states don't currently tax corporate income, we see this as a way to begin to limit the amount of taxes *individuals* pay to the federal government because the states can pick up more revenue by taxing corporations. And since investors love to receive dividends, and dividends are paid on profits, the corporations will be less likely to underreport profits just to avoid the tax."

Kennedy was unimpressed. "Larry, that's just another new tax, which is the opposite of where we need to go this year. Plus, it's a technical argument nobody's going to understand. You need to get back into the election-year politics—or we're screwed here! Republican governors may be supporting that idea, but Senator Roth and the conservative members of Congress are saying we should stop this 'common-ist proposal.' Roth gets lots of applause—and support—when he says the United States should abolish the personal federal income tax altogether. He says he'd replace the income tax with a national sales tax of 10 percent based upon the Consumer Price Index, though his top economic adviser says it might be 15 percent."

His voice rising, Kennedy continued. "And I can't believe none of us were smart enough to see that 'pun-based' attack on our proposal! 'Common-ist!' Christ! What were we thinking? I hate to say it, guys, but I'm starting to wonder, if we get corporate income taxed at a progressively higher rate in each state, maybe we should out-Roth Roth and drop federal personal income taxes altogether, do a national sales tax, but with a twist. Ken Galbraith showed me a thesis paper from a graduate student of his showing how we could provide a year-end tax credit that would negate more than half the sales taxes regular workers paid on average during the year. Plus, a sales tax could be easier to administer as it runs directly from merchants' cash registers and—"

Yarborough interrupted the President, barely concealing his rage at such a proposal. "Mr. President! This is lahk a fox askin' ta take over the chicken house if we substitute a sales tax for an income tax. Big Ken tried that 'twist' on me, too, but Ah ain't buyin' it! What—ya pay a federal sales tax on your car and your house?! Just try addin' 15 percent to those 'little items' if you're makin' just above minimum wage—and then ya gotta wait till next April 15—tax day—to get a ree-bate. And ya still gotta fig'a out who's lyin' 'bout his annual income to get that credit, so ya don't cut the bureaucracy hardly at all. Damn pointy-headed eee-con-a-mists!"

Looking around the room, Yarborough realized that most of the group, with the exception of Reuther, failed to understand the *real* politics of taxes, as he told his wife later that night. He stood up and spoke to the assembled group. "Now, fellas, lemme take a stab at tellin' y'all what's bad 'bout sales taxes so we get this outta our mah-nds raht now. First off, most Republicans and businessmen lahk the sales tax—and that should tell us all sum'thin' is bad raht there! A sales tax's *burden* falls more heavily on workin' folks 'cause they gotta shell out extra money in taxes raht they-ah for e'ry'thin' they buy. Rich folks, howevah, can't possibly buy enough things to make the sales tax a burden on them, even when they buy fancy china an' Cadillacs an' what not. That's why rich folks *love* sales taxes since they get the biggest break!

"Now the income tax, especially a progressive one, is the only tax that gets at the money the rich folks have so much of! My God, boys, the top 1 percent still owns 26 percent of our country's wealth, an' the top 20 percent owns almost half the wealth in the en-tire USA! Ya think it's good to put a *federal* sales tax on a candy bar some li'l paperboy buys instead o' taxin' the income o' the chairman o' General Motors?"

Yarborough sat down and looked at Reuther, who smiled approvingly.

"But, Ralph," O'Donnell asked Yarborough after the vice president sat down, "what about the flax-tax proposal this right-wing Illinois congressman, Phil Crane, is proposing? Won't that be a better way to compromise with Roth and the Republicans—and some Democrats, since we know that most of the rich people don't pay the top rates unless they have incompetent accountants?"

Yarborough flushed with anger and stood up again, determined to teach these "young'ns a lesson." He was back in Austin, Texas, now, "soapboxin'" as if it was 1937. "Kenny, this 'flat tax' talk is as big a bunch o' garbage as a sales tax—'cept there's a li'l flim-flam goin' on. When people think they want a flat tax, what they really mean, when ya start talkin' to 'em, is a *simplified* tax. But that ain't what those Ree-publicans mean, Ah'll tell ya that much."

Kennedy interrupted, "But Ralph, a flat tax is simple, isn't it?"

Yarborough replied curtly, "Bob, the damned IRS Code only's got *two pages* on tax *rates*—the rest o' dat football field o' pages is all that complex horse-hockey for rich folks that lets 'em evade those other two pages! Flattenin' the tax rate just turns two pages into one—and still keeps the football field o' pages for all the dee-ductions and othah stuff! If ya don't mah-nd mah sayin', what we need is tax *simplifyin'*, not flattenin' tax rates. Progressive tax rates ain't the problem! Heck, Ah'd rather scuttle this whole damned 'common corporate tax' than go flat or go sales taxin' little folks! *Ah mean it!* Corporations are still payin' 24 percent of all taxes by they'selves raht now, which is lower than it should be, but that's more than what they'll be payin' later if we start goin' down Roth's road!"[2]

Kennedy, noticing Yarborough had left "Passionate" at the train station and was steaming toward the town of "Belligerent," said, "Ralph, Ralph! Calm down! You're among friends here!" He was upset at Yarborough's tone, but he was also listening carefully. As he told Ethel later that night, "I need to be able to debate this with the press and with Reagan or Roth in the fall. I have to get educated on this stuff and then make it simple for people to get . . . I hope."

After waiting for Yarborough to sit back down, Kennedy, playing debate moderator, said, "Ralph, I just need to understand one thing about the flat tax: What's wrong with a straight 10 percent tax—just to keep our math easy—for everybody? I can't get past the argument that the guy making ten thousand dollars only pays *one* thousand dollars in taxes while the richer guy making one hundred thousand dollars pays a tax of *ten* thousand. The rate is flat, but the money paid . . . Well, it looks *progressive,* doesn't it, since the guy making a lot more pays more taxes, too. Right?"

Yarborough smiled, made a "click" sound with his mouth, and said, "Shucks, Mr. President, guess Ah got carried away there. Ah humbly apologize, 'specially for mah language an' all. May Ah, uh, answer that question you asked raht now?"

"Sure, Ralph, but don't stand up, okay? We can hear you fine sitting down, too." Kennedy spoke in a way that made clear he was not looking for any more of Ralph's "soapboxin'," just information.

Yarborough took a deep breath and said, "Okay, Mr. President, heah goes. When ya have a *progressive* income tax, then ya even out the *burden* o' the tax. The 'burden' is what ya *feel* when yo're payin' the tax. Now, take that example ya gave me. If the richer guy makin' a hundred thousand dollahs has to pay ten thousand, as you say, he still's got *ninety thousand dollahs left,* raht? Now that's a helluva lotta money he's still got, isn't it? That ten thousand in taxes don't hurt him none!

"Now compare that," continued Yarborough, "to the guy who only makes ten thousand dollahs all yee-ah—who then has ta pay 10 percent on *his* taxes. While that's only one thousand dollahs, that one thousand dollah tax payment hurts the li'l guy a helluva lot more. Why? 'Cause the li'l guy's got the rent due, food to feed some hungry mouths, and a monthly car payment. And that thousand dollahs was gonna pay for a nice, family dinner, an' a movie a few tahms a year, plus one vacation, but he ain't doin' mucha that now! The *burden's* a lot harder on him, ain't it? So that's why ya make the rich guy pay *more* in percentage *and* dollahs. The point is ta make him feel the *same burden* kinda lahk the li'l fella feels. 'Cause if ya don't, then the tax really ain't equal, is it?

"Now, Mr. President, may Ah say somethin' else heah? Thank ya. Now, Ah un'nerstan' the current problem with our country's income tax is that it covers too many li'l folks raht now—but that's thanks to unions and *your* administration helpin' workin' folks get more money when they join unions and collectively bargain with the bosses. If it wasn't for us and Walt's unions, the corporate exec-a-tives woulda kept most of the profits for themselves an' their big investors![3] As Ah said before, the income tax, not the sales tax, is where the rich folks' money is! Heck, if Ah really wanted to get rough, we'd just tax a hunne'rd percent on any income above a million dollars or make the rich folks pay reg'lar income taxes, not that cheap-y capital gains tax, on their stock and real estate profits! A worker makes investments with his *body* ev'ry day, but he don't get no low tax rate lahk the capital gains tax rate. Why does a rich fella who just 'invests' his play money get to have a lower, capital gains tax? Ah mean—"

Kennedy broke in, shaking his head, "Whoa, Ralph! We can't get anywhere near that sort of thing—especially not now!"

O'Donnell sat back in shock at Yarborough's radical proposals. This guy's crazy, he thought to himself.

Kennedy said soothingly to Yarborough, but now with a hint of tension in his voice, "Ralph, we understand what you're saying, but we have to deal with the here and now—not engage in an educational campaign."

Then, turning more to the O Boys than either Yarborough or Reuther, Kennedy said, "Let's face facts, gentlemen. We must agree right now on *some* form of tax relief for working- and middle-class people in this country. The state common corporate tax proposal is more for the states to fight for than us—since we're running directly against Roth and Reagan—not so much Abrams—on the issue of federal tax cuts. The conundrum we face is that incomes are rising, and so are the taxes—and that's a *good* problem to have when we think about it. But if I was a working fellow and my taxes were going up because I was making more, I'd be thinking about going for one of those tax cutting guys, too!"

Reuther stayed quiet, but he was seething at the possible compromises Kennedy and O'Donnell were floating. He was starting to worry now, thinking Bob Kennedy might be off on another "metamorphosis." Reuther had loved the time Kennedy had gone to a mine in South America and told the workers he'd be a "Communist" too if he had to work in horrible conditions for slave-level wages. But was Kennedy now going to go from sympathizing with workers in mines to being a corporate toady?

Kennedy was not finished speaking, however. He continued, "We need to find a way to give a tax cut and somehow keep the same revenue stream, especially to fund our Bed-Sty programs that are now going on in city after city. And the only reason we're projecting a budget surplus this year is because we were able to cut the military budget now that we're out of Vietnam and almost out of NATO. We also saved on antiballistic missile spending after we signed the ABM Treaty. But we are still spending billions of dollars MIRVing our weapons—Senator Cranston in California says it's a lifeblood right now for defense workers in the West and South—and there are other weapons proposals, some of which we might still need . . . Let me put it this way. I don't want to win all the big policy battles only to lose the election on something as simple as the Republicans saying, 'Kennedy wants to keep your taxes high and we want to cut them!'"

Turning back to face Yarborough squarely, Kennedy said, "And Ralph, we need a sensible tax cut—and quick—to take the wind out of those Republican sails. Your points sound good for 1932, but not 1972—I'm sorry, Ralph, but we gotta think more strategically about this."

Yarborough, who knew he deserved this reprimand from Kennedy for his soapbox lecture, spoke more humbly this time. Remembering he was speaking with "a bunch o' Yankees," Yarborough said, "Ah un'nerstan', Mr. President. It's just that sometimes a compromise isn't really a compromise when it's on somethin' fundamental lahk who pays what in taxes an' who pays more than who. Your brother's cut in the income tax ten yeahs ago—didn't that cut help the lit'le folks more'n the big fishes?"

Kennedy, who frankly couldn't recall, nodded anyway.

"Well, then," said the vice president, "fust off, we shouldn't compromise with Roth or waste our time in an election yee-ah on some state common corporate tax. Let the Democrat *and Republican* gov'nahs push that some. The *real* difference we need to show the public this year is that the real question is what *kind* of tax each party supports or doesn't support—not who's for tax cuts and who isn't. An' maybe people'll notice that those states *only* relyin' on sales taxes—'cept Nevada with its gamblin'—tend to be worse off in social services than ones with an income tax! If ya wanna strategy, Ah'd go with a simplified income tax that cuts workers' taxes and makes the rich folks come out from bee-hind their dee-ductions and all those sorta things!"

"But—" said O'Brien, who didn't like "kamikaze" politics unless they were absolutely necessary. But his "but" was hushed up by Yarborough.

"But nothin', Larry. Jus' lemme finish heah! If we wanna fight back against Reagan and Roth, and dem Republicans, we gotta push for *tax simplification*. An' Ah ain't jus' sayin' this without thinkin' 'bout it. In fact, Ah've been talkin' over the last yeah with Ralph Nader"—O'Donnell rolled his eyes in disgust because he was getting tired of hearing Nader's name, mostly from business leaders who thought Nader's first name was "That bastard" or "That son of a bitch."

Yarborough was not stopping for O'Donnell's private thoughts, of course, as he continued to explain his strategy, "—and us two Ralphs, well, we gotta plan heah that's bein' introduced by Senator Proxmire—Larry knows what Ah'm talkin' about—Walt, too—that calls for lowered rates across the board—even for those rich fellas—but it takes away all the deductions and othah things, 'cept for a few dee-ductions for buying equipment an' such, plus some limited deductions for charity, the house mortgage interest deduction, an' the state an' local tax deductions—gotta keep them state gov'nahs happy. With no hidden goodies for rich folks, we just set six or seven tax rates that start at 10 percent for the bottom 60 percent of income earners, takin' into account the negative income tax for the poor. Then, startin' on marginal income increases, we go to 20 percent, then 30 percent, 35 percent, 40 percent, 50 percent, and 60 percent dependin' on the income ya earn. Now, the rates may be different, but the key is still simplification—meanin' almost no deductions and such. This way, the top income earners an' their accountants can't play their games behind the scenes anymore—or at least not too many games, way Ah see it!"

Kennedy rolled his eyes. "Ralph, you don't think that's gonna cause *more* screaming from the business community? You're talking about a *fundamental* change here, Ralph! That can't occur without a lot of blood on the floor—and that is a very bad thing to happen to an incumbent in an election year!"

Ralph smiled. "Mr. President, let 'em scream. The beauty o' this plan is that the argument's on *our* terms because the reg'lar folks are still getting' their tax cut—which is what you started out talkin' about. With a simplified tax, we're lowerin' the rich folks' rates too, so what do they have to complain about? You got it! Their dee-ductions and all that stuff that shows how they've gamed the tax system in the first place. We're just takin' away their goodies, accordin' to Mr. Nader. Plus, this simplified plan divides the big biz-ness fishies and the small biz-ness fishies in the Republican Party because, if ya talk to small biz-ness lobbyists over a few drinks, whatcha learn is they are really mad at big biz-nesses for getting' all those hidden tax breaks they can't get 'cause they don't make as much money as large biz-nesses. The Republicans are *already* playin' divide an' conquer against us. They're pittin' the better paid against the poorer paid workers with their tax cut plans. With this tax simplification plan, we grab back the one issue the Republicans think they're united on—cuttin' taxes—an' divide *them*! Then we make 'em think 'bout compromisin' with *us*! And remember, we're talkin' 'bout cuttin' all those millions o' pages in the tax code, not lahk Roth and Reagan, who only cut one page of tax rates."

Kennedy, still trying to think of something less drastic, said, "Ralph, we can't go for something fundamental on a complicated subject like taxes in the middle of a reelection campaign, as I said—"

Reuther, deciding he had been silent too long, chimed in. "Mr. President, if I may," and seeing Kennedy nod warily with approval, he spoke with a slight tone of caution in his voice. "I'd rather have us tell working people we didn't get *any* tax reform this year than let the Republicans get their cake and eat it too. I'd rather run a campaign like Ralph is saying here. We tell voters, 'Hey, the Republicans want to tax *you,* the workin' stiff, with a 'national sales tax' and *increase* your *taxes that will be needed at the state level*!' We get nothing from any compromise with Republicans on this issue whatsoever!

"And," continued Reuther, "if you don't mind, we keep avoiding the fact that we have to watch our left flank, not just the businessmen or labor rank-and-file. I'm talking about the civil rights groups, the radical unionists, and the student radicals who still talk like there's a revolution around the corner. They're saying we need to talk about having a Western European–style social democracy, with *higher* tax rates, even confiscatory, on people earning more than two hundred and fifty thousand dollars. That may not sound like much to some of us here, but that's more than what 99.5 percent of American workers currently earn. If that ain't rich, then we better redefine the word 'poor' to include a lot more people! Our left flank, and I agree with them more often than not, wants socialized medicine now. They want a national public transportation program—now! There's talk about how our Bed-Sty program doesn't go far enough because the Kerner Commission, after the riots, called for even more money to go into black and other minority neighborhoods! Worse, some in the civil rights community are upset that Bed-Sty programs keep us focused on self-help for the communities but neglect the housing and school integration efforts the Kerner Commission also called for. The radical elements in these groups are threatening to support the Peace and Freedom Party—they've gotten on the ballots in about thirty-three states, mostly *our* states. Their presidential candidate this year . . . so I've heard . . . may be David McReynolds, a real radical but very bright, and . . . well . . . years ago I remember trying to get people not to back Norman Thomas during the Roosevelt reelection campaigns, let alone Henry Wallace in 1948 against Truman and Dewey."

Kennedy, seething at the mention of placating radicals, asked in an icy tone, "Walt, what does all that have to do with a tax plan?"

Reuther, who was feeling testy himself, replied, "What I mean to say, Mr. President, is that we need to put forth a tax plan that's exciting to the radicals in our party who vote in high numbers. And it still has to be a plan where well-off union workers and small businesses feel like they get something out of it, too. And the only plan I see that does both is one that simplifies the tax code by lowering rates on those making less than sixty thousand and hits rich people making over two hundred and fifty thousand dollars a year with higher taxes—not because they pay a higher rate, but because we closed their loopholes." He paused to catch his breath before concluding. "Mr. President, with all my greatest respect for you and all that we've accomplished, I think talking 'fundamental' on taxes may be the *safest* course we can take."

Kennedy, still thinking about the radicals who always complained that he was never going far enough when businessmen were calling him "Commie Bobby," began a long, sharp tirade of his own. "Walt, with all due respect to *you*, I will *never* beg to a bunch of spoiled Reds who don't have to deal with the things Kenny, Larry, and I are hearing from almost-wealthy unionized workers and moderate business leaders every single goddamned day! Christ! You hear the same thing, too, Walt! The Republicans are starting to make inroads with some of the well-off workers in suburban areas on this tax-cutting talk. Those radicals had better realize that if we lose to the Republicans this year, that's the *end* of the revolution, damn it! Don't they get it? If some of these radicals would just infiltrate a country club, they'd hear—and maybe realize—we're more radical in what we've accomplished than anyone could imagine! Forget the foreign policy stuff for a moment—I know it's hard for some of us, but domestic issues are gonna come roaring back, which is why we're here today. Last year, we passed the negative income tax, remember? Now some radicals wanted a guaranteed income, but already we're putting money into poor people's hands with no welfare caseworker telling them how to live. Isn't that something to cheer about, especially for those radicals who claim to love the poor so much? Yes, we put work requirements in for community service as part of the Bed-Sty program, but getting people to work is what every program should be about. And jobs are plentiful, with the highest minimum wage rates ever—and Medicare coverage up to 150 percent of the annualized minimum wage! We have environmental laws that are the envy of the world, with worker retraining and new, government-subsidized companies that have given permanent jobs to some of the VISTA volunteers who were working for them on recycling and pushing solar and wind power! We're cleaning rivers and streams—and more important, we're revitalizing our cities, with blacks' unemployment levels going down to almost white levels, once you include government work programs. And last year we saw, per Sarge Shriver at HEW, a dramatic decline in out-of-wedlock births, plus a drastic improvement in infant live births among minorities. And this was done without riots in our cities—and all with white people seeing black people working hard for their communities, not trashing communities, and crime rates dropping from mid-1960s' highs back to almost 1950s' levels. And one more thing: The poverty rate is down to 7 percent—unheard of in American history, damn it! I don't mean to make a campaign speech, but every person in this administration better make that speech *everywhere,* especially at the colleges and in front of civil rights groups!"

Reuther realized he had hit a nerve with the president. He spoke in measured tones now, saying, "Mr. President, I *am* making that speech everywhere. By the time they're through hearing Reagan, Roth, or Abrams, we'll definitely keep most of the radicals in our camp. But I just want to say again that Ralph is onto something here. Senator Proxmire has already introduced Nader's—and Ralph's—bill. Proxmire says there's enough support on Capitol Hill to make a go of it—even if it seems somewhat . . . well, it is a departure from past tax policy." He knew he didn't want to say the word "radical" anymore in front of the president.

Reuther continued. "If we can officially get behind that bill, Mr. President, we can really turn this issue against the Republicans—and forget the politics for a moment. Don't all of us want a tax code that isn't subject to ridicule and cynicism? A simplified and still progressive system is what we should all want to see. Why not argue for that—especially when it's good politics, too!"

O'Brien, who had been getting "hammered" by Yarborough, Proxmire, and Nader for the past several weeks on the issue, shrugged his shoulders and said, "Mr. President, I think Ralph and now Walt are right on this one, even though I didn't quite see it before this meeting. What do we get by way of doing a 'me-too' on taxes with the Republicans, particularly Roth and Reagan? The Republicans used to call us 'deficit spenders,' which they admittedly muted with our latest new budget surplus projection. The Republicans finally figured out that people don't notice candidates who worry about budget deficits, but do notice politicians who say they will cut their taxes. Union polling says there's enough sentiment out there in the mostly white suburbs in New York, New Jersey, and California to break toward a Republican presidential candidate if we don't start selling real tax relief in a way that doesn't look like a defensive reaction to the Republicans."

O'Brien sighed and said, "I say we go with the Proxmire bill." Turning to Reuther, O'Brien added, "And Walt, you and Ralph made your case today with me. All along I thought we couldn't afford *not* to compromise. Now I see I had it backwards. What we can't afford to do is compromise—not on this tax stuff at least. We have to hit them hard on closing loopholes for the rich so we can give real cuts to poor and middle-class workers."

Yarborough smiled and said, "Just as Ah told Bob in the first election campaign, and a couple times since: Face your fears and make 'em the other fella's fears. That's the name o' the game, boys."

Kennedy smiled but was still wary. He'd speak to O'Brien and O'Donnell later, he thought. He let out one thought, however, to his immediate regret: "Ralph," he said with a sigh and a smile, "you're friggin' dangerous, you know that?" While the others laughed, Kennedy asked himself, Why do the crazies out there want *me* dead? Why isn't anyone shooting at—or at least threatening—Ralph Yarborough?

What the president didn't know is that everyone else in the room, except Ralph, was thinking the same exact thing at that very moment.

Kennedy ended the meeting saying, "Ralph, Walt, Larry, I think you've given me a solid proposal. I need to think about it overnight, though, since it's not something I thought about coming into this meeting today. It's risky, but maybe it's a bigger risk, as you guys say, if we don't do something like what you've said." He shook his head and sighed, and then said, "Meeting's over. Let's get some work done today, okay?"

Later that night, Yarborough spoke with his wife, Opal. He said, "Honey-pie, we had a helluva meetin' today, and maybe Ah went a bit too far. I was wavin' mah hands and arms more than an Eye-talian! But Ah wasn't gonna grovel lahk some sheep gettin' a shearin' when there was somethin' impor-tant to be decided. The president's got a good visionary head on his shoulders, and Ah think he'll come along with me on fightin' fire with fire on this tax-cuttin' nonsense. But if he plays rabbit, we're gonna have us a hel-luva time tryin' ta win this fall. At least, that's what Ah think."

Political War Games

In the Republican presidential primaries, General Abrams remained in the race, relying on those working-class Republicans who previously had sup-ported "Tailgunner" Joe McCarthy and General Douglas MacArthur. Abrams railed about the "surrender" in Vietnam and how "Commie Bobby" sold out America to the Viet Cong. He later added "sold out Chiang Kai-Shek for a bunch of murdering Communists in China."

The Republican primaries, however, were shaping up as one where Reagan and Roth mined the growing spectrum of corporate middle and sen-ior managers who made up the likeliest Republican primary voters in 1972. And then there were those union-paid polls showing a growing number of union families thinking they could "consider" voting for a Republican can-didate in the fall if that candidate stood for cutting their federal income taxes. All Abrams was doing, according to Republican and Democratic insiders, was increasing his chances to be a vice presidential candidate under either Reagan or Roth.

Reagan surprised the national press elite by proving to be an able debater, prone to catchy and persuasive one-liners. Savvy party activists also recog-nized that Reagan was the governor of California, a delegate rich state. All Reagan had to do was to remain competitive during the primary season through the California primary in June. Roth and Abrams had no chance of victory in California and all three candidates knew it. As of April, Reagan was remaining competitive and, therefore, was seen as being in the lead.

Roth kept himself in the headlines, however, by hammering on the common corporate tax bill from the Senate floor. He said over and over in campaign appearances, "Too many taxes on our corporations will send them overseas, along with *your* jobs! What President Kennedy doesn't understand is that we can only grow our nation's economy if we cut taxes for everyone!" Roth's deliv-ery was dull, and his looks were even duller. But he beat Reagan in New York and Connecticut and, of course, his home state of Delaware.

The Pennsylvania primary in late April was proving pivotal, as was the

New Jersey primary in June. Roth needed to win in Pennsylvania *and* New Jersey to offset Reagan's California primary win, said Roth's campaign manager, William Simon.

In closed sessions with business leaders, Roth scored major points by railing against union power creating a "profit squeeze" for business interests. He also said that reelecting Kennedy and that "out and out Communist" Yarborough was "an open invitation" to wage and price controls—especially price controls if the largest corporations tried to pass off the costs of environmental law compliance and union wage gains. "We need to restore the power of business leaders in this nation," Roth said as he pounded the tables of various boardrooms.

Kennedy, for his part, was desperately searching for a few business leaders to publicly support his reelection besides the venerable Tom Watson of IBM and a few fledgling computer industry executives. The conversion program was off the ground with the help, unexpectedly, of the French automaker Renault. Renault built and opened factories in the Washington, D.C. area, Bed-Sty, and the South Side of Chicago to build or refurbish public transportation lines and equipment in various American cities. "This will definitely tide us over until the conversion programs mature," said Defense Secretary Warnke to Vince Learson at Commerce. Kennedy enjoyed the "thread of history" of a Frenchman "designing Washington, D.C., one hundred and seventy years ago and now a French company building new public transportation facilities here."

American troops stationed with NATO in Europe were now on the verge of discharge from the military. Kennedy and the O Boys realized that this made the conversion program more urgent than ever. There appeared to be enough jobs for the time being, but any unexpected "hiccup" in the economy would throw many of the black, inner-city veterans out of work—and the inner cities were where Kennedy needed almost unanimous support to defeat the Republican nominee in such states as New York and Pennsylvania. Therefore, he decided to troll for some business support to see who might be interested in making money in the conversion program proposed by Learson and Warnke.

In late April 1972, just before the Pennsylvania primary, Kennedy invited to the White House the CEOs of about twenty of the top fifty of the Fortune 500 companies. It was to be an evening with the president, ostensibly to talk about American corporations entering into conversion programs through the federal government. Kennedy's more urgent purpose, however, was to gauge whether any corporate leaders would support him in the fall.

The president invited Learson, Warnke, and Treasury Secretary Lance to the meeting. Lance, who had been largely ignored by the president, concluded this was merely an "afterthought invite." Lance told his friend, Georgia state legislator Jimmy Carter, "He sees Ken Arrow at the Fed more than he sees me. If ya ask whether Ah should quit, Ah got that figgered out already. Ah'm jus' stayin' on through the election if for no othuh reason than to show loyalty if he loses, an' either way, Ah fatten mah connections an' contacts."

Lance was a decent fellow, overall, as Yarborough reminded the president from time to time. But Kennedy simply never warmed up to the young, quiet Southern gentleman.

Yarborough and Reuther were reluctantly invited to the dinner meeting, but Kennedy was stern with them: "Gentlemen, no speeches about equality and class-consciousness tonight, all right? These fellows need to be made comfortable this evening, if for no other reason than to get one or two of them to support us later this year."

After dinner, the president found the business leaders eager to "jawbone" with him over what they considered a "life and death" issue: the common state corporate income tax. Ironically, despite Kennedy's warning to Yarborough and Reuther, he quickly found himself in the "middle of a rumble," as he later told Ethel before enduring another mostly sleepless night—a regular occurrence for most presidents, including this one.

Lee Iacocca, president of the Ford Motor Company, admittedly was the first to raise the temperature of the conversation. He said, "I don't mean to be sharp or disrespectful, Mr. President, but if this corporate state income tax, the common tax, gets passed, it just means more inflation as businesses will simply pass the tax cost on to consumers. Forget whether we're moving any plants to Brazil, Japan, or Indonesia, for goodness sake. Ford has some plants in South America already, and we're thinking, regardless, we may have to move more plants there in the next decade. But please, Mr. President, we are not the enemy, after all."

Kennedy didn't like Iacocca's threat about moving jobs offshore. But he decided to ignore it and respond to the point about the tax cost pass-off. As he told Ethel and, later, the O Boys, "I just didn't like the arrogant huckster-ism of that Ford president. I liked Henry Ford, Ford Motor Company's chairman of the board, much better. I guess I lost it a little with Iacocca."

"*A little?*" O'Donnell almost screamed when Kennedy said the same thing the next day. "You might as well have flown the hammer and sickle over the White House last night!"

Kennedy, according to recollections from corporate leaders and some of the other participants at the evening get-together, began his response to Iacocca by saying that businesses should pay their fair share of taxes to society and not pass on workers' wage gains, taxes, or environmental regulation costs through their products. "Inflation, Mr. Iacocca, affects all of us, not simply your employees or their families. For example, your prices were affected, were they not, when grain prices went up during last year's drought? Didn't we help your business, and American consumers, when we ended the practice of paying small farmers *not* to grow and instead, paid them to grow grain again?"

Iacocca, angry with the president for signing legislation demanding car fuel mileage improvements, making seat belts mandatory, and requiring a five-year phase-in of air bags for cars and trucks, now relished this moment to explain, in his view, how "self-defeating" most government interventions were. "But, Mr. President, surely you agree that private enterprise, the free market and the laws of supply and demand can do a better job than government intervention in most situations, including farming."

Kennedy was irritated with Iacocca's condescending simplicity. He said to the Ford president, "Mr. Iacocca, sometimes a few companies in one industry, without government intervention, can raise prices for their own ends quite apart from the theory you put forth. May I remind you that my brother, when he was president, was faced with the steel makers running up the price of steel in 1962." Kennedy glanced around the room, remembering the president of U.S. Steel had sent his regrets, supposedly because of illness. Alcoa's president was there, however. Kennedy continued as carefully as he could. "The prices stabilized; but they did so not because of 'free markets' but because we had some hard, but friendly discussions with the steel companies. That was good for consumers and good for the car industry, which relies heavily on steel, am I right?"

Iacocca responded, "Mr. President, I anticipated your point, and if I may speak freely—"

"You may," said a tensing president.

"Your brother, the late President John Kennedy, who I voted for, I might add, had said the steel companies' labor costs were essentially flat, their materials costs were down, and that the cost to the military weapons industry, if the steel prices went up, was possibly in the hundreds of millions. But presently, we are seeing profits squeezed in major businesses due to the high labor costs and environmental regulations—in our industry particularly. The new fuel-efficiency standards, seat belts, and air bag phase-in are hurting our industry's profits, too. That's a whole lot different than what the steel companies were facing in 1962, if I may say so. Besides the hundreds of millions of dollars of dividends being lost to stockholders in *all* businesses, we don't even have enough to invest in new equipment or to expand."

Kennedy, starting to simmer, said, "Well, Mr. Iacocca, I'll speak freely too, if you don't mind. Our secretary of labor knows your auto industry quite well himself. He can tell you, but I will, that in the major industries, including automobiles, the costs of labor have been absorbed without significant price increases over the past twenty years. Further, the costs of environmental regulations are short term and are being implemented across the board so that no businesses, including your competitors, are adversely affected. I asked my secretary of commerce about this, who is a former executive at IBM, and he admitted it's not a dollar-for-dollar pass-through of costs, which further undermines your theory."

Commerce Secretary Learson, who highly valued his continued relationship with his former fellow corporate executives, said later he wanted to crawl under the table at this point in the meeting.

Kennedy wasn't done, though. "Consistent with our nation's policies since our founding, we've even put a new tariff on foreign products made without environmental regulations to protect your industry and other American businesses through this transition. Yet the Japanese auto companies, who were the most adversely affected by the tariffs, are now complying with our environmental laws, from what I've just heard. I also find it interesting that Secretaries Udall and Reuther, in a joint study by their departments, found that foreign auto makers from Japan, Germany, and Sweden are already ahead of American companies in complying with federal gas mileage and seat belt requirements— and they are introducing air bags into their cars as early as next year."

Iacocca lost it here, he admitted later. "The Japs are selling tiny boxes, not cars! And only the people around this table can afford the real cost of German and Swedish over-engineering! Foreign-based employees are making a helluva lot less an hour than our union workers, too!" he yelled. Iaccoca hated the Japanese auto companies with a passion—more than he hated the man he called "that socialist dictator in Washington."

Kennedy was barely controlling his own rage. He stuck his prosecution attorney's knife into the Ford corporate executive. "Yes, Japanese cars are *smaller,* Mr. Iacocca. I'm aware of that. But the Reuther-Udall report shows that labor costs are rising in Japan at a very high rate. The difference, I must say, is that the Japanese business leaders simply take less profits and income at the top to compete with American products. The foreign and trade ministers from Japan, whom I met with last month, confirmed this possibly 'cultural' fact. And you know what? My son wants a new Toyota—but I told him to buy American! But I must say that if you and the industry raise prices to take care of your executives at the top instead of redesigning your cars, you may lose your market share when the tariffs come down for Japan once they pay their workers well and follow environmental standards. Secretary Udall also reminded me the other day that the environmental regulations you complain of are still allowed to be deducted from your profit-and-loss statements, and the new equipment you invest in for cleaner production and recycling of materials is expected to lower your production costs in the long-term. Let's just call it a trickle-up effect on profits, which I see as much better than a trickle-down effect on workers' wages. In the end, you operate more efficiently and increase your bottom line!"

Yarborough, while pleased at Kennedy's understanding of "prairie populism" these past four years, knew Kennedy had gone too far with this audience. He said to himself, The boy's done forgot he was supposed ta convince these guys he's not me! Yarborough had tried earlier to tug at Kennedy's elbow to end the debate, but to no avail.

As Kennedy ended his response to Iaccoca, however, Iaccoca did something he immediately regretted, but couldn't help. He snorted at the president's remark about "efficiency" and "bottom line."

That was it for Kennedy. He stood up and pointed at Iacocca. "Now, Mr. Iacocca, I asked you—and the rest of you!—here because I wished to reiterate that the last thing I want to institute are wage and price controls. I won't allow any *foreign* power to threaten the United States with any military or economic blackmail. And I won't have it here from *American* businesses that know better than to say such things as brazenly as I've heard it said here tonight, about passing everything on to workers and their families, or shuttering local factories and taking jobs to far-off places—as if I wouldn't increase our tariffs then! I would remind you, gentlemen, that wage and price controls were a hot topic in Congress last fall during the grain price scare— and controls worked well when Professor Galbraith ran the Wage/Price Control Board in World War II. Galbraith is still in excellent health, and he tells me he can do it again in peacetime. Yet, I continue to fight *against* wage and price controls and against many people in Congress. And again, through negotiation and cooperation with grain producers, we lowered inflation to an almost acceptable level for all of us!"

Looking around the room at the shocked faces, Kennedy finally realized he had gone too far. He put his right hand in his pocket, sat back down, and said, "When all is said and done, gentlemen, it seems to me that, as civilized business leaders and civil servants in the most advanced and successful nation in the history of the world, we can work together—government and business—to make sure that in the major industries, from steel to oil to autos to aerospace, we can ensure that inflation remains at a decent level without wage and price controls. All the common corporate income tax does is organize state corporate income taxes in a more uniform way—and, according to West German Chancellor Willy Brandt, who was here last week, as you know, your taxes are still at a level *below* what many nations in Western Europe charge their own companies or wealthy citizens."

Iacocca, not taking any threat from anyone, not even the president of the United States, said quietly but firmly, "At least, Mr. President, the Japanese don't tax capital gains on dividends or other investments."[4]

Yarborough put his hand hard on Kennedy's shoulder to keep him from leaping from his chair. As Kennedy inhaled an angry breath, Reuther took that as his cue to speak. "Mr. Iacocca, Mr. President, I am sure we can all agree that maintaining a balanced perspective will help in this situation." He looked over to Commerce Secretary Learson with "eye language" and a hard nod that said to Learson, Help, Vince! Say *anything*!

Learson stood up among the business leaders, and reminding himself that he was once the president of IBM, confidently said, "Gentlemen, I must say,

listening to this interesting discussion, the president did not get the opportunity
to tell you some important and very positive news. The administration is very
likely to propose, as did the president's brother in the early 1960s, as I recall,
a shortening of the time for the depreciation on the purchase of environmental equipment and perhaps other capital equipment, something I believe the
Japanese also do. We are also looking into discussing with the Federal
Reserve Board a reduction in the lending rate in order to help you facilitate
your purchases."

Kennedy quietly cleared his throat, thankful for Learson's intervention.
Learson was not sure the president was thankful at the moment, so he added,
"Gentlemen, this is an election year with lots of union workers voting. As we
know, they generally outnumber us executives. Isn't this the way to go for at
least a start?"

As the executives around the table harrumphed and nodded in agreement,
Kennedy, trying to make amends, spoke as if he really believed that Learson's
statements represented actual policies. "Thank you, Vince. As you know,
Secretary Learson was president of IBM before joining our administration. I
know we are requesting Congress to reduce the time for the depreciation of
environmental equipment and most capital equipment so your companies
may write off their investments earlier and improve their bottom lines. I think
the IRS can issue such a change before the election, without the need for congressional approval. Um . . . why don't we change the subject for a while,
huh? I mean, how about that Jack Nicklaus? Think he'll sweep the golf tour-
naments this year? Isn't he amazing?"

Conversation about golf, as usual, diverted the attention of the executives,
who themselves were shivering at Iacocca's conduct. Most left the White
House that night wondering how badly business would fare as a result of
Iacocca's outburst. The head of Prudential said to Alcoa's president after they
left the White House, "We're going to need to do a lot of ass-kissing for the
rest of the year—and maybe longer unless we get the White House back.
Learson is the best person in Kennedy's cabinet, but frankly IBM's just like a
government contractor with all that whiz-bang computer shit!"

Alcoa's president said, "Well, I figure Kennedy's gonna win anyway. Might
as well sign up for the conversion program with Learson and Warnke. If we're
going to get more government control anyway, we might as well make money,
too. Iacocca may have shot Ford in the head tonight, though, and I figure that's
an advantage for us if they aren't in this conversion program and we are."

Henry Ford II, who also attended the meeting, reaffirmed his belief that
Iacocca was an arrogant hothead—not to mention a possible threat to his
authority in the publicly held stock company because he could sell things
"like a salesman." He also saw that Iacocca was going to be a liability to the
company if Kennedy won. In the limousine ride back to his hotel, Ford began
to realize it was better to let Iacocca go now, especially at a time when Ford's

profits were essentially flat. A few months later, Iacocca announced his resignation from Ford Motor Company. Iacocca, however, quickly landed a job at American Motors Corporation, a moribund competitor of Ford.

Kennedy's infamous jawboning session did, however, have one salient effect. It kept most of the Fortune 500 companies from raising prices that year. The companies feared wage and price controls administered by Kennedy's administration would be popular with many working-class and even some middle-class Americans—and therefore guarantee Kennedy's reelection.[5]

One industry, however, didn't get that message and paid dearly for it. Within a week after the Kennedy-Iacocca "debate," the airlines, one by one, decided to raise airline ticket prices. Kennedy went on the offensive a couple of days later, which only proved to the other businessmen why they did not wish to challenge the president.

Kennedy called a press conference on the subject and spoke at some length. He told the reporters and the nation, "One of our greatest founding fathers, John Adams, once observed that the 'internal intrigues of our monied and landed . . . aristocracies are and will be our ruin.' Now, one doesn't have to hold the radical views of our founders to realize that raising prices without a strong justification is inimical to our nation's well-being. The business press, from the *Wall Street Journal* to *Business Week,* has been constantly threatening American workers and consumers with the specter of price increases every time our administration attempts to promote fair play and a balanced economy. American working families deserve better than to see the wage gains they fought so hard for in union struggles go out the window when corporations jack up their prices. This is particularly so in industries such as the airline industry, which depend upon our government to provide them subsidies with public airports, government grants, and tax credits for research and development for modern passenger jets and the like. Such government-subsidized businesses, indeed, any large enterprise, should recognize the American working family fights hard for them in wars and buys their products in war and peace. They don't deserve a kick in the face in the form of price gouging."

With the dramatic increase in labor union membership, the lessening of Cold War tensions, the expansion of public television through Blair Clark institution of a more pro-worker economic slant to public television's nightly news—not to mention the continued success against poverty through the Bed-Sty program, among other programs—American culture was ingesting "community" rhetoric, as opposed to "business" rhetoric, more than at any time since the late 1930s. This change in American culture helped create an immediate and strong pressure on the airlines to roll back their price increases. Indeed, within three days after the press conference, one by one the airlines announced a rescinding of the price hikes.

In the first timeline, the rhetoric of business almost completely overpowered the rhetoric of labor or community. For example, most economists, media pundits, and politicians—and many Americans—were rarely sympathetic with workers who were on a labor strike. Most of the time the corporate-owned media covered a strike from the point of view of how it disrupted business and affected "consumers." And in that context, consumer did not mean "worker" because both businesses and consumers faced shortages of the affected product or service during the workers' strike. Thus, what looked like a balance between workers and business interests by reporters was more misleading than not.

It rarely occurred to most reporters or their bosses in such media that workers do not decide to go on strike the way a wealthy woman decides to go to a mall. There are reasons that are generally based upon an underlying unfairness that cause workers to risk not getting paid at all—or losing their jobs—than continue working. If consumer-workers heard these complaints more clearly, they might have developed a better sense of solidarity in the first timeline that was increasingly lost.

After awhile, most Americans also saw deep inequality in income and wealth as "natural"—and therefore beyond the power of government or politicians to ameliorate or solve. Practically speaking, this meant that any politician who proposed any policy to lessen inequality was seen as a hopeless dreamer and, thus, not taken seriously.

And in this political environment, there were related consequences. From the early 1970s under Republican President Nixon to the end of Democratic President Bill Clinton's term in office, the income of *corporate* chief executive officers went from 79 times the average workers' income to 411 times that income. Workers' incomes from 1970 to the beginning of the twenty-first century stagnated at best during that time, while the poor, through most of these years, fell behind.[6]

And yet, candidates in each election cycle became more and more passive, compared to the era before 1968, in terms of calling for government policies to directly assist workers and the poor—even as the government's reach grew in terms of prison building and business tax incentives or subsidies. By the 1990s, it became clear that Democratic president Bill Clinton was more "conservative" in economic matters than a liberal Republican like Nelson Rockefeller had been in the 1960s.[7]

The first timeline also saw the rise of a particular form of economic globalization where rules were codified to protect patent rights, but very little was done to protect the rights of labor or environment. It was a time when corporations could merely threaten to move factories—and workers' jobs—off U.S. shores in order to defeat unions or hold down wage gains. Further, the corporate dominated media ridiculed the notion of placing tariffs on products coming from low-wage, child labor, and slave wage countries—and candidates who disagreed with that media consensus, whether on the Left or Right, were themselves ridiculed and deprived of ever-important corporate funding for their election campaigns.

The effect of all this was to skew the political discussion further and further away from economic issues relating to union and community interests and toward the interests and culture of business. This left America at the start of the twenty-first century as more of a business culture than it had been at any time since the 1920s.

Back in the RFK timeline, however, most commentators and political insiders in the early spring of 1972 thought Kennedy would coast to victory in the fall. Despite Kennedy's concern about tax cuts, most of these observers remembered the 1970 midterm elections and the strong voter turnout from labor and inner city minorities. In a presidential election year, the commentators and insiders knew that the turnout was historically higher among these groups, which was good news for Kennedy.

Further, with the economy remaining strong, soldiers coming home from Europe, wanting jobs more than tax cuts, and the sense that Kennedy, not his Republican challengers, had the experience to lead the Free World, there was nothing to stop Kennedy's re-election . . . except maybe a scandal of some sort.

Chapter 27

THE MOTHER OF ALL SCANDALS

Robert Kennedy was feeling lucky at the beginning of May 1972. He had survived assassins in 1968 and 1971. He had survived nuclear alerts from Russia, nuclear threats from China, a host of politically charged disputes, and was ready to unveil a new tax reform proposal designed to blunt the Reagan-Roth-tax-cut juggernaut. He also remained favored to win reelection in the fall.

Then, on Sunday, May 7, his good luck suddenly turned bad. On that day, a feature article appeared in the *Manchester* (New Hampshire) *Union Leader,* which was a newspaper published and edited by William Loeb, a staunch right-wing Republican and John Birch Society supporter. The article appeared on the front page, under a bold, two-line headline that read:

"The President's Women: More Than You Know and Many Are Afraid to Ask."

Written by the newspaper's two leading political reporters and based on FBI leaks and confirmations from mostly unnamed individuals, the article depicted Robert Kennedy as a lothario, having affairs with various Hollywood starlets during the 1960s when he was serving as attorney general and as a senator from New York.

The article said the information had been "bouncing around for years throughout Washington, D.C., and within the corridors of power, both in business and in government. However, most of the American press has refused to report, until now, on what many call the 'private lives of our political leaders.'" The article also discussed the martyred John Kennedy's well-known—at least among the elite in the media and political world—affair with Marilyn Monroe, and also disclosed Robert Kennedy's affair with the now deceased sex symbol and actress. The article did not stop there. Hollywood starlets Kim Novak, Candace Bergen, and others, including Kristi Witker, a new anchorwoman for a local news show in New York, were identified as Kennedy's "paramours."

The *New York Times,* which was becoming more hostile to Kennedy's "knee-jerk support of labor unions" and refusal to support the federal abortion rights bill pending in Congress, waited two days to print its own story on the subject. When the *Times* confirmed the story with its own reporters and published their findings, reporters in Washington asked Jack Newfield, Kennedy's press secretary, for a comment. Newfield gave the memorable though ineffective response, "Thoreau once wrote in an essay, 'I believe that the mind can be permanently profaned by the habit of trivial things . . . Read not the *Times*. Read the Eternities.' Ladies and gentlemen, we do not comment on gossip, particularly malicious gossip."

William F. Buckley, in a widely reprinted column that spoke for many journalists and editors, wrote, "Mr. Newfield is to be commended for quoting someone with the historic importance of Thoreau. However, one cannot fail to notice that the essay the press secretary cited was entitled 'Life Without Principle.' Perhaps Mr. Newfield has engaged in a Freudian defense, where a denial is actually an admission."

The night of Newfield's remarks, CBS News, with a report from Dan Rather supported by none other than Walter Cronkite, played up the *Times* article. They also spoke to the *Union Leader* reporters who had "broken" the story. Reporter Rather at one point gravely intoned that the reporters had been "willing to risk their careers" to "hunt down the information now seeping into the light of day for the first time"—meaning, of course, the first time the Establishment media dared to publish such information.

The *Washington Post* refused to cover the story for several days, with editor Ben Bradlee initially in denial—"I've known Jack and Bob Kennedy for almost two decades! There can't be any truth to this filth!" Then, when faced with his own reporters' confirmation of many, but not all of the stories, Bradlee announced to the entire newsroom, "Respectable newspapers do not print gossip. We print *hard news* here—and if anyone doesn't like it, they can work for Bill Loeb's paper in New Hampshire or the *National Enquirer* down in Florida!"

Katherine "Kay" Graham, the *Post*'s publisher, called Bradlee a day after his solemn announcement in the newsroom. "Whether we like it or not, Ben, we may no longer be able to ignore this story. The latest edition of *Newsweek,* our sister publication, hits the stands tomorrow with an article on this scandalous matter. *Time* is already up and running on the story—and our newspaper is being criticized in many quarters for not covering it."

"But with all due respect, Mrs. Graham," said Bradlee, "if we start printing stories of politicians' extramarital dalliances, we won't be able to find room to print the scores of ball games, let alone hard news of wars, taxes, and labor strikes. Corporate businessmen mess around with their secretaries. And at business conventions, I hate to speak this way to you, Mrs. Graham, there are almost as many call girls as businessmen. I can understand if the president was going to a brothel attached to the Russian Embassy, kind of like that Christine Keeler–Lord Profumo scandal in England ten years ago. But the *Union Leader*'s follow-up story admits Kennedy has been completely faithful to his wife since the time of the assassination attempt in Los Angeles almost four years ago. This whole subject is not only gossip, it's *old* gossip!"

Bradlee was obviously very worried about setting a precedent for anyone else—especially starting with himself, for the respected and venerable *Post* editor was known to cheat regularly on his wife and was, at the time, just beginning a "relationship" with a young woman reporter who worked at the paper—a pretty blonde.

"Mr. Bradlee," intoned Graham, "this is the *president* we're talking about here! Not some small-town congressman or a corporate executive in the private world of business, however distasteful I have found such conduct over the years. I am personally as shocked about Bob—I mean, the president—as you are. For the past several years, even before he became president, he staked out this moral mantle on so many policy issues—more than his brother did, I must say—and yet he picked up where his brother left off with Marilyn Monroe—"

"We don't *know* that he did!" Bradlee said, voice rising. "So she called him a few times at the Justice Department in 1962. There is no evidence he spoke with her, or if he did, whether it was very long. The initial article said there was a long-term affair, but Monroe died in the summer of 1962, and Bob couldn't have seen her more than four times according to that second article by the *Union Leader* reporters—and our reporters confirmed this, too. I haven't been completely ignoring this story, Mrs. Graham. I just don't see its public value—"

"Ben," said an exasperated Graham, "I won't debate this, except to say the president's flings with other Hollywood starlets, especially Edgar Bergen's daughter when she was barely above legal age . . . Well, it shows him to be . . . Oh, I find it so *below* him! We are behind the others in covering this story, whether we like it or not, and there is a political connection to this—"

"What political connection?" Bradley shouted, forgetting for the moment who paid his salary.

"Ben, stop taking this so personally! Some are already saying it. The president, shall we say, hypocritically flaunts morality when it comes to money issues and abortion. It's legitimate to ask for some consistency in a public person's private life, I suppose. I bet some of those straight-laced, self-righteous union leaders and radicals are just as bad. While I recognize that this story may mean we are crossing the Rubicon . . . " She sighed with disdain. "I simply must go now, Ben. People, as usual, are waiting for me. The story runs. We will not fall behind on this again." Click.

The story on Bob Kennedy's sexual escapades in the 1960s ran in the *Post* the next morning. Front page.

The day after that, "the dam really broke," as Larry O'Brien put it decades later, with another front-page story in the *Union Leader* headlined: "Jackie and Bobby: More Than Friendly In-Laws?" The story was directly fed to Dan

Rather later that day for the *CBS Evening News*. The *Union Leader* reporters, now with near-celebrity status themselves, wrote that Jackie Kennedy, despondent over the murder of her husband, began spending more and more time alone with Robert Kennedy in 1964 and 1965. By 1965, according to witnesses, the two met at Jackie's apartment on a regular basis and were seen in public acting "like lovers." Most sensationally, "unnamed" sources said they were "lovers in fact" for almost a year. It was as if the *Union Leader* was daring Kennedy, a sitting president, to sue them for libel.

CBS lawyers edited the television report of the story over Rather's objections. Rather was merely allowed to tell viewers that the story was "confirmed with two of the unnamed sources, but we are not completely satisfied that we should disclose this information as a fact—other than to say the *Union Leader*, which has been on this story from the beginning, believes it is true."

CBS Chairman William Paley had told both Cronkite and Rather that he was very concerned about risking the wrath from the leader of the free world—and federal government agencies such as the FCC and the IRS—if CBS said anything more definitive. He told Cronkite that what had been reported was probably already too much. Paley was himself a serial adulterer and worried about the implications of this story if it went beyond the president.

Jackie, now married to Aristotle Onassis and living in Greece, would not comment on the assertion that she had an affair with Bob Kennedy. Her husband, known to intimates as "Ari," hated Bob Kennedy more than anyone on the planet. Ari Onassis let it be known to business intimates, and to one of the *Union Leader* reporters indirectly through an associate, that the stories were true. He told them, "It happened. And I bet she's still in love with the little runt."

When confronted publicly, the Greek magnate denied knowing anything about Jackie's private life before "she and I dated." He publicly denounced this "invasion of my wife's honor and privacy."

Over the next fortnight, American political polling data showed a marked decline in support for the president among women in Los Angeles, Chicago, New York City, and San Francisco who considered themselves "feminists." Such women, over the previous four years, had been most vocal against the continued double standard that allowed even pro-feminist men to treat women like sexual objects while women were constantly having to fight the "either/or" of virgin and harlot. The abortion issue crystallized the feminists' frustration over women's lack of personal autonomy and being able to control their own "bodies and destinies." The sex scandal, combined with Kennedy's refusal to support the federal abortion legislation, was now seen as consistent with the president's—and his administration's—hypocrisy and disrespect toward "womyn," as some feminists insisted on spelling the word.

Other women, mostly suburban housewives and religious women in smaller cities like Cleveland, Topeka, and into the Bible Belt, shrugged their shoulders regarding the scandal, according to the first Harris Poll on the subject. The

Harris organization, which was considered more liberal than the Gallup Poll, stated that "women among the poor and working class, and some in the middle class, are likely to say, 'Tell me something that most men haven't been doing forever in Hollywood, in politics, at their business conventions—and with that floozy down the street!'"

The few nationally syndicated female pundits were also divided. Ellen Goodman of the *Boston Globe* was of a mind to forgive and forget. She wrote, "I take a back seat to no feminists, even icons such as *Ms. Magazine* founder Gloria Steinem, who are almost ready to demand that the president should resign for his past indiscretions. The original modern feminist, Susan B. Anthony, if she were alive today, would more likely beg to differ with Ms. Steinem, though. Anthony said, in one of her many pronouncements, 'If a man's public record be a clear one, if he has kept his pledges before the world, I do not inquire what his private life may have been.' Robert Kennedy didn't run on a platform for or against abortion. He ran on a platform of ending America's military involvement in Vietnam and trying to make life better for working people and the poor. He has kept his pledge. We must inquire no further into this unpleasant subject."

Meg Greenfield, an up-and-coming executive at the *Washington Post,* was "champing at the bit," as some male reporters whispered, to attack Kennedy's indiscretions. When finally freed from Ben Bradlee's code that only "hard news" can be covered, Greenfield unleashed a scathing editorial. She wrote, "President Kennedy reveals himself as the worst sort of male chauvinist pig"—a popular slang phrase of women's liberationists at the time. "He moralizes his indecision on abortion rights while women continue to die in back-street alleys, according to abortion rights' advocates. Then in a different but nearby back room as attorney general and as a senator, he groped and took advantage of younger women as if he were the publisher of *Playboy* magazine, not one of America's leaders. At the end of the day, there is no nuance or any countervailing influence in this sordid saga. Perhaps, then, the more strident feminists are correct that the 'personal is political.' The president should resign now—or must we instead wait for further scandal?"

Betty Friedan, in a letter to the editor of the *Post,* asked, "What does Meg Greenfield make of Grover Cleveland's fathering an 'illegitimate' child, using the parlance of the late nineteenth century and into our own still benighted time? What of the mistresses of Franklin Roosevelt and Dwight Eisenhower? Is the answer always to resign? The personal is political, perhaps, but not in the way Meg Greenfield believes. It appears that if one politically opposes the president's policies, then one is inclined to demand he resign as a result of this 'personal' episode. As for myself, I am not sure what to make of this news of Robert Kennedy's past. Yet, it bears repeating that all we hear of are past indiscretions. It would behoove women journalists not to leave themselves open to stereotyping such as 'gossips,' 'groupies,' or 'black widows.'"

Kennedy could take little solace from this argument among women, for, in a Gallup poll following the Harris poll, quite a few of the housewives and religious women said they might have to "make up their minds" before deciding on whom they would vote for in the presidential election in the fall. The polling more ominously showed that women in the upper-middle and upper-income brackets, regardless of whether they considered themselves "feminists," were less likely to support Kennedy in the fall because of the sexual dalliances exposed in the press. The refusal of the Kennedy administration to support the federal abortion rights bill loomed behind the scandal, as did women's growing agreement with their husbands' view that people at their economic levels were paying too much in taxes.

First Lady Ethel Kennedy, for her part, had been seething with anger since the scandal broke, but not initially at her husband. As she told Betty Rollin, a television news reporter and friend of the family, she was "outraged" at the press and the "vast Republican, pro-abortion conspiracy to destroy my family!" She finally turned her rage on her husband when the Jackie O. story was reported on the *CBS Evening News* on May 14.

"Did you or didn't you?" she demanded of her husband as she ran into the bedroom where he was resting.

Kennedy hesitated.

That was enough for Ethel, who screamed, "Damn you! I always—*always!*—hated that . . . that *bitch!* How—how could you? I *trusted* you!" Ethel ran out of their bedroom and slammed the door. Later that night, she stayed in little Rose's room, crying softly on and off for several hours, doing her best not to wake the toddler.

Seeing the polling, and his wife's reaction, Kennedy was now in a full panic. He called the O Boys for a late-evening meeting at the White House. They arrived at the Oval Office in less than half an hour after he called. Kennedy was standing and pacing as he spoke.

"I don't know for sure what Ethel just screamed at me about, but I know it's gotta be that new story tonight. Why does everyone—even Ethel for chrissakes!—listen to that friggin' crazy asshole bastard Loeb!? The *Times,* CBS, the television networks, the *Post,* all of them! Loeb's worse than the *National Enquirer!* I barely had anything to do with most of these women, guys! And no matter how many times I could tell Ethel that I didn't have sex with Jackie, well . . . Damn it! You know it—and I know it that we're—I'm in big trouble here. What really pisses me off is, here I've been a goddamned monk for *four goddamned years*—you think I have *time* to . . . to fool around . . . after working here all day and dealing with a wife and eleven children nearly every day and night?! Hell! For most of the last year, I've been cooped up *here* most of the time because Ethel and you guys think someone's gunning for me out there! And now right in the middle of the primary season, *this shit* comes down on us! We gotta control this—nah, it's friggin' *hopeless!*"

O'Donnell and O'Brien were numb from thinking about how they were going to make this go away without the administration going away as well. O'Brien, wanting to make sure his boss didn't just quit right there, said, "Bob, we're working on something that will get this off the front page. Really. We can't overreact here. Just stay focused on the country!"

O'Donnell said glumly, "I hope you're right, Larry."

Kennedy added sardonically, "Larry, I doubt a nuclear war in Asia could get this off the front page now . . . "

O'Brien, again trying to keep some perspective, said, "Mr. President, I'm taking a risk with you right now, but I'm going to say it: You need to speak out to the public on this—fast. And with Ethel at your side shedding a tear . . . with a look of love for you like nobody's business."

"That's just it, it's nobody's business, damn it!" yelled Kennedy. "And after tonight, I don't know if Ethel's going to leave me for Dan Friggin' Rather! I was hoping people would give Reagan a hard time for being divorced, but you can throw that shit out the window! He's a—"

O'Donnell said, "Snap out of it, Bob! I mean it! I've been living with the 'worst that happens' scenario for five days now, and kind of like Yarborough once said—Say, hasn't he been sorta quiet? I'm thinking he's not being—"

Kennedy put up his hand to stop O'Donnell. "Ralph called me on the first day and said to go public. He's not being a fair-weather supporter, Kenny. He's been pretty damned loyal," said a more-depressed-by-the-minute Kennedy. "I told him I'd see what the reaction is after a week. He said I might be sorry if I waited. Well, he's right."

"He's *damn* right, Mr. President," said O'Donnell. "I'll ask Helen," O'Donnell's wife, "to talk with Ethel. Look, we're already digging up dirt on lots of Republican congressmen and senators—we also got the goods on some of the top corporate guys. But this Jackie thing . . . well, that's a tough one . . . "

"'They all do it' is our leading argument?" Kennedy asked with an air of disgust.

"Um, Mr. President," said O'Brien, eyeing his boss in disbelief, "that's our *only* argument—and it includes you expressing your regret, remorse, contrition, and anything else that sounds good. You got somethin' better? I'm working on a different scandal concerning Ronald Reagan that's a doozy. It's financial, is all I'm gonna say . . . "

Kennedy shrugged his shoulders, deep in dark thoughts about whether he and the country would have been better off if he were "martyred' in February 1971 when that second nut went after him at the Press Club. He said to O'Brien, "A financial scandal? That doesn't sound very interesting to me . . . which means it'll bore the voters . . . But do what you can, Larry. Now, Kenny, tell me what I'm gonna say other than 'I quit.'"

After conferring until midnight with O'Donnell, Kennedy went to bed alone. The next morning he begged for forgiveness from Ethel. It was "painful beyond belief," said Kennedy to O'Donnell later that morning, "and she still didn't forgive me."

O'Donnell had his wife call Ethel, who listened politely, but Ethel was not any further along the road to forgiveness than when her husband had left her that morning for a strategy session with O'Donnell and Yarborough. Helen O'Donnell was known as a "quiet drunk," and Ethel, while supportive of and friendly with her, was not going to take advice from Helen on anything this significant.

The Kennedy matriarch, Rose, was deeply upset at the latest turn in the continuing scandal. Tired of trying not to interfere, she finally decided to pay a visit to Ethel that same morning. Rose had been living in Washington, D.C., since her husband passed away in November 1969.[1] "Ethel," said the Kennedy matriarch, "I've come to see you, if you'll speak with me. I'm not here for Bob—I haven't spoken with him in days. I am calling you to say one thing. If you are half as angry as I am about all this, I would presume you aren't talking to my son right now. But you *have* to stay strong and *support* your husband. He was a very bad boy, I know, but he was nothing compared to my husband, as you may know by now. Times have changed, dear, as we've discussed on occasion, and your husband, my Bobby, he's changed, too—better than most men, as you may also know. And he deserves some credit—"

Ethel began to cry. Through her tears she said, "I did *everything* for him—and *her*—after Jack . . . I was so *trusting!* How could she? *How could he?*"

Rose replied, "Ethel, I'm not sure of any of this gossip, but I am sure, as I said, your husband needs you, and he's been good to you since you spoke with him after . . . Los Angeles. After Bobby's father passed on—I never said this to you, but I will now. Bobby talked with me about his father and he said, 'Mother, I also strayed from time to time with other women since I've been married. I don't do it anymore, though.' There's nothing, nothing at all out there that says otherwise," although Rose and Ethel both thought to themselves, "yet."

Rose concluded, "This morning you're more angry—I can tell—about the 'who' than the 'what,' and I understand. I've lived long enough, though, to know you and Bob share a bond that shouldn't be broken, not now, and certainly not now for the country's sake. You have to go to him—"

"But—"

"*Go to him!* Ethel, it is up to you to—not forgive him, I admire your courage in confronting him, dear, but go to him. And tell him you'll be right there with him—always. I assume, even though I'm just considered a little old biddie and not a political operative, that he's going to make a public statement today or tomorrow . . . Right?"

Ethel, who was no slouch in political strategy, either, after all these years, sniffed some tears away and said, "Well, I assume so. I . . . guess . . . I got . . . I must have . . . "

"You 'must' is correct, Ethel. You must stand by Bob. There's a whole world out there that wants him to lose and a few who . . . well . . . you . . . *You* need to be there *with* him, not just *for* him."

After some silence, and a formal, but pleasant goodbye to the mother-in-law she revered, Ethel walked over to the Oval Office and into the meeting with Kennedy, O'Donnell, and Yarborough. She demanded more than said, "Kenny, Ralph, a few minutes alone, please. Thank you."

O'Donnell and Yarborough left, and O'Donnell immediately called his wife for whatever news he could get about Ethel's emotional state.

Left alone, the First Husband and First Wife talked. As they did so, Ethel realized the hurt would last a long time, but she also realized she loved him . . . or at least, she told herself caustically, she recognized the political importance of acting like she was still in love with him. The most important thing Ethel said was this:

"Bob, this thing with Jackie—no, Bob. No denials! I shouldn't have trusted her—or you—even if you keep telling me you didn't do anything! This wound is going to take awhile to heal. But you're a good father, and for the past few years you've been the best husband I could ask for. I can't throw that away. If you need to make a confession to the public, I'll be there."

At the end of their discussion, the First Wife kissed the First Husband, but the kiss was almost perfunctory, on the cheek near his upper lip. With this kiss, macho-tough-as-nails Bob Kennedy choked on his tears and shook his head to keep them from escaping. All the emotional toll of being president, of his guilt over Jack's murder, his past marital indiscretions, and the conflicted feelings about his father hit him all at once.

Ethel, the "dutiful" wife, as she later told her sister, Georgeann, cradled her husband's head against her breast and shoulder. My heart might heal after all, Ethel thought to herself. She let out a loud sigh, but thought to herself again, as she often had throughout her life: Men!

Kennedy called Yarborough and O'Donnell back to his office. With Ethel present, he announced, "Gentlemen, we go public this evening."

"That's the spirit, son," said Yarborough.

O'Donnell smiled but wondered if they'd be scripted enough to deliver an effective speech that night.

Jack Newfield alerted reporters that the president would speak to the nation at 8 P.M. Eastern Time about the reports on his private conduct during the 1960s.

That evening in the White House pressroom, Kennedy stood, ready to speak. Ethel was just off to one side, standing almost next to him from the camera's viewpoint, her face visible within camera range of the president.

Vice President Yarborough was standing behind and to the left of Kennedy, along with Senators Hubert Humphrey and George McGovern, and Congressman Tip O'Neill, who had just been elected Speaker of the House of Representatives a few months before. O'Brien called them for the occasion, and since none of them except O'Neill were running for office that year, they obliged. O'Neill told O'Brien he'd be there. "I'd take a bullet for Bob. Of course I'll stand by him. He's my Irish blood-brother."

Robert Kennedy, humble but not begging, spoke to the nation. He acknowledged the reports about his affairs during the 1960s and said, "I could argue about particular facts and particular persons, but there is no need to dwell further on private facts. The basic facts are true. Although I have been married to one person, my wife, Ethel, for over twenty years—twenty-two years next month, to be exact—I was not faithful to her during a relatively short period in my life. I am not, unfortunately, the first husband who was unfaithful to his wife. I'd like to think I could be the last. But that's not how life is. It is, however, how my life is and will be from now on, with my wife, Ethel.

"For too many years, and I've had some time to reflect these past few days, some of us men, whether we are in public life, private business, or wherever, have treated women as mere objects, and not persons for whom we have respect. At different points in our marriages, we have not respected our brides, our wives. We think we are not hurting our loved ones when we act this way . . . " He paused to make sure he didn't let a tear out, "but we do. And we have." He turned around to look at Ethel.

Ethel, recalling that moment years later, said she "almost lost it right there." The camera captured a shiver from Ethel as she shook her head mildly in affirming her husband's words.

Kennedy turned back to the reporters and the television cameras and spoke again. "If we say 'others have done this,' it doesn't make it right even if it answers those who imply that I alone have engaged in this kind of conduct. But I hope that my coming forward will become an example for other husbands, whether they are corporate executives, Democrat or Republican—many of them fathers, too, I might add. Each of us must show more respect and love for the women we committed to love, honor, and cherish. I have apologized to my wife in the privacy, what little there is, of our lives. I do not think, as the president of the United States, that saying 'I'm sorry' in private is enough."

Departing suddenly from the scripted speech, Kennedy turned to Ethel and said, "Ethel, I'm sorry for hurting you."

Ethel, hearing this, could no longer control her emotions. She began to cry, and Kennedy reached out and took her hand, repeating, "I'm sorry." The camera had moved to the left to catch this scene. Kennedy's words were barely audible but were played over and over by the networks just after the press conference.

Ethel later told her eldest daughter, Kathleen, "I wanted to scream into the cameras, 'You leave us alone—all of you!'" But Ethel didn't say anything, while several reporters present agreed that they felt as if they were more akin to "peeping Toms" at that moment.

The reaction by people across the country was one of sympathy for the First Couple, but a few—and only a few—Republicans and anti-Kennedy elements began to question whether the hand-holding had been "staged." The sex scandal had also caused certain network reporters and pundits to overcome their previous hesitation in personally attacking the president.

James J. Kilpatrick, a longtime southern columnist who loathed the Kennedys, wrote, "Why is it that liberals always denied Nixon the right to be sentimental about his wife, his family, or his dog, Checkers?[2] Yet, when Bobby and Ethel Kennedy slobber on national television, we're supposed to shut up and leave these poor people alone? Rubbish. The man should quit before the entire country is scandalized forever."

Tom Wicker, a southerner supportive of the Kennedy administration, was disgusted by such anti-Kennedy attacks. In one of his last columns in the *New York Times*—he was leaving the *Times* to write for the *Washington Post*—Wicker wrote, "The president did nothing that most politicians, and they know I know who they are, haven't done for years. Unlike those politicians—and businessmen, I might add—the president renewed his vow to his wife four years ago and kept his word. Next month the president and Mrs. Kennedy will celebrate twenty-two years together as husband and wife. Those who oppose Preseident Kennedy should do so for reasons having to do with public—and I repeat, public—issues such as his support for labor unions, civil rights, or his dealings in foreign affairs. His wife has apparently been doing a good job keeping him personally honest with her these last few years, and we in the press, especially, *who have our own skeletons,* ought to know better than to continue to print this sort of private gossip regarding our national leaders."

The *Times'* editor excised the italicized portion of that last sentence.

The battle lines were thus drawn and the arguing continued. Kennedy's slippage in the polls stopped, and his positive ratings began to rise above 50 percent again. In early June, however, when asked whom they would vote for if the election were held at that time, just below 50 percent of respondents chose Kennedy. The Gallup Poll showed, most ominously, that Kennedy would barely beat Senator Roth and might lose to Governor Reagan. Amidst all the coverage of Kennedy's scandal, Abrams bowed out at the end of May, pledging his support to Reagan.

The strangest thing, noted Walter Dean Burnham, a political scientist at the Massachusetts Institute of Technology (MIT), was that the Eastern European governments of Poland, Czechoslovakia, and Bulgaria were either collapsing to anti-Communist forces or electing non-Communists to office during Kennedy's sex scandal. In mid-June 1972, the Berlin Wall came down, and the people of East Germany voted for the reunification of Germany. There was drinking and singing in the streets of a newly and fully united Germany. Even German Jews, the few who were left, celebrated with the new German chancellor, Social Democrat Party leader Willy Brandt.

By July 1972, all of the Eastern European states had become independent of the Soviet Union. Brandt, pledging that Germany would "forever remain anti-militarist and in favor of economic development," declared to the people of the former East Germany and to the newly freed nations of Eastern Europe that "the answer to freedom and stability is neither fully socialist, capitalist, or communist. Freedom and stability come with a mixed economy that emphasizes the social contract between people in a tolerant and loving community."

Western Europeans also realized they were wealthy enough on their own to help their Eastern European neighbors with a Marshall Plan strategy. The European Union headquarters in Brussels became an important clearing-house for donating aid to the Eastern Europeans. Brandt convinced the Conservative British prime minister, Edward Heath, that the British, French, and Germans should take the lead in providing this aid. The plan for restoration of Eastern Europe was formally known as "The Free Europe Plan," although many on the European continent called it the Brandt Plan.

Although some word of this seeped into the news coverage in the United States, the nation remained focused on the nature and meaning of Robert Kennedy's sexual conduct during the 1960s and the "loss of innocence" that was inherent in the revelation of this information.

Not receiving more than cursory coverage in the U.S. media were the series of small electoral and other relatively bloodless revolutions in Latin and Central America. In Brazil, just eight years after a U.S.-supported military coup, a revolution nearly occurred after general strikes began in São Paolo. The strike was led by a young militant leader of the metalworkers union, Luis Ignacio Lula da Silva. When the strikes spread to other cities and then to the capital, Brasilia, some in the State Department advised that the United States should back repressive measures by the president, General Ernesto Geisel. However, the administration's support of labor rights abroad and at home interfered with foreign policy's "business as usual." Secretary of State Bowles, instead, told Geisel to negotiate with the union. Geisel initially refused because, he said, there would be an "immediate" military coup if he did that. Most Brazilian military leaders were longtime supporters of the interests of the families who controlled Brazil and represented the top 5 percent of the nation in terms of wealth.

Secretary Bowles spoke with Secretary Warnke, and, with the approval of Kennedy, the United States sent battleships to the eastern shores of Brazil and arms to General Geisel. Geisel thereafter secured support from a prominent military leader, General Joao Figueiredo, to begin negotiations with the union leader, Lula. A coup was immediately attempted, as Geisel had feared, but Brazil put down the revolt with the help of U.S. Navy ships, which shelled the coup leaders' main military post. Geisel, feeling empowered, began a larger and more significant program of land reform and nationalized private oil interests near and dear to the Brazilian "families" and Occidental, an American oil company that had a substantial investment in that nation. And, after the initial "revolutionary" fervor settled, Brazil asked for U.S. economic assistance. In return for the assistance, Brazil was told to "cool it," as Bowles said publicly, on further nationalization. In private, Bowles added, "At least for a while." The Catholic Church proved to be a major supporter of the reforms, which Kennedy, as a Catholic, heartily approved.

In El Salvador, an "election revolution" occurred just as the sex scandal hit Kennedy. José Napoleon Duarte, a Socialist, ran on a "unity-reform ticket" with a conservative businessman named Manuel Ungo. The two won, respectively, the presidency and vice presidency, defeating the traditional ruling party that represented what were called the "fourteen families"—referring to the families who "owned" the nation known in English translation as "The Savior."

Chet Bowles called Defense Secretary Warnke after hearing the El Salvadoran military was thinking of staging a coup to prevent the reformers from taking office. Warnke, acting on Bowles' suggestion—or essentially on his own, as he later said to a chagrined Kennedy—sent the Seventh Fleet to the coast of El Salvador with a warning to its military that the United States supported Duarte and Ungo. A coup was avoided, and shortly thereafter the would-be coup leaders were arrested by the civilian government and the military leaders who remained loyal to that government.[3]

Kennedy had heard criticism from Clark Clifford, Dean Rusk, and others in the permanent Cold War establishment when he had approved the use of military force in Brazil. After hearing that Warnke and Bowles had sent the Seventh Fleet to the coast of El Salvador, Kennedy told Bowles and Warnke, "I don't want us sending our military every time some nation votes for some Socialists or land reformers. I understand we don't want any more Vietnams, fellas, but let's not hasten revolutions around here!"

Then, lowering his voice a bit, he said, "I've taken a lot of shit, in case you don't know, from Clark Clifford, who may or may not still be my friend, and Bob Strauss, who's already talking about the Democratic Party 'post-Kennedy,' since he now believes we're going to lose to Reagan or Roth this fall. Between him, Dean Rusk, McCloy, and others, we have more than enough enemies in our own party. You guys don't deal with the hardcore political shit like the O Boys, Yarborough, or Reuther. You see, I'm getting hammered on this sex thing. There's talk the Democratic Cold Warriors are quietly shifting to Reagan because we're supposedly undoing 'Pax America'—" Raising his voice again, he said, "But we're not! Our foreign policy will remain cautious, gentlemen! Cautious! We need to get the Establishment back on our side—at least the Democrats!"

Bowles thought to himself, *Remain* cautious? If we're going to be 'cautious,' that would be a *change* in our policy!

Chapter 28

DOUBLE-EDGED SWORDS, PART I

Days before Kennedy's "wifey" speech, as some pro-Republican commentators called it, Republican presidential candidate Ronald Reagan accepted the endorsement of his former rival, General Abrams. Abrams thought he could hold out and be a dark horse at the convention, but leaders of the Republican Party told him, "Our tracking polls show you are perceived more as a MacArthur than an Eisenhower. Go with Reagan or Roth or you're out." Reagan, trying to create momentum for his nomination against his remaining opponent, Roth, defied tradition and announced in May 1972 that Abrams would be his vice-presidential choice at the Republican Party convention to be held in August.

Although it was not settled as to whether Reagan or Roth would win the Republican nomination, O'Brien was sure it would be Reagan. In an effort to derail the California governor and deflect attention from the sex scandal involving his boss, O'Brien was gathering background information on Reagan. O'Brien kept telling himself Reagan had to be corrupt in some way. O'Brien spoke first with reporter Ward Just of the *Post* to ask if he had picked up anything about Reagan on the "campaign trail." Just referred O'Brien to Lou Cannon, a reporter recently starting with the *Washington Post* after covering Reagan for many years for the *Sacramento Bee*. Cannon hesitated to speak to O'Brien about Reagan. He simply said, "Why don't you check the 1962 grand jury investigation over the sweetheart deal Reagan did with the Hollywood talent agency, MCA, while he was Screen Actors Guild president? You might find that interesting, Mr. O'Brien. There's no sex scandal with Ronald Reagan, if that's what you're looking for. Ron and Nancy Reagan are two intertwined souls. Ron calls Nancy 'Mommy,' which to some modern minds sounds kinky, but it's really an old-fashioned way of saying he loves her."

O'Brien was led, through more contacts, to a former Justice Department Anti-Trust Division attorney who would not directly comment as to the conclusions of the government's investigation. However, the attorney did give O'Brien leads on people to speak with. O'Brien spoke with various witnesses regarding Reagan's relationship with MCA.

O'Brien learned that MCA had been a large theatrical agency in the 1950s. As a result of being allowed a waiver from the Screen Actors Guild, a waiver no other agency received, it simultaneously developed into a production company. By the early 1960s, it had swallowed up most of Universal Studios to become one of the largest production companies of its time. Reagan, as president of the Screen Actors Guild in the 1950s, and under a talent contract with MCA, secured the special waiver for MCA.

In 1961, after MCA had purchased much of Universal Studios' assets, the antitrust division of the U.S. Justice Department stepped up its investigation of MCA and its spectacular rise since the 1950s. The investigation had begun under the Eisenhower administration and continued in the Kennedy administration. The antitrust investigation eventually led to Ronald Reagan being called as a witness in 1962 before a federal grand jury that was working on the investigation with the Justice Department. Reagan was asked why only MCA had received a blanket waiver from the rule that prohibited a studio or agency from representing actors and producing their films. Reagan claimed other studios or talent agencies could have asked, but the investigators quickly discounted this response after discussions with other studios and agencies showed this was an iron-clad separation that only MCA was able to penetrate.

During his testimony, Reagan said "I don't know" or "I don't remember" more than fifty times in "responding" to various questions, including questions dealing with whether there was a potential payback from MCA to Reagan in the form of acting work and other remuneration. The Justice Department may have thought about adding Reagan as a party to the investigation, but its lead lawyers may also have concluded Reagan was a stooge or a dupe for MCA.[1]

It took O'Brien more time than he had expected it would, but he finally secured several of the Justice Department's confidential reports regarding the MCA investigation. One of the reports said that Reagan's grant of a sweetheart deal for MCA was "the central fact of MCA's whole rise to power" during the 1950s and 1960s. The evidence from the investigation also revealed that MCA had deep ties to organized crime.

The investigators further noted that Reagan, whose acting career had been on the skids since the late 1940s, suddenly emerged as a television star after the MCA waiver was granted. He became the star on "General Electric Theater," which in turn landed Reagan positions as a corporate spokesman for GE and another large corporation. In these positions, Reagan was paid to travel around the country to rail against atheistic Communism and union activities—a surprising turn for a man who was still the president of a union for actors. The timing of his rise to fame in television and the granting of the blanket waiver to MCA seemed more than a coincidence.

Lucrative real estate deals also came Reagan's way in the 1950s and 1960s, and particularly after his successful run for governor of California in 1966. In one deal in the late 1960s, a major Hollywood studio bought various portions of Reagan's property in Malibu Canyon at exorbitant prices compared to other properties in the area. The deal was completed with the assistance of Sid Korshak, a longtime Mob lawyer who also happened to represent MCA. The studio that bought the property said it was going to use it for movie-making purposes, but never did. About seven or eight years later, the studio sold the land to the state of California for just one-eighth the price it paid Reagan. Yet, the 1960s and 1970s were a time, at least in California, when land values were soaring. Reagan was also the beneficiary of another similar land sale in Riverside County, California. The property deals helped propel Reagan well into "millionaire" status.

O'Brien spoke with several Hollywood actors who recalled Reagan's sell-out of actors at the end of the 1960 actors strike while he was still the union president. Politically liberal and conservative actors alike called Reagan's settlement with the studios "the great giveaway." Reagan, defying custom in the actors union, had remained as president during the strike, even though he was more a producer than an actor by that point. Reagan worked with—who else?—Sid Korshak in settling the strike.

This was a true scandal, thought O'Brien, because it would show workers that Reagan, no matter what he said, would sell out workers to big business for his own self-gratification. Money trumps sex if you're thinking about your pocketbook and tax-cutting schemes, thought O'Brien. At least, he hoped it would.[2]

O'Brien had only two concerns, one large and one relatively small. The large one was that there were two prominent Democrats who could be tarred with this scandal: the California State Democratic Party Chairman, Lew Wasserman, who was also—gulp!—president of MCA, and prominent liberal Democratic Party donor, Paul Ziffren. Wasserman was Reagan's agent at MCA during the 1950s and through the early 1960s. Ziffren was a lawyer whose law partner was none other than Sid Korshak. O'Brien's investigation also led him to understand how the MCA-Universal anti-trust investigation ended: with a settlement and Wasserman agreeing to become a major donor to the Democratic Party.

O'Brien, to a lesser extent, was also cautious about "messing" with any scandal leading to "the Mob." O'Brien knew Kennedy was no longer interested in leading any "crusades" against organized crime. As Kennedy told O'Brien at the start of his presidency, "We have more than enough other issues to deal with, Larry. I am past that phase of my life. Organized crime is still a problem, I agree. However, we can't afford to stir up old enemies when we have to get our nation out of Vietnam, finish the war on poverty, and help both the blacks and the unions, not just in the South. I already told Ramsey Clark to take a 'hands-off' approach so that local attorney general office prosecutions don't rise to become national issues. We can't allow any diversions from our other tasks. We can worry about the Mob after we do the larger things we need to do." Clark, for his part, said this was the most disappointing aspect about Bob Kennedy's policies overall.

O'Brien talked with Kenny O'Donnell about his findings regarding Reagan on the morning of the "wifey" speech. "Should we go to Bob with this, Ken? I think there's a chance it will fall back on certain mucky-mucks in the Democratic Party like Wasserman and Ziffren—and maybe hit Jack Valenti, who was Johnson's friend and is now a spokesman for the Hollywood studios. They've been generous Democratic Party donors, we have to admit. It could also lead to charges of corruption against Bob—which was why the Justice Department he ran settled with MCA and never charged Reagan for what he did."

Kenny O'Donnell was in no mood at that moment to worry about a possible charge of a weak settlement. "Larry, we can blame the settlement on Jack. I hate to do that, but we're desperate here. But all I have is one question. Does anything you found show that Bob had *any* contact with the Mobsters—other than . . . you know . . . Cuba, the CIA . . . "

"No—but Kenny, what are you talking about? I'm talking about the Mob, Bob's biggest enemy! What's Cuba and the CIA have to do with any—"

"Never mind, Larry. All I want to know is . . . Let me put it this way. Is there anything that makes you doubt anything about Bob's hostility to organized criminals?"

"No, Ken. Bob's clean . . . here, I mean." O'Brien was wondering, Am I out of the loop on something?

O'Donnell was firm now, hoping to shake O'Brien off the trail that led to CIA connections with the Mob while trying to overthrow Castro during John Kennedy's administration. "Just run with the Reagan stuff, Larry. Bob may get angry with us, but if this scandal hits Reagan, we can always fall on our swords. Roth is the weakest candidate. Without Reagan, the Republicans will have a harder time winning California, which may be key for us this fall. Maybe Sorensen, McNamara, or someone else can take over our jobs if we have to go. If anything, maybe Bob will finally do something he hasn't done since he became president—crack down on organized crime. It might be a good policy in an election year, and the timing might be good for us—you know, law and order and that stuff always plays to a certain section of the electorate, even when the crime rate is low . . . "

The O Boys only saw the immediate crisis of the sex scandals and the chance to tar Reagan with a financial scandal that called into question Reagan's "nice guy" integrity.

O'Brien, acting without Kennedy's knowledge, called up Roger Ailes and said, "Roger, you might want to meet me at the Jaworski law firm office . . . again. You know, it's been a long time, buddy. You and me should have a talk, if you know what I mean."

"Why would I want to talk with you? You and your guy are toast! You're going down—and there isn't anything you can blackmail my candidate with this time around!"

"That's what you think, young fella. Jaworski's law office? Or do you want to read about it in the *Washington Post?*"

Ailes realized something might be up. He said to O'Brien, "I'll call you back. But it won't be Jaworski's place, asshole." Click.

Ailes conferred with Reagan campaign attorneys William French Smith and Ed Meese. Neither could think of what O'Brien could be hinting at, but they berated Ailes for not asking what it might be. Ailes called back with instructions to meet at a "neutral" location, the law firm of Latham and Watkins. The firm had been more Republican-oriented but had also hired, in recent years, some older Jack Kennedy–era Justice Department lawyers with expertise in tax, import-export, and antitrust laws.

Ailes, who wasn't going to miss another opportunity to learn what might be up before the meeting, asked O'Brien in the second call, "And what information should I be so concerned about, Larry? I've got business in D.C. already, but I don't want to waste my valuable time with the likes of you. What's the 'big story' you have on my guy? It can't be a sex scandal because my guy doesn't cheat on *his* wife—and he was an actor in Hollywood with plenty of opportunities. That shit about 'everyone does it' doesn't apply to Ronnie Reagan, pal!"

O'Brien said, "You'll see, punk. Better yet, why don't you ask Governor Reagan's personal lawyer, Bill Smith, to come along for the meeting? That's all your people will need to know as to what this is about." Click.

Ailes relayed the conversation to Smith and Meese. After Ailes left the room, Meese said to Smith, "What do you think it's about, Bill?"

Smith said, "I don't know, Ed. I can't imagine what it could be."

But Smith not only "imagined" what it could be, he *knew* it was about MCA, the land deals, Sid Korshak . . . and the Mob, for it was Smith who had personally represented Reagan in many of those friendly land deals. Smith immediately called Reagan and told him the Kennedy camp had some "interesting information" that Smith may have to "investigate." Reagan, without asking what the information was, simply said, "Bill, just do what you think best. Nancy's not here now, but if you want to, you can call her later."

Smith replied, "I'll get back to you if I need to, Governor. Thank you."

Smith went into action, calling Korshak, who, in turn, called former MCA board chairman, Jules Stein, and MCA president, Lew Wasserman. The quartet discussed the situation and determined their strategy. The strategy was to "nip this in the bud" by confronting O'Brien at the meeting. If that didn't work, they would take this directly to President Kennedy for a private meeting. And if that didn't work, they would undertake leaking information to friendly reporters on a variety of "related" matters, all embarrassing incidents related to Bob Kennedy, Jack Kennedy, and the patriarch, Joseph P. Kennedy.

"If we go down, *everyone's* going down!" said Stein. "But they'll back down. They're bluffing! They gotta be!"

Ailes was informed of the strategy and filled in on some of the details surrounding his candidate. Ailes was very pleased with what he heard. Still smarting from his last meeting with O'Brien in 1968, Ailes was prepared for what he called "payback time."

O'Brien arrived at the meeting as confident as he had been in 1968. He brought two envelopes that contained his findings. After exchanging pleasantries with Smith and Ailes, O'Brien said, "Gentlemen, I have some news for you. Governor Reagan is going to have a bad day when he sees this stuff. And, as always, gentlemen, don't think this is all we have. There's more. And I suggest that if you don't want to see another investigating news reporter become the latest celebrity, you might think about calling Senator Roth, who at least is honest about his ties to all of his corporate buddies. You can have your Ronnie be the pleasant bearer of good tidings to Roth that Roth is going to be the next Republican Party nominee. Meanwhile, Ronnie Reagan will simply ride his high horse back to California, finish his gubernatorial term, and fade into the Santa Barbara sunset." O'Brien thought to himself, I'm so brilliant, I'm poetic to boot.

Smith was irked at what he viewed as O'Brien's unprofessional demeanor, yet he remained cool. He responded, "Mr. O'Brien, thank you for your opening remarks. We'll just read this information before we respond to the contents of what you have provided us—if at all."

After Smith and Ailes read the information, Ailes could barely contain himself, thinking, This is just what we expected! We've got these bastards now.

Smith smiled at O'Brien and said, "Well, Mr. O'Brien, I am not terribly impressed. All you have are hearsay, speculation, and things that have already been investigated—and, I may add, with Governor Reagan being completely exonerated."

O'Brien said, "He was exonerated because people thought he was just a dumb actor. Well, now he's been a governor of one of the biggest states in the country and is running for president. He won't get away with the dumb-actor routine anymore. We'll see what the reporters and public think if—"

Ailes broke in now, no longer able to contain himself. "Not this time, O'Brien! You take on Ron Reagan with this issue, then you also take on, just for starters, Reagan's former agent, Lou Wasserman. You know Lou, don't you? He's the current chairman of the California Democratic Party. And there are lots of people who'll go down, too, especially in *your* party, not ours! You—not us—will open up what your president's *father* did with those *same* Mob figures, and the Murder Incorporated your president and his brother ran—and we'll open brother Jack's love life to the point that nobody will see your president's older brother as anything other than . . . other than a rock and roll star with groupies! Unlike your little manila envelope, we could put a whole book together on the Kennedys playing footsie with the Mob! How do you like that, *Master* O'Brien? You are so desperate, O'Brien, that you don't even *know* what you're opening up here!"

Smith winced, realizing it was a mistake to give out too much information to Ailes. But he realized it was not a problem as he watched O'Brien turn ashen at what was said.

O'Brien remembered O'Donnell's initial reaction about the CIA and Cuba, and now Ailes had put it all together. O'Brien had already gone into this meeting without the president's approval. Maybe a strategic retreat was a good idea. He quickly took back the manila envelopes and reports. "Well, gentlemen, I'll give you one more chance to reflect on this, and I'll call you in two days. If you have something to say to me in the meantime, you know where to find me."

Ailes, while happy for pushing O'Brien back, was nonetheless nervous after O'Brien left. "I think O'Brien's stupid enough to go forward on this. . . . Do you think he was only bluffing at the end there?"

Smith smiled with condescension at the still young and portly Ailes. "Of course, he's bluffing, son. He's going to call *us* one more time, remember? If he was going to the press, he'd be giving us a deadline to call *him*. You must always keep in mind various negotiation strategies, Roger, and not get carried away with the particular facts of a particular case. O'Brien's probably running back to the president. The only aspect of this that baffles me is why Kennedy would think we would fall for such a bluff. 'Desperate' may be the right word here, Roger, but even Kennedy doesn't want to destroy his brother's and his family's legacy."

"We're gonna win this election, Mr. Smith. I can just feel it!"

"Maybe," said Smith. "But I remember Jess Unruh and the Democrats came much closer to beating Governor Reagan two years ago in the governor's reelection campaign than I would have thought. The unions are out in force, and have been for some time, registering people and promising them rides to the polls this fall. I never count out the Democrats and especially a Kennedy—"

"Why not expose *their* corruption then?"

"As you just noticed, that's likely to be a double-edged sword with a public that knows so little. One never knows which side of the sword is more deadly and to whom it is the deadliest."

After the meeting, O'Brien went to O'Donnell and both decided to speak with the president the next morning. O'Brien told Kennedy, "The corrupt Reagan land deals and the Mob connection with MCA hits too many targets. Reagan's corrupt, but the backfiring potential is even greater to a host of other people—and you can't just keep apologizing for what happened during your brother's presidency—"

"Yeah, I know," said Kennedy. "With Cuba, what pisses me off is we were following Eisenhower's and Nixon's policies—at least that's what we thought we were doing . . . And frankly, I don't recall much about the MCA anti-trust case . . . "

"Bottom line, Mr. President, is we're on our own this time. Maybe your speech last night will get this monkey off our backs. I can still picture us on the stump this fall having to keep answering questions about your past sex life—sorry, to be so blunt, sir."

Kennedy, looking more despondent than ever, said, "You know who I hate in all this? I don't hate Reagan. Reagan's not a bad fellow. A bit daft in his views that's all—and his land deal corruption is probably what a lot of middle-class politicians do to become millionaires—either that or you skim your campaign contributions or get a slush fund from businessmen, kind of like Nixon did. Nah, the guy I hate . . . well, you know. That's the guy who leaked the sex stuff in the first place. Reagan's lawyer, Smith, and his campaign guru, Ailes, they didn't leak the sex stuff. We know that."

O'Brien realized right then whom he needed to "get." In a late 1980s interview with a Harvard graduate student conducting an oral history of Robert Kennedy's presidency, O'Brien said, "I knew at that point we had to get J. Edgar Hoover. I felt, at the time, that Kennedy was more likely to go down in defeat than win a second term. Tax-cutting fever was running high due to the Republican primary, with Reagan and Roth both pushing that agenda. And the sex scandal was still gonna be a problem no matter what anyone said. You know, we actually thought we'd run Bob as the family man against Hollywood Reagan before that scandal hit! I just figured, if Bob was going down, we might as well bring down Hoover, too. That bastard would stay on with Reagan and then really let loose a police-state dictatorship, I thought to myself. I didn't share the view, like Bob did, that Reagan was so nice. I knew who was around Reagan and that he could be a mean son of a bitch when he wanted to be."

And so, without permission—again—O'Brien decided to "investigate" J. Edgar Hoover, known as "the Chief" of the Federal Bureau of Investigation.

Chapter 29

DOUBLE-EDGED SWORDS, PART II

Larry O'Brien's first call was to William W. Turner, a former agent who, in 1970, wrote a highly critical and fairly well publicized book on Hoover called *Hoover's FBI*. In speaking with Turner, O'Brien began to see there was plenty of fertile grist to be found, not the least of which concerned Hoover's relationship with his longtime close friend and assistant, Clyde Tolson. Turner referred O'Brien to Joseph Shimon, a Washington, D.C., special inspector, for more information on the private lives of Hoover and Tolson.

O'Brien, realizing he was enjoying being an investigative reporter, soon had names and confirming stories regarding the duo. Ready with information, O'Brien called Ben Bradlee at the *Post* on June 10, 1972, as Bradlee recalled in his RFK timeline autobiography written during the late 1990s.

"Ben," asked O'Brien, "since the press, and maybe the country, is starting to think the private lives of officials are so important, why doesn't anyone inquire into the private affairs of another prominent federal official, who we both know has had a longtime relationship with another man who is a subordinate of that official?"

Bradlee, still smarting over having to publish anything related to the Kennedy sex scandal, said, "Larry, Bob's gonna be okay. He's still the odds-on favorite to win reelection. Why do you want to take on that *other* guy? Isn't he leaving at the end of Bob's first term? I don't want to turn the *Post* into a gossip rag!"

O'Brien said, "See, Ben? You *knew* who I was talking about! Ben, I don't see Bob winning right now—even though anything can happen. Reagan is dirty, damn it, and I won't tell you why. For that, you can talk with Lou Cannon, who just started working for you. The press needs to take the *real* story on this *other* guy, and I mean hit it hard—and this is the time! I mean, both the *Post* and the *Times* are still telling us how important it is to expose 'moral hypocrisy' at the highest levels of government. If you don't do this, then the press guys ought to investigate *themselves* for hypocrisy."

Bradlee was not amused. "Larry, I ought to hang up on you right now. Get some sleep, man, and I'll try to forget this conversation—"

"Sorry, Ben—" O'Brien knew he had gone too far. "You're right, I do need some sleep. But I have a list of names of people who are willing to talk about

Hoover's sex life. Some will talk on the record, too. Ben, if Reagan wins, he'll unleash Hoover—not make him retire. And if that's the case, it may imperil the freedom of the press, if not other freedoms."

"What other freedoms are left if you take us out?" asked a still insulted Bradlee. Bradlee, however, realized he shouldn't upset O'Brien, either. So he breathed deeply and said, "I'm not sure why we have to go after Hoover if you say that Reagan is dirty in some—"

"Ben, it's because Hoover has been playing God in this country for too damned-long. Publishing something on Reagan, that's just one election. If Bob Kennedy's administration is gonna go down, fine. But, damn it, I want someone to finally give Hoover the treatment he deserves—and that he gave to others, as you well know!"

Bradlee breathed audibly into the phone. "Okay, let me have the names." After hanging up, Bradlee sat and pondered the names. He recognized several of them. He called a couple of the people on the list himself. Surprisingly, they said it shouldn't be such a big deal to talk about Hoover—it's modern times and people need to stop being so closed-minded about things, they said in their own ways. Bradlee shook his head, saying to himself, Here is the second step we're taking on the road to becoming a gossip rag. . . . But maybe O'Brien's right. It's time we exposed that son of a bitch . . .

Bradlee decided to ask two young reporters, Bob Woodward and Carl Bernstein, to talk with the people on "the list" and find out who and how many would speak on the record. The reporters returned after less than twenty-four hours on the story. They breathlessly told Bradlee, "Almost everybody will talk on the record, sir. They'll really talk!"

In the first timeline, Hoover died in early May 1972. However, with Robert Kennedy as president, Hoover was feeling better health-wise because he was finally smiting his longtime enemy . . . Robert Kennedy. Bradlee, taking no chances, told Woodward and Bernstein to keep quiet about their investigation, including friends, family, and fellow workers at the Post. It was dangerous enough to risk having one of the sources leak anything to Hoover or his cronies. It didn't take long, though, for Hoover to hear about this investigation.

Hoover sent his publicity man, Cartha DeLoach, to Bradlee. DeLoach warned Bradley not to "print malicious gossip and lies. There will be consequences to national security and consequences to you and this newspaper, which has been a fine, supportive newspaper in our efforts against crime and Communism. You ought to know, Mr. Bradlee, that one of your reporters on this malicious story, a Mr. Bernstein, is a Communist—and so were his parents."

Bernstein, who admittedly leaned left and whose parents had been Communist Party members at one time, was ready to throttle "this Roach guy" and Hoover himself when Bradlee told the two reporters about his conversation with the FBI man. Bernstein said, "I'll sue them—the bastards! I ain't a Commie—I've fought my parents for years about their beliefs! I rebelled against them by coming to work here at the *Post!* God damn it! Uh, sorry, sir. I am very honored . . . really . . . honored to be at the *Post."*

Bradlee smiled at Bernstein and put his hand on the young man's shoulder. He said, "Carl, if we print this story and he sues us for libel, then you go ahead and sue him right back. But let's see if he sues—and let's see if we can even publish this yet. They're afraid. At least I think they are. And see if our sources are still willing to talk on the record, though."

Bradlee spoke the next day with publisher Kay Graham. Contrary to her earlier decision about publishing stories regarding Kennedy's sex life, she initially rejected the idea of running a story on Hoover's personal life as being "beneath us." Bradlee flew into a rage. "This is outrageous, Mrs. Graham! We can print sex stories about the president because he's so important, but it's beneath us when it comes to the FBI director? I don't get it! Are we saying the director of the FBI is so important he can't be touched? Or is it that he's somehow less important? What is it?" Before allowing her to answer, Bradlee added, "You said Kennedy was a hypocrite—well, what about Hoover? He made a career out of attacking homosexuals, and look what we have with on-the-record sources!"

"The sources regarding Mr. Hoover have recanted."

"Not all of them. But fine. Let some of 'em recant. We have most of them on the record—I had the boys record them on tape, whether they knew it or not." He meant Woodward and Bernstein when speaking of "the boys."

"Your *young* reporters! Ben, what were you doing risking their careers like this? Were you *that* upset at the coverage on your friend last month—"

"He is *your* friend, too, Katherine, or *was*—" At that moment, Bradlee didn't care if she fired him. "Our lawyers say Hoover would have to prove malice on our part in publishing these stories, not just whether the statements were false—"

"Well, we know *you* don't like Mr. Hoover very much, to say the least."

"If Hoover sues, these people who recanted will tell the truth that they told our reporters. They won't challenge the tapes as made up, will they? We run this story or I quit. Better yet, let's run the stories and I promise you I'll resign if we can't make them stick. It's that simple. We have to run this story if we want to be fair about why we ran the other stories on the president."

"Life isn't fair, Ben, and you of all people should know that. I'm not putting our newspaper at risk—"

"Damn it, we didn't think that when we went after the president! I'll say it again. Are we saying the head of the FBI is above the president—and too important to expose any hypocrisy on his part? Is that what we're saying? That should be the biggest part of our story—why we've all heard this information for years and we wouldn't investigate—"

"And that's all we need for our credibility—" Mrs. Graham was fast losing patience with her editor.

"Kay, people have claimed they knew about Kennedy's indiscretions, even if I didn't—"

"Ben, I will speak with our lawyers about the latest and greatest in libel law. If I am satisfied that Mr. Hoover will have a difficult time with a lawsuit, I'll go along. You better hope Kennedy wins reelection because, if he doesn't, *and* if Mr. Hoover stays around, we'll have hell to pay!"

The lawyers confirmed that Hoover needed to prove falsity plus malicious intent, which would be hard with the audiotaped statements. The audiotapes that were made without authorization, however, might pose a problem with certain judges interested in "privacy" rights in common law, though there was no law yet to stop such recordings by private investigators.

The *Post* ran the story on Sunday, June 18.

The night before, an argument ensued between the editor and the publisher as to where the story would be placed in the paper. Bradlee prevailed, saying, "If we're going to be sued, we might as well play this on the front page!"

Mrs. Graham reluctantly relented.

She would not quite admit that she, too, had heard the stories over the years regarding J. Edgar Hoover and Clyde Tolson. Also, by her own observations, she didn't much doubt that there was something peculiar about the Hoover-Tolson relationship.

The article, "Hoover's Secrets," was a bombshell. The story was even-handed despite the title and subject matter. It quoted on-the-record witnesses who discussed details of Hoover's relationship with Tolson, how the two frequented clubs together, rarely with women, and went to known homosexual hideout "bungalows" near or at the Del Mar, California, racetrack. Hoover himself often went to the bungalows without Tolson to meet other, younger men, said these sources.

The article quoted people who had known Hoover and Tolson, or had met them on various occasions. Ethel Merman, a friend of Hoover's, was quoted at some length. Merman said, "Listen, some of my best friends are homosexuals. Everybody knows about J. Edgar Hoover, but he's the best chief the FBI ever had. A lot of people are homosexual, even Mr. Hoover. To each his own. They don't bother me." Merman also said, "And if you don't believe a great man can't be a homosexual, just ask Joe Pasternak. He's not a homosexual, but he can back what I'm saying about Mr. Hoover."

Pasternak was a film producer who confirmed several specific stories regarding Hoover, including an incident in which a policeman caught Hoover with a young boy back in the 1940s. The story was suppressed at the time, said Pasternak. "I guess it's time this came out—I mean, there are homos in lots of places, and they're starting to come out of the closet now. Might as well let it all hang out, as the kids used to say some years ago."

A former fashion model, Luisa Stuart, told of her evening with Hoover and Tolson. "They held hands most of the night. I didn't think that was normal. My boyfriend at the time, Art Arthur—he was a colleague of Walter Winchell—well, he laughed when I asked him about it. He said, 'Don't you know? They're . . . ' Well, he used a word that meant homosexual, but it wasn't the F word . . . It started with a Q."

Special Inspector Shimon spoke of seeing Hoover and Tolson kissing each other and "grabbing each other's asses," although the word "asses" wasn't printed in the story, of course. Hoover, after finding out Shimon had spoken to the reporters, pulled his usual strings to fire Shimon for the latter's refusal to recant what he said. Before the story was published, Shimon called the reporters and added more details. "I'm not afraid of Hoover. I respected the man for years, but I will no longer lie about his homosexuality. Let him sue!"

An underworld figure, Seymour Pollack, confirmed the stories—off-the-record—of seeing Hoover at the Del Mar track with Tolson and other "boys." He confirmed others' testimonies about Hoover and Tolson holding hands. Pollack had been an associate of Meyer Lansky, a famous mobster of the 1940s and 1950s. Lansky was still alive and well in 1972 and would live until 1983. Pollack said, "That's all I'm gonna say—and it's off-the-record, understand? You don't wanna know anymore if you know what's good for you."

Harry Hay, a founder of a trailblazing homosexual rights group, the Mattachine Society, said, on the record, "I'd see Tolson and Hoover in the audience boxes at the Del Mar race track. They were in boxes gay men owned and rented. Everyone I ever asked about them said Hoover and Tolson were lovers. I just wish he'd acknowledge himself. He would be doing a great thing for our cause. My goodness, this is so ridiculous to deny what is obvious to everyone! I also want to say that, after we gay men stood up to the police at the Stonewall nightclub in New York in 1969, a story that most newspapers haven't bothered to publish in any meaningful way, it is high time for all homosexuals to leave the closet. We're in government and business, let me tell you—and you'd be just *shocked* to know who I mean!" The last two sentences were not included in the article, spiked on Bradlee's orders.

The two reporters went to Bradlee the night before the story was released. They were upset at Bradlee's "censorship." Bradlee barked at them, "We're not going to get too far into this gossip—not if I can help it! And don't tell me I'm a censor—as if that's always a bad thing!"

Shimon talked of wild parties at Hoover's house, which mostly included other homosexuals—and some agents who went along to get along. This was upsetting to Shimon. He said, "I mean, I just feel uncomfortable talking about this, but it's what I've heard and seen. I didn't go to the parties, but Guy Hottel, who was close to me and to Hoover, told me about the parties."

Lots of agents, said Shimon, would call the two men "J. Edna" and "Mother

Tolson." "We knew what we meant—it was just one of those things that makes life . . . complicated." Hottel wouldn't respond to inquiries from the *Post*, but other former agents had heard Hottel talk among agents of such goings-on. Hottel resigned from the Bureau the day before the story ran in the *Post*, even though he'd been close to Hoover for more than forty years. Hoover had been best man at one of Hottel's weddings—he was married four times. Hottel never went on the record to confirm or deny Hoover's sexual proclivities.

The *Post* also said several other people had further details related to Hoover's homosexuality. However, said the article, these witnesses later recanted their stories. One witness, who went on the record but was not included in the *Post* article, was a high-society woman who claimed she saw Hoover in a dress at a party on one occasion. Bradlee spiked that part. "Let's not go overboard, even if you fellas believe it, which I sorta doubt," he said to Woodward and Bernstein.

Jack Newfield held up a copy of the *Post* to the pressroom reporters the morning the article appeared. "Well, well, well. J. Edgar Hoover and his kissing boyfriend. Isn't this a fine mess he's gotten into? Couldn't happen to a better guy! That's off-the-record fellas—and ladies—or no more leaks for any of you!" Nobody quoted Newfield's remarks.

Hoover's public comment was immediate. "The *Washington Post* has succumbed to lies and Communist propaganda in this malicious attack on the director of the Federal Bureau of Investigation. Each of these people is either deluded or a liar and in any event unreliable. One such person is Harry Hay, a longtime Communist homosexual.[1] And one of the *Post*'s reporters who authored this story of lies is one Carl Bernstein. Mr. Bernstein is a child of Communists. He attended Communist camps where he was indoctrinated into the Communist way of lie—I mean life. Well, I mean lying, too. The other reporter, Robert Woodward, was a willing dupe who, during his time with naval intelligence, should have known better than to be associated with Communists. What is truly horrible is that these attacks are also made against Clyde Tolson, who is recovering from a stroke. Mr. Tolson is too ill to comment, but his thoughts are the same. This is a scurrilous lie planted by dupes and deviants, Communists, and enemies of America."

Bradlee was unconcerned about either Hay or even Bernstein—and quite pleased by the article, which received much attention in the national press and broadcast media. He told Mrs. Graham, "I'm talking with a whole bunch of people who are now willing to come forward. Those young reporters may be bigger stars than the reporters from that podunk paper in New Hampshire!"

Kennedy was trying to make sure he said nothing—nothing at all. Inside, his joy was as great as if he had already won the reelection. He called Ken Galbraith to see what he thought. Galbraith said, "I'm glad that son of a bitch is getting his, I must say. He ruined the career of one of the greatest diplomats of our century, Sumner Welles. I knew Welles during the 1940s. Yes, Welles was a homosexual—maybe bisexual. He was married, and seemingly happy, too. I hate to be so vitriolic, but Hoover is a menace, and I hope they run him out on a rail . . . although perhaps we should all be more tolerant toward those who are . . . ahem, deviant."

Suddenly, on June 24, on the eve of filing a libel suit, Hoover died of a heart attack. Conservative—and Republican—columnists and writers immediately attacked the *Post* and other newspapers and television networks for their coverage on Hoover. "Our gossiping press has finally killed a high-ranking official. It's finally come to that," said Ernest van den Haag, a conservative law professor, in the *Wall Street Journal.*

Conservative journalist Andrew Tully, a longtime Hoover supporter, said that Hoover's death was the "passing of a great man in our nation's long history of freedom. It is time for patriotic Americans to fight back against Communists and their many agents in our once proud nation. J. Edgar Hoover was a man of principle."

Later in his editorial, published in many newspapers around the nation, Tully wrote, "Mr. Hoover was not a homosexual, as some anti-American writers and reporters are saying." In a pathetic attempt to defend the man, Tully noted that Hoover read *Playboy* magazine "from time to time." This was a leak to Tully, courtesy of one of Hoover's supporters within the FBI. As comedian George Carlin said in response to Tully's column, "Yes, but did he look at the pictures?"

Other journalists were almost sacrilegious in their discussion of the dead. "One hates to be mean-spirited," said Jack Anderson, a liberal investigative journalist with a nationwide column, "but our democracy is strengthened with J. Edgar Hoover no longer in charge of the FBI."

Just after Hoover's death, the *National Enquirer* reported the story the *Post* would not print: the testimony of the woman who claimed she had seen Hoover in a dress. The press, already having a field day, and with Hoover dead—thus posing no threat of libel under the law—pounced on the story for the elitist reason that she was a high-society woman, not a "money-hungry" poor person.

Hoover was replaced at the FBI with a longtime Hoover aide but secret critic, William Sullivan. In a meeting with President Kennedy, Sullivan apologized for the leaks regarding Kennedy's sex life that had come from Hoover's office. He told Kennedy the leaks came from his rival, Cartha DeLoach, who vehemently denied the allegation. DeLoach said the leaks might have come from another Hoover assistant, Mark Felt, but more likely Sullivan himself. Felt and Sullivan, no allies to each other, each denied DeLoach's claim.

Kennedy, however, told Sullivan, "There will be no reprisals, no vindictiveness. There will be Christian charity. This applies across the board. We will, however, have a change in some of the policies of the FBI. If you are to take this position, it would perhaps be a good idea for you to consider hiring an assistant who has been with the FBI, but who has been willing in the past to be publicly critical of its excesses." He then handed Sullivan a piece of paper. Sullivan's eyes bulged out when he read who Kennedy suggested as his assistant: William Turner.

Kennedy continued, "Mr. Sullivan, as part of this change in policy, the FBI is being reorganized as to where it will be reporting. It will be formally returned to its original place in the government's hierarchy; that is, under the Justice Department. Starting today, should you accept the position, you will be reporting to Attorney General Clark. No political investigations or wiretaps on anyone but the most hardened *criminals* will be undertaken without written authorization of Ramsey Clark. I need to know now, Mr. Sullivan. Is there any problem with this?"

"No, sir," said a still shocked and chastened Sullivan.

After the meeting, Sullivan met with Larry O'Brien. O'Brien said, "The president is in a forgiving mood, but I'm not. There are some congressional hearings that are going to come down over this. If you expect any protection, Mr. Sullivan, you better clean your friggin' house over there. I want Tolson out, as well as DeLoach, Felt, Mohr, Wes Grapp in L.A., and some others. Just talk with Bill Turner—today. He's expecting your call. You do this and you'll find that Bill's stay with the bureau will be temporary. We could put in L. Patrick Gray to run the bureau if you decline—we're told Gray has one career motto: 'Aye, aye, Captain.' But, Bill, we think you're the best man for the job. Don't let us down."

O'Brien put his arm around Sullivan, giving Sullivan what he perceived to be a menacing smile. Sullivan, who had always waited for the moment when he would succeed "the Chief," wondered to himself: Am I in an episode of *The Twilight Zone?* What am I going to be "the chief" of?

Meanwhile, Hoover's longtime administrative secretary, Mrs. Grandy, had misplaced—some said removed—from Hoover's office some dossiers on various famous people during what Frank Sinatra once sang about as the "wee small hours of the morning" of Hoover's death. Sullivan asked his most trusted aide to block the entrance to the office later that morning. Afterward, no other dossiers were "misplaced."

Sullivan spoke to Mark Felt, lead administrator under Hoover, about the files that were missing. Felt said, "Big deal. So some files were lost."

Sullivan told him "to get lost" immediately. By the time Sullivan went down the hall to face another Hoover favorite, Cartha DeLoach, the latter had already packed up his personal files and office pictures.

DeLoach said, "Good luck working under the Commies, Bill!"

Sullivan tried to ignore what DeLoach said.

DeLoach kept at him, though, saying, "Well, it looks like you were the best guy after all for this job—at least *now* you are, *comrade*!" DeLoach's laugh signaled outright contempt. Sullivan asked another agent to escort DeLoach out of the FBI building.

Sullivan called Clyde Tolson at home to say his services were no longer needed. Tolson, largely incapacitated by his strokes, and more than seventy years old, said haltingly to Sullivan, "You killed him, and you're trying to kill me."

Sullivan, tired of these attacks from Hoover supporters, just said, "Be well, Clyde. It was nice knowing you." Then he hung up. Sullivan couldn't believe Tolson could be that paranoid to believe such a thing, although some Hoover supporters, who believed anything bad must have been the work of Communists, did wonder at the timing of Hoover's death.

With the house cleaning, the morale of the FBI was thought to be one of depression, according to conservative columnists such as Andrew Tully, Bob Novak, and James Kilpatrick. O'Brien, in response, convinced Sullivan to allow reporters to talk with any agents they wished about "life after Hoover." Contrary to these pundits, who had been relying on the ones who were "cleaned out," most agents proudly told the reporters they were happier than ever now that Hoover, Tolson, and the rest were gone. "Maybe we can finally go after mobsters and real criminals instead of academics, black activists, and union organizers," said one agent in the D.C. office.

Sullivan, who had penned the infamous threat letter to Martin Luther King Jr., now began a strong "affirmative action" program to bring blacks, Latinos, and even "liberals" on board as FBI agents, researchers, and administrators. Sullivan stopped the COINTEL program and also stopped investigations against most of the Black Panthers, though, with Attorney General Clark's approval, some surveillance continued on a few unrepentant and militant Panthers.

Sullivan met every day with his assistant, Bill Turner, and with Attorney General Clark to discuss reorienting FBI agents to report to Justice Department attorneys and to coordinate with state and local officials in New York, Chicago, and other major cities where organized crime was still flourishing.

However, in late July 1972, President Kennedy told Clark, "Ramsey, let's not get too excited this year, at least, with prosecuting organized crime. We have time for this after the election." Clark obeyed, even though he was surprised at Kennedy's statement that assumed he would win. Kennedy was now, in July, ahead in the polls, but Clark noted the president's standings in the polls had been more down than up for the previous two months.

Kennedy, not quite thinking he would win, nonetheless sent the O Boys to meet with certain pro-FBI Republican conservatives at the Washington home of Republican congressional leader Gerald Ford. The purpose of the meeting was to gauge Republican opposition to a proposed bill to reform the FBI. Barry Goldwater was kept from the meeting because it was believed that "he wouldn't keep his mouth shut," according to a longtime aide to Ford. Larry O'Brien heartily agreed with that assessment, although Kennedy did not like the idea of excluding Goldwater.

At the meeting, O'Brien said, "Some of the toughest critics of the FBI in Congress, including Democratic Congressman Don Edwards, a former FBI agent himself, and Senator Dick Clark, are itching to begin hearings into the FBI abuses. Considering the gossip we all read about recently, we have to assume people will be very interested to know of the files Hoover kept on innocent people. Did you guys know that Hoover compiled a three-foot-thick dossier on the late Helen Keller? Gotta keep track of those deaf and blind subversives, I always say. And why? Because of her feminist, socialist, and pacifist speeches during the 1920s and '30s. How'd you like that blasted across America's television screens this summer?"

Phil Crane, a hard-right Republican congressman, said, "We can stand that heat, Mr. O'Brien. The question is whether Democrats can stand bringing out the information the FBI discovered in its investigations on the subversive and sexual activities of the late Dr. Martin Luther King Jr. I just heard about."

O'Brien smiled and said, "Yes, we understand there was some sex stuff going on between women and Martin Luther King Jr. But King was no Commie, and you guys will look really ridiculous trying to make that stick at this point in the game. But, gentlemen, I doubt any of us want to alienate black voters, particularly black business leaders, at election time, do we?" That response quieted the room, for in the RFK timeline, Ronald Reagan was actively wooing both black and white businessmen around the nation.

O'Brien then offered a proposal to reform the FBI that would, he said, be a "win-win." But Ford, believing Reagan was going to win the election, was in no mood for any compromise with the Kennedy administration. Contrary to his *later* reputation in the first timeline, Ford was known in the 1960s as a hard-right Republican who had been elected in the Republican juggernaut of 1946. In 1970, in both timelines, Ford, almost alone in Congress, introduced a bill to impeach Supreme Court Justice William Douglas.

Ford protested to O'Brien that Hoover's FBI activities against Helen Keller and other celebrities were not abuses but legitimate forms of surveillance against Communist subversion. Ford intoned, as only a congressman can, "Your reforms will politicize the FBI by placing its authority completely under a political executive office, which in this administration has not shown much concern about the menace of Communism."

"Gerry," said O'Brien, "this is 1972. The Russians have just given up Eastern Europe without a fight—even with their own puppets screaming for help. They signed a peace treaty on antiballistic missiles with us, and they have just announced they will agree to significant nuclear arms limitations. Bill Sullivan, who you know and are friendly with, wrote a memo to Hoover last year saying the Ku Klux Klan was a far bigger danger to this country than any Communists. I can have Sullivan send you the memo if you want. And even Sullivan says the FBI has been weak on the Mob for decades. Look, Gerry, I came here with Kenny O'Donnell to make peace with you guys, not rehash old arguments. There are a lot of people calling for abolishing the FBI, just like Congress did with the House Un-American Activities Committee. As for the politicization of the FBI, the problem is that the FBI under Hoover had a politics all its own that was, and still is a danger to our democracy—"

Ford said, "I don't buy that line. Not at all. You and your kind are out to destroy the FBI and let criminals roam free across state lines. And I happen to know quite a bit about your president, more than what the press has told—"

O'Donnell's "Irish dander" exploded like lava from a volcano. "Now you cut that shit right now, buddy! You wanna play rough? Fine. We have it on good authority that you were the snitch to the FBI while you were on the Warren Commission! And that you've been a stoolie for Hoover and his little gang of roaches! How about that? Your friends here probably knew that already, but now you know *we* know! You want to be the first political casualty of being too close to a faggot like Hoover? Just try us!"

O'Donnell had gone beyond any planned "bad cop" to O'Brien's "good cop." O'Brien quickly stood up and motioned to O'Donnell to quiet down. Enough of the bad cop, thought O'Brien. I just hope it isn't too late for the good cop.

Smiling at the stunned and angry Republicans, O'Brien said, "Look, we didn't come here to threaten. Don't we all want this scandal regarding Hoover, and the FBI's failure to fight organized crime, to be history? What would people in the heartland say? Does anyone want it known they kowtowed to a homo? Left-wing Democrats like Don Edwards and McGovern are gonna be the only ones smelling like a rose here—even Reagan gave information to Hoover while he was the Screen Actors Guild president. How do we know? Sullivan told us. Guys, we don't have to like each other here if we're gonna save the FBI. Between our party's radicals and your party's so-called libertarians, they might just abolish the whole FBI! It's now or never, guys. Now, Kenny and I are going to take a walk around this lovely neighborhood. You've got fifteen minutes to make your speeches to each other and come to a consensus. Okay? This is the last chance for . . . what's that phrase? Yeah, 'the vital center' to save the FBI, the way I see it."

Left alone in Ford's dining room, the Republicans caucused and cursed the O Boys, Kennedy, and all those "liberal Commies." Then they agreed on what must be done and called O'Brien and O'Donnell back into the house and Ford's dining room. They agreed to support the reforms the president was seeking for the FBI.

The next step was to keep Goldwater from filibustering against the reforms with "Neanderthals" such as Stennis or Thurmond. Kennedy invited Goldwater to dinner at the White House with FBI Director Sullivan. Goldwater was stunned to hear Sullivan talk about the various Hoover schemes, the abuses inherent in the COINTEL program, the threats against Martin Luther King Jr., the wiretaps without any approval, judicial or otherwise, the laxness in dealing with organized crime, and so on.

Goldwater said to Sullivan, more than to Kennedy, that he knew Hoover was sometimes a bit arrogant, but he had no idea of his hold over presidents and his corrupt ways. Turning to Kennedy, Goldwater said, "I always thought that *you* wanted to wiretap King, Mr. President. It sure looked that way to me from what Mr. Hoover said a few years ago."

Kennedy, a bit defensive, said, "Barry, when it's just us, it's always Bob. Yes, I can understand. But, Barry, I didn't want to tap King at the outset. I went along because I couldn't defend King anymore against Hoover and his minions. I approved it, yes, but only after King wouldn't get rid of Levinson, his white aide who was a Communist at one time. I wanted to prove King wasn't a Red. The taps proved King was somewhat radical in his views, but he was a loyal American, Barry, and that's the truth. That was never enough for Hoover, though—and a few months later, Jack's dead, Lyndon Johnson is running the White House, and I'm no longer attorney general. Barry, I understand your comment in the press the other day that the FBI should be above politics. But if we let a guy run his department without any executive oversight, even though the oversight is political, that department can often become a bigger dictator than the executive. At least the executive has to stand for election every few years."

"How about the FBI director being elected, fellas, just like a district attorney is in a lot of places?" Goldwater was serious.

After almost choking on his dessert, Kennedy said, "Barry, name me one federal executive administrator who we put up for election besides the president?"

"Well, I know you and your radical economists at the Fed are telling some bankers that one day the Federal Reserve Board chairman might be elected, not appointed," said Goldwater, with some relish in his tone.

"That's going nowhere—and no, Barry, I'm not here to deal. The point is I'm trying to spare the nation from hearing all the horrible things the FBI did under Hoover. We can't have the nation lose faith in our law enforcement, wouldn't you agree?"

"Yes, I agree, but . . . " Goldwater paused, "I must say, I've learned a lot this time in the Senate, starting with that Vietnam thing. Who'd a thought the Viet Cong would be our best stopgap against the North Vietnamese? Things are changing, all right. I just wish you'd stop giving in to organized labor, who I frankly don't see as all that different from organized crime. Sorry, it's what I think, anyway." Then, smiling with some mischief in his eyes, Goldwater said, "Now, Bob, don't be thinking I'm gonna vote for you, even if I go along on this FBI reform. I strongly believe Mr. Reagan is capable of creating the kind of government I'd like to see—one that's limited to what the Constitution says."

"Oh, come on, Barry!" laughed Kennedy. "I once got a look at *your* Constitution. The first thing I noticed was that it had the words 'general welfare' cut out so it only said the government would provide for the 'common defence.' And don't go telling me you don't know what the founding fathers meant when they talked about 'welfare'!"

Goldwater laughed, saying, "I know they didn't mean Medicare, Mr. President. Hey, I oughta tell Reagan that one!"

"Then tell Governor Reagan to read Federalist Paper Number 37, where Madison made clear the document was vague on purpose—partly as a result of unbridgeable differences, but also to make sure the Constitution could adapt to different situations like Chief Justice Marshall wrote in *McCulloch v. Maryland* back around 1820. You oughta remember that, Barry, because that's what Archie Cox told you during his confirmation hearings for the Supreme Court," said a smiling Bob Kennedy.

Goldwater smiled back. "Well, it's all a matter of interpretation, Mr. President."

Goldwater agreed that night not to filibuster against the FBI reform legislation and to not actively oppose it. But he was going to offer amendments if he thought the venerable bureau would be "unduly hamstrung by the radicals who want to undermine it."

Gerald Ford cosponsored the reform legislation with Representative Bob Michel, a Republican from Illinois, Democratic Congressman Don Edwards of California, and Senator Dick Clark of Iowa. This sent a strong message to other Republicans and conservative Democrats not to actively oppose the bill. The White House, for its part, sent a message to other liberal critics that destroying the FBI was "suicide" in an election year.

Perfunctory, limited hearings on the reform legislation were held in the House, but in the Senate, Thurmond threatened a filibuster. A quick cloture vote aborted that attempt. The Senate simply read the report prepared by the House and conducted no hearings in that chamber of the legislature.

The reforms included the following:

1. Informants would no longer be dispatched against any individual or group without a federal judge or magistrate approving the use of an informant. Informants could not "wear a wire" without a federal judge or magistrate approving it beforehand, either.

2. The FBI's charter was narrowed to crimes against persons or property as its main function, and the FBI would, except on approval of the United States Attorney General, agree to play a subordinate role to state authorities. Any investigations concerning "national security" would have to be directly approved by the president and the leading members of the House and Senate Intelligence Committees before any investigation could be undertaken.

3. A committee of congressional representatives, senators, and persons appointed by the president would oversee the bureau and report on its efforts, and review any citizen complaints against the bureau, on an annual basis.

4. As part of the reforms, which included reforms to the Freedom of Information Act of 1968, dossiers were to be catalogued on individuals who were only on file for non-violent political activities. Then the FBI was to contact each individual by a certified, return-receipt-requested letter. In the letter, the FBI would invite the person to come to Washington, D.C., to review the file and to take personal possession of the file. If a person was not interested in reviewing the file, the file would be immediately destroyed.

The legislation passed in mid-August 1972, with front-page coverage in the nation's press and broadcast media. With the vote almost unanimous, most people shrugged their shoulders and said, "Oh well. Things are probably okay now." A few dissenters, more on the left, said the reforms were "window dressing" and that the bureau should have been abolished, joining the now-defunct House Un-American Activities Committee. Most far-right writers accepted the reforms, with only a couple believing the FBI had been destroyed under the "guise of reform." Paul Harvey, a conservative nationwide radio host, said to his listeners, "The inmates of subversion are running the FBI's asylum."

President Kennedy's standing improved in the polls, hitting almost 55 percent by the beginning of August. The worst seemed to be over for Kennedy, as Americans realized that others, especially Hoover, were far worse than the president in committing what was still called "deviant conduct" or "sin."

After the scandals involving Kennedy and Hoover, the press decided that questions regarding the private conduct of a politician should be raised only for high-ranking officials and only if someone had kept doing "it" through the time of the press investigation. The first casualty of this unwritten rule was National Security Council Chairman Daniel Ellsberg. Ellsberg was a "serial adulterer" despite being married to the wealthy, fairly attractive daughter of the founder of the Marx Toy Company. He said to friends before the Kennedy scandal broke, "Hank Kissinger told me last year at a Harvard conference that 'power is an aphrodisiac.' Well, it is! And who am I to say no to so many charming and beautiful women?"

On July 13, 1972, Ellsberg resigned his position, just before publication of an article in the *New York Times* detailing his sex-capades. He claimed to the public that with the cooling down of various hot spots around the world, he was resigning to "spend time with his family." The story about his sexual adventures never ran in the *Times* or most other papers. The *Manchester Union Leader* ran the story, but the story never had "legs." Replacing Ellsberg at the NSC was a bright young aide, Roger Morris, who quickly became a favorite of Secretary of State Bowles.

Other casualties of this rule over the next couple of years included two powerful members of Congress, Wayne Hays, Democrat of Ohio, who had a mistress on the payroll; and Wilbur Mills, Democrat of Arkansas, who was arrested for drunk driving while coming home from a strippers bar with one of the "girls."

Kennedy was protected from further scandal after a couple of women came forward, in mid-July 1972, claiming they had had sex with him within the past two years. Although the *Union Leader* published their accusations, the *Washington Post* found that at least one of the women could not have been with Kennedy at the time she said she was—he was in the White House at the time, while she was in Rockville, Illinois. The other woman simply did not produce enough corroboration for her story for any of the lawyers representing the various newspapers that considered her claim.

Chapter 30

REELECTION, PART II

On April 20, 1972, Secretary of State Bowles made his first trip to Peking to meet with Chou En-Lai. In a photo opportunity meeting with peasants in eastern China, near the Great Wall, Bowles endorsed Confucian or Eastern thought as a form of anger control and as a means to pursue community values. Late-night television talk show host Johnny Carson joked about Bowles endorsing the wisdom of Confucius. "We have just learned that Secretary of State Bowles, when he returns to the States, is expected to announce his support for legislation to make our national bird Ganesha the elephant!"[1]

Bowles returned shortly before Kennedy's sex scandal erupted. When the scandal struck, Kennedy wanted to cancel his trip to Peking scheduled for the middle of July. The O Boys and Yarborough told the president, in Yarborough's words, "to make the trip, stay strong, and look presidential as all hell!" It proved to be good, if lucky, advice. By early July, Hoover was exposed as a homosexual and, more important, was dead. The primary season was over, and it was clear the Democratic Party's national convention was united to give Kennedy "Four More Years!" This was the slogan his campaign advertisers had devised. And it was now the right time for a sequel to the 1968 "looking presidential" foreign trip.

Kennedy left on July 14 for the first presidential visit to China since before World War II. On the recommendation of Bowles, Kennedy had been reading some writings attributed to Confucius and found them fascinating. A day after arriving in Peking, Kennedy delivered a speech before half a million people in Tiananmen Square in which he quoted from Confucius:

> We of the West and those of the East have much in common and more importantly, we have some interest in each other's culture and history. I am, for example, particularly intrigued with a story concerning Confucius, China's great philosopher. It seems he was once traveling with a companion to the town of Wei. Confucius noticed the town was overpopulated. He asked his companion if this was indeed the case. The companion replied, "Yes, Master, there are too many people. But what can we do?" Confucius said, "First, my

friend, we must enrich the people in this community with virtue. Then we must educate them and allow them, not force them, to be productive." Confucius understood the importance of education, of the need for public virtue in creating a caring society, and of the duty to be productive with our lives, as farmers, as workers, and as political leaders. Confucius also said, on many occasions, that leaders have a duty to secure the rights of the people they serve. We of the West believe in all these things and more, of course. The East and West, therefore, may be closer than we think, at least in terms of our goals and our spirit. We can only live in peace with each other as long as we cooperate, in open and friendly dialogue, in meeting those same goals.

Chou, in a private meeting after the meeting, told Kennedy obliquely that Mao, up until his second stroke, had "from time to time" shown an interest in women "from a more than political standpoint." After Mao's death in 1976, it was revealed that Mao was no different than any sultan or feudal king in terms of sexually satisfying himself with "young maidens."[2]

In attempting to show sympathy with the president's recent scandal, Chou was consistent with other world leaders, including European leaders, who, in the words of French philosopher Jean-Paul Sartre, saw the scandal surrounding the president's sexual activities as "indicative of the infantilism of American culture."

Kennedy's critics in the United States were astounded that the president could travel to Red China in an election year, after having endured a major sex scandal, and come out looking presidential to the public. William Buckley, in his magazine, the *National Review*, said, "The greatest sacrifice for the good of the nation would be if the president decided to stay with his friends in Communist China." The magazine's China expert, Brian Crozier, was only slightly less hostile. He wrote, "What the president did not say was that Confucius was a supporter of that great oxymoron, benevolent dictatorships. Yes, there are similarities between Confucius and Westerners, but only perhaps between Confucius and the Marxists—and Robert Kennedy."[3]

As a portent of what Kennedy was likely to face in the fall election, feminist Gloria Steinem criticized Kennedy's Red China speech from a different stance than the Republican conservatives. "Confucius," said Steinhem, "was idolized during a time when Chinese culture required women to bind their feet and were treated as property. It is typical of this president to support, by implication, the patriarchal tradition of oppressing women instead of calling upon China to embrace modern principles of equality."

Steinem had already become a dedicated foe of the president in 1972. During the time of the president's unfolding sex scandal, she appeared on the "high-brow" late-night television talk program hosted by Dick Cavett.

Speaking with Cavett, she said the president should resign for his patriarchal "hypocrisy" and "chauvinist treatment of women." Steinem had been attacking Kennedy for over a year before the scandal because of his continuing refusal to support abortion rights and his support for the modification of the language of then proposed Equal Rights Amendment to the Constitution, as discussed later in this chapter.

Despite the criticism from Republicans and other Kennedy critics, Kennedy's trip abroad, which also included his triumphant return to the unified city of Berlin on the way back to the United States, restored him to his usual heights in the polls. By the time he returned from his trip, the president's approval ratings in the polls were averaging just over 65 percent, with 55 percent saying they would vote for him in the fall. In Berlin, in a very brief address to the press, the president smiled into the cameras and at reporters while acknowledging his 1968 speech about the Berlin Wall coming down "sooner rather than later."

The Republicans were frustrated by Kennedy's rise in the polls, but they were still very confident going into the fall elections. Their strategy was already in place, and determined business leaders across the nation were raising monies by the millions. The Republicans envisioned a three-pronged attack on President Kennedy. First and foremost, Republicans would run on a platform to cut income taxes and cut spending on "socialist" programs. In light of the Russians' departure from Eastern Europe and the collapse of Communist China, the Red-baiting was now going to be based less on accusing Democrats of "treason" than on making the more practical argument that the Great Society programs were not responsible for lowering poverty to 7 percent. The campaign mantra was going to be that private enterprise could do a better job than "a lumbering, wasteful, bureaucratic Soviet-style government." That poverty had never gone much below 20 percent before the recent antipoverty government programs was, however, a hard fact for the Republicans to rebut without a bunch of statistical and philosophical arguments.

Second, the Republicans believed they were likely to win the presidency with the votes of people in white-collar middle-management positions in the Northeast and the West, including California. Such voters resented the various labor strikes that had taken place the previous four years, and they resented the fact that they seemed to make precious little more—in their view—than "garbage men" and "construction workers."

Business leaders, who had ingested the "ideology of freedom and liberty" in regard to tax cuts and opposition to the welfare state, also ingested some of the hippies' ideology against sexual hypocrisy and in favor of drug legalization and abortion. More and more country club golf course conversations included comments that if poor women were to have free access to abortion, there would be less need for antipoverty programs. "More abortion, less welfare—and less socialism!" became a cry among the Young Americans for Freedom, a conservative student group closely aligned with the Republican Party. A "hippie Republican," *Harvard Lampoon* writer P. J. O'Rourke, wrote what he called a "half-serious satire" in which he proposed a "cheap and effective poor people's program" for the inner cities. "Let 'em have all the drugs they want. That'll keep 'em happy and complacent. It's cheaper than welfare and all these 'Bed-Sty' socialist programs, especially if we let the pharmaceutical companies sell the stuff like Mary Kay cosmetics!"

Many business-oriented Republicans also supported population control and government-backed bank loans as a means of stemming the tide of poverty in the third world. Professor Paul Ehrlich, a leading population-control advocate, found a sounding board in the Republican Party. Democrats such as Stewart Udall, Walter Reuther, and left-wing environmentalist Barry Commoner rejected such "doomsday scenarios." As Commoner said, "Ehrlich lets the unequal capitalist distribution of resources and money off the hook for the problems of overpopulation. For example, India had no population control problem before the British arrived. But when the British required India to stop growing its own food in favor of cotton, silk, and opium, then poverty and overpopulation problems resulted."[4]

The Republicans firmly believed that their economically libertarian but culturally liberal stances were going to find favor among suburban whites, who still were voting in higher percentages than blacks and other minorities. Republicans also hoped to gain voters among bohemians and culturally liberal business-oriented people of all races in cosmopolitan areas. "Let the Democrats deal with the yahoos in the South," said Ed Rollins, a rising young Republican campaign consultant.

The third prong of the Republican strategy was the most risky, but potentially the most rewarding. The Republicans knew that more workers and minorities would be voting in 1972 than in any previous election year as a result of expanded registration efforts by the civil rights movement and the unions. To counter this, it was not enough to appeal to "liberty and freedom." In short, the Republicans needed to "nurture," in the words of Rollins, a split in the ranks of the working people.

Part of the strategy was to have southern business leaders, through intermediaries, financially assist the small racially motivated populist political party started by George Wallace in 1968 known as the American Independent Party. The 1972 standard-bearers for that party, now that Wallace had "gone soft with blacks and unions," were Lester Maddox, a former governor of Georgia, and Congressman John Schmitz, a John Birch Society member from Orange County, California. The strategy was to help the American Independent Party siphon votes of religious, white workers from the Democrats. Pro-racist mailers were carefully designed either to discourage such voters from going to the polls or to vote instead for presidential candidate Maddox and vice presidential candidate Schmitz.

In the North, the same would be done in liberal or radical college areas through the nascent Peace and Freedom Party, now led by the charismatic socialist David McReynolds. With little regulation of campaign financing, some business—and Republican—money found its way into that "other third party." The socialists in the Peace and Freedom Party were upset at "the snail's pace of change" and Kennedy's "essentially reactionary stances" in the face of "rapacious corporations." As one of the sons of Wal-Mart founder Sam Walton said after the old man passed on, "My father was one of those businessmen who put money into the hands of those socialist agitators. He told me, 'Son, a vote against Kennedy this year is as important as a vote for Reagan when it comes to dividing those union lovers.'"

When the sex scandal broke against Kennedy in May 1972, the Republicans began to create a series of ads for the fall about Kennedy's "sexual deviance" to be run in the Midwest and the South, and his "sexual hypocrisy" to be played in the San Francisco and New York markets.

Reagan's candidacy fit perfectly into this strategy of an economic commitment to liberty for corporate America and a cultural commitment to liberty for individuals. Reagan, for example, had signed the most liberal abortion rights law in his first term as California's governor (in both the original and RFK timelines). He also supported the original language of the Equal Rights Amendment (ERA). Thus, he was able to attract interest from traditional Republicans who saw the Democrats as no better than socialists, but also modern thinking feminists such as Gloria Steinhem, who at one time or another supported socialist ideals.

Steinhem and several other prominent feminists were angry at President Kennedy for his continued failure to support the federal abortion rights bill pending in Congress. Their anger then turned to outrage when Kennedy, along with the First Lady, supported a modification of the ERA in early 1972. The modification was proposed by the Kennedy White House in order to secure its passage among culturally conservative legislators who were becoming concerned that the ERA, in its original form, could be interpreted to mean putting women into combat, mandating unisex bathrooms, promoting homosexuality as a "civil right," and conferring a constitutional right to an abortion. Democrats and some Republicans in Congress quickly voted to modify the ERA to specifically state that the proposed amendment did not mean anything of the sort in these particular areas.[5]

Most feminists, including those who supported Kennedy, were upset chiefly because the modification required ERA proponents to restart the State approval process. But it became clear that the modified language was likely to pass the more than thirty-eight State legislatures required to amend the United States Constitution. Kate Millet, a prominent feminist, said, "This ERA will pass, but it provides us with very little, if any, protection for our fight against patriarchy."

In late May 1972, as Kennedy's sex scandal was still simmering and the modified ERA was being ratified by various states, Reagan met Steinem and some other feminists at his ranch in California. He told the gathered feminists that as governor, he had already signed a state version of the ERA as an amendment to the California State Constitution. His ERA law had no limitation on abortion, but it did have limitations against unisex bathrooms, military combat, and homosexuality. He also reminded his guests that he had signed into law the most liberal abortion law ever enacted in the United States in his first term as governor. The feminists, to quote Roger Ailes, "swooned."

Senator Roth was also given an opportunity to speak with Steinhem. But he told aides he was uncomfortable speaking with "bra burners" such as Steinem. He confirmed, however, that he supported the federal abortion rights bill. Steinem was furious when she heard from a Reagan spy in Roth's camp about Roth's bra burners' remark. Raising her hand above her head, she exclaimed, "I have had it up to here with the lie that we burned our bras—*anywhere!* We never burned our bras! All we did in Atlantic City, when the Miss America pageant was held, was throw our bras into a garbage can. A reporter suggested we burn them, but we didn't want the fire marshal to accuse us of violating safety laws. Burning our bras wasn't even on our minds!"

Nancy Reagan, hearing this directly from Steinem, put her hand on Steinem's shoulder and said, "We both know how the press distorts things, and against women especially."

Afterward, Steinem said to "sister" feminist Kate Millet, "You know, I like Nancy Reagan. She is one tough woman—and sharp!"

Reagan swept the June 1972 Republican presidential primaries against Senator Roth, and thereafter secured the Republican nomination for president. The Republican Party's national convention in San Diego, set for early August, was going to be unified for the first time in more than a decade.

Reagan, however, was not free of political wounds after undergoing a very competitive primary. Roth and Abrams' supporters, during the primaries, had used the typical argument against governors running for president: As a "mere" governor, Reagan was "untested" nationally and lacked experience in foreign affairs. Kennedy supporters would use this in the fall as well. It was, said O'Brien, "a natural. You'd be committing political-campaign malpractice if you didn't use it against a governor running for president!"

The Roth campaign did some damage to Reagan in the integrity department by highlighting his inconsistencies. First, Reagan the libertarian, small government candidate supported subsidies for tobacco farmers in North Carolina. Then Reagan suggested in Texas that the government repeal the minimum wage, even though he had signed legislation to increase the minimum wage in California—*above* the federal level—two years before.

Roth's favorite attack on Reagan concerned his flip-flop on taxes early in his tenure as governor of California. Roth also took advantage of Reagan's more recent flip-flop on the common state income tax proposal. In 1971, Reagan initially failed to oppose the common income tax for states. He hoped that it would pass because California already had a state sales tax and a state income tax.

Most moderate Republicans in the Golden State supported the common income tax in order to make California more competitive for business development compared with non–income tax states such as Arizona and states in the South. In New Hampshire, Reagan formally announced his opposition to any common tax for states "just in time to run in the presidential primaries," as Roth said over and over. Reagan supporters said this was a breach of Roth's pledge not to personally attack other candidates, but Roth said this was a fundamental issue of policy. Roth said he had a right to show that Reagan was a "fair-weather friend of the taxpayer."[6]

In the Ohio primary, one of Roth's aides, subsequently fired by Roth, attacked Reagan for being the head of the Hollywood actors union, which showed, said the aide, that Reagan was a "fair-weather friend of business interests."

Abrams' and Roth's supporters attacked Reagan during the primary for being a "dumb Hollywood movie actor." While Abrams joked about Reagan's intelligence a few times on the trail with reporters, Roth's complete refusal to descend to this level of personal attack did him no good, according to most political consultants reviewing the primary campaign. In fact, *Washington Post* pundit Nicholas von Hoffman said Roth's failure to attack Reagan for being "dumb" was a sign of Roth's "terminal dullness." Von Hoffman admitted, however, that "Roth's schoolmarm manner did not prevent him from wondering whether Reagan had the 'cojones' to lead the tax-cutting and antiunion revolt of the 'haves' against the 'starting to haves.'"

Ironically, Reagan's perceived "limited intelligence quotient" proved to be quite damning, more because of Reagan's own statements than anything else. Reagan had once said, in response to the environmental legislation crafted by the Democrats and Kennedy, that "trees cause more pollution than factories." Further, arguing against the Antiballistic Missile Treaty, Reagan said, "We can win a nuclear war with our traditional 'duck and cover' strategy and digging small holes in the ground." On the campaign trail, Reagan was specifically asked if he supported a New York Republican state senator's bill decriminalizing marijuana and cocaine. Reagan, not directly saying he'd support the bill, quipped, "Well, when I was a boy, Coca-Cola was still putting cocaine in its sodas—with no problem in society, I might add."[7] Adding to the perception of inconsistency, Reagan's campaign said he was quoted "out of context" and that he did not support such a "radical bill."

Despite these gaffes and the inconsistencies, the reporters who covered Reagan liked him for his libertarian instinct. It appealed to the reporters' sense of the "freedom of the press," Democratic pollster Peter Hart told Ralph Yarborough. That Reagan was choreographed and kept far away from the "boys on the press bus" did not harm his relationship with reporters because Kennedy was almost completely unavailable, supposedly because of security concerns. Hart warned Yarborough, "With Reagan's charm, even in places where he lost, very little seems to have stuck to him. His opponents' attacks were pretty right on, but they seemed to slide off the guy, even the attack on Reagan's tax increases in his first term as governor. Reagan has a way of connecting to people when he speaks. He's awfully sincere in his mannerisms. Bob better prepare to debate him in the fall no matter what the polls say. He can't hide from Reagan. And that's a fact."

In the 1972 election campaign, race became less of an issue, reversing a trend that had begun during the 1950s' civil rights movement. In the RFK timeline, there was less fear of "black male criminals," a fear that gripped white America in the first timeline and never let go from the late 1960s onward. There was now a more genuine—though not full—acceptance of blacks as "equal Americans" that began to take hold, due principally to the media success stories from the Bed-Sty programs across the nation.

When white people from the suburbs visited the cities, they found them thriving economically. New jobs had been created in the French-owned public transportation factories; the nascent computer industry, thanks to Hewlett-Packard, Intel, and IBM (Tom Watson even told an executive board meeting of the Chamber of Commerce that he found black workers "more grateful and more productive in their jobs."); and new factories—environmentally sensitive, relatively speaking—from such corporate stalwarts as Alcoa and Ford Motor Company. The Prudential Insurance Company gave new high school and junior college educated blacks a chance to sell insurance to each other and to enter the ranks of new "black-collar" middle-management jobs. With housing values going up in the inner cities, renters secured federal loans to buy the homes they were renting, and then borrowed from banks for second mortgages to remodel their new homes.

Kennedy's administration, with little fanfare, hired Dr. Harry Edwards, a sociologist from the University of California at Berkeley, to assist in reforming schools in various ghettoes. Edwards had become somewhat infamous for influencing three U.S. black athletes at the 1968 Olympics to give the black power salute when being awarded their medals. Edwards knew that even a Kennedy-led government would not be able to provide enough money or tools for the task. But rather than despair about it, Edwards traveled to Hollywood and secured the backing of Bill Cosby, Sidney Poitier, Harry Belafonte, Paul Newman, Warren Beatty, and other well-connected Hollywood actors and producers to support scholarships and other financial aid packages to give black students an incentive to go to college. Edwards also enlisted athletes Rafer Johnson, Rosey Grier, Arthur Ashe, and Muhammad Ali to convince students to stay in school as opposed to risking everything to join the National Basketball Association or other major professional sports leagues. Edwards' famous study showing that the chance of a black student reaching the NBA was not much better than a black man going to the moon resonated in the soon-to-be-former ghettoes.

Edwards also demanded the athletes and entertainers donate their time as well as their money to mentor students. These stars, combined with the black and Latino/Hispanic lawyers, doctors, and accountants who came back to their communities after securing their degrees, did as much for rebuilding neighborhoods as the government and private dollars. Bill Cosby did note in an interview in the *Village Voice,* however, "Without the government programs created through this administration of Robert Kennedy, we'd probably just be peeing into the wind."

The government was providing jobs in counseling, literacy programs, and other social work, as well as through a building rehabilitation department and an expanded sanitation department in every distressed municipality. These employment bases paved the way for the development of hardware shops, grocery stores, restaurants, bicycle repair shops, and a host of other small businesses. With the lessening of poverty, culture thrived. For example, music and dancing now tended toward traditional techniques rather than techniques designed to shock audiences. Jazz was revered and classical music developed a following among blacks not seen since before the Harlem Renaissance. The black-dominated inner cities developed highly regarded cultural organizations, with the best-known example being the Harlem Orchestra and Ballet, which played to sold-out, racially integrated audiences nearly every night after its opening in April 1971. The audience included white people from Queens and Brooklyn, traditionally white boroughs of New York City, who were losing their fear of blacks and Latinos.

Latinos were also flexing their political muscle in the wake of Bed-Sty programs in Texas, the Southwest, and California. Latinos were so successful that when Edmund G. "Gerry" Brown won his campaign for governor in 1974, it was said he won on the "coattails" of his running mate for lieutenant governor, Cesar Chavez. Latinos made up a fairly large minority in southern and central California in the early to mid-1970s. The key was to get the Latinos to vote on Election Day, which they did in large numbers.

For whites who lived near or in the cities, the most important benefits of the Kennedy administration antipoverty programs were the increased safety and livability of the cities. The money that was spent in the first timeline on "prisons and anticrime socialism" was spent on much less expensive community policing programs and boot camps in the forests—far away from the cities—for young gang members and other violent offenders.[8] Although the jobs, education, and social work programs had caused the first three fiscal years' annual deficits to total twenty billion dollars, the strengthening of these communities created a near-balanced federal budget for fiscal 1973 as the economy continued to improve for most Americans.

In the RFK timeline, New York City Mayor John Lindsay became a Democrat while running for reelection in 1970. Under his stewardship, the city received more than enough money in federal subsidies to finance redevelopment projects. Lindsay eventually defeated Republican Senator Jacob Javits in 1974 to join the other former-Republican-turned-Democrat from New York, Senator Charles Goodell.

Welfare as a government program essentially disappeared, having been replaced by the negative income tax. Single mothers, who, in order to stay on welfare, had to remain unmarried, now had an incentive to marry, particularly when the men secured decent-paying jobs. Poverty plummeted, as did welfare rolls.[9] Reduced expenditures for prisons and welfare programs (welfare programs were expensive because a bureaucracy was needed to constantly update who was poor enough to receive welfare) allowed money to be spent on more community-oriented programs. The resulting economic benefits brought even more tax money to government coffers.

By 1972, urban conditions were looking so positive that a National Board of Realtors study found that 29 percent of whites living in the suburbs were interested in moving back to the cities, even if it meant living in a city with black municipal leadership. Surprising sociologists, most whites in the survey claimed they wouldn't mind living in a city dominated by black municipal officials if they had to move there for one reason or another.

Integration in the South proceeded without much racial strife because working-class blacks and whites already lived close together by "tradition." Living close meant there was no need for busing students to distant schools for integration purposes. Further, there was little need to enforce as many "open and equal housing" laws once people accepted the idea that blacks and whites had more in common with each other as workers than either did with their bosses. With government support for labor organizing, through the pro-worker National Labor Relations Board, and with the merger of the civil rights and union movements, more racial harmony prevailed in the South than anyone could have anticipated just four years earlier. Exceptions remained in some rural areas of Mississippi, Georgia, Louisiana, and South Carolina, where whites, in the words of Southern newspaper editor Hodding Carter, "were too damned dumb for their own good. Too many of these people would rather put on hoods and dance around a Ku Klux Klan bonfire than have a new factory come to town that might employ them and some black folks."

In short, most white Americans were less afraid of black and brown Americans, even if they still had reservations about intermarriage—at least for the time being.

Reagan, in a very early campaign appearance in Philadelphia, Mississippi, in October 1971, had tested and then rejected the Nixon strategy of directly using code words with regard to race. Speaking to a crowd of mostly white people at a county fair, Reagan said, "I support states' rights." "States' rights" was, at the time, a southern code phrase for segregationist policies.[10]

Reagan backed off this strategy after learning black business leaders in the South and the North were just as opposed to Kennedy and labor unions as white business leaders. He and his advisers also realized that such racial appeals might hurt him in most white suburbs where people vehemently denied the latent racism that may have led them to move to the suburbs in the first place. Southern businessman Roger Milliken, a major Reagan supporter, told Reagan that Republicans would not prevail nationally by making racial appeals. "We need," said Milliken, "to preserve the Old South's *business* traditions more than its racial traditions. One of mah younger white managers told me that th' other day, an' Ah think he's right. An' you can't afford to mess up the support we'll need up north, where they lahk to think they aren't 'racist' lahk us folks down heah—arrogant Yankees, tha's what they are! Plus, it didn't get Nixon nowhere last time. Leave the racist stuff to Maddox—let 'im steal some white trash votes from Kennedy an' Yarborough."

Chapter 31

THE HOME STRETCH

Reagan entered a unified Republican convention in early August 1972. At the end of "a staged convention that looked more like an Oscars' ceremony than a political convention," according to Tom Wicker of the *Washington Post,* Reagan pulled briefly ahead of Kennedy in the national polls. But Reagan fell slightly behind Kennedy when it was learned that Reagan was not the "tax cutter" he claimed to be.

Reagan had said throughout the primary that he regretted his initial raising of sales, income, and corporate taxes in his first term as California governor. He said he was now a tax cutter, and to prove it, he pointed to his lowering of property taxes in 1971, overcoming the initial objections of a liberal, Democratic state legislature. While Roth and Abrams were content to let Reagan slide on this, the *Sacramento Bee,* just in time for Reagan's nomination, studied the effect of the property tax reduction. The study revealed the property tax cuts were skewed toward the richest homeowning Californians. The story was then picked up in the national media, which played into the Democrats' line that Reagan was a tool for the interests of the rich.

Kennedy, however, was not sanguine about Reagan hitting a pothole in the road to the White House. From studying the polls, Kennedy realized that he was not as much ahead of Reagan as much as Reagan had fallen behind. The president realized he needed to reestablish himself with swing voters. He also knew that Reagan would not be afraid to debate. Kennedy, therefore, agreed to two debates with Reagan in the month of October, just weeks before Election Day.

Kennedy had been having problems not only with swing voters, but also with the small, but potentially significant radical voters who were supporting the tiny, but growing Peace and Freedom third-party candidate, David McReynolds. McReynolds had risen to almost 5 percent in the polls, with support from radicals and left-wing feminists who were opposed to Kennedy's moral hypocrisy and failure to usher in true socialism in America. Yarborough told Kennedy, "You take care of the swing voters, and let me handle them radicals who don' understand what we're up against with Reagan and them *Ree*-publicans."

Yarborough enlisted Labor Secretary Reuther, and together, they sent black, leftist labor leader Mike Hamlin, social activist Michael Harrington,

Black Panther Bobby Seale (now a state assemblyman in California), and Chicago alderman Thomas Hayden to radical enclaves in Ann Arbor, Berkeley, San Francisco, and New York, where McReynolds' support was most pronounced. The promises made to Peace and Freedom Party supporters would loom large in Kennedy's next term, assuming he defeated the formidable Reagan.

Anti-Kennedy ads, paid for by "independent" businesspeople, filled the airwaves with attacks on Kennedy's integrity, "America's slide into socialism," and "excessive taxes." Reagan ads were softer, with one showing Reagan saying that it was time for "a truce in the war between organized labor and honest business enterprises. As someone with experience with both labor and management, we can, together, bring peace within our borders and, I might add, around the world."

In a whistle-stop train-riding campaign (he was still getting over his fear of flying), Reagan brought audiences to a state of teary-eyed patriotism as he spoke of America as a "shining city on the hill and a beacon of hope in a cruel and chaotic world." Vice presidential candidate General Abrams spoke at various rallies about the continued menace of Communism abroad and at home. He gravely intoned that the Soviet Union withdrew from Eastern Europe "only for the short run against China" and that "the Kennedy administration's weakness in the face of the world Communist menace will hurt us in the long run when the Russian bear awakens from its false slumber."

Worse for Kennedy, his relationship with several influential feminists had collapsed after Gloria Steinem officially switched her support from Kennedy and the Democrats to Reagan and the Republicans. For Steinem, the failure of the Democrats to pass a federal abortion rights bill was as bad as "the failure of Harry Truman to pass an antilynching bill for blacks in the 1940s, or worse!" Responding to those who claimed that Reagan represented a threat to larger societal interests and the economic well-being of workers, Steinem told one interviewer, "Workers are fine even if Reagan wins. He was a labor leader, for goodness sakes! The most ignored issue in this election is women's reproductive rights and the right of women to make as much money as men. We need to stop seeing feminism as somehow 'socialist!' We need to see feminism as having more to do with personal liberty and self-actualization."

Joining Steinhem in the nascent "Feminists for Reagan" movement were Kate Millet, Ellen Gould Davis, and several other feminist radicals, or as Larry O'Brien caustically whispered, the "pro-lesbian contingent." However, others stayed with the Kennedy-Yarborough ticket. Those particular feminists included Ellis Willis, Ruth Rosen, Bella Abzug, Shirley Chisholm, and Barbara Ehrenreich. As Ruth Rosen wrote later in her memoirs, "The split between various feminists starting in 1972 was more about economics than culture. Those of us who stayed inside the Democratic Party, and with President Robert Kennedy, had tied our feminism more to our support for unions, collective interests, an egalitarian community, and economic justice than our need for 'self-acutalization.'"

Ms. Magazine, the feminist magazine Steinem had founded, split apart at the masthead, with several of the Kennedy-Yarborough supporters quitting in protest against Steinem's endorsement of Reagan. Ehrenreich and Rosen founded a competing feminist magazine, which they christened *Mother Worker.* The name, they said, more strongly emphasized their belief in a woman having a choice to work outside or inside the home—or both. Ehrenreich wrote in the editorial page of the first issue that her experience with women union workers heroically balancing their homemaker and outside work activities had inspired the magazine's motto: "Mothers are workers. Period."

Despite these problems, most polls showed Kennedy ahead of Reagan at the end of September, 48 to 40 percent. Kennedy's union support, which had grown to almost 50 percent of the voters, was almost unanimous. This support was strong not only for economic reasons, but also because the administration refused to undermine gun ownership and endorse the federal abortion rights bill. These two issues were becoming important to the most religious of rank-and-file union families, who voted in slightly higher numbers than less religious union voters. On the other hand, there were many voters claiming to "be less than firm in their choice," which Kennedy attributed to his personal scandal earlier in the year. McReynolds and Maddox were at 3 percent each, with the remainder undecided. Pollsters and commentators, therefore, saw the first debate as potentially a "make or break" debate for either Kennedy or Reagan.

The first debate went forward on Tuesday, October 3, 1972. According to Theodore White, in his book, *Making of the President, 1972,* the most memorable part of the first debate was the argument between Reagan and Kennedy on the subject of taxes. Kennedy, before the Democratic convention, reiterated his support for a simplified tax system with lower rates for all. He had announced his support for such a plan in early May, but the scandal wiped out any institutional memory among the media and the public. Most of the media wrongly said Kennedy had made a "convention conversion" to support tax cutting. As White wrote in his book, the media was less than fair, but not completely unfair. For, as White noted, "a May announcement was perhaps not a convention conversion, but it could certainly be seen as an election-year conversion."

Reagan, with a media blitz, and the unanimity of Republican leaders supporting him, was becoming known as "Mr. Tax Cut," particularly compared to Kennedy. In the debate, when one of the three reporter-panelists asked the question on taxes, most reporters saw the question as a "softball" for Reagan. They had heard Reagan's stump speech so many times some joked that they could recite the answer themselves in the two minutes allotted to the candidate.

In his stump speeches, Reagan had become fond of saying that his tax cut would not necessarily mean less revenue for the government because "Americans will have more money to invest in the private sector. And these investments will raise more tax dollars than our government will know what to do with!" Like Roth, Reagan was willing to undermine the traditional Republican message of fiscal discipline and balanced budgets by saying America could have tax cuts without necessarily having to cut spending.

Two days before the debate, Reagan drew a distinction between his tax-cutting plan and the president's tax-simplification plan. Reagan said in a speech in Los Angeles that only *his* plan actually cut taxes for all taxpayers, which was technically true for those who earned enough to pay federal income taxes. But Reagan failed to emphasize that under his plan, the wealthiest taxpayers gained the most because, in addition to the tax rate cuts, they kept the deductions, exemptions, and credits they always had to lessen the pain of a more progressive income tax system.

Kennedy's plan, while it also cut income tax *rates* for all taxpayers, wound up requiring the top income earners to pay *more* in taxes to the extent it removed the deductions, exemptions, and credits that were mostly utilized by these wealthiest members of society. In effect, Kennedy's tax cut plan was a tax break for working class earners first and foremost, with those making at or near the minimum wage no longer paying any federal income taxes whatsoever. It was in effect, however, a tax increase on the wealthiest.

If Reagan, in his Los Angeles campaign speech, meant to draw this distinction between his and Kennedy's tax plans, it was, his aides realized, a double-edged sword, for the Congressional Budget Office, and even some pro-Republican, fiscally conservative economists, had recently concluded that Reagan's tax cuts could lead to greater deficits unless government *spending* was also cut. Only Kennedy's tax cut plan, by limiting and in many cases ending deductions, exemptions, credits, and other "goodies" in the tax system for rich people, kept the revenues flowing at the same or greater levels, at least according to the CBO report.

In the debate, the tax cut question was directed at Reagan, and he therefore was given the first opportunity to speak. Reagan answered the question with his usual grace and charm about the need for tax-cut relief, oppressed taxpayers footing the bill for socialist schemes, and his latest claim that only his tax plan cut everyone's taxes. When Kennedy heard that last part, a smile spread across his face. When it was his turn to respond, Kennedy looked directly into the camera and, using the old debater's trick of slightly twisting an opponent's words, said, "Governor Reagan said that only his plan cuts the tax rates of every taxpayer. That is simply wrong."

Then, turning to the governor, Kennedy said, "Governor Reagan, the plan I have proposed and supported throughout this year cuts everyone's tax rates, from the rich down to the poor. There is a difference, however, between our tax-cutting plans. The difference is that only *my* plan *simplifies* the tax system. Your plan cuts tax rates for the wealthiest income earners but lets those richest people keep all the special deductions, exemptions, and credits that most Americans don't receive—and likely never will. And that's unfair. My plan *simplifies* the tax system so the workers and even the richest people in this country receive a tax cut in the rates they currently pay. But the rich would also pay their fair share and will no longer be able to hide behind hidden or special-interest deductions. According to the Congressional Budget Office, which has objectively analyzed both our plans, your plan gives the most money to the rich and could cause our entire government debt to more than double in size, which would also create the largest annual deficit we've ever had! My plan is fair, responsible, and practical. It also brings in the necessary revenue for our basic needs as a nation, including our continued military preparedness."

"That was ninety seconds of pure gold!" exclaimed O'Brien backstage.

Reagan, unable to answer further under the rigid rules of the so-called debate, in which each candidate received only one chance to answer each reporter-panelist's question, decided to break the rules. After all, he was behind in the polls and needed to deliver a knockout blow against Kennedy. Reagan smiled into the camera and, in his usual folksy manner, said, "Well, there he goes again. Trying to bog us down in a world of economists contradicting each other. My plan, Mr. Kennedy, rewards those who take the largest risks with their money to create the jobs that make this nation the shining city on the hill it is to every other nation in the world."

In that rejoinder, Reagan showed his critics, once again, that if he was an idiot, he was an idiot savant. He understood perfectly what he needed to say to defend against the charge that he was "coddling the rich."

Kennedy, on the other hand, was determined to make Reagan pay for his support for the richest Americans. He had heard Reagan use the line "There he goes again" during an early primary debate against Roth and Abrams. Kennedy snapped back at Reagan, "Mr. Reagan, you tell me 'There I go again.' Well, sir, I'm not *going* anywhere tonight. If you think I'm wrong somehow, you ought to tell me so. Is it true or isn't it that your plan does nothing to end unfair deductions for the richest Americans?"

"Well," Reagan stammered, "um, no, it's not unfair—"

Kennedy, now in his prosecution attorney attack-mode, verbally jabbed Reagan, saying, "I have read your plan, sir, and it does nothing to remove deductions or exemptions. It merely cuts tax *rates*—which take up only two pages of the *million* pages of the tax code. The deductions and the exemptions are in the rest of those million—"

At this point, the debate moderator, Howard K. Smith, stopped the candidates from engaging in an actual debate. Smith said, "Gentlemen, this dialogue is outside the parameters of tonight's rules. I appreciate your enthusiasm, but I must break it up." After the debate, Kennedy's camp said Smith was biased because he protected Reagan from being exposed as being ignorant of his own policy proposal. Reagan's camp said Smith was biased because he saved Kennedy from being revealed as a pint-sized bully. Smith was biased, though, but not in the way either candidate's supporters alleged. The bias Smith possessed was the usual media elitism against any "messy" or "partisan sounding" debates.

With less than one month until the election, and with heavy news coverage of that debate sequence, Reagan found, for the first time, that a charge began to stick to him. The charge was Reagan's fealty to the rich at the expense of the rest of society. And the Republicans' charge that the "old, ruthless Bobby has returned" had a positive, not negative, effect with "swing voters." These voters tended to be lower- to middle-class workers who were nonunion. They saw Kennedy's tough questioning and posturing as evidence of strength and knowledge, an important "issue" for people who do not generally follow policy disputes. They also saw that Kennedy was going to cut *their* taxes but make sure "rich people" lost various special tax breaks. These voters liked that element of revenge in the tax plan.[1]

The question political commentators asked after the first debate was whether swing voters had been watching. Nielsen ratings measuring the number of television viewers for the first debate showed a larger audience, proportionately, than the audience for the Jack Kennedy–Richard Nixon debates in 1960. However, as with that 1960 debate, the number of people who claimed to have watched the Kennedy–Reagan debate increased as the news coverage continued in the days following the event.

Among the media commentators, the second most discussed sequences were Reagan's closing remarks, in which he said that Kennedy's policies were leading "this great nation of ours down the road to Communist serfdom. We Americans, who love our liberty and freedom, must stand tall at this moment in our history and send Washington, D.C., a message that we will not be whittled down, bogged down, or torn down with regulations and taxes."

Kennedy's closing remarks were also widely reported. He said, "Under my administration, more people are making more money than they have ever before in the history of the world. Our urban revitalization programs, designed to do for our inner cities what was done for the nations of Western Europe after World War II, continue to earn dividends for all of our communities, urban and rural, around our nation. Farmers and businessmen have more customers to sell to as a result of the increased purchasing power of city dwellers. Mr. Reagan's policies would turn back the clock to a nation that was one-third ill-fed, ill-clothed, and ill-housed, to use the words of the greatest president in our century, Franklin D. Roosevelt. Mr. Reagan opposed our peace in Vietnam and our policy of constructive engagement with the Soviets, as if more war would create a safer and better world. I pledge to each of you, and each of your families, that Ralph Yarborough and I will continue to support all Americans, and to promote unity, peace, prosperity, and, and most important, freedom in our nation and our world."

The Kennedy-Reagan debates were striking, at least for historians and political scientists, for the two candidates' contrasting world views that would either move the nation back to a pre–New Deal era of supporting business interests over labor if Reagan were elected, or toward Western European–style social democracy if Kennedy were reelected.

The second debate had its own dynamic and highlights. In Kennedy's opening statement, he cited the success of 1960s' programs such as Head Start, which included parenting classes that lowered the incidence of child abuse among the poor. Kennedy also spoke of a recent HEW study showing that poor people now had more incentive to work because of the negative income tax and a rising minimum wage itself. "The unemployment rate is down to 2.1 percent, the lowest on record since World War II," he said.[2]

Kennedy was questioned, early on, about the continued poverty that still existed in 1972. He responded, "The latest poverty figures show a mere 6 percent of people—parents and children—living in poverty, a level never achieved in the history of our nation. And to those who say our figures include so-called government 'make-work,' I say that cleaning streets and repairing neighborhood buildings is no more make-work than building airports, cars, office buildings, and factories. All are part of what constitutes a truly civilized and advanced society."

Reagan answered with more facts and figures than he usually did and provided a vision of an alternative future where entrepreneurs turned the latest technology into mass products for everyone and where government stepped out of the way to allow "America's natural creativity to flourish."

Reagan was strong in this debate, but it was not enough to "win" in the eyes of the reporters and "experts" commenting in the instant after-the-debate analysis on the five national television networks—including the expanded Public Broadcasting network and the new American Broadcasting Service (ABS), founded by several black entertainers and athletes, and backed with private philanthropic and government money. Most of the analysts concluded that President Kennedy presented his case for reelection with "skill and confidence" while Reagan was given "points" for presenting a new vision for America.

Walter Cronkite, the venerable anchor at the dominant news network of the time, CBS, said in his authoritative, yet comforting tone, "Governor

Reagan needed to hit a home run tonight in this second debate against the president. And in boxing, a tie goes to the champ, in this case, the incumbent. Would anyone disagree that there was no knockout by the challenger this evening?" Everyone in the studio, of course, agreed with Cronkite—as did the other networks. And, as often happens in such post-debate analysis, the challenger is held to a standard fit for boxing, but not for a democracy or a republic.[3]

In the only vice-presidential debate between Abrams and Yarborough, Abrams was asked to cite the difference between his vision for the American economy and Yarborough's vision. Abrams answered by repeating the Reaganite mantra of business knows best and how government is the main problem holding back economic growth. He then cited the failures of the "socialist" economy of the Soviet Union, "which can't even provide wheat to its own people." He concluded, "And socialism as practiced by the Kennedy-Yarborough administration won't work here, either!"

Yarborough, enjoying his moment of engaging in a soapbox "dee-bate," responded, "General, I guess ya haven't noticed the billions in federal government subsidies to American farmers over the past few decades that even people in your own party support. I guess ya'd call that socialism, too, though Ah've noticed with that socialism, as ya'd call it, we not only feed ourselves, but most o' the rest o' the world. Now if ya can't see the difference between what we've been doin' for America and what's gone on in Russia, well, sir, you oughta get around more."

Late in the debate, when each candidate was asked to describe his overall political philosophy, Abrams recited the famous quote often attributed to the legendary British leader Winston Churchill: "If you're not a liberal at twenty, you haven't got a heart. If you're not a conservative at forty, you haven't got any brains."

Theodore White described what happened next as follows: "There was a big gulp from the audience when Abrams finished his answer. People thought Yarborough, who was well into his sixties, might be angry at Abrams' remark. But when the debate audience looked immediately back to Yarborough, the vice president was smiling as he began his famous response:

"'And General, by the time ya hit sixty, lahk Ah have, ya realize that 'liberal' and 'conservative' don't mean a darn thing! The only real thing we gotta ask ev'ry time is this: Does a government policy help the workin' folks or doesn't it? That's it, isn't it? Sometimes a policy that's good for the workin' folks is gonna be lib'ral and sometimes it's gonna be conserv'tive. But Ah won't hold that silly remark against Mr. Churchill or you, General, since we were all in the big war together!'"

This response, like the Reagan-Kennedy exchange on tax-cut proposals, was played over and over in the media. Reagan's campaign manager, Roger Ailes, after Yarborough's quip, felt like stabbing himself through the heart with his Bic pen. Swing voters were going to stick with the incumbents, thought Ailes.

Worse for Ailes and his candidate, pollsters found the Kennedy-Yarbrough advertisements, which Ailes told Nancy Reagan were "corny," were working. Kennedy and Yarborough, said one advertisement, "work well together despite being from different parts of the nation. Together, they have united America in order to better serve us all in creating peace and prosperity."

In another ad, Kennedy stood alone, with the melody of "America the Beautiful" playing softly in the background, saying simply that he had kept his promise to "free us of our strife that resulted from a divisive war, to make the world a more peaceful place, and continue to help every American, in every part of our land, have the opportunity to take part in our economy— and in a way that benefits us all."

After the second debate, in late October, the Reagan camp faced another problem they wouldn't have anticipated "in a million years!" as Ailes told *Washington Post* reporter Lou Cannon after the election. On October 19, a southern fundamentalist minister named Jerry Falwell from a small town in Virginia with an evil-sounding name, Lynchburg, released a political pamphlet about Reagan. Falwell had strongly opposed Robert Kennedy's election in 1968 because of Kennedy's "radicalism," including Kennedy's positions on civil rights for black Americans. However, Falwell became pro-Kennedy once he realized he could now successfully minister to integrated audiences in a South where integrated unions were becoming stronger and stronger every year. Plus, Kennedy's refusal to support the abortion rights bill, which bill Falwell vehemently opposed, caused Falwell to change his mind about Kennedy.

To show his support for the president, Falwell prepared a pamphlet entitled "Mr. 666 Is Coming After You." The pamphlet explained that "Ronald Wilson Reagan" has six letters in each name. For many Christian Americans, "666" was the sign of the devil. In the pamphlet, Falwell wrote that the more he saw of "that slick Hollywood politician," as he described Reagan, the more he opposed him. In one memorable passage, Falwell wrote, "This Hollywood actor wants to kill little babies in their mommy's wombs in order to keep the rich from paying their fair share in our society." He also said that Reagan "had the support of prominent homosexual deviants in New York and Hollywood who want the first 'Hollywood president' to pass laws legalizing homosexuals to teach in your children's schools."

The phrase Falwell used for Reagan, "Mr. 666," swept like a prairie wildfire among evangelical groups in the South and the southern section of the Midwest. The major media never reported this story or this epithet against Reagan because, in the words of *New York Times* publisher Arthur Sulzberger, "We don't report on the ravings of some uncouth, backwater preacher." Governor Reagan wanted to sue Falwell for libel, but his advisers convinced him—well, really, Nancy Reagan—that this would only force the national media to report the accusation. Also, with the Supreme Court rulings on libel law from the 1960s (before Robert Kennedy became president), there was little chance Reagan would prevail. As Reagan strategist John Sears said to Nancy Reagan, "Nancy, you and I know that we'll be lucky to carry any state in the Deep South anyway. The game is in the Midwest, the Pacific Northwest, the Southwest, and the Northeast. Remember, the Deep South is where cousins marry cousins!"

After the intervention of Yarborough—and George Wallace, who was now openly supporting Kennedy and the labor unions against the "country-club-golf-playin' Republican biz-nessmen"—Falwell issued an apology for his pamphlet. But as a bitter Nancy Reagan said for years after the 1972 election, the damage was already done.

Kennedy's soon-to-be-departing press secretary, Jack Newfield, rather liked the analogy that Republicans such as Reagan were "devil inspired." He told Ralph Yarborough that the analogy was "fair enough, considering how, for thirty years, Republicans called plenty of liberal Democrats 'atheistic Communists' for wanting to help working people."

"Well," said Yarborough, "at least we look lahk fair players in gettin' that preacher ta apologize, but we still got the benefit o' that funny li'l phrase!"

Kennedy, who worried about such "demonizing" politics—because he had long been personally attacked himself—was adamant that his supporters never repeat the Reverend Falwell's words in any campaign appearance. He told the O Boys to get the word out, saying, "Anyone using anything like that phrase regarding Reagan will be fired! Got that? There's no second chance here!" Counting the letters in his own name, Kennedy breathed a sigh of relief. He then thought to himself, If we let this kind of attack continue, who knows what'll be made up about me?

Chapter 32

ELECTION DISSECTIONS

The results of the 1972 presidential election were not surprising to most observers—after the fact, of course. Bob Kennedy beat Ronald Reagan 53 percent to 40 percent. He also won in the electoral college vote with more than 380 delegates, which was almost a landslide. What stunned the pollsters was the percentage of registered voters coming out to vote on election day in 1972, which was more than 80 percent—the highest figure since the 1930s.

The racist-oriented Maddox-Schmitz ticket received just over 4 percent of the national vote. However, eliminating the states of Mississippi and Georgia, the only states in which Maddox-Schmitz scored somewhat significant vote counts, the percentage dropped to less than 1 percent of the national vote. Pollsters found that Maddox voters were people who detested Kennedy but didn't like the Republicans either. In other words, Maddox mostly brought out people who likely would have otherwise stayed home. David McReynolds of the Peace and Freedom Party received less than 3 percent of the vote, with many of those coming from people who would have otherwise supported Kennedy.

In a turnaround from 1968, Kennedy won most of the South. Mississippi was the anomaly because, between 1970 and 1972, many blacks left the state for better jobs in other parts of the nation. White workers undermined their own union organizing because they were still more concerned with "white pride" than better pay. While this all proved bad for Kennedy-Yarborough, it was a gift to Mississippi's Senator James Eastland, who easily won reelection.

In Maddox's home state of Georgia, the Maddox-Schmitz ticket finished second behind Kennedy-Yarborough, with Reagan-Abrams coming in a very distant third. For Kennedy-Yarborough, the winning difference was the white workers who were becoming unionized in integrated unions, along with the unanimous support from black voters.

Kennedy won New York, New Jersey, Pennsylvania, Maryland, Massachusetts, and Rhode Island, but lost to Reagan in Connecticut, Maine, Vermont, and New Hampshire. Kennedy won by "a nose hair," to use Yarborough's phrase, in California, due exclusively to white union voters and the black and Latino vote. Kennedy's labor-friendly environmental policies allowed him to win in the Northwest states of Washington and Oregon. In those states, Reagan's hostility to environmental laws and unions, while consistent with his business-libertarian stance, was fatal to his campaign.

Reagan's allegedly antienvironment stance, however, helped him win in the cattle-ranching states of Colorado, Wyoming, and Montana. Reagan also won in Nevada, where the Mob influence was still strong, and in the weak-union and mining state of Arizona. In the only other election day anomaly, Reagan-Abrams squeaked out a victory in Wisconsin. In that otherwise progressive state, David McReynolds, with support from radical college students, professors, and assorted bohemians, played a spoiler's role.

Union households voted overwhelmingly for the Kennedy-Yarborough ticket, making up a significant percentage of Kennedy's vote totals. With the reforms enacted under the Kennedy-Yarborough administration and the successful organizing occurring in the South, unions reversed their late 1950s' and 1960s' decline in membership. Union workers now accounted for more than 36 percent of workers nationwide, perhaps the highest level ever in America.

As Reuther said to Kennedy a few days before the election, "Mr. President, the key to ensuring the passing of important social legislation is to have almost forty percent of the workers unionized and voting in solidarity for pro-worker candidates."

Kennedy nodded and answered, "Well, Walt, you're the expert on that subject. Let's hope you're right. I still don't trust the polling unless we get those voters out to vote!" And they did, which, more than any other factor, led to Kennedy's reelection.

According to post-election pollsters, swing voters had moved into the Kennedy column in droves, largely because of the "sound bites" from the debates. In the Midwest and the South, the "Mr. 666" pamphlet, despite Reverend Falwell's apology, etched itself into religious voters' memories. With the economy still strong, despite more than sixteen billion dollars in deficits added to the national debt in four years, people stayed with the Kennedy-Yarborough administration.[1] It also helped that, by the end of 1971, most union battles in much of the country—outside the South—were resolved. There were hardly any strikes during the 1972 election year because employers had made the unions sign multiyear contracts to avoid further labor strikes or strife. This, ironically, helped blunt any criticism of unions by either nonunion workers or middle managers since things were fairly quiet—and content—on the workers' front.

American Jews, who, in the early 1970s were an important voting bloc in populous states such as New York, New Jersey, and California, voted for Kennedy at a rate of 70 percent, which was low for a post-FDR Democratic Party candidate. Reagan was able to get 30 percent of the Jewish vote primarily because of two factors: First, Reagan took a strong pro-Israel stance—typical of a nonincumbent politician seeking to win the presidency in the late twentieth century. Second, Reagan's tax-cutting plan and his pro–abortion rights stand helped him with a majority of well-off Jewish women and upper-class Jews. As most Jews were now glad that Israel had made peace with Egypt, however, the remaining super majority remained faithful to Kennedy and the Democratic Party.

Most voters, once the sex scandal faded in the fall campaign, believed Kennedy had a strong advantage over his Republican challenger due to Kennedy's successful foreign policy initiatives with the Soviet Union and his "skillful" avoidance of nuclear war with China. Pollsters found most Americans were willing to trust Bob Kennedy for a second term when it came to governing "the world," although some polling data indicated that this may not have been a primary motivating factor for a majority of voters. On the other hand, a review of polls just before the election indicated that voters perceived Reagan as "untested in foreign policy," which hurt him with working-class swing voters—who by then were looking for an excuse not to vote for him. General Abrams' vice-presidential candidacy failed to stem that concern because enough people believed Abrams was an inflexible military man, unlike the perception of General and later President Eisenhower.

Political scientists who studied the 1972 election, including Theodore Lowi and Walter Dean Burnham, among others, concluded that Reagan was too culturally liberal for the American people. One often cited example of Reagan's cultural liberalism concerned the issue of homosexuality. In 1972, homosexuality began to become a political issue in places such as New York City and San Francisco. Kennedy and Yarborough completely avoided the issue, with Kennedy saying in San Francisco, "Society has some long and difficult thinking to do on this subject. Experimental laws in this area may not be proper for our society at this time." Homosexuals and sexual hedonists such as Gore Vidal and pro-homosexual organizations such as the Mattachine Society were furious with Kennedy for his refusal to recognize homosexual rights.

Many prominent homosexuals, mostly from the theater and literature worlds, thereupon became strong supporters of Reagan. Reagan, as a Hollywood actor, publicly stated he was willing to broach the issue in terms of his "pro-liberty" philosophy. He said homosexuals have the right to "be left alone" and to "their own privacy." He said that he would consider having the U.S. Civil Rights Commission look into discrimination against homosexuals in the workplace. "We ought to find out if someone was fired for flaunting their homosexuality or talking about it. If they weren't flaunting or talking about their sexuality at the office, who are we to tattle on other people? We've had enough personal scandal this year, haven't we?" This statement was designed to shore up libertarian-Republican votes, while reminding culturally conservative voters of Kennedy's scandal and hypocrisy.

But the hammer of controversy fell on Reagan's head for a few days, with the mostly male, black leadership complaining that it was "obscene" to view homosexuals and blacks as equally needing "civil rights."

Reagan, unlike Kennedy, also supported ending the requirement for men to enter either the military or public service through VISTA or the Peace Corps. In a total reversal from four years earlier, the requirement of military or other public service, known as "the draft," had become highly popular. Kennedy's quick success in ending military involvement in Vietnam, with no subsequent long-term military intervention, and the opening of alternatives to military service through the Peace Corps and VISTA, were the main reasons for that reversal. There was a catch, however: Civilian public service in the Peace Corps/VISTA was eighteen months longer than the three-year military commitment.

Kennedy's success in melding together the peace movement, the civil rights movement, the labor movement, and government social work, brought patriotism back into style, particularly among young people. Reagan's call for ending the draft and replacing it with a "voluntary, paid professional army" only made him look less than fully patriotic. Worse, pro-Kennedy pundits and historians immediately criticized the concept of a voluntary, professional military idea as reeking of fascism.

With the rise in patriotic fervor, Kennedy was also able to end the college deferment exemption, so often used by more privileged young men to avoid service in the Vietnam War during the 1960s. More and more, employers reported that military, Peace Corps, and VISTA "graduates" had more poise, real-life experience, and common sense than the typical college graduates who had used the deferment exemption a few years before.

When General Abrams refused to agree to a voluntary professional army, the Reagan campaign, in August 1972, dropped all mention of ending the draft. As Roger Ailes told Nancy Reagan, "The governor's view appeals to no significant constituency. If anything, his position only hurts us—and it's a minor issue!" Nancy agreed and advised her husband "to forget all about it," which he did. In fact, at a rally in Colorado in the closing days of the election campaign, Reagan said he never supported ending the draft. As usual, Reagan meant it the moment he said it. If he were to change his mind again, he would mean that, too. That was one of Reagan's many gifts as a public speaker.

Despite his brilliant delivery, the political, cultural, and economic dynamics simply were not on Reagan's side in this RFK timeline. Reagan gained little, for example, with his support for a pure and unchanged Equal Rights Amendment. Bob and Ethel Kennedy's astute embrace of the modified language of the ERA was crucial to Congress' passing the modified ERA in early 1972 and the quick ratification, in the spring and summer of 1972, of the Amendment by the necessary thirty-eight state legislatures. Even before Kennedy signed the Amendment in October 1972, the ERA stopped being an issue in the campaign.

Reagan's leading campaign adviser, Roger Ailes, in a postmortem interview in December 1972, said, "We were hoping the ERA wouldn't pass until after the election so the governor could show women in the largest cities and states that his support for a 'pure' and 'original' Amendment meant he was better on women's rights than Kennedy, even apart from Kennedy's moral hypocrisy. Kennedy and the Democrats knew this, too, and that's why they rushed through the modified version. The women who were most supportive of abortion rights stayed with us, but not the rest of the women, particularly the working-class women. They stayed with Kennedy—kind of like battered women stay with an abusive, cheating husband."

In the Kennedy administration's first legal opinion on the meaning of the ERA, Attorney General Ramsey Clark said the Amendment did not require women to enter the military as long as there was a civilian alternative such as the Peace Corps or VISTA. Even within the military, women could be legally kept out of combat if the president and Congress approved the prohibition. This opinion was considered theoretical since most women overwhelmingly chose the civilian public services, at least in the first few years following the passage of the ERA.

In the 1972 presidential election, gun control became a dicey issue for both parties, but more so for the Republicans. With crime down in the major cities and Democrats relying on the pro-gun working class throughout the nation, many Democrats dropped their support for gun control "quicker 'n quicksand," said Yarborough. Gun control advocates in Congress tended to come from wealthier suburban communities that were near the largest cities, sometimes more Republican than Democrat in their voter registration. Reagan voters in the Mountain States and the Southwest, however, believed more in the Second Amendment than the First Amendment to the Constitution and were accurately described by political strategists as gun lovers. This forced Reagan and the Republicans to straddle the political fence on the issue.

Reagan, when running for president in 1972, reached an uneasy truce in the war over gun control by simply calling for a federal law that set a five-day waiting period for the purchase of a gun. Kennedy and Yarborough, who both had endorsed gun control as recently as 1969, agreed with Reagan's proposal. This allowed both sides to drop the matter as something they agreed upon already. In the election of 1972, gun control was more of a local issue in congressional campaigns, and it remained a local issue thereafter.

In his analysis of the 1972 presidential election, political science professor, Theodore Lowi, concluded, "It would have been difficult to predict, at the start of President Kennedy's administration in January 1969, that the Republican Party would, less than four years later, take up the mantle of supporting cultural liberalism. Even more difficult to predict was the split that opened wide in 1972 among feminists and, more generally, between the cultural Left and the economic Left. Economic leftists believed it was better to allow certain cultural trends to lag than risk alienating working-class voters. Some cultural leftists believed it was better to make common cause with culturally liberal pro-business elements in the Republican Party. Reviewing the results of the 1972 election, those leftists who stressed the importance of meeting the economic needs of working class Americans have won the initial skirmish in what could be a longer-term battle among the liberal-left as they attempt to consolidate their victory over the conservatives."

Peter Edelman, the general counsel for the Department of Health, Education, and Welfare, showed Lowi's analysis to Vice President Yarborough shortly after it appeared. Yarborough snorted after reading a bit of it and said, "Son, Ah coulda saved that pointy-headed professor a lotta time. Ah always knew what he thinks is *so . . . pro-found,* to use that college talk. Why d'ya think Reuther and Ah told Bob the first thing we needed to do was labor reform? Ya gotta bring people together first as workin' folks before ya start talkin' 'bout their culture and what not. And lemme tell ya somethin' else, son. We are nowhere ne-ah ready for a homosex'al civil rahts movement! We're still jus' gettin' started on a civil rights movement for the ladies—and Ah hope we don' hav-ta argue 'bout getting' rid-a ladies' and men's rooms, eithah!"

Chapter 33

SECOND HELPINGS

New Faces in the Congress and the Administration

The near-miraculous turnaround of Kennedy's fortunes in the South further strengthened his policy mandate as voters in that region elected more economic populists to Congress. In Texas, for example, Willie Morris, editor of the highly esteemed journal called the *Texas Observer,* defeated incumbent Republican Senator John Tower. In North Carolina, a Democratic Party firebrand, John Ingram, defeated the well-financed American Independent Party candidate, Jesse Helms. Helms, a former Democratic Party Senate aide, was also a well-known political commentator and an ardent "racial traditionalist," as he liked to call himself. The socially-liberal Republican candidate finished a very distant third in that North Carolina race.

Helms had the backing of Roger Milliken, executives of the J. P. Stevens Company, and other textile and tobacco kings. While Milliken had told Reagan not to go racist nationally, he realized, during the North Carolina Senate race, that Reagan-style libertarianism was not going to be a successful strategy in certain states in the South. He and other textile merchants, therefore, embraced the more "traditional" southern candidate in North Carolina— Helms. They still failed to defeat the Democrats, who were, as usual, aided by the growing labor forces and the rising number of black voters.

Despite the results in Texas and North Carolina, most incumbents in the Senate, Democratic and Republican, kept their seats. In Colorado, for example, Republican Senator Wayne Allard beat back Democratic Party challenger Floyd Haskell. Local pundits in Delaware gave "coattail" credit to Senator Roth for the close victory of incumbent Republican Senator Jim Boggs against the young "upstart," Democratic Congressman Joe Biden. Biden, however, was later nominated and confirmed for a federal appeals court position in the prestigious D.C. Circuit Court of Appeals, where he served for the rest of his life.

In a surprise move, more for its timing than anything else, Oregon Republican Senator Mark Hatfield switched to the Democratic Party for his reelection campaign in 1972. Reuther said Hatfield switched because he "didn't want to have to run against Wayne Morse, who wanted to avenge his close loss in 1968 to Republican Senator Bob Packwood. Everyone, including Hatfield, knew that both environmentalists and labor unions would be out in force for the Democratic Party candidate, particularly a liberal candidate. Hatfield made a deal with the Oregon AFL-CIO chapter that he could run as a Democrat, but only after publicly stating he would support labor's agenda. Being a good politician, Hatfield heartily agreed to the union association's demand. Running ahead of Kennedy in Oregon, Hatfield easily defeated his Republican challenger, Congressman John Richard Dellenback. While one could say the incumbent won in Oregon, the Republicans still lost another seat.

Senior Republican Party officials were disappointed with the election results but consoled themselves by saying that in states Reagan won in 1972, including Montana, Colorado, Nevada, and Arizona, Senate Democrats would be up for reelection in 1974. Republicans, therefore, looked forward to Republican Senate gains in those states two years hence.

In the House of Representatives, the picture was brighter for the Democrats. The Democratic Party gained seats in most regions of the nation where the Kennedy-Yarborough ticket had won, gaining fifteen more seats overall. Democrats, however, lost a seat in the Miami area as a result of the almost unanimous support of Cuban American voters for a strong anti-Communist Republican candidate. In Palm Beach, well-off Jewish retirees voted for a socially liberal, pro-business Republican candidate. But again, those were anomalies in a solidly pro-Kennedy-Yarborough South.

In the *New York Times* election analysis of November 10, 1972, the writers said the "most ominous aspect" of the election fell on corporations, for the Democratic Party was now, more than ever, most consistently "in favor of unions and government intervention in the economy on behalf of the working class and the environment. In other words, North, South, East, and West Congressional Democrats are carbon copies of the Kennedy-Yarborough national ticket." The august newspaper concluded that the largest corporations and the Republicans had "their work cut out for them to stop the juggernaut toward Western European–style socialism being pursued by the Kennedy administration."

At the start of Kennedy's second term, a few new faces graced various cabinet or executive-level departments and offices. To nobody's surprise, Bert Lance resigned as treasury secretary immediately after the election. Recognizing that Kennedy had hardly noticed Lance for four years, not many people were willing to take over the position. After a fruitless search for a replacement, Kennedy personally persuaded longtime Kennedy economic adviser Walter Heller to take the position in February 1973.

Jules Witcover, a veteran reporter and columnist for the *Baltimore Sun* newspaper, who had admired Kennedy since Kennedy's senate days, replaced Jack Newfield as press secretary. Newfield, in turn, became editor of the flagship newspaper the AFL-CIO purchased in the summer of 1972, the *Washington*

Star. Newfield made his own "inaugural address" to the staff of the *Star,* saying, "This newspaper, as with its future sister union papers across the nation, will be a newspaper of the workers, by the workers, and for the workers."

Peter Edelman succeeded Ted Sorensen as White House counsel after Sorensen resigned to become general counsel with Chase Manhattan Bank. Chase Chairman David Rockefeller was reported to have told a friendly Federal Reserve banker that he wanted to have someone close to the Kennedy administration on the theory that "one must keep one's enemy close to the vest in order to take effective action when necessary."

Kennedy also tapped Julian Bond to become secretary of health, education, and welfare after Sargent Shriver became commissioner of Major League Baseball. United Nations Ambassador Andrew Young resigned to return to his native state of Georgia to prepare for his run for governor in 1974. Texas Congresswoman Barbara Jordan, a dynamic speaker and brilliant legal mind, became the new United Nations ambassador.

In the only preelection change, Admiral Thomas Moorer replaced General Earle Wheeler as the chairman of the Joint Chiefs of Staff. Wheeler, watching with angry frustration as Kennedy appeared to survive the sex scandal, quit in a highly emotional press conference in August 1972. Wheeler announced his support for Reagan, and especially his "old friend, General Creighton Abrams," and said, "a new direction is needed to protect military readiness and integrity in our country." Kennedy, in a move that surprised nobody, chose General Hackworth to replace Wheeler as the army representative on the Joint Chiefs.

On January 20, 1972, Kennedy gave what many pundits and historians have called a "programmatic" Inaugural Address. It contained no unifying theme such as "threads of history." Instead, he spoke of the need to pass his "simplified tax-reform plan that allows everyone to pay according to his ability" and "with no hidden special deductions or exemptions from everyone's duty to our nation."

Kennedy spoke of building a "state-of-the-art" public transportation system in the main urban areas of the nation, a military conversion program to develop home computers that "will revolutionize the way we communicate with each other, increase productivity, create new jobs along with these new technologies—and still have military uses that will add to our strength as a leading world superpower."

Kennedy also used the occasion to call for "a policy of national health care and child care in order to give choice to Americans, particularly American women, as either homemakers, outside workers, or both. For it is the women in our society, and our children, who face the most immediate and often dire consequences when there is no available medical care and no one available to care for the children when mom is away at work." In the most discussed passage of his address, Kennedy, attempting to shore up support from women in his second term of office, particularly in the metropolitan areas of the nation, said:

> The essence of freedom and liberty is choice. Many women have entered the workplace in recent years, out of their own desires or due to circumstances that force them into the workplace. Often, they struggle to find care for their children. We cannot say there is 'choice' for any American, particularly women, if our government does not provide equal and proper means to help them decide upon that choice. Just as union workers understand there is no freedom if one does not have enough to eat, or earns too little to provide for basic needs, so, too, do our mothers, our sisters, and our daughters understand that freedom is meaningless if our society does not provide them with access to adequate and nurturing child care.

The next day the administration tapped Ruth Rosen, coeditor of *Mother Worker* magazine, to be cochair, with Ethel Kennedy, of the newly created Commission on Child Care. The commission was designed, said Larry O'Brien, to create "grassroots" support among women for government-sponsored child care programs. The commission more specifically targeted women whose daughters were going to college for a degree and a job—which daughters, after marriage, were most likely to need adequate and reliable child care.

The economist Herbert Stein, in the pages of the *Wall Street Journal*, complained in an editorial two days after the Inaugural Address that Kennedy would bust the budget and have to enact onerous taxes to pay for all his programs, from military conversion to environmental legislation and now medical coverage and child care. "Soaking the rich without their consent is the opposite of choice, if one may paraphrase the president. President Kennedy's programs, if only some are passed, will surely require onerous and oppressive taxation from more than the rich—unless the administration decides that middle-income earners are to be redefined, Orwellian-style, as 'rich.'"

Secretary of Labor Walter Reuther responded to Stein's column in an op ed piece published in the *Wall Street Journal* on February 1, 1973. He wrote, "Professor Stein, in his pro-business zeal, worries far too much about short-term deficits. Just as private businesses borrow money for investment in capital equipment and buildings, our administration is proposing to invest in the future infrastructure of our nation. Our administration's conversion program and the rebuilding of our cities, among other programs, create wealth. And with that wealth, there will be more than enough money to pay for those programs, unlike tax cuts with no target for particular areas of investment."

That last remark, of course, was more an attack on Reagan and Roth than the traditional, antideficit spending Professor Stein.

Reuther also wrote that Stein "ignores the likely effect of our proposed simplified tax legislation. Once passed, our government will receive more, not less, revenue as loopholes previously benefiting the richest Americans will be closed."

Finally, Reuther took on the *Wall Street Journal,* Stein, and anyone who doubted the "wisdom" of a national health insurance program. Wrote Reuther:

> The professor's view that a national health insurance program requires excessive taxation is also off-the-mark. Professor Stein forgets one salient fact in his discussion of our proposed national health care program: Americans, whether in business or as employees, *already* pay billions of dollars to private insurers in the form of deductibles, copayments, and premiums. When we pass our proposed legislation for national government insurance, Americans will no longer have to pay such enormous sums to the more than two thousand private insurance companies, who each must pay a battery of salespeople, marketers, executives, accountants, and especially lawyers. Americans will pay, yes, Professor, a tax, but that tax will result in *less money leaving the pockets of most American taxpayers compared to the "private" tax they currently pay to insurance companies.* Unlike the private insurers' overhead costs of lawyers, accountants, salespeople, etc., there are far fewer overhead costs with government-run insurance—and enough money to pay doctors and nurses for treating all Americans when they are ill.
>
> There is also a benefit to private enterprise for two reasons: First, employers will no longer have to pay directly for employee health care benefits, as they do under our current system. Our current 'non-system' rewards bad employers who do not provide for such coverage and punishes good employers who carry the burden of covering their employees' health insurance. Second, when we achieve national medical insurance for all Americans, we can finally limit the need for workers' compensation insurance except for pure disability payments when necessary, for it would no longer matter whether one is hurt at work or at home: Everyone is covered for medical insurance. It is time for the *Wall Street Journal* and Professor Stein to join the rest of America in demanding a national health insurance program—and for America to join the rest of the civilized world in having such a program.

Kennedy smiled as he read Reuther's response, and he said to himself, Maybe the next four years will be easier than the previous four . . .

The Complication of Tax Simplification

On June 14, 1973, the Congress passed, and President Kennedy signed, the Tax Simplification Act. Most Democrats supported it, as did a few Republican "renegades," as the *Wall Street Journal* called Republicans who sometimes voted with the Kennedy-Yarborough administration. Just before the president signed the law, Yarborough, with his usual bluntness, said on the Sunday morning television program *Meet the Press*: "This heah new tax law is designed to make sure the top taxpayers feel the pain o' taxes that the lunch-bucket folks feel. More important, it raises enough revenue to support our cities and public infrastructure, helps our family farmers produce food at a profit for themselves, and allows every person the opp'tunity to earn a good income. As the president made clear in his Inaugural Address earlier this yeah, it shore ain't freedom if yo're tryin' to get by on an empty stomach while the other fella is buyin' his second yacht."

When the Tax Simplification Act of 1973 passed, even critics said the event was as historic as the passage of the first modern income tax in 1913. The reform resulted in the repeal of a host of deductions, exemptions, and credits that had been used largely by wealthier persons and companies to avoid higher tax rates. The main tax deductions left were those for a first home mortgage interest, money given to charities, and payment of state and local taxes. But to keep the top income earners from using these remaining "loopholes" to avoid paying their "just" share, the charity and home mortgage deductions were allowable only to the extent one's income did not go above a certain sum, essentially the income of those in the top 1 percent of earners. From that point on, for every one thousand dollars in extra income, that wealthy taxpayer lost a dollar of deduction savings.

Despite Democratic control of the Congress, the Kennedy administration, in an effort to garner some Republican Party support, agreed to a variety of compromises.

First among these compromises was a phaseout of consumer interest deductions, as opposed to ending the deduction altogether. Business lobbyists pushed for this compromise with many Democrats' support because they were afraid that a complete loss of this deduction would undermine business sales that depended on people using their credit cards.

Another compromise concerned the number of tax rates in the simplified system. Although the Kennedy administration originally wanted at least ten varied tax rates, they found the drive for "simplicity" forced them to agree to limit the number to five, plus a surtax for the uppermost income earners. The lowest level, which was to begin on the margin at double the poverty level, was set at a tax rate of 10 percent, one-third less than the usual rate of 15 percent. The next percentage change on the margin was 15 percent at three times the poverty level. The remaining tax rates at various ascending levels of income were 25 percent, 40 percent, and 50 percent for those making more than one hundred and seventy-five thousand dollars a year. A special surtax of 55 percent was set for the top 1 percent of income earners. Many Democrats were pushing for higher taxes on the margin, including some talking of a 100 percent tax on incomes over one million dollars, but Kennedy made clear he would never support such a tax rate, no matter how exorbitant.

On the other hand, Yarborough and Reuther led the administration and their allies on Capitol Hill in ending the "coddling of trust fund babies" by limiting the applicability of the lower capital gains tax on investment income. Under the new Tax Act, after the first one hundred thousand dollars in annual income from investments, whether in interest, stock dividends, or the like, ordinary income tax rates, not the lower capital gains tax, would be applied. Certain Kennedy family members who lived on trust fund interest income were outraged as their relative, President "Bob," allowed this provision to be signed into law with the rest of the tax package.

Reading the mainstream press or listening to broadcast news when Kennedy signed the bill into law, one would conclude that the tax system was completely simplified. Obviously, that characterization was misleading. Adding to the "complication of simplification," the Kennedy administration, bowing to political pressure from Republicans and certain Democrats in marginally pro-Democratic districts, retained the ability of most businesses to deduct business expenses from their taxes. In a midnight bargain with liberal Republicans, expense deductions were maintained but were only allowed up to the 50 percent margin rate for individual businesses or corporations. Above that margin, business expenses would no longer be deductible.

The *Wall Street Journal* called this compromise the "fig leaf used by certain weak-kneed renegade Republicans to vote for this draconian law." The effect of the compromise complicated, rather than simplified, the tax code for the largest corporations. The compromise forced wealthy corporations to determine, through even more complicated accounting rules, the deductible business expenses incurred before yearly income reached the 50 percent tax rate margin and those nondeductible expenses incurred after the highest tax rate kicked in. As Walter Reuther quipped, "We had to give the Big Eight accounting firms something to do for their big corporation clients!"

Scared by Republicans into initially opposing the tax bill, small business owners screamed against "the socialistic Democrat tax plan"—until they spoke with their local accountants. Many of those small-time accountants, after reading some of the plan features, assured their customers, quite correctly, that the new act protected their expense deductions, simply because so few small businesses made more than an upper-middle-class employee's income in either timeline.[1]

Meanwhile, working-class taxpayers rejoiced at receiving a tax break in the form of lower tax rates. While they weren't happy that the credit card deductions would go away over the next few years, they were amazed that their taxes were going down, not up for the first time in years. Consumer confidence, therefore, pushed up consumer spending in 1973 and into 1974, the year of midterm elections. As a result, automakers and manufacturers of other durable goods achieved excellent financial results, and profits—regardless of having increased tax margins.

The Tax Simplification Act, in subsequent years, raised more revenue from the richest Americans and the leading corporations than the old, more cumbersome system of income taxation.

Converting the Converted

By the end of 1972, the military conversion program was starting to take off in terms of spending. Seasoned politicians in Congress realized as much as Kennedy that the return of NATO troops and their entrance into the civilian work force translated into a need for more money for the conversion program and less for military spending on troops in general. Kennedy, noticing that Congress was filling up with converted doves, knew he needed to take a more hawkish position for some balance. As he told his cabinet in their first meeting after the 1972 election, "Gentlemen, we still need to continually modernize our weapons so that we remain the most advanced—and best prepared—military force in the world."

Several top business leaders, who understood the election results, agreed to join the military conversion effort after a "private sector summit" between business leaders and State Secretary Bowles, Defense Secretary Warnke, and Commerce Secretary Learson. The business leaders, including Ford Motor Company Chairman Henry Ford II, agreed that the nation must not be allowed to fall into a recession now that troops were coming home from Europe and beginning to come home from parts of Asia.

In return for their support of the conversion program, Commerce Secretary Learson, with backing from Reuther and a more skeptical Yarborough, threw a couple of bones to corporations during the later debate over tax simplification. First, Congress officially endorsed the continuation of the IRS rules allowing for faster depreciation for corporate purchases of environmentally sensitive capital equipment that was also purchased to improve efficiency within factories.

Second, Learson was able to convince the Federal Reserve Board to lower interest rates for business borrowing, known among business folks as "the cost of money." This lessened the tax crunch on the cost of doing business, and allowed for more cash for corporations to expand production to meet increased demand and fund the purchase of the new environmental and labor saving equipment.

Some radicals to the left of the Kennedy administration complained that this "secret" deal brokered by Learson—which was not really secret at all—

was a betrayal of Kennedy's pro-worker philosophy. Kennedy was under-mining "class solidarity" by allowing businesses to develop any labor-saving devices, noted the radical magazine *Ramparts*. Radical unionists feared that labor-saving devices would eventually put working people on the street and "bid down wages and benefits." Said a prominent labor leader in a GM plant in Van Nuys, California, "One day we're gonna run out of whiz-bang stuff to make and the machines will do everything!" Such fears were, of course, a long, long way off, and politicians and other people being what they are, decided it was not worth pondering at that point.

Commerce Secretary Learson convinced Vice President Yarborough and Labor Secretary Reuther that the purpose of creating a new industry of envi-ronmental products and services, as well as the development of the computer industry, was to increase worker participation in "clean" industries and still allow the United States to maintain its dominance in the traditional "smoke-stack" industries. Kennedy, too, was convinced of the soundness of Learson's position. With Kennedy, Reuther, and Yarborough on board, the radical labor union criticism disappeared from the realm of the mainstream media, even among the union newspapers where "Joe Six-Pack" commentators railed that "any tax break for big business breaks the bones of labor."

Kennedy's success did not yet extend to his pet goal of creating a public transportation system for the nation. Much to his frustration, he found that Americans were still in love with their cars. Worse, as with any auto indus-try executive, unions in the auto industry were as adamantly opposed to anything that might lessen car use.

Speaking with radical journalists and activists in a meeting set up by Allard Lowenstein of VISTA, Kennedy said, "As FDR used to say to union leaders and reformers, you have to go out and agitate and get public support for your proposals. For example, we need some agitation and coalition build-ing to support our proposal for public transportation, or for national medical care and child care programs. Aren't these areas of important public policy we can agree on?"

"But what about the inequality of wealth of the top 5 percent compared to the rest of the people?" asked Michael Harrington. "Public transportation or national health care does not adequately address the fact that the top 5 percent still own almost 27 percent of the wealth in the richest country on the planet."

"Michael," said the president in a soothing voice, "if I address that issue the way you want me to, we're going nowhere, aren't we? Let the Peace and Freedom Party agitate on that while we move forward toward a similar goal through our programs. Romans didn't build Rome in a day, after all—or do I need to finish my thoughts here?"

"No, Mr. President," said a disappointed Harrington. Harrington, how-ever, was going to follow Kennedy's first piece of advice and find a way to agitate—and bring what he called democratic socialism, with workers cooperatives, to America.

While Harrington continued to gladly work with Kennedy's administration, other radicals were dissatisfied with Kennedy's "advice" and his call for patience. Such radicals became divided as to whether to continue working with the Kennedy administration or take to the streets in demonstrations. When Allard Lowenstein told this to Kennedy, the president smiled and said, "Good. Those who work with us will make us stronger, particularly with developing public transportation or national health care. The others can bitch and moan, and even demonstrate—and, as I have noticed, make us look like the moderates!"

Oil's Well

Kennedy, already assured of passage of the tax simplification bill, was more and more concerned about promoting public transportation. The more he thought about it, the more he thought about gasoline prices, about cars, about the environment, about oil-producing nations in the Middle East and Latin America, about Libya, and especially about oil companies. It's all connected, he realized after thinking through the "politics" of the subject.

Kennedy had initially balked when the oil companies sent lobbyists to the White House to protect the oil depletion allowance during the tax simplification debates. But after he signed the Tax Simplification Act, a reporter from the *Washington Star* noticed a rider Louisiana Senator Russell Long had attached that kept the oil depletion allowance in place. When the reporter informed Kennedy about this "midnight rider," Kennedy publicly scorned the "last-minute parliamentary maneuvering that happens all too often in our Congress. We'll have to look into this, but not this year. We have other issues we need to address."

Privately, Kennedy admitted he knew it was there when he signed it. As he told Kenny O'Donnell, "Kenny, for better or worse, we have to help our major oil companies against the rising radicalism of oil-producing nations such as Libya and Iraq. Worse, one of our best allies in the area, the shah of Iran, is joining the hard-liners. Chet Bowles is now very concerned the rest of the Organization of Petroleum Exporting Countries—OPEC—could organize a worldwide oil embargo against the West. Although higher gasoline prices might create an incentive for our public transportation program, Walt Reuther keeps reminding me that our nation runs on oil and gasoline—and we can't take a chance that everything comes to a screeching halt if oil and gas prices go sky high."

Three liberal Democratic senators—James Abourzek and George McGovern of South Dakota, and Albert Gore of Tennessee—were outraged at Kennedy's realpolitik with the oil companies, but only because they heard

Kennedy was leaning toward helping the *largest* oil companies known as the "majors." These three senators had long been interested in breaking up the five largest U.S. oil companies and, at the same time, were highly supportive of smaller oil companies such as Amerada Hess, Occidental, Bunker Hunt, and Continental Oil. These "small" independents, however, lacked the crude oil reserves of the majors. Worse, as Kennedy told Senator Gore when confronted, they lacked worldwide refining and distribution capacities that Kennedy saw as a crucial wedge against radicals in the oil-producing nations in the third world.

The independents were particularly distressed in the spring of 1973. Since 1970, the independents had essentially lost the two largest oil-producing nations that most catered to their interests: Venezuela and Libya. In Venezuela, new and more radical political and labor leaders wanted a bigger piece of the pie for their socialist programs than previous, more compliant, leaders. Bribery still worked some magic with Venezuela's socialist leaders, but it took more of the independents' money to lessen the actual effect of "sharing the wealth" with that nation.

The situation in Libya was even worse from the perspective of the independent oil companies. Before the Muslim military dictator Muammar al-Qadaffi overthrew King Idris in September 1969, the north African nation was a reliable source of oil for American independents. King Idris was always willing to produce more oil no matter what the economic conditions. Then Qadaffi took over and within a few months began to purposefully limit production in order to increase market prices for Libya's low-sulfur oil, which was highly prized in Europe and the northeastern United States. When Libya moved to nationalize some major oil companies' oil fields in 1971, the majors essentially said nothing. According to oil industry sources, there were three reasons for the relative silence: (1) the majors' Libyan holdings were relatively small; (2) they claimed the Kennedy administration was unlikely to help them, which was probably true at the time; and (3) oil company relations with the Middle East oil-producing nations continued to be friendly, so why make a large fuss about Qadaffi? To the independents, however, it looked as if Qadaffi, while nationalizing the oil fields in his country, was also doing the bidding of the majors in making it harder for the independents to compete against the majors.

In short, the independents had found themselves more and more reliant on oil and gas purchases from the Middle East, an area of the world most tied to the largest oil companies.

Kennedy, now spurred by Bowles, Reuther, and the three pro-independent oil company senators, read the Senate report from 1971 on monopolistic practices in the oil industry. Bowles and Reuther told Kennedy that, in their opinion, the most important aspect of the report was not the question of whether already low oil prices could be even lower if there was more competition among the major oil companies, but the fact that various oil producing nations around the world, and particularly the Middle East, were starting to become politically unstable. Oil executives, alerted to Kennedy's sudden interest through their interlocking directorships in the auto industry, were only too glad to help Bowles and Reuther make a case for U.S. government assistance—in the interests of national security, of course.

On May 16, Kennedy and Secretary of State Bowles met with M. A. Wright, vice president of Exxon, and John J. McCloy, one of the original Cold Warriors who was now representing the oil companies in Washington, D.C. It was here that the oil companies secured Kennedy's promise that even with tax simplification, the oil companies would retain their oil depletion tax allowance from the federal government. In return for agreeing to maintain the oil depletion allowance, however, Kennedy extracted a couple of concessions from the major oil companies.

Kennedy first demanded that the majors begin "some serious domestic oil drilling" to counteract any significant cutback in oil production by the oil-producing radical nations—Libya, Iraq, and now Iran. He pointedly said he did not want the United States to become "addicted to foreign oil," or else, in a crisis, he "would not hesitate to order that oil be drilled inside America," meaning through federal government control. Wright and McCloy quickly agreed that domestic drilling would start immediately.[2]

Kennedy also demanded that the oil companies promise that they would counteract any OPEC attempt to embargo or limit the production of oil. McCloy and Wright were pleased that Kennedy understood their concerns about OPEC, and his willingness to support them even against the independents. As McCloy told Wright after the meeting, "You fellas are doing a lot better here than my friend at IT&T, John McCone, was able to do regarding Chile, I'll say that much. Maybe Kennedy's growing up, finally."

A few days after the meeting, Kennedy went over to visit Secretary Stewart Udall at the Interior Department. After Udall provided Kennedy with an update on the latest department initiatives, Kennedy nonchalantly told him that if he saw permits for oil drilling coming in, he was to help "move those along quickly. I secured a concession from the oil companies that they would resume some drilling here in the States."

Udall was shocked by this news. Forgetting he was speaking to his boss, Udall said sharply, "That is not a concession from the oil companies! It's a capitulation *to* the oil companies! More oil drilling means more air pollution, more water contamination. I can't believe we did this! Why wasn't I consulted before you made this decision?"

Kennedy, realizing he was a fool not to have anticipated Udall's reaction, responded sympathetically. "Stewart, I . . . I'm sorry. I should have known you'd be upset. But please see beyond the environment for a second here. Oil and foreign affairs have always been intertwined, and this was more of a

State Department matter to me. The more I think about all this, Stew, the more I see we need to promote public transportation and alternative fuel sources to lessen air and water pollution. But right now, letting our oil companies drill in America is our only course of action. Too many oil-producing nations are becoming unstable in ways that we are not yet prepared to deal with. We need to increase our oil reserves for a rainy day. You know they're low; even Chet knew that over at State. What you may not know is the oil-producing nations in Africa, Latin America, and the Middle East are getting aggressive in cutting back production. We can't be held hostage to foreign oil. Just let your friends in the environmental movement know this is only temporary. Okay, Stewart?"

Udall nodded and said, abruptly, "Um, sir, I have a meeting I have to get to." There was no meeting, of course, and both men knew it. Udall walked out of the Interior Department building rehearsing in his mind his press conference announcing his resignation and his opposition to expanded domestic oil drilling. Midway through his thoughts, though, he remembered that Kennedy had undermined him at the start of the first term, too. Udall knew then that resignation was not the answer. He simply had to do what he did before. He had to organize support among governors in the larger states and in Congress for developing alternative, renewable energy sources such as wind, water, and solar power. He had to help Kennedy push public transportation in order to lessen the need for oil and gas to operate millions and millions of individually owned cars. He was also going to have to sell Reuther and Yarborough on the point that building and maintaining public transportation would create enough jobs to overcome any jobs lost in the American auto industry. That was going to be one tough sell, he realized, but there was a way . . . There had to be.

Kennedy's concerns about OPEC hard-liners using oil as a weapon proved prescient. In late summer, the most radical members of OPEC—Libya, Iraq, and, as the CIA had warned Kennedy in March, Iran—completely stopped their oil production. They called it an oil production "strike." They did this to raise prices in the market and to secure more concessions from the major oil companies. The majors deftly undermined the embargo because they had already increased their drilling in known American oil deposits and had also secured increased production commitments from pro-Western oil producers such as Saudi Arabia and Mexico. This more than made up for the actions of the OPEC hard-liners and Kennedy was able to say to Stewart Udall and others in the administration that he was glad the oil companies kept their part of the bargain.[3]

Golden Thoughts

In late May 1973, Undersecretary of State William Attwood finished his white paper on the gold standard, which had taken him almost two years to complete. The report had been ordered by Chester Bowles, and approved by Kennedy, after Ken Galbraith and Ken Arrow had discussed the need for America to increase its declining gold reserves—or to consider ending America's dependence on gold as a standard. Attwood's report explained the history of the gold standard for determining the value of a nation's currency. He considered issues such as whether the United States should stay on the gold standard; what staying on or going off the gold standard meant in terms of American domestic policies and foreign relations; and finally, which nations owned the most gold and the implications of that ownership. The report was written in cooperation with Jim Tobin of the Federal Reserve and the Treasury Department.

In his report, Attwood reached several conclusions. First, the two nations who owned the most gold were the Soviet Union and the Republic of South Africa. South Africa was not a threat to the United States, but the Soviets might still be a threat in the near future if gold prices rose because, among other consequences, they would lessen their debt load with the West and be able to increase military spending without affecting the rest of their economy. Attwood admitted in the report that the Soviet's growing political unrest as a result of increased press freedoms and its failure to show any positive, tangible results from its economic "restructuring" had made the Soviets more and more dependent upon the West. Said Attwood, "A strong Soviet Union is a threat to world peace as it will again spark an arms race and proxy wars in places such as Africa, Asia, and Latin America."

As for the question of whether maintaining the gold standard was "good" for the United States, Attwood's report said the advantages of the gold system to the United States were not what they were in the mid-1940s, when the World Bank and the International Monetary Fund were created following various international conferences on finance and banking. By the late 1960s, Attwood noted, European central banks, particularly French banks, were recycling U.S. bonds and trading them into the U.S. Treasury Department for American gold. Attwood also found that, during the past four years, U.S. gold reserves had declined despite the fact that the Soviet Union paid in gold for U.S. grain and other durable goods.

The pro-gold-standard economists argued that having the gold standard kept governments from printing money beyond the value of their gold supply. According to their theories, printing money beyond a nation's gold supply resulted in inflation of currency. However, at the end of World War II and through the early 1950s, the United States had printed and spent far more money than it had gold, yet there was little if any inflation. In the 1960s, President Johnson fought the Vietnam War and the War on Poverty without significant inflation.

When Attwood was preparing his report, he spoke with pro-gold standard economists about these matters. They responded that the price of gold had been going down since 1971 as a result of the Soviets selling off gold in the world market. This "protected" the U.S. government from the effects of spending beyond its gold holdings. Attwood found this argument less than compelling as the Soviets still maintained substantial amounts of gold and further, there was no indication that U.S. gold reserves were going to dramatically increase in the short to middle term, if at all.

To his surprise, Attwood found that, unlike the gold-standard economists, most American and European bankers openly questioned whether gold prices were a "driver" for American inflation or deflation, let alone inflation or deflation in a mixed and varied international economy. Attwood noted it was mostly the French bankers who were interested in accumulating gold and who continually traded American bonds for gold. And the French were investing inside the United States, much more than other European allies, particularly with the nascent French owned public transportation factories. Germany, Sweden, and Great Britain were concentrating most of their investment efforts in Easter Europe in 1973.

Attwood spoke to a couple of French bankers who stopped in Washington, D.C., after visiting one of these public transportation factories. They admitted to him that if America stopped allowing other nations to redeem U.S. bonds for gold, France had more than enough gold—and confidence in its economic outlook—to weather that change.

The "bottom line," said Attwood at the end of his report, "is that it is better for America to go off the gold standard now than continuing to live under a standard based upon any metal, whether it is gold, silver, or copper. The notion of 'gold versus silver,' so important in the 1896 presidential election between William McKinley and William Jennings Bryan, is simply outdated in our modern economy. However, if our nation waited until gold prices went up, the world might see any U.S. decision to go off the gold standard as a decision made from a position of 'weakness.' Gold will then regain its magical power, which will be bad, at least in the short run, for the United States, and could lead to hyperinflation more from panic than anything 'real.' If, on the other hand, we went off the gold standard while gold prices were low, it would signal that the United States is confident in its own economy, and that gold and gold prices are an outmoded way of analyzing a nation's worth. Both conservative economist Milton Friedman and the legendary British economist John Maynard Keynes agree that gold is an outmoded basis for analyzing a nation's wealth. As Keynes said several decades ago, it is 'barbaric' to rely on a prehistoric metal for a modern economy."

Kennedy read the report with interest, but with also great concern, because this was completely out of his range of knowledge. In a later meeting with Bowles, Attwood, Galbraith, Walter Heller, and Jim Tobin, Kennedy asked, "Are we sure we know what we're doing here? There are a slew of tautologies in all this talk of the effect of gold prices—from economists on both sides of this battle. I think the whole thing is based upon perception—and I don't want to do anything that messes with the perception that our economy is doing well!"

Heller, a dedicated Keynesian economist, laughed a bit nervously at Kennedy's comments. He said, "Yes, Mr. President, there is a lot of smoke and mirrors in all this talk of gold standards. But that's why Keynes said a modern economy is better off getting rid of the gold standard. If we need to print currency, the key is whether people believe in our policies or not. Without gold to buy as a hedge, people might well think more about sticking together and riding out any bumps in the road, if I may mix a couple of metaphors."

Bowles said, "I agree with Walter, but I come at it from a different perspective, perhaps. If our administration passes national health care, national child care, and public transportation programs, why do we want to risk having to rely on gold reserves from bankers who oppose our policies, if we hit a pothole in the road, to use that last metaphor? Worse, do we want France or some other nation—possibly a more economically sound Soviet Union— holding much more gold than us and then telling us they won't buy our bonds unless there's gold to back it? If we go off the gold standard now, gold will no longer be a standard because our country still sets the economic standard in the world. The Soviets haven't shown they want to do anything but *sell* gold, not hoard it right now. And once the magic surrounding gold is gone, it is very unlikely, in my view, that most nations will be able to revive that magic."

Kennedy was silent for a few moments. Finally, he said, "You know, Chet, you're probably right. But what about the inflationary effect if we print money that goes well beyond our gold capacity—"

Galbraith interrupted, saying, "Mr. Attwood's report already showed we defied that theory at least twice in the past thirty years. I don't see inflation rising simply because we go off the gold standard. Multinational corporations passing off their costs are far more likely to be the cause of any new inflation. Or perhaps a run-up in the price of oil if the OPEC nations become more radicalized. Or a grain shortage like we saw in 1971. The gold-standard economists use gold as a sort of talisman against the very programs your administration has pursued—investing government funds in rebuilding cities, minimum incomes through negative income taxes, or your new initiatives, such as national health care and increased public transportation. These are mostly the same economists who claim government spending is inherently inflationary and that the gold standard keeps governments from spending."

"I get that last part, Ken, at least I get the political part of it," said a chastened Kennedy. He thought again to himself, *I just wish I knew what I was doing here from a financial standpoint.*

After more discussion, Kennedy closed the meeting, saying, "Okay, fellas, let me sleep on this. I might want to talk again, though I am leaning toward getting us off this gold standard. Let's keep it under our hats, too. I would, though, like to hear what at least one prominent banker in the United States thinks of this—just to get another viewpoint outside our world of politics . . ."

Galbraith and Tobin came back a few days later saying American banking leaders were already acting as if Kennedy and the U.S. government were off the gold standard. If anything, these bankers complained that the administration needed to *officially* announce the new policy because French bankers were telling third world nations that France was a "better bet" because the United States was "spending its gold reserves to purchase socialism."

The French bankers' statements outraged David Rockefeller of Chase Manhattan Bank. As he sarcastically said to Tobin, "—as if the French economy were the height of 'laissez-faire capitalism!'"

Tobin told this to Kennedy, who was meeting at the time with Galbraith. Kennedy immediately asked Tobin, "Would Rockefeller meet us here at the White House to talk about this issue of going off the gold standard?"

Galbraith, hearing this, thought this a bit naïve on Kennedy's part. He said, however, "If you wish, sir. But giving him such information might give his bank an undue advantage—"

"It sounds as if he knows more than we do, or at least I did; and he's known for quite a while. Bring him here. I'd like to hear from the head of one of America's leading banks on this subject that he, unlike me, deals with every day."

David Rockefeller was on a plane for D.C. the next morning for a meeting with the president, Secretaries Bowles and Heller, and economic advisers Tobin and Galbraith. At the meeting, Rockefeller told Kennedy, "Our financial institutions have found that we are making a lot of money by investing in poor communities in the United States, but the government must continue to provide the seed money, as you have, to more or less guarantee adequate returns on the credit we provide. We must also further expand our markets overseas as the European bankers already are. But, Mr. President, you ask me my opinion of the gold standard. Well, sir, allow me to put it this way. If the U.S. government's bonds suddenly became even close to worthless, then gold will only last us so long in any event. It's like a company in a downward spiral that has cash on hand. It's fine to have the cash—or in this case, gold, but it doesn't last too long if other measures aren't taken from an overall structural standpoint."

Kennedy responded, "I never thought of it quite that way, Mr. Rockefeller. What has been driving me away from the gold standard was that our country could possibly get squeezed by foreign banks and foreign countries—as opposed to going completely broke—if we run too low on gold, after failing to go off the standard while we were riding high. I just don't want to get into a bind with outsiders telling us what to do—as if I'd let that happen if that crisis was upon us." He gave Rockefeller a raised eyebrow as if to say, And you bankers better not try it either!

David Rockefeller raised both his eyebrows, realizing he should keep to the subject at hand. He asked rhetorically, "Could we as a nation 'get squeezed,' as you put it? I guess it's possible, but again, you've already said it, Mr. President, in so many words. We are the greatest military and economic power on earth."

"I guess that's really it, isn't it?" said Kennedy. "Now is our opportunity to knock gold off its pedestal because, even with all our economic and military power, we still don't have the gold the Soviets or the South Africans do—and having all that gold isn't helping them, right? I mean, I hear most bankers don't care whether the dollar's backed with enough gold—"

Rockefeller looked around the room, wondering if he could afford to be blunt. He decided he could be. "Yes, Mr. President. We truly don't care all that much. We do worry about, quite frankly, your health care initiatives and other such plans, but that has less to do with gold standards than with overall government spending—and government borrowing crowding out the ability of private capital to raise money."

Kennedy ignored Rockefeller's political commentary and said, "So, what you're saying, in essence, is 'Why don't we just stop the charade of having a gold standard we don't really mean to follow?'"

David Rockefeller smiled as wide a smile as any banker ever did, saying, "Yes, Mr. President."

Kennedy said, "David—if I may call you that—you have made me a very happy man this morning. I didn't want to do anything that looked technical but could be devastating if we were wrong. But now I see why I was having trouble. There really is nothing there but *expectations* on gold prices, which is no way to run a railroad, as my Dad used to say—"

"My grandfather just said, 'No way to run *any* business,'" said Rockefeller.

"Okay. Let's announce it today since your banker friends need help in their overseas investments. I figure we can do for the world what we did in Bed-Sty and—"

Galbraith interrupted, "Mr. President, please! Let's wait a minute here! We're going to announce this? Just like that? With no preparation?"

Kennedy said, nodding to Rockefeller, "Mr. Rockefeller now has what the Securities and Exchange Commission calls 'inside' information. I think we need to quickly tell the world, before Mr. Rockefeller leaves here, that the United States has recognized the reality that the gold standard is no longer—"

Now it was Bowles' turn to interrupt. He said, "But, sir, we've been asking the German government to buy our bonds and hold off asking for any exchange of gold, while the French continue to redeem our bonds in gold—" Bowles was stammering, which left Kennedy open to interrupt right back.

"But, Chet! You're missing the point. The Germans aren't the ones screwed over this. If anyone is, it's the French holding gold at prices that are already low. And the Soviets may not be happy either, since gold will no longer be the key source for currencies if we say it isn't."

Rockefeller nodded in agreement, smiling at his financial "pupil." Galbraith smiled, too, thinking about how his friend Bill Buckley was going to respond to this. First, Vatican II liberalizes the Roman Catholic Mass, and now Bobby Kennedy and the bankers decree that the United States is going off the gold standard! Galbraith chuckled out loud at the thought of Buckley's likely horrified response.

"All right, Chet," said Kennedy. "We'll announce it tomorrow. But, David, you're staying here tonight, and you can't make any phone calls. Seriously, if Chase sells any more gold holdings today than they usually do, I'm directing the SEC or the FBI or whoever to investigate, and it won't be pretty. We can't look like we're helping out one bank as opposed to other banks." Knowing he was already sounding naïve, he went to the extreme of being a schoolmarm: "It isn't fair."

David Rockefeller gravely nodded his head. "Mr. President, I'm just glad you're on the side of American business when it comes to the rest of the world." Then he smiled and thought, At least this time.

Kennedy was worried again. He thought to himself, Rockefeller's agreeing with me. Do I really know what I'm doing here?

The next morning, with Federal Reserve Board Chairman Kenneth Arrow, economic adviser Galbraith, and Secretaries Bowles and Heller behind him, President Kennedy spoke to the American people and told them why the United States no longer needed to rely on the gold standard. "*We* are the standard, not some metal that our ancestors worshipped like an animal god. *Our* standard is in the technological advances we are pursuing in home computers, our world-leading products and services, our continued medical breakthroughs, not to mention our high standard of living. We make this decision now to help those areas of the planet where there is little gold and at a time when the price of gold is already low, lower than it's been for decades. There is no reason to tie our modern economy, or anyone's economy, to a metal more properly used for necklaces or rings. Gold is no longer the commodity that defines our worth, as our bankers are already living without it. And today we merely acknowledge this changed circumstance."

When a reporter who had talked with a gold-standard economist before the press conference asked if the president was a disciple of economist John Maynard Keynes, Kennedy replied, "In the modern world, we are all Keynesians now."[4]

Predictably, gold-standard economists were furious. Robert Mundell from the University of Chicago, nearly sputtering, said, "Kennedy can speak for himself. There are plenty of people who are not Keynesians now—or ever. Kennedy has decided to take this drastic step because he knows he cannot fund his massive spending proposals without taking us off the gold standard.

It is the key to his leading us down the road to socialism and economic ruin. The only other thing I'm going to say is, watch out for the price of oil!"

The French foreign minister ridiculed the president, saying, "If President Kennedy doesn't care about gold, let him give America's gold to us—or give it away to everyone else!" As the minister knew, Kennedy, as part of his decision, had banned foreign banks from any further redemption of U.S. bonds for gold.

Following Kennedy's announcement, there was some concern that the gold standard adherents might be correct. The market for U.S. government bonds dropped by 18 percent in the first three days. However, within ten days, the bond market recovered as skeptics saw the U.S. economy was not going to fall apart as a result of this decision. As with most highly technical financial stories, the U.S. media failed to cover it with any in-depth analysis, and so it did not resonate with the American public, either.

American bankers and manufacturers themselves shrugged their shoulders at the change, ignoring the gold-standard and other capitalist economists. At the exclusive country club golf courses, a common refrain among corporate leaders was heard: "When was the last time anybody saw a bar of gold—or even cared?"

The only people as upset as gold-standard economists were the Soviets, who now saw gold prices drop further after an initial increase following Kennedy's announcement. Dobrynin lodged a "protest" to Kennedy for not consulting the Soviets and acting "unilaterally." Kennedy, who realized Dobrynin was right, was also less than candid when he told Dobrynin he didn't believe gold prices mattered much to any nation's currencies.

Kennedy said to Dobrynin, "If the Soviet Union runs into any problems economically, you know we in the United States will do our best to help you."

Dobrynin was unmoved by such vague promises and somewhat angry at the condescension in the remark. "Mr. President, this could have grave consequences for my country. I am very concerned about our relations and what might happen if we are unable to purchase grain or secure funding to rebuild and modernize our economy."

Kennedy realized now that Dobrynin was very, very serious. The president left his desk and went over to the Soviet ambassador. Putting his arm around Dobrynin, Kennedy said, "I mean what I say. We are committed to helping you transition to a mixed economy, Anatoly, just as we are moving toward a mixed economy from our side of the economic divide. I can't emphasize this enough. Please tell Moscow that!"

Dobrynin shook his head with a weary half-smile. "Mr. President, I have learned to take you at your word. Your word with both the Politburo and me is worth . . . " He paused now, a more natural smile brightening his face. " . . . more than gold." It was Dobrynin's best performance as a diplomat. For deep inside, Dobyrnin knew, he said later, that going off the gold standard was not good news for the Soviet Union.

Chapter 34

CULTURE, COURTS, AND COMPUTERS

In 1973 Kennedy continued to strategize as to how to pass public transit programs in the face of Democratic Party politicians who were fearful of upsetting both the auto companies and the UAW. Kennedy exclaimed to Reuther, "What's it gonna take, Walt, to get the UAW behind us on this project? Whether your workers are in automobile factories or building mass transit, it's still good, union-wage work!"

Reuther shook his head with respectful understanding but said, "But, sir, it's a complicated question. It really is."

Kennedy snorted, "I hear that crap all the time from you, Hamlin, Congressman Winpisinger, everyone. But funny, I have yet to hear what the complication is, other than, 'We don't want to do it.'"

Reuther could do nothing but start talking about another subject . . . such as national health insurance or child care legislation. "Let's go for health and child care first, Mr. President. That will give you the momentum for us to take on the UAW and the auto companies." And Kennedy wearily nodded and that was that . . . until the next time.

As Kennedy analyzed the politics of each member of Congress to see how he could get the votes he needed to pass these programs, he noticed, without initially looking for it, that there was a "disconnect" in American culture that was no longer based on generations.

Instead of a single generation gap, there were now a few different types of gaps that had developed or were developing. Besides the growing gap between Stew Udall's environmentalists, who were pushing public transportation to "kill" cars, and Reuther's autoworkers in the powerful unions, who were resisting any call for public transportation, there were gaps between culturally liberal, secular, upper-middle-class people and culturally conservative, religious, working-class people on growing political issues such as abortion, the death penalty, and homosexual rights. These gaps were starting to transcend regions and states, which, thought Kennedy, might eventually make it difficult to govern. Reuther and Yarborough kept saying the administration needed to go slower on the cultural issues and stay within the bosom of organized labor. That was fine for some things, thought Kennedy, but issues such as the environment were harder for him to ignore.

There was also an "action" gap that upset Kennedy the most. Speaking with John Gardner, who headed up a new group called Common Cause that was seeking to reform election campaign financing, Kennedy learned that the insurance companies were pouring loads of money into congressional campaigns to stop health care and child care reform measures. The insurance companies saw child care and health care legislation as two parts of a single threat. Gardner convinced Kennedy that this was what was causing congressional Democrats to wax their speeches with the need for such "care" programs but to find one reason after another to not pass any legislation.

Kennedy found himself more frustrated the more he thought of these various gaps. He thought to himself, We need an opening . . . anywhere. Well, not at the expense of the economy . . .

Supreme Surprises

Starting in the summer of 1973, the U.S. Supreme Court began to exacerbate the cultural gaps that worried the president, starting with the thorny issue of abortion.

In August, the Supreme Court held that there was a federal constitutional right to an abortion, but only during the first trimester of a pregnancy. The Court adopted, to a limited extent, the standard proposed by the American Medical Association's "friendly, expert brief" to the Supreme Court. The decision came in the case of *Doe v. Scott* (1973) 414 U.S. 103.[1]

Doe v. Scott was a 6-3 decision with the majority opinion written by Justice Archibald Cox. "Doe" was the pseudonym of a Wisconsin woman who procured an illegal abortion in Minneapolis, Minnesota. "Scott" was the name of the Hennepin County, Minnesota, district attorney whose office prosecuted her. Some antiabortion activists later said the whole case was a set-up because "Doe" sued the district attorney in federal court in order for the Federal Circuit Court of Appeals in that region to hear the matter as an appellate issue. The appellate court's most senior justice, Justice Harry Blackmun, was known to favor abortion rights from his days as legal counsel to the Mayo Clinic. President Eisenhower had appointed Blackmun to the region's appellate federal court in the 1950s.

When the case came before him and the other appellate justices, Blackmun asked the American Medical Association to intervene with its soon-to-be-famous legal brief. Through the brief, Blackmun developed the "trimester" analysis in delineating the respective rights of a pregnant woman with the fetus she carried.

With the federal abortion law pending in the U.S. Congress, nobody expected the Supreme Court to take the case for review. Once it did, the buzzing began among legal bees as to what the Court would do. Would it reject the case as too "political" and therefore not ripe for a judicial decision?

Or would the Court extend privacy protections to include abortion rights for the mother—or use the privacy doctrine to protect the unborn child?

The majority Supreme Court decision affirmed the appeals court in part and reversed it in part. The majority ruled that the constitutional right to privacy gave a woman some rights over her body when it came to terminating a pregnancy. But after "quickening," in common-law parlance, or, in more modern terms, the first trimester, it would be up to Congress to prohibit or allow abortions—or to allow state laws to continue to prohibit or allow abortions. The only limitation on federal and state legislatures was that they could not outlaw abortions within the first trimester, based upon the Court's review of common law history, the current state of medical technology, and the constitutional right to privacy.

The Court, in the companion case of *Doe v. Bolton* (1973) 414 U.S. 198, another 6-3 decision, held that the provisions of a Georgia statute requiring hospital committees to determine a woman's right to an abortion violated that woman's constitutional right to privacy. The Court, in that case, further refined the nature of the right to an abortion. It held that an abortion was constitutionally appropriate to save the life of a pregnant woman. The Court could not, on the other hand, decide if a woman had a full constitutional right to an abortion to protect her "mental or physical 'health.' Because the term 'health' is far more difficult to define in many circumstances," said the majority opinion, "we leave that issue to the legislatures to decide."

This refusal to protect a woman's "health" prompted Barbara Ehrenreich, in *Mother Worker*, to say it was "a distinction only men could devise. Why should we force any woman through a pregnancy if that woman suffers a loss of her health, whether temporary or permanent? How can a mother care for her baby when it's born if she is still suffering from adverse health effects?" The letters to the magazine kept up for almost a year after Ehrenreich's editorial. First Lady Ethel Kennedy herself wrote a letter to the editor of *Mother Worker*, saying in part, "As a mother of eleven children and a deeply religious person, I believe the decisions of the Supreme Court to allow abortions at all, especially in the face of nearly 50 state laws banning abortions, are an abomination."

The president, who respected Justice Cox's opinion even if he didn't agree with it, said to his wife, "Ethel, the Court only says a state cannot pass a law that outlaws abortions in the first trimester. It does not force you, or any woman, to undergo an abortion at any time, including that first trimester. That is no different than our freedom to be Catholic or not. It's up to each individual woman and her doctor to choose what she wants to do in the first three months of her pregnancy."

"It's not a *choice* I'm talking about—like *choosing* to buy chicken or steak at the store. This is about killing a baby, Bob! Would you have wanted any of our children abor—oh, let's not be clinical here!—*killed?*"

"No, Ethel, but that's *our choice,* if I understand the Court decision. Look, most of the state statutes against abortion are going to be easily changed to meet the Court's requirements. The decision says we could even pass a federal law that *outlaws* abortion after the first trimester of a pregnancy. And, Ethel, please remember this is the Supreme Court of the United States we're talking about here, not the Council of Bishops in Rome. Supreme Court decisions may be erroneous, but never 'an abomination.' I wish I had seen that letter before you sent it—"

"It *is* an abomination, Bob, and you know it. Archie Cox should be ashamed of himself!"

"Ethel, we must deal with the here and now. And the here and now is that the federal bill to *expand* abortions is still stuck in the House and Senate conference committee. That bill allows for abortions with no restrictions in the first and second trimesters. It also allows abortions in the *third* trimester when a woman's life or physical or mental health is affected."

"But, Bob, who cares about the federal bill? You were going to veto that bill if it came to you, right?" She saw a hint of doubt on her husband's face. She raised her voice almost to a shout. *"Right?! You would veto that bill, wouldn't you?!"*

"Yes, yes, Ethel, I was . . . going to . . . veto that bill! Sure! I was!" said the dutiful husband, wondering if he would have vetoed that bill or not. Kennedy was still trying to figure out the political angles.

As it turned out, abortion-rights' supporters had not anticipated the consequences of "winning." Initially applauding the decision, politicians waited only a few weeks before telling abortion-rights' activists they were better off going to the states to have states define the meaning of the word "health" than bring the federal abortion bill to a vote. As Gloria Steinem later wrote in *Ms. Magazine, "Doe v. Scott* was not a victory for women's rights. If anything, it stalled our momentum."

One thing was certain, though. It was going to be a long time before Ethel Kennedy spoke kindly of Archie Cox again.

To further complicate Kennedy's view toward his Supreme Court appointees, the Supreme Court held, in November 1973, that most state death penalty statutes were a violation of the Eighth Amendment because the death penalty constituted "cruel and unusual punishment." In the 7-2 opinion written by Chief Justice Brennan, the Court stated that most of Europe, except for the Soviet Union, had long outlawed the death penalty. The crime rate, the Court noted empirically, had sharply declined in recent years, and juries were becoming less likely than ever to vote for the death penalty. Said the Court, "The death penalty, as the New York Public Defenders' amicus brief has shown, is fast coming to be seen as a barbaric ritual that can never afford a mistake, though mistakes have continued to occur into our own time." The two dissenters in that case were Justices White and Stewart.

Kennedy was furious with his appointees for this decision, although the Pope, from the Vatican in Rome, hailed the decision, contrasting it with the Court's "immoral" decision on abortion. Kennedy, who had been silent on the abortion decisions other than to say that the Supreme Court decisions "are the law of the land," now announced his support for a constitutional amendment to allow for reinstatement of the death penalty. To provide some balance on behalf of the black civil rights establishment and cultural liberals still in the Democratic Party, Kennedy required that the amendment include procedural reforms in death penalty cases. The procedural reforms included a requirement for federally-funded attorneys for all state law death penalty defendants, an automatic appeal for all capital defendants, and the establishment of a commission to investigate and monitor race- and class-based biases in the death penalty "system."

Kennedy, in supporting this proposed constitutional amendment but not the one to overturn the abortion decisions, found himself in "hot water" with the First Lady, as he put it to the O Boys.

Ethel told her husband, "Our church, Bob, is opposed to the reinstitution of the death penalty *and* the Supreme Court's abortion decisions. How can you call yourself a Catholic when you support reinstating the death penalty and opposing the pro-life amendment? I will not, if asked, support your short-term political thinking on this—I'm glad you can't run again, that's for sure!"

"Ethel, the death penalty is still supported by most Americans, in theory. What most people, including me, didn't like was the Supreme Court taking away our choice to order the death penalty in a given case. The abortion decisions are different because the Court didn't tell you that you and other women had to have an abortion. The majority of justices simply said a woman should have the right to choose—"

"You are at your worst, you know, when you fall into legalisms! And I hate that word—*choose!* The murderer you want to murder through the electric chair chose to kill and that's why you say he should die. The baby didn't hurt anyone and yet a woman can 'choose' to kill that baby—"

"Ethel, you can argue this all you want. Americans, when pressed, want to have the right to *choose* to institute the death penalty in particular cases, and again, when pressed, the right to choose first-trimester abortions—which is why most of the abortions are performed in the first trimester. This was true even when abortions were illegal, at least according to medical studies on this issue. I don't have any patience with theoretical arguments about the sanctity of life when there are a lot of real and burning issues out there, including health care, child care, third world debt, and things like that. If we keep debating these frankly smaller questions without dealing with the larger ones that affect life *every day,* we'll be in deeper trouble than you can ever imagine!"

Ethel, upset at that last condescending remark, stormed out of the room, but not before saying, "If the Republicans weren't worse than you on this, Robert Kennedy, I'd be looking to change parties!"

Meanwhile, Kennedy encountered other irritants in his quest to expand the scope of public policy questions. Attorney General Ramsey Clark and others in law enforcement, including the revitalized FBI, wanted Kennedy to prosecute organized crime syndicates. Kennedy told Clark that he could not justify spending resources in that area "at this time." Kennedy then said, "Ramsey, if we're going to do anything right now, let's prosecute the Teamsters now that the nation understands what a violent, dangerous union they've been over the years. The problem in prosecuting the Mob directly right now is that it is so intertwined with so many legitimate businesses. We have plenty of laws to prosecute businesses with, starting with the environmental laws. Let's just use those laws against bad companies that are tight with organized crime, maybe next year. I know you've read what I've read in any event about organized crime. The syndicates may be playing themselves out, especially during the last gangland wars in 1969 and 1970. The mobsters seem to be getting exhausted, as I interpret the Justice Department reports."

When Kennedy referred to the Teamsters as "violent" and "dangerous," he was referring to the July 1973 gangland-style slaying at the Teamsters' headquarters, in which a self-described "goon" of Teamsters' chief Frank Fitzsimmons shot and killed a young Teamsters' reformer, Ron Carey. Almost immediately, the "goon" plea-bargained with the federal government and claimed he was acting on the orders of Fitzsimmons. This opened the way for Secretary of Labor Reuther and the Kennedy administration to place the Teamsters' union into a trusteeship and on the road to reform, even though Fitzsimmons was subsequently acquitted on all charges.[2]

Under the receivership the U.S. government instituted against the Teamsters, the Teamsters conducted its first relatively free elections in mid-1974. The "reform" slate, which called itself the Teamsters for a Democratic Union (TDU), won with 55 percent of the vote. Upon its victory, the TDU promised to join the AFL-CIO and, most important for Kennedy, said it would support "pro-worker" Democrats instead of Republicans, as the Teamsters' old guard had done for decades.

When Fitzsimmons was acquitted, Kennedy said to Clark, "Now you see why I haven't bothered attacking the Mob directly, Ramsey. We can't afford high-profile losses *anywhere*. The Mob was hurt more by our Bed-Sty programs and the receivership over the Teamsters than by the criminal prosecution of Fitzsimmons or anyone else you would have wanted."

As Clark continually told his subordinates at the Justice Department, while he refused to accept Kennedy's reasoning about not prosecuting more Mob cases, he was staying on as attorney general because he believed in Robert Kennedy and agreed with him on nearly every other major issue the administration was pursuing.

Computer Conversions, Part I

The Kennedy administration, relying on the government's role in supporting the atomic bomb program in the 1940s, the national highway program of the 1950s and '60s, and the space program of the 1960s, poured seven billion dollars in 1972 and 1973 into the research and development of a home-computer system that would be designed to be a "super-typewriter," a means of communication through "electronic mail," and a way to create home information systems through something computer scientists called a "cyber-web" of electronic connections.

The system was being developed in government-sponsored-and-supported joint ventures with Intel, Hewlett-Packard, Xerox (made up of former Bell Labs' personnel), IBM, and an upstart known as Compaq Computer Systems. Once developed, the home computer was able to perform not only calculations for consumers balancing their checkbooks, but also more difficult computations for accountants and businesses. The money spent on these ventures went into workers' hands as wages, contractors' hands for buildings and supplies, and to restaurant owners, realtors, and a host of other businesses who were nearby where these other people lived and worked.

Secretary of Commerce Vince Learson spent much of his time from 1972 on coordinating the creation of the home computer. In early 1973, he read an article in the *Washington Star* about two young men who had managed to create a technology in a small box that allowed them to make long-distance calls without having to pay AT&T, also known as "Ma Bell." The youths had not been arrested yet because Attorney General Clark wanted to use them as "friendly witnesses" against the "ringmaster," an older gentleman named Draper. AT&T wanted all persons connected with the scheme to be prosecuted and had been pressuring the attorney general's office to arrest the young men.

Learson, however, saw an opportunity. He called in the young men, both named "Steve." One had the last name of Wozniak and the other, oddly enough, Jobs. "Is that your real name or a stage name?" Learson asked.

"Jobs is my real name, man!" said the long-haired youth as he stood up and leaned a bit over Learson's desk. "As in, 'take this job and shove it,' pal!" Jobs used a graphic gesture as he said that last sentence. Then, he and Wozniak giggled as Jobs flopped back down in a chair in Learson's office. Learson thought, These guys are right out of 1967! He shuddered at the thought.

Jobs wasn't finished, though. "And who are *you,* man?"

"I'm Vince Learson, secretary of commerce."

"Yeah, I heard that, man. So what were you before that? Dog catcher?" The two Steves exchanged "high-fives" as if they were 1950s' jazz musicians.

"Oh, I was president of a little company. I don't know if you've heard of it. It only had three letters in its name as far as most people might be concerned . . . I-B-M."

The two Steves sat up at attention now. Jobs said, a bit more respectfully, "So, you're gonna arrest us, too? I mean, Big Mama Bell is already after us. Why not IBM?"

Learson smiled. "Oh, no. I'm not arresting you. But Attorney General Clark—he's down the street. He's *very* interested in prosecuting you, as you know. The government is likely to send you to jail just to get Ma Bell off Attorney General Clark's back. He figures it's the least he can do since he's suing them for being too big—bigger than IBM." He paused again to reaffirm they were listening. "I called both of you in here," he said with a touch of parental authority, "because I have a proposition for you that might be more palatable than, say, jail."

The two Steves gulped. But Jobs, realizing he looked too interested in the proposition, slid down into his chair a bit, as he said afterwards to his friend Wozniak, "to look like I didn't care. Gotta be cool when dealing with suits, man."

"Boys," said Learson, "how would each of you like your own government-paid laboratory to see if you can build a home computer that's smaller than one of those long-distance telephone boxes you've been fooling with? I've checked your records, such as they are, and your interview with the FBI that concerned your . . . 'work' with Mr. Draper—"

"What's gonna happen to him, man?" demanded Jobs.

"Never mind him, son. He's not going to the electric chair or anything of the sort, but he is going to jail. I can't do anything about that, I'm afraid—and neither can you. So, again, let me ask you both. Are you willing to work under me and for the federal government in your own computer lab, in exchange for not being arrested? There's only one catch. I expect results, and I'll know—because I'll be working with you very closely on this. I have a hunch you two wouldn't work well with regular engineers, but I think you'll find something our engineers still haven't quite found yet—"

Wozniak was ready to say "Like what?" when Learson, reading his mind, put up a hand to interrupt.

Learson said, "You don't need to know what the problem is. I just need to let you two build a small computer that regular people can use that isn't complicated. Any questions so far?" He waited. No questions were asked. "Good. Why don't you think about it for a day or two and come—"

Wozniak was not waiting. "I'm in—I don't care what it is. I've always wanted to be an engineer and build a computer. I'm going to jail unless I agree, right? Or are we going to jail anyway?"

"It may be 'anyway,' but if I have my way—and I have some pull, as you can imagine—it will probably be 'unless you agree.'" Learson glanced over at Jobs, who was still thinking about whether it might be cool to be a martyr. Jobs thought better of it after speaking privately to Wozniak in the hallway for a few minutes. Jobs was in, too.

Learson said, "Boys, go home to your parents, if you have any, and we'll call you. Just leave the numbers you'll be at. We could find you anyway, but why make us angry?" He said it with just enough malevolence that the two Steves wrote down, in clear penmanship, every phone number where they might be staying.

As Learson said in his memoirs, the "boys" as he called them, were "my greatest discovery in my entire career." Working outside normal government and business channels, "the Woz" and Jobs, using existing research and development from the government-business partnerships, created, with a few other "out-of-the-box" engineers, a seventeen-inch monitor connected to a separate, larger computer box that held all the "hardware" gear. In the separate box, there was an open slot that allowed for insertion of a "floppy disk" that contained what the engineers called "software." The software ran the programs the computer "played." Jobs came up with what he called, somewhat pretentiously, "user-friendly windows" that popped up and allowed a "regular" person—per Jobs, "the usual idiot"—to perform multiple tasks without turning the machine on and off. In the process, Learson became their mentor. "Boys," he told them in late 1974, "when this thing rolls out to the public, we're going back into the private sector—and we're gonna be rich enough to bitch about taxes! Big time!"

The first home computer was produced and marketed in 1975, launched in a White House Rose Garden ceremony in which Kennedy gingerly operated the computer. IBM, along with Compaq, produced the computer boxes, and Intel and Xerox produced the circuits.[3] The computer hardware system was designed for various programs that could be created by "anyone with half a brain," said Jobs with the general sneer of a computer engineer. He called the system an "open system" because anyone could reconfigure or redesign it for improvements on the basic model. Jobs said, "We wanted to design these contraptions to see how much memory and speed can be stored or produced. That's what makes it open, too!"

Because the system was designed from the start to be an open system, IBM, Intel, Compaq, and Xerox demanded a "monopoly" for ten years on the product before anyone besides them could *commercially* redesign the hardware system, add memory capability, the amount of "bytes" it could handle in a software program, or any other changes, including the appearance of the computer. Ralph Nader and Michael Harrington, when they heard about this proposal, ran screaming into Learson's office. They strongly urged Learson to make sure the government received a "part of the gross," as Nader said, for allowing the private enterprises their "monopoly."

"These behemoths should have no monopoly whatsoever, Secretary Learson. It's as if you're all throwing out eighty years of antitrust law!" said Nader.

"Why shouldn't the government market this itself?" asked Harrington. "This will be sold first to schools and government offices before many businesses and citizens buy it."

Learson, after the two activists threatened to go to the public and to the president himself, decided to ask Attorney General Clark for three years instead of ten to avoid Nader's threat of an antitrust action. He then went privately to Kennedy to push for five years. Nader and Harrington went to Yarborough for help before going directly to the president. As a result of Yarborough's pleading with the president and Learson, the government required that 25 percent of the gross profits the private companies generated from the sale of every computer and basic software program would go into the government's coffers during the five-year monopoly period. To protect against the companies' passing on this tax as a cost, they agreed to price regulation by the Federal Trade Commission.

Kennedy chuckled at Yarborough's insistence on the 25 percent profit—not because it was too high, but because Kennedy knew that no matter what, part of that sum would wind up being a "hidden sales tax," as he put it to Yarborough. "I thought you didn't like sales taxes, Ralph!"

"Ah know it's lahk a sales tax," Yarborough responded, a bit defensively, "but this way we can get a direct profit off our government's investment on top o' getting a bite outta the companies' reg'lar taxes!"

Kennedy laughed and said, "I don't know, Ralph. Sounds like you're becoming a capitalist in your old age!"

Ralph made a noise like he was spitting and said, "Yeah, maybe Ah'm just makin' a li'l profit for the people o' the USA. But Ah ain't makin' a thin dime! And don't call me old—Ah can still race ya 'round the block and back ag'in!"

Learson recounted his "adventures" with Yarborough and Clark on one side and the businessmen on the other as he grew closer to Steve Jobs. "Steve," said Learson, "the radicals and the traditional businessmen are missing the boat—as usual. The real money is going to be in the software, not the hardware. Once a person buys a computer, that person is likely to hold it for a few years, like a television set. The hardware will probably undergo only small changes over a long period of time. On the other hand, people can buy new and different software programs for a variety of games, spreadsheets, and anything else we can imagine—*over and over again!* And that's where we're going into business before the year is out."

"Far out!" said Jobs. Jobs, though, decided he wasn't ready to venture into the software business. He wanted to keep tinkering with the hardware for a while. I want to redesign the hardware, too, he thought. The money, he decided, could wait.

Learson wound up waiting himself because of reasons relating to Jobs' desire to tinker with the hardware. Learson's assumption about the stability and reliability of the hardware was quickly proven to be optimistic as "computer hackers"—mostly college students—were able to immediately update or change, for the better, the computer system created by the joint efforts of the high-technology companies and the government. When corporate or government investigators caught hackers trying to sell their innovations without giving the open-source redesigns—and profits—to the "five-year monopolists," the media treated the "hacker-preneurs" as martyrs, not criminals. Attorney General Ramsey Clark, thinking of the Jobs-Wozniak precedent, often, and successfully, pressured the private high-tech companies to hire the hackers and let them design ways around the hacking and improve the overall capabilities of the computers. This had the salutary effect of compressing the innovation timeline the monopolists had assumed in those first few years.

Computer Conversions, Part II

President Kennedy, in the same Rose Garden ceremony where he introduced the personal computer, had also introduced another new technological innovation, courtesy of a private-public venture: the new U.S. Post Office electronic mail system that a person used over his or her new personal computer.[4] "E-mail," for short, was a civilian application of the ARPANET program first introduced in 1971 under the auspices of the Department of Defense. With the new e-mail system of communication, said Kennedy, "people will now be able to send text messages through their computers. And in about a year or so, we expect to be able to send pictures to each other. The Post Office will charge a flat fee of five dollars a month for what you might liken to a modern telegraph machine!"

The system initially worked like this: Every time the computer was turned on, the Post Office software noted any e-mail usage; and like Pitney Bowes' postage-meter system, the letter carrier, once a month, collected the five-dollar charge after inspecting the computer.

Almost immediately, however, postal delivery personnel complained about lugging the inspection machine that kept track of the e-mail usage. Postal union head Moe Biller, who kept insisting beforehand that his workers could handle the extra load, demanded that "postal delivery assistants" be added to routes. The Post Office officials rejected that proposal just as quickly, and Moe made noises about a strike. Then came the first robbery along a postal delivery route. What nobody in power positions in the government or industry had considered was how someone who carried loads of money—five dollars in cash from a lot of individuals added up pretty quickly—could become an easy target for nearly any criminal. When Moe Biller suggested arming the postal workers with guns in response to the first reported robbery, Kennedy told Learson and the postmaster general, "This is getting ridiculous. Figure something out—and fast! And tell Moe, or I will, that if he strikes over this, he won't get any other unions to support him—I'll make sure of it!"

Learson, seizing the moment on behalf of private enterprise, convinced the Post Office to turn over the collection of the monthly payments to the credit card companies. The companies would receive fifty cents of each five-dollar payment for administering the monthly payments. This proved a win-win solution for government coffers and the credit card companies because the companies were eager to further expand the use of such cards by Americans, and the government was able to maintain its new revenue source. Moe Biller was convinced to stay aboard the win-win train because more money to the Post Office meant more money that could go into the pockets of postal workers.

At a speech before the National Manufacturers Association luncheon in New York on December 5, 1975, Kansas Republican Senator Robert Dole cried out, "How does Kennedy keep moving our nation toward socialism and still buy off businessmen? When you think about it, Kennedy's doing a better job than Lenin in selling lynching rope to businessmen! He's engaged in guerilla warfare without guns—two steps toward socialism and one step back to capitalism—just like he did with the Post Office's e-mail program!" The audience laughed somewhat nervously, but also knew until they won back the White House and gained more congressional seats, cutting deals with the government was the best they could do.

But everything was not settled at the Post Office, either. Another problem the Post Office faced was the same problem computer manufacturers faced: hacking. This time, there was no simple "credit card" solution waiting in the wings. Instead, the problem took on the nature of an "arms race" in which software engineers for the government and the private companies in the joint venture pitted themselves against hackers who hacked for the pure sport of it.

The five-year monopolists issued anti-hacking software packages nearly every six months, but within each six-month period, one or more hackers were generally able to strike again—and publish their results on the cyber-web in encrypted software the hackers developed. This, in turn, inspired a race for secrecy under the guise of encryption, which began to overtake the open system the government founders had originally embraced. To allow engineers to respond to this unexpected expertise in the "hinterlands"— meaning outside government and corporate laboratories—the government had to cut into its own profits to pay for these unanticipated costs. Moe Biller, who didn't understand computers and e-mail, but understood money and power, was not amused to say the least. But he felt as helpless as the computer scientists and software engineers in their battle against the hackers.

Nader's response throughout the hacker arms race was, "Let the monopolists pay for these engineers to combat hackers. The public has paid enough!" Members of Congress were calling press conferences to say they agreed with Nader. The high-tech companies, the postmaster general, and their respective unions pleaded with Learson to speak to Kennedy to save their profits and wage increases.

For Learson, this was the moment he had been waiting for. Speaking with a lobbyist from the chamber of commerce, Learson had confirmed that he had been outraged at Nader for quite some time. He railed against Nader's "reckless indifference to private enterprise, except when it comes to private lawyers suing big corporations in their own twisted form of capitalism." Learson, now armed with complaints from business, labor, and other government departments, now went directly to the president. He said, "Mr. President, do you want this entire computer project to fail over what, for the government, are mere revenue crumbs? Remember, the companies' profits already come back in the form of taxes, as I keep trying to remind everyone! We can't listen to Ralph Nader on a subject on which he has no expertise!"

"That's not entirely true, Vince. I tried that out on Nader when I saw him the other day. He says if these costs were borne by the private companies, they would be deductible as expenses that lower corporate income, which in turn, means less taxes for them to pay."

"That's mixing up different parts of business accounting, Mr. President—"

"Look, Vince, it's true enough, but your other point has validity, too. Why fight over, as you say, 'crumbs' for something nobody thought could happen so quickly . . . or . . . easily. Who knew we had college kids so quick with mastering these new technologies? Tell your business friends we'll back them—and let's step up hiring these kids. It's like we say in politics—better to have them pissing outside the tent than inside."

The president signed the executive order that required the government to pay the costs of engineers responding to the hacking of Web sites and computers. Kennedy dared the congressional Democrats and Nader supporters to override him with a resolution or a law. Yarborough, realizing this was a battle between labor and Naderite forces, decided he had bigger fish to fry. He therefore backed Kennedy.

As usual, Congress failed to challenge the president's authority, though the carping of the most radical Democrats in Congress continued against "corporate sell-outs" within the Kennedy administration; that is, Learson.

By the beginning of the nation's bicentennial in 1976, the sales of computers were soaring. Besides the new software programs, which consisted mostly of games such as "Pong," among others, people realized how much "fun" it was to have text-based instant communication with friends and relatives across the nation. All one needed was access to the new computers—whether in one's own home, a neighbor's home, or in a community center or library where people waited in line to use computers that contained the new e-mail system. Like the television craze of the early 1950s, everyone had to have a computer and get "on-line."

There was another unexpected glitch, this time the result of too much success. The sale of large numbers of computers led to an upsurge in the use of telephone lines for e-mail and the cyber-web, which was starting to gain its own momentum. This put a strain on the copper-wire systems in many communities outside metropolitan areas. Ironically, this technological "traffic jam" inspired Attorney General Clark to find a solution to the six-year-old antitrust case against AT&T. After intense settlement negotiations with AT&T before a federal magistrate, AT&T agreed to the following proposal from the government: AT&T could essentially retain its potentially monopolistic position in return for agreeing to lower its "reasonable return of profit" and further regulation of its annual expenditures.

Apart from that, Clark, directly inspired by Learson, added an additional "technologically-related" proposal: AT&T, instead of paying a fine or damages for any antitrust conduct, would pay 75 percent of the cost of rewiring the nation using fiber-optic technology. Learson convinced Clark that fiber optics would smooth out the development of the government's computer program and cyber-web or Internet development. The government issued Treasury bonds to pay for the remaining 25 percent share of the anticipated costs.

Fiber optics, said Learson to Clark and the president, provided more room, or "bandwidth," than the old copper telephone lines for both telephone and computer usage. Further, fiber optics would speed the electronic transfer of voice, data (words and numbers), and, eventually, pictures. It was another "win-win" solution for the Kennedy administration. The government would make more money from the increased sales of computers, which in turn would generate more jobs for workers at union rates and more tax revenue for the government. The increase in jobs would enable other businesses to increase their purchases of labor-saving equipment to cut costs without having to send workers to the unemployment rolls.

The development of the personal computer and the Internet outpaced the development of cable television and audio compact discs during the period of the RFK presidency. The phenomenal growth of electronic and telephone operation bandwidth, due to the government-business partnership, simply leaped over those first-timeline technologies. Fiber-optic networks allowed sound and pictures to be sent through e-mail and the Internet, and this was, in the words of Paul Newman, chairman of the National Endowment of the Arts, "revolutionary for the arts."

It might be thought that Republicans were silent during this time of technological adjustment, but they were not. In 1976, the Republicans in Congress, especially the libertarians, put together a coalition with some of the most socialistically inclined Democrats to score a rare legislative victory: passage of a law that prohibited wiretaps against people's computers. The victory, however, proved to be short-lived. Five years later, in 1981, the law was repealed because the prohibition against computer wiretaps allowed for the rise of "electronic crime" in the form of financial scams and the stealing of people's "private" information. Many of the same Republicans who had supported the original law signed on to the partial repeal that allowed computers to be "wiretapped" in the same way as telephones.

As political, technical, and economic problems kept arising in the first years after the introduction of the new personal computers, e-mail, and the Internet, Commerce Secretary Learson realized he needed to stay on through the end of the Kennedy administration in order to guide the industry through the perils of "the monopolists, the unionists, and the socialists," as he called them. "I feel like the President of Computers," he told Jobs, "and this project is my baby, no matter what anyone says. I can't leave it to these socialists who might just take over the whole thing if I left. We'll have to wait until after the election. We're still early enough in this game to call our own shots with all the contacts we have and the prestige we'll have built up in guiding this ship forward."

With Learson staying in government, Jobs decided to stay with Compaq as he was still more interested in the hardware side of computers. Compaq had made him vice president of engineering, and he was very happy to stay on top of the hardware innovations before joining forces with Learson in the software world. This time, everything worked according to plan for Learson and Jobs. In January 1977, Learson quit the government for good, or as he told the president, "My term of public service is done."

Within days of Learson's announcement, Learson, Jobs, and Wozniak founded a new software company they called Apple. The name was Jobs' idea but it also appealed to Learson's love of Issac Newton and Edward Bernays—that is, apples equals gravity equals scientific endeavors . . . equals great market branding!

Apple eventually became a powerful software manufacturer that dominated the market. In 1981, Apple rescued a smaller software company known as Microsoft from a hostile takeover by IBM. The young twenty-something founder of Microsoft, William Gates Jr., eventually made the trio of Learson, Wozniak, and Jobs into a quartet. Together, they would, even after a significant business interruption during the mid-1980s, grow Apple into a Fortune Top 50 Company, particularly after they purchased a controlling interest in, and then merged with, Disney, which was ripe for the takeover in 1984 after suffering deep losses in a disastrous attempt to create its own software division.

The Political Economy of Computers and Software

Personal computers often broke down or had technical glitches, especially in the first years after their wide introduction through the federal government–private enterprise joint venture. Republicans and other capitalist critics of the joint venture complained that "technological socialism" explained the seemingly constant computer problems. They complained despite the fact that private enterprise had been a partner in the creation of the home computer, electronic mail, and the Internet. All problems, they theorized, were the result of government meddling.[5]

Jude Wanniski, the self-proclaimed computer geek and *Wall Street Journal* editorialist, wrote in that pro-business newspaper on May 4, 1976, "The government and their pampered monopolist business friends are always telling us to turn our computers on and off again if something is wrong, something they call 'rebooting.' Every time it happens to me, I think more of a government 'jackboot' oppressing me and wasting my hard-earned time. If rebooting is all it takes, why can't they fix the thing in the first place so we don't have to turn it on and off? Leave it to the government to create such a computer system as the one we are forced to live with until the hardware monopoly runs out— or probably beyond that point because of this government-inspired stifling of innovation."

Milton Friedman, the libertarian economics professor at the University of Chicago, wrote an entire chapter in one of his pro-capitalist economics books that "proved," through economic metrics, that if the government left the computer industry alone, private enterprise would have produced a computer that would run smoothly with little or no breakdowns.

Of course, the problems Wanniski and Friedman complained about in the RFK timeline also occurred in the far more capitalistic environment of the first timeline—thus, begging the question of whether economics is mostly political advocacy masquerading as a "science."

Steve Jobs, who lived deep within the world of the government-private enterprise venture, caustically responded to such critics and anyone else who claimed the system broke down too often. He would say, over and over, that this was the essence of any machine that handled a whole range of outside software programs under an "open system." Jobs did agree with Professor Friedman on one thing: The five-year monopoly was a mistake because "there are only so many things any individual engineer, including me, can figure out or fix."

President Kennedy was impressed after reading Jobs' reply to Wanniski in the *Wall Street Journal*. He said to Labor Secretary Reuther, "That Jobs kid is pretty smart. He's rich—and we gave him his start. I get so pissed off when people say we didn't allow the capitalist spirit to develop during my terms of office!"

Reuther responded, "I never bought that crap, either, Mr. President. Unions and government help foster growth and wealth, and we've proven that year after year after year. That's what I don't like about any of those ivory-tower types, whether it's Milton Friedman or even my pal Mike Harrington. What people with an economic or political ideology don't get is that reality is a whole lot more complicated than any theory, and that 'private' and 'public' are constantly blurring into each other. Maybe we just need to balance things out from time to time—but let's keep labor unions strong and people like us governing!"

Kennedy looked out the window of the White House and, feeling the warming sunrays of a spring day in late May 1976, smiled at Reuther's unifying theory of politics and government. He was starting to think of his own legacy and thought, I may not have done everything my brother might have done, but I've done a helluva lot.

Chapter 35

FOREIGN AND OTHER AFFAIRS

The Revolutions Against "The Revolution"

Just as first timeline President George Herbert Walker Bush watched the Soviet Union collapse in 1991, so, too, did President Robert Kennedy watch the Soviet Union collapse in 1974. The sequence of events leading to the collapse was different, of course, but the collapse occurred just the same.

In 1974 the Soviet Union leadership lost the will to maintain its power. The collapse of China, the smooth integration of Eastern Europe with the social democratic governments in Western Europe, and the successful foreign policies the Kennedy administration was pursuing in the third world left the Soviet Union leadership with no outside enemies to blame in order to justify their dictatorship. Worse for the Politburo, the Soviets had more difficulty than the Americans in finding jobs for their soldiers returning from Europe. And with gold no longer underpinning modern currencies, the Soviets received very little for their vast gold reserves.

Soviet citizens, with the opening up of the press, quickly learned how to express their frustration and anger. The newspapers, more than the broadcast media, constantly castigated the Soviet leadership for refusing to allow free elections with true opposition parties, as in Eastern Europe and the United States.

Prominent Soviet dissident Andrei Sakharov said, "We must end the corruption of Misha bartering bread to get shoes from Sasha. If the Americans can have some socialism under President Kennedy, why can't the Soviet Union have some market capitalism? Why can't we follow at least the Swedish people in having a mixed economy?" The problem was that, contrary to "pure" minds such as Sakharov's, many Soviet citizens wanted to end such bartering only for the "other guy."

KGB director and Politburo member Yuri Andropov, in early March 1974, finally joined Leonid Brezhnev and Constantin Chernenko in calling for a crackdown on "impudent, counterrevolutionary dissidents." As Andropov said during a Politburo meeting announcing his support of a strong response to critics including Sakharov, "How can we call our leading Soviet newspaper *Pravda*"—meaning "Truth"—"any longer if we allow daily slanders against our country to be published?"

President Alexei Kosygin asked, "Is it *all* a slander, Comrade Yuri Vladmirovich? Or is there truth beneath the emotional charges against our policies to justify the people's frustrations?"

Mikhail Suslov remained quiet. He had been spending less and less time with Andropov, his protégé, and more time with the mayor of Moscow, Mikhail Gorbachev, since the autumn of 1973. Suslov also had grave, depressing talks with Defense Minister Rodion Malinovsky about what he called "the decline of the East." "We had such hopes, Comrade Minister," said Suslov. "I wonder where it all ends . . . "

Suslov did not have to wait long to find out. General strikes gripped Moscow, Leningrad, and the Crimean region in May 1974. On June 17, 1974, the Politburo met and decided that it was necessary to send troops not merely to quell the strikes, but to begin a massive "crackdown" on dissent. Moscow Mayor Gorbachev received word of this and realized it meant civil war and a possible return to Stalinism. He marched over to the main Soviet television station in Moscow, ordered the technicians to broadcast his impending message throughout the Soviet Union, and, when the red light lit on the camera facing him, Gorbachev spoke to the nation.

He told his fellow Soviet citizens of the Politburo's plans, and noted that the Politburo had not made this decision unanimously. "That," he said, "is a sign that this is a gravely wrong decision. It is time for the Soviet Union and the people to emulate their brothers and sisters in the Eastern European nations and create a modern socialism to reflect our times. Russia no longer fears its enemies. China to the south of us is still mired in the chaos that followed its civil war of just a few years ago. We cannot allow civil war to be our future. But that will be our future if we accept the Politburo's divided decision. There is another way, comrades. And that other way involves our willingness to work with each other for a new Soviet, and a new world."

Speaking directly to the military, Gorbachev said, "My fellow soldiers, we cannot fire on our own workers who cry for bread on their kitchen tables and a decent wage for their hard work. We reveal only weakness, not strength, when we fire our weapons against our brave brothers and sisters in the factories. I beseech you, in the name of Lenin, in the name of Marx and Engels, in the name of the 1917 revolutionary ideals for which so much blood—too much blood!—has been spent! Let us begin anew. I do not care what happens to me now. I only care that we do what we can to avoid a descent into the madness of choosing between civil war and Stalin's worst oppression!"

The Politburo, after finally reaching the appropriate person at the Soviet television station, ordered Gorbachev's address cut at that point. However, Defense Minister Malinovsky and Comrade Suslov, who left the Politburo immediately afterward and headed to the Defense Ministry, decided that Gorbachev was right. "We cannot afford a civil war, Mikhail Andreenovich," said Malinovsky.

Suslov asked, "Then, Comrade Defense Minister, if I may quote our beloved founder, 'What is to be done?'"

Malinovsky responded, "We will see, Comrade Mihail Andreenovich, we will see. My troops will refuse to fight the workers, that much is certain. If Andropov and Brezhnev persist in their call for action against what is called 'counterrevolutionary' conduct by what is surely our proletariat, we must follow Mayor Gorbachev, I suppose. We must go to Comrade Mikhail at the television station if we are to protect him from forces that may wish to liquidate him. Any attempt against his life will bring on the civil war regardless of what we think, I am most convinced."

Suslov agreed with this assessment. "The entire Soviet Union itself may be liquidated if there is civil war this time around. We must surround the Politburo itself, Comrade Minister, and arrest the members if they persist. It is our only chance of saving the Soviet Union and the Revolution."

With that, Malinovsky ordered the military to surround the Politburo and dissolve its power. Replacing the military music and film of marching troops that was the usual mid-to-late-twentieth-century sign that martial law had been declared, Moscow Mayor Gorbachev appeared again in front of the cameras to address the Soviet nation. This time he stood in front of Defense Minister Malinovsky and Politburo member Suslov. Gorbachev said that all soldiers were to stay in their barracks or on base and not intervene against the workers on strike in the three cities. The workers in those cities were asked to meet to form provisional local governments. As for the other cities and towns, the commissars were asked to set elections for July 21, 1974, to elect representatives to a new Soviet parliament modeled along the lines of Western European governments. Soviet workers were asked to "work hard to keep our factories and services running in the meantime."

But Gorbachev and the elite who rallied behind him were unprepared for the reaction of workers and peasants in the western and southern regions of the Soviet empire. As in the first timeline, those regions rebelled and demanded not a federation with the Soviet Union, as Gorbachev and the "reform Communists" proposed, but complete freedom and independence. Lithuania, Latvia, Estonia, Chechnya, Azerbaijan, Georgia, and other regions overthrew their Communist commissars—some with no bloodshed to speak of, some with unspeakable bloodshed.

Gorbachev, Suslov, and Malinovsky refused to intervene for fear of losing the heart of Mother Russia itself in the cauldron of civil war. Malinovsky said to the other members of the triumvirate, "We gave up these lands during the Revolution of 1917 in the face of adversity. We do so again. Europe is not in the grip of chaos, as in the 1920s and 1930s, and America is becoming less bourgeois and imperialist. We must save Mother Russia from the fate of China."

During the winter of 1974 and early 1975, the Soviet Union dissolved, with the main region of Russia retaking its traditional name. The Kennedy administration, despite earlier promises to Ambassador Dobrynin to keep the Soviets from collapsing into chaos, could not stave off the collapse itself. In January 1975, the United States announced a foreign aid package to help the former Soviet citizens through the harsh winter and into the spring. Kennedy also asked UN Ambassador Barbara Jordan to coordinate a United Nations' effort for the former Soviet citizens. With food becoming scarce in many parts of Russia and in the old Soviet empire, Gorbachev was glad to have American assistance. He told his aides at the time, "The United States has saved us from a reversion to cannibalism."

In the first elections in post-Communist Russia, the Russian people voted for Gorbachev as president and Boris Yeltsin as vice president. Malinovsky remained as head of the armed forces of Russia, while Suslov retired from the government and was given amnesty for any Soviet-era crimes against humanity. Gorbachev followed Nelson Mandela's call for a Soviet Truth Commission like the one Mandela had established in South Africa. In return for truthful testimony and cooperation in securing the written records behind that truth, amnesty would be given to the former Soviet leadership and various commissars around the nation. However, some peasants simply killed their local commissars without waiting for any truth commission, particularly in the border communities of Mother Russia. As one peasant told an American freelance reporter who was present for a vigilante hanging of a local official, "We already know the truth! And this bastard deserves to die!"

As the Soviet, or now Russian, leaders, recognized as their own empire collapsed, things had gone badly for the Chinese Communist leadership. The death of Lin Piao, Mao's continuing feebleness, and the success of the Eastern Europeans in overthrowing Communism caused many Chinese citizens to see that the Communist monolith was not much more than what Chou had once called the United States—"a paper tiger." In the spring of 1973, Chou En-Lai, Liu Shao-Chi, and Teng Shao-Ping announced their support for a democratically elected, decentralized—almost federalist—system, and allowed for market capitalism that was limited to China itself, with no importing of Western businesses or technology.

China, under the specific tutelage of Minister Teng, embarked on what most historians later concluded was a disastrous flirtation with capitalism, as China tried to become the "new and bigger" Hong Kong. This "cold turkey" experiment immediately set into motion a plethora of financial corruption, opium dens, and prostitution rings. Worse, these crime rings included many former commissars who then engaged in gang wars that were similar to old-style feudal wars. In an attempt to stem the tide of this rising criminal element, the central government in Peking attempted to "shut down" the experiment in political and economic freedom. Instead, there was a descent into chaos and a renewed civil war in November 1973.

With Mao in a coma, Tibet and other southern and western provinces broke from the Peking government. As Chet Bowles grimly said to Kennedy, "Mao's desire in the mid-1960s for a 'permanent revolution' continues in ways even he could not have predicted."

After the fall of China, and then the Soviet Union, reunification finally took place between North and South Vietnam. The South, in a much stronger economic position under former Viet Cong guerilla Truong, was now in a position to dictate to the North that it open up its society. The North, facing a shortage of rice, capitulated, but only after begging Truong to set up a truth commission to save, as U.S. Ambassador Vann said, "their miserable souls."[1]

With North and South Vietnam enjoying relative peace since 1970 and a full peace by 1975, Cambodia was able to maintain some stability under Prince Norodom Sihanouk. In 1976, however, the prince, while visiting Paris, was overthrown in a "peaceful coup" led by a coalition of the longtime democratic opposition and the military. The Cambodian Communists known as the Khmer Rouge were easily dispatched when they attempted a putsch of sorts during the interim period between the coup and the nation's first modern democratic elections.

For the residents of Thailand, the loss of the U.S. military "protection" and war in their region of Southeast Asia meant two things. First, Thailand's radicalized students managed to gain the support of business and the military and turned the king of Thailand into a figurehead, serving as a titular head of a parliamentary system, much like the British monarch. Second, without the continued presence of U.S. troops, the nation did not become overrun with whorehouses, as it did in the first timeline of the late twentieth century and early twenty-first century.

Secretary Bowles, reviewing the news at the latest announcements from the new Cambodian government, and remarking at the changes in Southeast Asia over the past two years, said to Secretary Warnke, "I guess there really were dominoes after all."

Warnke answered, "Yes, Chet. I agree. But they were different dominoes than John Foster Dulles, Bob MacNamara, and others thought they would be."

Even a Rose Bush Has Thorns

The Israeli government, while claiming to want peace with the Palestinians, nonetheless continued its rapid expansion of settlements, particularly to house former Soviet Jews in Israel who now numbered more than one million. These former Soviet Jews would soon become their own political force, first within the Labor Party and then, in 1977, within the Likud Party, which had been considered "fascist" when it first began in 1948. Although some Soviet Jews—the "lucky" ones, said some Israelis—were able to secure visas to the United States, the most nationalistic Soviet Jews stayed in Israel and used their clout in that small nation to take a harder and harder line against the Palestinians, who supported the Soviet Union until the Soviet Union collapsed.

The Palestinian guerillas made matters worse for their people by refusing all entreaties of the United States to follow a strategy of civil disobedience as opposed to violent terror tactics. The Palestinians thought they could win by "armed struggle" because Arabs and the Arab nations outnumbered Jews and Israel. What they failed to understand was that Arab leaders such as Assad in Syria and Jordan's King Hussein were merely using the Palestinian struggle to keep attention focused away from their own regimes' lack of popular support.

Compounding the Palestinian fanatical violence, militant Jewish settlers, led by the religious group Gush Emunim and some Soviet Jews wishing to settle a cosmic score against all who have harmed Jews in any way, were more than willing to use terror tactics themselves. However, such settlers did not have to use violence very often, unlike their Palestinian counterparts. For the settlers had the Israeli army to use physical force against Palestinians and their property for reasons of "security."

Throughout the 1970s, each time it appeared a peaceful breakthrough was imminent, one or both sides' own fanatics would engage in some act of violence—although Palestinian guerillas would often produce the more dramatic actions against civilians. This would, in turn, undermine those advocating peace and send the diplomatic teams home from Paris, Geneva, Washington, or wherever the peace talks were being held.

The end result was that more settlements were built in the West Bank and Gaza during the Kennedy-Yarborough 1970s than in the Nixon-Ford-Carter 1970s, probably because more Soviet Jews arrived in Israel in the early 1970s instead of the early 1990s.

The Palestinian radicals mostly kept their violent tactics within the boundaries of Israel and the surrounding area. When they ventured out once in 1974, the results further undermined the Palestinian radicals' cause. In June of that year, the Palestinian radical Abu Nidal's splinter group hijacked an American Airlines' civilian airplane coming out of Rome. During a fight between the hijackers and the American pilots, two of whom were former Vietnam vets who carried guns—against regulations—the plane veered off course and crashed into the Adriatic Sea, killing all of the passengers, the crew, and the terrorists. The world was outraged by the actions of the Nidal group. Yassir Arafat, who had become by default the leader of the Palestinian secular guerillas, seized this opportunity to vanquish his most dangerous rival. He ordered his guerillas to kill Nidal in Lebanon and, this time, they succeeded.

Kennedy was not satisfied, however, even as he learned that Blee's CIA had secretly provided intelligence information to the Palestinians about Nidal's location, a favor that ensured Arafat's success. Kennedy ordered the

U.S. military to strafe terrorist hideouts in Lebanon, including those of a couple of Arafat's supporters. And, of course, Kennedy rode high in the American polls for taking that military action. Then Kennedy and Bowles, reacting to European resistance against any further military solutions, began to pressure the Israelis to reopen negotiations with the Palestinians. Peace talks began again—and failed again after a few months for the usual reasons of terror and violence among those on each side whose definition of "peace" was "you surrender and leave—or die."

This time, however, the violence that killed the prospects of peace came not from the secular Palestinian radicals, but from religious elements on the Palestinian side, particularly Islamic fundamentalists. Most of the "traditional" Palestinian guerilla leadership, starting with Arafat, was comprised of Arabs who were nominally Christian, if not secular, and had themselves opposed these religious radicals.

This development was initially greeted in Israeli military circles as possibly driving a further wedge between Palestinians. The Israelis assured the Americans that since the Israeli intelligence agencies had previously supported the Islamic clerics against Arafat's secular radicals, Israel might have more influence over the clerics in order to bring about a "realistic hope for peace," in the words of Prime Minister Yizhak Rabin.

However, Arafat saw things differently. In a long talk with the left-wing Australian journalist Wilfred Burchett, Arafat told of his fear of the religious zealots who, said Arafat, "have as much an argument against modernity as they do with Israel and the United States. Neither the Americans nor the Israelis will have any influence for peace with these zealots. I never understood why Israel would build up these Dark Age fanatics at my expense. Don't the Israelis listen to what these clerics are saying? They see the Jews of Israel as an outpost of Christian crusaders."

When Burchett asked Arafat why he didn't take the risk now for peace, and do what President Sadat of Egypt had done a few years before, Arafat replied, "Now is not the time for my suicide. If I move toward peace now, under these circumstances, I sign my death warrant. The Israelis cannot be so foolish as not to see this. When they do, they will embrace us and make it easier for us to make peace. On the other hand, if the Israelis do not approach me soon with a true and lasting offer of peace, the religious forces will swallow up our movement. And unlike you and me, the religious zealots are most happy to die . . . "

In late September 1974, as the latest round of peace talks in the Middle East was collapsing, the OPEC nations, acting in a surprisingly unified manner—with Saudi Arabia a very reluctant participant—began a worldwide embargo on oil. OPEC demanded that the Western oil companies increase their payments to the oil-producing nations and that the United Nations and the United States increase economic aid for development of their economies beyond simply producing oil.

As the embargo entered its second week and gasoline prices at the pump jumped 30 percent, Kennedy turned his anger directly against the three major oil companies, Exxon, Mobil, and Texaco, for failing to put a stop on the embargo as they had in 1956, 1967, and 1973. Vice President Yarborough, acting with the "plausible denial" of his boss, took to the media's airwaves to blame the major oil companies for not taking steps to protect America's oil interests.[2]

The oil companies responded, in ads placed in major newspapers and on television, that the united OPEC front, the nationalized oil fields, and the growing sophistication of the oil-producing nations explained why this embargo was different from previous embragoes. At the same time, they privately asked for a formal meeting with Kennedy at the Oval Office, which was what Kennedy hoped would happen following Yarborough's attack.

The oil company executives were well prepared for their meeting with the president. In response to Yarborough's accusation of a "breach of faith," Texaco's president said the Interior Department had been delaying permits for oil drilling since March. Added Exxon's new president, M. A. Wright, "This undermined domestic drilling at this critical juncture." Kennedy immediately telephoned Secretary of the Interior Udall, who angrily denied that claim. The Exxon president was undaunted and said, "Mr. President, I'll be glad to send you proof of the department's permit delays. I am sorry I didn't come to you sooner with these delays on permits, but the OPEC actions caught us by surprise."

Wright then angered Kennedy when he said that oil prices were still low compared to prices for other commodities, and that there was little to be done except to negotiate with OPEC. Kennedy responded, "We do not negotiate from weakness, Mr. Wright. We negotiate from strength! If the oil companies will not stand firm against OPEC as they have done in the past, we will have to consider alternative measures."

Wright responded, "Mr. President, several oil-producing nations have nationalized our oil fields over the years. If we do not wish to negotiate, our nation does have certain . . . ways to respond . . . ways a mere private company cannot."

Kennedy said, "Landing American troops in Saudi Arabia, Iran, and Libya to run the oil fields—or overthrowing those governments—is not my idea of a solution either, Mr. Wright."

The president of Mobil plaintively responded to Kennedy, "Mr. President, this is a very dangerous situation. If the United States does not exercise its military power, then we have little choice but to negotiate with OPEC. Prices will never come back to where they were. American consumers will have to accept this new situation, as we are learning to do at Mobil."

The meeting came hastily to a close as Kennedy said in a simmering tone that he would think about the views expressed in the meeting.

With the midterm elections of 1974 only six weeks away, Kennedy knew if he did not begin to do something in response to the oil embargo, the Democrats could find themselves punished at the polls. Long lines for gas had become commonplace since the start of the OPEC—and possibly the oil companies'—embargo. Inflation was already hitting the sectors most directly affected by oil and gas, particularly the food industry. As Treasury Secretary Heller warned Labor Secretary Reuther, "Inflation is going to be a queen bitch this winter, Walt. And then there'll be growing unemployment as people curtail their purchases and—well, we better enact whatever legislation we can, and soon!"

At Reuther's urging, Kennedy met with Reuther, the O Boys, Heller, Bowles, and Yarborough to formalize a response. The solution reached at that meeting, and successive meetings, was unveiled in Kennedy's address to the nation on October 13, 1974. In the address, Kennedy railed against the OPEC nations for hoarding oil against not merely the well-off Western nations, but also against "the poor nations that can do little or nothing to protect themselves." Kennedy, however, refused "to let our own oil companies off the hook. There are confirmed reports of tremendous oil company profits being generated as a result of this political, not natural, crisis. Such profligate conduct by American oil companies is not only affecting American consumers and workers, it is also undermining the profits of other businesses across America."

To protect the nation from being held hostage to "foreign oil and rapacious oil companies ever again," Kennedy announced a program for developing public transportation, with government contracts he granted the day before the speech to Renault, American Motors Corporation, and the Ford Motor Company. Kennedy also announced support for a special "excess profits" tax against the oil companies. The taxes, he said, would be used to partially fund the program. He also announced further regulations against the oil companies designed to "force them to disclose to the government where oil deposits are located in our own nation. We should not have to rely on profit-seeking oil companies, as we now do, to decide where and when to drill for oil."

Kennedy did not call for "nationalizing" the oil companies, as some members of Congress, particularly Senators Adlai Stevenson III of Illinois and George McGovern of South Dakota, suggested. He was concerned that the Supreme Court might block nationalization, as it had done when Truman nationalized steel companies during the Korean War in 1951. As Kennedy told a disappointed Senate Majority Leader Mike Mansfield, "I gave up long ago trying to read Supreme Court tea leaves."

In preparing the speech, Kennedy knew the two measures he proposed would take time. Therefore, he also stated in his speech that the nation "must pull together as a community" and begin to "ration oil and gas." First, motor vehicles whose license plates ended with an even number would be entitled to receive oil or gas on even-numbered days, while those with an odd number would receive gas and oil on odd-numbered days. Second, Kennedy called upon unions (Reuther had already secured a commitment from the AFL-CIO before the speech) and companies to create car-pooling arrangements to save gas, and he asked "communities across our land to devise ways to conserve oil and gas for the betterment of our nation."

At the end of his speech, and with a confidence in his voice that veiled his own doubts, Kennedy said to the people of the United States:

> My fellow citizens, we Americans have met many challenges in our history, and we will do so again. We met the challenge of the Soviet Union's space program in the late 1950s with our own science education programs, and developed a space program that led us to the moon in less than ten years. Our recent home computer program is going to be bearing its fruits in the coming months, something many critics thought could not be done in such a short time. We have set about alleviating poverty and in less than ten years are on our way to victory.
>
> We are a strong nation, a nation of people who thrive on both cooperation and competitiveness. We will prevail in this latest crisis, my friends. And most important, we will also succeed in building a public transportation program that will be as successful as our highway program of the 1950s and 1960s. We will also pursue an energy policy that protects the bounties of our planet and an economic program that will create new jobs and new technologies to help us all live better lives.

Kennedy then introduced the nation to Assistant Interior Secretary Barry Commoner, who Kennedy now called the nation's "energy coordinator." The business press and even the union press almost immediately began to call him the "energy czar." Commoner, whom Kennedy appointed after strong recommendations from Interior Secretary Udall and Labor Secretary Reuther, announced that the nation was "more than capable of weaning ourselves from fossil fuels such as gasoline and oil. We can and will create ways to harness renewable energy such as the wind, water, and the sun for energy use in our daily lives. We will do what Americans are so good at already—combining the best of Mother Nature and human ingenuity." Commoner said that windmill construction, and the harnessing of the wind to create energy, would begin "in the lakes that stir the wind of 'the Windy City' of Chicago, just as the Dutch have recently rediscovered with their wind energy program."

Commoner also said that the United States would step up its support of research and development of public and private enterprises pursuing solar energy in California and Arizona and introduce solar energy programs in Texas and New Mexico. In the Pacific Northwest, Commoner called for more dams to be built—despite later grousing by some environmentalists that salmon and other fish were being adversely affected. The problem of the survival of the salmon would wait for another day . . . or decade.

Commoner said the key would be to create renewable energy, in the case of wind and solar, and easily recyclable energy, in the case of water. In a prediction that he said he was determined to make happen, Commoner said, "I predict we will see an electric motor vehicle within the next seven years."

It is said that when Henry Ford II, watching television that evening, heard Commoner promise an electric car, he shattered his martini glass with his hand and was splattered with a wet "dry martini" and several drops of his own blood.

As Commoner ended his speech, Kennedy, with the cameras still rolling, went over to Commoner, put his arm on the scientist's right shoulder and, to the camera, gave Americans a "power" fist sign. Kennedy then said, "America, we *will* prevail and we *will* improve our lives—and continue to be a beacon of hope to the world!"

Reuther, watching the speech on television with Yarborough in Reuther's office, said, "Thank God for the oil companies! If we didn't find a way to implement a program involving alternative fuels and public transportation soon, those environmentalists, who forget there's jobs in the smokestack industries they hate, could have split apart the whole damned Democratic Party! There'll be some grousing by both sides—labor and environmentalists—but we can handle that. New jobs for building windmills, solar . . . panels, is it? Well, whatever. It's jobs, man, first and foremost."

Yarborough replied, "Ah jus' don't lahk what the inflation's doin' to us already, 'specially if people don't pull together. Let's pray this isn't elixir for the Republicans in the midterm elections next month. Ah don't want 1974 to be the ye-ah the Republicans took back Congress!" Then, doing his best to convince himself, the vice president said, "People will pull together, though. Gotta trust in people, tha's all." Standing up to face Reuther, Yarborough continued, "That's 'cause the unions are strong enough to make that type o' commitment work. Ah'm shor glad Bob listened to us back in '69, aren't you, Walt?"

Reuther nodded and said, "That's for damned sure, Ralph. This could have been a real mess if unions were on their backs. Everyone running 'round without their heads and doin' stuff in a panic. That only plays into the oil companies' and businesses' hands. But, like you say, it still might come to that anyway."

The two old warhorses need not have worried. The president had rallied the nation, and when rallied, voters stick with the incumbents, who were the Democrats, by and large. In the 1974 midterm elections, the Democrats held on to their strong majorities in Congress, in state legislatures, and in governors' offices around the country.

Meanwhile, Ralph Nader and his forces, whom Reuther increasingly referred to in less than friendly terms because of Nader's support of what Reuther called "short-term environmentalist and consumerist positions over long-term labor positions," pressured the oil companies in a creative, "capitalist" manner. Nader convinced some unions and various activists, particularly wealthy environmentalists, to buy stock in the oil companies just as oil company stock prices went down after the passage of the excess oil profits tax. The new stockholders pressured the leaders at stockholder meetings to invest in alternative renewable sources in a joint venture with the government. Exxon President Wright survived a particularly difficult annual meeting, at which the unions and environmentalist groups almost seated two directors on the board who could have "disrupted the company's business"—in the opinions expressed in the *Wall Street Journal* and *Business Week* magazine.

After that stockholders meeting, Wright, concerned about Nader's ability to organize so effectively against him, met again with Kennedy at the White House, along with other oil company executives, including some of the independents. At the February 11, 1975 meeting, in which Reuther, Heller, and Yarborough took part, it was agreed that the oil companies would invest their profits in renewable energy in exchange for Kennedy removing the excess profits tax. A joint announcement at the White House, with the three leading oil company executives standing behind the president, made this official, although the repeal of the oil profits tax did not get signed for weeks thereafter because of grumbling in Congress.

The grumbling of some activists and most unions ended when, ironically, oil company stock prices went up and the activists and unions who had invested when prices were low made an excellent profit!

The administration wasn't done, however, since the oil crisis was also a diplomatic crisis. Secretary of State Chet Bowles, acting often within his own discretion Kennedy had given him, rightly earned credit with many historians for his efforts to undermine the OPEC cartel. Two weeks after Kennedy's and Commoner's speeches in October 1974, Bowles embarked on a foreign trip to certain member nations of OPEC. In a series of meetings over five weeks, Bowles tried but initially failed to "make a crack in the cartel's wall," as he told Kennedy on his initial return to Washington.

Bowles requested and immediately received support from Kennedy to offer significant foreign aid, in the hundreds of millions of dollars annually, to those nations of OPEC who would be willing to break the embargo. Bowles again embarked on his "shuttle diplomacy." However, rather than wading into the muck of Saudi Arabia or Iran, he started close to home with Mexico.

Bowles, in a public statement in Mexico, spoke of how a nation can improve its economic conditions by "a prudent use of its main resource," in Mexico's case, "its current cash crop of oil. A nation, however, must use its monies earned from its single cash crop to invest in its people and develop other resources, natural and man-made. And the United States is willing to help in this endeavor." But first, said Bowles, "Mexico must end its embargo of oil against the United States and the other nations of the world who are suffering from a lack of oil."

This speech, and the subsequent debate among the Mexican elite in that less than democratically run nation, had its intended effect, not merely in Mexico but also in another oil-producing nation in Latin America, namely Venezuela. In March 1975, Mexico, and later Venezuela, significantly increased oil output in contravention of OPEC. As economic historians have discussed elsewhere, this was the beginning of the end of the embargo. The effect of the embargo lasting as long as it did, however, was increased momentum in the United States in support of Kennedy's (and Commoner's) call to activism and innovation.

Once the embargo was broken by March 1975, Kennedy's energy crisis initiatives, plus drilling for oil in Alaska and off the coasts of Florida and Southern California, quickly began to limit America's reliance on foreign oil and avoided significant depletion of oil inside the continental landmass of the United States. The initiatives also created new, well-paying jobs in ocean oil drilling rigs, environmental clean-up for inevitable spills, new capital equipment, and new public transportation vehicles. This was in addition to jobs created while constructing fiber-optics networks, computers, software products, and the rise of the new cable television industry—from cabling to production to selling of cable services. This more than made up for job losses in the traditional "smokestack" industries that came about as companies invested in automated, "environmentally friendly" equipment, and people bought fewer cars and turned increasingly to public transportation.

Unions, which were able to enter the new industries under the watchful gaze of a friendly United States president, were able, with philanthropic grants and government help, of course, to pay for retraining of workers transitioning from what sociologists called the "old" economy to the "new" economy. This lessened the pain of unemployment for those workers in transition from the smokestack industries to the new industries. The profits that would have normally entered the pockets of the richest executives and investors, as they did in the first timeline during the period from the 1970s through the early twenty-first century, were dispersed throughout the nation's communities under President Robert Kennedy.

Within a year of the end of the oil embargo, car pooling and refurbished public transportation had gained great popularity among union workers and city workers. Public transportation lessened auto traffic and pollution in the largest metropolitan areas as much as any conservation or pollution-control plans. In Los Angeles and other parts of Southern California, it became trendy to ride the new sleek and environmentally "clean" buses—and to ride in "super trains" that went eighty miles an hour from San Diego to Orange County and through parts of south and west Los Angeles.

Because most of Orange County and San Diego had not built much in the way of roads and freeways in the early 1970s, it was easier to design and implement public transportation programs initiated by the joint private-public partnership. Ford's aerospace factory in Orange County immediately became a center for developing public transportation, with another plant built in east San Diego. Renault and American Motors also built plants in Orange County and San Diego. This, in turn, gave political cover for the largely "pro-business" politicians in that area to support public transportation. The car culture of Southern California found itself reverting to the pre–World War II era, when a car was for "joyriding," not for getting to work or going shopping. Housing developers responded by making sure new developments had easy access to trains and buses. Large, centrally-located malls were developed, as opposed to the smaller "strip" malls.

The embargo, however, while it lasted, did cause economic pain in the form of inflation and uncertainty among many Americans. It was a sad and rough Christmas season in 1974 when the embargo was still going strong and the Kennedy initiatives were still developing. President Kennedy, on Christmas Eve, read "The Night Before Christmas" in a televised fireside chat geared to coincide with a nationwide "Christmas energy conservation sleep-over party," which involved people lowering their thermostats and going to friends' or relatives' homes to keep warm together. After reading the poem, the president reminded Americans that "our spirit of joy, our spirit of giving, and our spirit of innovation and ingenuity are already carrying us through these difficult times. I have said it before and I will say it again: We will prevail and we will be stronger, healthier, and more successful together as Americans!"

As retailers noted in their next quarter's results, pre-Christmas shopping was weak, but the post-Christmas sales of goods were strong, thanks in large part, they said, to the president's inspirational leadership. It also helped that money from the short-lived oil profits tax and government monies began to trickle into the new programs for public transportation and renewable energy research and development.

In a post-speech meeting with the O Boys on Christmas Eve, 1974, Kennedy thanked them and the voters—"and Santa Claus!" he exclaimed—for keeping the Democrats firmly in control of both houses of Congress in the

1974 midterm elections. As Americans across the country fell asleep at their Christmas Eve slumber parties, Kennedy told the O Boys, "Fellas, the businesspeople are working with us, however reluctantly, because we convinced them that they were just as screwed by the oil companies as working people or consumers. Plus, they, including the oil companies, knew we could have listened to the more radical members in Congress calling for more regulation or nationalization of the oil companies—and maybe the car companies if they fought us on public transportation. Even Lee Iacocca"—the president of American Motors—"was first in line to soak up federal dollars in our public transportation program two months ago," Kennedy chuckled. Then, he added, "You know what Bob Lekachman, our chairman of the Council of Economic Advisers, said to me at our Christmas luncheon yesterday?"

The O Boys nodded as Kennedy continued, "He told me that in the old days, when workers were afraid to strike or when government didn't get involved in the way we have, it would seem 'natural' for workers' wages to go down or stagnate when there was a crisis in the economy. Lekachman says we're getting close to what he called the 'later Marx'—not the Marx of the *Communist Manifesto*—where we use the power of democracy and unions to keep profits flowing through the workers—the producers, he says—and the community. I don't really understand all that economics stuff, but it sorta makes me wonder."

O'Donnell shrugged his shoulders and said, "Let your biographers wonder—or better yet, let our opponents wonder and never figure out how to beat us. Mr. President, it's Christmas Eve and it's only 1974. You've got two more years here. Let's just hope we leave this place on January 19, 1977, without anymore damned crises, okay? Remember, sir, it's week to week—no grand plans!"

Kennedy looked at O'Donnell and said, "Yes, Kenny, I remember. I just thought I could think about posterity, you know, the big questions, at least a little—at least on Christmas Eve." After a contented sigh, Kennedy said, "I don't know how you guys feel about it, but I can't wait to watch *It's a Wonderful Life* tomorrow with Jimmy Stewart. I never realized until last year how much I love that movie!"

O'Brien just rolled his eyes, while O'Donnell shrugged his shoulders.

Kennedy smiled and said, "Well, O Boys, Merry Christmas! I've gotta help Ethel. We've got gifts to wrap for eleven children. Kathleen and Joe Jr. are helping us gift-wrap for the younger ones this year, so it's not as bad as prior years."

With that, the president and his advisers called it a night—and another year.

Chapter 36

CLOSING IN ON THE RAINBOW

The last couple of years of Robert Kennedy's administration were not merely about "gee whiz" technological advances. There were important policy battles to face and win and there was the toll of price inflation as fallout from the oil crisis. Inflation's toll on the American economy from October 1974 through March 1975 was a high one. Inflation during those months went as high as 14 percent and averaged 9 percent in 1974 and 5 percent in 1975.

For the first time in years, businesses added most of the inflation costs onto their products and services without granting wage increases. The unions had been quiet during the two years before the oil embargo, seeking no significant wage or benefit increases. As the Council of Economic Advisers wrote in a report in the summer of 1974, "A union culture initially seeks wage increases for workers, but eventually, there is a stabilizing factor or equilibrium that occurs. The culture becomes more community and institution oriented. This, in turn, puts downward pressure on management salary increases and makes it easier for management to convince workers to support the institution by not continually demanding wage increases." This report was a result of private-sector studies from Europe, where this pattern was first discerned.

The report, however, failed to take oil embargoes into account. Thus, the report's conclusion was somewhat undermined in the summer of 1975 when workers went on strike across the cities and towns of America. The workers, angry at the effects of inflation on their paychecks, wanted wage increases to keep up with the price inflation that was largely the result of the oil embargo. The Kennedy administration, knowing where it's "political bread was buttered," as Reuther put it, supported the strikers. Kennedy, through emissaries, "hinted" to the business leaders that the administration might impose wage and price controls if they attempted to pass further wage gains on to the cost of products and services. The strikers won again, of course, restoring workers' pocketbook "power" over inflation with productivity gains from the overall economy: and with the continued threat of price controls, corporations failed again to pass on the costs to the consumer, which meant no further money going into executives' pockets.[1]

Public Financing of Elections

Unions, as they continued to buy up newspapers and television stations after the success of the *Washington Star,* began to demand "clean" elections—meaning public financing of elections and free broadcast time on radio and television for candidates. As record numbers of workers became unionized, and as the unions' power to persuade increased through their media holdings, union leaders realized that taking private money out of elections was a better idea than trying to keep up with corporations in terms of campaign donations. When all the corporations' contributions were added together against all union contributions, corporations tended to outspend unions by a factor of ten to one.

As AFL-CIO President Doug Fraser explained to Reuther and Kennedy, "We're getting our workers out to vote, and we now have media holdings to explain our position without pro-business filters. Remember how newspapers used to have a 'Business' page that included little about workers and nothing about their views? Well, now, even in the corporate press, there's a 'Workers' page included in Business sections, and we have Workers' sections throughout our newspapers. With public financing and free broadcast time, we save money overall for other pursuits, such as organizing—and getting every rank-and-filer to the polling booth, where it really counts!"

Kennedy had his own reason to support clean money reforms. He was particularly incensed at corporate leaders who were behind the secret funding of the racist American Independent Party and the radical Peace and Freedom Party in 1972—the secret having leaked out, as do most secrets. As part of the "clean elections" campaign reform, Kennedy demanded that the identity of campaign contributors be made public, a position also endorsed by unions, but not corporations.

Campaign finance reform, by late 1973, became a top priority for Kennedy—more than child care, at least according to Ethel Kennedy in a frustrated conversation she had with Ruth Rosen. The campaign finance reform passed and signed into law in May 1974 required public financing of federal elections, including the presidential race starting in 1976, to give the government time to set up the system. The law also required television and radio stations to provide free broadcast time for candidates in any political party that had received 5 percent of the national vote in the previous election, with each party deciding itself as to which candidates would receive that broadcast time in each primary election. Finally, it required that all campaign contributions be reported to the attorney general's office within seven days from receipt of the contribution. In 1978, after the rise of electronic mail and the Internet, Congress shortened this disclosure requirement to forty-eight hours.

The law had attempted to limit private spending by every candidate but in 1975, the Supreme Court held that provision was unconstitutional on First

Amendment grounds. Even without the private spending limit, the clean election laws changed the culture of elections. Candidates receiving only public money invariably said that an opponent's "private, special interest" funding made the opponent beholden to those interests, while the publicly financed candidate claimed to be able to "freely speak" his or her mind without offending large contributors. This new campaign culture tended to favor pro-worker candidates because now the candidates had to worry about who could turn out the biggest vote count, not who had the biggest wallet to buy advertising. A pro-corporate candidate could not rely on corporate money without facing the charge that he or she was being "bought."

Some corporate leaders had, ironically, applauded the new law when it first passed. Henry Ford II said, "Well, at least we don't have to spend so much corporate money on campaign contributions. The politicians shut off their own wellspring this time!" By the end of the 1976 election, however, Ford was devastated at not being able to directly support preferred candidates for fear of tainting them. "In retrospect, the 1974 campaign finance reforms leveled the field a bit too much," he said during a speech to the Automotive Association convention.

Medicare for Everyone

In 1974, with Congress and the unions understanding for the first time the need for public financing of elections, President Kennedy finally broke through the action gap in seeking a national health insurance system. Traveling and speaking around the nation, Kennedy, Yarborough, Reuther, and other cabinet members worked with unions, religious groups, and other civic organizations to push Congress into passing a government-sponsored health insurance system. Just before Labor Day 1974, Kennedy signed into law a national health insurance program.

The law expanded Medicare from a national medical insurance program for seniors to a program that provided health insurance for every American citizen. The new law replaced private medical insurers. Under this system, every person had the choice of his or her own doctor. The national insurance program included a five-dollar co-payment for each medical provider visit, a twenty-five-dollar co-payment for every hospital visit, and a prescription drug benefit with the same co-payment as for a medical provider visit. Instead of private insurance company premium charges and deductibles, the national insurance plan was paid through payroll taxes—on a progressive rate basis with no limits, so that the top income earners paid more into the system than poorer and middle-class families. For those who lived off interest income and dividends—mostly "the truly rich," as opposed to the highest-paid income earners—the government charged an insurance premium based upon a percentage of annual realized capital gains.

The national health program provided coverage for all physical ailments, a limited number of mental health ailments, and long-term nursing care, preferably home care, which a study had shown to be cheaper and more effective than nursing home care. The original bill, as signed by the president, did not include birth control and abortion because these were deemed similar to "cosmetic surgery" or "elective coverage." However, after the Supreme Court decision in *Roe v. Bond*, 434 U.S. 238 (1976), which held it was a violation of equal protection to deny birth control and abortion benefits while giving maternity benefits to women, Congress and the president added these benefits.

The national health insurance plan also called for assisting local hospitals, nurses, and doctors with the creation of "district health panels." The citizen-led panels would decide what to pay for doctors' and nurses' services subject to the advice, but not consent, of separate advisory boards consisting of doctors, nurses, and hospital administrators. As Yarborough said at the time of the debate over the national health insurance plan, "We're settin' up a system where the best-paid people in the system will be the ones who deliver the services, meanin' the doctors and nurses. The accountants, marketahs, lawyahs, and executives of insurance companies eat up way too much money in the current system. This heah new system will cover *ev'r'one* and do it for the same amount o' money or less!"

The advisory boards also provided advice—not orders—for hospital equipment purchases and the allocation of funds to fight different diseases or medical problems in various communities. They helped create, with the unions and consumer groups, preventive-health programs focusing on nutrition, exercise, and other "natural" ways to prevent cancer, heart disease, and the like. This, in turn, created a consciousness that, culturally at least, "required" food manufacturers to create less sugary cereals, healthier but better-tasting foods, and vegetarian "meats" that tasted like meat—well, almost. A growing health-club sector employed more people in the service industries, and the unions added body-builders and aerobic exercisers to their ranks. Bob Bergland at the Agriculture Department worked with the Commerce Department to help private individuals and businesses set up farm and grocery cooperatives for organic, vegetarian, and other nutrition-oriented markets.

To secure the support of the American Medical Association for passage of the health care legislation (the AMA had long opposed any "socialized" medicine), the president accepted a compromise in which claims of medical malpractice would be resolved through binding, nonjury arbitrations. This was not much different, said Yarborough, from union arbitrations. Ralph Nader and the trial lawyers' lobby were infuriated by this compromise and at one point had a majority of Congress rejecting any limits on lawsuits for medical malpractice. Kennedy, in a press conference, however, said bluntly, "I will veto any legislation that does not protect doctors from nuisance lawsuits under a national medical plan."

The O Boys argued in vain that this would risk the entire proposal, but Kennedy stood firm. "I made a deal, guys. And the doctors have been, for the past thirty years, the biggest obstacle to national health care—next to the insurance companies, of course. Congress doesn't have the votes to override me—and if they want me to sign national health care this year, they better support Jimmy McDermott's amendment for medical malpractice arbitrations." Jim McDermott, a Democrat from Washington State, was a doctor and former navy officer who was serving his first term as a member of Congress.

Further upsetting Nader and the trial attorneys, the new national health insurance legislation allowed for significant reforms in the workers' compensation system because, under the plan, it no longer mattered whether an employee was hurt at home or at work. What remained was simply a disability system in each state to pay for those workers who were unable to return to work for periods of more than a few weeks at a time or permanently. Kennedy did, however, allow a compromise within the compromise: A worker who could prove a serious and willful violation of state or federal safety rules could sue his or her employer in an arbitration proceeding. If unionized, the employee would simply use the arbitration grievance procedures.

Employers were overjoyed at no longer having to worry about expensive workers' compensation premiums and the bureaucracy connected with them. Small employers were relieved at no longer having to worry about the possibility of losing competent employees to larger companies because they couldn't afford health care group plans. Large employers and unions were glad to not have to bother with the paperwork and hassle of covering employees' medical insurance. Doctors, who had been hiring more and more staff to handle all the different insurance forms, rejoiced that they needed only one person to handle a single type of form and could now hire nurses, not administrators. The only ones not happy, of course, were the insurance companies.

The Republicans in Congress had attempted to convince the public that no *public* health insurance plan was needed. The Republicans' alternative national health care plan called upon every employer to pay 75 percent of every employee's family health coverage, a plan that drew immediate opposition from the small business lobby. The plan included the same coverage as the Democratic Party's plan, but unlike the Democrats' proposal, the Republicans explicitly included birth control and abortion.[2]

As Kennedy remarked to Larry O'Brien on the day he signed the national health insurance legislation, "It's amazing what we can achieve when we Americans get over the fear of the word 'socialism,' isn't it?"

O'Brien said, "I don't know. It looks more to me like we just put together a coalition wide enough to do in the insurance companies."

The insurance companies, on the day President Kennedy signed the bill into law, sued the federal government. The basis of the insurers' suit was that Congress refused to pay the private insurers any "just" or "reasonable" compensation for the loss of their business. The failure of Congress to pay the insurers was claimed to be the equivalent to a "taking" of private property without "due process," in violation of the Fifth Amendment to the Constitution.

In an expedited hearing before the Supreme Court, the Court, in a 7-2 opinion, rejected the private insurers' challenge. The Court majority held the insurance companies were entitled to *zero* compensation since, as part of the hearings on national health care, "the industry executives themselves admitted that only a small percentage of their profits were made on providing medical insurance. Insurance companies earn their money primarily on real estate and other investments, not medical insurance premiums. One may say, as did one senator, that the insurers are really in the real estate business, not the business of providing medical insurance coverage." The fact that the government set up a national health insurance business and decreed that insurance companies could no longer be in the medical insurance business was not a "taking." The reason, said the majority court opinion, was that the companies were still free to be in other insurance lines and could continue to buy or sell real estate or other like investments.

The Court also held public policy concerns "militated against the petitioners" because of the "need for the new health care system to use tax monies to set up the new system, not pay old debts to still-solvent insurers." The Court admitted there was a Fifth Amendment "taking" of the business of private medical insurers, but that "just or due compensation" was, in this particular case, "zero." The Court did note, against the backdrop of the oil crisis that began during the oral arguments on the case, that the insurers' petition was "a unique one that might not be appropriate for use as precedent for other decisions in this area of the law."

The two dissenting justices, Stewart and White, believed that the case should have been remanded to the federal district court to determine a reasonable "eight-figure compensation" to cover one to two years' premiums for the insurers. In other aspects, however, the dissenters agreed with the findings of the Court's majority.

Pro-business and Republican legal analysts were outraged by this "act of judicial communism," as Yale Law School Professor Robert Bork called it. Democrats, many of whom figured the Court would find some amount of compensation was due, were equally surprised that their position of "no compensation" was completely upheld. They quickly and happily defended the Court's decision.

In an article appearing in the *Washington Star,* Harvard Law School Professor Laurence Tribe wrote, "The Court understood the practicality of avoiding a monetary crisis to add to the very large oil embargo crisis. The Court also recognized the reality that private insurers make their money in real estate, not premiums. The government's plan did not force them out of the real estate business, just the business of having to provide medical insurance, which if the experience of many is correct, they did not like to do anyway. As the government's national insurance plan has significant start-up costs, but much lower maintenance costs once the plans are in full operation (unlike private insurers, there is little overhead in lawyers, accountants, marketers, and executive salaries needed), the Court, in deferring to the legislature, decided that no compensation was 'just compensation' under these circumstances. It may not have been a constitutionally pretty decision, but it was consistent with earlier Fifth Amendment compensation cases and, again, practically speaking, a sound decision."[3]

Vouching for Child Care

A national child care program for working women in America had a much more difficult time passing Congress. Unlike medical care, which everyone needed at some point, most Americans at the time believed that only mothers who worked outside the home and had preschool children needed child care assistance. This made it difficult for Kennedy to pose the policy question as a universal program, as he had been able to do with national health insurance. The inflation of 1974–75 also eroded support for any new government program that involved more government spending.

The issue would not die, however, because both political parties faced no significant ideological argument against having a national child care program. Before 1972 one would have expected the Republicans to oppose such a program. But with the influx of feminists into the party since 1972, the Republicans also supported a government-based child care program. The difference between the Democrats and Republicans was over the type of program to pass as a law. The Republicans sought a program based upon federal tax vouchers or credits that would be used for privately-funded and operated child care facilities. The Democrats' proposals centered on joint state and federally subsidized child care programs run by local towns and cities.

Up through 1974, most Democratic Party plans assumed the program would be available only for working women, whether married or not, and for single fathers who, because of the death or incapacity of the mother, were raising children themselves. However, after legal analyses regarding the impact of the Equal Rights Amendment, the Kennedy administration became convinced that it was unconstitutional to limit the program in that manner because the Democrats' program was akin to a welfare program. Said the Justice Department analysis, there could be no discrimination between families with a mother working outside the home and those with stay-at-home moms. This undermined cost analyses for the Democrats, which not only kept the proposal bottled up in congressional committees, but also played into the hands of the Republicans who promoted the voucher plan.

The Republican plan already applied to all parents, regardless of sex, who chose to use a voucher for a privately or publicly funded child care facility.

The Republican plan provided that the vouchers would be redeemable for one taxpayer claiming underage dependents, whether the tax filing was separate or joint. The Justice Department, relying upon tax law, said this was not discriminatory since it applied equally to everyone. And since it only applied to pay for expenses of child care, it was not a welfare program—or a right of citizenship—in the sense that the Democratic Party plan was.

At one point, Republican Senator Roth mused about a "child-raising" voucher, available to any parent whether the child was being raised at home or at a child care facility. He quickly rejected this after realizing it would, under the guise of a voucher, wind up lowering, or negating, the taxes on all but the wealthiest Americans. Like most pro-business politicians, Roth believed the main point of railing against taxes was to lower wealthy Americans' taxes more than everyone else's taxes.[4]

With the oil embargo lighting the fire of inflation and the Democrats becoming nervous about passing two large government programs in one year, more and more Democrats began to sign on to the Republican plan. But then, to complicate matters further, a new foe appeared. A traditionalist—at least in name—religious group, led by the Reverend Pat Robertson, came to Washington to testify before Congress *against* all child care legislation. Senator Robert Byrd, Democrat of West Virginia, invited the Reverend Robertson as a courtesy to Robertson's father, a former U.S. senator from Virginia during the 1950s. What Byrd did not say was that he wanted to derail both the Republicans and Kennedy—particularly Kennedy, for not supporting him when he was dethroned from his position as senate majority whip in early 1974.

The Reverend Robertson stated, as part of his testimony, "This proposed legislation o' puttin' children inta gum'int-sponsored so-called chahld-cayah fas-ilities—that's true whether the fas-ilities are run by gum'int or prahv-atley—will create a *puhverse* incentive ta push children away from hearth an' home—an' their mommas. This legislation will eventually, an' you mahrk mah words on this, undah-mayan the *traditional* family struct-chuh."

Senator Hightower, Democrat of Texas, responded, "Which *traditional* family are you referrin' to, Reverend?"

"Ah'm talkin' 'bout a *family* that has a mothah, a fathah, an' the childr'n all livin' togethah in one house, Senator!"

"Well, sir," said Hightower, "that sorta family only came to us around the end of World War II, which is why it's been called the '*nuclear* family.' Back in the old, traditional days, we had a mom, dad, grandparents, aunts, uncles, and all sorts o' folks, includin' neighbors, takin' care o' the kids. An' for a lot of families today, well, they don't have those extra relatives around. An' they need this legislation to hold their families together, way Ah see it. From what Ah see, these child care facilities are gonna be locally run with limited federal safety guidelines, which is sometimes a lot bettah than leavin' a kid in some-one's house who may not be able ta always watch what's happenin'. But, Reverend, let me ask ya anothah question, though. Ya say these facilities will undermine the family. Tell me, suh, how come schools around the nation don't undermine families, but somehow a preschool child care facility does?"

"Well, Senator, unlahk religious schools, *public* schools do undermine the family with all their so-called 'modern science' tahlk—"

"Reverend, Ah hate to interrupt, but where do you get the idea Darwin's theory is gonna be taught to three-year-olds in the child care centers?"

After some applause by some in the Senate gallery, Senator McGovern banged his gavel and warned against any more "gallery outbursts." Robertson replied, with a stronger Southern accent than he had when he started his verbal jousting with Hightower, "Senatah, this is off mah subject heah, but let me say that it's un-fay-ar ta only let the *secu-lah* chil' care cen-ters have at this, without the religious ones gettin' vouchahs for takin' care o' childrin—Ah mean, the *true* religious organizations, though we'd let the Jewish folks in, too."

There was a small, discernable gasp from the Senate gallery at Robertson's remark.

Hightower, who had been sympathetic to allowing vouchers to be used for religious schools, now saw why he could not allow *any* religious organiza-tions to be included. "Reverend, that's awfully Christian of you to allow Jewish temples to offer child care services. The problem, if Ah heah ya"—Hightower, too, decided to emphasize his Southern-ness—"is that you don't want any of them Buddhists, Hindus, or Muslims in heah—though there's hardly any heah in the U.S. Now, Reverend, there is no way Ah can agree with you on God's green earth! But Ah think you and me—well, let's put it this way. We would not want to let parents give their vouchahs to Satanic child care centers, would we? Ah mean, they acknowledge God all raht, and they'll pr'b'ly even put that in the application! But they jus' wanna pray to the other fella with the pitchfork!"

There was much laughter in the gallery, and McGovern banged his chair-man's gavel hard. Hightower waited for the laughter to subside, saying, "If ya don't my-ind, Reverend, Ah'll jus' stick with the non-religious, public chil' care centers raht now, kinda lahk we do for public schools." He sat back for a moment, then leaned into his microphone to say, "No more questions, Mr. Chairman. Thank you, Reverend."

Hightower's Democratic Party–sponsored plan for a federally chartered and operated child care program failed to attract enough votes after heated debates in the spring of 1975. Seeing that the Republican plan had momen-tum, Kennedy gave the signal to Democrats to support the Republican voucher-based plan. That plan passed with at least fifteen Democratic sena-tors voting in favor, although other Democrats continued to oppose it, waiting for another chance in 1976. Over the howls of protest within his administration and from many other Democrats, President Kennedy signed the child care voucher bill into law on May 30, 1975. Kennedy said to Yarborough, who was most upset at the decision, "I know how you feel on this, Ralph. But I think this is the best we're going to do under the circumstances. I don't want to lose any opportunity to help women who are entering the workforce get child care while we keep up this argument that looks more and more theoretical to me."

Yarborough, who knew when to fight and when to withdraw, stood silent at first. Then he said, "Yes, Mr. President. Ah unda-stan'. We've got othah things to get done, don't we?" He flashed his patented smile, and Kennedy smiled back. The president and the vice president, who were closer than any such pair in modern American political history, knew they had been through too much to risk their relationship over one issue.

Under the new federal voucher law, every family or person who reported anywhere from one to three preschool children as dependents received a yearly voucher for up to seven hundred dollars. Qualifying taxpayers could redeem the vouchers at a privately operated but federally chartered child care facility. Those eligible for a negative income tax also received a voucher in the form of a subsidy from the government, and those within 200 percent of the poverty line received a partial subsidy—again, as Yarborough said, "to keep lower-workin'-class folks from hatin' people on welfare. Thank God the Democrats who sided with the Republicans made them put that in!"

As a result of the legislation, private child care businesses sprouted overnight. Many of them came out of unions that hastily converted portions of union halls into child care centers. Unions also worked with industry to create child care centers at the workplaces of the larger employers, who were willing to gain a new expense item now that they no longer had to worry about medical insurance expenses. The Kennedy administration, with support from Yarborough, ironically, allowed businesses to deduct the child care expenses from pre-tax income, a benefit for both business and workers. Yarborough liked it because, he said, "Havin' General Motors, Ford, IBM, U.S. Steel, and Alcoa working with the unions to create a nationwide child care program ain't much different than the gum'mint doin' it."

Catering to small businesses that established cooperative relationships with each other, smaller child care centers were founded by formerly "stay-at-home" mothers and middle-manager fathers who decided they might as well get paid to raise other people's children besides their own. In 1979, legislation was passed allowing vouchers for after-school programs for working parents.

The unions, at first reluctant to embrace women workers wholeheartedly, found that women became the most thoughtful and hard-line unionists because they understood the importance of maintaining the institution as if it were a family. "Damn!" said Reuther at a gathering of Democratic leaders in

Congress when the after-school program law was passed. "I think in about five to ten years, we're gonna have a lady as AFL-CIO president! Maybe even a U.S. president!"

"Amen to both, brother," said Barbara Mikulski, the petite but tough-looking freshman senator from Maryland. Everyone laughed, but some of the male senators' wives cheered, as if to make the point that they could do their husbands' jobs as well or better if the opportunity to run ever arose.

"Quedarse Con Casa," Workers of Mexico!

In 1973, Kennedy began to hear that union workers, both white and black, and even some Mexican Americans, were upset that California and Arizona employers were illegally bringing in workers from Mexico to work in agricultural fields and on construction sites. Kennedy, after conferring with the legendary Cesar Chavez and other union leaders, mounted a mul-tipronged response.

First, Kennedy supported an amendment to the immigration laws that called for civil and criminal penalties against any employer who knowingly hired an illegal immigrant. The law was specifically limited, however, to agri-cultural and construction work. Some rich Hollywood Democrats, a dwindling few by 1973, had successfully lobbied Kennedy to make sure they could keep their Mexican maids and servants—something Republicans needed no lobbying on at all. Business leaders knew the Kennedy adminis-tration would not hesitate to imprison an employer for breaking this law. This caused what Walter Reuther called the "well of illegals" to dry up almost immediately.[5]

Kennedy also personally met with Mexico's President Luis Echeverria Alvarez, a leftist, though non-Communist, leader. The Mexican president was presiding over something of an "economic boom" at the time, but was wor-ried about a "brain drain" due to higher American wages and benefits. He was happy to "help keep Mexicans in Mexico," as he put it. Kennedy said that, in return for increased U.S. assistance to Mexico in the form of public works projects, educational projects, and, he hoped, business-to-business development to create a consumer class in Mexico, Echeverria must crack down on the corruption that had long characterized Mexican government and business. This put the Mexican president in a difficult position because he was a leader among leaders in such corruption—it's how one got ahead in the ruling party that had ruled Mexico without interruption since the 1930s.

Echeverria, recognizing that a refusal to support Kennedy might leave him politically vulnerable to others who might want to "please Uncle Sam," turned to his friends in Mexican businesses and government and said, "We're going straight, amigos—or else." This precipitated an assassination attempt against Echeverria, who, in turn, declared martial law. To placate Secretary of State Bowles, Echeverria promised new elections in October 1974—a year from the declaration of martial law—and imprisoned most of his former comrades on corruption and conspiracy charges.

Testimony regarding Echeverria himself did not appear in any trials because the judges knew that might lead to the judges themselves joining the defendants in highly dangerous and horribly maintained Mexican prisons. While "cleaning house," as union papers in the United States put it (corporate papers called it "another example of Stalinist purges and showtrials"), Echeverria turned to formerly radical elements in the Mexican ruling political party who had long sought clean government and, admittedly, socialist economic reforms.[6]

The AFL-CIO sent many emissaries to Mexico to train and support independent labor unions, at first over the objections of Echeverria, but then with his reluctant support after pressure from the Kennedy administration. As Echeverria learned to make peace with the independent unions by supporting their demands for better wages and benefits from government-owned industries and the relatively small private industries, he also clearly saw the benefits to himself in creating a consumer-worker society in Mexico.

American dollars flowed into Mexico. First, it was government money. Then as large-scale enterprises, including oil fields, became more profitable in late 1974, U.S. businesses cut their own deals with the Mexican president to build factories in Mexico. Mexicans would thus manufacture products they would purchase themselves—as opposed to exporting products back to American consumers. Economic development resulted in cleaner, more pleasant towns and cities, and Mexico became a popular destination for American tourists. This was particularly so after Mexico became the first of the OPEC nations to break from the cartel and began selling oil to the United States. It was deemed almost patriotic to support a nation "that was willing to sell oil to America," in the words of union radio talk show host Larry King.

Echeverria was overwhelmingly reelected in October 1974, which surprised many U.S. pundits who, as usual, were not following foreign affairs very closely. In 1976, confident he had the people on his side, Echeverria freed many former political comrades, who, upon "rehabilitation," began to enter the new economic world in Mexico. Just as one could never keep American Confederate leaders out of the political and economic arena in the nineteenth century following the American Civil War, these formerly imprisoned politicians and business leaders began to return to positions of power. A little less arrogant after spending some time in jail, they were, nonetheless, very agile in following any ideological party line, whether capitalist, socialist, or whatever. What they understood, like the elite in any society, was the will to amass and wield power.

Chapter 37

THE SPIRIT OF '76

A s President Kennedy entered his last full year of office in 1976, the top
1 percent of Americans now owned "only" 17 percent of the wealth
(compared with more than 30 percent in the first timeline in 1974—
and more than 40 percent at the turn of the first timeline twenty-first
century). Kennedy knew he had not accomplished as much as he wanted, but
he believed he had accomplished enough to give meaning to what he and
most Americans believed was his brother's idealized legacy.

1970's Culture, Kennedy Style:
   People who hated the Kennedy-Yarborough version of the Democratic
Party tended to fall into the following categories: (1) businesspeople who
were not earning loads of money through direct government intervention,
and quite a few—though not a majority—who were tied into government
programs (the latter for ideological reasons); (2) radical feminists who were
against state intervention on everything except abortion rights and antidiscrimination laws for women and homosexuals; (3) Cold Warriors who were
angry at Kennedy for "surrendering" to third world Communists even
though the Cold War with China and Russia was essentially over by 1974;
and (4) small groups of mostly white hate-mongers who created storefront
and community churches to counter more tolerant and union-oriented mainstream churches. The "theology" of the storefront churches was a hate-based
version of "end times," in which minorities and homosexuals represented
Sodom and Gomorrah and the harbinger of the Apocalypse. These groups
would not have registered on the political screen at all except for certain corporate executives who funded them. In the words of Wal-Mart's Sam Walton
and Coors Beer magnate, Joe Coors, who helped fund such churches, "We'll
take our strikebreakers or allies as we find them."
   The FBI, with no Communist conspiracies to investigate, the Soviet Union
no longer in existence, and Communist China sifting through the wreckage
of its civil war, had to find a new "internal enemy." The storefront religious
"haters" became the new target. Liberals in the Kennedy administration, who
quickly forgot about the abuses of the 1950s' Red Scare now that they controlled the FBI, unleashed informants and wiretaps on these barely employed,
mostly unhappy people.

When one of the groups, in Mississippi, allegedly plotted to assassinate President Kennedy, the FBI swooped in, killing one of the "conspirators" and arresting three others. At the trial, despite evidence showing the FBI informant who infiltrated the group may have encouraged their actions, the conspirators were sentenced to forty years, essentially life, in jail. One of the convicted conspirators, Bobby Lee Cherry, was killed in prison by an African American already serving a life term for the murder of a former Black Panther in Philadelphia. To some liberals, that African American was seen as a "hero," prompting James Kilpatrick to ask, "Where is the compassion of liberals and their sense of the need for civil liberties? Have their economic views of a 'mob'-ocracy carried over into their view of criminal justice?"

I. F. Stone, responding in his twice weekly *Los Angeles Times* column, observed, "This must be the first time I ever heard Jim Kilpatrick feel sorry for someone killed in prison. I don't recall him being upset when William Remington was killed or complaining about the dozens of others who are killed in our prisons every year. For those who may be too young to remember, Remington was convicted on flimsy evidence of being a Communist during the Red Scare of the 1950s. In the case of Mr. Cherry, one must conclude that, yes, those liberals who cheered his death are not worthy of the name 'liberal.' On the other hand, one must also conclude that Mr. Kilpatrick suffers from selective outrage." Such are the timeless wars of competing political commentators . . .

As the 1970s unfolded, those who hated the Kennedy administration became more and more isolated while most leftist "Sixties" radicals reentered mainstream society. Most of the leftist radicals had stopped using illegal drugs and alcohol and had become active members of their churches, synagogues, unions, and consumer or environmental groups. Men who had been in college in the '60s, now not so young and with families, had long ago cut their long hair (some to crew cuts, but most to early "Beatles" hair length) and shaved their beards, except for an occasional mustache. Their girlfriends and wives wore knee-length skirts or the "new professional woman's" pants.

This back-to-the-middle-class trend, said *Chicago Tribune* columnist Andy Rooney, "was the institutionalization of the 'Clean for Gene' McCarthy campaign from 1968. How utterly disappointing that these radicals worry about their families, their communities, and getting home from work by 5 P.M.—just like their parents, whom they once derided as 'dull.' What happened to 'free love' and rural communes? Now these former hippies are bowling every Friday night. Some of them are even bowling with . . . their parents!"

The 1970s were different in Bobby Kennedy's America, with little in the way of sexual and drug excesses—except, of course, among the Hollywood set and the "Buffys" and "Brads" of the wealthy elite from Beverly Hills to Grosse Point to the Hamptons. Incendiary rhetoric still flared from the Left on a few college campuses, but it was mostly ridiculed in the face of so many causes and opportunities to join the Peace Corps, VISTA, or labor organizing drives.[1]

If anything, incendiary, adversarial rhetoric arose more often among Republican-oriented college-age activists. In the words of Newt Gingrich, a young Arizona Republican firebrand who was originally a college teacher assistant from Georgia, these college activists hated the "Commie unions" and the "Red nerds" who wanted to turn America into the "mush of a nanny state." The killing, some said "murder," of right-wing and racist collegians in 1969 and 1970, during the union organizing that began in the South, had cooled any further attempts by pro-business or right-wing students to commit violent acts. They believed Kennedy's administration would not hesitate to shoot first and ask questions later, even if Attorney General Ramsey Clark was seen as a civil libertarian.

A scholarly and therefore detached libertarian movement developed on the college campuses of America, funded by reactionaries such as Richard Mellon Scaife, Mrs. Eli Lilly, and various trust-fund children. These scholarly conservative radicals quoted Ayn Rand and preached for a revolution along the lines of *Atlas Shrugged,* Rand's novel about the "revolution" of rich, "industrious" people who stop working in the face of socialist encroachment. In the right-wing organization Young Americans for Freedom, much time was spent lamenting the loss of a "business-oriented discourse in America." These college-educated youth wore t-shirts that read, "Cal Coolidge for President," immortalizing the thirtieth U.S. president, who once was reported to have said, "The business of America is business."[2] The most radical members of the group wore t-shirts with a picture of Franklin D. Roosevelt—the thirty-second president, who started the New Deal of pro-worker legislation—with a blood red slash across his photograph. Underneath the photo was the statement of John Wilkes Booth after he shot President Lincoln in 1865: "Sic Sempre Tyrannis." Nobody dared wear such a shirt with Bob Kennedy's picture because that might result in an immediate FBI arrest, particularly after the arrest and conviction of Bobby Lee Cherry and his co-conspirators.

The college educated right-wing radicals were often not religious, and were sometimes bohemian in a 1950s sort of way. While this lifestyle resonated well on some elite college campuses, it did nothing but turn off middle-class voters. These radicals tended to support not only the freedom to get rich, but the freedom to enjoy "free" sex and support the decriminalization of drugs such as marijuana, cocaine, and even morphine and heroin. Mrs. Lilly, though not Richard Scaife, soon withdrew funds from such "extreme" libertarians.

Corporate radio stations, listening to these cultural radicals, attempted to promote disco music during the 1970s to increase the purchase of clothes and accessories and divert interest from "social agitation." With many Bed-Sty communities developing highly sophisticated educational programs teaching jazz and classical music, disco music failed to inspire much interest. Even Motown music of the 1960s began to be looked upon as "plantation" music no longer worthy of lavish praise. Instead, jazz, classical music, and "pure" African folk music became the staple of many blacks in the urban centers and thereafter became the base for influencing the styles of mainstream pop music.[3]

Jimi Hendrix died in 1970 of a drug overdose (as he did in the first timeline). Yet, because of his intricate guitar technique, his music, along with that of jazz innovator Miles Davis, became a bridge between jazz musicians and the growing genre of classical-jazz-rock fusion recorded by European rock bands such as King Crimson, The Yes, Emerson, Lake & Palmer, Gentle Giant, P.F.M., Jethro Tull, and Genesis—and American rock icon Frank Zappa.[4]

Soon, racially-integrated inner-city bands began playing in this genre, starting with Mahavishnu Orchestra and Parliament led by George Clinton. "Music theory and application, not silly dancing, is our motto," said Mahavishnu drummer, Billy Cobham, an African American. George Clinton would later join forces with Genesis' Peter Gabriel to promote the union of this genre with ballet and theater, a movement that expanded to become "world music," an amalgamation of European, Asian, and African sounds and rhythms.

Union- and public-owned radio stations offered their airwaves to this new fusion music in the cosmopolitan areas. In more rural areas, particularly in the Southeast and the Midwest, a mix of country and western/rock, both soft and hard, was heard, starting with musically proficient country rock bands such as The Allman Brothers and The Charlie Daniels Band. Black-based rhythm and blues in turn influenced these country-rockers. An artistic benefit to having very few commercials compared to the first timeline was that artists created longer musical pieces, something that American teenagers definitely appreciated and enjoyed.

Union and public stations enjoyed an inherent advantage over corporate rock stations throughout the nation because, in the case of public stations, there were no advertisements at all. At the union stations, the ads were few but were nearly always couched in the language of a public cause to appeal to union households—even corporate ads on union radio were phrased in this way. Pro-capitalist writers and activists were particularly incensed at the lack of solidarity shown by corporations who advertised on union-owned radio, much as, in the first timeline, left-wing writers and activists railed against those who compromised in a culture dominated by corporations.

Corporate radio attempted to limit the number of commercials played, but found they could not easily compete with their low-profit public and union counterparts. Rock critics in the new music magazines also had a field day attacking corporate radio for pushing disco music. "Who wants to listen to corporate-backed music that sounds like the commercials they run?" asked *Rolling Stone* music critic Greil Marcus in a 1974 article. He and the other rock critics spoke for many American teenagers and those in their early twenties at the time.

The river of consequences of saving Bobby Kennedy had reached very far indeed, though its dynamic waters found nooks and crannies all its own.

A Queer Sort of Politics:

In the 1970s, Republican and especially libertarian radicals found they were hopelessly divided about homosexuals. Republican and libertarians in the largest cities and suburbs were more often social liberals as well as hardcore libertarians. Thus, they were likely to support both radical feminists and homosexual rights. This was not the case for rural and suburban Republicans who lived in less culturally stimulated or diverse areas.

The Democratic Party, particularly President Kennedy, simply ignored homosexuals in public statements. There were, however, plenty of "gays"—the new term for male homosexuals—in the Democratic Party, not simply the Republican Party. Most of the Democratic Party homosexuals were "in the closet," though. Kennedy, calling homosexual rights the "third rail of Democratic Party politics," left it to the Republican Party to openly fight over it.

Kennedy's "don't tell" stance on gays was shattered, however, when the *New York Times,* fearful that Allard Lowenstein might run for the open Senate seat in New York State in 1976, broke the story that Lowenstein, who was married and had children, had had several homosexual relationships or encounters. The story, which was published in December 1975, had started through leaks given to—who else?—William Loeb's newspaper in Manchester, New Hampshire, and the Quayle chain of newspapers in Indiana and Arizona.

Lowenstein, after initially denying the story, decided to admit the truth of some of the particular allegations. He also revealed that he had been separated from his wife for the past sixteen months. Robert Kennedy was now forced to say something publicly, since he was close to Lowenstein. Taking advantage of his lame-duck status, Kennedy said his "old friend, Allard Lowenstein" was "still the same person he always was. Whatever complications may exist in Al Lowenstein's private life, he has always been a great supporter of freedom in our land. His work for many Americans of all races, creeds, and classes stands taller than that of nearly any other American."

Democratic pundits, particularly in the union media, reminded their audience that those Republicans who tried to take advantage of the "scandal" of Lowenstein's private affairs were essentially the same people who had initially defended former FBI leaders Hoover and Tolson, now seen by everyone as homosexuals. The Republican Party leadership, however, was in a bind because their party, since the 1972 Reagan campaign, had developed strong ties with homosexuals. Their more limited goal was to undermine morale in the Democratic Party and see if they could whip up antihomosexual feelings among some rank-and-file union workers. Thus, the Republicans were unable to fully capitalize on the scandal.

"If we can only figure out how to take the 'yahoo-prayer-meeting' element from the Democrats and get them to support Republican, pro-business policies," said an exasperated Senator Bob Dole at a private Republican issues conference at the time of the Lowenstein scandal.

Senator Barry Goldwater answered, "Those antihomo people want to pass *laws* against homos. How's that consistent with our message of limiting government and allowing private enterprise to flourish? Either you're a libertarian or you're a statist, my aides tell me. But I admit that some of them say maybe a law against discrimination against homos wouldn't be so bad—kinda like laws against discriminating against black people."

Dole replied, "Pushing that type of law doesn't get us anywhere, if you haven't noticed, Barry. I don't know, though. There's gotta be a way to square the political circle. If we can get enough of those working-class religious people on our side, the Democrats would start to feel the heat, I bet."

The two men shrugged their shoulders at each other as they watched the Lowenstein scandal unfold . . . and fade.

Just as the first-timeline Republican Party constantly searched out marginally qualified blacks, Latinos, Asians, and women who spouted pro-corporate agendas, leaving Democrats who endorsed civil rights—and affirmative action programs—sputtering, the Democratic Party, under Kennedy's leadership highlighted the hypocrisy of any Republican opposing any public official because of homosexuality—in this case, Al Lowenstein. On the other hand, those Democratic pundits who most enjoyed attacking "limp-wristed Republican policies" over the last three years were secretly happy when Lowenstein resigned from his position as the director of VISTA on January 7, 1976.

First Lady Ethel Kennedy, who had become a barometer for religious women across the land, spoke with Barbara Walters on an ABC-TV special just after Lowenstein's resignation. She told Walters that she had always admired Lowenstein for his intelligence, drive, and, most of all, his loyalty to her husband. The first lady also said, "Don't each of us, when we search our families, or at least our friends' families, know someone who is a homosexual?" Ethel didn't identify anyone in particular, but years later she told her biographer, Cokie Roberts—herself a daughter of former Representative Hale Boggs, Democrat of Louisiana—that she was thinking of Martin McKenally, a close family friend, who was a closeted homosexual. Everyone in Ethel's family had wanted Martin to marry one of Ethel's sisters, Georgeann, during the 1950s and early 1960s, before they knew he was "hopelessly" homosexual.

Ethel also said in the interview with Walters, "Isn't life too short to hate people who are homosexual? I am not endorsing homosexual conduct by any means when I say that. But I think, especially over these past few weeks, that those of us who are Catholic, or whose religion teaches us not to be homosexual, ought to begin a dialogue about this subject among our families and our friends in private. We need to find out within our families how we love the sinner, but not the sin. I don't claim to have the answers. Bob and I have begun to discuss it, however painful it is to discuss. I can't speak for Bob on this, I don't think, but I think it is important that we in America solve this problem within our families first. This is about private conduct, not the color of one's skin—though if someone is kept from having a job because of private conduct—that doesn't hurt anyone, I mean—well, that seems wrong to me, too."

Nancy Reagan, watching Ethel on television that night, exclaimed, "I can't believe they crucified you, Ronnie, for saying the same thing four years ago! I despise that sanctimonious woman! I should say the *B* word, but I won't!"

Ronald Reagan, ever smiling, patted his wife's hand and said, "Don't be so harsh, now, Mommy. We had a good run, didn't we?" Reagan, after losing the election, had become a newspaper columnist, but found his columns less and less in demand, particularly after the Soviet Union fell. In 1976, he became the host of a game show called "The Match Game" and became a popular "speaking host" at various ceremonies around the nation and eventually the world.

Ethel, meanwhile, refused to talk about homosexuality any further in public. The media buried the story. Pundits, in a mantra from Democrat to Republican, agreed with the first lady, saying, "It shouldn't be discussed publicly. We should be discussing this among our families."

Ever the curmudgeon, journalist Nicholas von Hoffman mischievously remarked to one of his few Kennedy administration sources, "Don't be deluded into thinking we in the press are really listening to 'Fertile Myrtle Ethel' on this one. The reason the press doesn't want to talk about this is that our publishers and editors know too many homosexuals among their own set. Joe Alsop comes most easily to mind. And separate from the pundits, there's the president's former partner in Red-baiting, Roy Cohn. Now there's one really sick and corrupt homo. . . . I'm surprised Bobby Kennedy's people haven't gone after that little faggot, especially for the way he outmaneuvered Bobby with Joe McCarthy oh so many years ago! Anyway, the editors and publishers know all too well that fairy-hunting could easily get out of control if we start talking about who's just happy and who's really gay . . . "

Curmudgeons are usually on target, and this was no exception. It was a fact that most editors, publishers, and corporate media were concerned with protecting homosexuals among their own set. Therefore, most editors and publishers refused to follow up on a rumor that Kennedy had had a homosexual encounter with Rudolf Nureyev.[5]

As for Lowenstein, after leaving government service, he founded a non-profit program through the AFL-CIO designed to promote understanding for workers who are "gay, straight, or not quite sure." As Lowenstein said, "No matter what we do in private, we are all still working people dedicated to a greater and more prosperous America."

Lowenstein, in what some initially called a "suicide" move, ran for the open U.S. Senate seat in New Jersey in 1978. The incumbent, a liberal and pro-union Republican named Clifford Case, accepted the position of chancellor at Rutgers University, the State University of New Jersey, and did not stand for reelection. Lowenstein, surprising nearly every political observer, defeated Republican Bill Bradley, a former New York Knickerbockers basketball player and Rhodes scholar, in a very close race in 1978. While some pointed to the Lowenstein political organization as "second to none," others pointed to Bradley's elitist, pro-business positions with regard to economics and his dull performance during his debate with Lowenstein as dooming his candidacy.

During the debate, Lowenstein was seen as "scrappy" and dressed in his usual, "barely un-disheveled" suit. He spoke "as if he were a truck driver spouting 'poils' of wisdom," said Daniel Schorr in a post-debate commentary. Bradley's political consultant, Richard Morris, said after the election that Bradley lost because he refused to attack Lowenstein's homosexuality "to draw votes from Neanderthal union rank-and-filers." Morris, in a not-for-attribution quote given to the *New York Times* after the election, said that Bradley "lacked the killer instinct of a politician. Even if he won, he'd have compromised himself into oblivion." Bradley left politics for good, deciding instead to become an executive with the New York Knickerbockers basketball team. His second wife, a young culturally liberal Republican, the former Hillary Rodham, eventually ran, and lost, a Congressional race in New York State.

As for the homosexuals themselves, a very different trajectory developed compared with the first timeline. Although some homosexuals, mostly younger Republicans, descended into the "community" of bathhouses, drug abusers, and nightclubs featuring disco music—a community that exalted rampant sexual adventure and reckless behavior—many Republican and Democratic gays rejected that path.

In the RFK timeline, there were far fewer "disco queens" and more monogamous homosexuals, owing in part to different cultural trends and to the influence of Lowenstein's political activities. As a result, most homosexuals avoided the devastation of the spread of the disease known as Acquired Immune Deficiency Syndrome (AIDS), the disease that, in the United States, was concentrated among the mostly male homosexual community during the first timeline's 1980s and 1990s. Although many Democratic senators and members of Congress were too nervous to vote for gay marriage in the RFK timeline's 1970s and 1980s, such legislation eventually passed before the end of the twentieth century.

In other matters related to sex and death, the pro–death penalty and antiabortion constitutional amendments both failed to gain the requisite support by 1976 and were removed from active consideration. The death penalty amendment passed in twenty-nine states but failed to reach the requisite number, which was thirty-eight. The amendment stalled as juries became used to sending murderers to prison for life without parole—a stopgap measure passed by all fifty states in the wake of the anti–death penalty Supreme Court decision. Business leaders and union groups who analyzed the amendment decided that sending someone to the death chamber, particularly with the added procedural safeguards identified in the proposed amendment, was too expensive and, therefore, not worth pursuing.

The antiabortion constitutional amendment passed in only twenty-two states. No matter what polling data suggested, it appeared that, in the silence and privacy of the voting booths, women decided that three months to secure an abortion was enough time to deal with something they hoped didn't happen to them, but left the option open if it did.

Also undermining the antiabortion movement was the fact that the number of abortions declined dramatically to levels consistent with those in Western European nations that also had national health insurance, child care, and laws protecting women from employment discrimination. While women recognized the benefits of oral contraception, they also found that with well-employed husbands, they could decide to keep that "surprise" baby even if they were working. "That's what child care is for, isn't it?" said Ruth Rosen in an editorial in the October 1976 issue of *Mother Worker* magazine. Rosen, however, also said publicly what women said privately or to themselves in the cloistered voting booth: We want a safe abortion when we need it.

First Lady Ethel Kennedy was not to be bothered with such subtleties that she called hypocrisy. She continued to rail in public about the need to stop abortions, at least from a cultural, not political, position. This was her compromise with her husband, who demanded she not lead the battle for a constitutional amendment banning abortion.[6]

Despite her compromise, Ethel was angry that the amendment failed. The day the amendment was formally withdrawn for failure to achieve passage in enough states, Ethel said to her husband, with no small amount of sarcastic frustration, "Well, Mr. President, at least there are 'only' seventy thousand babies killed every year in our country rather than millions, as we initially thought. Heck, it's almost as low as the number of people killed in traffic accidents, something you care more about, I've noticed."

Her husband did not point out to Ethel that, although fifty thousand automobile-related deaths occurred annually during the 1960s and through part of his first term as president, the number of people killed in traffic accidents was significantly declining through the 1970s. Auto-related deaths were down to twenty-four thousand in 1975. This decline was related to the sharp increase in the use of public transportation, mandatory air bags and seat belts in passenger vehicles, and the lowering of speed limits during the energy crisis to fifty miles per hour maximum—sixty miles per hour in practice! The husband did not tell the wife any of these things. He was just happy to have kept morally complicated issues—the death penalty, homosexuality, and abortion—out of the political arena and closeted in the backdrop of American culture.

Chapter 38

YARBOROUGH STEPS FORWARD

Yarborough Steps Up to the Plate

Yarborough, to the surprise of nobody except the unknown fools who ran against him in the Democratic Party's election primary, became the Democratic Party's nominee for president in 1976. Yarborough had Kennedy's complete and unqualified approval, both publicly and privately. Yarborough selected Julian Bond, the popular health, education, and welfare secretary, as his vice presidential running mate. In 1976, picking a black man as vice president was a first for a major political party, but most observers did not consider Bond to be a risky choice.

Yarborough and Bond spoke to white, black, and Latino audiences, together and separately, with an economic populism that overcame most, but certainly not all, racist feelings remaining within some white workers. Historians have, in fact, rarely focused on Bond's status as a black man. Most historians have, instead, largely seen the election of 1976, in the words of one, as "one big patriotic circus, mostly staged by the Democrats."

The Democrats had a lot to be proud of that year, particularly because it coincided with the celebration of the two-hundredth anniversary of the signing of the Declaration of Independence. Some pro-business ideologues grumbled about the "sheer luck" of Democrats to run on their successes in that year, to quote the words of Princeton economist Alan Greenspan. The United States, under Kennedy-Yarborough, had weathered and defeated Communism and OPEC. The administration had also held back inflation, with gasoline prices hovered around forty cents a gallon through 1975 and 1976. Government taxes kept the price steady in order to increase the use of public transportation and ride-sharing in private vehicles. Kennedy had made taking public transportation a patriotic act during the oil crisis, and this carried through as more and more workers became involved in the development of public transit throughout the nation.

The public transit project, the research and development of solar and wind energy, and the computer industry produced economic growth that eclipsed that of the 1960s. As a result of the expansion of Medicare health insurance for all Americans, poor, single mothers no longer had to fear that getting remarried (or married) would result in losing formerly poor person's government paid health benefits. Thus, marriage rates rose to their highest levels in decades while divorce rates fell from previous 1960s' highs. Most important to Kennedy and his advisers, the poverty rate was down to 3 percent. Such a poverty rate was simply unheard of in the previous one hundred and twenty years—essentially since the rise of the modern corporation in the late nineteenth century.

Union membership in the U.S. workforce stood at about 45 percent in 1976, also a record in the nation, with nonunion workers receiving the benefit of excellent pay and other benefits from union-fearing employers. The distribution of wealth was more equal than it had been since the dawn of the industrial age, with the top 1 percent owning just over 14 percent of the wealth and the top 10 percent owning 28 percent.

Yarborough and Bond deftly melded the patriotic themes of the bicentennial celebration into the Democrats' economically populist platform. They quoted the Declaration of Independence's reference to "life, liberty, and the pursuit of happiness." However, unlike most Republican or extreme capitalist politicians, the Democrats emphasized the next sentence, which said: "That to secure these rights, Governments are instituted among Men, deriving their just powers by the consent of the governed."

Bond, and eventually Yarborough, would add "and women" after the part about "men" at public speeches around the country. Feminism had become a powerful force among unions and the Democrats, a development that suited both Yarborough and Bond "jus' fine," as Yarborough said. "Women organize bettah than men when they put their my-inds to it!"

Yarborough and Bond were seen at nearly every governmental bicentennial celebration across the nation. Republicans screamed, to no avail, that the celebrations were Democratic Party rallies in disguise, but this backfired as "Joe Six-Pack" union radio and television commentators branded the mostly libertarian critics as "loving international capitalism more than their own country." The libertarians often fell into this rhetorical trap when they constantly claimed that the government was the "enemy" or at least a "problem" they wished to "solve."

Yarborough and Bond easily defeated their Republican counterparts, Lowell Weicker and Robert Dole, in the presidential election of 1976. The Republicans thought they had a winning coalition based upon Weicker's so-called "moderate" libertarianism, coupled with more military spending for military contractors, and, with Kansas Senator Dole, a promise of additional farm subsidies for farmers and ranchers in the Midwest and Far West. Weicker had been the head of the Republican Leadership Council designed to "moderate" the culturally liberal fringes in the Republican Party on issues such as sex and drugs. Weicker was from a wealthy New England family and was known as highly principled, a maverick, or an arrogant jerk—depending upon whether you loved, liked or hated him.

Weicker chose Dole as his vice presidential running mate to win some votes from World War II veterans, who might be impressed by his war hero persona, and to secure support in the Midwest. As in the first timeline, Dole was asked to play the hard-line role against the "socialist" policies of the Democrats, but he was perceived by commentators, and eventually the public, as "too mean" during the vice presidential debate.

After the election, political analysts concluded that Weicker was simply a "bad luck" candidate regardless of Dole's public persona. Every time Weicker came up with something that might seem politically astute, it backfired. At one point in the campaign, for example, Weicker said that he'd like to consider the Republican freshman from Illinois, Congressman Jesse Jackson (who ran and won on a pro-business "black capitalism" platform in 1974) to be the first black secretary of state. Weicker had said this to appeal to black business leaders, who were feeling great pressure to endorse Yarborough-Bond. Union newspapers, and even some of the corporate papers, harrumphed that this was "racial pandering."

When Weicker called for ending the monopoly for the computer industry, "to unleash the wonders of free enterprise," as he said, business leaders in the computer industry, happy to be receiving government support, began to wonder whether it might be better if Weicker lost. Weicker repeated his theme of unleashing the "spirit of free enterprise" for other industries, including the airline industry. He intoned at a speech in California late in the campaign, "Airfares will be lower, the skies will be safer, competition more robust, and the profits greater in a deregulated airline industry!"

When Weicker called for deregulating the trucking industry, he became an eternal enemy of the Teamsters, who, for the first time in many decades, endorsed a Democrat for president—even though it was the Democrats, under Bob Kennedy, who had put their union into a trusteeship amid charges of Mob corruption. As the new Teamsters' president said, "Yarborough is pro-union—and he's not Bob Kennedy."

When Weicker called for the increased use of antitrust laws to break up the phone company into competing companies, he ran afoul of the Fortune 500 CEOs who noted, ironically, that at least "Pinko Yarborough" had little use for antitrust legislation. Yarborough had indeed supported private joint ventures with the government that often included companies that were supposed to be competitors. Yarborough added to this belief when he told a gathering of top CEOs at a Wall Street meeting that he personally preferred large enterprises because they responded better to union representation and, with economies of scale, were able to pay better wages "up and down the line."

Weicker's belief that antitrust proceedings would break up "sleeping giants" and "fuel the fire of innovation" pleased the Ayn Rand followers in the Young Americans for Freedom, economics and philosophy majors at the elite colleges, and capitalist-theory supporters in cafés who could recite Milton

Friedman as if he were a poet or a prophet, not an economist. However, such sentiments scared many sophisticated business leaders as they realized that such a change could set off too much instability, even if it gave businesses the ability to limit the power of "those damned unions," as David Rockefeller told fellow members of the Trilateral Commission. The Trilateral Commission was an organization Rockefeller helped form in 1973 to combat the creeping socialism and third world peasant lovers in the Kennedy administration.[1]

Weicker, flailing against the patriotic blanket in which Yarborough and Bond wrapped themselves, eventually threw away his original political game plan of not saying anything too "extreme" in favor of capitalism. "A 'me, too' strategy isn't going to work," he said to his skeptical campaign consultants after he began his new strategy of talking straight to the voters. Many post-election analysts, who are nothing if not a herd, said the problem with Weicker's strategy was that he mistook the excitement of speaking to and meeting with already converted crowds, particularly right-wing college activists, for the rest of America.

On the other hand, it is somewhat unfair to blame only Weicker for how he ran his campaign. There was also the pro-Republican experiment with so-called attack ads. Roger Ailes, hired directly by antienvironmentalist cattle ranchers, Southern textile merchant Roger Milliken, and Western beer maker Joseph Coors, created independently-funded attack ads designed to bring down Yarborough and Bond. These ads backfired, however, in a world of public financing of political campaigns. Most television and print pundits, including pro-corporate pundits who were more worried about being "consistent and fair" to gain the respect of a mostly working-class audience of Americans, denounced the coalition of "radical businessmen" for trying to "propagandize" and "corrupt" the electoral process with "personal attacks" against candidates. This echo chamber of denunciation convinced most Americans to also denounce the ads.

Ailes railed in an interview with the *Wall Street Journal* on October 22, 1976, "There's a double standard at work here. We're attacked for exposing unpleasant truths about the policies of Yarborough and Bond, but nobody attacks those candidates for wrapping themselves in the American flag to make it look like their opponents are less patriotic than they are. The union-backed media are particularly biased in this regard, yet their slogan is 'We report, you decide!' And, worse, most of the pro-business pundits—not the *Journal,* at least—act like a bunch of little nannies. They'd rather be 'pure' than win!"

Ailes, as usual, turned his clients' defeat into a personal gain when he landed a spot on the editorial page of the *Wall Street Journal* after the failed Weicker election campaign.[2]

Yarborough-Bond won a clean electoral victory with more than 57 percent of the vote, although voter participation dipped slightly to just below 80 percent. The Peace and Freedom Party won just 2 percent as a result of the strong flavor of economic populism in the Yarborough-Bond campaign. The American Independent Party received less than 1 percent, most of it coming in Mississippi and Utah, for reasons that were different for each state. The Republican Party ticket of Weicker-Dole finished with just over 40 percent of the vote overall.

There was not a great deal of celebrating among Democrats on the night of the election, however. As CBS national correspondent Dan Rather told news anchor Roger Mudd, "There are no coattails for Yarborough-Bond tonight." Rather's view was echoed throughout the media in the days following the election. For the Democrats in Congress, there were no net gains whatsoever, and the same held true for the state legislatures' and the governors' chairs. As Yarborough lamented to his longtime friend and former aide, Senator Jim Hightower, "An election based upon 'hip-hip-hooray,' which Ah admit Ah supported, does tend to favor incumbents. But we still got a majority, so let's get movin'!"

Yarborough Swings a Big Bat

In the weeks leading to Ralph Yarborough's inauguration, pundits speculated that the president-elect would deliver an inaugural speech that focused on the working family's interests and domestic policy issues. They were mostly wrong. Yes, it was true that Yarborough said America would continue to grow and prosper, and that "the men and women in unions and in the workplace are our greatest asset." But as most pundits said after the speech, forgetting their earlier and incorrect prognostications, Yarborough's inauguration theme was broader in scale than merely domestic concerns. Said the thirty-eighth president of the United States:

> Now that we have helped to greatly reduce poverty in our great land, it is tahm we began to fully implement a program of promoting justice, not merely charity, abroad. It is remarkable that our Peace Corps' workers have helped so many communities and villages, in country after country, promote healthy livin', irrigation, and dam projects and programs in education, and the delivery of medical services. But this is not enough if we are goin' to live in a world as safe for all o' humanity as it is for us heah in the U-nited States o' America, God's gift to the world!

With his Southern accent having faded a bit from his years in D.C. and especially on the road around the nation, Yarborough quoted a Brazilian priest who said, "'When Ah feed the poor, they call me a saint. When Ah ask why the poor are hungry, they call me a communist.' That priest is right, America! And we must make fightin' hunger and pestilence around the world *our* priority so that nobody has to be called a communist for wantin' to help people. Leave the bad stuff to the Communists, whoevah believes that point o' view anymore."

Yarborough ended his speech, shorter than Robert Kennedy's first Inaugural Address, saying, "The ancient Hebrew rabbis said, among many othah things, 'Justice, justice, shall you pursue.' Ah promise every American that we will continue to pursue justice heah in the USA, but we will also pursue 'justice, justice,'—sayin' the word twice as did the rabbis to emphasize our commitment—justice, Ah say, here and abroad, not simply charity. We will not jus' feed fish to the poorer folks in this world, as perhaps the greatest prophet, Jesus, once said. We are going to teach the world *how* to fish, ag'in lahk the prophet said. Ah thank you all very much for listenin', but now, it's tahm to get to work!"

It was, for many Americans, an eerie moment as Yarborough spoke while Robert Kennedy sat in his seat on the platform, watching with a passive serenity on his face. Some commentators thought they detected a look of relief on the face of now former First Lady Ethel Kennedy as she listened to Yarborough's address to the nation and the world. Ethel had told many intimates of her desire to leave what she called "the target of the limelight." From June 4, 1968, to January 20, 1977, the day of President Yarborough's inauguration, Robert Kennedy had survived two assassination attempts and four death threats. Each time, except for the Mississippi "conspirators," the assassins were cranky loners. The assassins each claimed a cause, whether it was the Middle East, communism, white rights, capitalism, environmentalism, or whatever, left them "no choice" but to seek to assassinate the president.

As if to test Bob Kennedy's gallows' humor about nobody wanting to assassinate his vice president, Ralph Yarborough just missed getting killed by a deranged former Charles Manson devotee, Squeaky Fromme, in October 1975, while Yarborough was visiting San Francisco. Fromme, who came within a couple feet of Yarborough before firing her gun and missing, had, in the first timeline, tried unsuccessfully to kill President Gerald Ford from close range as well. Manson devotees loved to think they were acting "politically," but they were simply murderous flakes and even more on the fringes in the RFK timeline than in the first timeline.

At the start of Robert Kennedy's last year in office, he made a personal campaign promise to his wife. He promised Ethel that, in the spring of 1977, he would take her and the family on a long, leisurely trip to southern France and Italy. When the time came, he kept his promise. Before beginning the trip abroad, Kennedy asked the leading magazine and newspaper publishers to give his family some "much needed private time" and "let others in the political world, whether Democrats or Republicans, have a chance to speak and act on behalf of our nation." The media, which, in any timeline can decide whether it wants to cover something, or someone, obeyed the wishes of the now former president. Kennedy simply disappeared from the news except for an article here and there, a television item in the local news, or a stray Web site news report.

In preparing for his departure from the world's stage, Kennedy refused to present a deeply philosophical farewell address to Congress. He went to the Capitol but surprised nearly everyone with a relatively short statement. Kennedy said he had spoken enough of his vision over the years and delivered enough speeches to "last past my grandchildren's lifetime." He did say that, of all his speeches, the ones that would remain most clear in his mind were his first Inaugural Address in 1969, his speech in the summer of 1968 at the Berlin Wall, and, "perhaps surprising many of you, a speech I delivered in March 1968. It was about the Gross National Product and what it tells us about America—and what it doesn't tell us about our country. I was going to redeliver that speech here today, but I thought, let the historians and journalists read it and see if they find it as compelling as I think it was—and is."

From that point, Kennedy used his appearance before Congress to thank the many members "who helped guide this nation through the crises and challenges over the years" and "made us stronger, more united, and more prosperous than any nation in the history of man—I mean, *human*kind. My daughter Kathleen reminds me all the time that it isn't just men around here!"

Kennedy then thanked each of the cabinet members who had served with him over his two terms, singling out Chester Bowles as "the greatest secretary of state since John Quincy Adams" and Walter Reuther as "the greatest labor secretary ever." He said, in closing, that "nobody comes better prepared to lead this nation than Vice President Ralph Yarborough. Ralph is one of the truly great Americans who knows how to lead and who loves his country as a *true* patriot. I know you'll work well with him over these next several years." He then turned around and shook hands with the speaker of the house and Vice President Yarborough, who were in their respective seats behind the lectern at the House of Representatives.

Television networks portrayed the president as a gallant warrior leaving the stage of world affairs. Daniel Schorr, anchor for the Union Broadcasting Network, summed it up this way:

"The once sandy brown hair of the president has turned mostly gray. Robert Kennedy, well clear of his late brothers' shadows, and casting his own taller and wider shadow, speaks with an aura of wisdom that seems to come from someone twice his just-over-fifty years. He appears beyond our time, as well as of it, almost as Lincoln did in the last year of his presidency. When Robert Kennedy began his tenure as president just eight years ago, he was already beginning to resolve a conflict in Vietnam that seemed without end. This son of an upper-class capitalist and schemer quickly ended our nation's involvement in that divisive war, and, surprising most observers, immediately embarked on a series of policies designed to increase labor union membership in the South and elsewhere in our nation. He also moved, less surprisingly but very successfully, to increase the scope of societal protections in a way not seen since the days of Franklin Delano Roosevelt.

"In eight years, President Kennedy's foreign policy, based upon a hard but practical idealism, helped bring about the demise of the Soviet Union and caused Red China to implode within its own Communist contradictions. During this time, President Kennedy, and his able Secretary of State, Chester Bowles, nurtured a variety of nations, such as Vietnam and El Salvador, into viable democracies, and helped exotic lands, such as Afghanistan, where the king nurtured a constitutional democracy modeled on Great Britain.[3] President Kennedy leaves office with an economy that is organized for the working classes of America in a way some founders might have applauded, but others might well have been horrified by. He has, as did Lincoln, remade the nation in his and his brother Jack's image."

Walter Cronkite, speaking as a commentator in one of his last broadcasts with the CBS network (he had just agreed to lead the public broadcasting network), slightly changed his usual nightly sign-off of "And that's the way it is." After Kennedy's farewell speech, he said, "And that's the way Robert Francis Kennedy has essentially ended his tenure as president of our nation: with grace, goodwill, and a strength of character that will be missed."

In the weeks leading to Yarborough's inauguration, the whispers among many of the Washington elite were that Yarborough was merely a folksy politician who would never compare to the grandeur of President Robert F. Kennedy. These permanent villagers of the nation's capital expected Yarborough to fail, and some rooted for him to fail. It wasn't so much their politics or ideology as much as it was their petty, gossipy, elitist ways.

This same elite had despised Truman for his rustic ways. They detested Nixon in every timeline for his middle-class sensibilities. And first-timeline President William J. Clinton also suffered the slings and arrows of the elite Washingtonians for not having tasteful extramarital relationships, unlike so many of the permanent Washington establishment. When Clinton's taste in various women was exposed, the villagers were so embarrassed that they simply wished Clinton would go away. Clinton's dogged tenacity did earn back some of this lost respect, but never enough to allow him to stay in the village after his presidency was over.

In short, Yarborough had his work cut out for him, a fact he knew better than the villagers who ran the permanent bureaucracy in and around the seat of the federal government. "Ah don't care whether they lahk me," he told his wife, Opal. "Ah only care whether we get our legislation passed. That's what Lyndon Johnson understood—and Bob Kennedy learned to understand more than his brother Jack."

Part III:

POST-BOB

Chapter 39

YARBOROUGH HITS TO
DEEP LEFT FIELD

The first subsection of the American elite to be surprised at Yarborough's effectiveness were those business leaders who held their breath and voted for him. These particular individuals expected Yarborough to work with business supporters after the campaign was over. Although he did work with them with regard to government contracts, his populist instincts remained strong. These business leaders soon learned to regret not taking a chance with the maverick Weicker.

Yarborough's first substantive post-election proposal was to pass "a truly progressive tax" system with a 100 percent confiscatory tax on personal income above the margin of five hundred thousand dollars. This was not limited to wages. It included "income from whatever source derived," which included interest income, dividends, gifts, and the like. As the new president said, "Makin' over five hundred thousand dollars a yee-ah, you're already makin' more than the othah ninety-nine and nine-tenths taxpayers. When people ask me, 'Well, where d'ya draw the line on who's rich enough?' Ah can only say, if ya can't draw it at less than one-tenth of one percent of the entire society, then ya can't be serious about the poor distribution of money in our country!"

As his vice president, Julian Bond, rhetorically asked on *Meet the Press*, "Why should a single corporate executive make more than the president, who makes 'only' two hundred thousand dollars a year? The president is still allowing that anomaly between a corporate executive and the leader of the Free World, but has decided, in a spirit of compromise, to draw the line at five hundred thousand. And remember, we're not saying we plan to take money out of a rich man's pocket and put it in another person's pocket. This maximum wage is designed to create a society where the differences between top and bottom are not horribly skewed and where the excess monies produced in any given enterprise are used to benefit everyone in the community."

Responding to the concerns raised by the Hollywood and music industry people, where one could starve for years and then make ten million dollars in one year, Yarborough said, "Undah our proposal, if any of us strikes it rich, the excess over five hundred thousand can be spread over more than one yeah, up to twenty years, jus' like those lucky few who win the Publishers

Clearinghouse contest. And really, bein' a big-shot Hollywood star or a rock an' roll star is kinda lahk winnin' a lottery, ain't it? Remembah, whether you're a rich singer or a poor movie director, we have good wages for most Americans, a strong national health insurance program, child care, and public transit systems. People don' need to have an infinite amount o' money on an individual basis lahk they used to, ain't that raht?"

At first, many Democrats were afraid to pursue this proposal, thinking it was too radical. Speaker of the House Tip O'Neill initially told reporters that Yarborough's plan was "dead on arrival," largely because, amidst all the patriotic hoopla, Yarborough had not been specific in his proposal during the campaign. The closest Yarborough had come to pushing such a policy was while he was speaking at a union hall in Ohio. There, he said he wanted to put a "a big tax on the wealthiest income makers—you know who Ah mean, those international plutocrats living on interest and dividends!"

If O'Neill didn't believe the plan could be passed even in a Democratic Congress, the Republicans were taking no chances. Republicans tried to immediately derail the plan, but not by fighting on the wrong side of the class war. Instead they used a strategy thought up by Senator Bob Dole. Dole held a press conference at which he said Yarborough's plan exempted corporations. "Now why is the president going to punish real human beings, who already pay a load of taxes in this simplified system, but not corporations?"

The strategy worked initially, as Americans immediately asked themselves the same question. But Yarborough took that argument on in his usual direct manner. He explained at his own press conference that "corporations need profits to invest in equipment and stuff for their companies. What's that coupon-clipper, livin' off dividends, doin' with his money? Ah have no beef with private corporations makin' some profit that they reinvest in their businesses. They pay 40 percent of total taxes already, as Senator Dole usually tells us when he's not fightin' for the plutocrat coupon-clippers. Heck, he must think Ah'm a socialist or sum'thin'. Ah'm not. Ah'm just an 'merican wantin' some balance o' liberty and equality." He smiled when saying that last sentence.

Yarborough's response was effective, but it also caused Democrats in Congress to tighten the plan away from the loophole of rich people incorporating themselves to avoid the maximum wage tax. The tax proposal was therefore amended to apply to individuals, professional corporations (such as those formed by doctors, lawyers, accountants, and the like), and to closely held corporations that did not produce "a reasonably identifiable" product or service. The tax lawyers licked their chops at that deliciously ambiguous phrase, said a tax attorney on Senator Roth's staff.

Meanwhile, Yarborough and Bond hit the airwaves to promote their proposal. Soon the echo chamber of talk shows on the increasingly pro-union media "talked up" the proposal. Out of Flint, Michigan, a new, young, pro-union radio and Internet host named Michael Moore told his listeners over and over again, "Don't let those plutocrats get away with not paying their fair share! No self-respecting American should fight against this bill! Even after it passes, you still have the right to earn more than 99 percent of us! Anyone calling that socialism is smoking more than your lawn! Am I right, folks—or am I right?"

The tax reform soon "gained not only feet but wings," said Secretary of the Treasury Robert Lekachman. Within less than three months, the Democratic Party–dominated Congress passed the bill and Yarborough proudly signed it into law. However, by the time the bill hit Yarborough's desk, the 100 percent marginal rate started at the level of one million dollars in annual income, not five hundred thousand. In return for that compromise, Yarborough demanded and received in the bill a new wealth tax for those whose possessions were valued at more than one million dollars.

On the day the bill became law, the *Wall Street Journal* editorialized that the rich should emigrate, or at least find ways to shelter money outside the country. But Yarborough was "fast on the draw," as Senator Jim Hightower put it. He clamped down, through the Federal Reserve Bank, with regulations designed to limit the amount of money one could take from the country, and ordered the U.S. Navy to begin military exercises in the corrupt, so-called tax havens such as the Bahamas and the Cayman Islands. Like first-timeline presidents dealing with "rogue" nations such as Cuba, the Dominican Republic, Grenada, and Nicaragua from the 1960s through the 1980s, Yarborough found a little naval threat went a long way when the target was small, vulnerable, anti-American nations.

The United States succeeded in exposing many a bank account in those tax havens after the naval exercises and a little "public diplomacy," as Yarborough's new secretary of state, Robert Span Browne, called it.[1] The Bahamas and the Cayman Islands soon found they could no longer stash money for wealthy individuals and criminals as effectively as they had in the past. The government's in-house experts in computer and encryption cracking, many of whom had gained expertise during the Kennedy build-up of the civilian computer industry, were extremely valuable in limiting the rise of other tax havens.

The *Journal* had also suggested bankers and wealthy business leaders invest monies in Singapore or Indonesia, but again, U.S. military "exercises" in that region of the world put pressure on those nations to avoid becoming tax-dodging or "rogue nations," as Senator George McGovern put it in hearings on the subject. The United States also directly provided grants to Singapore and Indonesia, which reduced their incentive to run afoul of U.S. tax laws.

Various American trust fund "babies," meaning adults who lived off trust fund investments, decided to form "cooperative investment" corporations in an attempt to evade the tax law's income limits by turning income into "perks" such as cars, boats, and the like. In working hard to make sure they acted as a legitimate business, the cooperative corporations quickly turned into homegrown investment banking houses, with many of the trust fund babies taking an active role in their operation. This development prompted John Kenneth Galbraith to quip to his friend William F. Buckley Jr., "Well, Bill, one of the many salutary effects of this legislation is that it finally got some of your lazier trust fund babies off their asses to work at better sheltering their money! When you think about it, the negative income tax got poor women off welfare, and Yarborough's income limits law got trust fund babies off 'mater and pater' welfare!" Buckley, a trust fund baby who was nonetheless a hard-working writer, was not amused at Galbraith's remark.

As part of Yarborough's overall labor and macroeconomic policy, his administration strengthened the International Labor Organization, an organization older than the United Nations. Yarborough and Browne pushed for all nations to sign its charter supporting strong labor union organizing rights, the right to decent wages and benefits, and a limited program for sharing the wealth among workers and farmers within each nation. Yarborough's goal was nothing short of a more equal level of development within poorer nations, as opposed to allowing international financiers, corporate leaders and the military to reap most of the profits of any economic growth or expansion.

As the U.S. government continued to reap revenue benefits from the technology revolution—a balanced budget was passed in fiscal year 1977—the Yarborough administration increased foreign aid. For fiscal year 1978, for the first time since the mid-1950s, the United States spent as much on foreign aid as any nation in Europe based upon a percentage of gross national product.

Secretary of State Browne, in a speech before the World Affairs Council in Los Angeles, said the United States would concentrate on providing economic aid to Latin America, Africa, and South Asia, areas of the world that Browne said "have been, until very recently, neglected by those of us in the West except as places to export military weapons."

Yarborough's most interesting decision in his first year of office was his successful push to have Michael Harrington replace Robert McNamara as the head of the U.S.-dominated World Bank. Harrington was a known "democratic socialist," a phrase not considered as contradictory in the RFK timeline as in the first one. Harrington, a middle-class child of a teacher and a lawyer, proved to be very effective in his dealings with business leaders. He combined a rationalist, linear way of thinking with a moral fervor developed during the 1950s while working with Dorothy Day and the Catholic Worker movement. McNamara did not feel his work was "completed" and silently bristled at Yarborough's lobbying for Harrington to replace him. However, ever the dutiful soldier, McNamara resigned his office after being offered the opportunity to run Harvard University, a position he held until his death some thirty years later.

Harrington, in one of his first acts as World Bank president, convinced Yarborough to demand, with hints of otherwise passing new federal regulations or laws, that U.S. banks write off third world debts. The debt-forgiveness idea was called the Jubilee Program, after the debt cancellation celebrations common among certain religious groups in ancient societies. As one banker admitted to *Business Week* magazine, "We made more money on our balance sheets after writing off the old debt than waiting forever hoping to get a portion of that debt paid back. With so few tax shelters open to us, we figured it was the best way to go." Such are the rationalizations of accounting and taxation in nearly every timeline.

Harrington thereafter began cultivating a working relationship with large corporations and banks. He listened to their concerns about the bottom line, and he reminded them that to make money, they, too, had to "take some risks." They soon began calling Harrington "an honorary capitalist" as a form of wary affection.

With union prodding, Secretary of Labor Reuther—he stayed on to work with Yarborough rather than retire—convinced U.S. automobile makers and steel makers to expand operations to these poor countries, backed with U.S. government guarantees, of course. The point was to build cars for consumption in those countries, not merely assemble cars for export back to America.

Editorials in the *Wall Street Journal, Business Week, Fortune,* and especially *Forbes* magazine proclaimed their outrage at the actions of U.S. business leaders. The editor of *Forbes,* Malcolm Forbes, thundered, "How dare the bankers and industrialists go along with their own demise and invest, along with the government, in nations who can't even spell f-r-e-e m-a-r-k-e-t, let alone understand one?" After that outburst, his magazine faced a deluge of canceled subscriptions. Forbes, frustrated by the "lack of courage on the part of business leaders to stand up to American home-grown socialists," turned the magazine over to his son, Steven, whom David Rockefeller recalled as being "rather dull." The senior Forbes then voluntarily "came out of the closet" as a homosexual and, with his latest young boyfriend, decided to take his yacht, the *Highlander,* around the world.

Henry Ford II did not miss, or care much about, Malcolm Forbes. At an exclusive party at the Grosse Pointe Country Club in Michigan shortly after Malcolm Forbes resigned from *Forbes* magazine, Henry Ford II said, "What practical businessmen always understand, even if capitalist ideologues—especially the queer ones—do not, is that businessmen simply want to know what the rules are for making money and operating their businesses. We don't really care what the laws are in any place or whether there is a dictator in place or not—truth be told. And we only care whether the laws are applied across the board against our competitors and not just our company. On the other hand, if we can get away with changing laws to promote our interests in profit making, all the better. We'll take—and take and take—what we can and where we can. But the way the system is in our country, and now around the world, we just play by the rules that govern us—most of the time, of course." That last remark was accompanied by a wink to an attractive young woman standing nearby.

Thus, the bankers and large corporations increased their investment in third world nations, which investments they saw as safe because the government was also investing money alongside them—and provided significant though not full guarantees. As John Quincy Adams, Alexander Hamilton, and other early American leaders always knew—but most early-twenty-first-century first-timeline leaders did not—building a nation's infrastructure is a key element for economic progress, and it is most often accomplished with government organizing the development, not through haphazard business investments.

Corporations continued to be interested in hiring Peace Corps veterans because of their "natural business savvy in getting things done under difficult circumstances," as Exxon's CEO told *Fortune* magazine. Such veterans continued to find their way into corporations as liaisons between the home corporate office and the foreign factories and offices in many countries. The Peace Corps veterans helped to create an institutional understanding inside corporations for joint public-private partnerships and investments in local communities. The Peace Corps vets themselves also found it was "okay" to want to make a profit on long-term investments. As General Motors vice president and former Peace Corps director Rennie Davis said in a speech to that company's stockholders, "In my younger, purist, but rustic days as Peace Corps director, and certainly before that during the Vietnam War, my friends and I often disparaged making any profit as if it was something evil. Now we know better and are proud to work in corporations or in government where we know we can act on our best principles, at least at most times."

Surprising most pro-business economists, American corporate dividends went up in the first eighteen months of the Yarborough administration. With no need to pay corporate leaders anything above one million dollars, the new maximum income law kept many executives' compensation in the four-hundred-thousand to five-hundred-thousand-dollar range. As a consequence of limiting bonuses and other perks—the latter often counted as compensation, but not always—there was more than enough money left to pay out more dividends to stockholders.

Yarborough was disappointed that the government was not gaining much in direct revenue under his new tax reform. However, as Treasury Secretary Lekachman explained, "We get the money indirectly through taxes on dividends. More importantly, our nation gains because the money is filtered through public and private investments that are broad-based. Remember, Mr. President, our goal was limiting the massive amounts of dollars that flowed into a few people's pockets. And we succeeded. Also, there's something else I noticed after talking with Secretary Reuther. It seems the corporate executives took no increase in pay this year. The executives used this fact to argue—successfully, Reuther admitted—that workers' wages should also not go up. I hate to say it, but having a maximum income is a good anti-inflationary device. It forces business executives to think institutionally. They don't fall into a spiral of desire, if I may wax poetic, trying to make unlimited money for themselves, as in the Gilded Age of the nineteenth century."

Yarborough was somewhat comforted by Lekachman's remarks. Like every president since Johnson, Yarborough feared the word "inflation" more than just about any other word when it came to domestic policy—although he would have added that he feared the word "unemployment" more.

Unions, meanwhile, were expanding their horizons in a world that was friendly to their growth. Realizing their political and economic power, and with a revitalized leadership that understood what 1930s' radical unionists had understood, they now went beyond mere bread-and-butter concerns. Thinking long-term, they sent young union members who showed "promise" to attend labor-management schools, or what used to be called "business schools." The point, said AFL-CIO leader Doug Fraser, would be to teach the world of high finance and business understanding to young men and women who would be the labor leaders of tomorrow, "even if we lose a few to management." Unions, said Fraser, "recognize that the continuation of institutions, once they are geared toward fairness and equality, is the most important priority we can pursue."

The "business schools" themselves changed their curriculum, not merely their name. Out went simplistic views of cost cutting through labor cutbacks and in came courses that stressed the need to understand the continual interplay between government and business; the importance of developing poor neighborhoods, villages, and nations; and the benefits of investing in equipment that would be ecologically sensitive and productive.

The rebirth of internally led union apprenticeships also increased union efficiency and institutional concern. The unions were able to fund these programs with the wealth they gained from their media holdings, the savings they realized as a result of publicly financed elections, and the increased dues from their expanding membership. In an essay in *Time* magazine, Peter Drucker noted that this was a "win-win" for business because business no longer had to pay for training costs in a variety of industries, especially the new computer industries. (What he did not note, because it only showed up in the first timeline, was that corporations did not have to hire expensive training managers, in-house labor lawyers, and human resources managers in a world of functioning labor unions. Such human training and management of workers was performed directly and more efficiently by union liaisons known as "business agents" and by the unions themselves.)

When these developments were added together with the union's stock purchases through the Employee Stock Ownership Program, a more cooperative, as opposed to confrontational, union culture began to develop within American society. Management and labor still had their fights when contracts were being renewed, but the overall focus of the relationship between labor executives and management executives was on balancing worker rights and institutional needs.

However, increasing criticism came from consumer groups, led by Ralph Nader, who believed that "whether they are union led or corporate led, companies produce too many defective products that injure too many people." In 1978, President Yarborough, with support from labor and business interests, signed a law that stated that any product approved by the Consumer Product Safety Commission (CPSC) could not be challenged in a civil suit, but only through the commission's arbitration program. This was designed to limit conflicting decisions among the fifty states, said Yarborough. To appease Naderites, who opposed the bill as a giveaway to companies that undermined the rights of injured litigants, Yarborough selected Mark Green, an original "Nader raider," as the new chairman of the CPSC. Green was a Connecticut congressman who had resigned his seat to run unsuccessfully for the Senate in 1976.

The development of poorer countries ironically, but not surprisingly contributed to some environmental degradation as the decade of the 1970s came to a close. Interior Secretary Barry Commoner, following his president's lead, tried to limit such degradation by emphasizing small-farm ownership in third world nations after land reform programs were implemented; the use of biodegradable chemicals except in rare cases (Africa proved to need DDT, for example, in fighting a malaria outbreak in 1978); the construction of public transportation systems; and the manufacture of high-tech products for use in emerging post-agricultural societies. Medical schools, established through the Peace Corps, and other professional schools helped stimulate what Secretary of State Browne called "the brain remain"—as opposed to the "brain drain" that had started in third world nations during the 1960s, but had stopped during Bob Kennedy's second term and Yarborough's presidency.

Some of the destruction of the rain forest in South America and other natural wonders was avoided thanks to more ecologically sensitive approaches to development, along with high-tech innovations, medical advances, land reform, and cooperation among U.S. and European governments and institutions such as the ILO, the World Bank, and the International Monetary Fund. Progress in preserving the environment was not as significant as many would have hoped, however. There was still a significant "stink" of air and water pollution that seemed to be an inevitable corollary of the development of modern civilization, much to some environmentalists' dismay.

The rise of business opportunities for U.S. corporations abroad, designed to create local consumers in those poorer nations, kept American workers supportive of international trade efforts. Michael Harrington, as president of the World Bank, ordered a systematic change in first world lending practices to third world nations. Instead of forcing a third world country to develop a single "cash" crop or holding down wages to provide foreign investment for exporting products, Harrington worked with developing nations to create a diverse set of industries and services in a domestic oriented—not export oriented—economy. In a speech to the United Nations, Harrington called this policy a marriage of Alexander Hamilton and Karl Marx. He said that once a nation established its own infrastructure and economy for its citizens, it could then look to take part in a global economy where there was more equality among the trading partners.

Harrington also refuted a favorite theory of capitalist economists known as "comparative advantage" where it was posited that one nation was "naturally" suited to produce this or that product or service. As a more mature Marx or, again, Alexander Hamilton understood, *social forces as developed through government policies* played a significant role in a nation's comparative "advantage." Harrington concluded that the goal of public policy should be to create more positive "human-made" consequences.

Harrington supported nations developing a national medical insurance program, state ownership of utilities (electricity, gas, oil, water), public transportation, and child care. He even supported state ownership of a nation's most important commodity, whether it was coffee, steel, diamonds, or other natural resources. Other than that, as long as workers had the right to organize, Harrington believed local and international businesses could invest and develop independently or with government subsidies, on an as-needed basis. He also, by his conduct, and in rare private conversations, issued an ultimatum to existing and would-be dictators: Open your political system or face isolation—or replacement when we of the civilized world support a revolution against you. Some dubbed Harrington's position the "TINA" principle: There Is No Alternative.

As Secretary of State Browne quipped to the retired State Department consultant George Kennan, "Dictators are far more worried that Harrington and President Yarborough mean what they say—even more than they did with John Foster Dulles under Eisenhower. Who would have thought *that?*"

Kennan, however, replied with a wary smile, "Yes, Mr. Secretary, that does seem somewhat surprising. Mr. Dulles, however, was not an interventionist in many ways. For example, he was what some called an 'apologist' for the Japanese warlords and Hitler during the 1930s—and he and his brother, Allen, opposed our entry into World War II until after Pearl Harbor. As secretary of state under President Eisenhower in the 1950s, Mr. Dulles refused to help Hungarian revolutionaries against the Soviet Union because, if he valued anything, he valued stability—even over democracy, despite his statements and speeches that opposed Communism. On the other hand, I worry somewhat that Mr. Harrington may not be as respecting of elite interests as he should be. Elite people often reach the top of a society for a good reason, and we need to keep that in mind lest we become mired in constantly seeking perfect utopias—which create more instability than we can ever imagine."

Browne rubbed his chin and thought, Kennan may be right. But he said, "George, that's certainly food for thought, but Michael seems to be doing well so far."

Kennan's wary smile returned, and he said, "So far, at least."

Certain university-based Marxists, especially in foreign universities in the very nations Harrington sought to help, thought Harrington was too solicitous of business interests and of the local elite. They viciously derided him as a "bourgeois" FDR-era New Dealer more than a true Marxist or socialist. Harrington laughed and said at a public forum in Kenya in 1979, "I am often glad to receive the opprobrium of Marxist professors. For those who believe such armchair radicals hurt our cause, however, let me say in response: If there is no Left, there is no progress. If there is no progress, there is only a fight among the forces of reaction, whether in the military, in the corporate world, or, yes, even among certain reactionary religious clerics who have stood in the way of progress in terms of pluralism and tolerance. Without an active Left, any one of these forces of reaction could hijack the pain of peasants and of workers for their own reactionary and often violent ends."

In an interview in *The Nation* magazine just before his death from cancer in 1998, Harrington said he had never felt as energized as when he ran the World Bank from 1977 through 1989.[2]

With American corporations building and selling products abroad and, as with the Marshall Plan in Europe after World War II, more money finding its way back to the United States, Yarborough now had the excuse to push for what he had always wanted for American workers: a reduction in the number of mandatory hours in a workweek.

At the beginning of the twentieth century, workers worked twelve-hour days and six-day weeks at a minimum—a workday and -week deemed "natural" by the economists and elite of the day. Through state and federal legislation, the workweek was reduced over the decades following 1900 to eight hours a day for five days a week. Starting in the late 1960s, economists and sociologists debated when the workweek would be further reduced. In 1979, Yarborough, acting in concert with socialist governments in Europe, especially France, called for instituting the thirty-two-hour workweek. After a couple of hearings and very little debate—most large businesses were doing well enough that they could not easily justify being against it—Congress approved the bill and Yarborough signed it into law. The law provided for a mandatory thirty-two-hour workweek, with 90 percent of the pay that workers had earned during the forty-hour week. Overtime would begin on the thirty-third hour as opposed to the forty-first hour. Business executives sucked in their breath—small businesses screamed in rank frustration—and the culture began to adapt to the change.

For women who worked outside the home and who wanted to spend more time with their children, the change was most welcome. *Mother Worker* magazine named Yarborough its "Person of the Year" in 1979, the first man to receive the award in the seven-year history of the magazine.

Efficiencies inside business increased as managers had to figure out how to make sure the work done in forty hours could be done in thirty-two. As usual, this simply meant less time at the water cooler for employees. When some employees complained to the unions, union leaders, under "suggestions" (read "orders") from Yarborough and Reuther, answered, "That's the price of progress, folks. Let's make sure we get our work done, and you can enjoy yourself afterward!"

As business consultant Robert Townsend said in a column he wrote for *Business Week* dated November 10, 1979, "Who better than the unions to enforce discipline and efficiency in order to make sure the four-day work-week will succeed?"

The technological advances in computers during the late 1970s also allowed for businesses to invest, with tax deductions still in place, in new computer equipment that allowed more work to be done in less time. In this timeline, the culture of strong unions and businesses were able to focus on the goal of getting more work done in less time, as opposed to business leaders unilaterally pushing fewer workers to work longer hours. The now legally mandated three-day weekend ironically produced more business—at least for businesses dealing with leisure. Certain businesses, mostly smaller ones such as organic and health food restaurants and health spas, expanded their work forces to meet the demand for "healthy living," "leisure," and "fun."

Nonetheless, Republicans and capitalist intellectuals tried to convince Americans that the new four-day week led to the failure of many small businesses. But most mainstream economists, after studying the matter, said it was doubtful whether the cut in hours had any true adverse effect on the rate of small business failures because previous studies over many decades had shown small businesses mostly fail within two years of their startup.

With regard to national environmental policy, despite carping from environmentalists that Yarborough was more pro-labor than pro-environment, windmills and solar panels popped up throughout the Southwest and even in the Midwest. By 1978, energy costs were drastically reduced, which led public utility commissions to begin to order cuts in regulated utilities' charges to consumers. Use of public transportation, which increasingly relied on electricity for trains and subways, created significant oil gluts. The Yarborough administration angered the Nader forces, who wanted a rollback of gas taxes and prices—a position that put Nadarities in concert with business. Yarborough said, "We will not go back to being dependent on fossil fuels by allowing oil prices to drop through the floor." He added he was surprised Nader would support big business instead of environmentalists and consumers on such a proposition. Republicans gained a few seats in 1978 as a result of the calls for cutting gasoline taxes. Yarborough, in a bow to the oil industry after the 1978 midterm elections, instead allowed for massive mergers of oil companies, independents as well as a couple of the majors.

With the four-day week and stable gas and oil prices, traffic snarled on the weekends for those who worshipped their cars. Most other people, however, serenely watched the traffic while sitting in luxurious air-conditioned trains or buses riding to the mountains, the lakes, or the beach.

The first electric vehicles, developed with an international (essentially Japanese, French, and American) joint venture of auto companies, rolled off the assembly lines in 1979. They could travel distances of only seventy-five miles at a maximum speed of forty-five miles per hour, which some experts believed would limit their sales. However, electric cars made sense, given a federally mandated speed limit of fifty miles per hour, the development of public transportation, and a commercial environment characterized by a few centrally located shopping centers as opposed to widely scattered strip malls. It didn't hurt that the government gave consumers a tax credit of one thousand dollars to purchase the vehicles—on top of the government helping to subsidize the costs of production. As the president of Toyota said (and as Henry Ford II reluctantly agreed), "Private industry could not have made these electric vehicles this quickly without government subsidies and encouragement."

With the U.S. government giving more subsidies to solar and wind power later that year during the oil embargo, private utilities limited and then abandoned their development of nuclear power plants in the United States. The environmentalists in both the Republican and Democratic parties convinced the utility companies that Americans, particularly in the Southwest, would strongly resist such plants as being too dangerous. Reports of higher infant mortality rates around nuclear plants killed off whatever enthusiasm remained.[3]   On the other hand, Interior Secretary Commoner continued to expand some coal mining operations by providing "environmental waivers," which in turn outraged environmentalists from Denis Hayes, who was still close to the Democratic Party, to David McTaggart, heading Greenpeace, the international environmental activist group.

In 1980, the Department of Interior announced that it had harnessed enough solar power during the summer months in Maine—one of the coldest places in the country—to meet half that state's winter heating needs. Government money and research, combined with the efforts of heavily regulated private-sector utilities, spurred this development. Fear of another oil embargo was a motivating factor, and the initiative was also helped by the availability of funds freed from costly nuclear development and maintenance plans. The success of the solar energy program lowered home heating costs in the Northeast to levels not seen for fifty years.

During Yarborough's first term, a couple of other notable events took place:

Yarborough nominated the first woman Supreme Court justice in 1979 when Thurgood Marshall, the first black American to sit on the Supreme Court, announced his retirement. Said Marshall, "I'd like to be able to speak publicly about political issues again and maybe try a few more lawsuits before I can't think straight any longer." Yarborough nominated a black woman, Solicitor General Marian Wright Edelman, to replace Marshall. The U.S. Senate quickly confirmed her. Marshall, whose sensibilities were strictly from the 1950s, congratulated Edelman and said, "My dear, your confirmation hearing was so easy, it was more like a debutante ball!"

Cardinal Joseph Bernardin became the first American pope in 1978, taking the name John Paul I, after the two previous popes, John XXIII and Paul VI. Six months after assuming the position, there was an attempt on Bernardin's life. A deranged Italian conservative Catholic, who had become a cook at the Vatican kitchen, attempted to poison the pope's food. The cook was caught by a janitor who saw him put arsenic in the dinner soup. The cook was arrested and, under Italian law, placed in a mental institution after being adjudged insane. Some conspiracy theorists noted the cook was a member of the ultra-conservative Catholic organization known as the Opus Dei, but the pope refused to allow any further investigation of the cook's ties to the organization.

The population of the United States continued to increase during the 1970s, though at a slower pace than in the first timeline. In this Kennedy-Yarborough timeline, sociologists noted that those who were once poor had fewer children than they might have had if they stayed poor. On the other hand, religious women still had more children than secular-minded women— regardless of race. They also took the greatest advantage of the child care voucher system and the four-day workweek as they entered the work force in greater and greater numbers.

Other factors contributed to the slower growth rate. During the administrations of Robert Kennedy and Ralph Yarborough, no "boat people" arrived on U.S. shores from Southeast Asia because, instead of "killing fields," American foreign policies led to peace and development in that part of the world. Economic development in other parts of the third world also minimized immigration from such nations as Mexico and India.

As a consequence, even as the U.S. population grew slightly, it was less diverse than in the first timeline. The only significant immigration was that of white people from South Africa and Rhodesia. Many formerly privileged whites did not enjoy life as a minority population in a new black-dominated southern Africa and, therefore, left for the United States, where whites remained in the majority.

In the 1980 presidential election, Yarborough was reelected while running a campaign that resembled the one in Election '76. But this time, the "feeling great about America" campaign did not work as well. Yarborough lost the popular vote in the 1980 election by one percentage point to the Republican candidate, but he "won" reelection because he carried the electoral college vote.

It didn't take a political scientist to see why Yarborough lost the popular vote. The main reason was that David McReynolds' Peace and Freedom Party garnered 9 percent of the vote nationwide. McReynolds even played a spoiler role in Wisconsin and Oregon, causing both states to go Republican. Almost all the McReynolds' votes had gone to the Democrats in the past.

During the campaign, McReynolds castigated Yarborough for being too busy spreading "bourgeois New Deals around the world instead of building socialism at home." McReynolds also charged that "boss" labor leaders and big business had blocked environmental legislation that was needed to "end the culture of the car."

Yarborough's campaign manager, Robert Shrum, discussed the campaign in an oral history sponsored by the University of Texas at Austin at the turn of the twenty-first century. He said the reason Yarborough wound up "winning ugly"—meaning through the electoral college voting system—was because McReynolds had been allowed to enter the debates normally restricted to only the Democratic and Republican candidates for president. The Republican candidate had shrewdly argued that the Socialist McReynolds belonged in the debate so that Americans could hear all "legitimate, if disagreeable" voices. Shrum argued with Yarborough that he should insist on including the racist American Independent Party candidate in the debates to counter McReynolds. He told Yarborough, "We need to scare our radicals into realizing there are enough yahoos out there who will vote for those idiot racists in the American Independent Party—votes that will hurt the Democrats more than they will!"

Yarborough refused, saying, "Ah'm more worried 'bout settin' racism on fire again if we let the American Independent folks in. Those are *our* votes, too, as you admit. Ah think Ah can handle that Republican reverend and that wild-eyed radical McReynolds, too!"

And who was the "Republican reverend" presidential candidate in the 1980 election? Why, none other than the only Republican congressman in the city and outskirts of Chicago, the Reverend Jesse "Black Capitalism Works!" Jackson. In mid- to late 1979, nearly every established Republican decided to sit out the election against Yarborough because they saw him as unbeatable in a still-thriving economy. Jackson, sensing an opportunity, stepped forward to "make history," as he put it in his announcement. Most pundits scoffed at Jackson's announcement, saying that black Americans would continue to support the Yarborough-Bond ticket, particularly because Vice President Bond was black.

Yet Jackson persisted. He soon convinced various major industrialists and bankers in the Republican Party that he could "split" the black vote, dig into the Latino vote, and make "capitalism popular again" with his rhetoric of passion and religiosity. He also agreed to support Republican positions on abortion and homosexual rights, which put him in the camp of feminists and cultural liberals, a strange stance, some said, for a minister. But to Jackson it was all about, as he put it, "the morality of tolerance, respect, and love."

As Jackson predicted, he did garner half the black vote as a result of what Shrum and other Democratic advisers said was nothing more than "black pride." He did not receive many votes from Latinos in California and Texas, who stayed with the preferred union candidate, Yarborough. But on store-fronts owned by Latino businesspeople around the country, "Jackson for President" signs were seen more often than not. White businesspeople strongly supported Jackson in the primaries, drawn by his ability to sound religious and moral when describing their business pursuits. They were ecstatic when Jackson caused a commotion in the National Association for the Advancement of Colored People and other civil rights organizations still accustomed to voting for Democrats for president.

Jackson ran on a platform of being pro-business, pro–minority "empowerment"—he meant in the world of business, since unions and politics had long nurtured black leaders—and for tax cuts. Speaking privately with top corporate executives, he called several times for the repeal of the "socialist" progressive income tax. Jackson's most quoted stump speech went like this: "We have had enough of the nanny state. Those of us in the so-called baby boom generation are no longer babies, and we don't need any more nannies tellin' us what to do or how to do it. And this goes for those of us who used to be called 'minorities.' We must now begin to leave nanny behind and embrace the strength that is within each of us. And live! And work! And do our *own* thing!"

While this argument was resonating more and more with suburban voters used to voting Republican, for many union rank-and-filers, and religious people throughout the nation, such talk was still considered unpatriotic and radical. After all, the Democrats had managed to turn the dictum "Ask not what your country can do for you. Ask what you can do for your country" into something of a communal experience.

As Republican strategists and capitalist theoreticians began to realize, they had to loosen that spirit of community to combat rampant unionism and government social programs. Individualism provided the means to loosen that spirit.

Jackson's vice presidential running mate in 1980 was another former Democrat turned Republican, Senator Patricia Schroeder of Colorado. Schroeder, who had worked for insurance companies as a claims adjuster while going to college during the 1960s, was a major supporter of abortion rights and ending the military draft. She had, with other more culturally progressive feminists, broken with the Democrats during Kennedy's sex scandal in 1972.

Although some political strategists believed that a black male presidential candidate and a female vice presidential candidate constituted a losing ticket for "traditional" white, male voters—a very large portion of the electorate—both the corporate and union media reporters saw Jackson and Schroeder as articulate and witty, which they were. This "hipness" obviously helped them among the feminists and the still largely white, male business interests in the Republican Party. But surprisingly to most political observers, it also helped them make further inroads into the increasingly prosperous union households in certain metropolitan suburbs, whose members also wanted to be "with it"—and to use their money to purchase "freedom," not duties to society.

The irony for Yarborough and Bond was that it was the white racist vote coming out of the woodwork that helped them win in the electoral college. Gallup and Harris pollsters noted that people who identified themselves as worried about blacks seeking "too much" equality voted overwhelmingly for Yarborough. They did not care what Yarborough stood for or that a black man, Julian Bond, was his vice presidential running mate. They voted for Yarborough because, in the words of the Ku Klux Klan Web site, "If the nigger Jackson wins, he'll turn the White House into a Black House, a fate worse than what the British did to the White House during the War of 1812!" The Klan and other racists downplayed Julian Bond's African American heritage by saying he was "very light-skinned for a nigger," something the few remaining black nationalist radicals noticed, too. Such are the minutia of racist "analyses" coming from people of any skin color.

In what proved to be key victories on election night of 1980, the Democrats won the states of Mississippi and Utah for the first time in decades. The racist vote won it for Yarborough in Mississippi and the antifeminist vote won it in Utah. "A woman's place is in the home," noted many Mormon leaders who looked with disgust upon the cultural liberalism of nearby Colorado.

With the victory in Mississippi, the Democrats won every state in the South that year. Losing California was not as significant that year because California had not increased its population lead as much as it did in the first timeline. A more balanced economic growth throughout the nation kept many "internal" immigrants from moving to California or other states in the Southwest.

Yarborough told Shrum he was "mah-ty glad" about at least one result of the 1980 election, which was that the Democratic Party's complete victory in the South had killed off for good the American Independent Party. In that election, the AIP received less than 0.5 percent of the vote nationwide. "Ironically," noted Southern newspaper editor Hodding Carter, "The Reverend Jackson's candidacy, even as he lost, did more to undermine the last vestiges of organized racism in the two main political parties than any other politician around today."

Yarborough never attacked Jackson on racial grounds, but, of course, how could he with Julian Bond as his vice president? Yarborough even fired one staffer from South Carolina named Lee Atwater for floating a trial balloon of race-baiting in a single mailer to whites in one district in that state.

The main criticism among insiders against Yarborough was that his "feel good about America" campaign in 1980 caused some workers to just stay home. The strong economy had been a double-edged sword. Some union rank-and-filers shrugged their shoulders and "forgot" to vote. In effect, said the AFL-CIO pollster, Patrick Cadell, some rank-and-file union members concluded unions were "strong enough" that no Republican could take away their gains. This complacency was something Yarborough had a hard time shaking, and, to be fair, if he did try to make the election more exciting, he might have sounded as "radical" as McReynolds and lost more votes than he gained. Voter participation in the 1980 election was down to 65 percent, which by then was considered extremely low for a presidential election year.

Calls to change the U.S. Constitution to do away with the electoral college system began in earnest in Republican-oriented journals and newspapers such as *National Review, U.S. News and World Report,* the *New York Times* and the *Washington Post.* However, as the noisiest calls to eliminate the electoral college system tended to be from those who had just lost because of that system, the winners ignored their pleas as naïve and not worth the effort. "Let's get on with governing," said most Democrats.

During the 1980 election campaign, Republicans continued to gripe on behalf of business leaders, and business leaders attacked Democrats and unions as "socialists." But after the elections, the corporations had no choice except to work with the Democrats. And Yarborough, who believed in the maxim "You get more with honey than with vinegar," never gloated. He knew that more than half the nation favored either him or a real socialist at this point. Business leaders knew that, too.

An interesting development that occurred in this timeline, beginning in the late 1970s, was the rise of politicians, particularly in the Republican ranks, who came from the business world. As the idea of holding an elected government office became respected—news media reports in this timeline consistently referred to government office holders as "public servants" as opposed to "bureaucrats"—more business leaders were interested in seizing the opportunity to wield power in the public as well as the private sector.

These business-politicians were, of course, supportive of tax breaks "in order to create more private-sector-led innovation." They were also fairly "liberal" on cultural matters. To the surprise and sometimes frustration of union Democrats, such former executives made inroads with some union-raised college students who were more interested in "helping the environment" than next year's union-management collective-bargaining negotiation. The new business-politicians' siren song was to call on the government to pay the total cost for environmental clean-ups for reasons of "natural national security." As freshman Connecticut senator Lee Iacocca (elected in 1976) said at the yearly convention of the Sierra Club in 1979, "The environment is like national defense and ought to be paid for by the government. Let's let business get on with business. And let's stop selfish union leaders, who are more intertwined with the Democratic Party than their own rank-and-file, from standing in the way of protecting our planet while we protect one unnecessary job for someone who can be trained to do something else!"[4]

Labor leaders and Democrats, in response to such arguments, reminded people that those very businesses, while making profits, had created the dirty rivers and air. They accused Iacocca and corporations of using "national security" as a cover to make the taxpayers—which included workers—pay for the mistakes and intentional misconduct of big business. They argued it was unfair to put the burden on the government, on top of health insurance, child care, and the like.

This put the Democrats on the defensive, however, because it allowed Republicans to reaffirm their position that these other social programs were "burdens" to the taxpayers and that the Democrats simply wanted to further punish private enterprise. The structure of this argument also highlighted the growing rift between environmentalists and the Democrats.

On the Democratic side, lawyers and labor union representatives had been running for office for several years now. Such successful candidates included former UAW local chapter leader turned California congressman Hank Lacayo, California U.S. Senator Delores Huerta, Chicago-area labor lawyer turned congressman, Thomas Geoghegan, labor lawyer turned New York governor Arthur Goldberg, and former International Machinists union president turned Florida congressman William Wimpisinger, among others.

The professional politician who was adept at raising money and avoiding economic questions other than calling for "tax cuts," "targeted spending programs" and trying to be "centrist"—in other words, all things to all people—did not develop in the RFK timeline. That didn't mean that politicians stopped lying. It was true that without the need to constantly raise money from the business elite, the politicians didn't have to lie to working Americans about trade deals that screwed them or wax eloquent about the debilitating effects of "mommy" welfare—while taking corporate money to protect "corporate" welfare. But politicians still danced about gun control, abortion, and homosexuality because anything having to do with "morality" that didn't cost money usually cut across party lines—and therefore was dangerous to any politician trying to build a winning coalition at election time.

Chapter 40

HOMERS ABROAD,
BUT OUT AT HOME

Foreign Reverberations

In foreign affairs, Yarborough continued to push for the development and building of schools, hospitals, roads for public transportation, and solar/wind energy initiatives in Latin America, Africa, and South Asia. With American and European bankers lending money, backed by U.S. and UN guarantees, local businesses began to develop within those nations, with unions and good wages for workers. Farm cooperatives and no-interest government loans helped maintain family farms, though many subsistence farmers nonetheless sold their land to more aggressive farmers or to business developers. Most important, however, enough food was now being grown to begin to feed the communities surrounding the farms.

In Africa, President Nelson Mandela of South Africa became the leader of the Organization of African Unity in 1974. Starting more during Yarborough's than Kennedy's presidency, the OAU developed a continental military to police disputes within Africa. Mandela said that militarism, tribal warfare, and poverty were the three scourges of Africa that must be overcome if Africa was to succeed as a continent. When revolutions rose up against Idi Amin in Uganda and against Mobutu Sese Seko in Zaire (the former Belgian Congo), the OAU provided military assistance to the rebels with support from the United States and the UN. To avoid protracted warfare in various emerging African nations, Mandela brokered new boundaries for such nations. For example, Angola was divided into two separate nations to resolve the infighting between the two Angolan leftist guerrilla groups—the MPLA, which was largely supported by the Mbundu tribe, and UNITA, which had support from the Ovimbundo tribe. Other nation-states had their boundaries redrawn, which overcame most tribal strife.

In Latin America, labor leader "Lula" ran for president in Brazil and won election in the late 1970s. Lula immediately implemented labor-law reforms for workers. Working with Michael Harrington at the World Bank, government aid programs from the United States, and the UN, he also revitalized the forest regions within Brazil and promoted a "slow development" designed to give

Brazilian farmers and peasants an opportunity to take part in creating their own wealth by growing crops and starting small businesses. He also chose, in the interest of his nation, to nationalize the copper industry and the banks, so that, in his words, "the profits stayed inside our house."

Yarborough's administration refused to criticize Lula's nationalizations. Secretary of State Browne said in response to a Republican congressman who denounced Lula as a Communist, "The Brazilians have had enough interference by American business or military interests over the years, particularly during the 1950s and 1960s. The president of Brazil has acted in what he says are the best interests of his nation and has promised just compensation to the affected non-Brazilian foreign entities. We believe that is enough for our large, powerful, and respected nation to accept from a large and respected nation in Latin America."

In various Latin American dictatorships, left-leaning military personnel began to stage coups that promised constitutional government and internal development. Discussing the matter with Secretary Browne, President Yarborough voiced concern about so much instability within these nations. Browne responded, "Mr. President, it is better to have the military wanting to go left than right. According to the white paper we have prepared for your review, the pattern is emerging that the military, so long in the pocket of right-wing dictators, now want to be heroes to the peasants by taking over and doling out land from the wealthy landowners. These military people don't know Karl Marx from Groucho Marx, which may or may not be good for American interests at some point. What they do know is where history's been going the past eight or nine years, and that's enough for them. Most importantly, compared to the 1950s and 1960s, there's very little blood being spilled. Also, when we send economic aid, that aid goes further than it did before because now, the church, military, and labor leaders—and even some businesspeople—are all on the same side. That makes a big difference in how effective our economic aid will be. And as we know from our experience of the previous few years, if economic aid is successful in laying the infrastructure of an economy, peace becomes permanent, and stability, in the form of economic and later political freedom, begins to allow for the creation of wealth."

In public speeches on this topic, Browne admitted there was still some political violence. In several nations where leftist military personnel stepped forward, militarists loyal to the economic elites attempted countercoups. Most of the time, the leftist military leaders, now able to hand out guns to farmers and peasants, quickly put down those attempts.

Sometimes, however, leftist military personnel were more aggressive in "preemptively neutralizing"—killing—recalcitrant military leaders and elite landowners. Browne explained how Latin Americans acted "preemptively" because of memories of right-wing coups where military leaders close to the wealthy landowners had violently seized and maintained power in Guatemala, the Dominican Republic, and other places. They also recalled, back in the 1930s, the successful Fascist counterrevolution in Spain led by General Francisco Franco against the Republican Spanish government.

Browne defended the Yarborough administration's foreign policy positions in testimony before Congress in the summer of 1978. He said that the United States had practiced a different gunboat diplomacy in Latin America and elsewhere during the 1920s through the 1960s, where the United States intervened on the side of reactionary generals and the landed aristocracy. These people, Browne noted, "were among the least democratic leaders around." The result was civil wars that shed lots of blood in places such as Guatemala and Bolivia, among other nations.[1] Worse, American and World Bank lending policies kept these nations mired in unequal economic growth as they were forced to rely on one or two crops or products for export purposes more than any other purpose. This, said Browne, was the context in which such "preemptive neutralization" (to use the leftist-inspired rhetoric) occurred in the 1970s.

Congressional Republican leaders, American business leaders, and pundits such as William Buckley, James Kilpatrick, Evans and Novak, James Reston, and others, who had previously endorsed American foreign policies that resulted in the mass murder of peasants throughout Latin America and Asia, now denounced these less far-reaching murder reprisals or "preemptive neutralizations." Reston, ignoring his own history of supporting mass murder by right-wing dictators, wrote in the *New York Times* that "America used to stand for freedom and democracy. But now, the Yarborough administration, much as Robert Kennedy did in his second term, is hell-bent on taking over from the old Soviet Union when it comes to endorsing armed, violent revolution around the world!"

Nicholas von Hoffman, who usually was content to be a contrarian critic of "the corny socialist" President Yarborough, now came to his rescue. Said von Hoffman in an essay in *Harper's Magazine*, "As at least a partial result of changes in American foreign policy over the past seven odd years, right-wing Congressmen and commentators have become very upset that those now being killed in third world nations are the landed aristocracy and reactionary-minded military officers. I do not, for myself, support these 'neutralizations,' as they are euphemistically called, but I do know that the Republicans and Cold Warriors used similar euphemisms when their so-called 'friendly' dictators committed much more horrible murders. Secretary Browne defends his current policies in the name of labor unions *über alles,* while the Republicans and Cold Warriors justified their support for mass murder in the name of fighting the evils of Communism. 'Plus ca change . . . ,' as a French diplomat might say."

Secretary Browne, in a widely reported speech before the World Affairs Council on the subject of American foreign policy, was not content to allow

Von Hoffman to be his defender. He said: "With the Soviet Union vanquished by their own people with the help of President Robert Kennedy and then Vice President Yarborough, our greatest evil to fight in the world today is *poverty*. And sometimes we have supported leaders who have the support of their own people in the international war against poverty, but who have also committed some highly unpleasant acts from time to time. To those who have suddenly become sentimental about 'human rights' and are looking for perfection in an imperfect world, they should know better than to attack those fighting against the evil of international poverty. When Franklin D. Roosevelt set forth the Four Freedoms, one of those freedoms was in fact, 'freedom from want' or freedom from poverty. What these suddenly sentimental critics of our foreign policy have never understood is that freedom on an empty stomach is often no freedom at all."

Contrary to Yarborough's and Browne's critics, even left-wing dictators were in danger of being overthrown, particularly in Latin America. In 1977, Cuban dictator Fidel Castro, disappointed that Robert Kennedy never recognized his regime, began to beg the United States for recognition. After a year of congressional and national debate—and an acrimonious debate it was—Yarborough signed a law authorizing him to recognize the nation of Cuba—with the proviso that Castro must "democratize" the political system inside Cuba.

In 1979, Yarborough opened relations with Cuba, thereby ending the embargo that had been in place for nearly twenty years. He did this after Castro issued an "order" to the press in Cuba to print what it wished and that open elections would be held the next year with no military leaders—except himself—eligible to run for office. The day before Castro's announcement, Castro arrested and jailed his brother, Raul, and several military leaders, claiming they were staging a "reactionary" coup.

In the election held a year later, Castro's charisma carried him to victory, a result that surprised American intelligence and most American pundits, including some in the union media. Castro managed to win despite weathering a full year of attacks in the press in Cuba, and in most American media, for running Cuba's economy into the ground during a disastrous experiment with "dictatorial Communism."

According to post-election analyses, the consensus was that it was a mistake for the Cuban American exile community in Miami to send the flamboyant Cuban exile (and ex-CIA agent) Felix Rodriguez to run against Castro for president of Cuba. Castro outmaneuvered Rodriguez at nearly every turn, largely because Rodriguez had been gone so long from Cuba that he seemed out of touch with the rhythm of the political pulse on the island. Upending Rodriguez's strategy of blaming Castro for the failure of his regime, Castro convinced the inhabitants that they were "heroes" for having stayed in Cuba all these years and "struggled successfully against the embargo"—as if the embargo was not against Castro but the people of Cuba, which, some noted, was perhaps true.

Rodriguez, running his campaign solely as an attack on Castro and Communism, found his strategy backfired as Cubans concluded such attacks were directed against them. Too many years of Castro saying he was Cuba and Cuba was him was not going to change overnight. It did not help that other exiles returning to Cuba with Rodriguez appeared arrogant to the Cuban population, according to post-election interviews with voters.

Castro, unlike Rodriguez, recognized all along that the election was about the *future,* not the past. Therefore, relying on Mexican President Echeverria's advice, Castro, at the same time he opened the press and called for elections, opened Cuba as a tourist destination for businesspeople and nonprofit organizations. The Mexican president told Castro that by beginning with the tourism industry, Castro would have more control over foreigners than if he started off by trying to lure factories and other businesses into his tiny nation. "Your country is in a different position than mine was. First, the tourists. Then, the factories will come," the Mexican president told Castro. Castro also pursued the development of a Cuban baseball team that he hoped to enter as a new team in the U.S. major leagues by 1981.

Shortly after his successful election campaign, Castro went to visit his brother, Raul, in jail. He told Raul, "My comrade brother, I did what I did to survive. As I sometimes like to say, I am Cuba and Cuba is me."

Raul spat at his brother and said, "You are nothing but a bourgeois movie star. That is why they like you in Hollywood. You might as well put on a dress, faggot!"

Castro laughed. "You know too well I like my women, Raul! Although maybe I am a movie star as you say. But I am free . . . and you are not. And nobody, not even the Yanqui Republicans and businessmen, cares about you!"

In 1982, the Havana Cyclones baseball team was admitted into the National League Eastern Division of major league baseball in the United States.[2] Castro never lived to see its first game against the New York Mets, however, because, on March 31, 1983, he was assassinated by a former Cuban American exile, Lozzaro Gonzalez. Gonzalez had lived in Miami since arriving from Cuba in the late 1960s. He had been a union worker for a while but had disputes with union officials, ran for a union office, and lost.

After the embargo ended, he returned to be with his family in Cuba, but he found it difficult to find permanent employment. Eventually, he had what his cousin Juan Miguel Gonzalez called a "nervous breakdown" and thereafter became convinced that he should run for office in Cuba—"to teach Cuba a lesson in real democracy," he said. Lozzaro Gonzalez ran with Felix Rodriguez's party and lost a local city council seat. He blamed Castro for his defeat, but, as his cousin said, "Nobody believed he would do something like shooting our beloved president!"

Another ironfisted dictator, the Shah of Iran, also found himself under attack during the late 1970s. In Iran, economics minister Abolhassan Bani-Sadr dared to run for prime minister over the shah's objections. The United States pressured the shah to allow for the election—even threatening to end all military aid to Iran and boycotting Iranian oil if the shah failed to comply. The United States was now in a position to make good on its threat to boycott oil from a foreign nation now that it had a nationwide, functioning public transit system; an energy system that increasingly used renewable energy such as solar, wind, and water; and high gasoline mileage requirements on cars and trucks.

After an overwhelming electoral victory in 1979, Bani-Sadr declared that the shah's rule "has come to an end." The U.S. military went on alert as the shah began to plan for a palace-led countercoup. However, the Iranian military decided to support Bani-Sadr after conferring with U.S. military and CIA personnel. In this timeline, the dreaded SAVAK, the shah's secret police, never developed as a strong force because Secretary of State Bowles, with CIA Director Blee, refused to fund its wide-ranging operations.[3] With the rise of the shah's hard-line tactics during the oil embargo, the CIA had developed, through the usual route of bribery, some very strong double-agents among the Iranian military. These contacts came in handy when Bani-Sadr announced the formation of a constitutional government against the shah's continued rule.

Bani-Sadr, an economist by training, subsidized Iranian students to attend college in Iran and abroad to secure degrees in engineering, medicine, and science. Bani-Sadr's successful use of Western loans and grants for land development helped return Iran to the position of being an effective exporter of agricultural products in addition to oil. With returning engineers, doctors, and scientists, Iran soon became a respected trading partner with the West in the fields of electronic communications and wireless transmissions of data and video.

Bani-Sadr said later that his inspiration for seizing leadership in Iran came from talks he had had with Sheik Ahmed Yamani, who in 1977 led a bloodless coup in Saudi Arabia. Yamani sided with and eventually led more liberal elements in the Saud family's dynasty against the reactionary and religious elements, who were "awash," said Yamani, in the "delusion of petrol-power." Yamani, who, like Bani-Sadr, had a Western university economics degree, recognized soon after Kennedy's anti-OPEC policies that the Middle East nations, to survive and prosper, needed to develop something besides oil fields.

Meanwhile, in "The Land of Milk and Honey," that is, the desert land of Israel and its immediate surrounding areas known as the occupied territories of the West Bank and Gaza, the Israelis continued to build settlements. The Israelis also continued their policy of attempting to weaken secular Palestinian radicals by subsidizing and supporting, through the Israeli equivalent of the CIA, religious clerics and religious groups among Palestinian Arabs, particularly Muslims. In the 1970s, internal Palestinian secular leaders' power struggles led to the death of various secular Palestinian guerrilla leaders. By 1980, however, followers of Islamic fundamentalists began to murder secular Palestinian leaders to the extent that the latter were soon fighting Islamic fundamentalists as well as the Israelis.

In a top-level secret report prepared by Israel's internal security service, Shin Bet, dated January 14, 1981, the Israeli government leaders were informed that the clerical groups' violence was now being directed against those secular Palestinians who were beginning to voice peaceful alternatives to the "armed struggle." Worse, the clerical groups were beginning to recruit and harbor students who, in their zeal for Palestinian rights, adopted the "holy war" rhetoric of Islamic fundamentalism much as the previous Arab student generation had once used the "class struggle" rhetoric of Marxism.

Worst of all, more and more violent confrontations between Arabs and Jews had been occurring at various holy sites, particularly at the location of what Jews called the Temple Mount and Palestinians called Al-Haram Al-Sharif. This shrine was considered the holiest in Jewish historic tradition and the third holiest in Islam's cultural tradition. On August 4, 1981, an event occurred that shocked all sides in the long-running dispute. The *Washington Post* provided a summary of the event that caused much soul-searching and despair:

> TEL AVIV, ISRAEL (August 6, 1981)—Israeli authorities have verified that the near total destruction of various religious shrines throughout the nation of Israel on Sunday night, August 4, 1981, was the result of a suicide pact between two young lovers, one an Israeli Jew and the other a Palestinian Muslim. Israeli intelligence sources have confirmed that Yasha Aron, a 21-year-old military pilot, was in love with his Palestinian girlfriend, 19-year-old Suha Fayed. Both their families, claiming to fear for the safety of the two lovers, were against any marriage plans and forbade them from seeing each other. An uncle of Suha had, in the weeks before the night of August 4, threatened her with physical harm if she continued her relationship with Yasha because, he now says, he feared possible reprisals against the family for her consorting with a Jew.
>
> On Sunday, August 4, the two young lovers, in a Middle Eastern bow to William Shakespeare, entered into a suicide pact that will not be easily forgotten in this troubled area of the world. Writing the same suicide note in Hebrew and Arabic, Yasha and Suha decried the hatred among the Arab and Israeli peoples that has "doomed true love among two innocent people." Citing the various disputes that

have developed among Jews and Muslims over various holy sites in and about Jerusalem and other Biblical cities and towns, the lovers wrote: "The religious places Jews and Muslims fight over are nothing but dirt and sand, and the buildings merely gold, metal, or wood. Religion is supposed to be about the love of all God's children and all other creatures, not the love of shrines. True religion can only flourish if, together, we build new shrines dedicated to loving one another. Then, and only then, will peace come to us all."

Unlike Shakespeare's play, this modern version of *Romeo and Juliet* did not end with a dose of poison and a sword. Authorities say that Yasha, after mailing the suicide notes to each of their parents, smuggled Suha aboard his assigned Israeli fighter jet. Instead of performing his usual Sunday night maneuvers, he and his lover embarked on what some are calling a cry of unrequited love expressed in violence and destruction. Yasha's jet immediately set a course for various religious sites in and around Jerusalem, starting with what Jews here call the Temple Mount—and Islamic Arabs call Al-Haram Al-Sharif. The sharp-shooting Israeli pilot destroyed the Temple Mount and three other holy shrines, killing ten parishioners and Israeli soldiers, before he and his lover met their fiery end as Yasha's jet crashed into the Golan Mountains. While the Israeli military claims to have shot down the jet, which then caused it to crash, other officials, off the record, state the Israeli military was slow to react. These sources state that before the Israeli air force was able to track down and fire on Yasha's jet, the aircraft, flying at full speed, crashed into the Golan Mountains and exploded upon impact.

Israeli Defense Minister Shimon Peres, in discussing the suicide note with reporters, confirmed rumors that the note referred to the holiday of Tisha Baav, a solemn Jewish holiday dedicated to remembering the Romans' destruction of the main Jewish temple in A.D. 70. The holiday occurs around this time each year. Although the defense minister would 'not speculate' on the meaning of the reference, an American rabbi, Harold Schulweis, said that on the holiday of Tisha Baav, the Book of Lamentations is read in every Jewish temple. In the Book of Lamentations, Jews are excoriated for forgetting their values, which led to the destruction of the main temple. The Book of Lamentations also contains the quote used by the United Nations that says that 'men shall turn swords into plowshares and neither shall they learn war any more.' The bodies of what Israeli authorities confirm are the two doomed lovers have been removed from the wreckage and are awaiting formal identification by their families.

Immediately, Arafat's remaining rival George Habash said there was one suicide and one murder, not two suicides. He issued a statement saying that Yasha
killed Suha by "polluting her mind with religious symbolism and Israeli propaganda that hides the intent of the Jews to annihilate the Palestinians."

Suha's mother, lamenting the loss of her "most precious jewel," at first
agreed with Habash. However, Egyptian journalist and diplomat
Mohammed Haikal, with the help of Israeli novelist Amos Oz, arranged a
meeting between the mothers of the doomed lovers. The mothers, recognizing their common grief, decided, ten days after their loss, to walk down the
street to the Knesset, Israel's parliament, hand in hand, to demand that the
PLO leader, Yasir Arafat, and Israeli Foreign Minister Moshe Arens meet to
negotiate what each called "a lasting peace." As usual, peace talks began,
with the help of Secretary of State Browne, but broke down when the rejec-
tionists on each side committed acts of violence. This sent the two sides back
to their "political corners," as Secretary of State Browne reported to
President Yarborough.

Browne did report one positive development to President Yarborough.
"Arens realizes the most dangerous threat to stability is now in the religious
communities of both sides. Arafat realizes this, too, but is simply not willing
'to take a bullet for nothing,' as he told me."

Yarborough answered, "Ah sometimes wish we could tell Arafat he needs
to take the chance to die for his country—in his case, a Palestine on the West
Bank. Why can't he be lahk Nathan Hale, for goodness sake?"

Browne rolled his eyes, something he had not done before with
Yarborough. He said, "I've hinted at that, Mr. President, and that's what
completely doomed the talks, although they were already breaking down
after that marketplace terror attack in Jaffa. The Israelis are beginning to
realize they are going to have a harder time making peace with Islamic religious fanatics than with Arafat. Arafat remains the only game in town for
peace, but he won't do what's necessary to take control of the movement
because he fears—maybe he knows—he doesn't have control any longer. I
must say that our acquiescence to Israel's settlement policy during the last ten
years and our support for their strategy of dividing the Palestinian radicals
against the religious elements have created what our intelligence people are
calling a 'blowback' effect. We won't be resolving this issue very soon, I fear."

Other areas of the world torn apart by ethnic and religious violence, such
as the Turkish and Greek populations on the island of Cyprus and the
Catholic and Protestant populations in Northern Ireland, attempted to move
forward toward peace. But ethnicity and religion remained powerful barriers
toward achieving that goal.

In Cyprus, Archbishop Makarios, who continually sought an independent biethnic federated republic for Greeks and Turks, was assassinated in 1978, after surviving four previous assassination attempts in the 1970s. A Greek right-wing militarist, who had entered the island unnoticed, killed Makarios at a political rally. With Makarios' assassination, the government of Turkey called for UN troops to protect Turkish Cypriots and threatened invasion if the UN didn't do so. The United States immediately led UN troops to the island, where they remained for two years while the United States called upon both sides to hold national elections designed to create a Cyprus independent of both Greece and Turkey. In 1980, elections were held amidst violent acts committed by Turkish and Greek "patriots." The Unity Party, led by a Greek Cypriot and a Turkish Cypriot, barely prevailed in the elections. The Greek was the former personal physician of the late archbishop and president, and a politician in his own right, Vassos Lyssardies. The Turkish Cypriot was Ozker Ozgur. Both survived assassination attempts shortly after the elections, though Ozgur was critically wounded and lost an arm in surgery.

UN, European, and American aid poured into Cyprus. American troops, with Cypriot government soldiers by their side, conducted raids against both Turkish and Greek Cypriot nationalists who were storing weapons. As Ozgur said, "We who know we are Cypriots first will continue to cooperate with each other to defeat those who want the island either all Greek or all Turk." It was to be a long struggle, and Americans would grow weary as several U.S. soldiers were killed by Turkish and Greek snipers. But the troops, few in number, stayed on through most of the 1980s.

The situation in Northern Ireland looked more hopeful as well. With former Secretary of State Bowles mediating, the Irish Republican Army and the British reached a tentative settlement of their differences in Northern Ireland in 1982. Bowles' proposal was to create a federation in Northern Ireland similar to what was being tried in Cyprus. There would be a coalition government designed, said Bowles, "to find out who wants to live with each other and who doesn't." The key provision was that IRA members would have to lay down their arms. Delay after delay, often punctuated by violence against Catholics but sometimes by extremists within the IRA itself, kept the IRA from complying with this provision.

By the end of 1983, the tentative agreement finally collapsed after three assassinations of local unity politicians in Ulster, Northern Ireland, two of them Protestants. The IRA and a new militant Protestant organization claimed responsibility for the murders. Bowles, weary of the continued strife, said, "We see again the extremes dictating to the majority who want to live peacefully with each other." However, he privately said to President Yarborough after returning from Northern Ireland one last time, "There is a growing part of me that believes the inertia of the larger population of

Catholics and Protestants is evidence of a desire on the part of each group for a final victory over the other side."

In February 1984, Chester Bowles collapsed from a stroke while shoveling snow from the driveway of his Chevy Chase, Maryland, home. He lingered, mostly unconscious, for several months before dying in May 1984, at the age of 83.[4] Bowles' last words, according to his son, were that he was proud to have worked with Robert Kennedy and most proud to have been able to spend most of his adult life serving his nation.

Bowles, of course, never knew what a difference he made as secretary of state in the RFK timeline. Unlike the situation in the first timeline, the Kennedy-Bowles-Yarborough foreign policy of the 1960s and 1970s helped save the lives of millions of people in the third world who did not die from unnecessary wars, revolutions, and starvation. Although the earlier collapse of the tyrannies in the Soviet Union and Red China also played a significant role in saving those lives, a major distinguishing factor was the refusal of Kennedy, Bowles, and Yarborough to support murderous regimes in Latin America, Africa, and Asia. Just as important, the United States, under Kennedy and Yarborough, sent mostly doctors, nurses, teachers, and construction contractors to third world nations as opposed to military hardware and forces.

The survival and election of Robert Kennedy as president in 1968 had not merely changed the future of the United States. It had also changed the future history of the world. The actions of the Kennedy-Yarborough administrations influenced the World Bank, the International Monetary Fund, and the growing global corporations, moving them to adopt a more humane approach toward developing third world nations. The policies pursued also influenced the people who stepped forward in those nations to lead their people.[5]

Because of the pursuit of a different foreign policy, the rise of a despairing religious fundamentalism in the third world was kept at bay. Third world secular liberals and radicals who, in the first timeline, were either killed or immigrated to Europe, Canada, and the United States, stayed instead and survived to take leadership in their own nations. On the other hand, some secular radicals remained a continuing threat within those nations through the early 1980s. Yet, over and over again, the diplomacy and policies pursued by Bowles and Browne abated the secular radical threat with what were often called "worldwide Marshall Plans," just as the original Marshall Plan had abated Communist threats in Europe after the devastation of World War II.

But the real world is not limited in its scope, unlike history books that emphasize one subject to the exclusion of others. Nor is the real world ever perfectly content or happy by any means. There were, in fact, *other* consequences that arose from saving Bobby Kennedy in 1968 that were less than expected or even desired by many of his supporters.

Chapter 41

THE BOOMERANG OF SUCCESS

Yarborough spent much of his second term traveling around the globe promoting his foreign policy initiatives. Like most presidents who spend too much time abroad, his domestic policies lagged. Some also noted that Yarborough, nearing eighty years old, should probably not have run for a second term. His age finally began to show—especially when he returned, exhausted, from his trips.

Military Contractors and Military Turf Wars

About the only new domestic policy initiative Yarborough actively sought, and achieved, in his second term was the nationalization of the military contractors' industry—something that was, ironically, relatively low on his list of "to do's." After the first federal government bailout of the military contractor Lockheed in 1974—in which President Robert Kennedy required that the government receive a controlling stake in the corporation as the price of the bailout—the Kennedy and Yarborough administrations allowed the remaining contractors to begin merging with each other. By 1981, only three companies remained—McDonnell-Northrup, General Motors' military contracting division (which included Hughes Aircraft, General Dynamics, and others), and Lockheed, which thrived after the bailout.

Yarborough appointed a task force, led by General David Hackworth, Admirals Hyman Rickover, and Averell Harriman, to research whether to nationalize the industry and how to provide just compensation for nationalization if that route was chosen.

Though Republicans and some Democrats screamed that the commission was "rigged" to favor nationalization, the commission continued its research and eventually presented its report. The report said, not surprisingly, "Nationalize." It did, however, suggest compensation in a sum equal to the net profits of the nationalized companies that had been generated in the two years before nationalization was to take place. Because the three remaining contractors claimed their military businesses made very little net profit—they were, after all, on "cost plus" contracts—they were in the awkward position of having to admit there was little to compensate. "Goodwill," that wonderful accounting intangible, could get them only so far, and everyone knew it.

The companies also glumly recalled the Supreme Court's decision with reference to the private medical insurers and quietly allowed the government to take them over in 1982.

The key reason for nationalization, said Rickover in interview after interview, was that the United States would finally end the "revolving door" conflict of interest whereby Defense Department workers and military brass would work for military contractors after leaving their government service—and executives of those companies would wind up in the Defense Department. Further, the nationalization ended the notorious "cost plus" contracts that led to so little reported profits. Those contracts, said Harriman in one interview in the *New York Times*, were an invitation to cost overruns and excessive costs for weapons.[1]

In addition to these "civilian-oriented" reasons for nationalization, the report noted a reason related to military readiness and efficiency. It provided example after example of how the profit motive undermined the development of effective weapons systems. The M-16 rifle and the F-16 fighter jet, for example, both had to endure "enhancements" that ultimately created defects in performance. The enhancements were more often designed to spread the wealth among various military contractors than what troops needed in battle. However, in *Aviation Week and Space Technology*, a pro–military contractor magazine, a critic of nationalization wrote that in the case of the M-16 rifle, the enhancements came as much from administrative turf wars within the military as from private contractors.

In fact, the turf battle among the military branches remained but had lessened significantly under the leadership of General Hackworth, who became chairman of the Joint Chiefs of Staff in 1977. Hackworth, a hero to "grunts" everywhere, immediately began to consolidate the various armed forces. "When we fight a war," he thundered in a speech at the War College in 1977, "we don't fight as the army, the navy, the marines, or the air force. We fight as American soldiers! If I hear any turf talk from anyone, he's outta here!"

Hackworth spent night and day consolidating the military and exerting pressure on high-ranking officers, whom he termed "perfumed princes," to give up their perks and live as their troops lived. He deftly used congressional hostility to military spending—as much from libertarian Republicans as radical Democrats—to cut bloated middle-management bureaucracies, to stop production of the B-1 bomber—which he saw as a "boondoggle"—and to stop accepting "anyone" just because an individual "chose" to join the military. He didn't end the draft, because that was clearly beyond his power, but he did use the 4-F designation rather "liberally," as he put it. He was quoted in more than one interview as saying, "I'd rather have a smaller force of strong, upright fighting personnel than a bunch of pencil pushers trying to make a 'career' in the military as if it was just another business!"

By 1980, the military had finally begun to be remade in Hackworth's image. Its arsenal included sleek new rifles that were deadly accurate and missiles that used the latest technologies to hit targets two thousand miles away. The military force was, in Hackworth's words, constantly well drilled and ready for war, if necessary.

Hackworth fought against "C-Cubed-Eye," or computer-based strategies (Command-Control-Communications-Intelligence networks), which made him some enemies in Congress among those Democrats and Republicans who were friendly with high-tech industry leaders. In one of his few "diplomatic" performances before Congress, Hackworth said, "I'm not against using computers for strategy, gentlemen—and ladies. It's just that we shouldn't get so focused on 'gee-whiz' computers to the point where we lose sight of what we need to do with a military force when we're in peacetime. And that's to continue our training sessions, make sure we always have extra rounds of ammunition available, and continually prepare every soldier to be ready to assume command during a battle. If our troops go into combat around the globe, it's not going to be with computers, at least for now. It's going to be in old-fashioned combat, whether in jungles or hills or even in cities—where the electricity needed to make C-Cubed-Eye work won't last five minutes!"

Hackworth promoted and demoted generals at will, which, in 1980, created a backlash when a few "middle-management" officers decided to seek a labor union for the military's "lifers"—themselves. Hackworth, who supported civilian labor unions as a matter of course, was outraged at this attack on his authority. Yarborough, to placate the general, quietly told the AFL-CIO to reject the union petition that had been made to it by the union-minded officers.

One of the generals who was somewhat sympathetic to the officers was General Norman Schwarzkopf, who resented having to give up his shoe shines, his special food, and other niceties. Schwarzkopf retired from the military in 1979 to join the famous private security (and union-busting) corporation known as Pinkerton Security.

One of Schwarzkopf's protégés was a tough-talking, risk-taking colonel named Robert Ignatius Herron. Herron, unlike Schwarzkopf, was savvy enough to follow Hackworth's orders to the letter, yet also build alliances within the military to ensure that he would be ready to lead if the opportunity presented itself. The officers' union movement, he quickly realized, might prove to be another opportunity to move up in the hierarchy. Herron's goal was to replace Hackworth, whom he considered to be a grandstanding maverick—at least that's what he would say in "highly confidential" company.

Talking with another young general, Colin Powell, who supposedly shared some of Herron's beliefs about Hackworth, Herron said, "If we're going to retain officers, we need to regain some of our perks from the time before Hackworth started in with this Communist 'everyone's equal' bullshit. Hackworth thinks we should all live like the Viet Cong!"

Herron was also among the few officers who remained bitter over the Kennedy-Yarborough withdrawal of support for South Vietnamese President Thieu in late 1968 and early 1969. On more than one occasion, Herron was quoted as saying, "I remember General Abrams tellin' me that the Viet Cong could have been defeated if we didn't push such early elections on President Thieu as Kennedy and Yarborough did."

Another way Herron maintained a power base in the military was by gravitating toward the C-Cubed-Eye program. This was popular among members of Congress whose districts relied on high-tech military as opposed to civilian programs, and Herron became, through his pro-union stance and his promotion of C-Cubed, an "untouchable" for Hackworth, who figured he had "bigger fish to fry"—and did.

Drifts and Splits

Apart from the nationalization of the private military contractors, and without consistent leadership from Yarborough, Congress was mired in arguments over further environmental regulations and, more important to left-leaning Democrats, whether to nationalize more industries or seek other methods of public control over increasingly international corporations. Yarborough took a passive approach to the environmental issues, saying "Let the boys and girls in Congress, with their sectional differences and differin' needs, figure this out."

On the other hand, Yarborough spent some precious political capital helping the movement of the wives of union rank-and-filers who joined with environmentalists in pushing local governments across the nation to use "eminent domain" proceedings to take over private golf courses and turn them into public parks. Yarborough, who had decided long ago that golf was a "rich man's game," publicly endorsed the "brave and conscientious moms across America" who wanted "this land to truly be *our* land, as Woody Guthrie sang."

With regard to the more serious question of nationalization of other industries, or other approaches to public control of capital, Yarborough found he could not commit to one approach or the other. As he told his press secretary, Molly Ivins, one evening, "It's hard when you agree with both sides and both sides are your friends." In the end he decided to take the same position he had taken with the environment: Let Congress sort it out. This frustrated Vice President Julian Bond, until Bond realized that if he sided with any one faction of Democrats, he risked inviting challenges to his natural ascension as the next presidential nominee. Although Bond knew other Democrats were afraid to challenge him, he did not want to risk a messy primary election season by expressing strong views regarding controversial issues within the party.

Bond remained concerned, however, because he realized that allowing union Democrats to join with corporations to halt further environmental regulations gave environmentalists more of an excuse to drift away from the mainstream of the Democratic Party. In government offices and in the hallways of Congress, environmentalists screamed at Democratic leaders who, in turn, screamed back that without Democratic Party initiatives such as government research on wind and solar power, regulations for higher gas mileage in motor vehicles, and the successful development of public transit, the environmentalists would be lost.

David Brower of the Sierra Club and David McTaggart of Greenpeace were so angry at the unions for opposing many environmental initiatives— sometimes more than business interests—that they decided to form a new party they christened the Green Party, after a new party of a similar philosophy that had formed in Germany.

The Peace and Freedom Party, hearing about the forming of a Green Party, quickly reached out to both Brower and McTaggart. McTaggart had never abandoned his roots as a pro-business Republican, and so he declined the offer to have the Peace and Freedom Party become the U.S. organ of the International Greens. The party did, however, manage to convince Brower to join forces with them, for Brower saw himself as a man of the Left as much as an environmentalist. This split between Brower and McTaggart delayed the Green Party's attempt at creating any immediate national presence.

Yarborough smiled at the infighting among the radicals and environmentalists as they attempted to drive a wedge into the Democrats. Speaking with Julian Bond on the telephone, Yarborough said, "Julian, them radicals may have just saved your political future. You gotta hit those radicals with ev'rythin' you got that *you're* the best way to equality, to freedom, and a healthy environment for ev'ryone. And always remember. All of us faced worse odds when we were fightin' for Bob Kennedy's ear—and mind—in the first year of his administration. Either way, though, Ah'm callin' Bob, 'cause we're still gonna need him at the convention this summer."

As Yarborough hung up the telephone, he wondered to himself, Will Robert Kennedy say yes to a request to appear at a political convention? Yarborough did not know the answer. Ethel Kennedy had worked hard to keep her husband away from much of the national political scene since 1977. She had moved her husband and their clan to a ranch in the mountains of Santa Barbara, far away from Washington, D.C. They purchased their ranch from, ironically, Ronald and Nancy Reagan. She also kept her husband on the road, with the two of them traveling to third world nations as unofficial ambassadors to the world. In that role, Bob and Ethel provided their legendary presence for "first digs" of new irrigation projects, new housing facilities, and new factories. It was politics, but the politics of luncheon receptions and cocktail parties, as Kennedy sometimes wistfully said.

When Yarborough called to ask Kennedy to appear at the 1984 Democratic convention in Los Angeles in order to help Julian Bond, Kennedy knew he had to appear for, as he told Yarborough, "I still read the papers, and I now have time to read the 'thoughtful'—or should I say 'thoughtless' journals out there always telling us how easy it is to pass legislation."

Robert Kennedy spoke at the Democratic Party convention in August 1984. His speech, which ended the convention, electrified the delegates gathered at the Inglewood, California, convention center and sports forum. He said little of substance, though, and basically demanded, in a fatherly way, that "people of good grace, good sense, and who stand for humane policies, must stay the course of freedom, for workers' rights and human rights." Kennedy then invited the Democratic presidential and vice presidential candidates to the podium and raised their hands with his. The presidential candidate was, unsurprisingly, Julian Bond. The vice presidential candidate, a surprise to many observers, was Yarborough's HEW secretary, Ruth Rosen.

Kennedy had, in the almost eight years since leaving the presidency, achieved legendary status by staying above party politics. He was so legendary, in fact, that people quoted him as if he was Jesus. Kennedy's appearance and endorsement were so powerful that Bond and Rosen received a major post-convention bounce that put Bond over 60 percent in polling for the first time that year.

Kennedy's endorsement had caused most people to forget, at least for a while, the infighting that plagued the Democratic Party. During the convention, the platform committee was the scene of argument after argument, and on a couple of occasions, those arguments broke out into fights among delegates.

The most significant philosophical split in the Democratic Party continued to be among those who would nationalize the top corporations (a small group on the edges of the Democratic Party and closer to the socialists at the Peace and Freedom Party); those who sought more regulation and employee stock ownership plans (Nader groups and unions such as the UAW); and those who, like Harrington, wanted to pursue workers' cooperative businesses and public ownership of stock. Harrington had been opposed to ESOPs as too limiting and subject to creating unnecessary divisions between workers in one sector and the rest of their fellow citizens—who were workers in other sectors. He also opposed wholesale industrial nationalization as potentially too costly and too divisive, considering American capitalist history.

Harrington had in mind Sweden's initial success in pursuing public stock ownership of former private companies, a program the Swedes called "the Meidner Plan," after Prime Minister Rudolf Meidner. Harrington wanted the United States to adopt an American version of that plan. Nader, on the other hand, angered left-leaning Democrats, including Harrington, when he remarked that all Democrats and Republicans should support ESOPs because they were the "socialism of capitalism." By implication, Nader threatened

Bond and other Democratic leaders earlier in the year when he said he "and others" would speak to those "outside the Democratic Party" if the Democrats were not interested in fully embracing ESOPs. To Harrington, who believed in working within the Democratic Party, no matter the policy differences, Nader's talk and conduct were akin to treason.

Harrington was also frustrated as he saw the AFL-CIO splitting over ESOPs versus an American Meidner plan. The UAW, which successfully bought controlling stock in American Motors Corporation, Ford Motor Company, and General Motors through the ESOPs, had come to the conclusion that a Meidner plan of public stock ownership—let alone nationalization—was "too radical." UAW President Mike Hamlin said during the 1984 Democratic Party convention platform hearings, "We are the automobile workers union. We know what to do to run the auto and other motor or electric vehicle business. I mean, no offense to the police union or the carpenters union, but what do they know about building cars, buses, or trains? We're the experts. We didn't end the management of the 'clean fingernails' class at Ford and GM just to give it away again to something called the 'public'!"

Nader had an additional, more long-standing beef with the Democrats. Nader had long blasted the Yarborough administration for refusing to enforce antitrust actions against the "Democratic Party's close friends," such as Apple Software, IBM, and the car and oil companies. Nader had said in a speech to the national convention of the Small Business Federation in April 1984, "Monopolies are bad whether they are engaged in by a small coterie of elitist businessmen, labor leaders, or in joint public-private ventures. Competition is the best way to introduce and innovate with new products. And public oversight, such as regulation and the important accountability weapon of antitrust litigation, is the best method of maintaining a level market field of play."[2]

Harrington was appalled at Nader's stance on antitrust enforcement. In a June 1984 interview with the Marxist-oriented *Monthly Review* magazine, Harrington said that Nader was "essentially a reactionary to worry about antitrust violations. The people who want to prosecute antitrust violators tend to be competitors of the entities violating antitrust laws, not real consumers or workers. To use an old Harry Truman phrase, Nader's complaints regarding antitrust enforcement are a 'red herring.'"

By the time of the Democratic Party convention, Harrington was worried not only about Nader, but also about the threat from environmentalists in the Greens and the socialists in the Peace and Freedom Party. To Harrington, Nader personified the lack of loyalty to the Democratic Party. Nader, for his part, saw his role as helping the Democrats "move beyond a static pro-labor type of policy analysis." As Nader also said, the Democrats needed to "broaden their public policy positions to include not only workers, but also workers and small business people as consumers. The party must treat the planet, including the air we breathe and the water we drink, as its own highly important constituency. For without air or water, we all—not merely the Democratic Party—could become the next dinosaurs."

On the last night of the convention, just before Julian Bond's nomination acceptance speech, Harrington and Nader, in front of several delegates and state political leaders, finally argued face to face in a hallway outside the convention arena. Harrington was drinking beer from a recycled can, while Nader was drinking spring water from a recycled plastic bottle. The argument started after Nader had been talking about consumer empowerment and taking companies, even the new ESOP-owned Ford and GM, to arbitration for defects in the electric car and for violations of health and safety laws at several factories.

Harrington, exasperated, said, "Ralph, the problem with you is you see people as either consumers or litigants. There's more to our society, and to life, than filing a lawsuit. Is that all you think people are? Litigants in a class-action lawsuit? I'll take the more traditional class struggle any day—"

Nader replied, "People are lots of things, Michael. They're not just litigants. They are, to begin with, citizens of a free country."

"Ralph, you keep using the same impersonal words! 'Citizen,' 'consumer,' 'litigant!' Where's 'father,' 'mother,' 'child,' 'grandmother,' 'Little League coach,' 'artist,' 'Rosary Society volunteer,' 'union member,' 'Boy or Girl Scout leader'? Where are the *community's* needs in all this? A sense of community spirit doesn't just spring out of the air and certainly not from a lawsuit!"

"That's ridiculous, Michael. You know darn—"

"Ralph, I never see you or your lawyers waving a flag on Flag Day. You don't want to walk in a parade on Columbus Day. You don't want to sing the national anthem or go to a ball game. Instead, you're up late on a Friday night at the office rather than playing in a bowling league or bridge club. Yet, you think a lawsuit will bring people together? What's important in life is class and community solidarity, through parades, songs, and ball games. That's what maintains the *spirit* of a community. Remember, starting in the 1950s, there was a growing excess of consumerism that was causing atomization, which accelerated in the 1960s—despite what we read about the free speech movement and the early antiwar movement. America's attempt to 'try on' the cloak of individualism was not confined to the rich and capitalist, but was beginning to permeate into the ranks of feminists and radical students dropping acid—and beginning to drop out altogether. Remember those slogans, 'Do your own thing!' or 'The personal is political'? That mindset is the opposite of community. If we had let that thinking continue along its path, people would have started thinking they could cut a better deal without unions or on their own. Eventually, that would have undermined worker solidarity. And that could have led to a vast increase in economic inequality—with all its attendant cultural consequences, including a rise in criminal elements and racial tensions—"

"Oh come on, Michael! That's as pathetic a 'parade of horribles' as I've heard. The '60s led to Bobby Kennedy getting elected! Listening to you, you'd think it was Nixon who was elected in 1968! And even if Nixon was elected, you think that would have eventually led to labor unions losing ground, or worse, workers losing solidarity? *Your* problem is your nineteenth-century Marxist jargon! Where do you think our class-action litigants come from anyway? From a laboratory—as if the trial lawyers are Dr. Frankenstein? Those litigants are, in fact, housewives, husbands, and fathers. That's how they wind up in litigation and become advocates for safer products, for cleaner air, and so on. The unions are doing very well for working people to gain direct power over their place of work—and I commend that as part of our nation's progress. But without consumer advocates, without trial lawyers, even businesses owned by labor unions through ESOPs can—and will—produce dangerous products or pollute the air and streams, and for the same reasons rich executives do: for short-term profit or a misguided notion of 'protecting' a factory or institution. Sometimes the collective, whether government or private, can be an enemy of freedom—and of life—with the environment, for example. The key is not simply whether institutions are open, as you have always said—and with which I wholeheartedly agree, by the way. But there's something else that you haven't discussed often enough. And that's the question of whether those institutions are truly accountable to those in the minority—or on an individual basis! That's a problem in corporations and in government."

Harrington responded with some irritation. "Ah, trial lawyers as the ultimate guardians of society! I don't buy that either, Ralph. And don't turn this into a chicken-and-egg argument or some kind of 'need for balance' argument. That's not what I'm talking about. If it were, I'd have already agreed. That's why democratic institutions are the key to any socialism—and it's why authoritarian corporate structures need public regulation and sometimes nationalization. What we're—or at least I'm—talking about is how to create a society where workers and the people as a whole can order their economic and political affairs. We create far more stability and room for civilized growth when we base our society on people being able to participate in the creation of laws, as Jefferson said in the Declaration of Independence. You know, '*governments* are instituted' for people to have a life, to have liberty, and to pursue happiness. The unions and a governmental legislature must be the vanguard of change, *not* lawyers and administrative law judges. We must work through the popular, or populist, institutions, such as the legislature or the presidency. Not elitist institutions, such as corporations or the judiciary where, even in jury trials, everything is pushed into a 'profit and loss line' for the litigant suing the company—"

"Wait, Michael! The last time I checked, jurors were *people!*"

"Sorry, Ralph, the judiciary isn't a populist institution, even in a jury case. My father was a lawyer, though not a trial lawyer—but I know enough about your profession and the jury system. Juries decide individual cases that are skewed by looking at one person's injuries or one business' damages. Even in class actions, there are limited remedies that are skewed by the requirement of looking at particular, and limited, facts. In a lawsuit, you rarely get to a panoramic view of a variety of possible alternatives and situations—and that's important for *legislative policy*. What you won't admit is that your trial lawyer friends have had a tough time these past few years when their 'business' in products liability and car accident cases dried up significantly after we passed national health insurance, child care, and expanded public transit. Plus, we hurt *your* business when we 'nationalized' product liability laws so that different laws in different states didn't trip up companies. With the expansion of unions, we didn't need to have lawyers to sue for us when our bosses gave us a raw deal. And inner-city job programs, training programs, and government-private investment undermined a lot of discrimination cases, I bet, since the blacks didn't need to run to the suburbs for a decent job.[3] You don't need to use the hammer of a court decision if you have representation elsewhere. It's bad for a democratic society to continually rely on the courts rather than legislatures for basic justice—"

"Michael, you're being too parochial in your Marxist views! A judiciary that's sensitive to an individual's needs as a consumer or worker is of equal importance—at least. And you know as well as I do that unions can choke off dissent as much as a corporation or a closed government—"

"That has happened, but with open union elections required under the labor reform law of 1969—and people being able to withhold monies for politics for either corporations or unions—there's far more debate within unions and more rank-and-file participation than anywhere else. And when the Soviet Union and Red China collapsed, we finally got past the usual distractions of calling someone a Communist. I am very proud of the unions in our country, Ralph, and if they don't want to constantly push for the most extreme laws on environmental matters, as you and your Raiders sometimes do—and elitist environmentalists such as McTaggart definitely do—that doesn't make this country a dictatorship—"

Nader sharply interrupted. "It makes it a dictatorship to those of us who know the earth needs more protection than we've given it for the last hundred years! And if we have to break with our friends from time to time, it's not fatal to our cause. It's called making a free choice in a democracy—"

Harrington, who had engaged in this debate precisely because he believed Nader might bolt from the Bond-Rosen ticket, threw down his can of beer in a rage. "Goddamn it, Ralph!" said the once-Catholic, now-atheist Harrington. "*You're* the one who's undermining this Democratic ticket! That's what you're really saying! Let's cut the bullshit and tell it like it is! You've been talking with the Greens, the Peace and Freedom Party—"

Nader, staggered at first by Harrington's violent act, regained his composure enough to respond with sarcastic contempt. "Go ahead, Mike, turn to the Stalinism or violence you always denounced! Yes, I even talked with the *Republicans* this year, I'm glad to say. I go where I can find the most viable coalition for moving our nation forward. But guess what? Despite your accusation, I'm staying with the Democrats this time around. This Republican candidate is calling himself some sort of a 'moral moderate,' trying to fool religious union voters. But he's as corporate and antilabor as they come—and I don't trust him on the need to protect the environment. Unlike you, Mike, I'm not a party guy in either the personal or political sense. But I consider Julian Bond to be, by far, the best candidate out there, whether you believe me or not."

"I don't," said a somewhat tipsy but seething Harrington. "You represent a virus of individualists who don't understand the need for people to stand together. A political party is not something one chooses or rejects like different brands of soap. It's like your country. You have to work within it to make it work. I could understand if the Democrats became corrupted by corporate influences and moved away from pro-worker economic policies, which would never happen. Maybe then, in that weird scenario, you might have to look for an alternative. But you think with your clever lawyerly arguments that I can't see what your *real* goal is—"

"What's my goal, Mike? Really, now, what's *my* goal? If you want an answer, I'll give it to you. But you have to answer that same question for yourself! At long last, Michael, what's *your* goal?"

Harrington abruptly walked—some said staggered—away, muttering something indiscernible. Some thought he called Nader a "fascist," while others said he called Nader an "anarchist." Either way, it was mostly a personal feud masquerading as a political one. Harrington was as angry as he'd been since his fights with college radicals in late 1967, before Robert Kennedy announced his intention to run for president. As it turned out, Harrington wrote to Nader the next day to apologize. But despite that apology, the crack in the Democrats' unity remained as the new Green Party and the socialist Peace and Freedom Party beckoned those who thought things had not "progressed" either far enough or fast enough.

Bond-Rosen, realizing their bounce was only temporary, focused on their strategy of holding together the Kennedy-Yarborough coalition. Bond, recalling how the Republicans demanded that McReynolds join the presidential debates in 1980, followed the Yarborough idea of facing your fear. He specifically stated he would be glad to debate both the Peace and Freedom candidate, McReynolds, and the Green Party candidate, McTaggart. Bond hoped to show that he was only moderate among the extremes of libertarian economic doctrine (the Republican candidate), environmentalism (McTaggart), and socialism

(McReynolds). The Republicans, remembering how they had almost elected Jesse Jackson in 1980, heartily agreed with no thought as to whether this could be a trap for them as well.

In the debates, Bond took on McReynolds by endorsing a public stock ownership program but said he would not mandate it as the only way. He said, "We have to experiment here since we are in uncharted territory. Let us continue with our ESOPs, find the right corporate vehicle for a public stock ownership program, and determine what type of program—whether it's ESOPs, government owning the stock, or government purchasing the stock and giving it to every American. We need to also consider strengthening cooperatives beyond simply the grocery store chains and the farmers. While we have already nationalized the military-contracting industry, there is no single answer for other industries in our nation, including allowing private enterprise to remain intact in various places."

McTaggart, quoting Edward Abbey and other radicals, gave many people the impression he liked plants and insects more than people, at least according to the responses pollsters gathered from "likely voters" after the debates. Meanwhile, McReynolds sounded the "old time religion" of pure prairie socialism, which had its own resonance for enough American voters in various states to make Bond nervous.

The Republican presidential candidate, Barry Sadler, first became famous in the 1960s for writing and singing the song "The Green Berets." He had served in the military with the Special Forces, which John F. Kennedy, while president, had christened the "Green Berets." He also served in Vietnam in 1963 and 1964. Sadler received an honorable discharge in 1967 and, riding high on his hit song, moved with his young family to Tucson, Arizona. After realizing he had little future in music as a writer or producer, Sadler turned to politics. Barry Goldwater was especially impressed with the high school dropout's intellect and mentored him. Sadler, with his rugged good looks and strong, but practical libertarian philosophies, rose in Arizona Republican ranks, eventually becoming governor of Arizona in 1980.

In 1984, Sadler was finishing his second and final term as governor. As governor, he organized Internet-based government filings and permits for businesses, auto license renewals, and other government services, including payment of taxes. He lowered the state's sales tax, which made him a hero to those who opposed sales taxes—for different reasons—on the left and the right wings of politics. He streamlined various laws in that state, saying, "Why duplicate, or worse, add further layers of restrictions to any laws the federal government already has? If anything, I'd like to tell Washington to do the same!"

Arizona, during Sadler's two terms as governor, saw increased business development at the expense of other states. Housing prices were lower, as were the costs of doing business. That Arizona was a beneficiary of federal government transit programs, water projects, and other programs was conveniently forgotten by most voters there.

When Sadler decided to run for president, he was quick to gather important business endorsements before he formally announced. He deftly outmaneuvered one of his Republican challengers for the nomination, Lee Iacocca, who thought he had the business vote locked up from the day he became the senator from Connecticut. But businessmen liked Sadler for his action-hero magnetism, his ability to emote, and his private promise to business leaders to "peel off" religious union voters with his message of "moral moderation."

By "moral moderation" he meant set views on the issues of abortion, homosexuals, and gun control. Specifically, Sadler was against any abortion after the third month, "as the Supreme Court has ruled—and the Supreme Court is the law of our great land, and must be obeyed." He was against homosexuals "getting married and adopting children," pointing to the "homosexual discos" and homosexuals' "natural" inability to have children of their own, which "must be for a reason." Breaking with suburban and urban Republicans, he also came out against gun control but promised "to vigorously enforce laws that require stiff sentences for those using a gun," although few of those laws existed at the time.

The strategy, according to Ed Rollins, Sadler's chief political adviser, was to lure Democratic union households into switching their votes to the Republicans on cultural issues, while holding on to Republicans desperate for a president not beholden to labor unions. He reasoned that with enough religious working-class votes, along with the usual Peace and Freedom and Green Party defections from the Democrats, Sadler could defeat Bond. Rollins later said, "I once heard that Yarborough told Bob Kennedy a politician must face his own fear and make it the other fella's fear, or something to that effect. I determined, and Sadler agreed with me, that the Democrats' fear was talking about these cultural issues. For too many years, we Republicans gave them a free ride because we kept pandering to our own cultural liberals. So we decided, let's be more moderate on the cultural issues so we don't scare away working-class voters. The hardest thing for us was whether we'd make it past the primary. If we did, we knew we were golden for November!"

Although the primary was tough, Sadler was also able to capitalize on the problems faced by his Republican primary opponents. Jesse Jackson, who ran again for the Republican presidential nomination, defeated himself more than Sadler defeated him. Jackson's argument for the 1984 race was that he had already won the popular vote in 1980 over Yarborough. But with the Democrats running a black for president—Julian Bond—Jackson's "split the minorities" strategy was far less appealing to the largely white Republican constituency this time around.

Jackson had also, by 1984, suffered twin scandals—one sexual and the other financial. He admitted to a sexual relationship with a young staffer after the woman involved admitted the story was true. The financial scandal, on the other hand, he consistently denied. It concerned allegations of misuse of funds in one of his nonprofit organizations. By the time the persons making the allegation were found, sued, and had recanted, the damage was done. Jackson received few endorsements, and the train for the presidential nomination had long left the station before Jackson could arrive for seating.

Sadler and Rollins smiled as Sadler's other business challenger, Iacocca, swooped up the endorsements of Hollywood homosexuals, radical libertarian feminists, and some bohemian elements at the edge of the Republican Party, including Frank Zappa. As Rollins told business supporters, "Our candidate's votes aren't in the rolls of our party right now. But they'll show up this year in the primary, and they'll be back in the fall, including votes coming directly from the Democrats." With Julian Bond running essentially unopposed for the Democratic nomination, the Arizona governor received, in state after state, votes from more than a few religious union rank-and-filers who switched to the Republican Party just to vote for him.

There was a rumor that Ethel Kennedy voted for Sadler in the California primary, which could not be proven one way or the other. First, Ethel hadn't talked to the press since 1977. Second, in 1983, California had passed an initiative, sponsored by libertarians and Republicans, that allowed people to vote for whomever they wanted, regardless of their party affiliation. Some said Ethel's refusal to say which way she voted, even as her husband spoke to the Democrats at their convention, meant she had voted for Sadler in the primary.

Sadler, like most Republicans of his time, took the position that environmental clean-ups were the government's responsibility, no different than issues of national security. With continued frustration at the Democrats, and with open talk of a new Green Party, this stance appealed to those environmentalists who saw organized labor as the bigger obstacle to further environmental laws. Plus, politicians knew that selling something as expensive as environmental clean-ups by claiming that it was for "national security" reasons is usually helpful in securing its passage. "Eisenhower did it with roads, and we can do it nationally—and save business a bundle from its own mistakes," said former American Airlines executive Bob Crandall, now a congressman from upstate New York.

Union media did their best to showcase Sadler's antiworker stances and his support of mining interests in Arizona against various environmentalist legislation. But Sadler's embrace of culturally "traditional" views of religious working-class voters proved effective at neutralizing those attacks. Meanwhile, the corporate media trumpeted Sadler's "moral moderation" in conjunction with his "forward-looking leadership" to the point that Iacocca complained that both the union and corporate media were biased against his own candidacy.

Iacocca, two weeks before the remaining state primaries in June 1984, knew he was beat. He contacted Sadler and offered his support in exchange for the vice presidential slot. Sadler readily agreed; polls showed that running with Iacocca would unite Republican environmentalists and bohemians behind the ticket, but still give Sadler room to fish for Democratic Party defectors.

The question the Republicans pondered through election day 1984 was, could they win enough electoral college votes against feuding Democrats, socialists (Peace and Freedom Party), and Greens?

The answer was, in short, yes, they could—and they did.

In a reverse of the 1980 election, the Republican ticket squeaked out an electoral college victory but lost the popular vote. The Democratic ticket of Bond-Rosen won 47 percent of the vote; the Republican ticket of Sadler-Iacocca won 46 percent. The Democrats were, in hindsight, punished for their failure to understand that the electoral college was a fickle system that could as easily punish as reward a political party. Under the system as it operated in most states at that time, a candidate who won by even one vote won *all* the electoral college votes for that state—even if the win came with less than 50 percent of the vote overall. The Republican ticket, taking advantage of the split among Democrats, socialists, and Greens, won several of the largest states' electoral college votes in the winner-take-all system.

The Peace and Freedom Party won only 5 percent of the vote, and the Green Party received 2 percent. Although voter turnout was 68 percent that year, higher than in 1980, it was still lower than during the Robert Kennedy era. MIT political science professor Walter Dean Burnham, the most revered political scientist during the 1970s and 1980s, concluded that if the voter turnout had averaged 75 percent, as in the Robert Kennedy years, Bond-Rosen might well have won the electoral college vote, too.

Robert Shrum, a longtime consultant to the Democrats, had a less sanguine analysis. He said that, because of Sadler's strategy of "moral moderation" and speaking out only against unnamed extremist elements in unions, the union members lacked sufficient incentive for their usual high turnout. Worse, Bond and Rosen, known among the activists and the media as leaning strongly toward cultural liberalism, were unable to convince certain religious union voters to stay within the Democratic Party fold—or vote at all. And in a close race, such voters were crucial for either side.

Finally, some wondered at the fact that in 1980 and 1984, the candidates who were the victims of the electoral college vote were both African Americans. In a close vote, it appeared the specter of racism may have played a role. The problem with this theory was that a review of the election results could not find any definite, let alone significant pattern of racially minded voting—though in a close race, one could argue that every vote is potentially the "winning" one.

Regardless, two days after the 1984 election, Robert Kennedy called President Yarborough to talk about the results. "Ralph," said Kennedy, "it was a helluva run. While I feel just terrible for Julian and Ruth, all in all it's not the end of the world, since the House and Senate remain strongly Democratic, and I'm not sure this fellow, Sadler, is up to doing anything very significant. How do you see it?"

"That's how Ah see it, too, Bob. Nothin' to worry 'bout, really."

Those who know the history of our nation from this point on, however, know that the two seasoned politicians could not have been more wrong. There was plenty to worry about. The only thing certain was that the Kennedy-Yarborough era had come to an end. Many changes lay ahead, and the legacy of that era, despite what would come next, would eventually survive—though not in ways most Americans could have anticipated or known at the time. For fate and history, even more than the electoral college system, are very fickle creatures, quick to punish those who believe they can avoid the law of unintended consequences derived from human actions.

APPENDIX

*"The Great Struggle and Beyond," address by Julian Lewis, Ph.D.
in American History, Philip S. Foner Chair, Columbia University,
September 6, 2011.*

(Editor's note: This is a transcript of a lecture by Professor Julian Lewis,
delivered at Columbia University on Tuesday, September 6, 2011, the day
after Labor Day. The lecture was reprinted, with an accompanying slide show
in the October 2011 online issue of *American Heritage* magazine.)

I apologize for starting late this morning. As our computer system is currently down, we cannot use the multimedia presentation I normally use for
my lectures. I will therefore risk some boredom by speaking without digital
photos and video, and other visual aids that accompany my lectures.

Yesterday was Labor Day, a secular but deeply sacred holiday for
American working people and their families. Labor Day, as we know from all
the celebrations that took place this past weekend, has more significance than
usual this year because we are celebrating the twenty-fifth anniversary of
what we commonly call the "Great Struggle." I am honored to speak today
before this incoming freshman class and their families here at Columbia
University because, as all of us know, our high school history classes often
give short shrift to the last forty years no matter what era one grows up in.
When I was in high school during the 1970s, we learned hardly anything
about World War II other than the Japanese government bombed Pearl
Harbor, Hitler was an evil person, and that some American general said he'd
"return" after losing an early battle to the Japanese—and he did return. Oh,
and, of course, we learned the phrase "six million" applied to the number of
Jews who the Nazis killed during that war. That scholars now believe the
number was 5.1 million is still deemed "too clinical" to discuss. As for events
after World War II, suffice it to say that if any of us students knew there was
a war in Korea in which Americans were involved, it was almost an accident.

I therefore will provide a summary of the immediate events that led to
Civil War II, as more cynical commentators call it, and what happened during the Great Struggle, as most Americans call it. We can then reflect on the
changes that came about as a result of the Struggle—I'll refrain from using
the word "Great" every time—and talk about some other interesting, if perhaps philosophical, and even trivial, things; for the act of reflection

encompasses the serious and the trivial, the practical and the philosophical, and both facts and speculation.

Before we begin our discussion of the Great Struggle, we should bear the following in mind: How one sees History is often limited by where one stands within the timeline of History. For example, if we were to look forward, say, from the 1960s toward the late 1980s and the outbreak of the Great Struggle, we likely would assume the Struggle was based upon the burning issues of the 1960s. Meaning, we'd assume the Struggle was an outgrowth of the civil rights movement for racial minorities and that it was a war in which racial hatred or hostility played a significant role. Or we might assume the Struggle resulted over the nature and extent of American intervention in foreign affairs that went back to the protests against the American invasion of Vietnam. Yet neither of those issues figured in the Struggle.

Even during great historical events, how one sees those events can often change. If you asked President Lincoln at the start of the first American Civil War of the 1860s, "Mr. President, what is this Civil War you're fighting all about?" he would say, "The preservation of the nation." The southern leaders, who represented those states seceding from the rest of the nation, almost to a man, would say it was about the issue of slavery. By the time the North defeated the South in April 1865, even Lincoln would concede that the war was as much about slavery as preserving the nation. The South, having itself freed the southern slaves in the waning days of the Civil War in a desperate attempt to stop northern forces, began to stress that the fight was about "states' rights," as opposed to slavery. We should therefore maintain some humility as we attempt to understand what any important event in History was "about" or "why" it happened.

Following the end of that war in 1865, there was the period most students of History recognize as "Reconstruction," meaning the reorganizing of the southern states away from a slave-holding society. The Reconstruction period saw important civil rights laws passed, and for a time it looked as if black Americans might see great political and economic gains. The southern "tradition," however, proved more resilient, in large part because of less virulent, but perhaps more effective, racism in the North. And, just over ten years after the end of the Civil War, we saw the rise of a movement to re-enslave black Americans under the guise of separation and discrimination; in other words, segregation. Now, where did the South get the idea of segregation? They learned it, ironically, from different cities and towns in the North, where darker-skinned people were separated from light-skinned people in both housing and education. This segregation in the North was not as widespread as some southern partisans would have us believe, but it was certainly present. And, of course, we know that segregation was imposed with as much violence as law.

What, you may ask, does all that have to do with the Great Struggle of 1986 and 1987? Well, I bring this up to suggest that the Great Struggle of the late 1980s was a kind of *reverse* of the first Civil War. In reviewing the events leading to the Struggle, we cannot fail to notice that our nation had a Reconstruction of the South *first*—and then we had our internal war that was anything but civil, as most civil wars tend to be. The "Second Reconstruction," in terms of securing black persons' political rights, was begun by the martyred President John F. Kennedy in the early 1960s and largely completed by President Lyndon Johnson in the mid- to late 1960s. Johnson's successor, President *Robert* Kennedy—John's younger brother— surprised many observers at the time by moving successfully to create a coalition of black and white workers in the South, especially through his support of AFL-CIO efforts to organize labor unions in that region. He also embarked on a program of government assistance to revitalize poor areas in the major cities of the United States, where many blacks had been languishing in poverty. As historian John Hope Franklin wrote many years ago, Robert Kennedy and Reverend Martin Luther King Jr. both understood that the true test of civil rights in America would be in the economic realm, not simply the political realm.

Thus, one may argue that Robert Kennedy's policies were perhaps the most important step to ensure the success of the Second American Reconstruction. Those policies made the South more like the rest of the nation and helped the South leave behind its insular, agrarian culture. Kennedy's policies in the North also overcame white people's fear of black, people, a fear we had begun to see among whites just after the mid-1960s race riots in many of the largest American cities. The election of Ralph Yarborough in 1976 was, to use a quaint phrase, "icing on the cake" in completing this Second Reconstruction, for reasons we can discuss another time.

Again, I go into this detail because I must say it is difficult for us, in 2011, to understand how significant it is that the Great Struggle was not about racial or ethnic warfare. As bad as the Second Civil War was in terms of lives lost, particularly civilian lives, I have, over years of studying American History and having lived through the era of the 1960s through the 1980s, been ever thankful that the Struggle was not about race. When one reads about American and Asian soldiers' racially-motivated killings and brutalities against each other in World War II, in Korea, and in Vietnam, or the racial hatred and violence throughout America during the civil rights movement of the 1950s and 1960s, we are relatively fortunate that our Second Civil War had very little in the way of racially-motivated murders; for nations that have racially- or ethnically-motivated civil wars often descend into ever deepening levels of brutality that end with one side being mostly if not completely annihilated.[1]

With that as an introduction, I wish to discuss the events of the Great Struggle. In my discussion, I hope I do not offend any veterans of the Great Struggle who may be present if I miss some important aspects. My goal is merely to provide an adequate summary for those largely unaware of the salient facts. I also hope not to bore those who have studied in detail this series of important historic events.

We must first recall that the presidential and national elections of 1984 created a strange result. The Democratic candidates for president and vice president that year won more votes but lost to the Republican candidates because of the so-called electoral college system, which after the Struggle was thankfully abolished. Before people think that the Republican president's victory was therefore "tainted" or "unfair" because the Democratic candidate received more votes, we must recall that the previous president, the legendary Ralph Yarborough, received fewer popular votes in his reelection campaign of 1980 than his Republican challenger, former congressman and later University of Chicago president Jesse Jackson. The Democrats had the opportunity to change, and even abolish, the electoral college system in 1981, but they refused. Some may therefore say that the Democrats would have saved themselves, and perhaps the country, from the subsequent events of the Struggle had the electoral college system been eliminated earlier. Another irony of History, I suppose.

Although the Democrats lost at the "top of their ticket," as we used to say, they retained control of Congress, both the House and Senate, in the 1984 elections. This was less comforting for the Democrats than one might think because the Democrats were themselves hopelessly divided at the time, particularly over the question of how to further neutralize excessive corporate power. Some Democrats wanted direct citizen ownership of stock, some wanted nationalization of various industries, and others wanted to actively assist employees in purchasing controlling stock in various companies.

The rest of Congress was composed of Republicans, mostly pro-corporate and culturally liberal, some Peace and Freedom members who called for nationalization or government ownership of "the means of production," and a couple of Green Party members who won races in a few scattered districts, mostly in the Midwest and on the West Coast. The Peace and Freedom and Green Parties' candidates were more eccentric than the mainstream party candidates. They ran the gamut from socialists who loved—I'll use a phrase of the time—"fish-killing dams" and nuclear power to extreme environmentalists who were highly capitalistic, or libertarian in the business sense of that political term.

In the parliamentary system we now have as a result of the Constitutional Convention of 1987, with a unicameral legislature and a president (who operates more as a prime minister) chosen from the members of the ruling party or coalition of parties, the 1984 electoral result simply would not occur. Our current system, in which political party platforms carry much more weight, is more inclined to a national perspective, and a more ideological perspective, I might add. The old Congress, on the other hand, had far more geographical than ideological biases in how its members voted. As the old, and long deceased, House of Representatives Speaker Tip O'Neill, once said, "All politics is local." This is somewhat true of our current system, but in a profoundly different way, which, unfortunately, again is beyond our scope today.

The official winner of the 1984 presidential election, Republican and former Green Beret Barry Sadler, had not held any national office before assuming the presidency. Sadler had been a highly successful governor of a relatively weak labor union state, Arizona, but was savvy enough to understand that he would only be able to pass his supposedly libertarian—essentially corporatist—agenda by directly challenging the Democrats and their union allies. This strategy was not as flawed as some historians believe, even though he obviously went too far in precipitating the Great Struggle.

But we need not consult Prince Machiavelli's cynical nostrums to see what Sadler saw as he attempted to change public policy and take advantage of his divided opposition. Sadler saw the Democrats did not have enough votes in Congress to override his rejections of proposed laws they sent to him as president. And he immediately and successfully used the power to reject or veto pro-worker legislation. Second, as president, he had some, but not complete, authority to issue "executive orders," which, though not written specifically into the old Constitution, had been a power exercised by presidents starting with George Washington. If the orders were not rejected by two-thirds of Congress—enough to override the president's order—and the orders were not overturned in the courts, the orders were as enforceable as any legislation Congress could pass. In the hands of someone such as Sadler, the veto and executive order powers were formidable.

Sadler loved the idea of confrontation. He saw it as a way "to roll back the extremist union leaders who really control the country"—as if he hadn't shown simply by winning that unions didn't have that much power. In any event, Sadler hoped to persuade Americans, with his "executive legislation," that his political party deserved more support in order to create, as he saw it, "a country based more on liberty than socialist equality."

To further his agenda, Sadler used his executive power to appoint people to the National Labor Relations Board who were far more sympathetic to businesses than to workers—or in his words, "balanced" in their view of labor-management relations. At the same time, Sadler began promoting an economic policy that he liked to call "creative chaos," which he claimed was "the mother of technological invention and innovation." This included having his cabinet and executive departments become more lax—more "reasonable," he said—in enforcing laws against businesses. This laxness applied not only to antimonopoly laws, but also to safety and health laws and some, but certainly not all, environmental laws.

To avoid a complete split with environmentalists who supported him, though, Sadler very adroitly increased the government's budget to have the government, not private businesses, pay for the costliest environmental cleanups. He reversed President Yarborough's policy of making businesses pay for most of the environmental harm they directly caused.

In his first significant antilabor move, President Sadler decided, in mid-1985, to challenge the Air Traffic Controllers Union, whose members, on a per capita basis, were the wealthiest members of any union in the country. Ironically, that union had endorsed Sadler during the election of 1984. In doing so, the union defied the AFL-CIO leadership and later that same year, left the venerable labor association. The Air Traffic Controllers Union, therefore, thought they had a friend in the White House. Instead, they became "lab rats" for Sadler's experiment in union busting.

After the air traffic controllers went on strike in early July 1985, Sadler, exercising a power that President Bob Kennedy and union interests mistakenly left in place while reforming other labor laws in 1969, "permanently replaced" striking air traffic controllers. In other words, he fired them.[2] This shocked the nation because, from the 1930s till then, no employer, especially corporate employers, had dared to use that power to permanently replace or fire workers who went on strike. According to Harvard professor Robert Kuttner, a leading historian of the period, most corporate leaders feared that politicians would support labor interests if a corporation acted so immorally as to fire workers who sought better wages or benefits for their families. Kuttner has persuasively argued that this was why the Democrats, in the 1969 labor reform law, never thought to prohibit an employer's right to "permanently replace" striking workers. Of course, our new Constitution flatly states it is illegal to fire workers in any labor union that goes on strike.

As Sadler fired the striking air traffic controllers, he also issued executive orders that deregulated the computer industry and the trucking industry. Although these orders did not take immediate effect, because of court injunctions and the appeals process, they had the effect of making people debate the issue. Sadler's executive orders also had what he called the "salutary effect" of diverting union resources and attention away from the air traffic control workers. Most inspiring to Sadler, however, was that his actions signaled to all bosses in both large and small corporations that here was a president willing to back them against workers in the major labor union contract negotiations of late 1985 and especially into 1986.

Corporate leaders, happy at the sight of squabbling Democrats and defensive labor leaders, leaped at the chance to support the president's policies. They immediately took a hard-line stance on that year's labor contract negotiations, and some were almost giddy at the prospect of permanently replacing labor leaders and their most vocal minions if there was a strike. As the *Wall Street Journal,* then a pro-business newspaper, exulted in an editorial, "The scent of labor discipline is in the air at last! May that scent now permeate through the entire nation and restore strength and resolve to employers everywhere against the forces of unionism."

The unions were indeed on the defensive, and for the first time in decades. Some union leaders feared that if their unions went on strike, the government might not be able or willing to support them—even though the Democrats still controlled Congress. In our previous Constitution's separation of the executive and legislative branches, the president had the power to send in troops and influence, if not determine, whose side those troops would be on. Again, this issue would not likely arise today under our parliamentary system in which the executive and legislative aspects of government function more harmoniously.

By the end of March 1986, the Ralph Nader supporters, unions, Harrington-ites, and many environment activists realized they had a common enemy in the White House. The call was heeded to organize a nationwide general strike in major American cities that would begin on Monday morning, April 7, 1986. That morning, aggressive strikers blocked major thoroughfares leading into major cities and also blocked public transportation to make sure people did not go to work that day. Fights broke out and so did some gun battles—battles that portended future events—between those supporting labor interests and those supporting the president. Surprising the president, and many observers at the time, the police refused to act in their then traditional role as strikebreakers. Instead, they largely stood with their "brothers and sisters" in the union-led general strike. Angrily, the president turned to the National Guard to disperse the strikers. He demanded that guard members "volunteer" to work for those employers facing strikes—in other words, scab on their fellow workers. In making this decision, Sadler cited the precedent of Democratic President Truman, who ordered the National Guard and soldiers to work in steel mills during the steel strike of 1951—though the Supreme Court at the time held that Truman acted outside of constitutional bounds.

President Sadler said this was necessary to quell the rebellion and anarchy that were brewing as a result of the general strike. To the president's shock, however, many in the National Guard, after being called out and armed to the teeth, suddenly refused to cross picket lines, let alone disperse union protesters. Most absolutely refused to take over another man's (or woman's, especially!) job. Instead, most of the guard, who were related to or neighbors of the strikers, joined the general strike within days of being called up by the president.

Seizing the opportunity presented by the police and the National Guard's defiance of the president, the Democrats in Congress, led by then Senator Jim Hightower of Texas, challenged the president's authority to call out the National Guard, and potentially any military, under these circumstances. Hightower introduced a bill to strip the president of authority to call up the National Guard or the military in situations involving labor unrest, absent congressional approval. The president said the Hightower bill was unconstitutional. He invoked the "separation of powers" doctrine and his constitutional power as president to take all necessary steps against any "rebellion" in the various states. Again, using precedents of Democratic Party leaders, Sadler reminded members of Congress that Robert Kennedy, as attorney general, unilaterally called up the National Guard to protect black students in the early '60s. In the late 1960s and early 1970s, as president, Robert Kennedy called in the guard to protect labor union strikers in the South. Outraged Democrats answered that Kennedy called out the guard to *protect* students and labor. In other words, real people, not non-human corporations.

In a speech to the nation, in which he derided the Hightower bill as un-American and unconstitutional, President Sadler declared a state of emergency. In his self-proclaimed role of commander in chief, Sadler now called on the American military to quell what he called "riots" in the major cities. At first, the disturbances were not riots at all, but they became more than riots after the military arrived. The military personnel, who were specifically told by the president that this was a warlike situation, were under orders to shoot to kill in case of any resistance to their commands to end the strikes.

The first military attacks against American strikers occurred in Los Angeles in mid-April 1986. There remains some dispute as to whether sniper attacks were directed against the military and whether that was the cause of the military's violent response. Regardless, union media were outraged and said that Sadler was committing treason against working people. Studs Turkel, America's most famous radio and Internet commentator of that time, spoke for many when he shouted over the nation's airwaves and the Internet, "This violent attack against American citizens is worse than any government attack on working men and women in the history of our great nation! It is worse than the militarist response to the sit-down strikes of the 1930s! This attack was as brutal as the murder of workers during the great general strikes of 1877 or Haymarket Square in the 1880s! No loyal American should tolerate the president's lawless and treasonous actions! If we do not stand up to this elitist and less-than-popularly-elected president, then we are not worthy of the word 'American'!"

Workers in city after city joined forces with local Democratic mayors and city councils to form what they called "strike councils," and, when the military engagements began in earnest, "workers councils." In those areas where the Republicans and pro-business interests dominated, such as Colorado and Connecticut, workers councils quickly became the new political order of the day; the workers, including the police, had more guns than the municipal governments. Concurrent with the rise of these councils, corporate leaders began forming vigilance committees, which included employees of the dreaded private security company, Pinkerton Security Corporation—now thankfully out of business. The vigilance committees were patterned after earlier committees that most old union men and women recalled as "lynching parties." Sadler told Vice

President Iacocca that he was glad to see the rise of the councils and committees because it proved his point that there was a rebellion in the United States that needed his executive and military authority to put down.

General David Hackworth had been in charge of the military's Joint Chiefs of Staff since Yarborough's first administration, but he resigned in protest when the president asked him to continue the orders of shooting to kill in order to stop the general strike. With Hackworth's resignation, Sadler went further in his exercise of emergency powers. He suspended the work of Congress and appointed Hackworth's intermilitary rival, General Robert Ignatius Herron, to lead the government—now, no booing here!

No matter what we think of Herron's subsequent conduct, we must remember that the military was deeply divided, not only as to whether to support the president or Congress, but also as to whether career military officers could form their own union. While we all regard Hackworth today as our second George Washington for his heroic actions during and after the Great Struggle, we should recall that the military's union movement began as a reaction against Hackworth's attempts to consolidate the various branches of the military and fire those officers and career members who did not want to accept the loss of corporate executive–type perquisites, such as free air flights and extra discounts on food and cosmetics.

And who was the main person in the military who led the fight on behalf of officer unionization, at least by 1986? It was, ironically, the same General Herron. Why did Herron side, then, with the antiunion president? Because, as Herron said in his war crimes trial after the Struggle, he believed he was acting under proper orders of his commander in chief, the president, in what by that point was clearly a breakdown in the authority of the United States government, regardless of how the nation had gotten there. That unions were leading the rebellion broke his heart, he said, but he believed his duty was to preserve the nation and support the president.

Hackworth—who maintained that soldiers "can't go on strike, damn it!"—resigned rather than continue to fire on American *civilian* workers whose only "crime," he said, was going on strike. As he memorably told the president, "That's no crime at all!" Hackworth also told President Sadler—and I'll read here from the official transcript that has since been released—"The last thing this country needs is a goddamned civil war with union guerillas! You're losing your mind if you think escalating this situation is the way to go. These union workers, a lot of them were trained in our military and have families in the military. You have no idea what you're getting into here! This could be like goddamned Vietnam!"

Sadler, who had served in Vietnam for a short tour in 1963 and 1964, said, "Fine, General. Except this time, I'm not gonna let the Viet Cong win like you and your friends did! *We're* gonna win this time!"

Hackworth answered, "Who's the 'we' here, buddy? Ah, forget it, man. I'm not arguing with a lunatic! If you think you're gonna 'win' anything here, all I can say is I'll see you in hell before this is over." Hackworth said later he wasn't sure what he meant when he said it, but he realized he was probably already thinking of creating his own counter-army against Sadler. Hackworth considered Sadler a military "wannabe," which Hackworth said was the worst type of civilian to ever have control over a military force.

Hackworth left Washington, D.C., and traveled west. He thought about *where* and *what* "the United States" was. Was it residing in the millions of striking workers or in the president? When the president, on April 24, 1986, ordered the Capitol surrounded by military troops, Hackworth knew the United States was *not* President Sadler.

Hackworth stopped in Chicago, realizing the time had come to challenge the president. He drove to the AFL-CIO chapter headquarters and, upon arriving, walked into the august labor headquarters. Hackworth asked if he might be able to contact Douglas Fraser, a longtime leader in the AFL-CIO. In one of those coincidences that History sometimes provides us, Fraser was himself visiting Chicago to check up on the condition of strikers there. Fraser had just come from the office of Mayor Thomas Hayden, whose support, along with the Chicago City Council, was so strong in favor of the strikers that there was no need for a separate workers council in the Windy City. Hackworth was led in to see Fraser and he introduced himself, as if he needed any introduction.

Fraser's recollection of the conversation, which I learned in an interview I did with him for an oral history project a few years after the Struggle, and which Hackworth has largely agreed with, goes as follows:

Hackworth said, and I quote, "I can't believe I'm doing this, but the president and his henchman, Herron, are turning this crisis into a real, live, and hot civil war—and they're coming after you and your union guys! I can put together more soldiers than those assholes can. Not as many officers, but most of their officers have forgotten how to fight! I figure I'll be commanding a lot of the sons of your labor union members or reservists who are union members. All I ask in return is one thing: After this thing is done—if we get out alive—you gotta agree there will be no labor union for the military. Otherwise, I'll continue to travel west, maybe to Idaho, and wait this shit out. I'll always support better civil service protection for my troops; but even then, command needs to weed out prima donnas that don't follow orders. You haven't got any time to argue this out in your committees, Doug, if I can call you that. Do you agree to my terms? Or do I keep heading west?"

As he told me years later in that oral history project, Fraser agreed, more because of the shocking news Hackworth gave him about Sadler's intentions than on the merits of having a military officers union. And as we know, Fraser's promise has been kept to this day.

Hackworth shook hands with Fraser and said, "Now, Doug, we gotta get rolling if we're gonna stop this Mussolini president and your former union buddy, General Herron. And I mean *now!*"

Angry with President Sadler's hasty choice of Herron, and after hearing rumors on military bases that Hackworth was assembling an army, navy, and air force to counter the president, Admiral Thomas Moorer resigned his commission to join Hackworth, as did a young general, Wesley Clark. Retired colonel and longtime presidential military adviser William Corson called Hackworth and offered his services, which Hackworth gladly accepted.

So here you have Hackworth, the so-called antiunion leader within the military, creating a rebel army of labor unionists against his own government. And you also have Herron, previously supporting the formation of an officers union, now leading government forces against rebellious labor unions. Again, one finds an eerie parallel in the First Civil War. In the First Civil War, Robert E. Lee was a man who detested slavery and was actually sympathetic to Lincoln. Lincoln had hoped Lee would lead the U.S. government troops as the crisis at Fort Sumter was escalating into a civil war. But Lee demurred, saying he had to stay loyal to Virginia, the state in which he had been born and raised.

And then there was northern General William Tecumseh Sherman, who had lived for a time in the South and sympathized with the South's position that slavery should remain legal. Sherman also believed that black Americans were intellectually inferior to white people. Yet, because he believed the United States must remain joined as one nation, Sherman reluctantly became a general under Lincoln, a man for whom he had little respect at the beginning of that Civil War. Despite Sherman's love of the South and the white people there, he would, before that war was over, instigate the first modern attack against civilians—on the very people whom he admired. If southern military forces had captured Sherman in the waning days of the Civil War, he would have most certainly been executed as a war criminal back when the death penalty was legal. In the Great Struggle and the First American Civil War—indeed, throughout History—we often find that real life has many surprising plot twists.

In any event, the Great Struggle began in earnest on April 29, 1986, when General Herron, with bombing raids reminiscent of America's conduct in Vietnam in the mid-1960s, fortified the Washington-Baltimore corridor. Scores of strikers were killed in the process. Herron knew he did not have the troops to match what Hackworth, Moorer, and Clark were amassing. He therefore used the military's most advanced weapons to bomb working-class districts where workers were arming themselves. Herron's actions, again, should not be judged in a vacuum. If we judge him harshly, then what should we make of General Sherman, who used the then latest technology to kill civilians and burn Atlanta to the ground during the First Civil War? I had relatives killed during the Herron-led attacks, so I do not make these comments lightly, I assure you!

I will not discuss any of the battles of the Great Struggle since military historian Gar Alperovitz has provided perhaps the best summary of those battles in his book on the Great Struggle. Suffice it to say that no major city was spared the consequences of the government's bombing campaign. During the first three months of the Struggle, it looked like Sadler and Herron would prevail.

Hackworth was forced to immediately employ guerilla warfare tactics, which, while very effective, gave Herron the excuse to bring the fighting—and more bombing—into civilian neighborhoods. Herron, after the Struggle, defended his bombing campaign by citing 1960s U.S. Defense Department memoranda on counterguerilla tactics. Such government-approved tactics included "stimulating" refugee situations that were "deliberately aimed at depriving" guerillas of a "recruiting base." The goal of counterinsurgency and mass bombing was to cause the civilian "sea" to "recede" from where the "guerilla fish swim."[3]

Herron believed he had no choice but to bomb union strongholds, even if there was, as he called it, "collateral damage" to civilians. Now I realize this sounds monstrous and criminal to our ears. However, if we are to be objective, we should emphasize again that Herron was following our own government's counterinsurgency techniques that had been used in South Vietnam—with the goal of preventing the guerillas from being able to operate within towns and cities. If this caused what our strategists called "collateral civilian damages," well, that was the price one paid for undermining guerilla threats to a village or community. In analyzing this over the years, I have had to consider the following: Unless we want to say that it's fine to do such things against other civilian populations in a time of civil war or rebellion, but not ours, then we should perhaps hesitate in being as righteously indignant as we usually are when we think of Herron's actions.

[A heckler called out that Lewis was a "corporate fascist apologist" and said Lewis should "leave America if you hate our country so much as to defend a war criminal!"]

Sir, I love our country, but History requires Truth and perspective that sometimes aren't pretty. Our children are now adults and must learn the truth in order to properly analyze policy issues when they hold public office or otherwise work in the real world. [A hearty, but not universal audience applause followed.]

And what I learned from my reading and discussion with those leaders who participated in the Vietnam War and the Great Struggle is that not only was Herron a war criminal, but also that many of our leaders during the '60s, in regard to their conduct in Vietnam, could be considered war criminals as well. [Groans, but also some tepid applause followed.]

Now, where were we? Oh, yes. Fitting the usual pattern of nations that have endured civil wars, after the Struggle, murderous reprisals continued even after the peace pipes were smoked and the war crimes trials were completed. Hackworth did his best to stop these reprisals from occurring, but he was largely unsuccessful. These occurred in nearly every town and hamlet across the nation and were difficult to control because of their local nature. Murderous scores were settled between the families of local business people and laborers, cultural liberals and religious zealots, environmentalists and hunters, neighbors who fought over too much noise coming from one house or the other, over adulterous affairs, etc. A prominent feminist once said in the late 1960s that the "personal was political." We could say, in reference to the Great Struggle, that the "political was personal . . . and deadly." Another one hundred and thirty thousand people were killed in these post-Struggle reprisals, not an insignificant number, I should say.

As we know from our history books, and they are largely correct in this, the Second American Civil War's eventual toll was more than four million American dead and sixteen million wounded.[4] President Sadler, during the early stages of the Struggle, often quoted the nineteenth-century financier, Jay Gould, to the effect that he would defeat the "unionists" because he could "hire one half of the working class to kill the other half." Sadler's civil war against workers, one could say, did prove at least part of Gould's point, for as many as one-third of the workers fought against their fellow workers. Why this is so has to do perhaps with the loyalty one naturally feels toward any president or leader, a question we may better leave to anthropologists or sociologists. And we are lucky more workers did not back the president, given the president's and General Herron's continual depiction of their side of the war as the side of patriotism and 100 percent Americanism. Luckily, for most Americans, the pro-union or pro-democracy forces prevailed.

As we know all too well, Miami, Charlotte, Washington, D.C., Baltimore, and greater Boston were essentially destroyed during the Great Struggle. Manhattan was partially spared, though outlying boroughs suffered tremendous bombing damage, mostly caused by the government's forces. On the West Coast, government forces bombed Seattle and San Francisco, both strong labor areas. Los Angeles was also largely destroyed, but more by street warfare than by bombings. Due to the unique, somewhat more horizontal layout of Los Angeles, most of the battles between labor and corporate-government forces were fought street by street, most notably in the Battle of the Miracle Mile—near downtown Los Angeles. That battle is mostly remembered for producing the famous Annie Leibovitz photograph of Maria and Joseph Flores, two union workers who were gunned down by Herron's troops while fleeing a burning apartment building. Maria Flores was pregnant with their first child, who was going to be called Marcia, according to family members. This added to the poignancy of the photograph, which showed them running moments before they were killed. The number of children I see every year named Marcia attests to the power of that photograph and the memory of the Struggle.

Chicago, the headquarters for Hackworth's war efforts, was bombed as much as the eastern cities, although Hackworth continued to elude and eventually outmaneuver Herron. Working in Hackworth's favor were not only his superior numbers, but also the fact that so many American males were already trained in the use of guns and military weaponry and equipment. This was the result of two facts: First, the draft had been retained in the United States, despite Republican-led attempts to repeal it. Second, Republican and Democratic members of Congress representing upper-middle-class suburban districts could never convince a majority of their colleagues to limit the sale or availability of guns. This meant many Americans owned and knew how to operate guns of many different types, from 22-caliber pistols to rifles and even assault weapons that were beginning to come into vogue for gun collectors.

For most military historians, and I agree with them, this explains the success of Hackworth's daring counterattack of July 3, 1986, in which his guerilla forces conducted surprise simultaneous assaults on many of the major U.S. military bases—particularly those bases with nuclear warheads, air capabilities, and technologically advanced equipment and weaponry. Many base commanders surrendered after some hard fighting, and some even joined Hackworth's forces, including Generals Colin Powell and John Shalikashvili, among others. The July 3 attack had the effect of taking out many, though by no means all, of the military cards Herron held. Hackworth's forces seized, along with the bases, most of the planes, guns, tanks, antiaircraft missiles, and artillery. And again, Hackworth's forces needed little beyond refresher courses in terms of training. Compare this, again, to the First American Civil War in which part of the reason the North took so long to defeat the South, despite numerical superiority, was because many northern troops lacked military training and were unfamiliar with the southern terrain.

From July 3 on, Herron was forced to conserve his weaponry. As Hackworth gained followers in his Unionist Army, Herron, who was beginning to voice disagreement with President Sadler, became somewhat cautious as to how much bombing inside the nation would be not only militarily appropriate, but morally appropriate. The United Nations, at that time meeting in Geneva, Switzerland, denounced the Sadler regime's bombing campaign.

Herron, in a deft propaganda move to diffuse that denunciation, let loose a rumor that Hackworth had cut a deal with Mexico to give California back to Mexico in return for some weapons and soldiers. Hackworth immediately took to the airwaves—and what remained of the Internet in the large cities—and contacted newspaper wire services to rebut that scurrilous claim. The disinformation definitely slowed down Hackworth's recruitment in California, Arizona, and Texas, which, in turn, prolonged the Struggle, according to military historian Edward Luttwak.

The Struggle, as autumn turned into winter, hit a stalemate of sorts, with each side attacking the other's less-protected areas. Each side now used more tactically designed—so-called "smart"—bombs against the other on the theory that less "collateral damage" was better than more. Hackworth, using his superior numbers, sent armed guerrillas and special forces teams into wealthy strongholds such as Grosse Pointe, Michigan; Newport Beach, California; and the Hamptons in New York, where corporate managers and executives lived. The purpose was to take their money and valued possessions to keep them from funding the government's war effort, disarm them, and inspire enough fear to neutralize their support for the Sadler regime. The massacre at Gross Pointe, one must say, was the low point of the American workers' side. While there is evidence to suggest that the people in Grosse Pointe were well armed and may have precipitated the events that followed there, I personally have reviewed such evidence. I must conclude the massacre was neither militarily nor morally justified.

On the other hand, Herron's worst moment, which led to his military war crimes trial in 1988, came when he bombed three nuclear silos and two bioresearch labs in the Midwest. At the trial, he asserted, as some of you know, that radical environmentalists had allegedly planned to strike out against "all of humanity" by setting off the intercontinental ballistic missiles in those silos and spreading the deadly viruses that were being experimented with at the labs. Herron's actions killed a million people in the Southeast and Midwest alone, and would continue to kill people over the succeeding twenty-five years through cancer, leukemia, and other diseases.

Considering the booing and comments we heard earlier, I'd like to talk a bit about Herron's war crimes trial. I'm not going to go into too many details, of course, but we should at least consider Herron's defense, even if we find it wanting. I don't recall his exact testimony, but it went something like this. Herron said, essentially, "If I didn't act to take out those silos and labs in Kansas and Missouri, those bio-weapons could have fallen into the hands of people who were true monsters, who hated all of humanity!" There was some, but not much, evidence that a radical group of environmentalists, called the Army of the Earth, had planned to hack into the computer-operated nuclear silos and detonate nuclear weapons over various areas of the United States. They wanted to rid the world of what they called "the stain of humanity."

As even revisionist scholars sympathetic to Herron admit, the Army of the Earth was a small group of holed-up Internet eccentrics who were, in any event, far, far away from any nuclear weapons base with little knowledge of how to gain entry to the nuclear computer systems. They communicated with each other mostly on the Web, and later short-wave radios, and had no troops to speak of. As Hackworth said in his war crimes testimony against Herron, the Army of the Earth was as much an enemy of Hackworth's military forces, but he viewed them "as right-wing, limp-wristed philosophy majors trying to sound tough during a war." Hackworth personally checked them out and found them, as he told me, "pathetically harmless."

In the defense portion of Herron's trial, documents proved he had no idea the bio-weapons would cause so much long-term damage as a result of what the prosecution conceded was very precise bombing. I do remember the final words of his testimony as though I was still there watching the proceedings that day. Herron said, "If I wanted to terrorize people, I would have carpet-bombed most of the nation, something the United States did every day in South Vietnam during the 1960s, as General Hackworth knows full well."

Herron's defense attorneys also reminded the military panel that, in the mid-1950s, the United States tested the use of LSD and disease-ridden mosquitoes on mostly nonconsenting Americans in Savannah, Georgia, in Florida, in the Mountain States, and in the West. The attorneys spoke of the so-called Tuskegee syphilis experiments against African Americans—who were told they were being treated for syphilis when they were instead being treated with placebos so that scientists could monitor the effects of syphilis. They cited our government's above-ground atomic tests in the mountain regions of the United States in the 1950s, which adversely affected infant mortality rates, cancer rates, and thyroid development of an entire generation of people born or living around that region. As Herron's attorney, Alan Dershowitz, stated in his closing argument, "Did General Herron do anything intentionally like that during this civil war? Where are the war crimes tribunals for that? Some of those people who committed those crimes are still alive—and supported the Unionist side, I might add! When those people killed civilians with their experiments, there wasn't any internal rebellion going on as we had here. If General Herron is a war criminal, then what does that make President—and former General—Eisenhower, who permitted many of these experiments to occur during his administration? And this tribunal dares to parse the motivations of General Herron's decisions made in the midst of an all-out war?" These were admittedly harsh, but powerful arguments.

Herron was, of course, convicted and sentenced to ten years in prison with no parole during that time. Many Americans thought this was too lenient, particularly those who appeared at the courthouse with severe burns, deformities, or newborn babies with missing or twisted limbs. However, as General Hackworth said in a speech to the public, "This was a military court, not a civilian one. We recognized that Herron was in a war situation and was, from his perspective—which we couldn't say was completely unjustified— quelling a rebellion. While we concluded his bombing of civilian cities and towns, and especially the three missile silos and those two chemical plants, went beyond the code of conduct in wartime, he did cooperate with authorities after the war. He also, during the trial, expressed remorse for the continued loss of life. That is why we concluded we could not justify life in prison, unlike President Sadler, who will remain in prison and cannot—and will not—be paroled."

As we know, President Sadler died of a heart attack in 1991 while still in solitary confinement.

The Unionist forces prevailed, as we also know, and General Hackworth stayed on as interim president until the elections that were held following the Constitutional Convention of 1987. Following Cincinnatus, the ancient general, Hackworth refused to run for political office or become the official president. In an interview I had with General Hackworth a decade ago, he told me, "That war was the most emotionally draining war I ever fought, because I never believed this could happen on our own soil. I personally learned how the Viet Cong *really* felt when dealing with those Thieu forces. You want to get revenge against them over and over—and forever! On the other hand, I knew the killing had to stop sometime, just as General Lee and General Grant knew things had to stop in April 1865, even with the atrocities Mosby's so-called Confederate Rangers were still committing in the border state regions."

In consideration of the death of Robert Kennedy earlier this year at the age of eighty-five, I ought to say a few words in *his* defense against those revisionist historians who claim he should have stayed in the United States while the Great Struggle raged for those long eighteen months. Just after the Great Struggle began, and as chaos engulfed our nation, Robert Kennedy, a symbol of everything the corporate elite hated, escaped with his wife, Ethel, his youngest son, Douglas, and youngest daughter, Rose, first to Mexico, and from there to Cuba, and eventually to South Africa. They had no intention of leaving, but Los Angeles Mayor Yvonne Burke knew the situation was dangerous. Fearing for the former president's life, she called upon two clergymen, who knew how to get around military convoys during times of civil strife, to travel to the Kennedy's Santa Barbara ranch to help the Kennedys: Congressman and civil rights–era legend, the Methodist Reverend Jim Lawson, and the then priest, and later Roman Catholic Cardinal of Los Angeles, John D'Quatro.

Kennedy eventually reached the Republic of South Africa, where he organized a world relief campaign for American Unionist forces. He regularly met with leaders from Europe, Africa, Latin America, Mexico, Canada, and Australia to maintain their support of the American Unionist forces. His joint broadcasts with South Africa President Nelson Mandela, which were smuggled into the United States on compact discs when not broadcast on short-wave radios, remain stunning, stirring, and electrifying to this day. As we know, Bob Kennedy was Hackworth's main civilian adviser during the interim period between the end of the Struggle and the elections of 1988.

To those who wrongly believe Robert Kennedy should have stayed in America, consider the fate of Ralph Yarborough, who was killed by a sniper early on in the war near his home in Austin, Texas. Kennedy was at least as tempting and symbolic a target as Yarborough! It is especially unfair to compare Bob Kennedy to the first post-Struggle president, Julian Bond, who joined the Hackworth-led military as a general for the Georgia contingent and served with distinction. We should also recall, however, as has military historian Richard Kohn, that Bond was young enough to be in "fighting" shape, and unlike Kennedy, had served in the civil disobedience "infantry" during the 1960s civil rights campaigns. Bond's civil disobedience skills made him an effective military strategist, though he always gave the most credit to his lieutenants and colonels who were trained military personnel.

The Unionist effort had countless heroes, but I should note our most recent former president, Ruth Rosen, who was fearless during that Struggle. Starting in the winter of 1986, Rosen formed a secret supply distribution center in Boston, which proved to be extremely effective throughout the war, and yet government forces never detected it.

As with any civil war, some families had people on both sides of the conflict. To take an obvious example, Robert Kennedy's large clan was no exception. Daughter Kathleen Kennedy Townsend, who long opposed what she called "arrogant unionism," consistently supported President Sadler. She denounced all violence as un-American, but always blamed the general strikers for precipitating the violence. After the war, she and her husband moved to Canada and have since led quiet lives, which perhaps is appropriate regardless of how one feels about her position during the Struggle.

Robert Kennedy Jr. and Joseph Kennedy Jr. loyally served in the Unionist forces. Robert Jr. was killed in the Battle of Bakersfield, where many migrant workers died at the hands of better-armed farmers. Adam Walinsky's book, *The Migrant's Struggle,* deals both perceptively and passionately with the younger Robert's leadership in the days leading up to and during the battle in that dusty California town. Joe Jr. was seriously wounded in the Battle of Roxbury, just south of Boston, but recovered and then became the first post-Struggle governor of Massachusetts in 1988.

Max Taylor Kennedy fought on the government's side as an aide to Herron. He was killed in the siege of the White House that ended with Sadler's failed suicide attempt, capture, and arrest as a war criminal.

Bob and Ethel Kennedy's "Mary" girls, Mary Courtney and Mary Kerry, were out of the country when the military engagements began. Mary Courtney was in Zimbabwe working with the International Labor Organization, and Mary Kerry was with a United Nations Economic Development mission in northern India. Both returned to the United States after the victory of Hackworth and the Unionist forces. Both, of course, went their separate ways in terms of their political views—but that's not necessary to discuss here.

And again, as everyone already knows, the workers and Hackworth's military forces prevailed in the Struggle. And contrary to President Sadler's claim at his war crimes trial, most of the fighting was done by military troops and union members, not radical agitators or socialist-leaning environmentalists. The proof in that pudding, if you will, was in the make-up of the delegates for the Constitutional Convention of 1987, in case anyone is interested.

I should also say a word about the Native Americans, or Indians, who revolted against white authority in the Dakotas and a couple of other plains states during the Struggle. Most scholars studying the Second Indian Wars have concluded that the Natives, as they call themselves, may have inhaled too deeply the rhetoric of "self-determination" from that saintly secretary of state, Chester Bowles. Unfortunately, following saints is often a risky business for a historically oppressed minority when civil strife breaks out. In the 1970s, Kennedy and Yarborough policies were helping Indian reservations become more prosperous with factory and other industrial work. However, those in the white communities throughout South Dakota and North Dakota who resented the "Indians," as they called them, became more resentful as the Natives became more successful in developing their reservations. At the start of the Great Struggle, some Native radicals convinced the Native communities to arm themselves for "protection." This played into the hands of anti-Natives in the white community, particularly in the government of South Dakota. The result was an attempt to wipe out "Indians" in a way not seen since the late 1800s.

The late United States Senator George McGovern, who had become very friendly with Natives, but who also supported the integration of Natives into white society, was killed by white anti-Native extremists when he attempted to mediate the situation in the spring of 1987, in the closing months of the larger Great Struggle. The Indian wars during the Great Struggle rarely register in the national consciousness, but they were, on a per-person basis, very bloody. In the affected states, more Natives were killed than whites—not really surprising, one should say—and the racial element here added to the level of brutality in the murders. But enough Natives survived to take over what we used to call North Dakota. After the Struggle, one of the first acts of Interim President Hackworth was to allow North Dakota to secede from the United States rather than create what he called "a Northern Ireland" situation. The remaining whites were given a military escort out of North Dakota and were resettled in other parts of the United States.

After the end of the Great Struggle, we saw the creation of a new Constitution with many of the same personal rights as enumerated in the older Constitution, but also new economic rights to medical insurance and child care facilities, among other basic economic rights. State governments were also reformed to merely administer federal programs and therefore avoid the overlapping and confusing former state laws. The Second Constitutional Convention also repealed the Federal Reserve Board and returned the country to a nationally-owned banking system, as many of our founders intended two hundred and thirty years ago.

The convention reformed the law of corporations by requiring individual stockholders, directors, and officers who lead corporations to be personally liable for corporate conduct. This repealed the late-nineteenth-century legal corruption of designating corporations as separate "persons" under the Fourteenth Amendment in the old Constitution.

To nobody's surprise, our involvement in world affairs during the period of the late 1980s through the late 1990s was very limited as we rebuilt our cities and our nation. The world, however, did not sit by and watch. While we were rebuilding, for example, what had been an intractable problem between Jews and Arabs in the Middle East reached a crescendo. In 1990, Palestinian radicals, tired of trying to overthrow Israel, coalesced with Jordanian peasants to overthrow King Hussein of Jordan and established a Palestinian state. The Israelis, in a stunning example of what the nineteenth-century diplomat Metternich called "real politics," immediately recognized the new Palestinian state. Israel also offered the Palestinian state much of the West Bank, which had nearly five hundred thousand Palestinians living in makeshift shacks, while keeping Jerusalem for itself, albeit with local control by both Arabs and Israelis.

The world also watched in horror as the English invaded Northern Ireland after a full-scale civil war broke out between Protestants and Catholics in that region. The English assisted their Protestant supporters in killing and expelling Catholics from Northern Ireland and pushing them into the rest of Ireland. As we know, English troops remain to this day in Northern Ireland as protective forces. Obviously, the relations between England and Ireland are still strained, unlike, ironically, the current relations between Israel and Palestine.

While China remains in the throes of what we could call "uncreative chaos," if we may paraphrase the hated Sadler, India has become an economic powerhouse that is essentially dominating the Asian region of our planet. India has become, next to the United States, a leading exporter of high-technology products and is working with the Japanese and Vietnamese in developing much of Asia, including various regions of China and those regions that had, long ago, been under the boot of Russian dictators, Czarist and Communist alike.

Russia and the Baltic States, meanwhile, have integrated themselves into the European Union of democratic-socialist nations. And, since the fall of the monstrously misnamed Soviet Union, Europe has enjoyed much peace and prosperity for its workers for almost forty years.[5]

As for our nation, we rebuilt ourselves relatively quickly and, from this distance of time, almost seamlessly. I recall Prime Minister Michael Foot of Great Britain coming to the United States in 1987 to speak to our nation—just before the Irish Republican Army's bombing of the English Parliament and the subsequent English invasion of Northern Ireland. He spoke to our new Congress and offered economic support from Europe. He also said the United States would emerge stronger than ever, as our cities would be rebuilt with the latest technologies. This was, of course, correct, and it is why so many American historians and politicians pay homage to Foot, despite some revisionist historians who dwell almost solely on his invasion of Northern Ireland.

In the last twenty-five years, we Americans have produced second-to-none wireless technologies, including wireless pocket computers for voice and data. We are world leaders in providing free educational content on the Internet from our universities and nonprofits for learning and discussion of science, the higher arts, and music. Consistent with Apple Company cofounder Vince Learson's prediction in the 1970s, what were once the television set, the telephone, and the computer have merged into the compufone we use today.

The victory of the union forces was also a victory for farming cooperatives against the old baron-like grain merchants, particularly Archer Daniels and Cargill. Our government and the farm co-ops are leading exporters of organic farm produce—though some human-made chemicals are always present and are used quite widely in Africa, among other places. The recent rejection, for example, of genetically modified food, such as that coming out of France and a few other nations, is a testament to the influence of the American organic and cooperative farm industry—or perhaps represents a lingering concern about the effects of the use of bio-weapons during the Struggle. The rather conservative position of the American farm co-ops at the International Labor Organization and the United Nations, as we know, is that there continues to be enough food to feed the planet, and that too much fooling with Mother Nature is neither necessary nor appropriate under the circumstances.

The same can be said for federal limitations on antibiotics in food. This goes back, of course, to the early 1980s, when Surgeon General T. Berry Brazelton, who was considered a liberal at the time, as were most Kennedy-Yarborough supporters—we call such people conservatives today, of course—campaigned in favor of strict federal guidelines limiting such additives. Brazelton argued persuasively that too much use of antibiotics might possibly endanger the effectiveness of existing antibiotics, particularly for children and the elderly.

The "co-op" or business cooperation movement received a major boost after the Great Struggle in the retail trades, including clothing, utilities, and software game makers. The utilities, being owned and operated as co-ops, embraced solar, wind, and water power, and often borrowed from European technologies before adding additional and more American-made innovations. However, the co-op movement has, for one reason or another, not expanded into heavier industries such as steel, lumber, and vehicles—whether those vehicles are gas, solar, or electric powered. Those industries continue to be employee-owned, though perhaps more in name as particular individual union members have exerted more influence in each industry as a result of what government officials call "speculative, predatory stock manipulation and practices." The oil companies, of course, were nationalized after the Struggle and remain government-owned today.

Public and union-owned media may be said to dominate our culture in ways that might have surprised those who were in the communications field during, say, the 1960s. There is, however, diversity in our commentators and newsreaders from the pro-labor to the pro-corporate or business viewpoints. Yes, there are those who conspiratorially complain that the commentary spectrum supposedly runs from hard socialist to soft capitalist, but if this is the case, it is perhaps due to what the often capitalist cynics must admit is a form of "supply and demand." Those cynical capitalist-oriented writers, who more often than not have little good to say about America and all it stands for, are not heard as often, I believe, because most people have concluded their arguments about creating a borderless capitalist society—which hearken back to the dreams of Calvin Coolidge and the 1920s—lack merit. Also, the moral relativism of capitalists, who value everything through money and the oxymoron of "bottom-line morality," further undermines their appeal.[6]

As a result of the first legislation to come from the revamped Congress after the Struggle, we have had for many years now a twenty-five-hour workweek that allows for more people to be employed. This policy, as economists tell us, does three important things for our society. First, it maintains a fairly equitable distribution of wealth. Second, it avoids unnecessary unemployment. And third, it promotes, say most anthropologists, wholesome community projects because people use their leisure time not merely to relax and enjoy themselves, but to help each other and their communities. Some, of course, believe we haven't gone far enough in limiting the workweek, while some believe we have gone too far, which is what public debate is all about, I suppose.

I should also add that we remain, despite our Struggle, the unquestioned leaders in the military arena since we quickly applied our high-tech advantage to rebuilding our military under the first post-Struggle war secretary, Ronald Dellums.[7] I should note, for those too young to recall, that we dropped the pretense of calling that particular position "secretary of defense." As part of the first Congress after the Struggle, we restored the nation's original designation of having a "war secretary" as a way to remind ourselves of the horrors of war. While some pacifists and capitalist critics complain about our current military budget, we have learned, in a few instances over the past twenty-five years, that having the most sophisticated bombs, rifles, and artillery, among other weapons of war, helps maintain our precious freedom. It also allows us to be in a position to protect others around the world from capitalists who attempt to bribe military leaders into reasserting control over the workers in various nations.

I also must state something that seems obvious as air to us, but might not be if we thought about other possibilities and scenarios in our History. It is a central fact that, since the Great Struggle, the United States has essentially implemented what former World Bank President Michael Harrington would call a reasonably democratic-socialist form of government. Our policies have also, over the decades, helped alleviate poverty throughout the country and the world. It is worth noting that even the more responsible proponents of the capitalist philosophy now support government-guaranteed health insurance, child care, housing subsidies, and public transportation—something that was unheard of before the Great Struggle.

No one—I mean no one in the mainstream of our political culture—disputes our legal limit in yearly income to two hundred thousand dollars, which, as we know, is the president's salary. However, back when President Yarborough called for a limit of one million dollars, or something like that, there was major opposition even within his own political party. For those of a utopian, libertarian bent, we should note that one's total wealth of up to five million dollars may be spread over a twenty-five year period, enough for people to do pretty much what they want to do. The societal effect of this limitation, of course, is that it reminds us that those who become rich must still live in the same society with everyone else. The policy of income limitations avoids what we used to see in certain Central and South American nations before their systems changed—things such as gated communities where the rich attempted to wall themselves off from the rest of society, private policing for corporations and wealthy individuals, and the like.

Some of you who know of my work in historical "focal points" may wonder if there was a focal point that could be changed that would have avoided the millions of deaths from the Great Struggle. Over the years, I have propounded two theories. The first and most obvious one would be stopping Barry Sadler from winning the election of 1984, but this is easier said than done. The split in Democratic Party forces in 1984 was difficult to avert at that time, and most Democrats did not want to repeal the electoral college system until it was too late.

Nearly every year, though, I have at least one student who suggests that if Sadler had been assassinated, then Vice President Iacocca might have heeded General Hackworth's warnings not to continue attacking the workers, which in turn would have avoided the Great Struggle. Iacocca was a former corporate leader who was not as hostile to unions, at least in the 1960s, who was not a military "wannabe," and who testified against Sadler in return for immunity during the war crimes trials. One should be very wary, however, of thinking a particular assassination—or perhaps avoiding an assassination—will solve one's "problem." For as George Kennan, probably America's leading State Department adviser during the twentieth century, reminded anyone who would listen, killing the heads of state can often undermine what he called, in his famous essay on the Great Struggle, "the moral fiction of authority." Once that authority is undermined, one is likely to replace one, perhaps worse, demagogue for another. Perhaps it is easier for me to support Kennan's position since the United States continues to have a very moral leadership—and had one starting with Robert Kennedy at least in the late 1960s.

My other theory over the years is that maybe Ralph Yarborough deserved to lose reelection in 1980 since he won merely on the quirk of the same electoral college vote that allowed Sadler to win four years later. The Republican Jesse Jackson showed no militarist sympathies and likely would not have done anything other than perhaps delay the onset of a democratic-socialist form of government in our nation. If, however, Jackson had acted as recklessly as Sadler, and there is some evidence that he may have endorsed Sadler's initial shoot-to-kill orders in the earliest stages of the Struggle, Jackson may himself have precipitated the Struggle. With Jackson being black, and white workers still not quite comfortable with black leaders, the outcome might have been worse for worker or union forces, who might have been more divided than they were in our time.

I have, in addition, given some thought as to whether it would have made a significant difference if Bob Kennedy had not survived the assassination attempts against him in February 1971 or June 1968. There is, I believe, an easy answer to that question. The answer is that it would *not* make a significant difference in either instance. If Kennedy had been killed in February 1971, we would have seen Yarborough ascend to the presidency earlier and with a stronger momentum, much like Lyndon Johnson had after Jack Kennedy's murder.

As for the earlier assassination attempt against Robert Kennedy in June 1968, this is also unlikely to have been significant if it had been, God forbid, successful. For even Humphrey was likely to beat Nixon in the 1968 presidential election, I believe. Nixon simply couldn't shake his "loser" image. Worse for Nixon was the lingering negative image of being "Tricky Dick" and his being the man with the perennial five o'clock shadow—trivial though that may seem. I spoke with one of Bob Kennedy's leading aides, Larry O'Brien, shortly before O'Brien's death in the early 1990s. When I asked about the importance of Bob Kennedy surviving in June 1968, he said that Kennedy could not have been a historical focal point because Humphrey would have taken the same strong stance against the Vietnam War and also beaten Nixon. Humphrey would have mended fences between old-guard machine politicians and the antiwar movement, for example, just as Bob Kennedy did. It was, said O'Brien, a "no-brainer" that Humphrey would have picked Yarborough for vice president in order to undermine the Wallace vote and win Texas and some border states. Thus, Bob Kennedy, though extremely important in our nation's history, would not likely be a focal point because we would still likely have had Yarborough as president in 1976 and again in 1980.[8]

I'd like to close this lecture with a discussion of the national anthem we have had for more than twenty years now. I thought of this as I was rereading the transcript of an interview I had a few years ago with Frank Mankiewicz, just before he passed on. Frank Mankiewicz reconfirmed what was long known to most observers; namely that the martyred Jack Newfield—who was killed on April 29, 1986, in the government's bombing of the building that housed the flagship union newspaper, the *Washington Star*—had asked Bob Kennedy to change the national anthem to Woody Guthrie's "This Land Is Your Land" if he won the presidency in 1968. In 1989, less than two years after the end of the Struggle, the new Congress voted to change the national anthem from "The Star Spangled Banner"—that national anthem had only been approved as such in the 1930s—to "This Land Is Your Land."

As any anthropologist or sociologist can tell us, a national song or anthem is often a very thick thread that binds a people into a nation. And as one who lived through that time, I believe that new anthem did more than just about anything else to unite most of our restored United States of America. It gave us a sense of unity, of a feeling that there *was,* in fact, a shared sense of belonging to our land and to each other that was, and is, vitally important to us at all times—but especially in those first years after the Struggle.

The beauty of the melody and the lyrics of this anthem also made it immensely popular over the years. This is so, even as our new anthem masked that other anthem that always sings, perennial and immutable. That other anthem is, of course, the anthem of faction and politics, which includes verses that sing of political deals among strange bedfellows, of dissent and loyalty, of dissension and cooperation, of betrayal and perhaps one day again, God forbid, revolt—as well as of unity. However, in this other and immutable anthem, one never really knows where the musical "bridges"—or focal points—are located, no matter where one stands in time. And playing with "space and time," if we should ever reach that stage, is likely to provide only more and certainly dangerous applications of what the Greeks called false pride tending toward tragedy, or, in the Greek's own word, hubris.

As a historian, I am here to tell you that History is more organized and rational in history classes, books, and media presentations than it is in real life. Life is, has been, and will always be, largely a mess. And if you don't learn that lesson in this class, you will learn it in your love lives, your membership in civic organizations or religious institutions, in your careers, and even in the families you create. For example, how often have we found ourselves attracted either platonically or romantically to someone who has political or religious views that we detest? And how often have we been personally repelled from those with whom we otherwise agree in matters of politics and religion? Those occasions are just a glimpse of what make History and life such a glorious and confounding . . . as I said, mess.

On the other hand, there have been many historic events that lead to clear consequences and from which we must learn—or else we are, as Karl Marx once said, condemned to repeat the tragedy of History as a farce.

Philosophers, poets, and novelists tell us that, with regard to human behavior and endeavors, Truth walks hand in hand with Falsehood. And Virtue walks hand in hand with Hypocrisy.

Yet, in many times and many places in human History, Truth is often found walking hand in hand with Hypocrisy. And Falsehood happily cavorts with Virtue. And we must add one additional dynamic neglected by most philosophers and historians, and that is this: The God of Change is mostly working in tandem with the Goddess of Stasis, each one simultaneously trying to double-cross the other in the struggle known as the Future.

And in some distant Future, our progeny's historians will tell us, "You people of the past! Couldn't you see? You were living in a Golden Age!" Or perhaps they will say, "How on earth could any of you have been happy? Didn't you know that you were living in a Dark Age?" Yet, if they would just look more closely, they would see that most of us, in every age, were just living—with all the joys and sorrows that occur in the lives of most human beings.

That's not all our progeny's historians will tell us. Oh, not at all! The future historians will also confidently tell us that those whom we call our heroes were actually villains—and that maybe our villains were really heroes. They will airbrush or digitalize away all the contradictions, the edges, and the subtleties of our best and worst leaders for the holidays they will invent or arguments they wish to win in *their* present time.

The arguments that radicals use in our time to seek change will, in the Future, be taken up by reactionaries to maintain the status quo. The policies that assist business interests will eventually be called upon to help the interests of labor. And the policies that initially brought peace will eventually be used to make war. And all that will occur over again in reverse.

Our progeny will confidently lecture and write that the Past's Future was always easy to foresee—just as their world is too complicated to accurately predict what will happen the next day in their time. They will haughtily laugh at our failure to accurately predict our Future and their Present—and at how wrong and often innocent we were. Many will even lament their loss of innocence that *we* supposedly had.

Our progeny will then triumphantly proclaim their superiority to us in their knowledge of us. And we of the simple Past will wearily sigh.

ENDNOTES

The following endnotes, which I hope give the book a "nonfiction feel," will provide a glimpse of the research involved and the threads of actual history I have stitched together to come up with this alternative historical weave.

I should also note that *A Disturbance of Fate* describes many "true" historical events not discussed further in the endnotes. I have chosen, instead, to note particular events or information that readers might see as less known, controversial, or both. Further, there are notes that explain what happened in the RFK timeline—just like a "real" history book.

Introduction: Robert F. Kennedy and Alternative History

1. Charles Whitman and Richard Speck were two mid-1960s mass murderers. Whitman shot people with a high-powered rifle from a tower at a Texas university. Speck used a knife to kill eight nurses in the Chicago area. See Gary M. Lavergne, *A Sniper in the Tower: The True Story of the Texas Tower Massacre* (Bantam, 1997, 1999); Dennis L. Breo and William J. Martin, *Crime of the Century: Richard Speck and the Murder of Eight Nurses* (Bantam, 1993). Sociologists, including Robert Merton and Emil Durkheim, have speculated that such killers arise from time to time when one mixes guns, freedom of movement, and the anomie of modern life.

2. Several books have been published on the subject of the assassination. The most respected are Robert Blair Kaiser's *R.F.K. Must Die!* (E.P. Dutton & Co., 1970); Philip H. Melanson's *The Robert F. Kennedy Assassination: New Revelations on the Conspiracy and Cover-Up, 1968–1991* (Shapolsky Publishers, 1991); and Dan Moldea's *The Killing of Robert Kennedy* (W.W. Norton, 1995).

3. Authors who believe RFK might well have won the nomination and then the presidency include Jules Witcover, *85 Days: The Last Campaign of Robert Kennedy* (Quill/William Morris updated edition, 1988) and Jack Newfield, *Robert Kennedy: A Memoir* (E.P. Dutton, 1969). The best work to strongly question whether RFK could have won either the nomination or the election is Ronald Steel's *In Love with Night* (Simon & Schuster, 2000). Though I disagree with Steel's conclusions on the subject of the nomination or fall election, his book, and Michael Knox Beran's *The Last Patrician: Robert Kennedy and the End of American Aristocracy* (St. Martin's Press, 1998), were thoughtful works that forced a reexamination of certain initial assumptions. I hope, however, that historians and political writers recognize that Steel's conclusions about why RFK could not have won the nomination or the presidency are no less speculative than what is contained in this novel. Further, I hope Mr. Beran sees at least some of

his views regarding Kennedy's liberal and conservative radicalism reflected in these pages.

4. For readers who believe having endnotes in a novel is unprecedented, please see Jack London's great social revolutionary novel, *The Iron Heel* (1907). More recent writers who have added notes in their novels include David Foster Wallace, *Infinite Jest* (Little, Brown and Company, 1996) and Sandra Cisneros, *Caramelo* (Knopf, 2002). See also: Robert Soble, *For Want of a Nail* (MacMillan, 1973), an alternative history assuming the British defeated the American colonies in the 1770s, which includes "alternative" footnotes.

Chapter 1: A Homicide at the Ambassador Hotel

1. A "primary" election is one where voters in each political party vote for delegates pledged to candidates seeking to become that party's nominee for particular federal or state political offices. At the nominating conventions, the delegates vote for their pledged candidates, with the winner becoming the nominee for each political office. Then, later in the election year, "general" elections are held where voters choose among the various parties' nominees.

2. Dan Moldea, *The Killing of Robert Kennedy* (W.W. Norton & Company, 1995), page 28.

3. Frankenheimer directed a number of films, including *The Manchurian Candidate* (1962), which was about a Korean War veteran who was hypnotized into becoming an assassin of a U.S. president. Historians and investigators of the Robert Kennedy assassination later argued about whether, like the character in the film, Sirhan was hypnotized or programmed to kill Robert Kennedy.

4. George Wallace had been a "traditional"—meaning racist—Southern Democrat who broke from the party to run for president under a political party known as the American Independent Party. See Marshall Frady, *Wallace* (Random House, 1998).

5. As with any successful or unsuccessful assassination of a famous person, conspiracy researchers speculated about the lapses that are typical in official investigations. In this new, RFK timeline, Cesar, in initial discussions with the police, failed to reveal his political support for George Wallace. Also, law enforcement authorities failed to follow up with Cesar as to why he waited to shoot Sirhan. Some assassination-attempt researchers, therefore, speculated that Cesar killed Sirhan to avoid having him "squeal" on others possibly involved in a conspiracy. As in the first timeline, Cesar never sued anyone who made nefarious allegations against him.

Chapter 2: Resurrection

1. Ironically, in the first timeline, in 1984, one of Daley's ward leaders in the black community, Harold Washington, ran and won against a white "Daley machine" candidate, becoming Chicago's first black mayor. See Gary Rivlin, *Fire on the Prairie: Chicago's Harold Washington and the Politics of Race* (Henry Holt, 1992).

2. For discussion of RFK's marital infidelity and Ethel's reactions, which ranged from anger to denial, see C. David Heyman, *R.F.K., A Candid Biography* (Dutton, 1998), pps. 472–474, and J. Randy Taraborrelli, *Jackie Ethel Joan: Women of Camelot* (Warner Books, 2000).

3. "Goy" is a Yiddish word meaning "non-Jewish." It is largely used in a negative context and often means someone not very intelligent.

4. RFK timeline: Before Sirhan's assassination attempt, Kennedy instructed an aide to call Lowenstein and ask him to formally join the Kennedy campaign. Lowenstein, who had been running for the Democratic nomination for a congressional seat in Long Island, New York, arrived in Washington, D.C., later in the week following Sirhan's death. He told Kennedy, "I'm with you all the way, Senator." Kennedy asked if he'd like to continue running for Congress or take part "in my administration, assuming I win." Lowenstein replied, "I'm quitting my race for Congress, Bob. I *know* you're going to win." Lowenstein was in with Kennedy for good—something McCarthy always suspected.

    First timeline: After RFK's assassination, Lowenstein won his seat in Congress in 1968. He lasted one term in Congress, losing in a close reelection campaign in 1970. Lowenstein, however, continued to remain active in politics during the 1970s and was an activist in environmental, labor, and consumer projects. Among his eccentric habits, however, was a penchant for befriending people who were emotionally needy and sometimes disturbed. On March 14, 1980, one of those acquaintances walked up to Lowenstein in his office and shot him dead. For a definitive biography of Lowenstein, that details his importance in the politics of the 1960s and 1970s, see William H. Chafe's *Never Stop Running: Allard Lowenstein and the Struggle to Save American Liberalism* (Harper Collins, 1993). There was an earlier biography written by Richard Cummings, *The Pied Piper: Allard K. Lowenstein and the Liberal Dream* (Grove Press, 1985). Cummings' book was subject to intense criticism from certain persons close to Lowenstein. See, for example, Hendrik Hertzberg's review of Cummings' book in the *New York Review of Books*, "The Second Assassination of Allard Lowenstein," October 10, 1985. See also Cummings' exchange with Hertzberg in that magazine, January 30, 1986.

5. First timeline: See C. David Heyman, *RFK: A Candid Biography*, op. cit., pages 493–494, interview with Ted Van Dyk.

6. Kennedy, in an attempt to assuage his wide coalition of supporters, made an obligatory appearance at the grounds of the Washington Monument, where the Poor People's Campaign was continuing in the summer of 1968. The campaign, originally proposed by Martin Luther King Jr., had lost its bearings after King's assassination on April 4, 1968. Kennedy's resurrection crowded out most news stories of the time, thereby further limiting coverage of the Poor People's Campaign, which was lucky for the campaign and poor people in general.

    First timeline: The campaign proved to be a disaster, with hastily built shanties that engendered sickness and despair among the poor the campaign was supposed to help. Worse, the mostly white working people around the nation, viewing the continuing scene on television in the first timeline, found yet another reason to run out of patience, from their perspective, with the "ungrateful poor."

Chapter 3: Trying Not to Lose

1. "Yippies" was the common name for the Youth International Movement founded by '60s radicals Jerry Rubin and Abbie Hoffman. "SDS" stood for Students for a Democratic Society, founded in 1960 in Michigan by several politically active students, including Tom Hayden.

2. Saul Alinsky was a grass-roots organizer in Chicago during the mid-twentieth century. He wrote a famous book entitled *Reveille for Radicals* (University of Chicago Press, 1946). He was active in civil rights boycotts and other acts of civil disobedience, including workers strikes and renters protests. Generations of activists and organizers admired Alinsky, and he was respected, though hated, by the powers that controlled Chicago.

Chapter 4: Daley Meets the Radicals

1. In the first timeline, Foran was the government prosecutor of the eight radicals— Hayden, Davis, Dellinger, Abbie Hoffman, Jerry Rubin, Bobby Seale, Lee Weiner, and John Froines—who were charged with disrupting the 1968 Democratic convention in Chicago.
2. Daley was referring to the Student Non-Violent Coordinating Committee, called "Snick" for its acronym SNCC. SNCC was behind many of the civil rights activities undertaken by young people in the late 1950s and 1960s, mostly in the American South.
3. I.F. "Izzy" Stone was a radical journalist, with his roots at the then liberal-left *New York Post* of the 1930s. Later, during the 1950s Red scare, Stone self-published a newsletter he called *I. F. Stone's Weekly*, with Albert Einstein as one of the charter subscribers. In the *Weekly*, Stone dissected the news and sometimes made startling discoveries through his careful reading of the *Congressional Record*, the official record of the proceedings of the United States Congress. Stone uncovered information relating to unsafe radiation levels around the world from nuclear testing and the mendacity of American officials concerning the Vietnam War. He wrote about '60s student radicals with a mixture of parental advice and respect. Stone had three children, two of whom also became fairly well known: Jeremy Stone, president of the American Federation of Scientists in the 1960s and 1970s, and Christopher Stone, a respected law professor in the area of environmental law. After the fall of the Soviet Union, there were allegations that Stone was a paid Soviet agent. One of the accusers, the late Eric Breindel, admitted Stone "significantly" deviated from the Soviet view on national and international issues, which in itself, undermined such an accusation. Further, Stone was a sharp critic of dictators, left and right. Finally, there was no indication of any Soviet Union monies passing to Stone. Stone was, in fact, the ultimate independent journalist whose writings are immortal in their prose and content. In the RFK timeline, Stone endorsed Robert Kennedy against Nixon in 1968.

Chapter 5: Looking Presidential

1. "Plastic People" was the name of the first song on Frank Zappa and the Mothers' second record album, *Absolutely Free* (1967). Mainstream American writers and political pundits considered Zappa a dangerous subversive, the same view shared, not so ironically, by Czechoslovakian Communist hard-liners. For a funny, but true story of the first days after the Communist collapse in Czechoslovakia, and the connection between Vaclav Havel and Frank Zappa, see Paul Berman's *A Tale of Two Utopias: The Political Journey of the Generation of 1968* (Norton, 1996). The Plastic People of the Universe had at least two English releases, *Passion Play* (Bozi Mlyn records, 1981) and *The Plastic People . . . Prague,*

aka Egon Bondy's Happy Hearts Club Banned (LTM/Bozi Mlyn records, 1978). The latter album includes notes and a booklet discussing the history of the band, including its involvement in protests against the Communist Czech government in the 1970s and 1980s.

2. In the United States, despite the infamous taunt, attributed to a student activist named Jack Weinberg, "Don't trust anybody over 30!" America's student radicals did trust several elders throughout the decade. They trusted Dave Dellinger, the fifty-year-old radical pacifist, and, to a lesser extent, Michael Harrington, the nearly forty-year-old anti-Communist socialist—and author of the book *The Other America,* which had spawned the Kennedy-Johnson "Great Society" programs. The student radicals respectfully read the writings of the old radical journalist I. F. "Izzy" Stone; Paul Goodman, who wrote one of the seminal books of modern American society, entitled *Growing Up Absurd,* (1960); and the late C. Wright Mills, whose work included books such as *The Power Elite* (1955) and *White Collar* (1951) and who died in 1962—before what most Americans call "the 60s" even began.

3. Dubcek's and Brezhnev's conversation was transcribed at the time and later released in the first timeline in the late 1990s following the fall of the Soviet Union.

4. Jan Masaryk was a deeply loved patriot of the Czech nation, as was his father, Thomas. Jan supported the coalition government in Czechoslovakia in 1945 and 1946 but became increasingly critical of Communist domination through the February 1948 Communist coup. The first official word from the Communist government, in May 1948, was that Masaryk had committed "suicide." While most rightly believe the Communist government murdered Masaryk, there has never been an "official" finding on the subject. See: the Web site for the Columbia Encyclopedia, entry under *Jan Masaryk,* among other sources.

5. In 1967, the United States largely wrote UN Resolution 242, with input from Israel and Jordan. It stated in pertinent part that the United Nations would not support the "acquisition of territory by war." It further said peace would be achieved with "(i) Withdrawal of Israeli armed forces from territories of recent conflict; (ii) Termination of all claims or states of belligerency and respect for acknowledgment of the sovereignty, territorial integrity, and political independence of every state in the area and their right to live in peace within secure and recognized boundaries free from threats or acts of force . . . " The resolution also called for "achieving a just settlement of the refugee problem," which was an apparent reference to Arabs and Jews displaced since the beginning of Israel's independence in 1947.

Chapter 6: Another Convention

1. Tonnage figures come from a survey of sources identified by Professor Barton Meyers in a paper entitled, *Vietnamese Defense Against Aerial Attack* (April 19, 1996, Center for the Study of the Vietnam Conflict). Meyers cites sources including military historians William Turley, James W. Gibson, and James P. Harrison, among others, in his paper. Meyers cautions, however, that figures for bombing in Indochina/Southeast Asia may be understated regarding actual American munitions tonnage dropped by the United States.

2. In the first timeline, Ronald Reagan was elected president in 1980 in part by saying he'd be tough on the Russians and terrorists. Yet, one of the first things

Reagan did upon assuming office in 1981 was to end the grain embargo his "weak" predecessor, Jimmy Carter, had placed on the Russians. Reagan also allowed Israel to send military arms to Iran, then identified by the United States as the leading "terrorist nation." Some alleged the Israeli arms were part of a deal Reagan's campaign brokered to allow American hostages held in Iran to come home on Reagan's Inauguration Day. Reagan also acquiesced in late 1981 to the Russians installing a military dictator, General Wojciech Jaruzelski, in Poland, dismaying human-rights activists around the world. See Garry Wills, *Reagan's America: Innocents at Home* (Doubleday, 1987), pps. 344-345, 353–355; Coral Bell, *Foreign Affairs*, "From Carter to Reagan" (Vol. 63, No. 3, 1984); Robert Parry, *Trick or Treason* (Sheridan Square, 1993).

3. McCarthy's quip may have been true regarding John Kennedy, but not Bobby. Bobby, despite not having talent according to his coaches and teammates, fought hard and played harder on his high school prep football team. Later in life, he would ride dangerous rapids and climb mountains. Still, he now felt he'd rather play football without a helmet than debate Nixon or anyone else, particularly after his lackluster performance against McCarthy during the primary.

4 This was Albert Gore Sr., senator from Tennessee in the 1950s and 1960s, not Al Gore, Jr., later a senator and then President Clinton's vice president in the first timeline. The senior Senator Al Gore had a strong though not perfect record on civil rights and was a fairly early opponent of the Vietnam War. He was also a solid supporter of labor interests in his last years. These factors—along with lots of money from the Republican Party specially earmarked to his opponent—contributed to his defeat in the first timeline in 1970.

5. RFK timeline: After the Democratic convention, Daley invited Hayden to stay in Chicago to run a key swing precinct bordering the white and black neighborhoods. Hayden accepted, having become tired of explaining himself to radicals in the SDS. Hayden worked hard to deliver the white and black vote for Kennedy in the November 1968 election. He became friendly with Daley's sons, Michael and Richard M. Daley during this time as well. Mayor Daley, who died in 1976, became so close to Hayden that he anointed him as his successor over both Jane Byrne and Ed Vrdolyak. He was going to anoint one of his sons, but both had personal problems at the time and were not considered strong enough to lead a coalition necessary to win a citywide election. Hayden became mayor of Chicago in 1977, serving as a bridge between blacks and ethnic whites. He married a local black educator named Marva Collins, who was instrumental in reforming Chicago's public schools.

Chapter 7: Nixon vs. Kennedy, the Sequel
1. In the first timeline, he lived to be ninety-three years old, dying on January 27, 1996.

Chapter 8: Checkmate
1. First timeline president Nixon and his foreign policy adviser, Henry Kissinger, essentially ignored this study. One of the study's authors, Daniel Ellsberg, became so frustrated, particularly at his former Harvard colleague, Kissinger, that he leaked the study to the *New York Times* in 1971. See Seymour Hersh, *The Price of Power* (Summit Books, 1983) pps. 325–329; Daniel Ellsberg, *Papers on the War* (Simon and Schuster, 1972).

2. First timeline: To defend himself against truthful charges that he received yearly income subsidies from a group of businessmen in the late 1940s and early 1950s, Nixon had made a nationwide speech in 1952 defending himself. In the speech, he said that one of his supporters also gave him Checkers the dog, which his children loved—and which he wasn't about to give back. Nixon evoked enough sympathy from the American voting public that Eisenhower kept him on the ticket as his vice presidential candidate in their successful run that year. Tom Wicker, *One of Us*, op. cit. Wicker believed a $15,000 a year stipend from businessmen to Nixon was inconsequential. However, the year 2002 equivalent would be approximately $100,000 a year, which is hardly inconsequential.

3. Larry O'Brien was referring to a few things here. First, Nixon had said to various newspaper editors that he didn't want to discuss in detail his plan to end the Vietnam War, which reporters, not Nixon, called "Nixon's secret plan." When one of the reporters asked him about his "secret plan," Nixon didn't challenge the use of the word "secret" and reaffirmed he did not want to discuss details of how he'd end the war. Nixon later explained his plan was similar to what was called "Vietnamizing the war," meaning letting the South Vietnamese infantry fight but with the United States merely supplying arms and advisers—ironically, the way Lyndon Johnson had campaigned on the issue in 1964. As for the Hiss reference, O'Brien was referring to Nixon's successful work with government prosecutors in proving in a court of law that Alger Hiss, a high-ranking New Dealer under Franklin D. Roosevelt, had lied in denying he was a Communist (and probably a spy for the Soviet Union). Earl Mazo and Stephen Hess, *Nixon* (Harper & Row, 1968); Tom Wicker, *One of Us* (Random House, 1991). Finally, Johnny Carson was a late-night television talk show host who told jokes in an opening monologue and asked movie star guests to talk about their new movies.

4. First timeline: For the Nixon-Thieu connection and sabotage of the 1968 peace talks in the first timeline, see, among others, Seymour Hersh, *The Price of Power*, op. cit., Anthony Summers, *The Arrogance of Power* (Viking Press, 2000), Stephen Ambrose, *Nixon: Triumph of a Politician* (Touchstone Books, 1989), and Anna Chennault's own account, *The Education of Anna* (Times Books, 1979). For Larry O'Brien's understanding of the Nixon-Greek military connection, and how it may relate to the Nixon administration's botched burglary of the Watergate Hotel in June 1972, see Christopher Hitchens' articles in *The Nation*, "Watergate—The Greek Connection," May 31, 1986, and "Nixon's Tapes & The Greek Connection," November 24, 1997.

5. New York Governor Thomas Dewey ran for president against incumbent Harry S. Truman in 1948. Polls consistently showed Dewey ahead in the race all through the campaign, and "everyone" assumed Dewey would win. On election day, a leading Chicago newspaper declared him the winner in an early edition of the paper. The next morning, when the results were in, Truman had surprisingly defeated Dewey.

Chapter 9: Restoration

1. In the first timeline, IBM was served with the federal government's antitrust lawsuit on the last day of the Johnson administration. The suit consumed IBM all through the 1970s and into the first days of the Reagan administration, where it was eventually settled under favorable terms to IBM. In the RFK timeline, Kennedy learned about the anti-trust lawsuit and killed it before it could be filed.

2. Mankiewicz never realized his dream of becoming the next Clark Clifford in either timeline. In the RFK timeline, Mankiewicz left Washington after a few years to become president of Columbia University in New York. In the first timeline, Mankiewicz remained in Washington and became vice chairman of the corporate client-oriented public relations firm, Hill & Knowlton.

3. In the first timeline, Blee did not become director of the CIA. However, under President Nixon, Blee became the head of the CIA's Soviet Division in 1971. There, he reformed the CIA's spying apparatus and was applauded in the CIA "community" for his efforts. See the obituary of David Henry Blee, *New York Times,* August 17, 2000.

4. Sam Brown, in the first timeline, served as Peace Corps director in the late 1970s under President Jimmy Carter.

5. Ellsberg had been such a Vietnam War booster in the mid-1960s that Lyndon Johnson's State Department sent him to debate antiwar activists at the teach-ins at the University of California at Berkeley and other campuses. In the 1950s, Ellsberg originated what became known as the "Madman theory"—making a leader's opponent think the leader is so crazy that the opponent comes quickly to the bargaining table to seek peace. Henry Kissinger, a fellow Harvard professor with Ellsberg during the 1950s, often advised President Nixon to follow this strategy. See Ellsberg, *Papers on the War,* op. cit.; Hersh, *The Price of Power,* op. cit. See also, Chapter 8, endnote 1, above.

6. Ironically, this is essentially what Nixon and Kissinger agreed to in the infamous "Paris Peace Accords" with the Communists in January 1973 in the first timeline. However, many more North Vietnamese troops were inside South Vietnam in 1973 than in 1969. Nixon's bombing of North and South Vietnam, and the bombing of Cambodia, failed to achieve much in the way of a negotiation advantage for the Americans. With the continued murder of South Vietnamese peasants as a result of the bombings, the reinforcements from the North made it more advantageous to the North Vietnamese to control the South once "peace was at hand," to use Kissinger's memorable phrase. See: Stanley Karnow, *Vietnam: A History,* op. cit., for discussion of North Vietnamese peace proposals to Nixon from 1969 through 1971. One notes similarities between the earlier proposals and the 1973 accords, particularly Articles 4 and 5 (U.S. withdrawal of its troops and military equipment from Vietnam in 60 days); 15 (reunification of the *sectors* known as northern and southern Vietnam per the 1954 Geneva Accords); and the failure to require the North Vietnamese to remove troops and materials from South Vietnam. For a hawkish, though similar, analysis of the 1973 peace accords, see: Larry Berman, *No Peace, No Honor: Nixon, Kissinger, and Betrayal in Vietnam* (Free Press, 2001).

7. For American support, protection, and recruitment of Nazis and fascists before, during, and after World War II, see Christopher Simpson, *Blowback* (Weidenfeld & Nicolson, 1988) and *Splendid Blond Beast* (Grove Press 1993). See also Charles Higham, *Trading with the Enemy* (Delacorte Press, 1983), detailing American business efforts on behalf of Fascist Italy and Nazi Germany, even after American entry in World War II in December 1941. Many Americans are still unaware that American business and political leaders have often been friendly with other leaders harboring Nazi and Fascist ideologies. For a summary of

General Suharto's bloody reign in Indonesia, starting with his military coup that killed almost 500,000 people in less than two months, see the Central Intelligence Agency report entitled *Indonesia 1965: The Coup That Backfired* (1968). In this first timeline report, the CIA said Suharto had committed one of the worst human rights crimes of the twentieth century. This is certainly significant considering the crimes of Hitler, Stalin, and Mao.

Chapter 10: The Politics of Peace

1. In the first timeline, the baby was named Rory.
2. American leaders weren't Nazis, of course. However, Telford Taylor, a former brigadier general and chief prosecutor at the Nuremberg Trials, suggested, in a book called *Nuremberg and Vietnam: An American Tragedy* (Quadrangle Books, 1970), that American leaders were subject to prosecution for war crimes in Vietnam. Professor Noam Chomsky, discussing Taylor's book, argued the same point more strongly in his essay, "The Rule of Force in International Affairs," originally published in the *Yale Law Journal* but subsequently published in Chomsky, *For Reasons of State* (Pantheon, 1973). See also Chapter 9, endnote 7, above. Also, in the first timline, Goldwater voiced outrage at fellow Republican and President Ronald Reagan for "violating international law" against Nicaragua and then for lying about it. See Robert Goldberg, *Goldwater* (Yale University Press, 1995).
3. First timeline: On January 23, 1968, the Communist regime in North Korea captured a U.S. military ship, the *Pueblo*. North Korea held the *Pueblo* crew in captivity for almost eleven months before being released on December 22, 1968. President Johnson asked for self-censorship by the American press to avoid sensationalizing the situation. The press dutifully followed Johnson's request. The reluctance of the press to make a daily issue out of the incident made it more difficult for candidates to criticize the president without looking divisive. Nixon tried to break through this self-censorship in his presidential nomination speech at the Republican national convention, saying: "I say to you tonight that when respect for the United States falls so low that a fourth-rate military power like [North] Korea will seize an American naval vessel on the high seas, it's time for new leadership to restore respect for the United States of America." Ironically, within four months of Nixon's assuming office, the North Koreans shot down an American military aircraft. Yet, the Nixon administration chose a diplomatic, not military solution, as Johnson did with the Pueblo incident. Hersh, *The Price of Power*, pages 69–77.

   RFK timeline and the *Pueblo* incident: Nixon did not mention anything relating to the *Pueblo* incident in his nomination speech. As he told John Ehrlichman, "We're running against an extreme, peace-at-all-costs candidate in Robert Kennedy. We don't have to say we're for war to get the pro-war vote. All we have to do is keep saying Bobby Kennedy will not bring peace with honor— and then use the old Teddy Roosevelt quote about 'speaking softly while carrying a big stick.' We must make it perfectly clear to the North Koreans and the rest of the Communists that we mean business when we get elected." Ehrlichman questioned whether that stance was aggressive enough for the campaign. Nixon replied, "With Johnson staying neutral and almost hostile to the Kennedy campaign, we simply can't afford to directly attack Johnson on this *Pueblo* thing." Yet, in the closing weeks of the campaign, Nixon spoke of the need for "new leadership to get tough with a fourth-rate power like North Korea." Some conservative commentators said this helped solidify support among hawks, but it was not enough to prevail in the election.

Chapter 11: Plan B in Saigon

1. In the delta province of Kien Hoa, in late 1968, American troops killed more than 11,000 villagers, including "at least" 5,000 "noncombatants," as admitted by official sources. After the mass killing, only 748 weapons were found. See first timeline exposé "Pacification's Deadly Price," by Christopher Buckley, *Newsweek,* June 19, 1972.

2. The Phoenix program was formally instituted in August 1968, though its methods had been honed since at least the early 1960s. The program was designed to kill people in the rural areas where the Viet Cong guerillas had taken control. This included not only bombing but also engaging in and directing widespread assassination and sometimes torture of those suspected to be guerillas, or sympathetic to the guerillas. The areas were euphemistically called "free-fire zones." American military and civilian officials paradoxically recognized that the program could result in intensifying support for the Viet Cong because it cast too wide a net over who was a sympathizer—and worse, it could increase the infiltration of North Vietnamese troops into South Vietnam to replace the guerillas and their supporters who were killed. Both consequences occurred, but the program continued until it was leaked to the media. The resulting outcry among even some pro-war hawks forced the discontinuance of the program in late 1969. The continued problem of peasant resistance, however, meant the program continued "informally," as it had before August 1968. For what may be the definitive book on the program, see Douglas Valentine, *The Phoenix Program* (William Morrow, 1990).

3. RFK timeline: See Walter Isaacson, *Kenny O'Donnell: Present at the Restoration,* (Simon & Schuster, 2005) for orchestration of the POW homecoming in January 1969. In the first timeline, the only known biography of O'Donnell was written in 1998, more than twenty years after O'Donnell's death, by his daughter, Helen, entitled *A Common Good* (William Morrow & Company, 1998). The book concerned her father's friendship with Robert Kennedy.

4. In first timeline 1969, Governor Ronald Reagan, in a speech before growers in Santa Barbara, California, said regarding universities having protests and strife: "If there's going to be a bloodbath, then let's get it over with." (See Ronnie Dugger, *On Reagan: The Man and the Presidency* (McGraw-Hill, 1982, p. 243). This was before the first timeline killings at Kent State University in Ohio and Jackson State University in Mississippi in 1970.

Chapter 12: The Threads of History

1. Some American soldiers died during the subsequent peace and election process under President Robert F. Kennedy, but they numbered fewer than twenty-five. Under President Richard M. Nixon, from 1969 through 1973, almost one million Southeast Asians, and another twenty-two thousand Americans, were killed.

I also thank Chuck and Jim Mangi, who run a Web site that lists the names of the American soldiers killed in Vietnam and the dates in which the soldiers' deaths are recorded. As Chuck told me in an e-mail on August 6, 2000, sometimes the dates are not accurate to the exact day. The Web site is called *Names on the Wall*, and the Web address is http://www.hereintown.com/warmemorials/notw/wallinfo.htm.

2. RFK timeline: During his time as president, Robert Kennedy never called upon Lyndon Johnson for advice. Ralph Yarborough did consult with Johnson from time to time, but never admitted it to Kennedy or nearly anyone else besides his wife, according to an oral history given by Opal Yarborough to Douglas Brinkley of Columbia University, 1992.

Chapter 13: Labor Pains

1. In the first timeline, Walter Reuther was killed in a mysterious crash of his privately-owned small aircraft. Leonard Woodcock, a close Reuther adviser, succeeded Reuther, even though Reuther appears to have been more partial to Fraser. After Woodcock became the leader of the UAW, the union returned to the AFL-CIO and bowed to Meany's leadership. See Nelson Lichtenstein, *The Most Dangerous Man in Detroit* (Basic Books, 1995).

   In the RFK timeline, Reuther did not die an early death, nor did he die in any plane or other vehicular crash.

2. Kennedy had a righteous vendetta against the Teamsters Union and its then-leader, Jimmy Hoffa, for their ties to organized crime. Kennedy had been the lead lawyer on the Senate committee investigating the union. See Robert Kennedy's *The Enemy Within* (Popular Library Press, 1960).

   RFK timeline: Surprising most observers, President Robert Kennedy showed little interest in ridding the nation of organized crime. He allowed certain prosecutions to take place, but always made clear to Ramsey Clark, his attorney general, that the Justice Department would not treat these cases in any "high profile" manner. That most of the cases ended in acquittal or dismissal for "lack of sufficient evidence" did not surprise the disappointed Attorney General Clark.

3. Warnke was intrigued with the "military conversion" analyses of Professor Seymour Melman of Columbia. Warnke, who knew of Melman's work for the government during the 1960s, and particularly during the Johnson administration, hired the professor to spearhead the study, under his and Admiral Moorer's command. Melman, in an effort to head off the military contractor industry's buy off of the unions connected to the industry, tapped William Winpisinger, president of the military contractor-oriented machinists' union, to become involved in the project.

4. As was often the case and known inside the Pentagon in most situations regarding military hardware, the Soviets were behind in MIRV technology in 1968. The point of limiting MIRV development, according to American arms control negotiators, was to stop the Soviets from MIRVing their missiles at all. In both timelines, the Soviets followed the United States and began MIRVing their missiles in the late 1960s and early 1970s. See, among other first-timeline works, Gerard C. Smith (Nixon's leading arms limitation negotiator), *Doubletalk: The*

Story of SALT I (Doubleday, 1980), and Thomas Powers, *The Man Who Kept the Secrets* (Alfred A. Knopf, 1979).

5.   Archibald "Archie" Cox was the solicitor general of the United States under Jack Kennedy. A famous and outspoken liberal attorney and Harvard law professor, Cox, in the first timeline, served as the first special prosecutor to investigate the Watergate scandal and the more serious related crimes of the Nixon administration.

6.   The new president made another decision that reneged on a promise made to a few supporters. Within days of his inauguration, Kennedy stated that he was not under any circumstances going to open the still-classified Warren Commission papers and exhibits. This decision bitterly disappointed New Orleans District Attorney Jim Garrison, JFK conspiracy writers such as Harold Weisberg and Mark Lane, and social satirist Mort Sahl, among others. The owners and editors of both the mainstream press and broadcast networks, not wanting to reopen anything about the JFK assassination for fear of giving an incentive to another potential assassin, suppressed anything relating to the Warren Commission critics, including most letters to the editor on the subject.

Chapter 14: Sailing into the Storm

1.   This holiday dinner argument was reported in the first-timeline books, *The New Left and Labor in the 1960's,* by Peter Levy (University of Illinois Press, 1994), and David Halberstam, *The Reckoning* (William Morrow, 1986).

2.   Goodman, Cheney, and Schwerner were the names of three civil rights workers (two Jews and one black) who, while on a civil rights Freedom Ride in 1964, were killed by Klansmen and local police in Philadelphia, Mississippi. For the most widely respected account of the civil rights movement, including this episode, see first-timeline book, Taylor Branch, *Pillar of Fire: America in the King Years 1963–1965* (Simon and Schuster, 1999).

Chapter 15: Saigon Bye-Gone, Hello Viet Cong

1.   RFK timeline: The Viet Cong leadership, as a compromise, chose Truong to lead the Viet Cong's National Liberation Front (NLF) Party. Those Viet Cong leaders closest to the North Vietnamese Communists believed that Thieu's forces would kill Truong before the election and therefore allowed him to be chosen. Thieu forces, however, believed they could not kill the person chosen to lead the NLF Party during the election for fear of undermining the hawks in Washington, D.C. Thieu learned, in his discussions with General Wheeler, that American hawks were fighting a rear-guard action against the new American administration. See RFK timeline book, Gloria Emerson, *A War and a Peace* (Holt, Reinhart and Winston, 1972).

2.   First timeline: In 1976, a former Chilean ambassador was killed on the streets of Washington, D.C., on orders from Chile's military dictator, Augusto Pinochet. Reagan, on his talk-radio show, strongly suggested the killing was by leftists opposing Pinochet who wanted to make one of their own a "martyr." See: Ronnie Dugger, *On Reagan,* op. cit., pages 521-523. When Reagan was president during the 1980s, he attributed many right-wing death squad atrocities to leftist guerillas, contradicting church investigation groups and international human rights organizations, as well as, later, U.S. government studies. In each of these

instances, Reagan was horribly wrong and made himself akin to an American Stalinist apologist from the 1930s or 1940s.

3. The Unity Party did not exist in the first timeline. In the RFK timeline, the Unity Party stressed the desire for "one Vietnam, North and South" but only after negotiation with the North, and full and free reunification elections in both the North and South, consistent with the Paris Accords. The Unity Party ran first in the cities of Saigon and Hue and made respectable showings in various smaller communities, particularly among Buddhists, who saw the Unity Party as a "lesser evil" compared with either the NLF or former President Thieu's National Party.

4. Tran Van Tra was born in the southern section of Vietnam but fled north in the 1950s. There he became a leading military figure. In the first timeline, after the fall of Saigon to the Vietnamese Communists in 1975, Tran ordered the dismantling of the NLF as an independent force. See: Truong's first-timeline autobiography, *A Viet Cong Memoir* (Vintage Books, 1986).

5. The CIA had a fairly accurate intelligence track record in Vietnam. It correctly identified strong support for Ho Chi Minh in 1955–1956 throughout the entire country of Vietnam (north and south) which led President Eisenhower to step up support of the newly created American entity known as South Vietnam. In Eisenhower's memoir, *Mandate for Change* (Doubleday, 1962), he said every "knowledgeable" person inside the government told him that Ho would have won any election during the 1950s with "possibly 80 percent" of the vote. Another example of the CIA's correct intelligence assessment occurred in the fall of 1967 when it warned the Johnson administration and U.S. General Westmoreland about the influx of Viet Cong forces into the areas surrounding Saigon. This build-up of forces occurred in the months leading up to the Communists' Tet Offensive in 1968. The warnings were ignored, however, which set off a turf battle between the United States military and intelligence departments. See Sam Adams, *War of Numbers: An Intelligence Memoir* (Steerforth Press, 1994), and Bob Brewin and Sydney Shaw, *Vietnam on Trial* (Atheneum, 1987).

Chapter 16: Southern Discomfort

1. The 1930s federal law prohibiting courts from hearing or issuing labor dispute injunctions had begun to be ignored by the United States Supreme Court in the late 1960s in both timelines. In the RFK timeline, however, Labor Secretary Reuther immediately added a reaffirmation of the law into the bill after reading the first of these decisions. Under the United States Constitution, Article III, Sections 1 and 2, Congress has the right to bar courts from hearing cases in any particular subject matter.

2. Reuther, however, demanded, as part of the compromise, that stockholders must pre-approve any corporate political donations. While corporations had been prohibited from giving donations to political candidates since 1907, the new law extended this prohibition to political action committees or any political research groups.

3. First timeline: Maurine Hedgepeth and Addie Jackson were two workers in southern textile factories who were active in union organizing in the early 1970s. Each was profiled in the pro-labor journal known as *Southern Exposure* during that time. Barry Bluestone, also in the first timeline, later became a prominent

economist and progressive and pro-union activist. There was, of course, no bombing of a church during the late 1960s or 1970s over union organizing. further, all three of these people continued to live and be heroic in their efforts on behalf of working people.

4. "Shiva" is the seven-day period of mourning observed by Jewish people when a child, sibling, or parent dies.

Chapter 17: A Small Step, a Hop, and a Leap

1. In the RFK timeline, Neil Armstrong was told that Robert Kennedy and William Buckley had collaborated on the phrase for the common good of America and humanity. Armstrong practiced the sentence over and over. Unlike in the first timeline, Armstrong flawlessly said the sentence to an excited world. Kennedy himself limited his own public comments, except to say that it was his "brother's dream to reach the stars. Now we have done so before the end of the decade in which he began to pursue his dream." Robert Scheer, writing his first column for the *Los Angeles Times* after radicals at *Ramparts* magazine removed him as editor, saw in Kennedy's comments "that the president does not appear to share his brother's passion for space exploration, preferring more earthly matters, including labor law reform and pursuing peaceful foreign policy initiatives."

2. RFK timeline: Meany stepped down with grace, amid a whitewashing tribute to his career as president of the AFL-CIO. Reuther commented to Fraser in Reuther's office after the AFL-CIO convention, "You know something, Doug? That bastard would have destroyed the union movement if he kept on as president of the AFL-CIO. I just feel that, even though I shouldn't say it at this point." See RFK-timeline biography *Reuther: Labor's Savior*, by Douglas Brinkley (Alfred Knopf Co., 2008).

3. Rather was referring to the scandal that broke out in the late spring of 1972, which is discussed in Chapter 27.

4. Martin fared no better under President Nixon in the first timeline. In 1970 Nixon replaced Martin with Arthur Burns, who was chairman of the Council for Economic Advisors under Eisenhower. Nixon chose Burns because, in 1960, Burns had urged Nixon to advise the Eisenhower administration and the Federal Reserve Board to stimulate the economy for Nixon's election campaign against Jack Kennedy. Eisenhower and his advisers refused that request. Nixon later concluded that the relatively weak economy played a significant role in his loss to Jack Kennedy in 1960. Stephen Ambrose, *Nixon: The Triumph of a Politician*, op. cit. and Tom Wicker, *One of Us*, op. cit., among other Nixon biographies, discuss this subject.

Chapter 18: Backing into Vietnam

1. RFK timeline: The Peace Corps was sometimes a dangerous organization in which to enlist. In Vietnam, several Peace Corps workers were killed, a few by land mines that were not cleared properly. A former North Vietnamese soldier, now living in the South, murdered a volunteer for "stealing" his girlfriend. Former Thieu regime military officers, in separate instances, killed two volunteers who had spoken "too brashly" of being antiwar veterans opposed to the previous South Vietnamese regimes. Other deaths occurred in Africa and Latin America because of weather conditions, such as floods or extreme heat, earthquakes or volcanic activity, or diseases

such as malaria. The deaths took place over a seventeen-month period from 1969 through 1971 and dampened some enthusiasm for serving in the Peace Corps. Although each of these deaths made headlines, sometimes for days, the Kennedy administration treated each death as one deserving of military-type honors. This muted the Republican criticism and helped keep the program a popular one overall. When one local conservative television commentator, Joe Pyne of Los Angeles, attacked the Peace Corps program as a "big-government, socialist conspiracy that causes senseless deaths of misguided American youth," he was suspended from his weekly commentary and forced by his management and advertisers to apologize for his "intemperate" remarks.

2. The "first" treason was when Southern Vietnamese leader Ngo Diem refused to support reunification elections in 1956 in Vietnam. Diem, as noted earlier in the text, had set up the separate nation of South Vietnam with American backing. See Stanley Karnow, *Vietnam: A History*, op. cit.; Peter A. Poole, *The United States and Indochina from FDR to Nixon* (Robert E. Krieger Publishing Company, 1976); George Mc.T. Kahin, *Intervention: How America Became Involved in Vietnam* (Alfred Knopf, 1986); and *The Pentagon Papers* (Bantam Books, 1971).

3. In the RFK timeline, Ted Kennedy never hosted a drinking party in Chappaquiddick, Massachusetts, for those who served in Bob Kennedy's last campaign of 1968. Mary Jo Kopechne did not drown nor did she ever have an affair with Ted Kennedy. Kopechne, however, could not completely deny her fate. She was killed by a drunk driver (not a politician) on May 22, 1980, while driving home from work one evening.

Chapter 19: Minding the World's Business

1. In both timelines, George Harrison of the Beatles took an active interest in Bangladesh and Kashmir, and his influence helped inspire many volunteers to join the Peace Corps missions there. It should also be noted that Europe agreed to provide economic aid to the region as well.

2. Meyer, in the first timeline, was also a high ranking official at the CIA during the early 1970s. He reluctantly followed Nixon's and Kissinger's order to destabilize Chile and convince the Chilean military to overthrow Allende. Meyer, in his autobiography, *Facing Reality* (Harper and Row, 1980), claimed he doubted the feasibility and morality of this order despite his participation in these policies. The coup, which occurred in 1973, resulted in the death of Allende, thousands of other Chileans, and some Americans living in Chile.

3. A review of transcripts of conversations among Politburo members revealed that they often called each other "comrade," followed by the first and middle names of the person addressed. In the first timeline, many Politburo transcripts were released after the fall of the Soviet Union in 1991.

Chapter 20: Rising with the Fall

1. Nader, in both timelines, worked closely with the NAACP in North Carolina and other southern states on lawsuits filed to oppose racial discrimination and barriers to union organizing in textile mills. Mazzocchi, also in both timelines, spearheaded labor's support for the Occupational Safety and Health Act (OSHA) and actively supported environmental protections for workers and consumers.

2. Reagan, in his first term as governor, raised sales, corporate, and income taxes in both timelines. While he later claimed to do so because he wished to provide some relief from property taxes, he also famously quipped at the time, " . . . taxes should hurt." For an authoritative first-timeline source, see Lou Cannon, *Reagan* (Putnam, 1982).

3. RFK timeline: A young Republican congressman and former professional football player, Jack Kemp, was especially intrigued by this plan. He asked Bond to come to his district in Buffalo to promote the same program. Bond and Kemp became friends and, as a result, Kemp pushed for greater and greater funding for Bond's program. Kemp, initially a believer in volunteer-based organizations, countered the influence of some labor lobbyists who believed that volunteer work undermined union wages and was akin to "slavery." Kemp later became a Democrat in 1974 and a strong advocate of the government-business partnership in improving housing and commercial construction throughout the nation.

4. In the first timeline, the Chicago police and the FBI murdered Fred Hampton in a pre-dawn raid of his home in 1969. See: *Search and Destroy: A Report by the Commission of Inquiry into the Black Panthers and the Police* (Metropolitan Applied Research Center, Inc., 1973); Wesley Swearingen, *F.B.I. Secrets: An Agent's Expose* (South End Press, 1995).

5. RFK timeline: In 1972, George Wallace had so reformed his image among blacks that he was able to win a close election to become Alabama's senator. In the first timeline, Wallace, by the late 1970s, also became more in favor of civil rights for minorities. See Frady, *Wallace*, op. cit. Some believed Wallace had merely returned to his "roots" because, as a judge in the mid-1950s, he had a reputation for fairness to black litigants and criminal defendants.

6. RFK timeline: Some of these white ethnic people became bitter opponents of the Democrats and the Kennedy administration, and therefore ardent Republicans.

7. In the first timeline, particularly during the 1980s, taking a position against deficit spending proved no better for the Democratic Party. The Democrats' opposition to deficits coincided with the movement of some upper middle-income and wealthier white professionals and corporate middle management into the Democratic Party. Such persons tended not to be racist, at least for the most part, but they also tended to oppose any significant government programs to economically assist vulnerable or working class people. Robert Lekachman, *Visions and Nightmares: America After Reagan* (MacMillan, 1987), Chapter 6; Kevin Phillips, *The Politics of Rich and Poor* (Random House, 1991), pages 40-41. Phillips, who predicted the rise of the Republican Party through its co-opting of George Wallace's racist constituency in the American South (see Phillips book, *The Emergence of The Republican Majority* (Arlington House, 1969)), has, since the mid-1980s, refocused his populist anger away from "wine and cheese liberals" and toward "free trade and religious conservatives." In the RFK timeline, however, Phillips merely faded away in bitterness, much like other right-wing populists of the 1960s who detested both union-based populism and corporate elitism.

8. RFK timeline: George Will, a little-known philosophy professor at Hillsdale College, wrote what some historians consider an excellent biography of Nelson Rockefeller entitled *Almost President: The Life of Nelson Rockefeller* (Kentucky University Press, 1998). In his book, Will stated, "In truth, Rockefeller's defeat

in the 1970 gubernatorial race should not have been surprising. Rockefeller's victories in previous races for governor were not overwhelming, and at least on one occasion, he won a mere plurality victory, mainly due to a third-party candidate. While a number of people in New York genuinely liked 'Rocky' as a person, his obvious presidential ambitions for 1972 caused people to wonder whether Rockefeller would adequately represent their interests as governor. Some say he might have won rather handily if he had concentrated on his reelection, but we must leave such views to the realm of speculation."

In the first timeline, Rockefeller defeated Goldberg in the gubernatorial election of 1970. In that timeline, Richard Nixon, a fellow Republican, was president, and Rockefeller was not planning to challenge an incumbent Republican president in 1972.

Chapter 21: A Strike in Gdansk

1. In the first timeline, Nixon and Kissinger attempted to keep the ABM issue alive as a bargaining chip. ABM development was eventually though only temporarily forestalled as a result of the anti-ABM treaty of 1972. Smith, *Doubletalk: The Story of SALT I*, op. cit.

2. "Finlandization" was a term American Cold Warriors used to describe what they believed would happen if the United States removed its troops from Western Europe. Finland was a free country that bordered the Soviet Union, yet Cold Warriors considered it to be essentially under Soviet occupation. The Soviets had invaded a pro-Fascist Finland in 1940, and there was admittedly some anxiety within some elements of Finnish society that the Soviets could easily invade again. But most Finns barely thought about the Soviets and did not hesitate to exercise their freedoms within their nation throughout most of the Cold War. A useful article on the subject is Peter Bottichelli, "Finland's Relations with the Soviet Union, 1940-1986," Spring-Fall 1986, *Loyola University's Student Historical Journal*.

3. Bowles and Kennedy had carefully read Soviet dissident Andrei Amalik's remarkably prescient book, *Will the Soviet Union Survive 1984?* (Harper & Row, 1969) before the book was formally released. The book, published in both timelines, was based upon a 1968 essay in Russian that was translated and published in 1969 in the United States in both timelines. Amalik wrote about what he saw as the fatal weaknesses in the Soviet system and the growing estrangement of the larger Muslim populations in the southern areas of the Soviet Union against the Russian leadership. Amalik's arguments were well known inside the Politburo, but in the first timeline Amalik's U.S. policy makers largely ignored the work. In the first timeline, talking about Russia's weakness was not profitable for that portion of the American elite seeking to increase budgets for military and intelligence spending, even as the Soviets were falling apart. See also: Andrew Cockburn, *The Threat* (Random House, 1983), which analyzed the pattern of such "threat inflation" promoted by the pro-military elite within the United States and Soviet Union.

Chapter 22: The Hits Keep Coming

1. In the first timeline, many Congressional Republicans in the early 1970s supported the idea of a negative income tax. President Nixon, steering a "moderate"

course between the negative income tax and a guaranteed minimum income sought by liberals, endorsed a guaranteed minimum income (called the "Family Assistance Plan") that was slightly lower than what many Democrats sought. The proposal died in Congress as a result of liberal and conservative bickering. See the first-timeline book *Nixon's Good Deed: Welfare Reform* (Columbia University Press, 1974), by Vincent J. and Vee Burke. However, there is also evidence Nixon cynically wanted the proposed legislation to fail, according to Nixon aide H.R. Haldeman's diaries of his discussions with Nixon. See H.R. Haldeman, *The Haldeman Diaries: Inside the Nixon White House* (Putnam, 1994).

2.   RFK timeline: In early 1970, after Congress failed to pass the first Family Assistance Program, which called for a guaranteed income of $3,000 a year to every American, President Kennedy sought and Congress approved the creation of a commission to study problems associated with welfare programs around the nation. The commission would also explore solutions including a guaranteed income and a negative income tax. Daniel Bell, a highly respected sociology professor who had written *The End of Ideology, The Coming of the Post-Industrial Society* and other analytical works, was asked to head the commission at the initial suggestion of economist John Kenneth Galbraith. "Bell is intrigued by the negative income tax idea but has also supported a guaranteed minimum income. He will be very objective on this, I believe, as well as practical and thoughtful." Finally, in both timelines, welfare advocate George Wiley died of a heart attack in 1972 and, thus, could not challenge Kennedy from the Left.

3.   In the first timeline, Casper Weinberger, who worked for the multinational corporation Bechtel and with other private-sector firms in his career, came to a similar conclusion after spending several years in government service in the Reagan administration in the 1980s. See Weinberger's autobiography, *Fighting for Peace* (Warner Books, 1990), Acknowledgments; C-Span cable television, *Booknotes*, May 17, 1990, interview with Weinberger.

4.   Seymour Melman made many of these points in his first-timeline articles and books, including *The Permanent War Economy* (Rev. ed. Touchstone Books, 1985). See other first-timeline military conversion books, including *Dismantling the Cold War Economy* (Basic Books, 1992) by Ann Markusen and Joel Yudken, who built their analyses on Melman's research.

5.   RFK timeline: Far-right journalist Westbrook Pegler, relying on certain CIA sources later discredited, attempted to argue that Gavenenko may have turned into a double agent for the Soviets. However, Gavenenko's record of pro-Nazi and anti-Communist statements was seen as too consistent for such a view to be tenable. To some on the Right, who, in this timeline, devolved more and more into conspiracy theories, this only meant the conspiracy was a well-planned Soviet "trick."

Chapter 23: The Cold War Twists in the Wind

1.   RFK timeline book, John K. Fairbank and Stephen Cohen, *Communist Battle-Lines: The Russian-Chinese Crisis, 1969-1973* (St. Martin's Press, 1994). Fairbank and Cohen were noted Western scholars regarding China and the Soviet Union, respectively, in both timelines.

2.   For first timeline (albeit Western) sources regarding the Chinese Cultural Revolution, one may wish to begin with John K. Fairbank, *The Great Chinese Revolution, 1800-1985* (HarperCollins, 1987) and Jonathan Spence, *The Search*

for Modern China (Reprint, W.W. Norton, 2001). It is also a useful exercise for anyone interested in modern China to read the article by Jonathan Mirsky in the *New York Review of Books*, May 30, 1991, in which he discusses and analyzes Western scholars' often dramatic misperceptions regarding Chinese politics, culture, and history. The book reviewed in the article is Steven W. Mosher's *China Misperceived: American Illusions and Chinese Reality* (Basic Books, 1990).

Chapter 24: More Twisting and Turning Around the Globe

1. RFK timeline: Bowles became concerned, from a foreign policy angle, about the level of United States' gold reserves. He therefore asked his undersecretary of state, William Attwood, to prepare a report on the subject of gold as the basis for exchange, its effect on the domestic economy and foreign affairs, which nations held the most gold, and any alternatives to using gold as a currency standard. Bowles suggested that Undersecretary Attwood work with Jim Tobin of the Federal Reserve Board and with Treasury Secretary Lance in preparing the report. Bowles told Attwood, "If the other departments of government want it as a joint project, so be it. This is complicated even for a businessman like me!" The report would not be completed until early 1973 (see Chapter 33, infra).

2. First timeline: Some economists and social commentators believed that Nixon's allowing grain sales to the Soviets in 1972 and the 1971-72 worldwide drought created inflation in food prices and then in the broader economy. This, along with oil and gas embargoes and shortages of the early- to mid-1970s, was far more responsible for 1970's inflation than labor wage demands or Nixon going off the gold standard in 1971. See first-timeline works, including Jeff Faux, "The Fed's Unnecessary Assault on Wages," Economic Policy Institute Issue Brief, Issue Brief #136, March 2, 2000; Mark Zandi, "The Economics of El Nino" (October 17, 1997, Economy.com); Edward Renshaw, "The Fed (Or Economy) Watchers' Handbook" (1996, Web site publication, Essay 11); Dan Morgan, *Merchants of Grain* (Viking Press, 1979); Michael Harrington, *Twilight of Capitalism*, (Touchstone, 1976) pp. 225–227; American Corn Growers Association report on *Food Prices v. General Prices, 2001*, as reported on the ACGA Web site, among other sources.

3. International observers could never understand how young revolutionaries could have penetrated the prison, considering the South African government's strong fortress set up in and around the prison. Years later, the South African government disclosed documents revealing that the secret police in South Africa had penetrated the group almost immediately. The documents also suggested the secret police hoped the plan would succeed in order to have Mandela leave the country. By 1971, the South African government realized that Mandela sitting in jail was a continuing embarrassment to them. In the first timeline in 1976, the government offered Mandela his freedom if he would simply renounce the use of violence in opposing the apartheid system. Mandela responded that he would refuse to leave prison as long as any conditions were attached to his freedom.

4. In the first time line, during the 1980s, prominent civil rights attorney Lani Guinier had suggested cumulative voting to help American minorities get attention from white politicians—or else let them vote "in black or Latino blocks."

When President Clinton nominated Guinier to lead the Justice Department's Civil Rights Division in 1993, nearly all conservatives denounced her ideas as "radical" and "un-American." See Lani Guinier, *The Tyranny of the Majority* (Free Press, 1994); Clint Bolick, "Clinton's Quota Queen," *Wall Street Journal,* April 30, 1993. Ironically, in the first time line, various conservatives, including *National Review* editor William F. Buckley, Jr., and Russell Kirk, supported the apartheid system in South Africa during the 1960s and 1970s, which system included a refusal to allow minorities to vote at all. See also: Lally Weymouth, *Washington Post,* July 15, 1993, where this moderate to conservative columnist discussed, in a positive way, the idea of cumulative or minority voting structures to protect white voters' interests in South Africa. Ironically, Weymouth was a harsh critic of Guinier, calling her anti-democratic. See Weymouth, *Washington Post,* May 25, 1993.

5. See endnote 7 in Chapter 5 for an explanation of Resolution 242. As for Sadat's peace offering, this also occurred in the first timeline. Sadat made this offer following a recommendation by Gunnar Jarring, the United Nations Special Representative to the Middle East. Israel, however, refused to accept this offer, a position backed by President Nixon and his adviser, Henry Kissinger. Israel's failure to accept Sadat's offer played a significant role in Sadat's decision to attack Israel in 1973, in what most people in America and Israel call "The Yom Kippur War." On the Jarring Mission, Sadat's peace offer, Israel's rejection, and the 1973 Egyptian attack on Israel, see, among others, Fred J. Khouri, *The Arab-Israeli Dilemma* (2nd ed., Syracuse University Press, 1976); Mohammed Heikal, *The Road to Ramadan* (Ballantine Books, 1976); Hersh, *The Price of Power,* op. cit.; and Noam Chomsky, *The Fateful Triangle* (South End Press, 1983). See also Walter Laqueur, *Confrontation: The Middle East War and World Politics* (Abacus, 1974), particularly pps. 24–37, where he discussed "missed opportunities" for peace between 1967 and 1972, mostly opportunities missed from the Israeli side. Laqueur did not see the February 1971 Sadat offer as significant as the other writers mentioned here, though he discusses other Egyptian offers on which Israel refused to follow up. Laqueur is a deeply committed Zionist who has written many works on Israel and world history.

6. For those readers shocked at some of the statements uttered by these Israeli leaders in the RFK timeline, please see the first-timeline book by Yossi Bellin, *Mehiro shel Ihud* (Revivim, 1985), which unfortunately has not been translated into English. Bellin, a prominent Israeli official, wrote this book on the history of the Israeli Labor Party in the first timeline. Surprisingly, he publicly quoted from various Israeli officials in his 1985 book when some of the participants were still alive. Noam Chomsky, who reads and speaks Hebrew, has translated several of these quotes into English in various articles and books he has written that deal in part with Middle East politics. See Chomsky's *Deterring Democracy* (Hill and Wang, 1991, Afterward), for example. In the first timeline, there is also evidence that Dayan supported Sadat's peace proposal, but was then isolated from Israeli Prime Minister Meir's Cabinet. Hersh, *The Price of Power,* op. cit. See also: Stephen Green, *Taking Sides: America's Secret Relations with a Militant Israel* (William Morrow, 1984), which includes a post–1967 war memo from Johnson's Secretary of State Dean Rusk regarding shift in Israeli leadership "from seeking

peace with no . . . territorial gains toward one of territorial expansion." A prominent historian, Michael Oren, has called the tone of Green's book "sensationalistic," referring more to the conclusions Green draws than his evidence. See further: Oren's *Six Days of War: June 1967 and the Marking of the Modern Middle East* (Oxford University Press, 2002), where Oren discusses the significance of the Israeli victory in the Six Day War in terms of the failure of the Israelis and Arabs to make peace with each other.

7. In the first timeline, when Soviet leader Mikhail Gorbachev allowed Jews in the Soviet Union to emigrate in 1989, the United States, with prodding from Israel and the American Jewish organizations, forced many of the Soviet Jews to go to Israel, despite the pleas of Soviet Jews who wanted to emigrate to America. See: Sheldon Richman, "Let the Soviet Jews Come to America," *The Cato Institute*, October 3, 1991; Andrew Kilgore, "Are Soviet Jews There to Stay or is Israel Just a Way Station to the U.S.?" *Washington Report on Middle East Affairs*, October/November, 1999.

8. In the first timeline, in 1971, Ellsberg's psychiatric records were stolen by Nixon's "plumbers," or burglars as part of the Nixon administration's efforts to smear Ellsberg for leaking, with Anthony Russo, the Pentagon Papers. See Jonathan Schell, *The Time of Illusion* (Vintage Books, 1976), among other books that deal with the Nixon administration and its political and constitutional scandals. The information about Ellsberg seeing a psychiatrist was not a secret among Washington gossipers, but the Nixon administration wanted more. As for Kennedy, a Washington-area psychiatrist named Leonard Duhl claimed, after Robert Kennedy's assassination in the first timeline, that he "treated" Kennedy on an "informal" basis from 1964 through 1967. Duhl was a high-ranking medical officer in the Peace Corps during the 1960s.

9. RFK timeline: Kennedy was becoming frustrated, he told Kenny O'Donnell, that college students found more and more "causes," particularly in foreign affairs matters, to fight for as he brought peace in Europe and in Vietnam. Students began supporting sanctions against right-wing military dictatorships in Guatemala, Nicaragua, Honduras, and Ecuador, among other countries, which nations had close relations with U.S. business and military interests. Conversely, many of these same students sought an end to the embargo against Fidel Castro's Communist dictatorship in Cuba on the basis that the dictatorship would likely be undermined if America opened trade and diplomatic relations with Cuba. These contradictory positions were easy to caricature, although they may not have been as inconsistent as they seemed. As usual, however, such protesting students were a minority within a minority as many students entered the Peace Corps, VISTA, or the military with pride in their hearts to serve their country.

10. First-timeline sources for Israeli funding of Islamic fundamentalists include Dilip Hiro, *Sharing the Promised Land* (Olive Branch Press, 1996) and *Intifada* by Ze'ev Shiff and Ehud Ya'ari (Simon & Schuster, 1990). Yehoshafat Harkabi later detailed his change from hawk to dove in his book, *Israel's Fateful Hour* (reprint, HarperCollins, 1989). See also: Amos Elon, "Israelis and Palestinians: What Went Wrong?" *New York Review of Books*, December 19, 2002.

11. RFK timeline: Nahum Goldmann wrote prodigiously in favor of Sadat's plan for peace between Egypt and Israel in the *Washington Post* on behalf of the administration. This made Goldmann a hated figure among many establishment Jewish organizations. Goldmann took the heat off Ellsberg and undermined the canard that one must be a left-wing self-hating Jew to be for peace. But Goldmann was essentially alone as a Jew in the mainstream press on this issue—unless one counted the *Los Angeles Times*' newest Washington columnist, Izzy Stone, who "everyone"—meaning the Jewish organization leaders—"knew" was a "left-wing self-hating Jew," although Stone was an unquestioning supporter of Israel up through the 1967 war. After that war, Stone began to doubt the wisdom or morality of building settlements in the areas won in that war, but never wavered in his support of Israel.

    First timeline: Goldmann supported Sadat's peace offerings of February 1971 and in 1977. Goldmann also criticized Israel's policies toward Palestinians, and just before his death in 1982, opposed the Israeli invasion of Lebanon earlier that year. When he died, the Israeli government officially ignored this towering figure in the history of Zionism. Noam Chomsky in *The Fateful Triangle* (South End Press, 1983), p. 97, cites the *Jerusalem Post* as one of his sources for this fact.

12. Rabbi Hecht, in the first timeline, used the Maimonides' quote to support the assassination of Prime Minister Yitzhak Rabin about three months *before* Rabin was assassinated in 1995. Rabin had been pursuing a peace plan with the Palestinians at the time. Hecht, however, came under heavy criticism after an Israeli rabbinical student assassinated Rabin. After a controversy ensued against Hecht, Hecht claimed to have apologized to Rabin just before the latter's assassination. See Robert Friedman, *New York Times,* October 9, 1995; *Anti-Defamation League* Web site article by Abraham Foxman, director, entitled "Responsible Democracy Requires Responsible Rhetoric" (1995).

Chapter 25: Russian Summer and Chinese Fall

1. RFK timeline: As scholars Cohen and Fairbank later wrote, this was "an example of a case in which Communist propaganda turned out to be the truth." See *Communist Battlelines,* op. cit. The authors also noted that Jack Newfield, after learning he was "out of the loop" regarding Ellsberg's no longer secret trip, told Kennedy he would stay through the 1972 election but did not wish to stay with the administration thereafter. "I think I already lasted longer than either of us expected," he told Kennedy. "I still admire you and respect you, but you know where I stand. I won't be a decoy for misinformation, pure and simple." Kennedy tried to cajole Newfield with gallows humor, saying, "I didn't know you were so optimistic!" When Newfield looked confused, Kennedy added, "You actually think the world will survive the year—and even more fantastic, you think I'm winning reelection this fall!" Newfield smiled. "It won't be easy to leave you, Bob," which drew a wry smile from the president. Cohen and Fairbank, ibid.

2. RFK timeline: Lin, in his last days, spoke with aides about seeking asylum in the Soviet Union but decided against it based upon the many anti-Soviet statements he had made as part of his strategy against Chou En-Lai. Lin also knew the Russians were aware that he considered dropping a single tactical nuclear weapon on the

Russian side of the Manchurian border. After hearing Mao's famous speech, Lin made the decision to use a nuclear weapon. However, Lin's chief science adviser, who admitted after the initial civil war that he was swayed by Mao's speech, lied to Lin about a change in the wind, saying a nuclear attack would "blow back" against them. Lin, relying upon his science adviser, then decided against using any such weapon. See Fairbank and Cohen, *Communist Battlelines*, op. cit.

3. Chen was a Taiwanese-born Chinese national who left Taiwan for Red China in 1966, convinced that Mao represented the future of China and Taiwan. In the first and second timelines, she escaped China in the mid-1970s and wrote of her experiences. In the first timeline, she wrote a book of short fictional stories, based upon real events during the Cultural Revolution, entitled *The Execution of Mayor Yin* (Indiana University Press, 1978).

4. For those who believe "pretext" is unfair to conservatives, it must be noted that most conservative pundits, as well as some liberal ones, applauded General Suharto while he was committing mass murder in Indonesia in 1965 and after, the Brazilian military's mass uprooting and murder of Brazilians and native Indians following a military coup in that nation in 1964, various Guatemalan military dictators soaking the land of Guatemala with blood over several decades in the mid-twentieth century, and . . . well, one could go on about such a subject.

5. Brian Crozier wrote an excellent first-timeline biography of General Chiang entitled *The Man Who Lost China* (Charles Scribner and Sons, 1976). In the RFK timeline, he also wrote a biography with the same name. See also Crozier's RFK-timeline article "Chiang's Last Stand," *National Review*, January 23, 1973.

6. RFK timeline books: Robert Dallek, *President Robert Kennedy: Many Are the Days* (Simon & Schuster, 2008). Schlesinger's RFK-timeline book, *Robert Kennedy and His Presidency* (Houghton-Mifflin, 1992), is considered far more sympathetic to Kennedy because of the historian's friendship with Kennedy. However, reviewers of Schlesinger's book concluded he was willing to entertain the belief that election year politics played a small role in Kennedy's decision to go public with the information.

7. In the first timeline, many American policymakers feared that Václav Havel would prove "too radical" a leader in post-Communist Czechoslovakia. By the time Czechoslovakia divided into the Czech Republic and Slovakia, those fears were proven wrong. And by the turn of the twenty-first century, President George "Dubya" Bush was praising Havel for his support for Bush's then policy toward Iraq. *Washington Times*, "Havel Endorses U.S. Line on Iraq," September 17, 2002.

Chapter 26: Reelection, Part 1

1. In a sign of the changing political culture, Republicans in the Senate split on the Wilkins' and Edelman nominations. Republican Senator Margaret Chase Smith from Maine, led the charge of "split" Republicans to support Wilkins and Edelman. Kansas Republican Robert Dole sided with Thurmond and other Republicans against Wilkins and Edelman—though he was known as a "split" Republican when it came to supporting farm subsidies and expanding the food stamp program. Dole said privately, "We don't have too many blacks or feminists in Kansas." The Senate confirmed Edelman's nomination as solicitor general 72-26, with two Democratic Southern senators, Ervin and Hollings, absent.

2. In the first timeline, corporate income taxes declined as a portion of federal revenue over the past fifty years. According to The Twentieth Century Fund (now called the Century Fund), in its first-timeline 1999 report entitled "The Basics of Tax Reform," the decline in corporate income taxes "has been made up by the increasing share of revenue from social insurance contributions, primarily the Social Security payroll tax. In 1943, corporate taxes comprised 39.8 percent of total federal revenues; social insurance contributions contributed 12.7 percent. By 1996, the situation was nearly reversed; social insurance contributions provided 35.1 percent of federal revenues, while corporate income taxes provided 11.8 percent. In 1994, corporate tax revenues amounted to just 2.5 percent of GDP."

    In the RFK timeline, corporate taxes as a percentage of overall taxes paid had declined from 38 percent to 24 percent because of RFK's expansion of investment tax credits, primarily for purchasing capital equipment designed to increase efficiency and promote a cleaner workplace and environment.

3. Yarborough was more correct than he might have known. In the first timeline in the United States during the 1980s and 1990s, a time when unions almost disappeared from the private business sector, most income gains went to the top 10 to 20 percent of income earners. This reversed a trend during more union friendly time periods in America such as the 1940s through the 1970s where workers shared more equitably in the overall income gains in American society. See Kevin Phillips, *The Politics of Rich and Poor*, op. cit. See also sources cited in Chapter 26, endnote 6 below.

4. Iacocca was partially correct in his statement. In both timelines, the Japanese government did not impose any taxes on long-term capital gains from investments. However, the Japanese government did tax short-term capital investment profits. Regardless, Japanese corporations in the 1960s through the 1980s were highly regulated and heavily taxed. In large corporations, Japanese employees received lifetime employment and benefits. In the first timeline, discussion of different aspects of the Japanese economic system can be found in Lester Thurow, *The Zero-Sum Society* (Basic Books, 1980) and *The Zero-Sum Solution* (Simon & Schuster, 1985); and Robert Kuttner, *The Revolt of the Haves* (Simon & Schuster, 1980) and *The Economic Illusion* (Houghton-Mifflin, 1984).

5. In the first timeline, in August 1971, President Nixon, fearing the Democrats would use the softening economic outlook against him in his reelection campaign in 1972, instituted wage and price controls. This was a major surprise since the Nixon administration had just stated a few weeks before that it opposed such controls. Traditional Republicans opposed Nixon's turnabout on wage and price controls, as did the AFL-CIO leadership (because it feared Nixon would control wages more than prices). Ironically, most business leaders applauded the move, as did, initially, most of the public. The controls worked at first to hold down what was already a growing inflation, but Nixon, trying to woo business support in 1972, began to allow prices to rise. Wages were tightly controlled in the first six months, as labor feared, but began to rise more slowly than prices until controls were lifted around the time of the first major oil embargoes and shortages in late 1973. See, among other studies on this subject, Robert M. Bleiberg, "Farewell to Wage and Price Controls," *Imprimis, The monthly journal of Hillsdale College*, July 1974, Vol. 3, No. 7; Daniel Yergin and Joseph Stanislaw,

The Commanding Heights (Simon and Schuster, 1998); Robert Hetzel, "Arthur Burns and Inflation," *Federal Reserve Board of Richmond Economic Quarterly*, Winter 1998, Vol. 84, No. 1.

6. First timeline: Depending upon which year is used in the period of comparing the early 1970s with the late 1990s or early 2000s, the numbers fluctuate in terms of the disparity of wealth between the top 0.5 percent to top 1 percent on the one hand, and nearly everyone else on the other. However, one conclusion is clear despite such relatively minor fluctuations in the percentages and numbers: The wealth and income gaps clearly favor an extremely small wealthy portion of the public. For a snapshot in 2002, see Paul Krugman's essay in the *New York Times Magazine*, "The End of Middle-Class America (and the Triumph of the Plutocrats)," October 20, 2002. See also: Edward Wolff, *Top Heavy: A Study of the Increasing Inequality in America* (New Press, 1996); Wolff's separate study for The Century Fund in April 2000 entitled "Recent Trends in Wealth Ownership", shows that over 75 percent of stocks and bonds are owned by the top 10 percent of income earners. Corporate-dominated media presentations often distort the nature and extent of stock ownership among the public.

   Other studies relevant to the distribution of wealth and income include: Thomas Piketty and Emmanuel Saez, *Income Inequality in the United States, 1913-1998* (Quarterly Journal of Economics, April 2002); Cavanagh, et al., *Executive Excess* (United for a Fair Economy, Institute of Policy Studies, September 2000); and the Republican Party-controlled Congressional Budget Office's study in 1997 that showed similarly disturbing wealth and income inequality trends. The Cavanugh report, *Executive Excess*, notes that corporate leaders made only twice the salary of the president of the United States in 1960, but *sixty-two times* that in the year 2000, even as the salary of the president *doubled* over that period. Finally, there is a highly useful Web site on the subject of the inequality of income and wealth in America, known as *Inequality.org*.

7. First timeline: Shortly after taking office as president, Bill Clinton admitted to advisers that despite his campaign rhetoric about "putting people first," he concluded he was forced to put financial interests and business interests first. He believed this was due to the structure of the American economy at that time and to his own compromises with business supporters. See Bob Woodward, *The Agenda* (Simon and Schuster, 1994). Other examples: Clinton passively accepted undermining "mommy welfare" while making barely a ripple of noise regarding government subsidies to robustly profitable corporations. Also compare Clinton's hard Congressional lobbying for business interests in passing corporate-dominated global trade treaties with his passively accepting defeat in the debate over providing health insurance for every American. See Michael Tomasky, *Left for Dead* (Free Press, 1996); John R. MacArthur, *The Selling of Free Trade: NAFTA, Washington and the Subversion of Democracy* (Hill and Wang, 2000). That Clinton's health care proposal was more conservative and capitalist in its approach than Nixon's health insurance proposal in the 1970s—let alone what President Truman proposed in 1948—is also significant. See Tomasky, op. cit. and Chapter 36, endnote 2. While one may rightly say that Clinton's personality and foibles were significant factors in his decisions, there is also something to be said

about the structure of a society in which a person elected president can almost immediately conclude he is helpless against financial and business interests.

Chapter 27: The Mother of All Scandals

1. RFK timeline: Joseph P. Kennedy, the patriarch of the Kennedy clan, died on November 17, 1969, after being largely incapacitated for almost seven years after a series of strokes. His death did not cause as much grief to Bob Kennedy as he himself thought it should. According to Arthur Schlesinger Jr., Kennedy told him, "My views are very different from my Dad's views. And he'd been so . . . out of it . . . for so long . . . I feel worse for not crying now than for his death, Arthur. I cried more after his first stroke, which is when, I guess, I felt I lost him." Schlesinger replied, "I understand, Mr. President. It is hard to disagree with one's father and not have it affect the relationship. It was very difficult for me, if you remember, when my father endorsed Frank Keating instead of you for the New York Senate race in '64. He died in '65. We never fully reconciled our differences on that and in some other areas before . . . he passed on." The two men looked down, not at each other. In doing so, they implicitly recognized that the "politics" of fathers and sons are best left to nineteenth-century Russian novelists.
2. See Chapter 8, endnote 2, for a discussion of Nixon's infamous "Checkers" speech.
3. In the first timeline, Duarte and Ungo were prevented from taking office because of a military coup backed by the Nixon administration. Ungo escaped to the hills of El Salvador and joined the left-wing rebels fighting the "14 families" who ran El Salvador. The military arrested Duarte and tortured him, causing him to lose two of his fingers. Duarte miraculously became president in late 1980, but this time he decided to work closely with the incoming Reagan administration by supporting the El Salvadoran military's merciless attacks on peasants during the guerilla warfare affecting that region. See William M. LeoGrande, *Our Own Backyard: the United States in Central America, 1977–1992* (University of North Carolina Press, 1998); Raymond Bonner, *Weakness and Deceit. U.S. Policy and El Salvador.* (The New York Times Book Company, 1984). Bonner was harshly criticized by Reagan administration officials in the early 1980s and driven from his foreign correspondent job with the *New York Times.* However, official investigations in the 1990s confirmed the accuracy of Bonner's reporting, particularly with regard to the El Salvadoran military's massacre of peasants in the El Salvadoran town of El Mazote. For an interesting take on former Reagan administration officials who were supportive of the military in El Salvador and other Central American nations, and later held prominent positions inside the early twenty-first century administration of George W. Bush, see Conn Hallinan, San Francisco Examiner, "[John] Negroponte and the War on Terrorism," October 20, 2001.

Chapter 28: Double-Edged Swords, Part I

1. Later in the first timeline, Reagan would also claim memory loss in his testimony during government prosecutions of his former aides for what were called the Iran-Contra scandals despite notes of his former secretaries of defense and state that revealed his knowledge and participation. The scandals involved selling arms to Iran, a nation Reagan's administration itself defined as "terrorist," and arming a terrorist guerrilla group fighting against a left-wing regime in Nicaragua.

Both actions by the Reagan Administration violated federal laws and regulations. For the best analysis of this scandal, see Theodore Draper's *A Very Thin Line* (Hill & Wang, 1991), and separately, the official report of Special Prosecutor Laurence Walsh. Years after his first timeline presidency and his court testimony in the Iran-Contra scandals, Reagan ironically developed Alzheimer's disease.

2. First timeline information on Reagan's land deals, grand jury testimony, and the 1960 studio strike appears in Lou Cannon, *Reagan*, op. cit., and Dan Moldea, *Dark Victory: Ronald Reagan, MCA and the Mob* (Viking, 1986).

Chapter 29: Double-Edged Swords, Part II

1. The information on Hoover and these witnesses can be found in Anthony Summers' controversial book, *Official and Confidential: The Secret Life of J. Edgar Hoover* (G. P. Putnam's Sons, 1993). For a counter to Summers, see Cartha DeLoach, *Hoover's FBI: The Inside Story by Hoover's Trusted Lieutenant* (Regnery, 1995). In William Turner's earlier and similarly named book, DeLoach is seen as Hoover's "enforcer" against any and all attacks, whether or not such attacks on Hoover were justified. Summers, Turner, and other writers, including Max Lowenthal, Fred Cook, and Hank Messick, have each written about the FBI's lax attitude toward the Mob and organized crime during Hoover's tenure.

Chapter 30: Reelection, Part II

1. Ganesha the elephant is a symbolic deity in the Hindu religion, which was not the main religion in China. Ignorance of other cultures is fairly typical for a society in its period of hegemony.

2. From the first timeline, see Dr. Zhisui Li (Mao's personal physician), *The Private Life of Chairman Mao* (Random House, 1996), and Philip Short, *Mao: A Life* (Henry Holt, 1999).

3. First timeline: The intellectual "marriage" of Confucius and Marx was, in fact, taken very seriously by Chinese scholars in the early twentieth century. Kuo Mo-Jo, who was president of China's Academy of Science in the 1960s, wrote an essay in 1925 called "Karl Marx Visits the Ancestral Temple of Confucius." The essay was a fantasy dialogue between Marx and Confucius comparing what they had in common, as well as some differences between them.

4. This political divide with regard to population control is consistent with past history. For example, Karl Marx and Frederich Engels were two of the harshest critics of the nineteenth century economist and original population control advocate, Thomas Malthus. See first-timeline book, Ronald Meek, *Marx and Engels on the Population Bomb* (Ramparts Press, 1971). Marxists and other economically oriented leftists tend to oppose the idea of "population control" because they see starvation and hunger as the result of corporate or government manipulation of supply and unequal distribution of food, not a lack of food for human consumption.

5. RFK timeline: Ethel Kennedy, no longer pregnant every year, came out of her shell to become a powerful force in not only passing the Equal Rights Amendment in 1972, but also supporting Title IX Amendments to the 1964 Civil Rights Act to protect women from discrimination in public and private education, including funding of women's sports. Ethel's "mommy" image allowed her

to moderate the feminist movement as she stuck to issues such as girls sports, child care, and equal pay for equal work. Ethel's antiabortion and ERA stances undermined the public career of conservative activist Phyllis Schlafly, who, in the RFK timeline, never became a leading opponent of the ERA or abortion. Instead, Schlafly, a Republican anti-Communist and anti-union ideologue, found herself disillusioned with a "libertine" Republican Party and a "socialist" Democratic Party and faded from the national scene.

6. In the first timeline, President Reagan cut federal income taxes in the early 1980s but almost simultaneously raised Social Security taxes, which had the effect of negating the meager income tax cuts for lower- and middle-income workers. The richest Americans wound up with the largest tax cut benefits during the 1980s. Government deficits also ballooned during Reagan's tenure as Reagan pushed for vast military spending increases at the same time the government was initially losing revenue from the tax cuts. In six of his eight years as president, Reagan showed no interest in balanced budgets as he proposed to spend *more* federal money than Congress originally proposed. The difference was mostly based upon Reagan wanting to spend less on so-called community-oriented programs and more on the military and business subsidies. See the following first timeline books: Kevin Phillips, *The Politics of Rich & Poor*, op. cit.; David Calleo, *The Bankrupting of America* (William Morrow, 1992); David Stockman, *The Triumph of Politics* (Harper & Row, 1986). Stockman, who headed the Office of Management and Budget for Reagan, concluded that Reagan's main advisers supported running up massive deficits because it politically undermined the ability of Democrats to seek new federal social programs.

    Those who claim Reagan's tax cuts fueled the mid- to late-1990s' economic gains during the Clinton administration forget there were five federal tax *increases* between the 1980s and mid-1990s: (1) Reagan's 1982 tax increase; (2) Reagan's 1983 payroll tax increase (see previous paragraph); (3) Reagan's 1986 tax reform, led by many "liberal" Democrats in Congress, which eliminated various tax shelters while admittedly lowering tax rates; (4) George H.W. Bush's general federal tax increases in 1990; and (5) Bill Clinton's 1993 tax increases that fell largely on the top earners. The 1990s recovery followed these tax increases, which should cause policy makers to wonder about the limited effect of taxation on economic growth or contraction.

    Some Reagan defenders, faced with this point, will often switch gears and admit that the effect of the tax increases, starting in the late 1980s and into the 1990s, negated much of the 1981 Reagan tax cuts in terms of total taxes Americans annually paid to the federal government. However, one must avoid using that statistic to conclude that everything became just like it was in 1979 in terms of who paid what taxes to the government. Because of the payroll tax increases in Social Security and Medicare that Reagan pushed through during the 1980s, middle-income and lower-income earners pay more in total taxes than they did before. And, as noted in Chapter 26, endnote 3, most income gains in the 1980s and 1990s, went to those who earned well above a median income.

    There is something else Reagan defenders don't like to mention: The federal government's national debt almost tripled during Reagan's two terms. Fiscal "conservatism," indeed!

For support for these propositions, see: David Calleo, *The Bankrupting of America*, op. cit.; David Stockman, *The Triumph of American Politics*, op. cit.; Harvard business school professor Michael G. Rukstad, *Macroeconomic Decision Making in the World Economy*, and more particularly his "case studies" of the Reagan and Clinton Economic policies (available on the Web at http://www.hbcollege.com/econ/rukstad); "A Vote for Clinton's Economic Program Becomes the Platform for Often-Misleading GOP Attacks," *Wall Street Journal*, October 26, 1994.

7. Coca-Cola removed cocaine in 1906, according to Oakley S. Ray and Charles Ksir, *Drugs, Society and Human Behavior*, (8th ed., McGraw-Hill, 1998). Reagan was born in 1911.

8. In the first timeline, keeping economically poor mothers and fathers in jail for drug violations cost society far more than creating jobs to clean up neighborhoods and educating parents and their children. Often non-violent drug offenders are jailed with violent criminals, despite first-timeline studies showing that prisons often teach people to become more violent. A variety of studies exist on this topic. See, for example, the "Debt to Society" series, *Mother Jones* On-line Special Report (July 10, 2001). More scholarly works include William Ryan, *Blaming the Victim* (Vintage Books, 1971), and two books from leading criminologist Elliot Currie, *Confronting Crime* (Pantheon, 1985) and *Reckoning: Drugs, the Cities and the American Future* (Hill and Wang, 1993).

9. In the first timeline, removing poor women from welfare rolls, known as "welfare reform," has had little effect on poverty rates. Welfare reform, in the first timeline, was designed to end "welfare as we know it," not "poverty as we know it," particularly among single mothers and their children. Even with a rise in marriages, as women with young children sought more support from men, families with two low-income earners were often unable to meet basic economic needs. First-timeline sources include "Two Parent Families Rise After Change in Welfare Laws" (*New York Times*, August 12, 2001); "Hardships in America: The Real Story of Working Families" (Economic Policy Institute, July 24, 2001); "Poverty Rate Among Single-Mother Working Families Remained Stagnant in Late 1990s Despite Strong Economy" (Center for Budget and Policy Priorities, August 16, 2001).

10. In the first timeline, Reagan opened his successful 1980 presidential campaign in Philadelphia, Mississippi, by exalting "states rights," which, since the 1950s, was "code" for entrenched racist interests. People still wonder why a California Republican opened his campaign in a small Southern town. The answer, of course, is that Philadelphia, Mississippi, had made the national news in 1964 when racists killed three civil rights workers there (see Chapter 14, endnote 2, identifying the names of the three civil rights workers). Reagan, in those remarks, was continuing the first-time- line Republican strategy of playing the "race card" to secure white Southern votes. See among other first timeline books: Lou Cannon's second biography of Reagan, *Ronald Reagan: Role of a Lifetime*" (Simon & Schuster, 1991); Kevin Phillips, *The Emerging Republican Majority*, op. cit. The scandal in late 2002 involving Trent Lott, the Mississippi Republican Majority Leader in the U.S. Senate, provided fresh evidence of this race-baiting strategy. See among other articles on the subject: Robert Scheer, "Lott's Love Affair with Racism," *The Nation*, December 17, 2002; Cathy Young, "Party

Purge: Republicans Move Beyond the Racist Past," *Reason Magazine,* December 24, 2002; Joe Conason, "Ashcroft and the Neo-Confederates," *Salon.com,* December 16, 2002. For other examples as to why black-skinned Americans have reason to oppose modern Republican Party leaders, see Laughlin McDonald, "The New Poll Tax: Republican-sponsored ballot security measures are being used to keep minorities from voting," *The American Prospect,* December 30, 2002; and Greg Palast, *The Best Democracy Money Can Buy* (Pluto Press, 2002), particularly Palast's discussion of the State of Florida's removal of black voters falsely identified as felons from voter registration rolls.

Chapter 31: The Home Stretch

1. In the first timeline, such voters liked the measure of revenge "welfare reform" brought against poor people who, with Medicaid and housing subsidies, made not much less than they did for not working at all.

2. First timeline: In October 1994, a study appeared in the *Industrial Labor Relations Review,* Vol. 48, No. 1, pps. 48-64, entitled "Child Poverty in Sweden and the United States: The Effect of Social Transfers and Parental Labor Force Participation." In that study, comparing poor, white Americans with poor people in the more racially homogenous Sweden, it found that the white American poor barely worked or if they did, hid that fact from the government. In Sweden, most poor people worked and almost as important, publicly reported working. The study's authors concluded the reason for this difference was because Sweden's socialist programs of health care, a minimum guaranteed income, and child care applied to everyone regardless of whether they worked or not. Plus, vacation and parental leave policies in the workplace created a *positive* incentive for the poor to work. In contrast, American "means-tested" programs emphasized the need to become poor in order to receive assistance. This also created an incentive to remain poor. And if the poor worked, they often worked under the taxman's radar. The study's authors concluded that universal, as opposed to means-tested programs create a strong incentive for the less fortunate to work as well as a more stable society. The first-timeline book, *The Economic Illusion,* by Robert Kuttner (Houghton-Mifflin, 1985), reached similar conclusions for all poor Americans, regardless of race, based upon government data and other private studies.

3. In the first timeline, President Reagan performed dismally in his first reelection debate in 1984 with Democratic Party candidate Walter Mondale. When Mondale thereafter began closing the gap in the polls against Reagan, media pundits set a new standard for the candidates: Mondale needed a second "knock-out," whereas Reagan merely had to meet the standard of "holding his own." As defined by the pundits, Mondale's failure to defeat Reagan in the second debate by the same "knockout" as the first was deemed a "win" for Reagan. This was the pundits' conclusion, despite Reagan's second-debate gaffes and his inability to complete his rambling closing remarks within the required period. As usual for first-timeline television pundits, they were more concerned about the "bags" under Mondale's eyes, much as such pundits used to obsess about Nixon's "five o'clock shadow." See the following first timeline books: Lou Cannon, *Ronald Reagan: Role of a Lifetime,* op. cit.; *On Bended Knee,* by Mark Hertsegaard (Farrar

Strauss Giroux, 1988); and on the Web, Cspan.org/campaign2000/archivede-bates.asp (video of debate in Kansas City, Missouri, October 24, 1984), which is the video recording of the second Reagan-Mondale debate.

Chapter 32: Election Dissections

1. In the first timeline, the annual deficits under President Nixon for the first four years totaled almost $60 billion. See David Calleo, *The Bankrupting of America*, op. cit., p. 110, table 6.2. Nixon-era deficits were largely the result of three factors: (1) expansion of the Vietnam War, and consequently increased military costs; (2) increased spending for police protection and prison building in the United States; and (3) the continued erosion of life in the inner cities, which increased welfare and other related antipoverty spending that did not increase employment or promote economic growth in those areas. Nixon's urban policy was often called a policy of "benign neglect," even though the author of that phrase, Nixon aide Daniel P. Moynihan, may have meant a policy of de-empha-sizing "race" in public policies for urban areas, not ignoring urban economic deprivation. See, among many books on the subject, William J. Wilson, *The Truly Disadvantaged* (University of Chicago Press, 1987).

Chapter 33: Second Helpings

1. In the first timeline, most small business groups opposed President Clinton's 1993 income tax hike for the top 5 percent of income earners. However, as the *Wall Street Journal* reported around the time the tax bill was passed, most small businesses did not earn sufficient income to be covered by Clinton's tax hike. This fact of small businesses producing income not much different than the median-family-income level has been largely consistent and steady throughout the first timeline in the twentieth and twenty-first centuries.
2. First timeline: Starting in 1968, before any significant environmental legislation passed the U.S. Congress, American oil companies had sharply curtailed drilling activities inside the United States. This had more to do with an oil glut and the majors' concerns about the rise of the independents than any environmental leg-islation. See John Blair, *The Control of Oil* (Pantheon, 1976). In both timelines, Republican pro-business politicians and economists, who tend to believe country club golf course chatter as if it were the gospel, often complained that it was "liberal" environmental policies that caused the drop in drilling.
3. In 1956 and 1967, the OPEC nations attempted an oil embargo against the United States and other Western nations, only to be foiled by oil companies for the same reasons. See the first timeline source Joe Stork, *Middle East Oil and the Energy Crisis* (Monthly Review Press, 1975), p. 211. For first timeline information on rela-tions between independent oil companies and the majors, and issues concerning Libya, see John Blair's *The Control of Oil*, op. cit., Chapter 9 of Blair's book.
4. President Nixon said essentially the same thing in the first timeline when, in 1971, he removed United States' currency from the gold standard. His decision followed fears in his administration that the United States was running out of gold at a time when the gold prices were rising. Tom Wicker, *One of Us*, op. cit. Inflation did eventually increase after Nixon's decision, but it is very questionable whether it was the result of Nixon's decision. Inflation from grain shortages and

increasing oil prices in 1972 and 1973 are more likely causes of the increased inflation. When the largely Arab OPEC nations began their oil embargo, the Arab nations said they acted in solidarity with Egypt's military attack against Israel in the so-called Yom Kippur War. See also Chapter 24, endnotes 2 and 5.

Chapter 34: Culture, Courts, and Computers

1. In the first timeline, the famous abortion rights' decision was called *Roe v. Wade* 410 U.S. 113 (1973).
2. RFK timeline: Kennedy's nemesis, former Teamsters' union president Jimmy Hoffa, was still in jail in 1973. Hoffa remained in jail through 1980, when he was finally paroled. Again, as in the first timeline, he was killed after his release from prison. That's the way things go in the world of the Teamsters and the Mob.
3. RFK timeline: Kennedy, wanting to promote economic development in the Appalachian and coal-mining areas, strongly suggested—some said ordered— that some computer factories be opened in Kentucky, Arkansas, and West Virginia.
4. The British Post Office, in the first timeline, was in the forefront of innovations in fiber optics, among other high-tech developments. Secretary of Commerce Learson was aware of British Post Office activities in fiber optics during the 1960s and supported using the U.S. Post Office as an additional "money funnel." Further, this was not the first time the United States undertook to create and fund technological advances. For example, the federal government, through a variety of public subsidies and other mechanisms, accelerated innovation in civilian and military airplanes. See the first-timeline book by Frank Kofsky, *Harry S. Truman and the War Scare of 1948* (St. Martin's Press, 1993), which includes a detailed discussion of the U.S. government's subsidizing and support for the airline indus- try. Other technological innovations and advances that resulted from the federal government's subsidies or support in the first timeline include computers, atomic energy, water projects, railroads, and space exploration—and the civilian appli- cations arising from those technological developments.
5. RFK timeline: There were also unexpected cultural issues that arose with the Internet. First, the record companies found themselves embroiled in litigation try- ing to stop music fans from sharing and downloading music off the Internet. But several leading artists, including Peter Gabriel, George Clinton, Chick Corea, and Elton John, undermined the companies' efforts when they opened an Internet company called *The Global Village*. The web-based company allowed musicians and singers, for a $50 fee, to upload their music and music videos at the Web site. Fans could then listen to the music for free, but voluntarily and directly pay the artists any amount they wanted—"Passing the hat world-wide," said Gabriel. Musicians immediately flocked to the site, as did fans, which eventually destroyed the traditional music companies as more of these Web sites proliferated. Musicians and businesspeople quickly realized that the real money had mostly been made with concerts, t-shirts, caps, and other accoutrements, and in turn, concentrated on those activities from that point on, particularly with a strong musicians' union which kept wages higher for musicians for live performances. See the second timeline book, Richard Cromelin, *Downloading the Record Companies,* (Harper & Row, 1982), in which Cromelin analyzed this phenomenon.

Second was the issue of pornography on the Web. Congress thought it found the solution against on-line porn when it required all companies operating on the Web to pay taxes. While this immediately shut down many for-profit pornography companies for awhile, it did not take pornographers long to offer their services for free and seek advertising from *other businesses* who wanted to reach the largely male porn "customers." However, with a more conservative and community-oriented culture, most advertisers did not want to risk customer boycotts for advertising at the sites. Further, Congress passed a law, upheld 5-4 in the Supreme Court, that banned what the Court called "pure" pornography. The ruling created a sub-industry for lawyers as prosecutions turned on how "pure" the pornography in question was, but the law nonetheless had the effect of limiting the depth and scope of pornography on the Web. See the second timeline book, Nadine Strossen, *Sex on the Web* (Touchstone, 1984).

Chapter 35: Foreign and Other Affairs

1. RFK timeline: Many writers on the political far right continued to demand World Court trials against Communist leaders like the Nuremberg Trials against German Nazis and Japanese Fascists after World War II. Longtime State Department sage George Kennan quickly disabused Kennedy of any thought of setting up a tribunal for the Communists. He said, "Our intervention in Vietnam might well have been a war crime, if one wished to begin making accusations, Mr. President. Also, you may wish to review Operation Paperclip, in which we brought Nazis into this country—far more than Werner von Braun and Nazi scientists, I admit. I would also hate to see our business leaders, such as Henry Ford II or Armand Hammer, get caught up in an ever-growing net of looking for those who collaborated around the globe with what moralists call 'war criminals.'" Kennan applauded the South African Truth Commissions, first proposed by Nelson Mandela, as being far more effective in protecting the elite from retribution by the masses and healing wounds in nations racked by civil war or revolutions. "Governing a nation," said Kennan, "is a most difficult task. The loss of power is enough punishment for most Nazi and Communist leaders in my view." After an off-the-record discussion between media executives and Secretary of State Bowles, in which Kennan's point about larger business interests and government credibility with the public was repeated, calls for Communist "Nuremberg Trials" disappeared from the mainstream media—in the name of "national security," of course. By the 1980s, only a few Web writers were interested in the subject.

2. RFK timeline: Robert Mundell, the pro–gold standard capitalist economist at the University of Chicago, cried in vain that the cause of the oil price increase was Kennedy's going off the gold standard in 1973. John Kenneth Galbraith, asked to comment by a reporter, said, "Even a stopped watch is right twice a day—but that doesn't mean there is a connection. This has been brewing for some time, even before the world went off the gold standard." In this RFK timeline, there was no Nobel Prize in economics for Professor Mundell, unlike the first timeline when he won the prize in 1999.

Chapter 36: Closing in on the Rainbow

1. In the first timeline, a similar process occurred in reverse. A wave of worker lay-offs would often inure to the economic benefit of corporate executives (and sometimes stockholders) and create a "natural" anti-inflationary effect by putting the fear in the worker, not the corporate executive. Few politicians reliant on political campaign donations from corporations would dare support a labor union or workers' strike or support policies designed to increase worker' bargaining power. Further, government laws allowing employers to fire workers who went on strike were a useful tool for business owners to keep workers from starting a union or considering a strike.

2. The Republicans' plan was, incidentally, the same plan proposed in 1974 by first-timeline Republican President Nixon, with Republican support in Congress. First timeline sources include Martin Plissner, "A Health-Care Bill Fantasy" (Slate.com, June 5, 2001), and Ambrose, *Nixon: Triumph of a Politician*, op. cit. Despite the title of Plissner's article, Plissner stated it was true that, in 1974, President Nixon called for a national health care plan that required all employers to cover their employees. Nixon's Health, Education, and Welfare Secretary Casper Weinberger said at the time: "Nothing should deter us from adding . . . comprehensive health insurance protection to the basic security guarantees that America offers" its citizens. The Democrats, who were fighting for a more socialized form of insurance coverage at the time and could taste overall political victory against the Watergate-beleaguered Nixon, opposed the Republicans' plan.

3. In the first timeline, the Supreme Court reached a similar "arbitrary" decision in *Bush v. Gore* (2000) Case #00-949. In that case, a five-member majority of justices who were often called "strict constructionists and states' rights conservatives" decided to *broadly* construe the Fourteenth Amendment and void the Florida Supreme Court's interpretation of its own state election laws in order to leave George Bush as the winner in Florida and, thus, the winner overall under the Electoral College system of electing presidents. The Supreme Court's interpretation went against previous and subsequent decisions by these same justices on questions of states' power and the Fourteenth Amendment. This led many to conclude the Court's decision was arbitrary and politically motivated. The Court further hurt its cause of impartiality when it said, in its ruling in *Bush v. Gore*, that although thirty-seven other state laws could be held unconstitutional for similar reasons, the Court's ruling should be considered limited to its specific facts. Liberals and leftists in the first timeline were outraged by such judicial fiat, while conservatives and right-wingers rejoiced at the "practicality" of the Court's decision ending the uncertainty of the Florida vote recount for each of the two major party candidates. Compare two first-timeline books: Alan Dershowitz, *Supreme Injustice* (Oxford University Press, 2001), and Richard Posner, *Breaking the Deadlock* (Princeton University Press, 2001), among other books on the subject.

4. In the first timeline, the *Wall Street Journal*, in an editorial entitled "The Non-Paying Class" (November 22, 2002), actually claimed that Republicans should seek to raise income taxes on the poor and middle class so that they feel more of a burden than the richest taxpayers allegedly do. The *Journal*'s argument, consistent with most Republican and American conservative ideology, refuses to recognize that the poor and middle-class are already more heavily burdened than the richest taxpayers with payroll taxes. In both timelines, Republicans and

American conservatives tended to rail against taxes in order to lighten tax burdens on their wealthiest supporters.

5. In the first timeline, employers were rarely sanctioned, civilly or criminally, for hiring illegal immigrants. On the other hand, striking American workers were often jailed for violating pro-employer court injunctions directed against striking American citizens. Worse, starting under first-timeline President Reagan, workers were fired from their jobs for going on strike at all.

6. First timeline: Echeverria and his fellow corrupt leaders conducted a "dirty" war against leftist radicals in Mexico during the mid-1970s, murdering thousands of Mexicans. According to Office of Economic Cooperation and Development (OECD) statistics, among other sources, however, Mexico enjoyed tremendous and widespread economic growth during the 1960s and 1970s, even during the "dirty" war. Then, with the rise of leaders pursuing pro-corporate trade policies, Mexico slashed its social services budget, increased the power of foreign and domestic businesses, and continued to suppress independent labor unions. Mexico's economic performance plummeted and a new round of political murders began that rivaled that of other third world nations in distress. As a result of Mexico's weakened economic situation and political instability, significant illegal immigration from Mexico to the United States began in the late 1970s and continued into the twenty-first century. This played a role in weakening wages in the United States and keeping Mexico from developing a more functional consumer society.

Chapter 37: The Spirit of '76

1. RFK timeline: This is not to say that sexually illicit conduct and drug or alcohol abuse did not occur. It's just that such conduct went back—somewhat—in the closet. For people believed they needed to be respectable in their civic organizations, which made hypocrisy seem more a virtue than it was for "free-loving" hippies. It wasn't a return to 1950s' moralism, however, as people were less morally righteous in denouncing those who went outside the bounds of proper conduct—unless someone was physically hurt, of course. In some ways, people began to understand what Jesus might have meant when saying, "Judge not, lest ye be judged."

2. Coolidge's actual comment was: "After all, the chief business of the American people is business." Coolidge stated this in a speech in 1925 to a gathering of newspaper editors. He also said, in the same speech, "Of course, the accumulation of wealth cannot be justified as the chief end of existence."

3. RFK timeline: It should be noted that starting around 1983, Motown music staged a comeback as a form of nostalgia among those who had been children during the 1960s. This was part of an overall nostalgia wave for 1960s' pop and rock. When it was realized that the 1960s' pop, rock, and Motown songs had the structure of "nursery rhymes," the songs of that era took on a new life. The difference, of course, was that nobody called the Rolling Stones or the Temptations "geniuses." They were simply singers of simple and largely cute songs. In this timeline, "genius" defined Miles Davis, Frank Zappa, Keith Emerson, and others.

4. In the second timeline, Frank Zappa, who was hostile to labor unions but a cultural and political anarchist, endorsed Reagan in 1972 and became affiliated with

the Republican Party's libertarian wing. His cultural "strangeness," however, made him as politically unpopular among the so-called mainstream listening audience as in the first timeline.

5.   Gore Vidal had heard this rumor in the first timeline, years after Bobby's actual assassination in 1968. See Gore Vidal's memoir, *Palimpsest* (Random House, 1995). In the RFK timeline, Vidal, when contacted by a young conservative reporter from a Quayle-owned paper in Indiana, said Nureyev confirmed it directly to him. The story died, however, when Nureyev was contacted and promptly denied it.

6.   Much to Bob Kennedy's chagrin, ex-Kennedy and Johnson aide Joe Califano was the leader of the pro-life (antiabortion) constitutional amendment. In the first timeline, Califano, a strong economic liberal, was President Jimmy Carter's Health, Education, and Welfare Secretary. During his confirmation hearing before Congress, he said he opposed abortion and that he would follow a recent federal law prohibiting federal funding of abortions—despite the fact that many observers at the time thought the law was unconstitutional. Califano's position on abortion was a disappointment to many cultural liberals in the Democratic Party, though President Carter continued to support him. See first timeline book, Joseph A. Califano Jr., *Governing America: An Insider's Report from the White House and the Cabinet* (Simon and Schuster, 1981).

Chapter 38: Yarborough Steps Forward

1.   The Trilateral Commission was an offshoot of the Council on Foreign Relations, itself founded in 1913 by a coalition of the elite in the business, political, and cultural spheres of U.S. society. In both timelines, the Trilateral Commission played an important role in providing a forum for the pro-business elite to exchange ideas and develop strategies against anticolonial movements and those poorer nations who dared to seek independent development as the United States itself had done during the nineteenth century. The Commission would fade and eventually break up during the Yarborough administration.

2.   In the first timeline, a similar pattern occurred, but in reverse, against the liberals and the Left. So-called liberal commentators in the broadcast media generally appeared weak because they looked more toward fairness than confidently stating substantive positions on economic policies to help the poor and middle class. The differences between liberal and conservative commentators more often appeared on cultural issues, such as abortion, homosexuality, the death penalty, and gun control, rather than economic issues. There were corporate liberals and corporate conservatives, and plenty of ethnic, racial, and sexual diversity in the corporate-dominated media. But in the end, the economic priorities favored corporate positions on issues of trade, union organization, national health insurance, child care programs, and the like. The wild card was often the environment, but there remained a corporate overlay in the way environmental issues were phrased or developed. Environmentalists often downplayed workers' fears about their jobs—or else displayed a "not in my backyard" mentality when appearing on most television and radio political programs. As this book goes to press, this subject is explored in Eric Alterman's latest book, *What Liberal Media? The Truth About Bias and the News* (Basic Books, 2003).

3.   RFK timeline: The king of Afghanistan, Zahir Shah, withstood a Communist coup in 1973 and a Muslim-cleric-led coup in 1983. In creating a constitutional

monarchy in early 1973, the king had turned over most day-to-day power to Prime Minister Musa Shafiq, a left-leaning but moderate politician, according to Bowles' State Department. Shafiq created business zones for foreign investment and worked with the World Bank—which, under Kennedy, did not pursue the budget-cutting "capitalist shock therapy." Shafiq used grant and loan monies to build community centers, hospitals, roads, and dams. He continued the king's policy of liberalizing women's rights, including their right not to remain veiled in public. Shafiq helped bring that nation into the growing Asian economic zone led by Japan. Japan also funneled money to that region, starting first with Pakistan, then Afghanistan, and then India, Bowles' favorite nation in the area. Japan served the United States as an effective surrogate in Pakistan, where Bowles feared American influence was considered less helpful than it was considered in India and Afghanistan.

Chapter 39: Yarborough Hits to Deep Left Field

1. Browne was a surprise choice to succeed Chet Bowles, but Yarborough fought hard to secure Browne's confirmation. Browne was a senator from Ohio, having defeated Republican incumbent William Saxbe in 1974. Saxbe had won a close race in 1968, a race in which he ran just slightly ahead of Republican presidential candidate Nixon in that state. As Democrats lined up to run against Saxbe in 1974, Browne won a plurality of the vote in the Democratic primary. Browne was an African American economist who had been active in the anti–Vietnam War movement—having married a Vietnamese woman in the 1950s—and later became a proponent of black urban business development. He had extensive contacts with world leaders, particularly in Africa during the 1960s and 1970s in both timelines. In the RFK timeline, Browne became a point man between the Senate and the United Nations for initiatives designed to assist poor nations in development. It was there that he caught the eye of Bowles, who in turn suggested to Yarborough that Browne would be an excellent choice to succeed him at the State Department. Bowles said, "Ralph, I'm just a little older than you, but I *feel* a lot older. I promised my wife I'd tend to our 'garden,' meaning our private lives. And I must make good on that promise." Bowles' daughter-in-law, Nancy, a Peace Corps veteran, was tapped by Yarborough to lead the Peace Corps program in 1977. Bowles, despite his promise to his wife, was later called back into service in the early 1980s to deal with the latest turn in the history of Northern Ireland.

2. In the first timeline, Harrington died of cancer in August 1989, a few months before the Berlin Wall fell and Eastern European Communism completely collapsed. Harrington was saddened at the end of his life by the loss of any socialist vision and how Soviet and related dictatorial-Communist experiences betrayed his democratic socialist ideal. See Harrington's final first-timeline book, *Socialism: Past and Future* (Arcade, 1989). Harrington's *Socialism* (Saturday Review Press, 1972) is the most astute analysis of Marx's overall writings and Marx's support of democratic values ever written.

3. The fact that nuclear power plants were successfully built in France, with little adverse effect on infant mortality, was an argument the nuclear industry, even with support from the Oil, Chemical, and Atomic Workers Union, could not succeed in making with the American public. Solar and wind energy proved far more

popular and alluring to most Americans. For a first-timeline book on the adverse effect of nuclear power plants on infant mortality rates in the United States, see University of Pittsburgh radioactive physics professor, Ernest J. Sternglass, *Secret Fallout: Low-Level Radiation from Hiroshima to Three Mile Island* (McGraw-Hill, 1981). Compare it, however, with Don Hopey, "Cancer Rate Near TMI Vitrually Unchanged," *Pittsburgh Post-Gazette,* November 1, 2002. The article discusses the University of Pittsburgh long-term study showing no increase in cancer rates, but a slight increase in other diseases such as lymphomas, leukemias, and blood-related disorders. The arguments continue in this regard.

4. Between the start of the twentieth century and the 1920s, Republican presidents Theodore Roosevelt, Warren Harding, and Calvin Coolidge supported government policies replanting and maintaining forests—forests that had been decimated by industrial development during the late nineteenth century. Theodore Roosevelt, in his speech entitled "The New Nationalism," (August 31, 1910), placed the environment within the realm of national security when he stated, "Conservation (of nature) involves the patriotic duty of ensuring safety and continuance of the nation (Parentheses added)." Theodore Roosevelt's conservation views and policies were an inspiration to many RFK-timeline Republicans.

Chapter 40: Homers Abroad, but Out at Home

1. In the first timeline, unbeknownst to Browne, this bloodshed went on for the rest of the century and beyond.
2. A few owners opposed bringing a government-owned team into major league sports. However, as Major League Commissioner Sargent Shriver said, "The Green Bay Packers of the National Football League is more of a publicly owned than privately owned team, and the NFL gets along fine. We'll do fine with Cuban baseball, particularly when their players get a load of America up close!"
3. First timeline comparison: During the late 1960s and through much of the 1970s, SAVAK, with the active support of the United States, carried out political executions of most secular opponents of the shah. Opponents of the regime who sought asylum in the United States were, on a few occasions, kidnapped and brought back to Iran for torture and execution. See Amnesty International reports on Iran (1974–1977). The CIA, in the first timeline, taught "torture techniques" to SAVAK based upon "Nazi torture techniques," according to Jesse Leaf, former CIA chief analyst in Iran. See March 5, 1992, *Congressional Record* remarks of Senator Alan Cranston (D-California), who in turn relied on the U.S. General Accounting Office report entitled, "Foreign Aid: Police Training and Assistance."
4. In the first timeline, Bowles lived until 1986.
5. In the first timeline, some capitalist and elitist pundits, particularly after the events of September 11, 2001, conceded that perhaps U.S. and Israeli support of Islamic fundamentalists in the last decade of the Soviet Union (which survived in the first timeline until 1991) might have been a "mistake," though still justifiable in the context of the Cold War. Even fewer voices found a reason to reconsider an American foreign policy toward third world nations that could be deemed to be, in a more objective sense, both anti-peasant and anti-worker. Most attempts

to revisit past United States' foreign policy actions were greeted with derisive accusations that the persons questioning these past actions were "justifying" the terrorist acts. It should be noted that there was no foreign-based September 11-type attack on American soil in the RFK timeline.

Chapter 41: The Boomerang of Success

1. RFK timeline: There was another reason why some in Congress supported nationalization. Libertarian Congressmen Ron Paul of Arizona and Ronald Dellums of California, in their own study of the private military contractor system, wrote that "The United States government will no longer be able to use private military contractors to sell weapons to other nations without the knowledge, consent, or approval of the American people." Elsewhere, they called private military contractors a "parody" of private enterprise.

2. In a first-timeline book entitled *The Challenge of Hidden Profits: Reducing Corporate Bureaucracy and Waste* (William Morrow & Company, 1985), Nader acolytes Mark Green and John Berry set forth similar points and arguments.

3. In the RFK timeline, so-called affirmative action programs designed to increase participation of blacks and other minorities, including women, in the work force, were rare. If anything, women found it somewhat harder to advance in this timeline, even after the advent of child care programs nationwide, than in the first timeline. This was due to a cultural lag where more women choose to stay at home as their union-member husbands made more money.

Appendix: "The Great Struggle and Beyond"

Introductory note to the Appendix: The notes in this Appendix do not purport to be by Professor Lewis. The endnotes are written by the author, as were the endnotes for the previous chapters.

1. Americans who cannot imagine inhumane behavior ever occurring in any protracted war among Americans might be interested in reading *The Guerrilla Conflict in Missouri During the American Civil War* (Oxford University Press, 1989) by Michael Fellman, and *April 1865* (HarperCollins Publishers, 2001) by Jay Winik. These books describe the gruesome violence committed by Unionists and Confederates during the American Civil War (1861-1865). This included various instances of brutality, terror, and betrayal, including the rape or murder of women and children, as well as escalating violent reprisals and recrimination.

2. In the first timeline, the same union endorsed Ronald Reagan in 1980. Then, in 1981, Reagan fired these same unionized air traffic control workers when they went on strike. From that point on, private corporate leaders in the first timeline cited Reagan's example to fire other striking workers and further weaken labor unions.

3. Lewis is quoting from memos or reports from, respectively, 1960s' Departments of Defense and State memoranda and analyses from the Rand Corporation and other government-oriented think tanks. An excellent analysis of such memoranda appears in Noam Chomsky's essay, "The Backroom Boys," *For Reasons of State*, op. cit.

4. In the first timeline, there were approximately three hundred thousand homicides in the United States from 1969 through 1988. Additionally, approximately fifteen

million abortions were performed in the United States during that time. One may also wish to add the millions of people around the globe who died, were murdered or otherwise killed as a result of first-timeline American foreign policy initiatives and decisions. See, for example, William Blum, *Killing Hope: U.S. Military and CIA Interventions Since World War II* (Common Courage Press, 1995; updated edition, 2000). Blum's book is highly controversial in many U.S. establishment quarters, if recognized at all. However, at least two mainstream commentators, A.J. Langguth and Thomas Powers, have praised Blum's book for its scope and wide-ranging research.

For a different perspective on the cause of human carnage during the twentieth century, there is an equally wide-ranging account of the crimes of Communist regimes around the world entitled *Black Book of Communism,* originally published in France and then translated and published by Harvard University Press in 1997. Unfortunately, the book takes exaggerated estimates of the number of people killed under Stalin, Mao, and other Communist regimes, and almost solely blames the Communists for the tens of millions of people who died or were killed in various famines and third world anti-colonial wars. The six authors of the *Black Book of Communism* (most of whom were former Communists) conclude that the death toll of eighty years of Communism is over one hundred million. Historians and political scientists, however, who have studied each of the nations where Communist dictatorships existed, have reached lower, though still horrible numbers of people who died, were murdered, or otherwise killed in various Communist-dominated nations. The figure nonetheless remains in the tens of millions and as much as sixty million, largely due to two particular Communist leaders, Russia's Stalin and China's Mao, which makes *Black Book of Communism* a still useful review overall of the Communist experience. For those who believe genocide mostly comes from politically left dictators, however, such persons should also recognize that if one applied the analytical structure of the four European ex-Communists to the Western powers, including America, one may also accuse the West (including America) of causing the death of tens of millions in various famines in India, Africa, and other places around the world, as well in the various twentieth century anti-colonial wars. Then, using almost the same eighty-year period, one could reasonably conclude that the number of those who died, were murdered, or otherwise killed by the West is closer to those suffering the same fate under the scourge of Communism.

Further, we American citizens may be wise to compare the United States government's genocide of the Native Americans in the nineteenth century when measuring the human holocausts that occurred under the tyrannies of the Soviet Union and Red China in the twentieth century. Each of these decades-long mass murders occurred as each nation was forming under its respective ideologies and in a time of massive change. This perspective allows one to recognize that simply because a nation is a democracy or a republic does not render it immune to at least some of the barbarity exhibited in dictatorships. For example, the similarities between our treatment of the "Indians" and Stalin's treatment of the "kulaks" are closer than we ordinarily imagine.

5. Lewis and most persons of the RFK timeline saw a democratically socialist and united Europe. They never saw the Balkan Wars of the 1990s and continued strife

in the old Soviet Union and its once far-reaching empire. Yugoslavia, which in the first timeline broke up into five different nation-states as the Cold War ended, developed in the RFK timeline a more class-based, democratic socialism. The Communist Yugoslav dictator, Marshal Tito, survived long enough with French and British military and economic aid to defer loosening up political freedoms. Following Tito's death in 1988, the economy in Yugoslavia was sufficiently strong to survive any attempt to revitalize ancient ethnic tensions. The motorcar known as the Yugo developed, in the RFK timeline, a reputation as being well built, particularly after Volvo, owned by the Swedish public, bought the state-owned Yugo factories in return for agreeing to provide lifetime employment and benefits similar to what Swedish workers had. The Swedes promised the Yugoslavs that after ten years, the Yugoslav employees would own their own company with an ESOP type of plan. The Swedes kept their promise, although Swedes remained in various management positions for a number of years thereafter.

6. It is unclear whom Professor Lewis is referring to here. It is possible he is refer-ring to capitalist intellectuals of the RFK timeline such as University of Pennsylvania law professor Benjamin Stein, or the novelist P. J. O'Rourke, known as much for his trenchant, though some say anti-American, political essays. Such writers, to the extent they are mentioned in respectable media, are usually attacked by Joe-Six-Pack commentators such as Michael Moore, Bill O'Reilly, Dana Owens (in the first timeline, Queen Latifa), and Sean Hannity. These commentators are partisan supporters of unions, Robert Kennedy, and lim-itations on income for high-income earners. They continually rail against utopian capitalists, plutocrats, and, in Hannity's words, "other anti-Americans who think nothing of crossing a picket line or worse, think it's wonderful to have a big dis-parity of wealth between the rich and the poor!" That Hannity and O'Reilly were not "socialists" or "unionists" in the original timeline is . . . well, let's just say it's another one of the many ironies of history.

7. Dellums wrote a first-timeline book, *Defense Sense* (Ballinger, 1983), in which he set forth a proposal for a lean, tough military that takes advantage of high technologies and a prudent use of military personnel. Dellums was considered a far left Congressman in the first timeline. Yet, he often allied himself with pro-business Republicans such as Congressman John Kasich (R-Ohio) and Senator Charles Grassley (R-Iowa) in challenging various "pork-barrel" military projects that bore little or no relation to military needs. Even with that left-right political alliance, how-ever, Congress overwhelmingly passed most such military weapons projects.

8. In the first timeline, Humphrey was unwilling to speak plainly against the war until the very end of the 1968 campaign. Instead of picking Texas Senator Yarborough for vice president, Humphrey chose a dull-speaking and elitist liberal U.S. senator from Maine, Edmund Muskie. Humphrey never bothered to deal with the student supporters of Robert Kennedy or Gene McCarthy. Humphrey further looked weak and indecisive as Daley and the police turned the nihilistic Yippie-led demonstrations in Chicago into a violent free-for-all—a "police riot," as later government-sponsored investigators called it. See Charles Kaiser, *1968* (Grove Press, 1988). Finally, Larry O'Brien, in the first timeline, and speaking years after RFK's murder, said it was inevitable that RFK would have lost the nomination to Humphrey had he lived. Ronald Steel, *In Love with Night*, op. cit.